THE BAST[illegible]
sweep an[illegible]
the Cont[illegible]
turbulent, glorious days [illegible]
the reign of Louis XIV. The central character is Gaston, Comte de Racon, who is lecherous, ruthless, brutal, but at the same time human and capable of the utmost tenderness. Father to an illegitimate son—whom he cruelly abandons in his youth—the Comte, at first hating the boy, eventually comes to recognise and love him. And bound to the lives of these two are the Comte's two legitimate sons and their mother, the fair, gentle Madeleine. These are the central figures—all powerful and vitally alive—but as well we encounter some of the famous and eccentric personalities of 17th Century France . . . Louis XIV, even in his youth showing signs of the evil genius that was to make him one of France's most omnipotent kings . . . La Vallière, and the Montespan, the king's ill-fated mistresses . . . Monsieur, the King's brother, painted and bewigged, seemingly a simpering fool but exercising a corrupt and decadent influence on the young men in his court.

THE BASTARD is a novel bursting with drama, intrigue, murder, savagery and love in all its manifestations. . . .

The story of THE BASTARD is told in two volumes, of which this is the second.

Also by BRIGITTE VON TESSIN

THE BASTARD VOL. I

and published by CORGI BOOKS

Brigitte Von Tessin

The Bastard

Translated by Mervyn Savill

Volume Two

Part Two and Part Three

CORGI BOOKS
A DIVISION OF TRANSWORLD PUBLISHERS LTD

THE BASTARD Volume Two

A CORGI BOOK 0 552 10216 4

Originally published in Great Britain
by Barrie & Rockliff

PRINTING HISTORY

Barrie and Rockliff edition published 1958
Corgi edition reprinted 1968
Corgi edition reprinted 1968
Corgi edition reprinted 1968
Corgi edition reprinted 1968
Corgi edition reprinted 1969
Corgi edition reprinted 1970
Corgi edition reprinted 1972
Corgi edition reprinted 1973
Corgi edition reissued 1976

This book is set in
Plantin 10/10½ pt.

Corgi Books are published by Transworld Publishers Ltd.,
Century House, 61–63 Uxbridge Rd., Ealing, London W5 5SA

Made and printed in Great Britain by
Richard Clay (The Chaucer Press), Ltd., Bungay, Suffolk

CONTENTS

Part Two

Part Three

CHARACTERS IN THE NOVEL

GASTON COMTE DE RACON, *Marquis de Brayonne*
MADELEINE COMTESSE DE RACON, *wife of the count*
RAOUL VICOMTE DE CLARMONT
GUY DE BRAYONNE } *sons of the count*
LOUISE, *daughter of the count*
MARTIN SAINT-JEAN, *the count's illegitimate son, 'The Bastard'*
THERESE DE DISMARAT, *the count's cousin*
FATHER TULIER, *father confessor to the Racon family*
DR. BOREL, *physician to the Racon family*
D'OUVILLE, *the count's master of the horse*
MADAME D'OUVILLE
GROUCHET, *the count's master of the hunt*
JOSQUIN
TONIO TENELLI } *tutors to the count's sons*
PIERRE, *the count's valet*
CHARLES, *the count's groom*
DENIS, *the countess's servant*
EMILIE, *the countess's lady's maid*
DOMINIQUE, *valet to the count's sons*
FRANÇOIS, *Martin's groom*
MADAME FOUILLARD, *bailiff's wife at Brayonne*
MAURICE DOURANEZ, *tenant farmer of Les Chênes*
LISON, *the farmer's daughter*
BICE, *Italian courtesan, the count's mistress*
AMARYLLIS, *an actress*
JEANNE, *peasant serf*
BLANCHE, *the count's 'plaything'*
GOVERNOR OF THE PROVINCE
GERARD COMTE DE MONTIGNON
VICOMTE DE LA PORTE-MURY } *cousins of the count*
DU LAC
DE FALLERON
DE VITRY } *officers in the count's regiment*

CHARACTERS

ANDRE BARON D'EPPONCOURT
ANGELIQUE BARONNE D'EPPONCOURT, *the baron's first wife*
MARGUERITE D'EPPONCOURT, *the baron's daughter by his first marriage*
BARONNE D'EPPONCOURT, *the baron's second wife*
CLAUDE *and* ANDRE, *the baron's sons by the second marriage*
CHARLES DE RIBERAC, *Marguerite d'Epponcourt's suitor*
ANNETTE, *the baroness's lady's maid*
JACQUELINE, *poultry maid at the baron's castle*
BARON DU TERNE, *friend of the Comte de Racon*
BARONNE DU TERNE
ARMAND MARQUIS DE CHASSIGNY, *friend of the Comte de Racon*
MARQUISE DE CHASSIGNY
NICOLAS DE CHASSIGNY, *son of the marquis*
LOUIS, COMTE DE SALVIEUX
CLAIRE-MARIE DE SALVIEUX, *his sister*
MONSIEUR BOQUELIN, *banker*
CONSTANT DU FAYEL, *boyhood friend of the Comte de Salvieux*

HISTORICAL PERSONAGES APPEARING IN THE NOVEL

LOUIS XIV, *King of France*
PHILIPPE DUC D'ORLEANS (*Monsieur*), *the king's brother*
DUCHESSE DE LA VALLIERE } *the king's mistresses*
MARQUISE DE MONTESPAN }
CHEVALIER DE LORRAINE, *the duc d'Orleans' minion*
LOUIS D'HUMIERES, *Marshal of France*
DUC DE LA ROCHEFOUCAULD
MARQUISE DE SEVIGNE
NINON DE LENCLOS

PART TWO

BROTHERLY HATRED

THE count stayed at Brayonne until August 1672, and then returned home by a devious route. He accompanied some of his guests to their estates, enjoying their hospitality for several days. On his departure from M. de Méril's castle, his retinue was reduced to the two young gentlemen, Constant du Fayel and Louis de Salvieux, and the actress Amaryllis, who had accepted his invitation to Grandval. They travelled fast and visited the wealthy Baron du Terne, who was pleased to join them, with his wife. The company reached Grandval one late afternoon in the beginning of September. On dismounting the count learned from the steward that M. d'Oubray had been a guest of the countess for three days.

As soon as the count had ordered Martin to fetch Raoul and Guy, in order to introduce them to the young gentlemen, he visited his wife's apartments. The countess was in her salon with Dr Borel, listening to M. d'Oubray's interpretation of a brightly painted zodiac. She had already been informed of her husband's return, but M. d'Oubray had considered it wise to wait quietly for him to appear in her salon.

The count was amazed to see the unruffled dignity with which they rose to their feet.

'I am surprised, M. d'Oubray, to find you here in my wife's apartments.'

'I am delighted to see you again,' replied the lawyer calmly. 'You have been greatly missed here.'

'I wrote to you, to Brayonne,' said the countess, 'telling you of M. d'Oubray's arrival. I expected the letter to be forwarded.'

The count glanced swiftly from one to the other.

'I should be grateful if, after so long an absence, I could be alone with my wife.'

D'Oubray gathered up his papers and said: 'I will leave you now.' He bowed to the company and left the room with the doctor.

The couple stood facing each other. The count looked his beautiful wife up and down. She wore a new gold dress and a yellow rose in her chestnut ringlets, which were tied back at the nape of her neck. Under his gaze a look of fear suddenly appeared in her large blue eyes. Clutching a lace handkerchief to her bosom she asked: 'Why do you remain silent, Monsieur?'

'I am looking at you, Madame. During the summer you have made a remarkable recovery and you have changed. Your complexion is radiant and your arms and hands are dazzlingly white. You have filled out, without becoming plump. I have never seen you so beautiful.'

The countess's lips parted in amazement. With a smile he took a step towards her.

'You are so beautiful, Madame, that I am inclined to think that you must be a little in love. What favours have you accorded to your admirer?'

'A single kiss,' replied the countess.

'I believe you. But before you give him a second one, accept one from me.'

She turned pale, but he was already at her side. He caught her ringlets with one hand and drew her towards him. He kissed her lips for a long time and gazed into her wide open eyes, which suddenly clouded over and closed. He fumbled with her dress and pressed his hand inside her bodice, until, breathless from kissing her, he released her and cried:

'Madeleine, you love me, although you don't know it. I am not too jealous of your admirer.'

Completely bewildered, she looked at him uncomprehendingly and, in her agitation, leaned for support against a small table. He laughed. 'Don't you think it's time we were reconciled? *I* once struck you with my whip and *you* left me to rot in Brayonne. Let us call it a closed chapter. You are well again, are you not?'

'Well?' she asked, obviously trying to collect her thoughts. 'No, I am not well.'

'Do you wish me to believe that such radiance is only a

sham? Whatever else I may believe, I won't believe that, Madeleine.'

Before she was aware of what was happening, he had carried her into the bedroom. Then, seized by sudden terror, the countess felt sick, which made her tempestuous husband think that she really was still an invalid. Disappointed and sobered, he apologised for his impulsiveness and left his wife as quickly as possible. The countess burst into tears and called for Emilie.

Martin and the two young visitors first met Master Tenelli, who gave him a hearty greeting and summed up his new pupils with a critical eye. He questioned them about their ages and their knowledge, and sent for Raoul and Guy to make their acquaitance. Raoul embraced Martin and said that he had missed him more every day. Guy remarked that Martin's new pea-green suit was of the best cloth, and that the whiteness of his simple shirt would have done no discredit to the count. Tenelli proposed that the newcomers should be shown the castle and the stables, and the five boys set out together.

Pierre caught them up and summoned Guy to the count's presence. They continued on their rounds and imagined that they would see him again at supper, but Guy was absent. Raoul found him in a pitiful condition up in his room. The count had given him an unmerciful thrashing and had apparently forgotten to give a reason for his punishment, for Guy was swearing about Martin and vowing to take a bloody revenge. Raoul fetched Martin, who assured Guy that he had never discussed him with the count. The boy shouted, and insisted that he had obviously repeated his conversation of the night when they had thought their father was dying. Martin denied it vigorously. Raoul supported him but Guy was not to be convinced. Martin was seething with rage. They quarrelled and abused each other, while Raoul tried to act as peacemaker. Guy suddenly gave way, saying that it was dangerous to arouse the enmity of a favourite and he would reserve his judgment. Martin replied that he was no favourite but the count's friend. Guy was speechless, and even Raoul was a little perturbed. He asked how Martin could remain his friend and at the same time a friend of his father's. Martin replied that it was quite simple because M. le Comte never cast a slur on his honour and did not take it amiss when he sometimes insisted upon remaining silent about something. The brothers were amazed. Raoul assured Martin of his trust, and took him off to join the two guests.

The countess stayed in bed for four days, giving rein to her sorrow, and refusing to see all visitors with the exception of the Baroness du Terne, whom she had to admit for the sake of politeness. The baroness had lost her beauty at an early age from repeated child-bearing and had just begun to recover her strength now that she was growing old. Her sole interests were domestic matters and her children's prospects; she exhausted the countess by extolling the virtues of her eldest daughter, who in a few years was to become the Vicomtesse de Clarmont.

Raoul and Guy soon grew used to Constant and Louis, who, for their part, found it difficult to submit to Master Tenelli's authority. M. de Méril had merely bothered about their manners, and allowed them to be given the barest rudiments of an education by an ancient, half-deaf schoolmaster, who ate the bread of charity in his house. Now they had to learn Italian, construe the Divine Comedy and draw plans of fortresses and Roman battles.

Louis took the lessons in his stride, but Constant groaned at the harshness of his existence. At the outset, the lazy, indifferent youth was teased unmercifully by his far younger comrade, Guy, on account of his stupidity, but, after receiving a few extremely powerful cuffs, Guy began to worship him almost as a god. Guy's main aim now was to be recognised by Constant, and to achieve this he embarked upon a series of outrageous and often rather dubious pranks. When a grin appeared on Constant's broad face, and a grudging 'not bad for a midget like you' was forthcoming, Guy's day was made. He would willingly take a thrashing from Master Tenelli for a word of praise from Constant. The Italian tutor had a poor opinion of Constant. He informed the count that the boy was a lazy good-for-nothing who put the minimum of effort into his training, relying on the advantages of his physical strength. Every horse began to foam and sweat under him, until the master of the horse gave him only the stubbornest horses with the hardest mouths. When he rode them, however, they displayed the most astonishing capabilities.

The Comte Louis de Salvieux made friends with the Vicomte de Clarmont. Raoul let him into the secret of the library key, and, since Louis had also learned Greek in the Jesuit school, Raoul's hopes were roused of one day being able to read the Iliad and the Odyssey. At first Louis refused to become Raoul's secret teacher, but the boy was so insistent that he finally took compassion on him and allowed himself to be lighted to the library like a diminutive schoolteacher. He enjoyed life at Grandval and considered himself fortunate in having found two such outstanding fencing masters as the Comte de Racon and Tonio Tenelli, both of whom assured him that he was not without talent. The count enjoyed relieving Tenelli at fencing practice, and this was an incentive to the boys. Guy wept tears of rage when Martin beat him in the presence of Constant. Constant, for his part, moaned that he had to mess about the whole day with a foil. Although he was sixteen, he received many a cuff and was often called an oaf or a clod, which did nothing to diminish Guy's admiration.

One sunny September morning, the countess went out for the first time into the park. M. d'Oubray, who had installed himself comfortably with a book on a stone seat, caught sight of her in the distance and immediately took the opportunity of joining her in one of the rose-covered arbours. She stopped as she saw him coming, and held out her hand for him to kiss.

'Madame, I have been very worried about you. Did the encounter with your husband have disagreeable consequences?'

'I'm not quite sure about that myself, M. d'Oubray.'

He looked at her intently with his grey eyes and asked: 'Where is that gay smile with which you so often gladdened my heart during those days when I was pleased to be able to call myself your sole guest?'

'I am trying to recover my spirits by enjoying the autumn beauty of the park.'

'Madame, I have longed for you. You once allowed me to kiss your soft lips, and I have longed ever since to repeat that pleasure. May I offer you my arm, Madame?'

'Yes, M. d'Oubray, for the length of this arboured walk.'

'Then let us walk up and down it several times.'

The countess took his arm but turned away when he bent towards her. 'Monsieur, I am no longer mistress of my lips. They have become enamoured of my husband and will not be converted. I am engaged in a struggle with myself, and hope to be victorious.'

'Madame, what are you saying?'

'Monsieur, I have wept for days and nights on end and am now capable of uttering a truth which is painful to me.'

'Do you love your husband?'

'Not I, but my body.'

'God be praised. I trembled at the thought that Diana could be attracted to a satyr.'

'Yes, Gaston is Pan . . . No human feelings in his case have any meaning. Where he is concerned, what do hate or love signify? Should one think him guilty when he is inconstant or heartless? What are the feelings of Pan? Can he be blamed if he chases the nymphs? Whoever falls in love with him is in love with a void, and whoever hates him hates a shadow. If Pan were to enter a church, sit down on the altar and begin to play his pipes, who could punish him? I am trying to extinguish all my feelings for him in order to recover my peace of mind. Do not disturb me in my attempt, M. d'Oubray.'

'I hardly recognise you, Madame,' said d'Oubray, deeply moved. 'Have I in any way disturbed your spirit?'

'Monsieur, in the future I shall value your letters more than your conversation, and I beg you not to take that amiss.'

'You are dismissing me, Madame, after having roused in me such great hopes.'

'Monsieur, you told me that, according to my horoscope, great changes were about to take place. I have changed a great deal in spirit.'

'And I have to pay the price.'

'Monsieur, I value your friendship more than ever.'

'And if my friendship changed to love?'

'Then I should have to mourn the loss of it. Please spare me this pain.'

'Madame, for your sake I will banish Eros and remain your friend.'

They walked together in silence for a while, until M.

d'Oubray asked gently:

'Shall I leave Grandval?'

'The presence of a friend is always a pleasure.'

'And the presence of an unattainable, beautiful woman is always a torture.'

'Monsieur, like my husband, you will have to accustom yourself to seeing in me a marble statue, the sight of which arouses the senses without ever being able to satisfy them. As you know, I am an ailing woman.'

'But mockery speaks from your beautiful eyes.'

'That may be. My illness is a source of strength, and in its protection I believe I shall rediscover my peace of mind. You conjured up a wealth of strange thoughts and pictures before my soul, and as a result the Bible became merely another book. I intend to read it once more from beginning to end, and I anticipate that it will help me to emerge triumphant from all the confusion you have caused me. I long for the divine truth which has been dimmed by my friend's mountebank tricks.'

'If at times you find me enigmatical, I beg you to question me. I have no greater wish than to aid you to recognise the truth.'

'Monsieur, you have no other wish than to lead me astray so that I cannot recognise the truth.'

'I do not accept that impeachment.'

'I did but jest, M. d'Oubray. I feel free because I no longer hate Gaston. I hope that I shall soon be able to see him for the mythical monster he really is.'

'Madame, do you look upon me as a man?'

'You are an enigma. Do not reveal your true self to me. Nothing fascinates a lonely woman more than riddles. Let us go into the sun. Are those not my guests coming with my husband? Is that enchanting creature with the tawny hair not the actress Amaryllis?'

'Yes, Madame, you are right.'

'Lead me to her. I am curious to meet the latest nymph.'

The countess picked a rose and appeared with M. d'Oubray on the sunny, gravelled path. Both the baron and the count stopped and watched her approach, while the actress tripped lightly towards her and exclaimed:

'Oh, Madame, at last I have seen you. The picture I had of

you pales before your regal beauty. You might be a heroine from out of one of Racine's magnificent plays.'

'And you are a charming flatterer, Mlle Amaryllis.'

'Oh, Madame, if you arouse admiration in women what paeans of praise must you not wring from men!'

M. d'Oubray said with a smile: 'Mlle Amaryllis, the Comtesse de Racon, does not care to hear hymns to her beauty, for compliments mean nothing to her.'

'So beauty and intelligence have combined in you. I beg you to forgive my erstwhile praise and to be gracious to me.'

'Which roles do you prefer to play, Mlle Amaryllis?' asked the countess. 'Hardly the tragic ones, I imagine?'

'You have guessed rightly, Madame. I swear by Molière and play the young lover in his plays.'

'It must be delightful to see you in such a role.'

'You will have that opportunity next winter.'

'Oh, I do not know whether I shall go to Paris this year.'

'Oh, Madame, you say that so calmly.'

'I have become so used to the country that I no longer miss Paris. But I should very much like to see one of Molière's plays.'

'Madame, would it amuse you to rehearse a scene from *Tartuffe* with me? One of the gentlemen—possibly M. d'Oubray—could play the old hypocrite, the Baron du Terne Orgon, you his wife and I his daughter, as I do in Paris. Tell me, would it amuse you?'

'What a delightful proposal. But I'm afraid I have no talent as an actress.'

'Oh, I do not believe that. Your expression is dignified but by no means frozen, and your movements are the perfection of grace. The son who resembles you so much could play the young lover.'

'You mean the Vicomte de Clarmont?'

'Yes, Madame. He is as fair as Adonis and will soon set all the women's hearts aflame.'

The countess bowed to the Baroness du Terne and the comte as they came up, and asked the actress: 'And what part have you intended for my husband?'

'None, Madame. The Comte de Racon could never play anyone but himself'

There was an exchange of greetings. Everyone enquired about the countess's health and they remained standing in a group on the gravelled path.

'Monsieur,' said Amaryllis, 'your wife has a whim to play Tartuffe with your guests and me.'

'I shall be delighted to watch.'

'Monsieur, the rehearsals will be in private. You can invite a number of guests for the performance. Shall we start today, Madame?'

'I am quite willing, Mademoiselle.'

'Does that mean,' cried the count, offended, 'that I am to be deprived of feminine beauty and to be locked out?'

'Only for a few hours each day.'

'I will consider whether I shall give my permission.'

'Monsieur, in our age, women rule. Do not swim against the stream. Even the Sun King has bowed the knee to us.'

'Well, as his servant, I cannot but do the same. But I beg you, my pretty Amaryllis, not to let me feel the touch of your sceptre too heavily.'

'What is happening?' interrupted the Baroness du Terne. They hastened to explain to her while they strolled slowly between the box hedges in the autumn sun. The count had offered his arm to the baroness and the countess took the arm of the genial baron. D'Oubray wanted to escort Amaryllis but the actress strayed from one couple to another lending a sparkle to everyone's conversation.

One cloudy Sunday, the five boys went to the fish pond to shoot duck. Guy had brought his two dogs and was furious with Martin because he had borrowed the count's best gun. The dogs were perfectly behaved, pointing at the game until the guns were within range. Scores of duck rose from the water, shots rang out, and their game bags were soon full. Constant, Guy and Martin were the best shots. Louis was too excited to aim properly, and Raoul was handicapped because of his short sight.

On the way home, the boys met a peasant lad with a russet mongrel coming out of the forest. 'He's come at the right time,' said Guy. 'He! Bastien, carry the game home for us.'

The boy approached hesitantly. They slung the knapsacks

over his back.

'What were you doing in the forest?' asked Guy.

'I was only taking a Sunday stroll, M. Guy.'

'With a hunting dog?'

'That is our watch dog, M. Guy.'

'He looks like a fox.'

'His sire was a fox, M. Guy.'

'Then he's a good hunter, eh?'

'I keep him on the leash.'

'Do you think I should find anything if I followed his trail back?'

'M. Guy, I haven't been poaching.'

'He says he hasn't been poaching.' Guy turned with a grin to his friends. 'Well, we'll have a look.' Guy whistled and his dogs rushed up. He set them on the tracks of the russet mongrel. 'Come on, all of you. You too, Bastien.'

The boys followed the dogs with interest, and noticed that the peasant lad was sweating with fear.

Behind the first tree in the forest they came across a tied sack hidden under dead leaves.

'Undo it,' ordered Guy.

Bastien obeyed, and a hare with its neck bitten through was brought to light. 'That will cost you fifty,' said Guy.

'Be merciful, M. Guy. I won't poach any more. Don't betray me.'

'What shall we do with him?' Guy asked his companions.

Raoul looked annoyed, and Martin said:

'Fifty lashes are far too much for a wretched hare.'

'But he must be punished,' said Louis.

'What do you think, Constant?' asked Guy. The boy shrugged his shoulders.

'Gentlemen,' Bastien started to plead, 'I am my parents' only son and there is so much work to be done in the autumn. Spare me . . . have pity . . . Put in a word for me, Martin.'

'I suggest that we should take away his dog and the hare, that is sufficient punishment.'

'Yes, that seems fair,' replied Raoul.

'Put it to the vote,' said Guy. 'I'm for denouncing him.'

'So am I,' said Constant.

Louis voted against this, and thus the two boys were overruled. The peasant boy thanked them and swore loudly that this hare would be his first and last. They set out with him to the castle.

When the park wall came in sight, the shepherd appeared with his flock. Little Lison was walking behind the sheep. Raoul nudged Martin.

'I've something to give the little girl which I've been carrying about with me all the summer. I don't want to meet her alone, and Guy's no use. Wait till the others have gone on ahead and then come with me.'

Guy, Constant and Louis discussed what should be done with the mongrel and paid no attention to Martin and Raoul when they left to join the little shepherdess. Lison pretended to have difficulty in keeping the flock together.

'Stay where you are, Lison,' called Raoul. The little girl obeyed, and with scarlet cheeks stared at the ground.

'Lison, I am acting on behalf of the count, who last spring ordered me to give you these coins. Open your hand.'

The girl's cheeks changed colour. 'Open your hand, Lison,' repeated Raoul. Lison did not stir a finger. Raoul dropped the money on the ground.

'You can take it or leave it, as you like. I've carried out my commission. Come, Martin.' Raoul walked on ahead with Martin and the flock went on its way.

'But you were once in love with the little girl, Vicomte Raoul.'

'Father tumbled her because he thought she was a serf . . . fortunately without any ill results.'

'But you flung the money at her feet!'

'Yes, because she wouldn't put out her hand. Don't let's talk about her any more.'

At this moment they heard a shrill, dismal howling from the direction of the other boys. Raoul and Martin involuntarily quickened their steps and soon saw the cause. Guy and Constant had tied the russet mongrel six feet above the ground to two trees, so that he was stretched between them. His belly had been slit open and the hounds were leaping up at him and pulling out the entrails. Guy was laughing and there was a grin on Constant's face.

'We're carrying out the execution,' Louis said to Martin and

Raoul. The peasant lad was standing there, almost weeping with rage and grief. The cries of the tortured beast grew ever shriller. Raoul curled his lip.

'As though you couldn't have thought of anything more intelligent!'

'His entrails are out now,' said Guy. 'We must lower him.'

At this the peasant rushed up, tore the bloody knife from Constant's hand and stabbed his dog.

'You've spoilt my fun, you dirty oaf,' screamed Guy. 'Now you'll get the fifty lashes.'

'By all the saints, M. Guy, spare me!'

'I shall denounce you as a poacher.'

Martin placed his hand on Guy's shoulder. 'M. Guy, you accepted the vote. We agreed that Bastien should be spared.'

'Nothing was agreed.'

'M. Guy, as a nobleman you have to keep your word.'

'Not to a serf.'

'To anyone.'

'No, never—and not to you either.'

Martin gave him two hard blows in the face. Guy fought back, but Martin was the stronger and began to give him such a drubbing that Raoul and Louis finally had to interfere to rescue the younger boy. Raoul caught hold of Martin, while Louis restrained Guy. But Martin was in such a rage that he knocked Raoul to the ground and went for Guy again. At this point Constant knocked him down with a single blow. When he rose to his feet, Raoul and Louis were protecting Guy, who was spitting blood and screaming: 'I'll denounce him. That is quite certain. And I'll settle with you when we get home!'

He looked for his gun, which Louis took away just in time.

'Pull yourself together, Guy,' said Raoul.

'Martin, you did not behave very nobly, for Guy is the youngest of us and far weaker than you.'

'He insulted my honour.'

'Yes, your bastard honour—you clod!'

Raoul and Constant had to hold Martin forcibly. Feeling safer, Guy croaked: 'You filthy peasant oaf, slimy favourite . . . misbegotten bastard . . . whoreson!'

'You wait,' cried Martin. 'I'll finish you if I lay my hands on you . . . and if you rot I shall feel no remorse!'

'Now stop taunting him, Guy,' Raoul cried angrily. 'Take back your insults.'

'Not on your life.'

'But we can't go on holding him for ever. He'll do what he says.'

Martin gnashed his teeth. 'I'll kill him.'

'Can you hold him till I fetch Master Tenelli?' Raoul asked Constant.

'Maybe, but not for certain.'

Raoul stepped between them. 'Now, Martin and Guy, listen to me. You must be reconciled and there mustn't be any fratricide. Martin, you gave Guy too bad a thrashing. Guy, you abused Martin too much. I think you can call it even. Come to your senses and shake hands.'

'I insist that he apologises for his insults,' said Martin.

'I wouldn't dream of it.'

Raoul reflected and said with great dignity:

'He is right, Guy. Apologise.'

'Never!'

'Do you want to murder each other?'

'With the greatest pleasure, if Louis will give me my gun.'

'Think of father, Guy . . .'

'M. le Comte shall decide,' said Martin.

'That would suit you,' jeered Guy. 'You know exactly whom he'd help, don't you?'

'No, M. le Comte is just.'

'I doubt that very much.'

'M. Guy, if you start insulting M. le Comte . . .'

'Be quiet,' shouted Raoul. 'Guy, there is no other arbitrator available. You will have to make do with Master Tenelli.'

'Master Tenelli will not do,' said Martin calmly, 'but he shall be present.'

'And mother too,' added Guy.

'Agreed. M. Constant, let me go.'

Constant released Martin, and Louis returned the gun to Guy, saying: 'But only to shoot duck with!' Guy shouldered his weapon and whistled to his dogs, which in the meantime had torn the mongrel to pieces.

'Where is the fellow with our ducks?' asked Louis.

But Bastien was nowhere to be seen. The full haversacks lay on the ground. Louis pointed to them with a smile. 'When two parties fall out, the third always profits.'

Guy slung a bag over his shoulder and said curtly: 'The bloodhounds will soon find him!' Martin controlled himself and held his tongue. Picking up their belongings, they made their way in outward amity towards the little gate in the park wall.

About this time the gentry were on the terrace crowding round Mlle Amaryllis, who was giving a superb reading in mime of Molière's *Tartuffe* and allotting the roles. Everyone had succumbed to theatrical fever, with the exception of the count, and the Baroness du Terne quarrelled with Mlle de Dismarat for the part of Pernelle, which Amaryllis had to shorten considerably because neither of the ladies could remember their lines. She had suggested that the two ladies should appear alternately in the same costume, but neither of them would give way to the other and the gentlemen were vastly amused.

At this moment the boys climbed the steps from the park. 'How many ducks have you bagged?' cried M. d'Oubray.

'Seventeen,' replied Louis.

'And how many did you shoot and not find?'

'Two hundred.' There was laughter.

'What is the matter with your face, Guy?' the countess asked anxiously. 'Did you fall on your nose?'

Raoul stepped forward and bowed. 'Ladies and gentlemen, I crave your attention for a few moments. We have had a dispute which we cannot settle, and we should like mother and father, along with Master Tenelli, to act as arbitrators.'

'How interesting,' cried Amaryllis. 'I will lay *Tartuffe* aside for the moment. I shall prepare for a judgment of Solomon.'

'Take your ducks to the kitchen, put away your guns and then come back here,' ordered the count. The boys obeyed. When they returned Raoul, as before, acted as spokesman. 'We should be grateful if we could state our case before the arbitrators alone.'

'Our guests wish otherwise,' replied the count, 'so begin.' The boys exchanged glances.

'Couldn't we postpone it, M. le Comte?' asked Martin.

'No. Speak up, Raoul. What happened?'

Raoul described their encounter with Bastien and gave all the details of the quarrel. He repeated each of Guy's insults and finally asked his comrades: 'Was that so, or not?' All of them confirmed his words.

The countess could not resist saying to her husband: 'You see how dangerous it is to let illegitimate children grow up with your own.' The count ignored her remark. 'Look,' she said, pointing at Guy, 'the poor boy's face is quite swollen.'

'One should always be chivalrous to a weaker foe,' the count said to Martin. Martin flushed scarlet, and the count turned to the other boys. 'Your quarrelling and fighting does not interest me, and I should send you packing had Guy not offended my honour by calling Martin a whoreson. Martin's mother was a woman to be respected. Guy, I shall expect you to refrain from using that word of abuse from today onwards. Make your apologies to me and to Martin.'

Guy did not hide his rage. He stepped towards his father, bowed deeply, and said: 'I apologise.'

'Good.'

Then he went over to Martin and, without bowing, hissed through his teeth: 'I apologise.'

Martin also said: 'Good, I accept,' and Guy returned to his place.

'I insist that Martin be punished for putting Guy in this state,' said the countess angrily.

'Are the other ladies of the same opinion?' asked the count, turning to the Baroness du Terne and to Amaryllis.

'Yes,' said the baroness.

'I'm sorry for the little bantam,' said Amaryllis.

'Very well,' said the count. 'I'll see that Martin's face is made just as swollen as Guy's. Come here, Martin.'

'M. le Comte,' pleaded Martin, 'not before the ladies, please.'

'But Guy has already apologised before them.'

Martin went over to the count, who stood up, and faced him. He gave him two mighty slaps and returned to his chair. Martin felt his nose bleeding, and searched desperately for something to wipe it on. The count noticed and threw him a lace-edged handkerchief, which saved Martin from his embarrassment. The guests looked very surprised at this extraordinary mark of favour, because such costly trifles were used for ornament alone. The boys were dismissed.

Hardly had they disappeared into the castle than the countess said to her husband. 'Monsieur, you yourself heard that Guy and Martin are at daggers drawn. Can't you see that Martin is a danger to your sons?'

'In anger one often threatens to kill someone.'

'Monsieur, Martin irritates Guy.'

'And Guy irritates Martin.'

'Could you not send your Martin away for a while?'

'I'd rather get rid of Guy in case something happens to me. Without Martin I should not have the pleasure today of enjoying such delightful company. M. de Méril has invited my various sons to spend the winter with him. I accepted but I shall keep Martin here. Are you satisfied?'

'Yes, to some extent.'

'Well, my pretty Amaryllis,' said the count, turning to the actress, 'what happens now to our Tartuffe?'

'He wants to seduce the lady of the house.'

'Have the two ladies decided about Mme Pernelle?'

'No,' replied the baroness. 'I am of the opinion that it would be very confusing to the audience to see two ladies playing the same role.'

'You are quite right, Madame. I feel that a judgment of Solomon is required here too. May we trouble you once more, Comte de Racon?'

'Why take all the trouble when these would serve?' said the baron, bringing out his dice. 'When anything is in doubt I usually rely upon the fall of the dice.'

His proposal was accepted. Mlle de Dismarat threw a six. The baroness replied with three, and looked very offended. Amaryllis tried to smooth the matter over by saying that she looked far too youthful to play the role of a grandmother. It was of no avail. The baroness suddenly remembered the fruit that was ripening in her garden at home and expressed doubts whether the jam making would be successful without her personal supervision. Mlle Amaryllis read out the names of the cast to see whether the baroness would accept another role, but since there were only servants' parts left, the good lady said huffily: 'A lady of quality should have sufficient good taste not to disguise herself as a maid.'

The count then saved the situation by turning to the baroness: 'But, Madame, I was looking forward to being allowed to watch the play at your side—and now apparently your jam means more to you than my company. I shall never be able to enjoy the delights of your cuisine any more.'

'Monsieur, it was not so intended.'

'Then please allow your future son-in-law to display his histrionic talent before you. Raoul would be delighted if you were to write a word of praise to his longed-for bride.'

The good lady smiled, quite appeased. 'My daughter would also be delighted. Please go on reading, my dear.'

Amaryllis continued to read and the company enjoyed her bird-like voice until the steward appeared and announced that dinner was served.

The same day, the runaway peasant lad, Bastien, was tracked by bloodhounds and given the customary fifty lashes for poaching. Louis, Guy and Constant watched the flogging. Raoul and Martin did not appear, the former because he did not care for such brutal scenes, and the latter out of anger and protest. Guy said later to Raoul that he had missed a great deal, but Raoul merely replied that when he became count he would introduce milder laws, and that at the moment he wished to be left in peace to study his part. Raoul was to play Valère, Louis Damis, and Constant the police official. There were no parts for Guy and Martin. Father Tulier was asked to act as prompter at the rehearsal and the performance, but the priest replied, with chilly politeness, that the church was against Molière, who had only the king to thank for his fame. For a priest, the church's ban on the insolent comedy, *Tartuffe*, still held good because in it even piety was mocked. These remarks caused long faces, and in future the company paid greater attention during Mass.

The ladies rehearsed very seriously, but the gentlemen were often out hunting. Amaryllis was on good terms with the countess and both ladies continued to express their mutual admiration. They avoided mentioning the count and laughed a great deal at M. d'Oubray, whom the part of Tartuffe suited admirably, although he was a very different person in real life. M. d'Oubray never knew whether they were joking or serious and was very reserved in the ladies' company. Tenelli had to play Cléante, the protagonist of healthy, human common sense, and had to copy out the parts. The vivacious actress captivated his heart ever more, but he had grown modest after his sad experience with Bice and contented himself with kisses stolen from the Baroness du Terne's pretty maid.

Since Tenelli had to appear at all the rehearsals, his five charges were left very much to themselves. They enjoyed this freedom and were always plotting something of which the steward would have undoubtedly disapproved. Recently they had been looking for treasure and had been exploring the vaulted cellars. They did not, however, visit the family crypt because they found the bronze or stone tombs, with the sculpted figures on them, rather sinister. Apart from this, they searched everywhere but found nothing except a mouldering human skeleton in one of the two oubliettes and, nearby, a closed iron door to which no one had a key. The steward declared that it led to a subterranean passage which had half collapsed. M. le Comte's father had ordered the door to be locked and the young gentlemen should not venture into the passage. The boys, however, ignored his warning, took a wax impression of the lock and ordered the village blacksmith to forge a key for them. Constant was the first to crawl with a lantern into the passage, which was only half the height of a man and ended in a pile of rubble, barring further progress. There was no sign of treasure, but the other boys crawled along the passage after Constant to show their courage before finally abandoning the search.

That evening, Guy took Martin aside and told him that in the passage he had noticed a loose stone in the wall. He had mentioned nothing to the others, for he suspected that a treasure was hidden behind the stone and he did not want to share it with so many. Would Martin help him loosen the stone? Martin asked why he in particular should help. Guy replied that he had come to the conclusion that a continued enmity between his father's friend and himself was pointless. The best thing would be to bury it by a joint escapade. Martin was even more surprised at this sudden change of attitude and said that they should at least take along the vicomte, since he had a better right to the treasure than himself. Guy made the excuse that Raoul would inherit Grandval and thus had no need of a hidden treasure, whereas he and Martin could very well make use of ten thousand gold pieces. How did Guy know that there were ten thousand? Guy replied that this sum had been mentioned in his grandfather's will but had never been found. According to the steward, their grandfather had been in the passage two years before his death and it was only too obvious why he had ordered it to be closed. Martin reflected, and the idea of the gold began to attract him. When did Guy want to descend with him? After supper, for then their absence would remain unnoticed.

After supper Guy and Martin left the dining-hall, where the last rehearsal was taking place, to carry out their mission. Raoul called Martin back. 'Why don't you watch? Tomorrow there will be two hundred and fifty guests and you won't be able to see anything except their heads.'

'I have something on with M. Guy.'

'What?'

'Oh, nothing special, Vicomte Raoul.'

'Is it a secret?'

'I'll tell you tomorrow.'

At this moment Amaryllis cried: 'Where is my beloved Valère? Where is the handsome vicomte hiding?'

'I'm here, Mademoiselle. Until tomorrow then, Martin.' The boy slipped away.

Guy was waiting for Martin with two lanterns, and hurried on ahead with his two dogs to the dungeon entrance. The boys descended the steep, damp stairs behind the dogs, and reached the iron door after passing through two vaulted chambers. Guy had the key and opened it. Martin lit the interior. 'Where did you see the loose stone, M. Guy?'

'Right at the end, to the right. Are you going to crawl on ahead?'

'I don't mind. Do you think we shall need any tools?'

'We can fetch some, if necessary.'

'We can't both go into the passage at the same time because it's too narrow to turn in. I'll crawl in.' After reaching the pile of rubble on all fours, he called over his shoulder: 'M. Guy, I can't find the loose stone. They're all quite firm.'

His voice echoed eerily under the low vaulting and he hurriedly crawled back. The soles of his feet touched the iron door and he noticed that he was locked in.

'Don't play any silly tricks, M. Guy. Open up.' There was no reply. An icy fear suddenly gripped Martin. He listened with bated breath but could hear no sound. 'M. Guy, M. Guy, let me out!' Silence. Martin kicked against the door. 'M. Guy, stop playing the fool with me. Open up!' He tried to stifle his fear with rage and made as much noise as he could by banging his heels against the iron door. Then he listened again, heard nothing, and began to plead again and to call Guy by name.

Despite his rage, Martin was intelligent enough not to utter any threats, and swore by all that was holy not to take his revenge on Guy, never to thrash him again and to forgive him everything that did not impugn the honour of his dead mother. Then he suddenly remembered the skeleton in the nearby oubliette and was overcome with terror. He began to shout for help as loudly as he could, until he grew hoarse. Then he noticed that the candle in his lantern was a mere stub. Forcing himself to remain calm, he crawled with the lantern to the pile of stones and tried to move them aside. The stones were heavy but he managed to lift them. Martin arranged them against the wall. When the pile grew lower there was an opening at the top through which he could see. He stretched his arm through with the lantern. He felt a cold draught and looked down into a hole filled with water. The passage seemed to continue on the other side, but it was stopped up with loose stones. Martin hastily threw the stones at his side into the water. They splashed and wetted him. Then there was a rumble above his head. He drew back quickly and a shower of stones rattled down into the depths. Quiet was restored at last and Martin looked out once more. The water level was now higher in the hole, and above yawned a cleft in the earth. Martin realised that there was no possibility of reaching the stopped-up passage on the far side, and crawled back with his lantern. He hoped vaguely that the iron door was now open, but it was closed as before. He began to call for help again, until the candle in his lantern went out. Now he was in pitch darkness. In wild rage he hit out with his fists, began to pray and weep and shout for the count. Each time he fell silent and listened, there was no sound. Despite the damp and cold he was sweating with fright. The echo of his own voice increased his fear, but when he stopped shouting and the silence seemed to be filled with noises, he could not keep calm and started to shout again until he had no strength left.

On the following morning, after Pierre had awakened the count, he went to Martin's room, thinking that for some reason the boy had overslept. But the room was empty and Martin's bed had not been slept in. Pierre reported this to his master, who was already growing impatient at not receiving his usual morning visit from his young friend, and was immediately sent to look for him. Pierre passed the orders on to the other servants, and the castle sprang to life. Martin could be found neither with Raoul, Louis, Constant nor Tenelli. The stable lads were asked, but no one had seen him.

The count said angrily that he did not appreciate sudden disappearances and, as soon as Martin turned up, he was to come and see him. Raoul remembered his conversation with Martin before the rehearsal the previous evening and went to the fencing room, where Constant and Louis were having a lesson, to ask Guy if he knew where Martin was.

'How should I know anything about him?'

'Because he said he had something on with you and would not tell me until this morning.'

Guy bent down and scratched his leg. 'We were in the orchard together and ate some plums.'

'Why didn't he tell me so?'

'We wanted to hollow out a marrow, put a light in it and frighten you and the others.'

'Why didn't you do it?'

'There were too many mosquitoes. The bites are still itching.'

'Did you come back with Martin?'

'Yes. He said he was going straight to bed.'

'And you watched the dress rehearsal. Guy, if I didn't know that you were Martin's bitter enemy I should feel happier about it.'

At this moment Tenelli called: 'Vicomte Raoul, start fencing with Comte Louis.' Raoul obeyed, and after a few bouts managed to win. He returned to Guy but the latter had to fence with Constant.

After this the tutor and the pupils went to the boys' living-room, where Tenelli explained fortifications from some of his own drawings. He did this on the orders of the count, who, the following spring, wanted to take the boys to the war zone to accustom them to their future profession. Guy remarked that Brayonne was terribly antiquated, but that one day he would have it rebuilt as a fortress.

'To do that you will have to get permission from the king,' replied Tenelli.

'Why?'

'Even the nobility cannot dispose of their castles and lands as they please. The king has assumed supreme power, and if any wars are to be waged it is only against the country's enemies. For example, the Comte de Racon cannot declare war on the Baron du Terne, as his grandfather could have done if it had pleased him. And that is why Grandval can no longer be given modern fortifications.'

'A pity,' said Guy.

'Modern fortifications,' continued Tenelli, 'eat up an enormous amount of money, which the king raises for the defence of France through the higher taxes.'

'Taxes which we do not have to pay,' said Guy saucily.

'Don't crow too soon, M. Guy. If the king should decide one day to revoke the nobility's freedom from taxes, you could do nothing about it.'

'Yes, we could. The entire French aristocracy would rise, as in the days of the Fronde, and Louis would be dethroned.'

'M. Guy, if you were grown up and I were to repeat your words, you would be put in the Bastille for high treason.'

In his alarm Guy looked from one to the other and asked: 'Master Tenelli, how can one storm one of these fortresses you have just drawn?'

'You have to shoot breaches into them and build up batteries for this purpose. Let us take this as the enemy position . . .' The four boys' heads bent forward. 'An attempt would be made to encircle it, then batteries would be brought up to the surrounding heights, and gradually advance along trenches, reducing their range. Breastworks would be built in front of the trenches, behind which new batteries would be placed to shoot with more effect at the fortress. Look, from this battery a trench runs forward under its protection. This is one of the fortress bastions, and that is the trench. Comte Louis, what is the meaning of those dots inside it?'

'I don't know, Master Tenelli.'

'Which of you knows?'

'I do,' said Constant. 'They are palissades to stop the attacking enemy.'

'Quite right. Vicomte Raoul, why have I drawn the fort in the shape of a star?'

'Because between the points of the star the enemy can be enfiladed.'

'Right. Now I let the enemy advance towards the breastwork.'

The boys looked at Tenelli's drawing attentively and Guy kept his mouth shut.

On their way to the midday meal, Guy said to Raoul: 'Raoul, I have something private to say to you. Come with me, quickly.'

Raoul followed him into an empty reception room which was already decorated for the expected guests.

'Raoul, when father asks which of us knows anything about Martin, please don't tell him that I was the last to be with him.'

'Really!'

'Be quiet, Raoul. I mean that father could suspect me and force a confession from me. I don't know anything, but father's methods are gruesome. From pain I could say something foolish and ruin myself, although I'm innocent. For God's sake don't breathe a word.'

'I don't trust you, Guy.'

'But I'm your brother, Raoul.'

'You wanted to shoot Martin.'

'That was only in anger. Martin threatened to kill me, and he wasn't serious either.'

'Yes . . . And yesterday evening you went and ate plums in the orchard alone as friends—or was someone else there?'

'Tenelli came later with some female.'

'Did he see you?'

'Yes. Stop, Raoul. Where are you going?'

'To Master Tenelli.'

'What for?'

'I'm going to ask him if he happened to see Martin.'

'He couldn't possibly have seen him because the moon was covered by a cloud and Martin was hiding in the branches of a tree.'

'Why? The branches can easily be reached from the ground.'

'The plums had already been picked from below.'

'That's a lie. They haven't yet started picking.'

'Raoul . . .'

'Guy, I don't trust you. I'm sorry, but I shall have to repeat what you've said to me.'

'I beg you to keep silent, Raoul. I admit that I've played a trick on Martin, but I swear that he'll appear again this evening, alive.'

'Is that so? Well, tell me where he's hiding.'

'No, I won't tell you. If you keep silent he'll appear this evening, provided that you don't spy on me.'

'What does that mean?'

'It means that I'm going to cover up for myself and try to avoid any unpleasant consequences.'

'Is he safe and sound, Guy?'

'I haven't touched a hair of his head.'

'Will you swear that?'

'Yes, by the Holy Virgin.'

'Have you locked him in somewhere?'

'Yes. Is that so dreadful?'

'No one heard him call out.'

'Will you keep silent now, or not?'

'Why don't you let him out now?'

'Because it doesn't suit me to.'

'And if I speak?'

'Then you'll only harm your friend Martin.'

'How?'

'It is in my power to kill him.'

'Are you mad, Guy?'

'Raoul, I'll tell you something. If I go and fetch Martin now, someone would see me and father would punish me afterwards. Tonight they're playing *Tartuffe*. The guests will be there and I shan't be conspicuous. Martin must swear to me to keep silent. That is why I'm waiting for nightfall, and demand the same oath of silence from you.'

'Very well. I'll swear to keep silent until after the play, but not a moment longer.'

'That's good enough for me. Thank you.'

They could hear voices from the dining-hall and the clatter of cutlery on the silver plates. Raoul and Guy slipped into their places. As expected, the count asked the boys for news of Martin. Each of them insisted that he knew nothing. The count ordered Martin's dirty washing to be fetched, so that the bloodhounds could search in the vicinity of the castle. He was in the blackest mood and hardly spoke to the ladies. The baron suggested that the boy might have gone out hunting on his own. The count replied angrily that the boy could not go hunting without permission, and that when he came home he would be taught a lesson.

'But Martin is your favourite,' said Amaryllis.

'Favouritism doesn't go as far as that.'

'He's only been away half a day.'

'He didn't sleep in his bed last night.'

'Perhaps he was in someone else's bed.'

There was a laugh, and the count forced himself to join in. 'My pretty Amaryllis,' he said, 'I have not yet noticed that Martin has fallen in love with anyone.'

'Oh, it can happen very suddenly, you know.'

'Then he would certainly be hungry and would long since have been here.'

'Monsieur, I hope that your guests mean enough to you for you to be able to do without your favourite for one whole day.'

'I'm not used to his being away, my beautiful Mademoiselle.'

' "My pretty birdie",' corrected the baron. 'Isn't that what you call her?'

' "Butterfly" would also suit her,' added the countess.

'Yes,' said d'Oubray, 'the countess is right. Why not "butterfly", Comte de Racon?'

'Because she is a tame birdie who eats out of my hand.'

'Does she really?'

'I can prove it.'

The count took a morsel from his plate and reached across the table to the actress. She stretched her neck and took the piece with pursed lips from his fingers.

'Enchanting,' cried the baron. 'Comte de Racon, does your little bird eat from your hand alone, or from anyone's?'

'I don't know. I only know that it is very particular and will not look at crumbs.'

They continued the meal amid laughter and gay jokes, and everyone seemed to have forgotten the vanished boy.

In the course of the afternoon the guests arrived, and that evening *Tartuffe* was performed. The countess, Amaryllis and M. d'Oubray received great applause. Raoul was unlucky enough to forget his words twice, although this had not happened to him at the dress rehearsal.

After the performance there was a banquet which lasted late into the night, at which the boys had to act as pages. Raoul caught Guy as he was handing a silver dish to one of the ladies.

'A word with you, Guy.'

'What do you want?'

'When are you going to fetch Martin?'

'You can see that I can't get away,' grumbled Guy, hurrying off with his dish.

At midnight the ladies retired, and the pages were finally released. Raoul caught hold of his brother in the corridor and said: 'Now come, Guy.'

'But the place is teeming with servants, Raoul. Wait until it's all quiet.'

'I tell you, Guy . . .'

'No, don't say anything. It suddenly struck me that he might have suffocated.'

'What?'

'For a joke I shut him in somewhere a trifle too enclosed.'

'And that suddenly occurs to you now! Come on, run as fast as you can. If the place is really too enclosed it's too late. You're a monster!'

'I'm very sorry, Raoul. I beg you not to betray me if he's dead.'

'Guy, you're to bring him here now, whether he's alive or dead. On my honour I won't wait a moment longer, and I swear to you that I won't remain silent. Is he in a chest?'

'Something like it.'

'Take me there.'

'No, I'm going alone . . . and I'm waiting until everyone's asleep.'

'Guy, I mean it!'

'Will you keep your mouth shut if he's alive?'

'I don't know.'

'Then he'll certainly be dead.'

'All right. If he's alive I'll keep silent, but only if he's alive.'

'Swear it?'

'I swear. But if you don't fetch him tonight I shall go early tomorrow morning to father.'

'He'll only punish you because you kept silent so long and lied at midday.'

'Even if he thrashes me to death I'll tell him everything . . . And so that you can't harm me I'll sleep tonight with Constant and Louis, instead of with you. You are the most infamous and treacherous swine to have committed such an atrocity!'

'Raoul, I'm full of remorse . . .'

'Get out of my sight!' Guy made himself scarce.

When the gentlemen were well on the way to intoxication the count unobtrusively left the table. Grouchet was waiting in an antechamber.

'I sent for you, Grouchet, although it does not seem much use. If the bloodhounds haven't found him, the hunting dogs won't either. I've already promised a large reward. Give me your advice. Have you any suspicions?'

'M. le Comte, I have had Bastien flogged. You are hated by the peasants. Perhaps they have taken their revenge on you by killing Martin.'

The count turned pale. 'Grouchet, but we should at least have found a trace.'

'Put Bastien on the rack. If anyone knows anything it must be Bastien.'

'Yes, Grouchet. Have Bastien brought here. I'll attend the proceedings.' Grouchet gave a military salute and left.

Two hours after midnight Guy made his way with two dogs, a lantern and a rush-light to the oubliettes. When he passed the torture chamber he heard the sound of groaning and screaming. Despite his curiosity he hurried past and reached the dungeon stairs unseen. Sending his dogs on ahead, he followed them slowly down the steps.

In the lowest vault he knocked on the iron door. No sound came from within. Opening it cautiously, he caught sight of Martin's feet. He tugged at them. Martin quivered and uttered a hoarse scream. Guy swiftly closed the iron door again, reflected for a moment and then reopened it.

'Martin, it's Guy de Brayonne. I've come to set you free.'

Martin kicked his feet and slipped slowly out on his stomach. He turned round and was about to stand up, but sank down on the ground at Guy's feet. 'Thank you,' he croaked, and looked up into the gleaming barrel of a cavalry pistol.

'I'll shoot you, Martin, if you don't swear what I want.'

Trembling, Martin lifted his stiff, torn hands.

'Swear that you'll tell no one where you were,' insisted Guy.

'I swear.'

'Swear that you'll tell no one who locked you in.'

'I swear.'

'Swear that you won't take your revenge on me.'

'I swear.'

'Swear it by your mother.'

'By my mother.'

'Repeat what you have sworn.'

Martin, who could scarcely speak, repeated: 'I'll take no revenge. I won't tell anyone where I was or who locked me in.'

'Good. You're free.'

Guy picked up the rush-light and ran up the steps with his dogs.

Martin took the lantern and staggered up the steps. When he reached the torture chamber one of the torturers came out.

'A ghost. M. le Comte . . . M. le Comte . . . it's Martin.'

'Stop,' ordered the count, and the torturer opened the door for him. Martin's lantern fell to the ground, broke and went out. The count stood in the brightly lit doorway. 'Martin . . .' the count caught him as he fell. 'Where were you, Martin? Where have you come from?'

The boy's clothes were torn to shreds at the knees and elbows and his flesh was bleeding. His hands were bruised and cut.

'Martin, you smell of the grave. Hi, you in there! Untie that lad and carry him back to the village. I'll see that he receives compensation. Can't you speak, Martin?'

'Water,' groaned the boy, and the count repeated: 'Water for Martin.' A cup was brought immediately. Martin drank greedily. 'Now tell me where you were.'

'I swore to remain silent, M. le Comte.'

'You swore?'

'I beg of you not to ask me.'

'I won't ask you any more.' The count returned to the room and said to one of the grooms: 'Set a dog on the trail and inform me. Call Pierre.'

He turned to Martin again, who stood leaning against him.

'Give me your hand.' He led the limping boy to the inhabited part of the castle, a groom preceding them with the light. Pierre came hurrying up.

'Here you are, Pierre. Clean him up and put him to bed. Tell Borel to bind his ankle. Give him a hot drink and something to eat. Then report to me. I'm going to bed.'

The count retired to bed, and a little later there was a knock on his door.

'Come in.' The old steward appeared.

'M. le Comte, the dog made for the sewers and wanted to go into the underground passage. The iron door has been closed since the death of your late father and there is no key, but I found it open and this key was in the lock.' He handed the newly forged key to the count.

'Ask both the castle smith and the village blacksmith who made it and who ordered it,' said the count, handing back the key.

'Tonight, M. le Comte?'

'Yes, immediately.'

The old man bowed and left the room, and a few moments later a groom was galloping towards the village.

After an hour there was a further knock on the count's door. He was still awake. 'Come in.' The steward reported:

'M. le Comte, the village blacksmith forged the key for the five young gentlemen from a wax impression.'

'All five of them?'

'Yes, M. le Comte. They all visited his smithy and watched him at his work.'

'Thank you. Lock the iron door and keep the key. You can go.' Once more there was a knock, and on his way out the steward met Pierre. 'What is it?' asked the count.

'Here is Martin, M. le Comte.'

The boy limped into the room and remained standing there. He was wearing a nightcap on his freshly washed and dried hair and nothing but a clean nightshirt.

'He did not want to stay in his room and followed me here,' explained Pierre.

'Why?'

'He's frightened of the dark.'

'Light the candles on the mantelpiece and put some wood on the fire. Martin, get into my bed.'

Martin was hampered by the bandages on his hands, elbows and knees, but he had soon crept under the count's blanket and pressed close to him.

'Why are you trembling like that, my boy?'

'Please have candles lit.'

'They're already alight—look! Has he eaten, Pierre?'

'Two bowls of soup, that's all.'

'Are those grazes deep?'

'Some are, M. le Comte.'

'But there's no need to worry?'

'I don't like it, M. le Comte. It seems as though . . .' The servant behind Martin's back tapped his forehead. The count gave a start.

'Pierre, bring a large jug of strong mulled wine.'

'Yes, M. le Comte.'

The count sat up beside Martin, who stared into the candlelight. 'Why don't you close your eyes?'

'Because then it would be dark.'

'Aren't you tired?'

'I dare not go to sleep.'

The count removed Martin's nightcap and felt his brow. 'You're a little feverish. Are you in pain?'

'Yes, my knees hurt when I touch them.'

'Lie still.'

Martin looked up at him and asked anxiously: 'Am I dreaming or are you really here?'

'No, this time it's no dream.' Martin smiled and touched him gently with his bandaged hands before staring again at the candlelight.

Pierre brought in the spiced wine and handed the count a glass, which he held out to Martin. 'Drink this, Martin, I'll hold your head.'

'I'm not thirsty any more, M. le Comte.'

'I want you to drink.'

Martin obeyed unwillingly.

'Fill it up again, Pierre.'

'M. le Comte, the wine is very strong,' said Pierre hesitantly.

'I am purposely making him drunk. Drink it up, Martin.'

The boy forced himself to swallow it, and the count ordered Pierre to fill the glass once more. Martin tried to refuse, but his resistance soon collapsed. He drank and began to wail: 'M. le Comte . . . everything's beginning to sway. Your bed is swaying. Please stop rocking it. M. le Comte!' The count dismissed the servant.

'Martin, why can't you say where you were locked in?'

'I swore . . . protect me . . . please protect me!'

'Why did you swear?'

'Because he threatened me with a pistol. M. le Comte, the left-hand candlestick is slipping off the mantelpiece . . .'

'Who was holding the pistol, Martin?'

'M. Guy held it, but he didn't shoot . . . Oh, I feel sick . . . Everywhere I look things are going round and round, and I dare not close my eyes or else it will be black night and when I reopen them you'll have disappeared and I shall be terrified again. Ah, God, I feel sick . . . I feel terribly sick. Where can I go? M. le Comte, I must be sick.'

The count gave him a push in the nick of time, so that he vomited on the floor, and called for the valet. Pierre saw the mess and ran to fetch a second servant. A dishevelled maid appeared with a pail and some rags. She wiped the floor and asked leave to retire.

'What shall we do with Martin now, M. le Comte?' asked Pierre.

'I'll keep him with me. You can go.' Pierre left.

'M. le Comte,' wailed Martin, 'I still feel giddy.'

'It doesn't matter. Lie still.'

'M. le Comte, the candles have grown shorter!'

'They're still long enough to burn until daybreak.'

'Are you certain they will burn so long.'

'I'm certain. You can rely upon me.'

'Is the door locked, M. le Comte?'

'It's not necessary.'

'But what if the skeleton appears . . .'

'No skeleton will come here.'

'M. le Comte, I can hear something.'

'It's Pierre snoring in the next room.'

'There was a creak as though someone were coming.'

'That was only the cupboard. It often creaks.'

'Please don't go to sleep, M. le Comte.'

'You go to sleep, Martin. I'll keep watch for you.'

'If I could only keep my eyes open so that I could see what was approaching. M. le Comte, the bedhangings. Look, they're moving. There's something behind them. There's a rustle in the folds. Protect me. Help, help!'

The count shook Martin to bring him to himself. Pierre looked into the room.

'Pierre, sponge him with cold water. Quick! He's lost consciousness.'

The valet hurried up with wet towels and did as he was bid. Martin gasped for air and grew calmer. The count took him in his arms and laid him out flat by his side. Martin stared at one of the candles until weariness overcame him and his eyelids closed.

An hour before dawn the count was woken up by ear-splitting screams. Martin was hitting out like a madman. The count threw him out of bed, stood up, took his riding crop and started to thrash him. Martin recognised him.

'I've done nothing wrong, M. le Comte.'

'You rampaged like a savage. Get into bed and turn your face to the wall, quickly.'

Martin obeyed. The count noticed that the bandage on Martin's left knee had become loose, and retied it.

'Now, are you going to lie quietly or not?'

'I'm lying quite still. Let me stay here.' The count got back to bed. 'M. le Comte, the candles are now mere stumps.'

'Do you want a beating?'

'No, no. I'll be quiet.' The man soon fell asleep once more, but Martin remained awake.

Outside, dawn was breaking. Martin sat cautiously up in bed and communed gently with the day. 'It's growing light. It's growing light again. Day is breaking and night has passed. Oh day, oh friendly, kindly day! I greet your light, your beautiful, kindly light. Thank you, day, for appearing.'

The count opened his eyes, and since Martin was sitting up quietly at his side he let him go on talking undisturbed until Pierre came in to wake them.

'Good morning, M. le Comte.'

'Good morning.'

'Thank you, Monsieur,' cried Martin, 'for keeping me here with you.'

'Are you no longer afraid?'

'No, it's daylight, now.'

'Do you trust yourself to sleep in the daytime?'

'Shall I?'

'Yes, you look green and hollow-eyed. You'll stay in bed today.'

'In your bed?'

'Yes, Pierre, you look after him and see to his needs. Call me if you think it necessary. Lie down again, Martin.' Martin lay down, watched the count get dressed, then suddenly fell asleep. The count tiptoed from the room.

Just as the four young gentlemen in the courtyard were about to set out for their morning ride with Tenelli, a lackey summoned them to wait upon the count without the tutor. He was in the dining-hall. The boys exchanged glances. Like everyone else in the castle, they knew that Martin had been locked in the underground passage, and that on account of the key they were all under suspicion of having committed the deed.

On the way to the dining-hall, Louis said to Raoul: 'I'm afraid your father will be very angry. Do you think he will believe our innocence?'

'I hope so, Louis.'

'I don't feel at all happy about this business, Raoul. I wish we'd never embarked upon that ridiculous treasure hunt. Why did Guy have to lose the key?'

'If only Martin has not lost his reason!' Raoul said with a sigh. 'Pierre loves telling stories which make your flesh creep. Let's hope he's exaggerated this time too.'

The count was standing by the french window looking into the park. When he heard the boys enter he turned round. 'What made you try to suffocate Martin?'

Louis stepped forward. 'Comte de Racon, your accusation is untrue. We did not lock Martin in.'

'You ordered the village blacksmith to forge the key.'

'Father,' interrupted Guy, 'I lost the key out riding a week ago.'

'Is that so!'

Guy looked his father straight in the eye.

'Are you speaking the truth, Guy?'

'I swear it, Father.'

The count's hand felt for the grip of his riding crop, but he controlled himself.

'Why are you so pale, Raoul? Do you know something?'

'No, Father. No more than Guy.'

'Come, Raoul, perhaps Guy knows something. What do you think?'

'I know nothing, Father,' replied the vicomte.

'You've started trembling. Why?'

'Because you frighten me. You know that I'm afraid of you.'

'Then you must have a guilty conscience. Perhaps you hid the key.'

'No, by all the saints, no!'

'You're all very ready to swear. Martin also took an oath. His brain is still confused by the terrible fright he was given. What is your opinion, Raoul? Do you think it's very difficult to make him drunk and then wring a confession from him without his being aware of it?'

Guy turned pale. The count looked at him out of the corner of his eyes and continued to address Raoul: 'Pierre is a gossip. He has perhaps already told you how drunk Martin was last night. I will be lenient to anyone who confesses his guilt. Has one of you something to say?'

Raoul broke down. 'Father, I rescued Martin because I happened to find out with whom he was last, two nights ago. I asked the person in question and learnt that he had locked Martin in. The guilty person refused to tell me the place and I was foolish enough to imagine that it was not dangerous. Only when he told me that Martin could suffocate did I grow afraid. I wanted to report the matter to you, but I was threatened that in this event Martin would be killed and I had to swear to keep silent. Martin is alive and I will not betray the guilty party.'

The count peered intently into the terror-stricken blue eyes. Almost hesitantly he asked: 'Raoul, must I force you to tell me the name of the guilty person?'

'Why should you destroy my honour, Father, when you can learn the name from Martin, unless you know it already? I will try to be steadfast, but I know that I should betray it. Father, please spare me this disgrace.' He flung himself at the count's feet. His father helped him to rise and said:

'Raoul I shall not abuse your honour, just as I have not abused Martin's. Take that as you like. Even if I knew who the guilty party was, I could not punish him now. Do you understand? Not now.' Guy breathed with relief and insolently thrust out a leg.

'Raoul,' continued the count, 'you saved Martin's life. You may ask a favour of me.'

'Let me go on reading, Father.'

'You can read by daylight, but not by candlelight, Raoul.'

'Very well, Father, I will only read by daylight in future. Thank you.'

' "In future". What does that mean?'

'I have been reading in secret,' replied Raoul.

'Where did you get the books?'

'I had a second key to the library forged.'

For the moment the count was speechless. Then he gave him a resounding box on the ears and said:

'Now be off with you to your riding lesson.' The boys ran out of the room into the corridor. The count walked out on to the terrace and made his way down the steps into the park, where his guests were enjoying themselves.

That evening, between five and six, the count visited Amaryllis in the luxuriously appointed room which Bice had once occupied. The actress was already dressed for supper and was sitting on the gilt bed; the yellow hangings billowed above her in artistic folds. The count knelt before her, took her tiny silk-clad foot in his right hand and an equally tiny shoe in his left.

'You poor birdie, the shoe is too small.'

'Oh, that oaf of a shoemaker. May he burn in the largest cauldron in hell! I shall get blisters when I dance—and I love dancing.'

'Can't you get the shoes on?'

'Just. I raise my foot in the air until it grows thin and then I can force it into the shoe.' She withdrew her foot, swung it on to the bed, and leant back against the pillows.

'Comte de Racon, it's going to rain. The fine weather in the country is over. Paris is awakening from her summer reverie. Paris is awakening and soon will be pulsating with life, remembering me, and waiting to fête me. The ladies of the Court are longing to shine in their boxes, with their diamonds and pearls, and the gentlemen hope this winter to win the favours of those dancers who refused them a year ago. I seem to hear the call: "Amaryllis, where is Amaryllis?" I am coming. I am coming, I shall wing my way towards you.' She spread out her arms and fluttered them.

'Little bird of passage,' said the count, 'Perhaps I will fly there after you.'

He sat on the bed and took one of her feet in his hands. 'It has already grown slimmer. What fragile, beautiful legs. Is your knee round or pointed?'

'Surely you know that by now, Comte de Racon.'

'I am so forgetful.'

She thrust his hands away. 'You are disturbing my dreams of Paris.'

'Amaryllis, I think you are a trifle displeased with me. Why?'

'I have learnt something.'

'Is it sad news?'

'Oh no, it concerns you, Comte de Racon.'

'Me?'

'Don't look so innocent.'

'You make me feel guilty, although I have no idea why.'

'There is a dark-haired peasant girl in the castle.'

'You mean Jeanne. She is merely a relief after all these polished gallantries—that's all.'

'Monsieur, I should not have thought that gallantry would be such a strain on you.'

'Sometimes,' he explained, 'I must have a simple girl to tumble.'

'Oh!' A shocked look appeared on her face. He smiled.

'This little foot, for instance, I cannot seize roughly.'

'I wonder what that would be like? Stop . . . you're crushing it. Now it will swell up and I shall never get it into my shoe!'

'Now you're angry, you see, yet you were curious.'

'Yes, I am angry with you—and I am still curious, M. le Comte. Are you by nature a savage or a gallant?'

'Different women think differently on that score.'

Amaryllis blinked coquettishly. 'I should very much like to know what you are really like.'

'According to Madeleine, I am like Pan.'

'Let me see you as Pan. Oh, my dress, you clumsy lout!'

'You wanted it that way.'

'No, I shall never want it again—at least not in this dress. Look, the spangles are torn here and the bow is quite crushed.'

He began to sing:

'Swallow, little swallow
Be not angry and forgive me
Give your little hand to kiss
I repent. Do let me stay!'

'You sang that very charmingly. What a pity you are a

count! You could have been a great success as a singer.'

'I am satisfied if I'm a success with you. Now why do you pout?'

'I'm angry with my dress now because it prevents me from enjoying your savagery.'

'Let us punish it by removing it.'

'But then I shall have no protection against you.'

'Don't be afraid, Jeanne is still alive.'

They both began to undo her bodice and their fingers hampered each other. There was a knock on the door. The count sat up, and the actress covered her bosom with a kerchief. 'Who's there?' she called petulantly.

Her plump maid appeared. 'Mademoiselle, Pierre wishes to speak to M. le Comte.' Before Amaryllis could reply, the count said:

'Let him in.'

Pierre entered the room and announced: 'M. le Comte, it's growing dark and Martin is crying for you.'

'Is he alone?'

'No, Dominique is with him.'

'That should be enough.'

'He's trembling with fear, M. le Comte. We have had to light six candles. He's terrified at every shadow.'

'I'll come. Please excuse me, Amaryllis.'

'What, Comte de Racon, are you leaving me?'

'Join the guests in the salon. They will be delighted to see you.' He followed the servant from the room.

Pierre's suspicions seemed justified, for Martin's nerves remained shattered. His grazes healed in a few days, but as soon as it grew dark, fear of the night, which for him was peopled with terror and ghosts, overcame him. The count realising that he could achieve nothing by sternness let Martin continue to sleep in his bed. He was unaware of the gossip to which this gave rise, and when Amaryllis hinted that in his anxiety for Martin he was behaving like a lover whose mistress was ill, he laughed at her for playing a comedy of jealousy. She must not take it amiss that he could no longer spend his nights as he pleased. In any case, Eros was by no means averse to daylight.

As soon as all the guests, with the exception of Mlle Amaryllis and M. d'Oubray had left, the count let Martin take part once more in the riding and fencing lessons with the young gentlemen. It soon became apparent that Martin had lost his former self-assurance. In the first bout with Guy he was defeated, and from now on was beaten constantly by all the other boys. In riding practice it was the same story. When he tried to make a stubborn horse obey, Guy jeered at him, and within a few minutes he was lying in the sand. Tenelli and M. d'Ouville were perplexed and informed the count.

The count took Martin away from his comrades and allowed only Raoul to look after him. Raoul confessed to his friend that he knew about Guy's misdeed. Martin burst into tears, embraced him and said that he found no pleasure in having been saved because, as any one could see, his courage was waning every day. He feared that one day the count would tire of this and banish him from his bed. Then he would be lost. Raoul consoled him and repeated Martin's fears to his father, who assured Martin that he would not leave his friend in the lurch. He took him for rides and practised fencing with him, but the slightest reprimand, the most friendly reproach, upset the boy so much that the count often had to break off the lesson. He could no longer allow Martin to ride his own horses as before, because he had no control over them. When a horse refused a jump for Martin, the count was forced to make him dismount and ride the horse over the obstacle himself. Martin suffered terribly. The count fell silent in his presence, and when he informed him one day that he would perhaps go to war that year, Martin felt that his fate was sealed because he realised, as well as the count did, that he would be useless on a campaign.

One fine autumn afternoon when the count had gone hunting with M. d'Oubray and the four boys, Martin went for a stroll on his own in the park. He avoided the shadows of the arboured walks and the tall hedges and remained on the sunny paths. He suddenly noticed the dark figures of the old spinster and Father Tulier, who had discovered him and were approaching with solicitude. Martin fled along a passage which led from the park into the orchard.

The pears were being picked. Martin stood and watched. The foliage of the trees had partially taken on autumnal tints. In the clear September sun the fruit glittered like gold. One of the maids climbed down from her ladder and went over to the boy. It was Jeanne, the prettiest maid in the castle.

'M. Martin,' she said, 'I have long wanted to ask a favour of M. le Comte, but I do not dare to ask it unless you are there. Will you greet him when he returns from the hunt?'

'No,' replied Martin, turning his head away.

'I beg you, M. Martin.'

'You can follow me when I leave the orchard. Maybe I shall meet him somewhere, but don't come into the castle with me. Your presence would only embarrass me.'

'Thank you, M. Martin.'

Jeanne returned to her pear tree, where one of the men was just climbing the ladder. Martin picked a few plums from a heavily laden tree, sat down in the grass and began to eat listlessly.

In the distance he could hear the sound of horns and the baying of hounds. Jeanne looked over at Martin, who did not stir. The huntsmen had returned. Martin continued to eat his plums. Suddenly, some chestnuts rattled down on his head from behind. He jumped up with a start and saw the four young gentlemen roaring with laughter. Guy threw another, and Martin ducked too late.

'Throw them back at him, Martin,' cried Raoul. The boy picked up two chestnuts and Guy took a step towards him.

'I forbid you to throw them.'

Martin let fall the chestnuts. 'Why do you stare at me as though I were Satan?' asked Guy. Martin did not reply.

'Look friendly, Martin.'

'I can look as I please.'

'And I can kill you.' Guy lowered his voice to a whisper: 'It is terrifying in the grave.'

Martin shivered. 'M. Guy, you mustn't murder me.'

'I was only joking. You know me, Martin. As a joke, I'll honour you with a touch of my whip. There!'

Martin seized the upraised arm, then the handle of his hunting knife. Guy grinned:

'Go on, attack me with the knife. No you don't dare, because you are afraid of me. The worms crawl in the grave. Look behind you—over there. A corpse's hand is springing out of the ground.'

Martin turned round with a start. Guy laughed uproariously and slapped his thighs. 'Ha, ha! Martin can see ghosts in broad daylight. Martin is cuckoo!'

Raoul stood beside Martin. 'Guy, leave us immediately.'

'I was only teasing him. How pale he is. Martin, the corpse's hand is waving.' Raoul lifted his riding crop. Guy sprang away with a laugh, taking the grinning Constant with him. Louis went over to Martin and Raoul.

'Why do you let yourself be terrorised, Martin?' he asked. The unfortunate boy covered his face with his hands.

'I can't help it, Comte Louis.'

Raoul put his arm round his shoulders. 'You're suffering from nerves, Martin, but it will pass.'

'Guy was disgusting. I shall tell him so,' said Louis. 'He doesn't behave like a gentleman.' A rotten apple suddenly burst in the grass close to Martin.

'That was Guy again,' cried Raoul. 'You just wait!' He ran off with Louis in the direction from which the apple had been thrown. Martin fled from the orchard, followed by Jeanne, the maid.

The count arrived from the kennels. Martin stopped. 'What have you been up to, Martin?'

'Nothing, M. le Comte.'

'That is too little.'

'Yes, Monsieur.'

'What is the matter? Are you crying?'

'No, Monsieur.'

'You look to me as if you were.'

'M. le Comte, I get frightened for no reason.'

'That will pass. What does Jeanne want?'

'She has a favour to ask of you.'

'Very well, Jeanne. Out with it.'

Martin stood aside. Jeanne looked appealingly across to him. Smoothing her apron, she began in a halting voice:

'M. le Comte, the tradesman's son, Gaspard, has promised to marry me and now he says he won't wait any longer. His parents want him to take cross-eyed Tinette because she has never been to the castle. M. le Comte, be gracious and give us permission to marry.'

The count looked her up and down. 'I see no good reason why I should send you home.'

'Heavens, M. le Comte, I shall soon not be slim any more.'

'You'll remain in the castle.'

'Then he'll take Tinette, M. le Comte.'

'That's all right as far as I'm concerned. I'll give you to someone else.'

'M. le Comte, it's been almost a week since you sent for me.'

'I'll send for you today or tomorrow.'

'M. le Comte, I'll drown myself if I don't get Gaspard.'

'The water will be far too cold. Go back to the kitchen.'

He turned his back on her, beckoned to Martin and walked off with him. Jeanne hid her face in her apron and, weeping bitterly, ran over the bridge into the castle.

At the end of September the count received a letter, which put him in the best of spirits. Immediately after the midday meal he retired to his study to write a reply, taking the greatest pains over his handwriting.

At this moment Pierre announced the countess. The count laid down his quill and rose to his feet:

'I'm honoured, Madame. Please sit down. You come at a most propitious time. The Marquis de Chassigny writes to me that the king mentioned my name during a hunt, and the Duc de Luxembourg suggested that he should give me a cavalry command. They have suffered great losses and the marshals are looking for capable officers to fill the gaps which have occurred. I have been given the remnants of a light horse regiment. That is better than nothing. In a few days I am going to headquarters. Have you come to see me on a very important matter, or will you allow me to finish my letter?'

The countess remained standing. 'Monsieur, I am surprised and overjoyed that once more the prospect of honour and glory lies open to you. I beg you to take Martin with you.'

'No, I can't use children in this war which looks like becoming a retreat. The Dutch have opened their dykes and flooded the country. It is hoped that the frosts will form ice bridges.

Martin will remain at Grandval with Raoul. I am sending Guy the day after tomorrow, with Tenelli, to the Court of the Duchesse de Bouillon. Chassigny writes that he has arranged a pageship for Raoul. I am giving the post to Guy to part him from Martin. As soon as Tenelli returns he is to take Raoul, Louis, Constant and Martin to M. de Méril. Would you like to go to Paris? My house there has been empty long enough. If you feel so inclined, go to Court and prepare for my return. I am convinced of your fidelity. Would you have the strength to become one of the queen's ladies-in-waiting?'

'Monsieur, what sudden changes you propose! But before I reply, please hear why I came to see you. I beg you most urgently either to take Martin with you or to part him from Raoul. My son has struck up a friendship with him, and you will probably understand why I am anxious to end this friendship.'

'Why? I do not understand you.'

'Monsieur, must I be more explicit.'

'I entreat you to be, Madame. I am in a hurry to complete my letter.'

'Monsieur, since, like Jupiter, you love a Ganymede, I am afraid that Ganymede might seduce Raoul to enjoy the same type of love.'

The count's dark face took on a deeper shade. 'Madame!'

'Please do not feign indignation, Monsieur.'

'I beg you to leave my study.'

He opened the door for her, but she stood firm.

'Monsieur, I refuse to leave until I have your consent that you will remove Martin for ever from my sons.'

'You have no proof.'

'Everyone knows that you have shared your bed for more than a week with Martin, whose character has changed remarkably.'

'Madame, Martin's nerves have been destroyed by being locked in the subterranean passage.'

'Or by you.'

'Leave me immediately!'

'Remove Martin, or I shall have to appeal to your cousin Gérard de Montignon for help.'

The count swept from the room, banging the door behind

him. The countess sat down on a chair and reflected. Pierre came in, removed the unfinished letter and the writing material from the table and left the room. After a while the countess followed.

That afternoon the count spent a long time with the master of the hunt and the bailiff. He despatched grooms to the post station, to his various villages and to the tenant farmers, demanding that they should pay their year's rent forthwith. Then he ordered supper to be sent up to his study for Martin and himself and spent a few hours with the actress, who congratulated him on his recent promotion, displayed some anxiety as to his safety and wooed him even more than usual with her gay charms. But his mood had been so soured that he behaved discourteously and tactlessly to Amaryllis, until she dubbed him a coarse soldier, took offence, and was glad when at last it was time for supper.

The count ate with Martin in his study, in a blaze of candlelight, without addressing a word to the boy. Martin was pale and on the verge of tears. He could hardly swallow his food and took great pains that this should pass unnoticed. Not until the count stood up from the table did he dare to ask what was to happen to him when he went to war. The count did not reply. Martin fell at his feet and implored him not to abandon him. The count left him lying there and ordered him to get into bed. Martin obeyed.

When the count retired a little later, he found Martin in tears. 'Yes, child, now you are howling. I don't know what to do with you. I really don't know, Martin.'

'Oh, Monsieur, without you I shall be completely lost.'

'So it would appear. Pierre has just told me that Father Tulier spent the afternoon with you. What did he say?'

'I had to confess. He asked me what you did with me at night, and I said to him that you kicked me away if I lay too close to you. He asked me if I had to kiss you.'

'And what did you reply?'

'I said I should be happy had I been allowed to, for I love you very much. He said that such a love was sinful. I told him that it was news to me that one was not allowed to love one's friend and father. Tell me, M. le Comte, are you still my friend, even though I am afraid of the dark?'

'I am still your friend. What did the Father reply?'

'He said I should return to my own bed, but I replied that I should be afraid. Then he offered to let me sleep in his room. I said it was very good of him but I would only do so if you sent me to him. Don't send me to Father Tulier, his room smells musty and the huge crucifix looks ghostly.'

'Martin, I can't make use of you in a war. I had intended to leave you here with Raoul, since Guy is going to the Duchesse de Bouillon's Court as a page. But this plan has been ruined for me today. How does Raoul behave to you.'

'He is always very friendly.'

'I'm afraid, Martin, you will have to accept the Father's offer, gracefully.'

'Oh, Monsieur, have pity! Take me with you.'

'Tell me, in what capacity?'

'As a stable boy . . as a servant, only let me remain with you.'

'Have you no pride left?'

'Monsieur, all that I have left is my love for you.'

The count laughed bitterly. 'And that love is sinful. If I could punish the rogue who locked you in, no chastisement would be severe enough . . . and yet it would not help you. Martin, I'll give you one more chance. If you sleep tonight without candlelight, I'll take you with me.'

'But, Monsieur, the fire in the grate does not always burn brightly.'

'Your future lies in your own hands.'

Martin climbed over the count and went over to the candelabra. The count watched him. The boy blew out the candles one after the other, then turned his back to the fire.

'M. le Comte, it's nearly dark. God, how black your bed-hangings are! Say something . . . say that you are there.'

'I'm here, Martin.'

'M. le Comte, I can't come to you. The corner has sprung to life. Look . . . two tall shadows are in front of me.'

'They're your legs.'

'When I move, everything moves, Oh God! Oh God! If the fire behind me goes out! The chimney is a pitch-black hole.'

At that moment a log fell into the embers. Martin gave a

start. The count sprang out of bed, lifted him up, carried him across the room and laid him in his former place against the wall.

'Calm yourself, Martin. I'll light all the candles again.'

'And you won't take me with you . . .?'

The man lit the candles on the mantelpiece and returned to Martin. 'Now everything's the same as it was before. Don't howl, I can't bear it. Be as affectionate as you like and don't think of tomorrow. We'll sleep on it.'

Martin hid his face in the count's raven hair and whispered: 'This is the only darkness of which I'm not afraid. Here I can sleep, but you usually kick me away.'

'I won't tonight.'

'Monsieur, when you were asleep, I often kissed you near your eyes, because the skin is soft there.'

'Do you know what the Father meant by sinful love?'

'Oh, a little. But I pretended not to understand.'

'So you have not lost your cunning.'

'Can I kiss you?'

'As far as I'm concerned.'

'Monsieur, I feel that my life has come to an end. Everything is burnt out in me. I feel that you are at my side, and as long as you are there my fear cannot kill me. Father Tulier said I should pray to the Virgin Mary so that I could find my courage again. But I told him that in that awful passage no one could have cried to her more fervently than I did. He replied that She had sent Raoul to save me. That may be so, but I cannot really believe it for Raoul is a doubter. I can't pray any more. Monsieur, if you cannot help me, then no one can. You are my sole salvation. You gave me permission to kiss you. I can think of nothing else except that I love you . . . and can feel nothing except that I am close to you. Thank you, Monsieur, I am happy.'

The boy kissed the count's temples, his pock-marked cheek, and then, very softly, his lips. He pressed his face against the fine linen shirt between his shoulder and neck and remained there motionless. The man caught hold of his thick, brown curly hair and fondled it for a while.

'Martin, suppose I wanted what the Father has forbidden?'

'I don't know exactly what it is but tell me. I would do

anything for you.'

'Take off your nightshirt, Martin.'

Martin knelt at his side, took off the garment without hesitation and remained in a kneeling position. The count folded his arms behind his neck and watched him dispassionately through half-closed lids. Martin had very broad shoulders, almost feminine in their roundness, a well arched chest with no trace of ribs despite his slimness and narrow hips reminiscent of a Greek torso.

'You are beautiful,' said the count. 'I did not know that you looked like that.'

He suddenly caught hold of the boy, and leant over him. Martin was not afraid. He looked calmly up at the man and his still childish mouth offered all its softness. The count clenched his teeth.

'Martin.'

'Yes, Monsieur.'

'To think that it would be so easy to destroy you utterly!'

'Monsieur, what I still am belongs to you.'

'Martin, you look at me as she did on her last day on earth. Are you—too—going to die on me?'

'What do you mean,' asked Martin. 'I am alive for you.'

'Yes, for me, with the last vestiges of your true self. Martin, what were you . . . and what have you become? And what could you become tomorrow? I'll make no girl of you.'

'Don't you want me?'

'Yes, I own you, yet I can't stand it any more. Everything I love perishes.'

'Do you love me then?'

'You ask that? I love you as I have never loved a woman. I love you, and yet I cannot help you.' The man shifted his weight and flung himself down on his back beside the boy.

'I didn't know you loved me,' Martin whispered. 'You never said so. Do you still love me?'

'Yes, I cannot rid myself of it. Had I known that it would end like this, I would have left you with the farmer. Today you're worthless. I realise it and I love you all the same. The fires of hell burn within me.'

'Monsieur, I will conquer my fear. Be a little patient. Tell me how I can do it.'

'What does one do with a horse that refuses a hurdle?' asked the count angrily.

'You take him by the rein,' replied Martin, 'show him the hurdle, coax him and finally make him jump it.'

'Yes, and once it has jumped it has conquered its fear. Now you know what you have to do. But until then you cannot do without the candles. Do not torture yourself with pointless attempts to please me. Perhaps time will heal you. Do not be sad.'

'Monsieur, I must go down to the dungeons again, and crawl into the passage. That is where fear took hold of me and there I will fight it. I must be worthy of your love. Monsieur, I must succeed.'

'Don't get excited. Don't overheat your poor brain any more. Lie still, Martin, and think of something else.'

'Monsieur, I shall think all night that you love me, and tomorrow I will go down into the passage. I'm not boasting, Monsieur. I am really doing it for you.'

'You might have tried to do it earlier and failed.'

'But then I did not know that you cared for me, Monsieur. I can hold fast to your love.'

'What are you doing?'

'I am putting on my nightshirt.'

'Lie in my arms and go to sleep.'

'You are very kind to me, Monsieur.'

Martin slept late, and, on the count's orders, Pierre did not wake him. The valet sat by the bed until he woke and informed him that the count had long since left for his morning ride. Martin got up, refused Pierre's offer of help to dress, got ready, and breakfasted in the study. He ate his soup and a slice of smoked meat before going down into the courtyard to wait for the count.

The new façade still lay in the shadow. Beyond the sunny postern gate the pollarded elms gleamed gold in the long avenue. Overhead the sky was as clear as deep blue glass. A fresh breeze sprang up and the leaves began to dance. At last the scarlet riding coats came into sight. The actress, in an enchanting rhinegrave, was riding a docile grey beside the count. M. d'Oubray followed, in a shabby brown velvet habit, and the four young gentlemen brought up the rear. The porter opened the gate and the horses' hooves rang out on the cobblestones. The grooms were already in attendance. The company dismounted and entered the castle through the new doorway. Martin noticed that the count was jesting with the actress, and remained where he was.

Guy turned round and came up to him: 'Well, Martin, how do you feel now? He didn't even glance at you.' Martin did not reply. Guy gave him a light tap on the head with his riding crop.

'Wake up. I've got an idea, Martin. Go and borrow a girl's dress so that you'll appeal to him more. I suggest a pale blue ribbon in your hair. Shall I get you some rose water? Hi, have you gone dumb?'

'Monsieur Guy, I have nothing to say to you.'

'Are you becoming insolent again?'

'Not yet?'

'What does that mean?'

Martin shrugged his shoulders. Raoul ran out of the castle at this moment and called from a distance: 'Martin, father sent me to fetch you. Hurry, he's changing.'

Martin ran up to the count's room and arrived out of breath. 'Good morning, M. le Comte, I have a favour to beg of you. I need the key to the underground passage.'

'It's with the steward. I should prefer that you gave up your intention.'

'Why do you want to stop me, M. le Comte?'

'Because I am frightened for you. I've encouraged you to commit a folly. I'll fence with you now in the park. Go and fetch the practice foils.'

The count fenced with Martin on a broad sunny path between two box-fringed beds of asters.

'Martin, you've never been so negligent as you are today. You're lunging blindly as though I were not there.'

'Monsieur, I want that key.'

'You're to pay attention. Things can't go on like this.'

'Forgive me, M. le Comte.'

'You're not trying. Here take my foil.'

'M. le Comte, I must go down that vault.'

'You deserve to be thrashed.'

'M. le Comte, tomorrow I will fence properly, I promise you. Please let me have the key.'

'Of all the impertinence!'

Martin thrust the foils into the gravel. 'M. le Comte, if you don't give me the key, I'll have one made.'

'Your tone has changed.'

'I know, M. le Comte, but things are different now. I'm tired of being afraid and that is why I must go down into that vault. Give me your permission.'

'Are you giving me orders?'

'M. le Comte, I'm ashamed that you should see me in this state. I can wait no longer. I would rather make an attempt.'

'And if you fail?'

'Then you'll have lost nothing.'

'You look almost like you did in Brayonne when I was sick. Full of energy—just as you really are.'

'No, as I was, M. le Comte.'

'My boy, you're taking on too much.'

'I entreat you most earnestly, Monsieur.'

'Very well, you shall have the key.'

Martin kissed his hand.

'Stop that. When do you want to go down?'

'At this very moment.'

A bell rang in the castle.

'That's for the midday meal,' said the count.

'Give me the key after we have eaten.'

'I'll think it over.'

'M. le Comte!'

'You shall have it.'

After the meal the countess tried to have a conversation with her husband. He put her off until the evening, beckoned to Martin and demanded the key from the steward. Martin expressed a wish that he should be left to carry out his plan alone, but the count insisted on having him accompanied, at least as far as the cellar door. He told him to fetch a lantern.

Lantern in hand, he walked swiftly ahead of the count and stopped outside the cellar door. Opening it, he peered into the depths.

'Have you any doubts?' asked the count.

'It's dark, but not as dark as before. Where shall I find you afterwards?'

'I'll wait here, Martin.'

'I may be a long time, Monsieur.'

'I'll be on the terrace or in the park.'

'Thank you, Monsieur, but please promise me that you won't send anyone down to fetch me and that you won't come down yourself.'

'I promise you.'

'Thank you.' Martin raised his lantern and climbed down the steps.

The count listened until the boy's footsteps had died away, and then leant against the stone wall. The door remained open. The count trod on a cockroach and unsuccessfully tried to open a warped window. He gave up the attempt and walked up and down, listening each time he came to the door that led to the dungeons. Not a sound could be heard.

The count lost patience. Waiting no longer, he took of his shoes and climbed down in his stockinged feet, feeling his way along the wall. At last he heard a dull muttering. Cautiously following the sound, he reached the iron door to the underground passage and found it ajar. The faint gleam of a candle could be seen through it. Martin was talking to himself. The count stood there motionless and listened.

'Things have changed now, you know,' Martin said. 'The door is open. I need not die of hunger and thirst, and he knows that I'm down here. That probably annoys you, but you have held me long enough in thrall. So this is where you live. It is a fitting place for you. I know that you are lurking there ready to crawl slowly towards me and envelop me, but you will never be able to reach me. Now you've grown smaller and you're on the alert. The candle is growing smaller, too, but this time I will not wait for it to go out by itself. I will blow you out, fear. I blow you out now that I can feel the brightness of his love around me and the darkness holds no terror. Yes, now I'm ready.'

The count heard a tinkle and the faint gleam died. 'Ah, now you're beginning to grow,' Martin went on. 'I have his love around me and you cannot penetrate it. You are upon me, above, below and all around me, and I am not afraid. His love is steadfast. You think that if something touched me now I should lose my reason. That is what you would like, but nothing touches me, and if it did it would be only a rat . . . a harmless living creature. Now you are weighing down on me. You make me cower but you cannot enter me, and even if you did, you cannot reach my heart. Now I am withdrawing into it for you are pressing me hard. I am sore beset. Fear, I say to you that if you drive me too hard, I will attack you. I will come out into the open; for you see, his love expands within me. Here are my hands, there are my feet and there is his love . . . and there you lurk. Let it remain like that. Now I stretch myself. Ah, so you would attack again. I retire once more. I am a flea compared with you, but I am not fighting for myself alone. I am fighting for him. You don't understand that. I can feel that you are embarrassed. Yes, had you had me alone you would long since have conquered. You are powerful but you cannot bear love. Now I am in the bowels of the earth, but I can love here below and his love remains here with me. You would not understand that. Where are you going? Go and cower somewhere. I will tell you what he said to me and you will be good enough to listen . . .'

The count withdrew noiselessly and climbed up the endless stairs. As soon as he had grown accustomed to the daylight, he put on his shoes and almost lost his balance. As he walked through the castle on to the bright sunny terrace he came face to face with the countess and Amaryllis.

'Ah, Monsieur,' said the countess. 'A fortunate meeting. Have you come to a decision?'

'No, Madame.'

'Monsieur, are you feverish?' asked Amaryllis. 'Your forehead is moist.'

He wiped his brow.

'Why don't you give Martin to Grouchet,' said the countess, 'before you leave Grandval? The master of the hunt is well disposed towards him and the hunting lodge will be a good place for him to recover. What do you think of my proposal?'

'Madame, I do not wish to discuss Martin now.'

'Why do you avoid the subject?'

'Please leave me in peace.'

'Where is your darling then?' asked Amaryllis.

'Down in the underground vaults. He is trying to master his fear. We must hope that he doesn't lose his reason.'

'Well, go to him.'

'I promised to leave him alone.

'How irresponsible of you.'

'Yes, it was irresponsible.'

'Be Jupiter and send your eagle to him in the guise of Pierre.'

'I was never other than Pan.'

'But you have no horns.'

'Perhaps M. d'Oubray will present me with a pair.'

The countess blushed. 'That was lacking in good taste, Monsieur.'

'Please do not demand any witty conversation from me at the moment. I beg your leave to withdraw.' He bowed and left the two ladies alone.

The cellar door remained open as before. The count listened for a long time and paced up and down outside. At last he heard footsteps.

'Martin.'

'Yes, Monsieur.'

The boy appeared far below.

'I have done it, M. le Comte.'

The count waited until Martin was outside and took him in his arms. 'You're pale and trembling.'

'I'm only cold, Monsieur.'

'Come into the sun.'

'Fancy, it is still day! I thought that night had long since fallen. Here is the key, but I forgot the lantern. I'll go back and fetch it.'

'No, leave it down below.'

They walked along the corridors together.

'Monsieur, I am as I was before. Are you pleased?'

'Yes.'

'You don't trust me. Go down and look. The lantern is in the corridor.'

'I believe you, Martin.'

'Why do you look so grave?'

'I was worried about you.'

'You thought of me?'

'Yes.'

'That must have helped. It was really not so difficult, and now I can go with you to the war.'

'Who said so?'

'You said so yesterday evening, but then I could not stand the dark. I can go now, can't I?'

'I'll think it over.'

'Oh, Monsieur!'

'Not even Raoul can come with me. If you are really cured you shall stay at Grandval.'

'How must I be so as to come with you?'

'No then, don't start ingratiating yourself.'

'Monsieur, I am frank with you, but you doubt me.'

'I will see how you are tonight.'

'I wish it were dark already.'

The terrace was deserted. They sat side by side on the broad, sunny steps in silence. Martin looked bright-eyed at the beautiful autumn-tinted park and gradually grew warm. M. d'Oubray and the ladies watched them from the salon window.

'Are you still cold, Martin?' asked the count.

'Only a little down my back.'

'Turn round.'

Martin slipped down two steps lower. When the count stretched out a hand to him he nestled with his face against the man's knee and turned his back to the sun. The count let him remain there in peace and stared over his head into the distance. Yellow and deep red petals were falling from the last roses. The fountains sparkled and the spectators at the window disappeared.

That evening the count ate alone once more with Martin because he wished to postpone his conversation with the countess. The boy sat opposite him, self-assured, and offered him dishes before Pierre could do so. Both of them were silent and seemed preoccupied with their food.

When the count stood up, Martin bowed and said: 'Good-night, Monsieur. Thank you for your kindness in having allowed me to sleep in your bed. I am going to my room now and wish you a restful night.'

The count offered him his hand without a word. When Martin looked up after the hand-kiss, the count could see a smile in his eyes. He bowed once more, took a rushlight and left. Pierre stared at him in amazement.

'Yes, Pierre,' said the count. 'It's a surprise to me, too. Can you find me a girl in the village who is pretty, no older than Martin and who has hardly any breasts?'

'You never wanted anything like that before!'

'I want something new.'

'Are you sending Jeanne home?'

'No, she's to remain.'

'M. le Comte, it won't be easy to find such a girl for you tonight, and you might easily stumble upon one of your own daughters.'

'I want the girl for tomorrow. Go and have a look at Martin.'

'Shall I fetch him?'

'No, just see what he's doing.'

Pierre left. The count cracked a few nuts and left the rest in the dish.

'He's sleeping without a light,' said Pierre on his return.

'How is he sleeping?'

'With his head on his arm.'

'Is he really asleep?'

'Yes, he didn't hear me. Do you want to go to bed?'

'Yes, I'm tired.' The count pushed back his chair so that the valet could take off his shoes. 'Pierre, there's talk in the castle that I abuse Martin. This chatter has got to stop, do you understand?'

'Yes, M. le Comte.'

'You are to report the first one to make a remark. I'll have him flogged and that will teach the others. Go and look at Martin again at midnight. If he's awake, tell him he can come to me, but don't wake him.'

'Yes, M. le Comte.'

The count stood up and Pierre finished undressing him.

At daybreak Martin was already awake. The count came into his room just as he had finished dressing.

'How did you sleep, Martin?'

'Well, M. le Comte, but why have you come to me?'

Instead of replying, the count embraced him so savagely that he cried out: 'You're crushing me.'

The count released him but caught him again immediately and shook him roughly. 'You're all right again, you young rascal! I could thrash you for joy. I'll fling you against the wall.'

He lifted Martin up and flung him on to the bed, so that the old truckle nearly broke. Martin jumped up and cried hilariously: 'M. le Comte, what do you propose to do with me now?'

'I'm riding with you. You take Cato and I'll take Mirabelle, and off we'll go over the jumps and hedges. God help you if Cato refuses. Come on.'

Martin ran after the count who was already in the corridor.

With a jingle of spurs they made their way down the north-west staircase. In their headlong descent the count looked out of one of the small mullioned windows.

'The weather will be glorious. I'll visit some of my good-for-nothing farmers and put the fear of God into them so that they will pay up. And then to the war. I'll have fifty horsemen here in two days.'

'Can I come, M. le Comte?'

'You'll remain at Grandval with Raoul, Constant and Louis, and in the spring you'll come with Tenelli to Flanders.'

'Why not until the spring, Monsieur?'

'Because I shan't have a full regiment till then. I can't use you children in a rabble of newly-impressed louts and plundering soldiers who have to be disciplined. Can you run fast?'

'Not very.'

'Run as fast as you can.'

Martin ran along the corridor with the count in pursuit. He caught the boy before he reached the door.

'You're still too short in the legs, my lad.'

'I wanted to wait for you here,' replied Martin, 'to let you pass.'

'Hm!'

'M. le Comte, I lied to you.'

'Pity that you admitted it. I should have liked to box your ears.'

The watchman opened the gate and they went into the courtyard where the horses were already saddled.

Whistling a great dane, the count mounted and trotted with

Martin, to the postern gate, followed by the dog. He left the avenue and galloped straight across country. The last wisps of mist dispersed. The morning sun grew brighter and the sky turned a radiant blue. The forest had put on its most beautiful autumn tints and the pasture land was a rich brown in a haze of gold. The count made for a hedge, looked round at Martin as he jumped, and saw the boy getting ready to follow.

'Good, Martin,' he cried, once they were both over the obstacle, 'now for the brook and then over the game paling.'

Cato shied at the brook but, using his spurs and whip, Martin landed next to the count who grabbed him by the hair in his delight. The paling was also taken in their stride and now they were galloping along the edge of the forest. Martin shouted for joy; the dog bayed; the game stampeded and a covey of partridges rose in the air.

When they came to a farm, the count threw the reins to Martin, dismounted and went into the house, where his sudden appearance caused great alarm. After a quarter of an hour he was once more in the saddle on the way to the next tenant. He found the peasant ploughing, gave the little boy who was driving the oxen a cut with his switch to make an impression on his father, threatened him with plunder by his horsemen, listened grimly to the promises of the kneeling man, insisted upon payment on the following day and trotted off with Martin. Skirting a heronry with a lake that glittered in the sun, he stopped in a village to visit the village headman and suddenly felt ravenously hungry. After ordering a country breakfast, he fixed new dates for the payment of taxes and rode on.

By midday the horses were so tired that the count had to leave them in one of the farmyards. They continued their ride on a couple of peasant nags; by the time these were worn out and the dog could hardly keep up, the horsemen decided that it was time to take a rest. They lay down on a sunny slope out of the wind, slept for an hour, bought blackberries from some children, shot a squirrel for fun and trotted on, changing horses once more until, towards evening, they reached the little castle of Fleury, which stood on a steep hill on the west bank of the river.

The count disturbed the steward and his family at supper, demanded to see the accounts and announced his intention of spending the night at the castle. The servants completely lost their heads, for the castle had not been lived in since the death of the former count and was in a state of utter neglect. The count gave orders for the main room to be got ready for the night and started to pore over the books. Martin went into the kitchen, ordered omelettes, and was shown over the castle by the steward's wife. The ground floor was occupied by the staff and there were only five rooms on the first floor, the centre one being a bedroom. The silk bed-hangings were faded and torn; rats and mice made their nests in the ancient mattress; the Spanish leather panelling had peeled away from the mouldy walls and hung down in strips; the crossed swords above the fireplace were rusty and the few chairs were worm-eaten. Martin opened the french window leading on to a small balcony and looked down at the neglected garden, which led in four broad terraces to the river. The shadow of the castle hill darkened the sluggish water in which the first stars were reflected.

In her anxiety the woman asked Martin what could be done. After ordering her to air and heat the room, he returned to the bailiff's parlour, where the count was eating with great gusto. After making his report, he too sat down to eat. The count remarked that it was like being at the war, where they often had to make their quarters in plundered castles. The servants were to fill sacks with straw and make a bed for him.

When the count retired to the bedroom, which in the meantime had been heated, he found that the leather panelling gave off a disgusting stench from the heat. He swore at the steward, calling him a rascal, took the candle from his hand and inspected the other four rooms. Doves were nesting in one of them, and the bats had taken up their quarters in the others. The count cursed the tottering old man, and once more was about to use his riding crop, when Martin tugged him by the arm.

'What is it?' asked the count.

'The night is so warm, M. le Comte, that we could easily sleep by the open window.'

'Yes, we'll do that, Martin.'

The count was pacified and the servants carried the bedding to the open door. Then he told them to go to hell and bolted the doors. He tried his pistols, let Martin take off his riding boots, and retired to bed.

Martin pushed his sack of straw near the bed and rustled so long that the count asked him coarsely whether he was about to have kittens.

'No,' replied Martin, 'I'm not having kittens, but I don't like it down here. Can you see the river and the stars?'

'No, I can't see the river because the balustrade is in the way. Are you afraid of the dark again?'

'How can you ask! If you wish, I will sleep in one of the rooms with the bats or down in the cellar.'

'That wouldn't be very wise. The steward is so furious that he would probably like to club us.'

'You should have brought a couple of horsemen.'

'Yes, but he can't surprise us while we're asleep; Hector is a good watch dog. I let the fellow off half the last year's rent for improvements, and now Fleury looks like a dovecote. I have doubled his rent now and he's got to pay it tomorrow at Grandval. I'm not tired yet. Tell me a story.'

'From down here, M. le Comte?'

'Aren't you comfortable?'

'I'm three times worse off than you.'

'Why?'

'Lower and harder.'

'And thirdly, I suppose, not fashionable enough?'

Martin did not reply.

'Begin the story,' said the count.

'I can't.'

'You won't, you mean.'

'Monsieur!'

'To hell with you, come into my bed.'

Martin called the dog, gave him his bed and slipped in with the count. He nestled close to him and said eagerly:

'I told you all the stories I knew in Brayonne. Which one do you want to hear?'

'None of them. A new one.'

'I don't know any.'

'Then invent one.'

'Can I ask you something first?'

'What?'

'Have you definitely made up your mind to leave me in Grandval?'

'Yes.'

'Monsieur, I am afraid for you when you're at war.'

'Fear?'

'Oh, yes, but another kind of fear.'

'Better forget it as well. Death can catch up with us at any time. That stone balustrade annoys me; it looks unsafe. I'll try and knock it into the garden.'

'I'll help you.'

They went from the head-end of the bed to the balcony, and pressed against the balustrade until it crashed with its small pillars into the courtyard.

'Good,' said the count, 'now I can see the river as I lie here.'

'And in the morning,' added Martin, 'we shall see the sunrise.' They climbed back into bed.

'Well, what about that fairy tale?' asked the count.

'It's no good. Perhaps you know one.'

'I?'

'Didn't they ever tell you one when you were small?'

'Yes, but I've forgotten. Do you know the story of the cockerel who was only half a bird?'

'What, only half a cock?'

'Yes, a cock and a half. This is how it came about. Two virtuous girls inherited nothing from their parents except a cockerel. One wanted to roast it and the other to spare it. So they cut it in two. The one ate her half crisply roasted, and the other prayed to St Martin to spare her half a cockerel. St Martin healed it and it began to crow and scrape. Since it had been spared it wanted to show its gratitude and find treasure for its mistress. It wandered away and found a purse containing a hundred gold louis. Since it was very heavy, to make it easier to carry, the half cockerel stuck the purse in its backside.' Martin laughed. 'It wandered further and then met a fox. No, I think the story went differently. A thief took the purse, and later the half cockerel had a wolf, a fox and a swarm of bees in his backside.'

'My God!'

'Yes, and they all turned out to be very useful to him, but I can't quite remember why. I thought I still knew it.'

'Monsieur, why not let your cockerel wander to Grandval and meet you?'

'Do you think it would greet me?'

'Of course. But tell me, how did it look from the side where the other half once was?'

'I don't know.'

'You don't know anything.'

'Ho, ho!'

'You're the most intelligent count in the world.'

'Where are your ears, you brat?'

'Here I am with my ears.'

The count suddenly found himself being embraced and kissed wildly.

'Stop Martin, not on the lips, those are meant for women.'

'I can't bear your women.'

The count pushed him away. 'Wait until you have one.'

'I don't want any.'

'Do you want to go into a monastery?'

'I want to go with you to the war.'

'And I want to go to sleep—goodnight!'

'Monsieur!'

A loud snore was the only reply. 'You're making a noise like a wild boar. I know perfectly well that you are awake.' The count turned over and made no further sound.

Then Martin said, with a sob in his throat: 'Monsieur, you said that you loved me, and now you want to be rid of me. You are embarrassed by my love, you find me too soft and not manly enough.'

'No, Martin, you are a proper boy. I thought you'd start begging again to go to war. I hate beggars.'

'You love me and yet I'm not allowed to kiss you.'

'Idiot. Give me a farewell kiss then.'

'Anywhere I like?'

'Yes, and then be satisfied.'

Martin gave him a swift, passionate yet childish kiss on the lips. 'Thank you, Monsieur.'

'Martin, you love me only as a younger friend.'

'Do I?'

'Yes. Father Tulier was badly informed about us, otherwise

he would not have plagued you to confess. Friends are allowed to kiss now and then.'

'But you never kissed me.'

'I don't much care for the custom. With a friend I want to ride and fence and go to war.'

'So do I.'

'Be patient until spring, then you can ride into battle with me.'

'I shall be your bodyguard.'

'You'll have the best weapons. Practise your levade. Go on fencing with Master Tenelli and become even more skilful than you are.'

'I am all right again. I'll fence with you in Granval. You'll be surprised.'

'I hope so. You rode very well today and now I'm really tired.'

At last they fell asleep.

A DAY OF DECEPTIONS

THE following evening, the count returned with Martin to Grandval in the gayest possible mood, and learnt that various farmers had paid their rent. Amaryllis was sulking, Jeanne had disappeared, but Pierre had found him the little girl he had ordered.

While shaving him next morning, Pierre asked his master whether he had been satisfied with his services. The count ignored the question and ordered him to return the child immediately to her parents. He preferred Jeanne. The valet said that Jeanne was nowhere to be found, not even in the village, and that her swain had come to ask the count's permission to marry another girl. The count said that Jeanne should be found. He gave the tradesman's son permission to take home the virtuous but hideous Tinette, and went at once to the fencing hall, where Martin had just forced Guy into a corner and given him a sound beating.

'Bravo!' cried Master Tenelli, 'bravo Martin! You can see the result of your lessons, M. le Comte. You did very well to take Martin away from the others for a time. He has made astonishing progress.'

Tenelli handed the count his practice foil. Martin stood there with a smile on his face and his hand on his hip.

'M. le Comte, am I to be honoured by a bout with you?'

'Yes.'

There was a clash of foils. Tenelli and the four boys watched the contest with increasing surprise.

'M. le Comte,' Tenelli cried enthusiastically, 'he has never fought so brilliantly before.'

Martin retreated, stepped quickly to one side, feinted and

went in again to the attack. He forced the count to pivot and attacked even more fiercely. Suddenly, he cried with delight: 'Touché.' Raoul and Louis applauded and the count flashed his white teeth. Martin leapt about the hall and the count had to follow him. Then he altered his tactics and suddenly attacked at the lightning speed which had made him famous and so much feared as a swordsman. Martin was hard-pressed, tried a feint which the count immediately parried, and felt the button of the foil on his chest.

'Bravo Martin,' cried Master Tenelli, clapping his hands. 'That was an honourable defeat. You certainly made the count take care. M. le Comte, I congratulate you on such a pupil. Gentlemen, take him as an example.'

The two contestants stood opposite each other with lowered foils. Then Martin let his fall and flung his arms round the man's neck, shouting with glee. The count caught him by the forelock and shook him off.

'Yes, you've recovered. Take him riding with you, Tenelli. I'm riding alone today. Stay where you are.'

Martin understood and obeyed. The count left the hall and Raoul walked over to Martin. 'I congratulate you, Martin.' With a smile the boy held out his hand to him.

Before the midday meal the count visited his wife's apartments. He found her in the salon with the actress and M. d'Oubray.

'Do you wish to speak to me alone, Monsieur?' she asked.

'Certainly not, Madame. What I have to say is for everyone's ears.'

He greeted the others curtly, sat down and immediately came to the point.

'Madame, you suspected me of abusing Martin because I allowed him in my bedroom while he was suffering from nerves. He is now completely cured and has gone back to his own room. I hope that you will realise that you were mistaken.'

'Have you tired of him?'

'Madame, he is completely happy and knows that he has my friendship. You can safely send the priest to him. Father Tulier will relieve you of your anxiety.'

'I am very relieved, Monsieur. Father Tulier has also questioned Raoul and learned nothing ill.'

'Will you allow Martin to remain in the castle with Raoul?'

'Yes, as long as I hear nothing evil.'

'I am grateful to you, Madame. I am leaving early tomorrow morning, and Guy is also travelling tomorrow.'

'Monsieur, Guy has a cold and is coughing. You must postpone his journey.'

'That is impossible I am afraid, Madame, for he and Martin are deadly enemies.'

'It is your duty, Monsieur, to see that nothing happens to Guy. Martin slapped him at breakfast after their ride.'

'Presumably Guy taunted him.'

'Tenelli had to part them with a stick.'

'I will give orders that, on this last day, they are not to be left alone together.'

'Please forbid Martin to touch Guy.'

'I shall forbid them to speak to each other.'

'Yes, that is best.'

'Are you pleased with me?'

'As far as this matter is concerned, yes.'

'I thank you.'

The count tried to kiss her hand, but she withdrew it.

'Why this coldness, Madame?'

'How can you ask, Monsieur?'

'But I have just convinced you that there was no foundation for your suspicions of Martin.'

'But something else has occurred.'

'Oh, yes, Madame, I had the little one returned to her village early this morning.'

'You should be ashamed of yourself.'

The count's dark face grew even darker. 'This eternal gossip. Madame, you are largely responsible for my latest misdeed. Your suspicions made me think that perhaps some pleasure was to be found in immaturity. I have satisfied my curiosity and discovered that it has no appeal for me. Please remain seated. I shall leave now, but before I go I must tell you something. The servants' gossip about Martin and myself has ceased since I threatened to use my whip. I do not wish to hear any more of this nonsense and insist that Martin's honour shall not be impugned. As far as I'm concerned the matter is closed, and is so for everyone in the castle. Good morning.'

After the count had left there was a moment's silence. Amaryllis opened her gold smelling flask and sniffed at it like a little rabbit.

'Madame,' M. d'Oubray said to the countess, 'I admire your courage in the face of this man, but you should not antagonise him. By disregarding his antics you will live in peace, for at heart he is afraid of you. However you have an opportunity for revenge, since he is leaving Martin here.'

'Monsieur, he knows that I should never take advantage of such an opportunity. Raoul defended Martin's virtue almost in tears, called him his friend and refuses to part from him. How could I deprive Raoul of a friend? He was like a lost soul all the summer and only came to life when Martin returned. I must be grateful that Gaston has not taken Raoul away from me too.'

'Madame, if you feel so dependent on him, this is all the more reason to overlook your husband's shortcomings.'

'Oh, M. d'Oubray, sometimes I forget that I am dealing with Pan and get enraged with the man.'

'Madame, I do not suggest that you should excuse everything. Christian teaching denies the existence of Pan and you are therefore dealing with the failings of an ordinary human being. One must protect oneself against wicked men.'

'M. d'Oubray, you are trying to incite me. Please do not do so. Mlle Amaryllis, you look tired today.'

The actress closed her flask and, raising her eyebrows wearily, leant back in her chair. 'I have a very bad headache, Madame. I am afraid we shall have a storm. I shall retire this afternoon. Would you object if I asked the vicomte to read me something from a romance?'

'Oh, no, Mademoiselle, certainly not. He reads with great expression and has a musical voice.'

'His father's voice, Madame.'

'The voice of Pan and the face of Apollo,' added d'Oubray. The countess was flattered, and smiled.

During the afternoon the sky clouded over and the first autumn storm broke. Raoul, much against his will, visited the actress on his mother's orders, while Tenelli gave the other boys an Italian lesson.

Amaryllis had drawn the curtains although it was still light, and received her young visitor by candlelight, lying on her ornate, perfumed bed. She offered him her hand wearily.

'Ah, my handsome Vicomte! My headache is the better for seeing you.'

Raoul perfunctorily kissed her scented fingers, and asked:

'Where is the book you want me to read to you?'

'Over there on the table.'

Raoul caught sight of a huge, thick volume.

'Sit down,' said Amaryllis. 'It is a love story.'

Raoul sat down and opened the book.

'Do you want me to start from the beginning?'

'No, no, Vicomte Raoul.' Amaryllis gave a silvery laugh. 'Don't be afraid. I shall not be able to listen very long for I always find it very tiring. There is a marker in it. Have you found it?'

'Yes,' said Raoul with relief. He began to read: ' "With a wildly beating heart, the young hero, regardless of danger, climbed the ladder and caught sight of Esmeralda lying on her couch. Although she was asleep she seemed to be having a vivid dream, for her coral red lips quivered and her veiled, snowy bosom rose and fell ecstatically . . ." Mademoiselle, I promised my father to read only by daylight. It is still light outside. May I open the curtains?'

'No, for then I should see the storm stripping the leaves from the trees in the avenue, and that would make me sad.'

'Mademoiselle, the print is very small. May I fetch one with larger print?'

'Why don't you want to read about Esmeralda? Don't you care for the sleeping beauty?'

'I am quite indifferent to her, Mademoiselle.'

'How can you say that! Were your eyes not so full of melancholy, I should be inclined to think that you had never been in love. Has life been cruel to you?'

Raoul was embarrassed. 'I don't know.'

'My handsome Vicomte, you have been unlucky in love.'

'How do you know that?'

'I can see it in your face, and I feel sorry for you. Was she faithless?'

Raoul flicked the pages of the book and did not reply. 'Did she accord you too little?'

'Mademoiselle, please allow me to fetch from the library a story book with large print.'

'Yes, if you insist, Vicomte, but please do me a favour before you leave. My maid is ironing lace down on the first floor. Please deputise for her and unloosen my bodice for me. I feel a trifle tight-laced and foolishly enough, my skirt fastens at the back.'

Raoul stood up politely and the actress gracefully turned her back to him. He untied a ribbon. 'Thank you, Vicomte. Loosen the string a little more. Stop, not too much. That's right. I already feel more comfortable.'

Then she began to cough violently. 'Vicomte, I have swallowed something. Pat my back.'

Raoul did as he was asked and the flower patterned silk dress slipped down. 'Your dress!' he cried in alarm.

Amaryllis turned to him and gave him a swift kiss on the cheek.

'Thank you for your help, Monsieur.'

Looking at her lovely, scarcely concealed breasts, Raoul retired to his seat. Amaryllis seized his hand. 'Come and sit by me. I can see that you don't like reading, and I won't pester you. Tell me of your sorrow. It will lighten your heart. Sit down, my shy, handsome Vicomte. It would make me so happy if I could cure you of your melancholy. Look upon me as your friend. Give me your confidence.'

Raoul remained standing, as steady as a rock. Without releasing his hand Amaryllis went on: 'From the very first day, I was attracted to you. No one understands your soul. Is that not true? Are you lonely?'

'Mademoiselle . . .'

'Call me Amaryllis. I, too, know the pangs of love.'

Raoul freed himself. 'I came here to read to you. I will fetch another book.'

'Listen to the storm, Vicomte Raoul. Stay with me until my maid returns.'

'I shall not be long.' He was already by the door and in the next moment was outside.

On the way to the library he met Martin, carrying an inkwell. 'Where are you off to, Vicomte Raoul?'

'To the library, Martin. Come with me.'

'I'm afraid I can't. Master Tenelli only let me go to fetch some ink. Have you finished reading?'

'Yes and no. It's hideous.'

'But you love reading.'

'Yes, for myself . . . but this person. Come with me and I'll tell you all about it.'

Full of curiosity, Martin followed Raoul.

In the library the vicomte explained the cause of his agitation. 'Martin, she wants to make me cuckold father. As though I would ever touch something that had already belonged to him! She let fall her dress and exposed half her bosom.'

'Was it beautiful, Vicomte Raoul?'

'Beautiful or not, I can't stand her.'

'Doesn't she smell nice?'

'On the contrary, her perfume is three times as strong as mother's. I can't get it out of my nostrils. How appalling these scents are! It reminded me of that day in the Duc d'Orléans' coach. I prefer a cow stall.'

'I like the smell of scent,' said Martin.

'You go to her, Martin, and take her a book.'

'It can't be done.'

'Why not? In any case I refuse to return to that whore.'

'You mustn't say such a thing.'

'What else is she? You told me yourself that she came to Brayonne with a marquis and then remained with my father.'

'She is not his mistress, but a guest.'

'That's one and the same thing.'

'Mme la Comtesse respects her highly.'

'My dear, good mother!' Raoul took a book from the shelf and blew the dust off it. 'Here are the stories in big print. Take her this with my compliments. Tell her that I have a belly ache from eating too many plums.'

Martin weighed the book and reflected. 'Go, Martin,' urged his friend.

'Then take the ink and tell Master Tenelli that I shall soon be back.'

'Agreed, Martin. Adieu.' Raoul ran off with the ink.

When Martin entered the actress's room, he forgot, in his amazement, to close the door. All the candles had been extinguished, except one, which was masked by a book standing on its end. In the mysterious darkness the whiteness of an enchanting bosom gleamed; the frailest hand was spraying a cloud of overpowering scent which rose like incense from a burning pan. The actress half concealed her nakedness with the handkerchief, stretched out her slim, beautiful arms to the visitor and cried gaily:

'Ah, you're back already, my handsome Vicomte. What have you brought me?'

Martin went over to her, without a word, and handed her the book.

She held it up to the candle, read the title and let forth a silvery peal of laughter.

' "The Golden Legend". How enchanting. Read to me about St Anthony. Sit on the bed where the candle throws its brightest beam.'

Feigning to give Martin the book, she let it fall. As he bent down to pick it up he felt her arms round his neck.

'Another kiss to thank you for the book.'

Martin was kissed and let himself be drawn on to the scented couch. The overpowering perfume numbed his senses and at the same time aroused them. The closeness of those white breasts confused and excited him.

Amaryllis kicked the book away and said: 'Let us abandon the reading, Vicomte. I want to console you, because no one else has done so as yet. Why were you so shy just now? Have you only just noticed how much you mean to me? I have fallen in love with your beautiful, sad blue eyes, which I should so much like to see shine with happiness. Are you angry with me that you hang your head?' He shook his head. 'Oh, Vicomte Raoul, if you only knew how enchanting you are, and I am foolish enough to tell you so. Love makes one so foolish. You must forget my words.'

Martin could not resist the desire to try the softness of her breasts with his cheek, and his boldness was well received. Amaryllis encouraged him tenderly, and while continuing to utter all manner of nonsense, led his hesitant, exploring hand on paths of which he had not yet dreamed. Whispering that it was too hot in the room, she removed his jacket with nimbly caressing fingers and divested him of everything which, in her opinion, could have hampered him. Martin's inherited passion was set aflame, but when he grew ruthless the lady defended herself, paused for reflection, and threatened to call her maid. Because of the threat, Martin was now in an even greater hurry to overcome this feigned resistance, and after he had conquered, pleaded for forgiveness in the intoxication of his happiness. Amaryllis wept a few tears. Martin suddenly remembered that she had taken him for another, and began to search for his clothes.

At this moment, from near at hand, they heard a carefully suppressed cough.

'Get out!' cried the actress, thrusting Martin from the couch and hastily covering herself. 'Hide in the closet.'

Martin had the presence of mind to gather his essential articles of clothing with him as he fled, leaving behind his jacket, shoes and stockings.

Guy, suffering from a bad cold, was the visitor. 'Please excuse me, Mademoiselle, your door was ajar.'

'Leave the room, immediately, Monsieur.'

'Why? If Martin can be happy, I want to be too.'

'It wasn't Martin.'

'Yes, it was. I recognised him by his broad shoulders, and this is the jacket of his new brown suit.'

The proof was conclusive. 'The shameless creature! He ravished me.'

'Insist that he be punished.'

'I certainly shall. Leave me, my maid is below. No one heard my cries for help.'

'Nor did I, Mademoiselle. You seem to have been most satisfied with Martin.'

'You saw nothing.'

'Yes, nearly everything, Mademoiselle. Accord me the same favours or I shall have something to talk about at table.'

'M. Guy, be a gentleman and don't expose a lady.'

'I like you when you're exposed. I insist upon my claim or else I'll betray you. You haven't long to think it over.'

'But you're still a child.'

'Not such a child as you think.'

Guy heard a noise next door and quickly bolted all the doors. The actress saw that he was serious, and asked with real anxiety:

'M. Guy, and if you do not keep silent . . .'

'I swear to keep silent.' He leaped on to the bed beside her.

The count was in his study sitting at his desk, busy sorting coins of various sizes into little piles, according to their value. There was a knock at the door: 'Come in. Ah, Martin. What do you want?'

'Nothing, if I'm disturbing you.'

'You're not disturbing me.'

'M. le Comte, I have a guilty conscience and have something to confess.'

'Have you thrashed Guy?'

'No, M. le Comte. But I haven't behaved correctly towards you.'

'I have not learned of anything.'

'It happened like this. The vicomte was sent to read to Mlle Amaryllis and fled. He gave me a book and sent me to deputise for him. In the dark she mistook me for the vicomte, was very tender, showed me much and permitted all.'

'What did she permit?'

'The same favours that she accorded to you, Monsieur.'

'To me? Did you prove your mettle?'

'Yes, I think so, M. le Comte.'

The count bent over his money.

Martin approached cautiously and bent down to try and see his expression.

'You're laughing!'

The count roared with laughter and pushed the table away. 'Oh, Martin,' he gasped, 'I have never met such an open-hearted rival before. I don't grudge you anything. You have no idea how pleased I am. Was it wonderful?'

'But aren't you angry with me?'

'No, Martin. I couldn't be angry with you. Tell me, was it wonderful?'

'Yes, wonderful, Monsieur, she smelt better than your

nightshirt and was soft all over and oh . . .'

'I can imagine the "Oh". And did you thank her afterwards.

'No, does one have to do that?'

'In this case, yes. A man should always cherish his first love.'

'But I don't love her in the least.'

'Oh, so you don't love her. She merely pleased you well.'

'I like the love-making better than the woman.'

'Martin, a gentleman would never say that. One always has to speak with respect of women.'

'Why should I lie?'

'You have no graces. Go back to her and say thank you.'

'M. le Comte, she mistook me for the vicomte and she might abuse me.'

'You deceived her atrociously but all the same you must thank her.'

'I don't want to.'

'I refuse to accept such an answer. You're to go.'

'M. le Comte, someone else is with her now.'

'Someone else?'

'M. Guy came into the room.'

'He too?' The count laughed heartily. 'I have some wonderful sons. I really ought to play the angry father. You insolent dog, you have poached on my preserves. Wait, you must have a thrashing.'

He jumped up, caught hold of his crop and rushed at Martin, who ran laughing round the table and then held the stool in front of him in defence.

'You young ruffian, by rights I ought to flog you.'

'I thought so too, when I came here.'

'Give me the stool, I've got to write.'

Martin pushed the stool towards him. The count sat down. Taking a sheet of paper he wrote the following words:

'The birdie brought me joy as well'
GASTON

He poured sand on to the paper, blew on it and folded it into a *billet*.

'I must give her a present.' He took a few pieces of gold from one of the piles, but then replaced them. 'No, they wouldn't do. Wait Martin. I've got something pretty for you to take her.' He stood up and went into his room. 'Look at this,' he said on his return. Martin barely glanced at the gold hair clip with three glittering diamonds. His face had clouded over. The count put the piece of jewellery in the letter and sealed it. 'Take it, and don't forget to say "thank you"!'

'Must I go to her now?'

'Yes, knock and wait until you are allowed in.'

Martin bit his lips and stalked from the room. The count sat down again, counted the individual piles, made a note of the sums and put the coins into little bags which he kept in his coffer. Pierre brought two candelabra, drew the curtains, put wood on the fire and left. The stormy wind blew through the chinks in the window, making the curtains billow. The fire flickered in the grate. With an almost melodious chink, the coins fell from the count's hands into the leather sack—louis d'or, pieces of silver and pathetic copper coin.

There was another knock and Martin returned.

'Well?'

'She abused me at first, then read the letter and wrote me a reply for you. Here it is, M. le Comte.' The count took it and read:

'You do well to console me for your churl.
I insist upon the severest punishment!'

The count looked at Martin with a smile. 'She calls you a churl and insists upon the severest punishment. How did you thank her?'

'I thanked her profusely for the service she had rendered me.'

'Service! Martin, that is too much. Come here and get your slap.'

'I won't come.'

'You've insulted her terribly.'

'I'm honest and I intend to remain so.'

'She is your first love.'

'M. le Comte, for me this adventure has nothing to do with love.'

'You don't mean to say, in all honesty, that you are entirely indifferent to her?'

'Yes, I am, Monsieur.'

'Then you're a swine.'

Martin raised his eyebrows and said nothing.

'Martin, the jest no longer amuses me.'

'Nor me, M. le Comte. It appears as though you wanted to divert my love for you to a whore. Yes, to a whore . . .'

The count stood up and was on the point of striking Martin, who embraced him before he could deliver the blow. 'Strike me, if you wish. You are striking my heart.'

'Martin, what is happening to you? I cannot really allow you to insult a lady.'

'If you will suffer my love, I will never insult another one. I want to be your friend and to remain so.'

'You are my friend and you will remain so.'

'Even when you're away.'

'Always, you ass. Partings make no difference.'

'Then it is all right.'

Martin released him and stepped back a few paces.

'You behave very oddly, Martin.'

'Monsieur, it is so. I preferred being in your arms than on her breast.'

'Even though she smelt far better than my nightshirt.'

'I do not love you with my nose. There's only one of you, but there must be thousands of ladies who smell nice and wear soft lace. I should like to take my pleasure often with women, but never again with one who belongs to you.'

'Martin, you are a gift from heaven.' The boy's face lit up.

The count went over to the window and pulled the curtain aside.

'It will be no pleasure to travel in this weather. As soon as the wind stops blowing it will rain.'

He turned round and asked with a smile: 'And what will you do until Master Tenelli returns?'

'I shall get up to all kinds of mischief, Monsieur.'

'I am afraid of that, but I have an idea. You will stay with Master Grouchet at the hunting lodge and let him train you to hunt. That will keep you healthy and away from the petticoats. You're too young to be chasing skirts. On my return I don't want to find you a pasty-faced boudoir hero who can't use a foil and gets thrown by a mettlesome steed.'

Martin bowed. 'I will try to follow the count's example in all things.'

The count cleared his throat. 'Grouchet is coming this evening. You're on good terms with him now, aren't you?'

'Yes, M. le Comte, since Brayonne.'

The count looked at the clock. 'I must go and visit a certain lady and try to raise her spirits. Will you stay here alone?'

'No, I'll go to the vicomte and have a talk with him.' They left the study.

Since the count wished to celebrate his departure, everyone appeared at table in his best attire. Amaryllis was wearing the new diamond clip in her Titian red hair. The countess suddenly noticed this. Turning to the count, she said in a sharp tone:

'Monsieur, Mlle Amaryllis is wearing a clip which I saw my dead friend Angélique d'Epponcourt wearing several times. Does it come from the coffer which has been deposited with you as part of the dowry of my future daughter-in-law, Marguerite?'

The count picked up a wing of goose, gnawed it fastidiously and replied:

'Your presumption is correct, Madame. I felt it my duty to show my admiration for the charming theatrical performance before I left, and since I had nothing else to hand, I borrowed the clip from the coffer. I will replace the piece of jewellery by another of the same value as soon as I have an opportunity of visiting a jeweller in Paris.'

'Monsieur, in the interests of Mlle d'Epponcourt, I insist that the clip is returned to its rightful place this very evening. I beg you, Mlle Amaryllis, to choose a piece of jewellery of the same value from my coffer.'

With a smile, Amaryllis removed the clip from her hair, and the russet lock fell down over her forehead. She handed the clip to the count who put it in his pocket and apologetically remarked: 'I should have preferred to borrow from the dead rather than from the living.'

The countess could scarcely conceal her rage. Martin looked down at his plate and the count avoided his eyes. There was an embarrassing silence, during which the only sounds to be heard were the storm and the rattling of the shutters.

'What an appalling night,' the actress said at last. 'I should hardly dare to walk along the corridors without an escort. The curtains all billow, the foliage rustles at the window, the flames flicker and gutter . . .'

Guy began to cough and spat over his shoulder on the floor. When he turned round, his eyes met the count's black ones and he turned pale. He had noticed the malicious grin in that glance.

'Madame,' said the count once more apparently gay, 'Martin has recently performed such an astonishing feat of courage that I'm sure he would not be afraid to wander alone through the uninhabited parts of a castle tonight. I wish to prove the courage of my legitimate sons and suggest that they make a tour through the lofts of the main building. How about it, Raoul and Guy?'

'I won't go alone,' cried Guy, in terror.

'Nor will I,' said Raoul.

'Are you so craven?'

'Monsieur, they are frightened of ghosts,' explained the countess. 'I beg you spare me any further irritation and stop plaguing the children before you leave.'

'Well, Guy,' continued the count, 'are you really a coward?'

'I wouldn't be afraid if I had my dogs with me.'

'You will go, without your dogs, from the south-west staircase, through the lofts, and to see that you really do it, you will take Raoul with you; he will give me his word of honour not to take any short cuts.'

'Comte de Racon,' asked Constant, 'may I accompany your sons? It will only be a walk for me.'

'You don't appear to be frightened of ghosts, so we can spare you this test of courage. What about Louis?'

'Monsieur, I do not wish to be considered a coward. I will go with them.'

'Good, but three together is too many. Louis you'll go with Martin in the opposite direction. You will meet at the north-east tower. The doors are open. Be careful of your candles.

Each pair is to take one and no more. Give me your word of honour, Raoul.'

Raoul stood up and said firmly: 'I give you my word of honour that I will accompany Guy round the lofts.'

'Well, off with you heroes.'

The four boys stood up and left the hall. The countess tried to ask her husband a question, but he had already engaged M. d'Ouville in conversation. Constant covered a slice of melon thickly with sugar, to enjoy it at his leisure.

The four boys climbed the south-west tower together and separated at the entrance to the huge lofts. Martin took Louis by the hand and held the rushlight to his right.

'Come, Comte Louis, we'll walk quickly, and you can sing a song. Then you won't hear the storm.'

'Martin, the weathercocks up here creak appallingly. How these cobwebs flutter. Look at everything around us!'

'Don't look round but keep your eyes on the floor because of the steps. Hi!' he called over his shoulder, 'sing loudly if you're afraid.'

The second rushlight had already disappeared round the corner. They heard Raoul cry: 'Thanks for your advice, Martin.'

Louis began to sing a marching song in his high-pitched voice, and hurried after Martin who was walking half a pace ahead of him. The dusty beams looked ghostly in the light of their candle as they passed. Piles of rubbish seemed to come to life. The roof tiles rattled. The song could not drown the storm which raged through all the crevices and howled along the roof.

The north-west tower was soon reached and they hurried on. When Louis stopped to catch his breath and broke off his song, Martin said:

'We should meet the others by the next tower, but they're probably going slower than we are.'

'Martin, I'm not in the least afraid with you, what test of courage did you undergo?'

'I went voluntarily for a second time down into the dungeons.'

'Oh, well, this must be a mere walk for you. Can't you ever tell who locked you in?'

'No, Comte Louis.'

'Pity, the fellow should be hanged. What was that, Martin?'

The boys stopped and listened. 'There it is again, Martin. It sounded like a scream.'

'Come on, Comte Louis,' said Martin, 'perhaps the others have had an accident. They must still be in the east wing or we should have seen the reflection of their light.'

Louis stumbled. 'Please don't go so fast, Martin.'

Martin held his hand tighter. 'We must run, Comte Louis.'

There was another cry. 'Hi, Vicomte Raoul, we're coming.'

Screams for help mingled with the howling of the storm. Louis' hand was hot and moist in Martin's strong one. The delicate boy began to pant. 'Please go slower, Martin.'

'Pull yourself together, Comte Louis, until we are round the next corner. Perhaps their light has gone out. Vicomte Raoul, we're coming, we're coming . . .'

At last they reached the north-east tower where some steps led up and down again. Now they heard a long-drawn-out scream.

'Help! Help!'

Then Louis also screamed and Martin stopped. Raoul came rushing towards them and nearly knocked Martin over.

'Be careful, Vicomte. Where is M. Guy?'

'He's gone off with the light. Run, run as fast as you can.'

'Vicomte, let me go. What has happened?'

'There's a ghost behind me.'

'I'll take a look at it.'

'No, Martin, stay here. I won't go back.'

'Vicomte, I'm holding the light. Take your paws away. Either stay here with the Comte Louis and wait for me, or come along.'

'We won't stay here without a light.'

Martin wrenched himself free, distributed a few cuffs and went firmly forward. The two boys behind him screamed with terror. He caught sight of a figure swinging above the floor, and came to a halt.

'Hi, you there,' he called. 'Answer, who are you?'

Raoul and Louis grabbed for the light but Martin thrust them back and continued to advance.

'Vicomte Raoul, Comte Louis, that's no ghost, it's only

someone who's hanged himself ... it's a woman! It looks like Jeanne. Yes, it is Jeanne. That is her scarf and she always wore that kind of dress. You cowards, the dead don't bite.'

Martin went over to the hanged woman and pulled off her scarf. 'Now do you believe me?'

Raoul and Louis, clinging tightly to each other, passed as far as possible from the corpse.

'A fine pair of heroes you are. Well, come on, perhaps we shall meet M. Guy somewhere.'

The three boys hurried at full speed to the south-east, and then to the south-west tower. There was no sign of Guy. They climbed down the spiral staircase and met the steward, to whom Martin reported his discovery. The three boys entered the dining-hall where the company were still at table. Guy was sitting as pale as a ghost, next to the countess, who had placed a protective arm round his shoulder.

'M. le Comte, we finished the tour,' reported Martin. 'Jeanne has hanged herself in the loft and this is her scarf. M. Guy, I give it to you as a present.'

Before anyone realised what he had in mind, he went over to Guy, and slapped him in the face with the scarf. Guy jumped up with a wild scream and, trying to avoid the blow, fell over with his stool. Mlle de Dismarat and Amaryllis both screamed. The countess took the scarf, rose from her seat and threw it into the fire. Then she went to Guy who was shivering and washing his face in a hand bowl.

'I insist,' she said to her husband, 'that Martin be punished.'

'Come here, Guy,' ordered the count. The boy approached. 'Guy, you left your brother in the lurch and fled with the light. Your behaviour has been despicable but I wish you to carry out the test. Either you cut down the dead woman and bring me a piece of her skirt, or I'll lock you up tonight in the crypt. Which do you prefer?'

At this, the women protested loudly so that no one could be heard. The count banged on the table until the silver plates rattled: 'Silence! I'm talking to Guy. Which do you prefer?' Guy's teeth were chattering. 'Which do you prefer?'

'Take a sword and cut through the rope, then you won't have to go too close,' advised Constant.

Guy cowered back towards his mother. The count stood up and seized him by the arms. 'So we're going to the crypt, eh?'

Guy flung himself to the floor. 'Monsieur,' cried the countess, 'Guy is my child, I will not tolerate his being locked in.'

The count ignored her, pulled Guy to his feet and dragged him to the door. 'Help, Mother.' The countess hurried up and caught her husband by the arm.

'Monsieur, I ask you again, spare Guy. I am not afraid of a scene. Spare Guy.'

'Madame, I warn you not to irritate me. This coward has deserved punishment. Go back to your seat.'

'Monsieur, I will not stir an inch from you, until you release Guy from his punishment.'

'Take your hand off my arm.'

'No.'

'Madame . . .'

D'Oubray leaped from his seat, but he was too late. The countess was flung several feet away on to the floor. Everyone rushed to her in terror; the priest and Dr Borel lifted her up. D'Oubray went over to the count and shouted at him:

'You are a savage, you disgust me.'

The count immediately drew his sword, d'Oubray drew back and looked amazed. Martin flung himself between them.

'M. le Comte, don't commit a murder.'

'Get out of my way!'

Guy seized the opportunity and tried to creep away through the door, but the count noticed it despite his rage.

'Lackey, stop that boy!' Guy was caught. Those present forced their way between M. d'Oubray and the count, who replaced his sword in its sheath.

'M. d'Oubray, will you be in the dining-room in half an hour?'

'Wherever you like, Monsieur, by day or by night.'

'We will discuss the details in the dining-hall.'

'I accept your challenge, Comte de Racon.'

The count looked around him. 'Where is Guy?'

'He's hiding behind the ladies,' said a servant. The ladies

closed in to give him further protection.

'Guy, are you coming with me or am I to fetch you?'

Then Martin approached the count once more. 'M. le Comte, I beg you to spare the coward.'

The count stared at him in amazement. 'You're pleading on behalf of Guy?'

Then Martin said softly so that no one else could hear: 'It's a question of your dignity, M. le Comte.'

The blood surged to the man's furious face. He gnashed his teeth and seemed about to strike the boy. Martin looked him straight in the eyes and did not flinch.

The count made an effort to control himself: 'I will spare the coward the crypt. Goodnight, ladies.' He made for the door.

'Father!' shouted Guy. The count turned round and Guy came towards him. 'Father, I'm going up to the loft. I'm no coward, and I spit on Martin's plea. Let him lend me his hunting knife. He is no braver than I am.'

Martin unfastened his knife and handed it to Guy without a word. There was general amazement.

At the door Guy turned once more to the count: 'Father, let someone go with me to the staircase so that you can have proof that I do not take my dogs to the loft.' The count beckoned to a servant to follow him. Then the door closed behind him.

'May I ask the ladies to return to their places,' said the count. They did as he asked. 'Has anyone any idea why the peasant girl hanged herself?' asked Mlle de Dismarat.

'Presumably,' said the priest, with emphasis, 'because, with the count's consent, her suitor took another woman.'

'Poor thing,' sighed Amaryllis, 'I should never have thought that a peasant would commit suicide for love.'

The count looked out of the corner of his eye at Martin, who had placed a stool by the wall and was sitting there with lowered head. Master Tenelli whispered to one of the servants to hand round the wine. The countess stared frozenly into space. She was so pale that Borel asked if he might count her pulse, but she thrust him away with a gesture.

At last Guy returned and handed the count a strip of Jeanne's blue skirt. 'She is lying on the floor, Father.' He returned the borrowed weapon to Martin, and at the same time gave him a look of triumphant hatred. The count stood up and threw the strip of cloth into the fire.

'Goodnight ladies. M. d'Oubray, pray be so kind.'

The company rose. For once, the two gentlemen left the room before the ladies. The count decided with M. d'Oubray that the duel should take place without seconds, for this would have required two days to arrange. They would meet the following morning near the gravel pit at six o'clock, in the presence of Borel. Then the count discussed with Grouchet the immediate future of Constant du Fayel, Louis de Salvieux, Raoul and Martin. Grouchet was prepared to take the boys to the hunting lodge, and tugged grimly at his red moustache. He insisted that the four young gentlemen would certainly make excellent hunters, and he would see to it that they became so. Could he subject them to military discipline? Certainly, replied the count, for in the spring he would take them all with him to the war, but he asked him to be lenient with the delicate Louis de Salvieux, so that his health would not be impaired.

When the count returned to his bedroom after his conversation with Grouchet, he sent Pierre to fetch Martin. When the boy arrived he was standing in front of the fireplace.

'Martin, you take too many liberties with me.'

'Forgive me, M. le Comte.'

'I want you to know that you irritate me.'

'Tomorrow you'll be rid of me.'

'And suppose I wish to be rid of you for good?'

'Monsieur, you are only speaking in anger.'

'Martin, I have ill-treated the countess, and tomorrow I shall kill d'Oubray. Tell me what you think of me.'

The boy looked him sadly but firmly in the eyes. 'You are a good man but you often behave evilly.'

'Do you consider that a good man can behave badly?'

'Monsieur, I often experience it with you. You are always kind to me and very seldom to the others.'

'I can also ill-treat you.'

'Of course you can, M. le Comte.'

'Aren't you in the least afraid of me, Martin?'

'Monsieur, thanks to you, I have overcome my fear. Why

should I be afraid of your bad moods when I know that they will pass by tomorrow?' And fixing his eyes on a picture, he added shyly: 'I am your younger friend and should like to look up to you.'

'You young puppy!'

Martin did not look at the count. 'Yes, Monsieur.'

'I'm beginning to dislike you.'

'Monsieur, you're only angry with yourself.'

'To hell with you!'

Martin bowed. 'Goodnight, M. le Comte.'

'Stay where you are.'

'But you've just dismissed me.'

'No. Martin, you make me relent. What do you want of me?'

'Nothing, Monsieur. Nothing in the world.'

'That is a lie.'

'Monsieur, a younger friend should not make demands. At best he should only express a wish.'

'What do you wish from me?'

'I've already told you and I can't repeat it. Can I go, M. le Comte?'

'Yes, you can go. Stop, Martin. I have another question to ask you. Why did you fling Jeanne's shawl in Guy's face?'

Martin flushed: 'M. le Comte, I behaved disgracefully and I'm truly sorry.'

'I advise you to become reconciled with Guy.'

'Monsieur, no reconciliation is possible.'

'Why?'

'I beg you to allow me to be silent on that score.'

'Martin, no one hates you apart from Guy. Therefore it was he who shut you in the underground passage. That is why I wanted to punish him today. Be silent, the matter is closed. Do you find my behaviour to the countess inexcusable?'

'Monsieur, there is no possible excuse for you.'

'You dare to say that to my face!'

'Monsieur, I had to say it. Beat me if you wish.'

The count bent down, picked up the poker and made the sparks fly. Then he returned it to its place and raised himself. His dark face was strangely frozen

'Martin, does the power you have over me come from your love?'

'I don't know, Monsieur. You helped me when I was on the point of losing my reason. Since then I believe in nothing, except you.'

'You believe in me as though I were a saint.'

Martin did not laugh. 'Yes, something like that, Monsieur. In spite of all.'

'Hm! You make the most edifying jests.'

'I was not jesting, Monsieur.'

'So I perceived. Thus I need only destroy your faith in me to be free of you. I am pleased to know that simple remedy.'

'Monsieur, you are free of me. I am only here because you sent for me.'

'I should like to be cruel to you.'

'Are you drunk?'

'Insult me a little more, Martin.'

'Monsieur, I beg you not to make me say anything more.'

'Have you second thoughts about defying me?'

'I do not wish to annoy you. You are as excitable as a horse that has been stung by a gadfly.'

'The comparison is not bad, my boy. Gadflies have to be squashed.'

'You are my friend.'

'Martin, you should never trust the friendship of the powerful. You are a bastard who has perhaps been raised to favourite, through a whim, and whom a whim can also banish. How do you know that I am serious in my friendship? Perhaps for me you are no more than a court jester, who is allowed to speak the truth for my pleasure, until one day he is superfluous. Could that not be the case?'

Martin turned pale. He raised his hands, his lips started to move but no words came out. His expression amused the count. 'You see how easily your faith in your saint collapses. Come here, my boy, I did not really mean it.'

Putting his arm round Martin, he said: 'In all friendship I was leading you by the nose to knock your strange saint from its unworthy plinth. Men are seldom to be trusted, and they die on you. Believe in yourself, or believe once more in the Holy Virgin and the other denizens of heaven.'

Martin burst into tears and caught hold of the silver-embroidered edge of the count's coat. 'I will learn. Let me believe in you as long as I can . . . just for a while.'

The count was forced to laugh. 'For a while. What is a while?'

'A year at the most.'

'You mean that I've got to behave impeccably for a year?'

'Oh, Monsieur!'

'Martin, you are fantastically stupid, but your stupidity is irresistible. I will grant your wish and try to put things in order.'

Martin flung his arms round his neck with real passion. 'I know why you tormented me. It's to make me strong and independent, so that I shall be a friend worthy of you. You meant well, Monsieur.'

'I am going to take you to the war with me. I shan't let you out of my sight, day or night.'

Martin freed himself in surprise. The count held him tighter and asked: 'Aren't you pleased?'

Instead of replying, Martin leant his forehead against his.

'You're not pleased.'

'Yes, M. le Comte, but . . .'

'What do you mean, "but"?'

'I do not know whether I could stand being with you continually.'

'I promise I won't confuse you any more.'

'Monsieur, do you think you could stand me the whole time?'

'That depends on you,' laughed the count.

'No, M. le Comte, not always.'

The count pulled his hair. 'Perhaps you are right, my very intelligent ass. I'll think it over until tomorrow. Go to bed.'

'In my room?'

'Yes. Otherwise we shall again fall under suspicion.'

As they parted, the count held out his hand to Martin. Martin kissed it twice and left.

The count left his place by the fire and opened a heavy oak chest. From a secret drawer he took out the jewel case of the late Baroness d'Epponcourt, opened it, extracted the list of contents which bore his signature, and returned to the fire. But he changed his mind, and instead of burning the paper, returned it to the chest. Placing it under his arm, he set out for the countess's apartments.

In the antechamber, Denis woke up abruptly and, opening the door to the salon for the count, cried: 'M. le Comte!' There was no one in the salon, although two candles were burning. There was a rustle in the bedroom and the door closed. The count found his wife still dressed, with her hair partly undone, as though she had intended to retire to bed without Emilie's help. Noticing the look of terror in her eyes, he hastened to reassure her.

'Forgive me, Madame, for bursting in on you so late. I have merely come to give you your dead friend's jewellery, which will be in safer custody than with me. Please compare the contents with the list. Only a pair of pearl earrings and a gold bracelet are missing, both of which can easily be replaced.' The countess took the coffer without a word and placed it on the commode.

'Do you intend to go to Court or not?' he asked abruptly.

'I shall remain at Grandval.'

'I prefer that, and you are to write to me for written permission before you take a journey. Despite your malady you are too beautiful for the Court, and also too beautiful for an admirer. You know that tomorrow morning, early, I am fighting a duel with M. d'Oubray. I had decided to kill him, but I do not wish to leave too bad an impression of myself before I leave. I have changed my mind. I suggest that I spare d'Oubray in return for a promise from you.'

'What do I have to promise?'

'That you will not see him as long as I am away.'

'I will give you my word, provided that you, for your part, promise not to wound him.'

'You seem to be more concerned with his safety than with your husband's. But that is quite comprehensible today. I promise I will not wound him.'

'And I promise not to receive him during your absence.'

'Madame, that means that he leaves Grandval with me and must not return without my personal invitation.'

'Monsieur, I accept your terms.'

'I am content, Madame. You have my full confidence. M. d'Oubray owes his life to this confidence. Have you a bruise on your elbow that you wear a bandage?'

'Yes.'

'I am ashamed, but I know that it is useless begging your forgiveness. I deeply regret having been brutal to you in my rage, and should prefer to fall to a bullet rather than offend you again in the same manner. You love charity. I am adding this purse to the coffer, so that you can indulge your generous impulses. I take my leave.' He bowed formally and left.

The countess sat on her bed and covered her face with her hands. A door opened gently and M. d'Oubray entered. 'Madeleine, how terrified I was for you. How easily he could have grown suspicious.'

He sat by her side and tried to embrace her, but she thrust him away. 'It is too late now, Monsieur.'

'What is too late, Madeleine? Why do you no longer call me Etienne?'

'Did you hear our conversation?'

'Yes, every word.'

'Then you know enough.'

'Madeleine, you don't intend to keep your promise to this man.'

'Yes, Etienne, his confidence obliges me to.'

'Madeleine!'

'I can do nothing else. Just think if he had come a little later. We should both have been lost.'

'Yes, Madeleine, but now he will not return and the goal of my longing is near at hand.'

Once more she thrust him away. 'I have told you, Monsieur, it is too late.'

'Madeleine, I have desired you from the first day I met you. By all the Gods, I will do anything you ask of me. I will leave Grandval for ever but do not now destroy my hopes of your love. Let me for this once possess you completely and you will belong to me wherever I may be. Madeleine, I am naught but an adventurer, a restless creature who may one day be killed in a brawl, die unnoticed and rot unmourned in some distant land. Madeleine, these are the last hours I am allowed to spend with you.'

'Etienne, I suffer more than you.'

'No, otherwise you would have pity on me. A short while ago you said that for me you would break the fetters of your fidelity, and now your virtue means more to you than your lover. How loveless, how icy is your heart.'

'Monsieur, he is capable of believing in my virtue. My conscience plagues me. I cannot deceive this man.'

'Madeleine, he threw you to the floor. A girl hanged herself on his account, and he has never been faithful to you.'

'Monsieur, he knows that he is evil, nevertheless he is not entirely so. He is Pan and he has no soul.'

'Yes, he has a soul. Martin loves him and he loves that boy.'

'Pan is incapable of love. He lusts after Martin.'

'No, otherwise he would take him tomorrow to the war.'

'Leave me, Etienne, I am bound to Gaston.'

'You are deluding yourself. Can't you see that he only simulated regret at this farewell in order to bind you more firmly in his toils? He is the devil and keeps his claws in your soul. Free yourself, Madeleine. This is your last chance to escape. Love me now, as you have long wanted to do and he will lose his power over you.'

The countess rose to her feet. 'Monsieur, it is the will of God that I belong to this man and God has now given me strength to resist temptation. Go now. In future our relationship must be confined to conversation and letters.'

D'Oubray rose to his feet. 'Madame I have not deserved such a farewell.'

'Monsieur, I shall place my future in the hands of God.'

She went to the commode and took the purse off the dead baroness's jewel case. 'Take this purse for your impoverished Huguenot friends. Do not reveal the name of the donor, for letters of thanks would only embarrass me.'

D'Oubray held the purse as though it were a relic, and replied: 'My letters will inform you of the recipients' joy, of the parents' tears of gratitude and the delight of the children.'

He was about to pocket the purse, when she said with a slight blush:

'I have just noticed that the purse is very pretty. I should like to have it back. Please transfer the contents into your own purse.'

D'Oubray's eyelids twitched as though he were in pain: 'Will Diana preserve a memento of Pan, and refuse one to her servant?'

She blushed even deeper and replied: 'My husband is off to a war which claims more and more victims every day. This bow from my dress is for you.' D'Oubray kissed the bow and hid it in his breast. Then he poured the gold coins into his own purse and returned the other.

'Madame, less than an hour ago you said that you would love me and desired to see me happy. If, tomorrow morning, I should be as skilful as my opponent, I will not spare his life. Sleep well.' He hurried from the room.

The count, M. d'Oubray and Dr Borel returned through the little park gate from the forest at eight o'clock next morning. Both sleeves of M. d'Oubray's coat were in tatters, but he was not wounded. The count had a small scratch on his head, the result of a lunge parried too late. He let himself be bandaged in his study in Martin's presence and informed the boy that he had decided not to take him to the war. He ordered their departure for ten o'clock, breakfasted in high spirits, took his leave of the ladies and was in the saddle punctually at the prescribed hour. M. d'Oubray, the four young gentlemen, Master Tenelli and Martin, rode with him out of the castle courtyard at the head of fifty horsemen. Mlle Amaryllis followed in one of the countess's coaches, which was to drive her to the next relay station. The storm had not abated.

They parted at the bridge. Raoul, Constant and Louis rode home. Guy and Tenelli branched off the road to the Duchesse de Bouillon's castle. The actress travelled with M. d'Oubray in the direction of Paris, and the count at the head of his troop went north-east. Martin was allowed to accompany him for one day's ride. The count showed his most attractive and friendly side to the boy, so that with each mile he grew sadder and sadder and finally begged not to be sent home. The count curtly refused his plea, telling him that he must write every week. With tears in his eyes Martin promised, and had to return to Grandval after a night of weeping in the inn. At the castle he was told that the young gentlemen had already moved into the hunting lodge. Martin reported his return to the countess and joined the other boys.

THE YEARS OF WAR

Master Grouchet treated the young gentlemen as he had treated his recruits in the old days as a corporal. Martin took the delicate Louis de Salvieux under his wing and occasionally persuaded Grouchet to excuse him from reconnoitring in bad weather. Constant twice rose too late, despite his comrades' attempts to wake him, and the third time, despite his sixteen years, was thrashed with a dog whip, whereupon he ran away. Grouchet was looking forward to thrashing him again on his return, for being absent without leave, when news came from the castle that Monsieur Constant du Fayel had taken his leave of the countess and was on his way home. Louis was furious at Constant's desertion, and also wanted to return home to escape this strenuous service. Raoul and Martin, however, persuaded him that a real nobleman had to be a capable hunter, and consoled him with the thought that Master Tenelli would soon return and that they would then be allowed to return to the castle. Louis let himself be persuaded and held out gallantly.

Tenelli duly arrived, and immediately began to quarrel with Master Grouchet. Grouchet maintained that the count had ordered him to train the young gentlemen to hunt until December, whereas Tenelli insisted that the count had expressly ordered him to teach them the Italian language and the art of war at Grandval. Grouchet would not give in, and Tenelli wrote a stormy letter to the count who, through Martin's letters, had been kept informed of the young gentlemen's progress as huntsmen.

One December day they set fox traps. The following night there was a fall of snow. Louis lost his way looking for the traps and was found half frozen. The following morning Grouchet sent him with a hound to find his trap. Martin insisted upon accompanying Louis, and the two boys searched for hours in all directions without finding the trap or a nearby earth. Louis said that the forest looked quite different in the snow. He no longer recognised it, and his toes were beginning to smart. Martin was more than glad to get him back to the hunting lodge and to rub his feet until life returned to them.

The countess received a letter from Guy. He was having a magnificent time at the Duchesse de Bouillon's Court. The days were a round of pleasure. He was in favour and had never been so happy before. A certain Monsieur de la Fontaine, who wrote the funniest fables in verse, was a member of the Court. The duchess had them read aloud and allotted the various parts; Guy as Reynard the Fox, had made them all laugh. But his best costume was too tight and his dear mother should be kind enough to send him 100 livres. The duchess's own tailor was a botcher, but since they were shortly leaving for Paris he would visit his father's tailor. His hounds had been a success and must have smarter collars—red with silver buckles. The countess was delighted with this gay letter and sent Guy 300 livres instead of 100, for she knew the prices charged by Parisian tailors. Each evening, in the presence of the snuff-taking, sneezing Mlle de Dismarat, she made Tenelli read to her from the Divine Comedy and wrote long letters to M. d'Oubray.

Finally, a letter arrived from the count addressed to his wife, in which, among other things, he wrote that the boys were well enough with Grouchet and that, after Christmas, Tenelli should continue to teach them at Monsieur de Méril's. Grouchet was jubilant. A letter was enclosed for Martin. His scrawl had pleased the count, but it was almost illegible. He must learn to write more clearly and more correctly. Martin was alternately happy and depressed by this. When his comrades were asleep he practised writing by the light of a candle, until his fingers were numb with cold, and wrote the count a long letter every Sunday, which the countess was kind enough to forward. One day before Christmas Grouchet dismissed his pupils with a short speech; he said that all three had been capable but that the noble art of hunting would benefit if the vicomte kept his eyes open when he fired.

After the Christmas festivities in Grandval the young

gentlemen travelled with Master Tenelli to M. de Méril, who suffered from gout, did little entertaining, and ran his household with great economy. He constantly sent his guests to hunt wolves, because his shepherds could not keep down these beasts and he demanded five gold louis compensation for an old hound accidentally shot by Raoul.

In the meanwhile, the count endured all the toil of the winter war in order to win his way back into the king's good graces. The Dutch defended their freedom with the courage of despair, and the hopes of the French army commanders remained unfulfilled. As they had hoped, the entire flooded area was covered with a thick layer of ice which allowed the king's regiments to make a rapid advance, but before they could consolidate their gains the thaw set in, and anyone unable to reach firm ground died an agonising death by drowning. The Comte de Racon lost all his baggage and three men. The total losses in guns, horses and men were enormous and appalled the Court.

The king had new troops and auxiliaries impressed as quickly as possible. He exhorted his commanders to double their efforts, promising them the highest honours and piles of gold if they succeeded in defeating the Netherlands Republic before the end of the year.

At the end of February 1673 Louis, Raoul and Martin, now close friends, returned to Grandval to wait there for the count, who, to the grief of the countess, proposed to take them that spring to the Netherlands. Martin received a letter ordering him to ride with a groom and meet the count.

Out of his senses with joy, Martin rode off without a groom and, after two days, met the count on the Baron du Terne's lands. The count greeted him affectionately and cursed him for having exhausted his horse. Martin replied that he felt no remorse. His frank innocence pleased the count, who asked him whether he had any conquests of his own to boast of. Martin said happily that he hoped to make some conquests in the Low Countries. He could leave that to Maréchal Turenne and the Duc de Luxembourg, was the reply. Had he had any success with the ladies? At Master Grouchet's and at M. de

Méril's there had been no women about, but Emilie had been very friendly.

The count laughed and replied that she was nearly old enough to be his mother. Martin agreed, but said that she was allowed to wear the countess's cast-off lace underwear and secretly used her scent. And what if the armourer discovered it? Then there would be a duel. Did Martin love Emilie? He loved lace and silk, the contents were far less important. The count took Martin by the ear and the boy embraced him. After this, he gave up playing the custodian of his morals. They rode together, allowing their horses their heads, and reached Grandval three days later.

Impulsive as in everything he did, the count checked the administration of his extensive domain in barely two weeks, travelled to Brayonne with Martin for the same purpose, returned, and after a brilliant farewell feast left for the war with the three young gentlemen, Master Tenelli and a fair-haired mistress. As colonel of his light horse regiment, he wore a scarlet cloak with gold braid and had dressed his fifty riders, now in full complement again, in grey and red, to comply with the Minister of War's penchant for uniformity. He travelled as fast as the horses allowed, conversed with Martin and paid not the slightest attention to the comfort of his mistress, who was consoled in secret by the ever obliging Tonio Tenelli.

On reaching his regiment the count ordered a roll call, sent the sick to the devil, made one man run the gauntlet, hanged two more, gave them their arrears of pay and, with the aid of his corporals, restored discipline in no time. Officers and cadets reported daily to him; some he confirmed in their former rank, others were recommended to different regiments. He rode from time to time from his quarters to visit the Duc de Luxembourg who invariably received him graciously and invited him to his table. Thanks to a certain affinity, an uneasy friendship sprang up between the duke and the count, which the latter used to his advantage. He knew that the favour of the duke would very soon bring him back into the good graces of the king.

The enemy did not remain idle. They made every effort to disturb the French preparations and, with the help of the allied powers, launched furious counter attacks. The count's regiment was soon in action in various parts of the line. Both armies inflicted grievous wounds upon each other, but it never came to a decisive battle.

The count had given the boys strict instructions not to get under fire and had made Tenelli responsible for their safety. The Italian often cursed his difficult position, for both Louis and Martin longed to get into the fray and constantly found an opportunity of giving him the slip. On one occasion, when riding along the sea shore with his charges, they met a Brandenburg patrol, and since both the boys immediately fired their pistols instead of wisely taking to their heels, he found himself forced to fight for his life. Fortunately, the shots had been heard by some French Grenadiers behind the dunes; they hurried to the rescue with wild shouts, whereupon the Brandenburgers, in a hail of bullets, fled, leaving two dead behind them in the sand. Tenelli cursed and swore, but this had no effect on either of the boys, who boasted of their deed. Louis had received a slight graze from a bullet and Martin's horse was so badly wounded that it had to be killed the same evening. The count deemed it necessary to punish not only Martin but Louis, and thrashed both of them; this, however, would have been of no avail had he not threatened that, on Tenelli's next complaint, he would send them home with ignominy. Louis and Martin both promised on their honour that in future they would obey their tutor. The count accepted their word, and from then onwards bothered no further about the three boys.

The Duc de Luxembourg was anxious to save his infantry for big battles and generally used his cavalry for small skirmishes. The Comte de Racon's light horse were constantly in action and won several minor victories. The count liked to lead his best squadrons and distinguished himself by the lightning swiftness of his attacks. Although the duke constantly honoured him at his drinking bouts and invited him to attend his councils of war, the count displayed little interest in the cumbersome plans of full scale operations and much preferred to act on the spur of the moment, at the same time not infrequently overstepping his orders in the process. The duke appreciated the independence of Colonel de Racon, who was intelligent enough not to boast of his success but on every occasion to extol the duke as his incomparable teacher and as the king's greatest army commander.

One cloudy, late summer afternoon, Tenelli, with his three young charges, was observing from a safe distance a siege led in person by the great Vauban, architect and fortification expert. Among a group of engineer officers, Louis suddenly discovered Guy, who was still supposed to be at the Court of the Duchess de Bouillon. Guy pretended not to recognise his former comrades, but Louis, Raoul and Tenelli rode over to him and he was thus forced to greet them. He reluctantly admitted that he had run away from the duchess's castle and was now a page in the service of a well-born engineer officer. He said there was more opportunity for advancement in the field than elsewhere, and this must suffice his father as an excuse. To the officer's amusement, Tenelli explained that he was M. de Brayonne's tutor, and forced Guy under duress to join his other charges.

In the meantime, Martin, on horseback, had joined the group of high-ranking officers and their ladies, who were watching some heavy guns being brought up, when suddenly they came under strong artillery fire from the fortress. The intention had been to bring the guns into position behind a breastwork, so that their fire could be brought to bear on the opposite enemy gate. However, at that instant the drawbridge was lowered and a strong enemy column, its commanding officer at the head, emerged from the fortress. In no time, the forward trenches had been bridged and, while the fire from the fortress ceased, the assault force charged and tried to rush the French artillery emplacements, which the French gun crews fought desperately to protect.

Around Martin, orders rang out, orderlies galloped off, and the ladies fled. Foot soldiers were brought up at the double, only to have their own guns turned on them by the victorious enemy. Panic ensued. Then the sounds of shots could be heard drawing close from the opposite direction. As it happened, the defenders from the high battlements of the fortress, had observed a relief force approaching the beleaguered fortress and had accordingly timed their surprise sortie.

Martin heard Tenelli calling and at the same time saw the Comte de Racon's regiment of light horse galloping up at full speed. Martin's good resolutions were forgotten. Spurring his horse, he found himself advancing with the troop at full tilt and a little later among the captured guns which were still thundering. His horse reared and fell over backwards. Fortunately, he was thrown clear. Jumping up, he caught a riderless grey by the rein, swung himself into the saddle and leaped over the twitching bodies of dying horses and screaming soldiers into the fray where, despite the gunpowder and the swirling dust, he recognised the count on his black charger.

It was a short, sharp encounter. The guns were recaptured and the enemy pursued back to the fortress. Martin galloped in the van of the pursuers, outstripped them and blazed away with his pistols into the backs of the fleeing enemy. Suddenly he felt himself caught by the left foot and, before he was aware of it, pulled from his horse, disarmed and taken prisoner. A few other hotheads suffered the same fate, and when he heard the cannon balls from the fortress whining over his head he realised that there was now no hope of escape. Looking back, he caught sight of the count's red coat disappearing into the sunlight behind a blue cloud of powder. The walls of the fortress closed about him and a jeering Spaniard flung him into a dark casemate.

The count, with his victorious horsemen, retreated out of range of the guns and despatched men to search for Martin among the dead and wounded. When a blood-stained corporal reported that he had seen Martin riding ahead of him in the pursuit, the count realised that he had either been taken prisoner or lay wounded under fire. An advance at this moment would have been suicide. The count hastened his retreat, leaving the transport of the wounded to the infantry which had just arrived. Rallying his regiment, he led it against the enemy reinforcements which were already engaged with a regiment of musketeers. Both sides fought with equal bravery, but superiority lay with the king's troops and on the same day the Duc de Luxembourg was able to despatch a courier to the royal headquarters with the news of victory.

The unfortunate Tonio Tenelli, who was not to blame for Martin's misfortune, bore the brunt of the count's rage and was carried, half strangled from his tent. Guy was soundly thrashed, but after writing a letter of apology to the Duchesse de Bouillon, was allowed to remain with the army; the engineer officer's praise enabled him to get back into his father's good graces. Raoul was in complete disgrace. He had told his father that at a distance he could not distinguish the enemy flags from their own and could only recognise the cockades at twenty paces. The count abandoned the idea of making a soldier out of him and sent him with Tenelli to replace Guy at the Duchesse de Bouillon's Court where his good looks and wit soon won everyone's heart.

The siege dragged on despite the presence of Vauban. After fourteen days, on the insistence of the Comte de Racon, an exchange of prisoners was proposed to the enemy commander; the Dutch accepted on condition that there should be a three days' truce. Since the besiegers had taken less prisoners than the besieged, Martin was not among those released, who told of the appalling hunger reigning in the completely encircled garrison. The count at least learned that Martin was safe and sound and, although he knew that he was starving, was powerless to help him.

Firing continued on both sides. Vauban threw up a succession of earthworks and the noose grew ever tighter. At last the attackers managed to drive two breaches in the walls; the infantry stormed through both but were repulsed. The losses were appalling. Then came the news that the Prince of Orange was approaching. The duke's troops were in no state to give battle and, completely exhausted, waited for reinforcements. Fearing a break-through, the duke gave the order to retire, with a view to launching a new attack later. Vauban implored him to wait another two days, for then the fortress would be cracked like a nut and captured without difficulty. The duke had already ordered the guns to be loaded on their carriages at nightfall, when a fluttering white flag appeared on the tallest bastion. After a short parley the fortress surrendered, driven to do so by hunger. The emaciated prisoners were released from the casemates. The courageous garrison defenders were sent to the galleys; the commanding officer and his high-ranking subordinates were received with honour by the duke and taken under escort to a fortress, safely in French hands and well behind the lines.

Like his fellow sufferers, Martin had been without water for two days and was almost too weak to stand. Pierre brought him to the count, who, by way of greeting, boxed his ears, lifted him up and embraced him so wildly that he nearly crushed his ribs. Martin would take no food until he had been forgiven and, needless to say, the count immediately forgave him.

No decision was reached that year in the war which had started in such a blaze of glory in the spring, and the king began to give up hope of a total conquest of the Low Countries. The strength of his allied opponents continued to increase and England deserted him. The Imperial Commander, Montecuccoli, and the Prince of Orange, pressed forward with such superiority of numbers, despite a spirited defence, that Turenne was forced to give the Duc de Luxembourg orders to retreat. The duke's prudence and intelligence enabled him to lead his troops back in good order. They were given the opportunity of recuperating their losses by plunder. The Comte de Racon and other cavalry commanders who had to fight a rearguard action to cover the endless convoy, engaged the enemy every day. He ensured for himself a rich portion of the booty and saw to it that the country they covered was utterly laid waste. The atrocities were appalling and the duke permitted the troops to give free rein to their savagery. On account of the danger, the count would allow none of the young gentlemen to ride with him, but contrived that Guy should remain separated from Martin. Louis and Martin were detailed to join his baggage train, while Guy was attached to one of Vauban's engineer officers.

One November evening the count summoned the three boys. Guy was the first to arrive at the tent, which had been pitched out of the wind next to a blackened wall, all that remained of a ravaged farm. The count sat on his camp bed, shivering in his fur coat, warming his feet by a little smouldering fire, the smoke from which went up through a hole in the tent. The captain, who, in addition to a lieutenant, shared the tent with him, retired to bed and wrapped himself in his blankets. The count could not offer Guy a seat for there was no second camp bed.

'Guy, I have enquired about you several times and I am pleased with your behaviour. You avoid rushing into unnecessary danger but when the occasion arises you show courage. Every aspect of the art of war seems to interest you and you never miss an opportunity of learning. I am sending you tomorrow with the baggage and an escort to Grandval. There you will find Tenelli, who has taken Raoul to the Duchess de Bouillon. You will leave with him for Paris and enter the military school. I have great hopes of your future and I believe you have sufficient ambition not to disappoint me. You ran away from the duchess's Court, but I suppose you know that if you run away from the military school it is tantamount to desertion. At sixteen, you will do your service with the king's musketeers, and thus you will spend three years at the school. Your mother will equip you in Grandval. Take this letter to her. Adieu.'

Guy pocketed the letter and kissed his father's gloved hand.

'Thank you, Father, you have granted my dearest wish, and I promise that you will not regret your decision.'

As Guy left the tent, the reflection of distant fires flickered on the canvas. The snorting and stamping of horses tethered together in the lines, and the gossip of the soldiers round the camp fires invaded the tent.

A few moments later the corporal of the watch announced the Comte de Salvieux and Martin. When the two boys entered the tent the count barely greeted them, and announced without preliminaries:

'Guy is riding back to Grandval tomorrow with the baggage and you will ride with him, Louis. Have you news of your uncle?'

'No, Comte de Racon.'

'Do you know what his intentions are for you during the winter?'

'No.'

'Write to him as soon as you can. Guy is going to the military school. Perhaps you will be allowed to go with him.'

'Monsieur, I have recently had doubts as to whether I possess the qualifications necessary for a soldier. I could perhaps put my studies to better use in a different field.'

'What do you want to become?'

'A diplomat, Comte de Racon.'

'Not bad for a former pupil of the Jesuit Fathers,' smiled the count. 'Very well, write to M. de Méril and take an escort of four grooms with you when you leave Grandval. Martin, you cannot travel in company with Guy, but I should like you to spend the winter at the hunting lodge with Grouchet.'

'M. le Comte, in what way would that help me?'

'What have you in mind?'

'To remain with the army and become an officer of the king as soon as possible.'

'Shall I post you to winter quarters as a recruit?'

'As a corporal, M. le Comte, not as a recruit.'

'Are you serious?'

'Were I your son, I should ask you to buy me the rank of corporal and let me command a handful of horsemen. I do not know what a younger friend is entitled to ask.'

'Would you like to accompany me to Paris as my page?'

'M. le Comte, you have noble pages there who would look down on me. I should be out of place in Paris before I became an officer.'

'Ho, ho, so you're dissatisfied with your status, my princeling!'

'M. le Comte, I find your mockery hard to bear. You made me your sons' companion, but now playtime is at an end. I have grown used to feeling at home in a society to which I do not belong until I have won the right to do so. It would be painful for a Martin Saint-Jean to sit at your table at which a Lieutenant Saint-Jean would gladly sit. I do not wish to accompany you to Paris and should like to remain with the army.'

'I can see that you are no longer a child. You shall have your wish. You will winter with the Marquis de Chassigny's dragoons who are already in winter quarters behind the lines. Aide!'

The lieutenant rose from his camp bed. 'At your orders, Colonel.'

'I need my writing materials.'

The lieutenant rummaged in a saddle-bag, handed the count paper and ink and set the inkwell before him on the floor. The count removed his right glove and wrote a few lines.

'Here you are, Martin. Hand this to the Marquis de Chassigny with my greetings. He will give you the rank of corporal and put you under a capable sergeant. Take this purse for your equipment. Write to me at Grandval until you receive news of me. Keep away from women with the pox and bad company. Don't get into the habit of gambling and drinking. It will be a hard winter for you, but you're strong and you'll survive.'

'M. le Comte, can I serve under you in the spring?'

'No, not until you've been promoted to sergeant with the dragoons, and that will take a few years.'

Martin gave a start. 'Shan't I see you for all that time?'

'You can come and visit me in my Paris house during the winter.'

Martin lowered his head and stared at the ground.

'Our friendship has now got to be on the footing of a friendship between men; a parting is therefore rather useful.'

'But you just said that I was no longer a child, M. le Comte.'

'Are you infected with lice?'

'Yes, somewhat.'

'That's all part and parcel of a soldier's life. Adieu, Louis.'

Louis de Salvieux took his leave and the count held out his hand to Martin.

'We shall meet again sometime. Until then you must fend for yourself. Off you go. Adieu and goodnight.'

Louis and Martin left the tent. The count continued to sit there for a while, lost in thought, his dark, haggard face lit up by thc fire. At his whistle Pierre came in and made his bed with blankets and furs.

Winter with the dragoons was not as hard for Martin as the count had maintained, for his training with Master Grouchet had been severe in the extreme. Recommended to the officers by the Marquis de Chassigny, the sergeants also treated him with consideration, and when they discovered how well he rode he was appointed instructor to the recruits, who idolised him. As usual, he took the part of the weak and was not too brutal with the cowards. The officers appreciated his frankness, were not too proud to learn a few fencing tricks from him, and often, to the general envy, invited him to their table. Not being rich, he avoided gambling, and since he was fastidious, had little to do with the not precisely appetising trollops who, under the watchful eye of some worthy dame, solaced the lives of soldiers who had been parted from their sweethearts and wives.

Martin wrote long letters to the count, who could not bear his circumlocutions and solecisms and often criticised him sharply. As a result, Martin in time acquired the clear and natural style of expression peculiar to ladies and gentlemen of high society. He had no idea that the count was intentionally grooming him in their correspondence for the natural tone now prevailing in Paris salons. The count usually wrote only a few lines, but insisted upon full reports from Martin. 'Write to me as though I were there and you had a great deal to say to me!' Martin told him everything.

On the 26th February 1674, at four o'clock in the afternoon, the Comte de Racon was in the salon of Ninon de Lenclos who, in spite of her frivolous past, was still one of the most famous ladies in society. The count did not have to wait long. The eternally youthful Ninon entered in an enchanting green dress: 'M. le Comte, you dare to visit me, although I gave orders you were not to be admitted.'

'Forgive my audacity, Mademoiselle. I am returning to the war tomorrow with the Duc de Luxembourg, and have therefore only today to be of service to you.'

'You have not made the slightest effort in my interest.'

'I shall do so this evening at the Louvre, and should have liked a little promise from you in return.'

'Ah, now we are coming to the point. Come into my boudoir. You are lucky that the man I am waiting for is so disgustingly unpunctual.'

The count followed Ninon and caught sight of a well-laid table for two. 'Mademoiselle, the happy youth will most certainly overeat himself.'

'And what if he does, M. le Comte? That is why I shall not offer you a bite.'

The count smiled as though Ninon had said something flattering. 'Mademoiselle, I seem to remember having eaten with you at the same table.'

Ninon raised her hands in mock defence. 'Heaven preserve

me from yesterday's meats.'

'Ninon, I will recommend the young man of your heart to the Duc de Luxembourg as a presentable lad, if you persuade your ex-lover the Maréchal that he is once more the only receiver of your favours. Beg him to recommend my promotion to the king.'

'I thought the duke had already recommended you.'

'I need recommendations from all sides.'

'Why did you not tell me that until today? My poor boy is quite desperate and is probably at this moment hanging himself. I must look and see if he is coming.' Ninon hurried out, and the count had leisure to examine the elegant appointments of the boudoir.

Ninon returned. 'No sign of him, Monsieur. If my lamb has hanged himself I shall take my revenge by confessing that I committed perjury some years ago, and you will be beheaded.'

The count looked at her in amazement. 'I thought you did not care for yesterday's meats?'

Ninon laughed and subsided gracefully into a chair. 'M. le Comte, I have just forgiven you. Please sit down. If that ill-mannered cub is not here by five o'clock you can eat with me.'

'Mademoiselle, my dearest wish is that the devil has flown away with him.'

'I see that you have remained a beast. You will not be given any dessert.'

'Only fools bang their heads against a brick wall,' said the count, making himself comfortable. 'But since you are capricious, perhaps your tastes will change once again. I still hope to appear at your table as yesterday's roast.'

'Ugh, roast devil must be very tough. What change of taste have you noticed here?'

'Your flame-red couch of the old days is now draped in a dignified violet, and your eternal charms are more discreetly veiled than they used to be.'

'I like to show a change of face to the world, and in secret I am already in mourning for my last love.'

'Your last love? Can such things be?'

'I am not immortal, Monsieur.'

'Ninon, you'll be still in love on your deathbed.'

'Be silent, I do not wish to hear of death. If the priests did not constantly frighten us with it, life on earth would be thrice as gay. We should stop the mouths of the black crows. Do you remember how, wrapped in my scarlet silk coverlet, you terrified two gallants, making them think you were a cardinal? I can still hear your sermon. You were wonderful, Count.'

'And so were you, although you were sitting on my clothes and my blue hat, which did the ribbons and feathers no good.'

'I pricked myself on your spurs.'

'Do you still feel that rowelling?'

'Comte de Racon, let us begin eating and discuss the present. Have you recent letters from your favourite?'

'A whole bundle, Mademoiselle.'

'Let me see them, Count.'

The count handed her a bundle of letters and they sat down at the table. Ninon undid the string and continued chattering amiably.

'The Marquise de Sévigneé thanks you. She reads Martin's letters with the same pleasure that I do. I have every hope of seeing your favourite here one day. He must be quite charming. Please help yourself. I'm sure the lobster is delicious, for he was still alive when cooked.' The count helped himself, and Ninon began reading.

20th December 1673.

MONSIEUR,

Your letter made me very happy because it came from you, and very sad because you expressed a wish to see me in your Paris house at Christmas. Why do you always try these days to make me break my word and demean my honour? Please forgive me if I do not ask for leave. I shall never mention again how much I long to see you. I now have five comrades, the highest in rank being a bourgeois ensign. We can trust each other and we are never treacherous. Without comradeship one would die here, and comrades make life far gayer. Thank you for your generous offer but please do not send me more than ten francs. That is enough for a meal with my friends; anything that remains over is sure to be stolen. The colonel has entrusted me with his Spanish horse and I am to train it in the levade. Please think of me on Christmas day and do not lead me into temptation any more.

Your devoted and grateful young friend,

MARTIN SAINT-JEAN

'Oh dear,' said Ninon, 'the poor boy is miserable. Was he here at Christmas?'

'No, he never appeared.'

'What astounding pride! Give me a little more of that lobster. Compassion always gives me an appetite.' Ninon unfolded the second letter.

3rd January 1674.

MONSIEUR,

The regimental writer threw me out today. I want you to judge whether he was right. His wife always fed me well, particularly with ham and eggs, but her sauces were terribly spicy, and would have made me as randy as a bull, had our sergeant not constantly kept us on the move while the marquis was on his way here. I finally said to her that I could not swallow the stuff any more. She then suggested that when her husband was out drinking with his companions she could offer me something better. Hardly had the old man left, and I was off duty, than she started pressing home her attack—but the comestible was no less spicy!

Monsieur, if I could describe to you what a stinking baggage she is, you would understand why I behaved as Joseph did with Potiphar's wife. But you have always insisted that, on the king's example, I should express myself politely to all the female sex, so I told the lady that I was secretly betrothed and could not break my oath of fidelity, and that my lieutenant was waiting for me.

I left the house, and that night found the door locked. When I arrived next morning the writer told me that I had eaten more than my board, and that he had been forced to give my room to an officer. I was to pack my things but he would continue to be at my disposal on all matters of orthography.

I should have liked to smash him in the face, for the billets are so overcrowded that even two officers have to share a bed. My lieutenant, who is poor but ambitious, offered me quarters with him in the hope of some gratitude, because he knows who my noble friend is. He seems to have smelt the money you send, for which I thank you. M. le Marquis arrived the night before last and handed it to me. There was no letter from you. I gave the lieutenant twelve *livres,* for which I have the right to sleep on a pallet by his bedside. It reminds me of the night at Fleury when you told me the story of the half chicken. I am writing in my new billet, which unfortunately has no fireplace, and shall try to continue with my letter in the tavern. Perhaps I shall find a corner where I can write undisturbed. Adieu, Monsieur,

Your grateful,
MARTIN SAINT-JEAN

Ninon eagerly opened the third letter.

6th January 1674.

MONSIEUR,

I beg you to forgive me for having gambled away your gracious gift as soon as I had received it. I should have preferred to remain silent about this, had not the Marquis de Chassigny on his rounds been gracious enough to notice me on sentry duty. He said that I should hurry up and become a fop so that I should be worthy to sit at the Comte de Racon's table. I replied that this would be too great an honour for me and that I had no intention of ever becoming a fop. He banged me on the shoulder and said that I must not be a fool, but go as quickly as possible to the tailor. He gave me leave and I had to confess my irresponsibility. He merely laughed, gave me fifteen pistoles and said he would come tomorrow and watch my prowess as a riding-master. I must pray to God that none of them will be thrown! Please don't laugh at me too, and do not be angry.

Your remorseful,
MARTIN SAINT-JEAN

Ninon laughed loudly and ate the titbit the count laid on her plate. She continued to eat while she read.

11th January 1674.

MONSIEUR,

Thank you a thousand times for your letter. You were at Court and thought of me all the same. Thank you. I am giving fencing lessons to two officers and insist that they pay in advance, because otherwise the gentlemen mislay their purses. All the secret duellists are in a hurry to improve their skill. Now at last I know why some of them walk about wearing a bandage, maintaining that they have fallen off their horse. At the great farewell banquet so much was drunk that there were a number of brawls. The Marquis de Chassigny himself separated two of the gentlemen and ordered several of them to be locked up until the following morning. After the riding exercise on Monday, he praised me in public before the officers, saying that I was an excellent riding-master. I wonder whether he told you. I am sure you would have been pleased.

The service now demands that horses and harness should be spared. The mounts are too fat, and the harness and saddles are wearing out. The fall-in is sounded repeatedly. We are swiftly mustered and dismissed. My lieutenant says that in February we shall have to cut hazel wands because the men begin then to desert.

Monsieur, there is nothing doing with the peasant girls. They will only look at sergeants, but a beautiful lady's maid, who has now left with her employers, accorded me her favours. The pretty trollops are too expensive for me and I leave the ugly ones to the others. I am,

your grateful and devoted pupil,

MARTIN SAINT-JEAN

'Grateful pupil,' commented Ninon with a laugh. 'That has a delightful ring when he tells of a success with a lady's maid.'

'I taught him to fence,' explained the count.

'I know, Comte de Racon. Your favourite diverts me so

much that he makes me forget my faithless rogue.' Martin's next letter read as follows:

14th January 1674.

MONSIEUR,

My dragoon with the poisoned foot died yesterday. The other men in the hut could not bear his groans any more and laid him outside the door at night. He froze to death. I wanted to let him sleep in the stable but my lieutenant would make no exceptions to the regulations. I had not enough courage to stand up for the poor fellow and I feel very remorseful. He was a magnificent horseman. The regimental doctor says that, in any case, he would have died in a few days from blood poisoning. With my lieutenant's permission, I made the men stand to attention for an hour in the bitter cold and cuffed anyone who moved his feet. They will never put anyone outside again and leave him to freeze. The man with the itch has been sent home at last.

I am writing this letter in the priest's pigsty, for that is what his room is like. He keeps his pig in the room and his geese under the bed, because the dragoons rob all the barns since supplies have been delayed and we get nothing to eat but mouldy bread and rancid cheese. I met the reverend gentleman on his visit to the sick and today he invited me to supper with him. His cockerel has just dirtied my sleeve.

The priest started to probe into my life and I was frank with him. I should have kept my mouth shut for he started to talk about my conscience, and would still be doing so had I not told him that I had to write to you today. I do not care to think of God, heaven and salvation, since I was locked up in that dungeon, but for you I could become a saint. Would you like that? I'm sure you would not. You ask too little of me. The priest said I should visit him often, but I have no intention of doing so.

Your devoted,
MARTIN SAINT-JEAN

'The boy would become a monk for you, Count,' cried Ninon. 'Why don't you write to him, for a jest, and tell him that he will have to wear the cowl and pray for you in a monastery?'

The count swallowed an oyster and, while choosing the next, replied: 'Martin does not appreciate jests. He would put on the cowl.'

'I don't believe it.'

'I swear to you that he would.'

'Let us wager, Comte de Racon.'

'I don't wager about Martin.'

'Why not?'

'It would confuse him.'

'It's a pity. I should have won that wager.' Ninon replaced the letter and opened the next one.

19th January 1674.

MONSIEUR,

I have had no letter from you and I have been dogged by misfortune. Yesterday it was bitterly cold and I was writing to you at night in the tavern. I sat down between two peacefully drinking sergeants, who treat me as an equal because the marquis occasionally addresses me. Three lieutenants came in, one of whom had recently been degraded. They were already drunk and spoiling for a fight. After terrorising a few soldiers, one of them came over to my table and asked what I was writing. I replied that I was writing to an important nobleman. He laughed and insisted that I had no such acquaintance. I was not to boast but to admit that I was writing a love letter. I replied that he should be good enough to leave me in peace. Then he prodded my coat and asked why I was so padded. I replied that I wore a fur waistcoat underneath it, but it was your letters, Monsieur. I usually carry them on me because, in my new quarters, my belongings are constantly searched and the others pester me to write to you and ask for money to spend on them. I therefore hid your letters and pretended that you were no longer so well disposed.

You once told me that you don't like beggars and I have no wish to embarrass you. Soldiers always have debts. The lieutenant did not believe that I had a fur jacket. He caught me suddenly and held me over the table, knocking over the inkwell. He called the others and, although I defended myself, they ripped off my coat and discovered the letters. One of them stood on a stool and began to read out the letter in which you addressed me as 'my boy' advising me to scour the country for a cow maid rather than get poxed by one of the garrison whores. They laughed at the broad-mindedness of my sweetheart, but when the reader came to your name he looked pretty foolish.

One of them guffawed and suggested that she must be a married woman using a pseudonym. I tore myself free, smashed a pitcher over his head and was thrashed by his two friends. My comrades did not dare to lift their hands to the officers, but they cried out that they should spare me because my patron was a friend of the colonel. At this they let me go. I was in a rage and demanded satisfaction from the lieutenants, one of whom was unconscious. I was thrashed once more for my insolence and had to be bandaged by the sergeants and taken away. I managed to save your letters and threw them into the fire. Then one of the officers, who was still holding the letter he had read, cried out that I was probably a spy in the pay of the Spaniards, and that I had been giving away information. My comrades tried to rescue your letters as a proof that this was untrue, but they had all been burned.

You can imagine from where I am writing to you. I have been given writing materials to describe the incident and ask for a pardon. I have addressed both to the colonel, although I was advised to write direct to M. le Marquis de Chassigny. This I do not dare to do, because I should feel ashamed of appearing before him as a delinquent. My lieutenant visited me and said that my behaviour had merited the gauntlet and that had I been anyone else I should have been put to the torture, under suspicion of espionage.

Monsieur, I did not want anyone else to read your letters and that is why I burnt them. You know that I am no spy. I beg you to put in a word for me. I am in despair for I might cause you difficulties. I beg you, do not be ashamed of me. I shall certainly not incur more disgrace because, rather than run the gauntlet, I will slash my veins with a knife. Have I lost your friendship? I had to defend myself, Monsieur? I have always tried to be a credit to you. Am I in disgrace for ever? If only I could be a noble for a few days so that those three well-born dogs could not ignore my challenge.

I am no criminal. The three lieutenants should be hanged. Monsieur, please do not despise me for being in a cell. Do not abandon me, and speak to the marquis. You are his friend. If it is too painful for you to know a delinquent, then do not bother any more about me. You are the Comte de Racon. I am Martin Saint-Jean and have no right to call upon my father for help. If you can find it in your heart to do so, continue to love me, remember how much you cared for me and write what you think of me now. I have had no letter from you.

MARTIN SAINT-JEAN

'Monsieur, what happened to Martin?' asked Ninon in great excitement.

'Go on reading.'

'You're eating and I am alarmed.'

'My fears are over. I was at Court, wolf-hunting for ten days, and received Martin's letter somewhat late.'

'The poor boy, but you have such a good appetite that I think he must be alive. Give me another plateful. Is the bottle already empty?'

'I've opened the second bottle, Mademoiselle.'

Ninon drank and continued to read.

28th January 1674.

MONSIEUR,

I still do not know what will happen to me and I am still a prisoner. I have been told that in my case the decision rests entirely with the marquis, and I have been advised to ask you for money. I am writing this because I am being watched as I write. I need no money for in no circumstances will I try to escape, however much they incite me or try to frighten me. The Marquis de Chassigny is your friend and what he decides will be carried out, for he will do nothing to offend you. They say that even the marquis has to listen to his fellow officers. I do not believe that and have great hopes in you. I am certain that you still love me and wait patiently for your letter. I know that you will write to me. I dreamed of you.

Your MARTIN SAINT-JEAN

6th February 1674.

MONSIEUR,

You sent Charles to me! Oh, thank you. You spoke to the marquis who told you he would keep me under close arrest until the 10th February, so that in future I should not flout my superiors, and thus I shall be free in four days. The three lieutenants visited you and apologised for having insulted you indirectly. My honour has been saved. I am the happiest man in the world. I also thank you for the purse and the fur coverlet which Charles brought, and for the cloak. Now, I no longer have to jump up and down like a crazy ape in my cell, to prevent myself from freezing. I can also order myself mulled wine. I shall be released without being degraded. Monsieur, I am infinitely happy. Charles says that he is in a hurry so I will say adieu, with all my thanks. I do not dare to thank the marquis in person, but I have enclosed a letter of thanks to him which perhaps you will forward, if you think right. Where should I be today if I did not enjoy your friendship? Any other soldier would have been tortured and made to run the gauntlet. How I should like to kiss your hand! I thank you once more. I am eternally grateful, Monsieur.

MARTIN SAINT-JEAN

10th February 1674.

MONSIEUR,

I have been released. I have been given better quarters. The three lieutenants are no longer here. My case has become so well known that all the officers treat me with respect. The gentlemen whom I teach to fence have invited me to supper tonight. Tomorrow I am arranging a dinner for my comrades because they expect it of me. And tomorrow I have to march four men to be executed. If only they, too, could be given their freedom! To help his father out of the debtor's jail, one stole from the officer to whom he acted as orderly. The second, in a drunken frenzy, thrashed a cadet. The other two are deserters. Oh, Monsieur, and I still enjoy life!

Your eternally grateful,
MARTIN SAINT-JEAN

13th February 1674.

MONSIEUR,

In three weeks we're off campaigning. The equipment order has already arrived. Our regiment too has to dress uniformly in cream coloured coats with blue facings, brown hose and the leather trappings black whenever possible. Your red coats look much finer. Please write to me when you leave and tell me what route you are taking. Perhaps I shall meet you on the march.

Monsieur, before we leave, the marquis is holding a parade to promote officers and distribute decorations. I hope my lieutenant will be made a captain. He has really earned it. I also know that the marquis would be prepared to make me a sergeant if you requested him to do so. But you would not agree because I did not come to you in Paris. Very well, I'll remain a corporal until you forgive my obstinacy, or, because of my feats, the marquis promotes me against your wishes! And then you must let me serve in your regiment, unless you intend to break your word. I would rather be a cavalryman fighting at your side than have to bite the dust as a dragoon. I have just won a wager by jumping my horse over a gate into a hut and then over two benches and out by the other door. It does not sound much on paper but the hut was low and narrow. A cadet tried to copy me but his horse broke its neck and he is now under arrest. If only we were allowed to hold a riding display, but now the orders are to spare the horses, spare the harness, spare our hose and make the men's lives hell.

Thank you for your gift and your few words. My

weapons are in good order. I need nothing except two new shirts which would not take long to make. My new uniform is in hand. The bugle has just sounded . . .

The nightly practice alert is over. I can't tell you how I'm looking forward to the war. Are you asleep at this hour? I hope I shall dream of you.

Your devoted and grateful friend,

MARTIN SAINT-JEAN

Ninon de Lenclos had picked up Martin's last letter when she heard a rustle in the antechamber. She jumped up and ran into a dandified young nobleman at the door.

'Ah, so there you are, you monster, you faithless dog, you hideous deceiver. Come in. Yes, you can now see that the Comte de Racon has left you nothing to eat.'

The young man stuttered out his excuses, which Ninon brushed aside. 'Comte de Racon, I don't think you should recommend him, he has not deserved it.' The count rose with a smile.

'Mademoiselle, I think we should be lenient with him. If he reports tonight at nine o'clock to the lieutenant of the watch, outside the clock tower of the Louvre, I will introduce him to the Duc de Luxembourg as a very talented cavalier.'

Ninon took the young man by the ears. 'Do you hear, my lamb, my golden-haired love? Promise me immediately that you will be there punctually by the clock tower.' The young man flung himself at her feet.

'Forgive me, my goddess.'

'I don't want to hear anything about forgiveness. Will you be punctual?'

'Yes, of course, I swear it.'

Ninon turned round. 'Comte de Racon, my marshal will recommend you. Write me one of your spicy letters from the field and take care that you do not receive a bullet. I will look after Martin's letters for you like a relic.'

The count kissed her hand and heard the young man cry out in an outburst of jealousy: 'What did the Comte de Racon want? Who is your marshal? What are those letters?'

The Comte de Racon gave a farewell party in his Paris

house, at which many officers met for the last time before joining their regiments. The Marquis de Chassigny joined his dragoons, where he immediately held a grand parade. He promoted officers who had distinguished themselves in the previous year's retreat, and handed Martin a package containing 300 livres and a letter from the count. He asked Martin's captain for a report on Corporal Saint-Jean, and seemed pleased with the glowing reply. The regiment left and was detailed to the Prince de Condé's army. Martin had many an opportunity of showing his courage, and fought like a Turk. Whenever possible he tended the wounded, without losing his joy of battle at the sight of their wounds. On the 11th of August his regiment was in action at Seneffe and aided the Prince de Condé to win a magnificent victory over the allied forces of Spain, Holland and Austria. The Comte de Racon was wounded in the same battle and had to retire from the war for a few months. Martin could not obtain leave to visit him and had to nurse his fears until the autumn. He wrote first to Grandval, because he did not know the whereabouts of the wounded man, and received the desired address from the countess. From then on he wrote to Pierre, who answered all his questions through the count's doctor. The count recovered, and Martin was delighted when he received the first few lines in his own hand.

After the great victory, the Marquis de Chassigny's dragoons fought the same year on the Rhine and retired to winter quarters at the end of December for a well-earned rest. Martin was now granted leave, but once more remained with the regiment because the count was already on his way to Paris.

The following spring—1675—Martin was promoted sergeant and, at his request, the Marquis de Chassigny released him to join the Comte de Racon's regiment of light horse. The count had already been made a general. The meeting of these friends of different rank took place in bad weather on a parade ground where the count, with a few officers, was inspecting the drill of several squadrons. Martin gave a start on catching sight of the count, who unconsciously ran his hand over the left side of his face, as though trying to wipe away the fresh bright pink scar, which ran from temple to cheek. Ashamed of his anxiety, Martin kissed the scar at the graciously accorded embrace. The count told him that he could now serve under him, although his prospects of promotion were far less than with the marquis, since he could be shown no favouritism. Martin replied that he expected no unearned reward and that M. le Comte would be as just to him as he had always been in the past.

The year 1675 brought the Sun King the irreparable loss of his two most famous generals. Turenne fell at Sassbach, in Baden, and the ageing Condé had to retire to his estate owing to his failing health. The Duc de Luxembourg was made a marshal, but he was unsuccessful in defeating a superior enemy force. Louis began to sue for peace, and France breathed with relief in the hope that the king's diplomatic skill would be more successful than his commanders had been in war.

On a broiling July day in 1676, one of the Comte de Racon's light horse regiments, weary after a skirmish, encamped for the afternoon in a Flanders wood, through which meandered a shallow stream. Outside the wood, the sun beat down on unsown weed-strewn fields and on the brown back of the count who was lying on his belly sunning himself like a lizard. About thirty paces away a living human head stared at him from a mound of earth, while a hundred paces behind it the view was masked by a tall cluster of oaks, in the shade of which an occasional glimpse could be seen of a sentry's red coat.

The eighteen-year-old Martin, in shirt and hose, came out of the wood carrying an armful of beech branches. He was now fully grown, and, although he had broad, powerful shoulders, he was not particularly tall. He approached the count as he lay there sunning himself. 'Monsieur, I've come to pay you a visit and have brought something to protect myself from getting sunstroke.' A growl was the only reply. 'Do you want to sleep?' asked Martin.

'I'm listening to the crickets; can't you hear their pretty music?'

'No, I've got used to them.'

Martin stuck a few branches into the cracked soil to the left of the count, and retired with the rest towards the human head. 'There, you've got some shade, too. Where's the gold?'

'I don't know,' screamed the head. 'Dig me out, dig me out!'

'Shut your mouth! The general will shoot you if you don't confess, or he'll have you buried alive.'

'I know nothing.'

Martin gave the head a blow with one of the branches, returned to the count and lay down beside him. Settling down in the shade of the branches, he said: 'The fellow still refuses to speak.'

'Your merciful measures won't work this time. Later I'll have him questioned in the old familiar way.'

'Monsieur, I'm convinced that he was only digging for roots with his hoe. The entire population is starving.'

'There are no roots near rubbish heaps. He was certainly looking for the treasure he had previously hidden.'

'You have no proof. Let the poor devil go.'

'You're becoming tiresome with your eternal compassion, and you're making yourself unpopular with the men. They like to torture people and I don't begrudge them that pleasure.'

'Monsieur, brutality should not inflict more wounds than a battle does. There are men hanging from the trees everywhere as over there on that oak, or being tortured. I have fired more bullets to put them out of their misery than against the enemy. The Maréchal de Luxembourg should forbid such cruelty.'

'I don't agree. The enemy must be made to fear us, and cruelty increases fear. I'll order the men to dig the fellow out and allow them to torture him slowly. You'll be surprised how quickly he'll confess.'

'Be patient a little, Monsieur, there is nothing worse than to feel buried alive. I've experienced it myself. If he knows of a treasure he will certainly betray it, and if he doesn't, torture will be of no avail and he will be a cripple for life.'

'Very well. I'll be patient a little longer.'

The count turned over on his back, yawned and stretched and turned over once more on his belly.

'You bear a queer resemblance to the dark brown plundered corpses rotting everywhere in the heat,' said Martin.

'That is a charming compliment, I must say.'

Martin was unperturbed. 'From the back, you would look quite well if you weren't so bony. You have no backside.'

'You watch after your own looks. When you're my age, you'll be as fat as a pig.'

'Why? I haven't an ounce of fat on me.'

'You'll soon get fat when you have a few days' rest and there are no pretty skirts around.'

'I can't bear ugly women. Incidentally, how is it that you have so much success with the women, despite that scar on your cheek? Or do you brag when you exchange memories with your officers in Paris?'

'I have no need to brag.'

'How do you make the women fall in love with you?'

The count laughed. 'My God, what sort of a conversation is this for a hot day? Shut up! I'd rather listen to the crickets.'

'But I'd like to learn from you how to make a lady fall in love, in case I ever meet one.'

'You can't learn that from someone else.'

'Well, give me a little advice.'

'Cleanliness is very important.'

'So that is why you always wear fresh linen and wash more than the others?'

'Quite right, but don't repeat it. My rivals never guess why the women prefer me. They think I possess a love philtre, pills made out of goats' droppings and suchlike.'

Martin roared with laughter. 'Tell me, Monsieur, what first gave you the idea of striving to be clean?'

'An accident. At the age of fifteen, with my fresh pock marks, I became page to the Grande Mademoiselle at the Court. It was purgatory, I tell you. Every snotty-nosed boy could boast of some lady who favoured him; everyone laughed at me and I was not granted the least favour. Only the old women were charitable, but they did not attract me. I frequented the trollops and was constantly in debt. Then one day I was lucky enough to fall off my horse and was covered with slime. I had to have my head washed and I took a bath in a tub. When I got out of it, I was handed fresh linen. That evening I went to Court. The ladies noticed my freshly washed hair and my snow-white lace. I was aware of favourable glances, plucked up courage, and that very night, experienced a pleasure which exceeded my wildest dreams. I thought at first it was a miracle, then suddenly I saw the light, and since then I have always been successful.'

'Thank you for telling me this story, Monsieur.'

'You're welcome, my friend.'

'I envy you very much,' said Martin, after a short silence.

'You have no occasion to do so here in Flanders.'

'Oh, yes, Monsieur, for you get letters from a couple of ladies.'

'You are a Paul Pry.'

'Monsieur, you're always dropping your letters. Some of them have even been picked up by the soldiers.'

'They can't read.'

'What have you done with my letters?'

'A certain lady is keeping them for me. She wants to meet you, although she already knows you from your letters.'

'Monsieur, those letters were intended for you and for no one else.'

'They were too charming for a single reader.'

'I shan't write to you any more.'

'I should be offended.'

'You've offended me too, Monsieur.'

'You mustn't be offended.'

'But I am.'

'If you knew the lady you would not be.'

'Is she a lady of quality?'

'She's a perfect lady.'

'Is she beautiful?'

'Her charms are unsurpassed.'

'Is she young?'

'She is ageless.'

'So she is old. I find it difficult to believe that you, at the age of forty-three, can find your pleasure with old women of fifty.'

The count's shoulder muscles shook with laughter. 'I admit that I was never very lucky with the young girls. I don't think much of well-born girls and content myself with the virgins from my villages.'

'Sour grapes, Monsieur.'

'No, well-bred girls do not fall in love unless you appear to them as a demi-god adorned with virtues, which is terribly tiring. Then they give you their devotion and have nothing to offer except a brief pleasure and an endless chain of boredom. Only one thing remains to you and that is flight. You can't understand that. My interest is usually aroused by newly married, disillusioned, childish women who are just beginning to realise that they are a bore. At first they fight shy of me, but I play the tactful friend. They grow trusting and tell me their sorrows. I console them patiently. Young women's need for tenderness is very great. As soon as I become tender, they forget my ugly face. I achieve my goal, make an unfortunate woman happy, give her back her lost self-confidence so that later she is capable of entertaining her husband delightfully. I think I have patched up many a marriage.'

'Did my mother bore you?'

'Don't question me about her.'

'Monsieur, in my opinion, you look for nothing but pleasure in women and do not really love them. I find that despicable, if you will forgive my expression.'

The count turned over on his back once more and looked up into the blue, shimmering sky. 'Now and then I have really loved, but even after the greatest fulfilment there remained a desire for something inexplicable. There is no perfect happiness in true love. It always leaves a bitter taste.'

'Monsieur, I think that is true. When I had to be parted from you for a year, I could sometimes hardly bear it. Then when I was with you again I wanted to remain with you constantly, and now that, as a cadet, I can even be your tent companion, I finally realise that it is not your presence but your conversation which makes me happy. I should like to talk to you day and night, even in this heat. And I know that I often talk rubbish.'

'You must visit Ninon de Lenclos's salon in Paris. There one learns the art of conversation.'

'I will not go to Paris until I'm a lieutenant. I have no wish to fall in love with a lady of quality who would only look down on me.'

'I only hope that a clever lady falls in love with you and makes a gentleman out of you.'

'Monsieur, can the love of a woman be more wonderful than our friendship?'

'That depends on the woman. There are women who know you through and through and are capable of loving you all the same. That is a magnificent boon. And there are women whom you value so greatly that you would like to place a hundred lions to keep watch outside their door.'

'For me, women are necessary but rather incomprehensible creatures,' said Martin, thoughtfully. 'Presumably they don't think and feel in the same way that we do.'

'Yes, and no. A very intelligent lady once said to me that nearly all women had something masculine, and nearly all men something feminine in them. On this basis, men and women could occasionally understand each other.'

Martin laughed.

'Why are you laughing?'

'I was thinking of our moustachioed sutler who used to beat her husband black and blue. There was something definitely masculine about her.'

'And there's something feminine about you with your gentle compassion. You must get rid of it.'

'Do you consider your vanity is a masculine virtue?'

'Oh, Martin, if you were a woman I should be madly in love with you.'

'And I with you, and there would be a terrible end.'

'Why?'

'You wouldn't remain faithful to me for a month and I could not bear that. But it is wonderful as it is; we never know what this war holds in store for us, but I know that this moment is wonderful; if only it were a little cooler. The branches don't give much shade. Couldn't you go and lie under that elder for a change?'

'I like the heat.'

Martin sighed and fanned himself with a branch.

The count blinked up at the sun. 'It's midday. I would rather hear a shepherd's horn blowing in the distance than the noise of those fellows in the wood.'

'Monsieur, it would be marvellous now in Brayonne. Do you remember the stag hunt, the cornfields and the dancing peasants? The splashing fountains in the castle courtyard, and the ladies strumming their lutes? It is a long time since you sang a song. Yes, it was marvellous in Brayonne.'

'The war is making no progress since the Duc de Luxembourg replaced the Great Condé,' said the count with a sigh. 'He never does anything decisive and wastes his strength in small skirmishes. I am only allowed to stop the enemy advance and never to pursue him further than the lines which the duke has graciously traced on his map. I am tired of this ravaged landscape with its crickets and crows and this eternal stench of corpses. Every village has been burnt and abandoned. I could relinquish my command to Colonel du Lac, plead illness and go hunting with you in Brayonne.'

'No, you can't do that. You would be considered unreliable. How do you expect to get your marshal's baton?'

'Don't worry, I shall remain at my post.'

'Monsieur, the world is full of injustices. No one would punish you if you rode home, but a soldier would have to run the gauntlet.'

'I find that quite in order.'

'I don't, but that's how it is. I'm thirsty and I'm going off to plunge my head in the brook. Please give me a little time off.'

'All right, but come back quickly.'

Martin made his way to the forest where officers and men were sleeping beside their horses or enjoying a noisy bathe. Clothes, riding-boots and saddles were scattered about everywhere. And yet it was only an apparent disorder. Everyone knew where to find his horse and weapons, and a blast on the trumpet would transform the resting regiment into a fighting contingent within a few minutes.

Martin returned with a silver beaker to the count who was still sunning his back.

'Are you thirsty, Monsieur?'

'No, thank you.'

Martin turned to the head of the buried man and then looked down at the count, who had laid his head in his arms. Making up his mind, Martin slipped over to the head, unnoticed. 'If you tell me where your treasure is, I'll give you some water.'

'I don't know.'

'Don't shout. Here, drink.' The head drank greedily with rolling eyes.

There was a whistle and Martin rose to his feet. 'Hi!' called the count, 'what are you doing over there?'

'I'm questioning him.'

'Bring me the water.'

Martin dawdled and pointed to the half-filled beaker.

'Pour it out.'

Martin splashed the cold water over his back. The naked man leapt into the air. 'You midden spawn.'

Martin ran away like a deer, jumped over the head and made for the oaks. But the count had longer legs, caught him by the shirt and at the same moment gave vent to a yell. 'What's the matter?'

'I've trodden on a thistle.'

'A general shouldn't run about barefooted. Show me your foot.'

The count held on to Martin, who removed the thorns.

'Good, now look down on the ground.' The count gave him a kick that sent him sprawling.

'That was a despicable thing to do. The place is full of thistles.'

'That was for splashing me.'

Martin stood up, scarlet with rage, and said as calmly as he could: 'Monsieur, are you at this moment my superior or my friend?'

'Your friend, naturally.'

'I'm taking you at your word.'

Stepping back a few paces, he rushed with such force against the count that he knocked him over. 'Long live the king! You only fell on stones.'

He helped the count to his feet. 'I hope I didn't hurt you.'

'You've shamed me in front of the sentry.'

'Good heavens, I'd forgotten him.'

The count rubbed his back and clenched his teeth. 'To save my honour I must degrade you for at least three months to the rank of corporal.'

Martin turned pale. 'And,' continued the count, 'the sentence will be: loss of rank for knocking a general over. Mitigating circumstances: the general was unrecognisable shince he was stark naked. Good material for a lampoon.'

'For Heaven's sake, I did not really wish to make you look

ridiculous.'

'I believe you, ensign. We jested, and our jests are our own private affair. But I refuse to be made to look small. I am going to even the score. Turn your backside for me to kick it.'

Martin laughed with relief and bent over. 'And don't miss the mark, Schoolmaster.'

The count slapped him three times on his leather-padded hose. 'That's enough. The sentry saw it. Now I'll go and question the oracle again.'

The count went over to the head and bent down to it. 'Where is the gold?'

'I know nothing.'

The count took a beech twig and showed to the head the broken-off pointed end. 'Do you see this? I'll gouge out one of your eyes if you don't tell.'

'I wasn't digging for gold. I was looking for roots.'

The count raised the right eyelid of the helpless victim and plunged the point into his eye ball. A hideous scream of pain made Martin run up. The count then threw a handful of earth into the open mouth, and the wailing ceased.

'Monsieur,' said Martin, 'you really are a fiend!'

'Don't interrupt me. Shall I gouge out your other eye, or are you going to show me the gold? Yes or no?'

Spitting out earth, the head nodded; the remaining eye stared at the count in horror. 'Will you reveal the hiding place?' Another nod.

The count stood up and said to Martin: 'Give orders for the fellow to be dug out, and send Pierre to me.'

Martin ran towards the forest and could be heard calling for the servant.

Pierre soon appeared with a handful of soldiers, one of whom relieved the sentry. Within two minutes the count was fully dressed, and gave orders for his Spanish chestnut to be brought. He mounted. The soldiers led away the earth-stained man, who to their amusement, kept spitting. Pointing with his riding-crop, the count ordered: 'Forward to the rubbish heap.' He rode off and dug his spurs into the horse, which tried to rear.

With a few officers, Martin waited in the wood for the

the same as I. Virtue passes with youth. Until then, nurse your gentle conscience and be content!' He replaced the ring in his pocket, brushed a gadfly off his horse's neck and looked up at the sky. 'There'll be no storm until this evening.'

He rode his horse at walking pace towards the cluster of oaks. 'I want to take a look at the country behind the trees. A squadron of Imperial Horse and five hundred Spanish musketeers are supposed to have assembled behind that ruined mill. The fellows certainly won't expect an attack in this heat. I think I will attack.'

'Has the enemy any guns?'

'My patrols could not discover.'

'You should have sent me.'

'If the enemy has any artillery, I'll retire. We had enough losses this morning. Hi, you there!'

The sentry came running up. 'Can you see the enemy out-post?'

'Yes, your Grace.'

The count dismounted. 'Show it to me.' The man led the count through the undergrowth. Martin held his horse until he reappeared. 'Martin, I'm going to attack. Colonel du Lac and Captain Falleron are to report to me.'

Martin rode off and, a little later, the colonel and the captain came up at the gallop. The rested battalion assembled smartly on the field, while the count conferred with his officers beneath the oaks. The battalion was split in two in order to attack from both sides. The soldiers were in fine fettle. 'That's just like the Black Racon; he'll bowl them over like sunstroke.'

Here and there, the latest ditty rang out until the trumpets sounded. Martin carried the standard of the Falleron squadron and pressed forward after his captain who galloped away with the count. The song of the crickets was silenced by the thunder of hooves, and they only began to chirp again when firing started in the distance.

The one-eyed man groaned and washed his bloody socket in the forest brook. Then he pulled himself together and searched the trampled forest floor for crusts of bread and other edible scraps. A riderless horse sped past and collapsed on the ground. The one-eyed man hurried up swiftly, smashed its head with an axe and cut a strip of flesh from its quivering flank with his knife. The crickets chirped, the firing died away and the sun was still high in the sky.

During the year 1676, the Maréchal de Luxembourg's military enterprises still led to no decision. Exhaustion overtook both the French and the Hispano-Dutch army and its allies, while Louis XIV negotiated tirelessly with the enemy governments for a favourable peace treaty, designed to bring a last minute salvation from poverty and danger to his sorely pressed land.

The following year, the Comte de Racon and Martin Saint-Jean took part in the storming of the Fribourg fortress. Martin was wounded in the thigh. The count sent him to Grandval with a good surgeon, sufficient money and an escort. After a long and wearisome journey, he arrived there in a sorry state.

The countess, who was at first very reserved towards him, gradually accepted him, and eventually wrote his letters to the count when he was too weak to do so himself. At last, Martin's wound began to heal and he recovered his strength. In the winter of 1677–1678 he rode into the winter quarters of the Comte de Racon's light horse, and from there to a royal stud to carry out a remount order. This task brought him recognition from his superiors.

As usual, the count spent part of the season at Court. Raoul was in Rome as second secretary to the French ambassador; Guy and Louis de Salvieux were on the grand tour in Italy and, in the spring of 1678, joined the army in the king's musketeers. That spring, Martin was promoted lieutenant.

On the 14th August, four days after the longed-for Peace Treaty of Nijmegen, the Comte de Racon's regiment took part in the battle of Saint-Denis, in which the Duc de Luxembourg, in a last desperate effort, tried to destroy the army of the Prince of Orange. The enemy, however, fought with the same dauntless courage as the French. The battle was indecisive, and the Dutch Republic, after seven years of war, was lost to the glory-seeking king, despite all the heroism displayed and the victories won by his troops.

In one of the last forays, Martin was wounded for the

second time, but on this occasion only slightly in the shoulder. Since the war was now over, the count travelled with him in great comfort to Brayonne, where he spent his time at parties and hunting, while Martin was cared for by Pierre and Madame Fouillard. At the first autumn rains, the count suddenly tired of Brayonne and travelled to Paris without visiting Grandval. Before leaving, he told Martin, who had not yet entirely recovered, that as soon as he was well enough he should go to Grandval, collect the rents and bring them to Paris. Lieutenant Saint-Jean could find no reason this time for avoiding Paris in the winter.

HÔTEL DE RACON, PARIS

On the 4th December 1678 Martin, who was now twenty-two, arrived in Paris early in the afternoon riding a dappled grey Spanish barb. His retinue consisted of his orderly, six heavily-armed grooms, and three ordinary stable lads riding the two pack horses and Martin's spare mount. The young lieutenant was in a hurry to reach the Hôtel de Racon and was blind to the gay street scenes, the magnificence of the buildings and the gilded carriages of the nobility. At last, one of the grooms pointed out an old grey building in a narrow side street bearing the Racon coat of arms. The high gateway was open, but the vaulted corridor to the inner courtyard was blocked by a waiting coach.

'Hi!' Martin's orderly called to the oafish coachman on the box. 'Either draw inside or drive out. Make way for Lieutenant Saint-Jean!' The coachman and three lackeys burst out laughing until the rafters rang.

'This is a Palais Royal coach. The lieutenant must dismount outside.'

'Before my master soils his riding-boots in your Paris pigsty, we'll thrash you.'

'It's clear you're from the provinces and don't know your manners.'

Martin lost patience. 'Three men dismount! François, get up on the box and drive that crate into the courtyard.'

The order was carried out with such speed that the dazed coachman was unaware of his defeat until François threw the reins back at him.

Martin dismounted in front of the entrance. 'Carry up my chest,' he said, rushing up the steps. Pierre appeared at one of the doors. 'Hullo Pierre! Where is M. le Comte?'

'Still at Court, M. Saint-Jean.'

'What time will he be back?'

'About eight o'clock, M. Saint-Jean. He is expecting guests this evening. M. le Vicomte is here.'

'Announce me to him.' Pierre preceded him into the house.

Martin was shown into a room and found Raoul, who freed himself from four agitated ladies, and, with a bandage round his face, hurried over to him.

'Martin!'

'What has happened, Vicomte?' They embraced each other.

'Do be careful,' cried one of the ladies, 'you mustn't make any violent movement, Vicomte.'

'Do sit down again, Vicomte,' pleaded another. The third lady caught Martin by the arm.

'I beg you to be considerate of the Vicomte de Clarmont's condition.'

'Ladies!' cried Raoul, 'may I present my friend Lieutenant Saint-Jean.'

Martin bowed deeply and turned anxiously to Raoul. 'Have you had an accident?' he asked. Raoul suddenly began to sway.

'I have terrible toothache.'

Martin helped him to a chair and said to the ladies: 'I think the vicomte needs rest. Will you be kind enough to leave him for today?'

The fourth lady held up a small gold box. 'I will leave my toothache pastilles here.'

'Ladies, you are all too good to me,' said Raoul, in a dying voice. One of them scented his forehead, while the second tried to undo his lace cravat. 'Please do not crowd me,' cried Raoul, closing his eyes as though about to faint. Martin caught sight of Dominique who had just popped his head through the door. 'Don't stand there gaping!' he shouted, 'help the vicomte to bed. I beg you ladies to take your leave of us.'

Shrill, excited, almost sobbing voices echoed in the room and vanished through the door. Martin, with a series of bows, drove the swarm along the corridor to the steps and then hurried back to the room.

Raoul was standing at the window and had just removed the bandage from his head. 'God be praised you came,' he laughed.

Martin looked bewildered.

'Are you all right?'

'Of course. But, for your information, I'm officially suffering from an abscess of the gum.'

'Why?'

'Because from time to time I cannot stand the atmosphere of the Palais Royal. They are all in love with me . . . Monsieur and the ladies.'

'Monsieur?'

'The Duc d'Orléans, the king's brother. The Chevalier de Lorraine looks daggers at me, and Madame treats me with contempt.'

'But you have a brilliant post at Madame's court! The countess told me that Madame is a German and a very admirable woman.'

'So she is, Martin. Madame herself would be easy to bear, although she sometimes has fits of violent temper. She constantly goes hunting with the king and I like to accompany her. But when she is at home, Monsieur pesters me by visiting Madame on the slightest pretext, and the women make declarations of love to me, so that I no longer know where to flee. I cannot bear these scented women with their powder and patches; so Monsieur insists that I am abnormal, like him, and offers me honours and money. This makes me terribly embarrassed. But I cannot let father know because he insists that I feather my nest at Monsieur's Court. Monsieur and my father are two fires between which I am being slowly suffocated.'

'I thought you were happy, Vicomte.'

'I was happy in Italy. There I had a feeling of freedom and got to know real beauty—only to find myself forced to turn my back on both of them. You have come from Grandval. How is my mother?'

'She is well. She gave me a letter for you.'

'Why didn't you tell me before? Give it to me.'

Martin pulled the letter from the inner pocket of his uniform and handed it to the young vicomte, who tore it open and began to read. Martin gazed at his half-brother, whom he had not seen for five years, with admiration. Raoul was now as tall as his father, and remained just as slender without appearing thin. His wavy, raven-blue hair contrasted admirably with his fair skin and his mother's dark blue eyes. He had his father's beautiful hands but the skin was almost white. When he let the paper fall, Martin said: 'Vicomte, you are the most handsome man I've ever seen. I can quite understand Monsieur and the ladies.'

'Oh, please don't talk like that. Here, read my mother's letter.'

'Vicomte, may I draw your attention to the fact that I am an officer and I should be addressed by my surname.'

Raoul flushed scarlet.

'Forgive me, it was pure habit. Although we have not met for five years, my feelings for you have remained the same. Had I been the elder, I should have suggested that we dropped the formality.' It was now Martin's turn to blush.

'Monsieur, had you not been so very much above me in station, I should gladly have proposed it.'

Raoul held out his hand. 'Let us then, Martin.'

Martin took his hand and they embraced.

'Now read the letter, Martin.'

He sat down and began to read:

MY DEAR SON,

You know what anxiety all your letters cause me, and I beg you today once more not to lose courage. I know the world of the Court and realize how difficult it is to preserve one's integrity there. But you will clearly recognise evil for what it is and not be dazzled by outward appearances, which conceal vice under a cloak of virtue. If only, in addition to this happy gift, you were able to be a trifle more amiable to people. You are inclined to see only the bad in them and doubt the good. People feel it and are cold towards you.

How different Martin is from you! Since you parted he came here twice, and just as you have preserved the purity of your soul at Court, so has he preserved his at the war. While he was here last year, wounded, I wrote and told you how much I had learned in conversation with him. He does not see only the evil in men, like you do, but the good, and that is why he is loved by everyone. I tried to learn to see things with his eyes and I find myself almost understanding his love for your father.

Recently, I drove with him to one of our tenant farms. The November mist hid the view. It was damp and cold. I was shivering in spite of my furs. Suddenly the mist lifted ahead of us and in the pallid light a few lean cows appeared on the shorn meadows. 'Look, the sun, Madame,' said Martin. At that moment I suddenly understood him perfectly, and thanked God that I had brought him to Grandval seven years ago.

In the old days, I did Martin an injustice because I saw in him a danger to you and Guy, but his honour is unstained by any false ambitions. He is intelligent enough to recognise his position clearly and does not long for that to which he has no right. He is a friend in need. I beg you most earnestly to shrink from no effort to get on better with your father. Try not to irritate him. Like Martin, I am convinced that he worries in the best sense about his sons' future. Believe me, it has cost him great effort and much money to get you into the Palais Royal and Guy into the musketeers. He has opened the path to a brilliant future for you both, and even I, who despise worldly honours, can look with pride upon your position. But I have written to you so often in this vein, and your replies are always bitter and increase my anxiety. My dearest son, now that Martin is with you, I am comforted. I was beginning to worry about you. Your melancholy troubled my soul and I fear lest some disaster overtake you. May Martin avert it! I am pinning all my hopes on him. I know that it is asking too much of him for something which only you yourself can achieve—the curing of your melancholy. But perhaps my intuition is right and God will send you the necessary aid through him. Greet him affectionately from me, and accept your mother's deepest love.

MADELEINE, COMTESSE DE RACON

The embarrassed Martin returned the letter to Raoul and said, 'Your noble mother holds too high an opinion of me, because she does not know me well enough. She does not know, for example, of my backstairs relationship with her maid, who is married to the count's armourer.'

'Do not let us destroy my dear mother's belief in your virtue,' replied Raoul with a smile. 'I have not seen her for three years. Is she still beautiful?'

'More beautiful and more dignified than ever.'

'How envious I am that you saw her! Did she often visit you when you were ill?'

'At first she enquired through Denis, but later she came herself and I had to tell her about the war. Then she wrote to M. le Comte for me, and finally she told me the story of David and Saul, which she allowed me to read in secret, in her Bible.'

'So you share a secret with her?'

'The same secret as you, and I have not confessed it. I cannot see why people should be hostile to heretics. Thanks to your mother, I have become a believer again.'

'How remarkable, Martin. Have you also read the gospels?'

'Yes, I often read them when I was bored. It is a very good thing to consider once in a while, what is right, so as to avoid doing too much evil. Usually one behaves badly, but it can sometimes be avoided.'

There was a knock at the door. 'Come in,' called Raoul. The servant brought lighted candles since it was beginning to grow dark.

The steward appeared and asked politely if M. Saint-Jean would like something to eat. Martin accepted and, within a few moments, the servant brought in a tray of cold meat, wine, bread and fruit. Martin ate with appetite and Raoul consumed two oranges. Suddenly a great noise of squabbling and shouting came from below. Martin listened.

'What is that?' he asked.

'Oh, probably some creditors, they come nearly every day.'

'Has the count debts?'

'Yes, but you needn't be worried. One has to pay one's gambling debts, but tailors, cobblers, saddlers and Jews have to wait.'

'But the count doesn't like gambling.'

'At Court he is obliged to play. It is all part of the entertainment. The king insists that people stake large sums to give the game a cachet. Since everyone cheats, it neither harms nor benefits anyone. Father also has to grease a lot of palms to further his ambitions and, in order to create an impression, has to live far beyond his means now that he no longer has any prospect of war booty. It would not surprise me to learn one day that he was ruined.'

'Ruined?'

'Yes, that can happen to anyone here. Occasionally the king has pity and gives them a helping hand, but he can also be very stingy.'

Martin jumped up. 'I can hear horses!' he cried. He ran over to the window and opened it quickly. Raoul also looked out, and said with a smile:

'It is not father but the Comte de Salvieux. He is staying with us this winter.'

Disappointed, Martin closed the window and returned to his seat. It was not long before Louis came in.

'Good evening, gentlemen. M. Saint-Jean, how did you come by such a magnificent horse? I saw it in the stable and I can hardly wait to admire it tomorrow in the daylight. A Lippizaner with Arab blood . . . that small noble head with the tiny ears and those broad withers . . . I'm sure it has slender hocks and a thoroughbred gait. Did you buy the horse for the Comte de Racon.'

'No, Comte de Salvieux, it belongs to me.'

'It must be worth a fortune. Comte de Racon's chestnut cannot compare with it. Raoul, your Phaeton is a nag compared with the grey.'

'Who gave you this fabulous beast, Martin? My father?' asked Raoul.

'No.'

'A princess must have given it to him,' said Louis with a laugh.

'You are very near the truth, Comte de Salvieux.'

'Won't you tell us the fairy tale?'

'No, I'll tell you the truth.'

The young men made themselves comfortable before the fire, and Martin began: 'After the battle of Saint-Denis, our regiment was pursuing the fleeing Spanish troops. We drove a large body of infantrymen into a village and cut them down among the houses. We left part of our company to clean up the sharp-shooters who were still firing. Then, between two walls, we discovered an unharnessed carriage which bore the crest of some high ranking person. Now it was ours, together with its contents, which consisted of two ladies. One was young and extraordinarily beautiful, the other old and yellow, like a wrinkled lemon. For months we had seen no women except worn-out whores, and you can imagine the effect this young beauty had on us. An officer pulled the girl out of the coach and defended her with his sword against a fellow officer of the same rank, until one of his superiors arrived. The girl had to be handed over to him and despite her cries, was dragged away into a nearby barn. I was sorry for the unfortunate creature. Since I remembered being promised a large share of booty, I followed the officer and begged him to give me the girl as my portion. The man was generous enough not to refuse my request, but demanded to be the next in turn. I asked him to leave. As soon as he left, the beautiful girl embraced my knees in terror and implored me, in French, to spare her. I told her that I intended to rescue her and begged her not to hamper me. I called to a soldier and ordered him to strip the uniform off one of our dead and bring it to me. The uniform was brought; the lady unloosed her hair, changed clothes and—you can laugh gentlemen—like an Amazon mounted a spare horse which proceeded to run away with her! I followed in hot pursuit and managed to chase the horse in a big sweep towards the enemy lines. For no apparent reason the girl fell into a thicket and the horse was done. She had scratched herself, and began to beg and entreat me once more in tones that would have moved a heart of stone. So, like a cavalier, I put her on my horse, slowly skirted our village, avoiding a hot engagement, until I saw a pair of Spanish barrel hose. I began to wave a handkerchief. The wearer of the hose noticed me and came up with lowered rapier. I lifted the disguised cavalryman from the saddle, and explained to the Spanish lieutenant what had brought me there. He bowed, asked my name and respectfully took his leave. I galloped back and returned just in time to receive a wound in the final melée.

'The following day, as I lay in the Comte de Racon's tent—he was as furious with my condition as I—I was greatly surprised when a Spanish delegation arrived bringing me the horse as a token of gratitude, the very horse you have just seen in the stable, Comte de Salvieux. The girl was the daughter of a Spanish commander and the fiancée of a Spanish grandee, who at the time was indispensable to the Netherlands. Had I been in his place I should have left my bride at home in Spain until times were less dangerous.'

'A charming story,' said Raoul. 'If anyone other than you had told it I should not have believed them. I must go at once and have a look at the Lippizaner. Will you come with me?'

'With pleasure.' Martin proudly led his friends to the stables.

When, after their visit to the stables, the three young gentlemen were together once more, Martin asked the Comte de Salvieux to tell him of his experiences during the last years. Louis described his journeys and his stay in Italy and announced that in the spring he would be travelling to Madrid, in the retinue of the French ambassador. Politics were his vocation and he hoped one day to play an important part in them. He knew how to carry out secret missions and, as a result of his discretion, enjoyed the confidence of people in high positions, whose names he could not mention. Martin seemed impressed by the Comte de Salvieux's successful rise, and sat there lost in thought. Since Raoul was also silent, Louis began to feel bored, and said that he would like to go and visit Guy for a while.

Martin looked up. 'Is M. de Brayonne here in the house?'

'No,' replied Raoul, 'he's living with Tenelli and the count's pages over at the Hôtel de Brayonne. My father has forbidden him to set foot in the Hôtel de Racon as long as you are here. Tenelli is very keen to test your prowess in fencing and will visit you as soon as he knows you have arrived.'

'M. de Brayonne is not very well-disposed towards you, M. Saint-Jean,' said Louis, rising to his feet, 'and your magnificent charger will certainly not endear you any more to him.'

'Please give my regards to Master Tenelli,' said Martin.

'I shall see to it. Good evening.'

Louis was still in the doorway when a noise of rattling

harness, horses' hooves and shouts came to their ears. Martin rushed once more to the window, opened it, looked out and cried: 'This time it is the Comte de Racon.' He rushed along the corridor, past Louis, and stood frozen to stone on the top of the stairs. The count was wearing a large wig, in which Martin had never seen him before, and was hurrying up the stairs in his diamond-studded Court attire. Martin rushed forward to embrace him but was thrust aside so violently by the apparently furious man that he hit his newly healed shoulder against the painted wall.

Two small pages swept past him behind the count. One of them dared to ask a question. Two cuffs rang out and a door banged . . . Martin clutched on to the banister and rubbed his shoulder, while the two pages rushed past him down the stairs and out into the courtyard. Comte Louis sauntered down the stairs, and said in an amused voice to Martin: 'Well, M. Saint-Jean, that was a nice reception.'

Martin bit his lips.

'Is your shoulder hurting you?' asked Louis.

'I have a scar. Do you know a good tavern where one can eat decently here?'

'Monsieur, in Paris one does not eat in taverns, but with one's acquaintances. So many noble houses are open to me that I know absolutely nothing of taverns, but my equerry can give you the names of several.'

'One will be enough.'

'Come with me, M. Saint-Jean.'

Martin followed Louis and ordered his horse to be brought round. When they were already mounted in the gateway, Pierre came rushing down.

'M. Saint-Jean, M. le Comte has sent for you.'

'Tell him that I will wait on him tomorrow morning.'

'But Monsieur, you won't ride away now?'

'As you see, I am already on my way.' Martin rode out of the gate on Louis's left. Pierre ran out into the street after him.

'M. Saint-Jean, the count is expecting you.'

Martin pretended to be deaf and trotted on. Then Pierre shouted at the top of his voice: 'M. Saint-Jean, the count is ill.'

At this, Martin pulled his horse round so suddenly that it nearly slipped in the mire, and rode back to the house. 'You idiot, you should have said so at once.'

Martin jumped off his horse, rushed up the steps and called out: 'Which is the door to his room?'

'The third to the left, M. Saint-Jean.'

Martin knocked and entered. The count was sitting without his wig and jacket, in shirt sleeves, at his table, upon which stood the various chests Martin had brought. 'Why didn't you come, eh?' he roared. 'Have I got to open the locks with my teeth? How much is there?'

'Here are the keys and here is a letter from Madame la Comtesse.'

Martin handed him the keys and the letter and noticed how the brown hands trembled as he opened it. The countess had written only a few lines to her husband.

> MONSIEUR,
>
> I send you by Martin, 81,400 livres interest and rents with an accurate list and 53,500 livres from the mines. I beg you not to ask for more until next autumn. The peasants are in dire distress.
>
> MADELEINE

The count rolled the letter into a ball and flung it into the fire. 'That's a drop in the ocean. Not even 100,000 from my properties! You're not fit to be sent on such an errand. I need 200,000 and I wrote to her quite plainly. She'll have to give me some of her jewellery. Open the chests and count!'

'Monsieur, shall I call Pierre to undress you?'

'Leave the dolt outside.'

'You shouldn't get excited if you are ill. You should lie down.'

'Why should you think I'm ill?'

'Aren't you?'

'It's the first I've heard of it. I've had trouble at Court. That's all.'

'Oh!' Martin stepped back a pace. 'Monsieur, if you are not ill, you can open the coffers yourself. I have fulfilled my errand and beg to be allowed to return to my regiment.'

'You are to remain in Paris.'

'Are you giving me orders as a general?'

'Lieutenant Saint-Jean, I have been waiting for you fourteen days.'

'I could not travel faster.'

'How is your shoulder?'

'It was all right until just now.'

'Did you hit it on the stairs?'

'Yes.'

'Forgive me, I forgot your wound and was too angry to greet you. Let us make up for that now.'

The count stretched out his arms and Martin ran over to him. They embraced each other. 'Your hair is damp, Monsieur,' said Martin.

'That's from the heat of the wig.'

'Are you really not feverish?'

'Certainly not.'

Martin unbuttoned his waistcoat and felt his chest under the soaked shirt. 'Your heart is beating furiously. You must get undressed.'

The count tore himself loose and began to pace up and down.

'Martin, I am in a furious rage. If only I could hang that carrion!'

'Whom do you want to hang?'

'The Montespan, that lying, painted hussy.'

'Monsieur, as far as I know, the Marquise de Montespan is the king's mistress.'

'Yes, and she still has him under her thumb. If only he would throw her out! May she catch the plague and the pox. Don't repeat what I've said. The slightest word against her is dangerous. Anyone who mentions her name in connection with the poison rumours disappears into jail.'

'Has the marquise poisoned someone?'

'Her enemies all succumb to a mysterious illness, and when the king has a bellyache people mutter that it is probably caused by her love philtres.'

'If I have the bellyache,' laughed Martin, 'I don't feel like making love.'

'You can laugh. I have overplayed my hand.'

'How do you mean?'

'Another courtier is being given the command of the Light Horse of the Guard. The appointment has just become vacant.'

'Why are you no longer satisfied with your regiment?'

'Because the Guard accompanies the king, and his presence is worth more to me than ten frontier regiments. Oh, Martin, if only I still had money! Let me tell you about the Montespan's latest piece of malice.'

'Why don't you lie down and tell me?'

'Hell, don't tyrannise me!'

'You should be rubbed down.'

'No, I'm too excited.'

Martin saw a red dressing-gown hanging on the bed-post, took it down and helped the count into it.

'Well, go on, tell me about it.'

The count sat on the edge of the table and went on with his tale. 'The weather was mild this morning and the whole court drove to Versailles to see the new fountain play for the first time. The party strolled at its usual slow speed, the king ahead. We gathered round the fountain in admiration. Madame, gay as ever in the presence of the king, laughed at the goldfish which a boy shook from a silver bowl into the fountain. Then the Montespan turned to me. I gave her my usual respectful bow and she beckoned to me. I approached, expecting to hear something of my hoped-for transfer, when the creature said, so that everyone could hear: "I believe that your wife is still a Protestant?" Hell, I thought, somebody who wants to see my downfall must have whispered it in her ear. Trying hard to remain calm, I replied: "Unfortunately you have been correctly informed, Madame, but the example set by so many ladies of quality will, I am sure, convert her." With a compassionate smile, she replied: "It grieves me that you have so little influence over your wife." Her studied compassion told me I had lost. It was not easy to remain composed, but I succeeded. I remarked that the spray of water behind her enhanced her beauty like a halo. Then she let fall her handkerchief. I picked it up. She pretended not to be able to reach it and let it fall a second time. Her play-acting was repeated and it fell to the ground a third time. I heard a titter behind me and could have stabbed her. Then I turned round, and said in a voice loud enough for all to hear: "I am surprised that no one, apart from myself, is ready to render the marquise a service." The whole pack rushed forward and fought like wolves for the wretched rag. I stepped aside and saved my honour. The marquise's glance was anything but friendly. Sit down, Martin. I managed to approach my friend, the Maréchal, in the Louvre. I asked as casually as I could when the appointment of the Commander of the Light Horse of the Guard was to be announced. He was clearly embarrassed and said that certain last-minute information had decided the king to keep the gentlemen under consideration waiting a little longer. Someone has spoiled me with the king.'

In his rage, the count jumped up and started pacing the room again. 'That charming couple! Montespan wears the earrings I gave her and the duke rides gaily on my chestnut. God knows what presents the others must have given them! If I could only find out their names. Chassigny swears he has no interest in the post. I know four of them. I must rely once again on the Maréchal d'Humières and Ninon de Lenclos. I wonder if the Duc de Luxembourg is a secret enemy after all? I have suddenly remembered something, Martin; do you recall the quarrel I had last year with him in front of all the generals at headquarters, when he tried to make a scapegoat of me in public?'

'I was not there,' replied Martin, 'but I remember that you were out of favour with the duke for a long time.'

'Yes, because I refused to accept his accusation of having disrupted the enemy line of battle by too hasty an attack, thus forcing him to retreat prematurely. As though the enemy would ever have thought of giving battle once he had realised that our infantry outnumbered him! Our musketeers had to attack at the double, and to encourage them I flung myself on the enemy before the Spaniards sounded the retreat. The dragoons were on the spot, but not the infantry, thus the enemy was able to disengage and withdraw his main body, fobbing us off with paltry skirmishes. I shall see that the king is informed of this affair and I'll find someone who'll give him the true version. Let some infantry general lose his post! I want command of the Light Horse of the Guard and, I tell you, I'll get it.'

'Don't overtax your nerves, Monsieur. In the last few years you have accomplished a great deal and still greater success will only add to your burdens. I cannot imagine that a guards' regiment will satisfy you. You love your independence. Could you tolerate the exalted presence of the king, day after day, year after year, for the rest of your life?'

'You understand nothing of Court service. Anyone clever enough is even freer. From time to time I shall have the gout, like the king, and enjoy a rest on my estates. Tell me about Grandval!'

'Willingly, as soon as you lie down.'

'That's blackmail.'

'You must forgive me, but I'm worried about your health. I never thought that Paris could be so exciting. You're quite yellow in the face.'

The count suddenly went over to Martin, who rose from his stool, and said in a quiet, vicious voice: 'My cousin wrote to me three days before her death that you went driving alone with my wife. Was she telling the truth?'

'Yes, Comte de Racon, Madame la Comtesse drove alone with me.'

'Are you in love with her?'

Martin turned fiery red. 'Monsieur, I hope that this is the first and last time you will ask such a question. My respect for Madame la Comtesse is boundless. I love her as I love the Holy Virgin and am happy that I enjoy her respect.'

'Why did you drive alone with her?'

'Mlle de Dismarat had attacks of giddiness, which were the precursors of her stroke. Mme d'Ouville was suffering with asthma.'

'What about Borel?'

'Dr Borel cannot stand the rattling of the coach on account of his stomach.'

'And Father Tulier?'

'Mme la Comtesse does not hold him in great esteem.'

'Did my wife have any guests?'

'Yes, every day.'

'Really! My late-lamented cousin gave me no word of that.

Who were they?'

'I cannot recall their names, but there were about twenty-three girls and sixteen boys, between the ages of five and twelve, the ugliest of whom bore a great resemblance to the Comte de Racon. They ate in the cold dining-hall and sat in rows on the carpet in the warm salon, singing songs. These guests came in the morning and left in the evening. A hospital had been set up for a further twenty, and the countess attended the little girls herself. A man looked after the boys.'

'Martin, is it true that my wife's charities eat up large sums of money?'

'I don't know the details of her household books. The little girls wore blue woollen dresses and the boys brown serviceable coats, which, taken all together, could not have cost a fraction of your court dress . . . And they all wore wooden sabots, which clattered up the stairs like a roll of drums.'

The count retired to bed and covered himself with the dressing-gown. Martin sat beside him, took off his shoes, felt his heart and said with a smile: 'Now, at last I've got you where I wanted you. Your heart is still beating too fast.'

'Martin, I'll ride with you round the city tomorrow and show you the fortifications. Have you seen the Louvre yet?'

'No, I was in a hurry to greet you.'

'Which I turned into a jostling match,' added the count. 'Could you ring the little bell there, so that Blanche can come in?'

Before Martin could ask any questions or fulfil the request, a hidden door opened in the panelling and an enchantingly dressed doll-like creature of not more than fifteen appeared. Martin stared in amazement at the white, child-like face with its huge dark eyes set wide apart, the tiny hands and feet and the suggestion of little breasts seen through the silver lace. Her dark, wavy hair was artificially curled and adorned. The child was carrying a lute and, looking questioningly at the count, pointed to the strings.

'Yes,' said the count. 'Play me something. This gentleman is Lieutenant Saint-Jean, my friend and the Vicomte de Clarmont's half-brother. Greet him politely.'

The charming child curtsied, without looking at the young man, and began to play softly, standing by the door in the wall. Martin could not take his eyes from her. The count noticed his surprise and asked:

'Does she please you?'

'Monsieur, you have never had such a beautiful mistress.'

'She is not my mistress, but she belongs to me like a Turkish slave. I found her on a journey to the Marquis de Chassigny's estate where she grew up as a foundling. The marquis sold her to me for a ridiculous sum because she's dumb. I tell you it is a wonderful relaxation to come home from the chatter of the Court and find a dumb little slave like her. I suspected, from her graceful movements, that she had a talent for dancing and took her with me to the opera. She was delighted by the ballet and the music. I gave her lessons from a ballet master and a lute player and she has made wonderful progress. What have you learned today?' he asked. The child blushed, looked at Martin, and shook her head, a pleading look in her eyes.

'Don't you want to dance for him?'

The girl repeated her gesture.

'She's still very shy,' the count explained. 'When I bought her, she was so frightened and timorous that I thought her dumbness must have led to mental derangement, but after three days she summoned up a smile, and after a week she began to laugh. Do you ever weep?'

The child shook her head, with such a radiant smile that Martin caught his breath. The count undid his garters. 'You obviously like it better here with me than with the marquis, or would you rather go back to him?'

A look of terror came into her dark eyes and she made a gesture of horror and disgust. 'I will keep you, Blanche,' said the count consolingly. 'Our good Armand de Chassigny clearly did not know how to treat you. She's rather too small for me but the most adaptable of little trollops you can possibly imagine. How's your monkey?'

Blanche laughed, showing her small even teeth, and mimicked a nervous, nut-cracking monkey. Martin laughed aloud. 'Monsieur, how enchanting!'

'Isn't she? I'm delighted to hear the little monkey has recovered. She gives me pleasure day in and day out and I guard her like a precious jewel. I lock her away from Guy and Louis, but Raoul teaches her to read and write. Blanche, come over here.'

Martin stood up and moved a few paces away from the bed, whereupon the child flitted over and took his place at the count's silk-stockinged feet. She conjured a few shy tones from her lute and, when the count said nothing, continued playing softly. Martin stared at her until she stopped playing and let the instrument slip to the floor. Martin noticed that the count was fast asleep. He stepped forward and said: 'Mademoiselle, please don't wake him.'

Blanche turned to him, placed a finger gravely to her lips, folded her hands as though in prayer and pointed to the door. Martin bowed and quietly left the room.

Pierre grinned at him from the valet's room. 'How is he, M. Saint-Jean?'

'If you lie to me again, I'll give you a box on the ear. Don't wake him.'

'M. Saint-Jean, the guests have arrived.'

'The vicomte will deputise for M. le Comte.'

'Can I refer that order to you?'

'Yes.'

'Very good.'

Martin changed and went down to the new dining-hall; its walls were now covered with magnificent new Gobelins. The bluff Marquis de Chassigny, fat old Baron du Terne, Captain de Falleron, the Comte de Salvieux and the Vicomte de Clarmont were already sitting round the fire.

At Martin's entrance there was a loud guffaw of laughter. 'Count Saint-Jean,' cried the captain, 'where did you get your most elegant coat?'

The blood rushed to Martin's cheeks, and he replied: 'M. de Falleron, though you may be my captain, I will not allow you to mock me. Withdraw that mocking title or I shall challenge you to a duel. I have paid long enough for my stupidity.'

'I quite agree with you, my good Saint-Jean. Let us bury the hatchet and wish each other good evening.'

After a short hesitation, Martin took the proffered hand and then greeted the old baron and the marquis, with whose dragoons he had served from corporal to sergeant. 'Gentlemen, as soon as I can I shall visit a Paris tailor, and I beg you to accept me as I am today. My suit was made in Grandval where they have no knowledge of fashion.'

'You are welcome, Saint-Jean, in any garb,' cried the Marquis de Chassigny, 'but where is our host?'

'He is very exhausted,' replied Martin, 'and begs to be excused for this evening.'

The marquis winked. 'Has he found better company?'

The baron banged the arm of his chair and cried: 'That was going rather far for his son's future father-in-law.'

'Gentlemen,' cried Martin, 'I have not lied to you and beg you not to impugn my honour.'

'Good, good,' said the marquis, 'I do not begrudge my friend a little rest. Sit down Saint-Jean, so that your splendid suit shan't dazzle us in the candlelight.'

To the accompaniment of renewed laughter, Martin took a chair next to Raoul who beckoned to a footman.

A few minutes later the double doors were opened on the brightly lit dining-hall and the company sat down to table. Since the baron, at the start of the meal, engaged the marquis and M. de Falleron in conversation, the three young gentlemen could gossip undisturbed. Louis asked why the captain had bestowed the title of count on Martin. Though Martin was annoyed by the question, he explained: 'Since, like the Comte de Clarmont, you are a gentleman, you will not abuse my confidence. I told you how I acquired my Lippizaner. I could not resist the temptation of letting the lady and the Spanish officer call me Comte Saint-Jean, for my behaviour had been chivalrous and I felt like a king. How could I suspect that they would come and give me this token of their gratitude? Naturally, there was no Comte Saint-Jean in the whole regiment, and had I not been wounded, everyone would have chaffed me. I have never felt so ashamed in my life and shall never again assume a false title. Only the count acted as if he knew nothing of my *faux pas*, and behaved to me as usual. For that I am eternally grateful to him.'

'I never heard a word of this story,' said Raoul.

'Nor did I,' assured Louis.

'Raoul, I heard in Grandval that your future bride has the measles. How long can you still remain a bachelor?' Martin asked.

'Until February, I believe, and then next winter it will be Guy's turn.'

'Have you seen the little Mlle d'Epponcourt again?'

'No, but one hears nothing good of her family. I believe her father has married a second time and is in financial straits, but, of course, her dowry is assured. Has anyone thought of a match for you?'

Martin laughed, 'No, thank God. A Martin Saint-Jean can find a wife for himself. I'll take my time. Incidentally, the count has an enchanting little girl.'

'He has indeed. When I'm teaching her to read and write, I often have to laugh, for we're a dumb girl and a blind man and lack only a cripple.'

'I'll play that part for you willingly. When I'm tired, I feel the old wound in my thigh and start limping.'

'I have long wished to see the little treasure,' said Louis.

'You're not quite to be trusted, but with us she is safe,' said Raoul.

'Only because your father looks on you as a woman hater and because Martin is his friend. If he could only see your Nicolette!'

'Be silent Louis, the very idea makes me sick.'

'Do you love a lady of quality?' asked Martin. Raoul blushed and Louis said with oafish gravity: 'Nicolette is the most beautiful and most virtuous laundress in all Paris. The vicomte seduced her, but she blabbed to her good parents and the vicomte had to pay astronomical sums of money.'

'Alas, alas!' cried Martin. 'Raoul, I fear you've got into the toils of a pimp.'

Louis roared with laughter. 'He agrees with me. Don't be angry, Raoul. Isn't it true, M. Saint-Jean, we both have faith in the true love of sweet Nicolette?'

'Let us say,' said Martin with a smile, 'that she is worthy of so noble and handsome a lover.'

Raoul changed the conversation by asking for details of Martin's stay at Grandval. The two old officers were laughing heartily at one of the baron's coarser jests. The doors were suddenly flung open and the count appeared, looking pale and haggard. 'Gentlemen, excuse my late appearance. A joke has been played on me. Martin, how dared you give orders to let me go on sleeping!'

'I felt responsible for your health, Monsieur,' said Martin, rising to his feet.

'I'll teach you to give orders in my house. Has your success gone completely to your head?'

'I shall leave your house at once.'

'You will remain here.'

'You are insulting me before these gentlemen.'

'You insulted them by letting me go on sleeping.'

'I do not share that view.'

Martin was already at the door and tried to pass the count, but he caught him by the arm: 'We must have a word or two together. Excuse us for a few moments, gentlemen.' The door closed behind them.

The guests continued their meal. 'Poor boy,' said the Marquis de Chassigny, 'this time he has gone too far.'

'Wait, Marquis,' said M. de Falleron. 'You'll see, in a few minutes they'll come back the best of friends. I've shared their tent too often not to know their ways. They often quarrel, but before it comes to a break one of them gives way and they're immediately reconciled. If by some chance they happen to be angry with each other for a whole day, they're both miserable and the whole regiment has to suffer the count's ill-temper until they're seen riding off together again.'

'Did the young Saint-Jean show the same excessive bravery under your command as he did with me as a dragoon?' asked the marquis.

The captain laughed. 'Excessive bravery, that's the right description. When some enemy sharp-shooters persisted in firing from an isolated barn, although the main body had long since been scattered to the winds, all one had to do was to order Saint-Jean to silence them. Anyone else would have tried to avoid the duty, but Saint-Jean would take five men and make a gallant frontal assault. When he returned he'd report the barn cleaned up, as though he had just come back from a routine patrol. I once asked him if he knew that people were rarely given a decoration for such heroic but trivial actions and this was his reply: "In a battle it does not matter to me whether or not I acquit myself well before a high-ranking officer, provided I satisfy myself." What do you say to that, gentlemen?'

'Very honourable and very foolish,' replied the marquis.

'I agree,' said the Baron du Terne.

'He's incredibly proud,' said Raoul. 'Ambition can make a slave of anyone.'

The company laughed. 'That's pure philosophy,' replied the marquis.

'Yes, Monsieur, and it's the truth.'

'In any case, Vicomte de Clarmont,' de Falleron added gravely, 'too much pride and independence are far more likely to bring you to an early grave than lead to wealth and honours.'

The doors opened again and the count came in with Martin, in the best of moods. 'Gentlemen, please excuse us both. My friend acted with the most honourable intentions and will not repeat his mistake.'

Captain de Falleron clapped his hands. 'Bravo! Long live friendship!'

The count sat down. 'I'm as hungry as a hunter, and shall eat while you go on drinking. How are things, Baron? Am I to take you to the Marquise de Montespan tomorrow?'

'No, thank you, Comte de Racon. I have thought matters over and decided to return home the day after tomorrow. At Court you lose your money to no purpose, and apparently your health as well. I have never seen you look so yellow as you do in Paris. Do you suffer from liver?'

'Not that I know of.'

The baron emptied his glass. 'My dear Count, I survived the great reception this morning. I've had enough of that sort of pleasure to last me the rest of my life. What on earth do you hope to achieve by remaining so long at Court?'

The count replied evasively, and took a slice of roast. 'Anyone familiar with life at Court hates it, but can never escape its toils. You always think you might be missing something when you are away from it.'

With good-natured mockery, the marquis asked: 'How would you feel, you old rebel, if, like many a duke, you had to spend the whole summer in an attic in Versailles in order to remain near the bright sun?'

The count shook his head. 'No, I could never do that.'

'But aren't the gentlemen in waiting given suitable accommodation at Versailles?' enquired the baron in surprise.

The marquis laughed: 'A room under the eaves costs more than the largest castle in the provinces. Versailles is becoming enormous, but more men live there than there are ants in an ant-heap. Where can they be squeezed in? Snugly beneath the roof until it bursts!'

The baron leant back comfortably in his chair. 'Gentlemen, I am a country squire and will remain one. I stood on my feet for five hours this morning without a rest, and saw the king only for five minutes. That's the last time. Where were you hiding, Count?'

'I had the honour of accompanying his Majesty in the park.'

'Did you have to stand as long as the rest?'

'Why should I be an exception?'

'You will eventually become a hunchback.' There was general laughter. 'But I mean it,' the baron continued. 'You're no longer as young as you were, Comte de Racon. Be careful you don't get that strange crick in the back from which most of the old courtiers suffer. They all develop a pathetic stoop. Isn't that a drawback in bed?'

The laughter grew uproarious. 'I haven't noticed it, Baron, in the case of my friend,' retorted the marquis. 'He recently bought the prettiest little filly from me.'

'Well, and how goes it, Count?' asked the baron.

'I am still quite pleased with myself. Haven't you taken a young mistress yet to spare your ageing wife?'

'No, I'm rather mean. Mistresses are too expensive.'

'Ha, ha,' cried the count. 'That explanation sounds suspicious to me. I believe you've reached the stage when you get more pleasure from your food than from a pretty wench.'

The baron slapped his enormous stomach. 'Bellies are deceptive, Monsieur.' More laughter.

'Would anyone mind if I lit my pipe?' asked M. de Falleron.

'Do you mind sitting at the end of the table and blowing

your smoke into the air?' replied the count.

'With pleasure, Monsieur.'

The captain changed places and lit the long churchwarden he had brought back from the Low Countries. The baron took a pinch of snuff and gave a gargantuan sneeze. The servants went on filling their glasses. Martin grew sleepy and the count found it more and more difficult to keep awake.

The Marquis de Chassigny suddenly turned to the baron. 'Monsieur, I admire the frankness with which you speak of life at Court, but what's wrong with Paris that you want to leave it before you've really settled down?'

'What can I do in Paris, Marquis? I look like a fop in my fashionable coat and I'm bored to death in the salons. I have never been witty and have no intention of becoming so. I can buy myself all I want. I have everything at home. I love security and prefer to invest my money in some business which I know in advance will bring me a profit, such as supplying the army. What does the king's favour signify? Today, a robe of honour, tomorrow the Bastille. The nobility is being destroyed at Court.'

'Those are strong words, Monsieur.'

'I'll tell you why I hold these views. In my day, you came to Court once a year and the king was honoured that you came. Today, if you want to make a name, you have to be at Versailles or the Louvre year in, year out, day and night. Both you and the Comte de Racon fought with the Fronde. How powerful the noble was in those days! What is he today? We are no longer needed. All the important posts are held by bourgeois because they can be relied on. How many bourgeois officers are there today? According to the king, the nobility is only good enough to shed its blood for him in a war and to surround him with a brilliant tinsel retinue. I say "tinsel" because everyone at Versailles is heading for ruin. The pomp insisted on by the king turns everyone eventually into a petitioner for a pension. I have warned my sons and appealed to their pride. Is it not better to live the life of a free gentleman on a rich estate in the provinces than to light the king to bed at night and hand him his hose in the morning? What do you say, Comte de Racon?'

'You cannot win honour in the provinces.'

'What do you call honour?'

With an effort the count raised his heavy eyelids and stared at the baron in surprise. 'What is honour? It is, for instance, the proximity of the king.'

'According to you, then, endless standing and waiting and bowing and scraping and flattering.'

The count was suddenly wide awake. 'Baron, what are you hinting at this evening?'

'I want a son-in-law who doesn't squander my daughter's fortune.'

'If I had my way, Baron,' put in Raoul, 'I should like to retire to the country as you do and never set foot in Paris, Saint Cloud or Versailles again.'

'Really!' said the count in a strange tone.

'Comte de Racon,' said the baron, obviously pleased, 'let the vicomte travel with me so that I may have the opportunity of becoming better acquainted with him.'

'Yes, Father,' cried Raoul. 'Let me accompany the baron.'

'You'll remain here. Baron, I realise to my shame that I cannot keep up with you tonight. Please do not take it amiss if I retire. Goodnight, gentlemen.'

'Hi, Gaston,' the Marquis de Chassigny called after him, 'you are my guest the day after tomorrow for supper.'

'I shan't forget.'

'Bring along my little dumb girl, of whom you have such marvellous things to tell.'

'No, she'll remain here, or else you'll want her back, Armand.'

'Don't make me envious, you sly devil. I'm beginning to regret the bargain and I'll steal her from you yet.'

'Try it!'

The marquis stood up and followed the count to the door. 'Where is she hiding?'

'Now don't try to search or you'll burn your fingers.'

'I want to see her.'

'She's asleep.'

'I'll wake her up.'

'Go home to your mistress, or send for her to come here at once if the sap's rising to your head.'

'Why did you have no surprise for me today?'

'I forgot to order a strumpet for you. I'll have one for you next time.' The count gave the heavily-built man a friendly jab in the chest, making him stagger back towards the table, and left the hall. A servant closed the door behind him and the drinking party went on.

THE SUFFERINGS OF THE VICOMTE DE CLARMONT

EARLY next morning, Martin went as usual to the count's room and found him dressing for a ride. 'Good morning, Monsieur.'

'Good morning, my friend, I am glad you are wearing your uniform again. You can give that new coat to your groom. When we come back you must go to my tailor and order a wine-coloured suit with ribbons to match. I think wine-red would suit you.'

'I hoped you'd come with me and give me the benefit of your advice.'

'I don't want to appear at Master Volin's, for if I do the suit will never be ready. Don't tell him you know me, and pay for the material in cash. On the table there you'll find your pay, which you asked me to keep for you.'

'How much will I need?'

'Nearly all of it.'

'My God, wouldn't it be better to go to a cheaper tailor?'

'Out of the question. I want to introduce you to the Paris salons.'

'How wonderful, Monsieur! I shall look forward to meeting the ladies. Tell me, wouldn't a rhinegrave suit me?'

The count patted Martin's powerful stocky figure. 'You're too broad-chested for a rhinegrave and, besides, they're going out of fashion.'

'What a pity. I always envied you and your sons in them.'

The count smiled. 'You've got to be tall and slim to wear one.'

'Yes, like you. I can see that. Good Heavens, that's a monster!'

Martin lifted the huge court wig from its stand and placed it on his head. 'How heavy it is,' he said, going over to a Venetian mirror. 'I look like a shaggy bear. But it makes you taller and enhances your dignity. You walked in like a tower yesterday. But, with your fine hair, is such a contraption really necessary?'

'You look conspicuous at Court if you wear your own hair.'

'But your own dark locks are far more attractive than this black, shaggy horror.'

'I'm going grey at the temples.'

The count raised a few strands of hair so that Martin could see for himself. 'Yes, you are, but grey hair suits elderly gentlemen.'

'Thank you, for the "elderly gentlemen".'

'Do you want to appear younger than you really are?'

'I am usually taken to be younger than the king, although Louis is forty and I'm forty-five. I have all my teeth whereas his mouth is full of stumps.'

'I thought he was as handsome as a god.'

'His poise is incomparable. Put that thing back on its stand.'

Martin obeyed, lifted the stand, and began to make it swing. 'Just imagine if it appeared to you in the night. You could easily mistake it for a ghost.'

'What a child you are!'

'I see that you are moderately good-humoured today.'

'It's better than being moderately ill-tempered.'

'I quite agree. I am looking forward to a good gallop with you.'

Martin continued to chatter while Pierre shaved the count. Master Tenelli was announced and Martin hurried over to greet his old tutor.

After their ride, Martin, instead of visiting the count's tailor, paid a visit to the Marquis de Chassigny, whom he found at breakfast. He offered to sell the astonished marquis his Lippizaner, on the grounds that it distressed him to own a more beautiful horse than the Comte de Racon. Knowing the story of 'Count Saint-Jean', the marquis showed his understanding and advised Martin to sell the extraordinarily handsome horse for at least 20,000 livres to the Duc de Luxembourg. Martin thanked him for his advice and immediately went to the marshal's palace. His mission was successful and he returned to the Hôtel de Racon with 20,000 livres. He arrived in time to share the count's midday meal. He offered his friend the money, begging him to make use of it, since he himself would not need it for at least the next two years. Then he asked the count to accompany him to the tailor to help him choose the material. The count did so and paid a part of his debt, whereupon the delighted tailor promised by all the saints to deliver Martins suits—the count had advised him to order two—to the Hôtel de Racon within four days.

They returned late in the afternoon, to be greeted by the strains of music. 'Incidentally, do you know how to dance?' asked the count.

'No, I never had a chance to learn.'

'Then take part in Blanche's dancing lesson.'

The count led Martin to the brilliantly lit salon where the little dumb girl, in a flowered pinned-up dress, was dancing in the presence of her elderly maid. A retired, tottering ballet master beat time on the floor with a stick, while two ancient musicians accompanied on the flute and the violin. On catching sight of the count, Blanche stopped, tripped over to him on her toes and curtsied gracefully in time to the music.

'Well done, little Blanche,' praised the count, 'but don't dance as stiffly as your teacher.'

Blanche smiled and began to dance round the room, pretending that her legs were of wood. Then, changing suddenly, she became light as a feather and seemed to hover like a moth. The ballet master whistled through his teeth and said: 'M. le Comte, I have not taught her that. She has known it from the cradle. She is a miracle and would earn a fortune at the opera.'

'Blanche,' the count asked in his gayest mood, 'would you like to dance one day on the boards?'

The girl stared and shook her head vehemently. She began to pirouette.

The count then turned to the ballet master. 'This young gentleman cannot dance, and will take lessons with Blanche. Stop! Play a minuet. Martin, I'll show you the latest fashion in dancing.'

A rosy flush appeared on Blanche's face. She quickly uncount's return. The regimental jester, a pink-faced ensign, began to sing:

'Tirondon, Tirondon,
Our leader is the Comte de Racon,
Only one stood up to him
His little ensign Martin,
Who gave him a clout, and laid him out.
Who'll make the boy see reason?
None other than General Racon
Did he have him hanged?
Oh dear me no!
He merely kicked his arse,
Tirondon . . .'

The song was taken up by several voices, to the accompaniment of loud laughter. Martin blushed but joined in the laughter.

The count soon returned with the soldiers, having found what he had been looking for. A corporal was despatched into the woods, with orders that Ensign Saint-Jean was to report on horseback. Martin swiftly put on his uniform while his horse was being brought up. Leaping into the saddle, he galloped out of the shade into the searing sunlight.

The count was practising his stubborn chestnut in the levade until Martin rode up. 'Look, my boy, we found this too,' he said, showing Martin a sparkling ring. 'Would you like it?'

'No, thank you. You once told me that rings did not look well on my podgy paws.'

'You can sell it or give it away.'

Martin bowed with a smile. 'Thank you for the magnificent gift. Allow me to present it to you.'

'Why the malice?'

'Monsieur, you need money in Paris, for Paris is a bottomless pit. You must continue to amass booty, to exploit and plunder, and you cannot afford to give presents.'

'Do you take me for a robber captain?'

'You have all the makings of one, Comte de Racon.'

The count's dark face broadened into a grin. 'I enjoy playing at robbers. You mark my words, in a few years you'll be pinned her pretty dress, which fell to her ankles, and assumed a graceful pose. At the first notes of the minuet, the count walked towards her, bowed low as if before a lady, caught her little hand and led her nimbly and without hesitation through one figure after another. He danced, as was his wont, with a slight soldierly disdain that showed off his masculinity to the best advantage.

'Hi, Martin, watch me, not Blanche. Try and learn the steps.'

'Monsieur, she is like a child compared with you! She's so small.'

'Spare me your comparisons. Here, take her paw. Blanche, what does this mean?'

The girl had swiftly withdrawn her little hand from the count's and folded her arms behind her back.

'Give me your hand. You met the gentleman yesterday and you must be polite to him.'

'Monsieur,' cried Martin, 'she is on the verge of tears. Please don't ask her to do anything distasteful to her.'

'I can't understand why she is afraid of you. Blanche, don't be a ninny and dance with him. He will be as chivalrous to you as the Vicomte de Clarmont.'

His last words seemed to have a soothing effect. Blanche held out her hand to Martin and summoned up a shy smile. The elderly musicians repeated the minuet and the ballet master showed Martin the steps. At first it was obvious that Martin would have preferred to be elsewhere, but once he began to dance in tune, his face cleared and he was soon thoroughly enjoying himself.

The count sat in a chair and watched.

'You're far from clumsy, Martin. You look very well. Master, when can I show off your pupil?'

'In my opinion, after eight or ten lessons, M. le Comte.'

'Good, in a week then. No, that's wrong again. Blanche, show him the turn.'

Blanche proudly showed him her skill. Martin attentively followed her tiny feet and avoided her dark eyes which were once more sparkling and focussed continually on the count. The latter stood up. 'Martin, you can go on practising alone. Come, Blanche.'

The child immediately went over to him. She reached barely to his chest. Placing his arm round her shoulders, he led her quickly from the hall. Martin noticed how she nestled against his hip, and stood still. The door closed.

'Pay attention, please, Monsieur,' piped the ballet master. 'Turn your toes out. One, two, three and bow. No, no, that was too stiff. Not like that. Like this.'

Although Master Volin had promised to deliver Martin's suits in four days, he did not keep his word, and since Martin could not appear in society in his shabby uniform and both the count and the vicomte were often absent, the young man was frequently left to his own devices. But he was not bored. He often rode alone through Paris or walked through the streets if the weather was fine. From the banks of the Seine he admired the Louvre and tried in vain, in the dim twilight of Nôtre Dame, to discover one of the standards he had captured among those the Maréchal de Luxembourg had presented to the cathedral in honour of the Virgin Mary; he explored the booths of Saint-Germain, went to the tennis courts in the morning and to the theatre in the evening. He was delighted with his new experiences. At the Jeu de Paume he made the acquaintance of some officers of his own rank and age, and with them visited the fencing halls and taverns.

In the Hôtel de Racon, he often kept little Blanche company. With the count's permission he was allowed to enter her play-room, where she kept a monkey, a squirrel, three perpetually yapping lapdogs, a canary and two indolent cats. This little 'zoo', as Martin christened the room, smelt appallingly and he found it quite understandable that the count had forbidden Blanche to take a single one of her pets into her elegant bedroom. She was allowed to go for a drive once a day with her old maid, and her large escort of armed grooms gave the impression that she was a young girl of quality whose virtue had to be preserved. For exercise, Blanche had to dance and she did this not only during her lessons but continuously when she was not actually sitting or standing. She danced up and down the stairs, danced in front of her pets, and danced before Martin and Raoul. On the count's orders the vicomte taught her to read and write, and she began to forget the agony of being dumb. She copied out tirelessly everything that Raoul wrote for her and, when he was absent, Martin had to replace him, although, like the count, his orthography was not very brilliant and the vicomte had to correct a great number of mistakes on his return. The most frequent questions she asked Martin were: 'Where is the Comte de Racon? When is the count coming?'

Martin had to tell her all about the count's life, until she knew as much of it as he did, although his tact prevented the mention of any woman other than the countess.

Blanche began to write the count little *billets doux*. The first one Martin handed to him said in huge letters: 'I love the Comte Gaston de Racon.'

When the count laughed heartily at this declaration, Martin was furious. He insisted that there was nothing ridiculous about her great love and that there was probably no other female creature at the moment who loved him so deeply and genuinely as Blanche.

Martin had come to Paris with a great desire to find a well-born love—and all he had found was the enchanting, dumb Blanche, who belonged to the count. He purposely avoided looking at her or touching her more than necessary, and never took her hand except when they were dancing. But continence did not agree with him and it was difficult to get advice on this subject. He did not like cheap trollops and the expensive ones were far beyond his means. He envied Raoul who always had a host of feminine admirers. The ladies did not hesitate to visit him when he pretended to have toothache, and were constantly sending him scented love-letters.

Since Martin noticed that the most frequent visitors were no longer in their prime, and rarely young and attractive, he decided that the unseen letter writers must be ravishing beauties. Raoul noticed Martin's interest and suggested that he should serve as a messenger and deliver his polite refusals. Martin accepted enthusiastically and, in this way, was given an entrée to many a noble lady's antechamber, from where, for a young man of the world, it was not very far to the boudoir. He often came home in great excitement and told Raoul that he had been fortunate. His method was very simple. He told the maid that the letter entrusted to him was so important that he must hand it to the lady in person. He was shown in to her mistress, who learned from the note that the messenger was the vicomte's half-brother and trusted friend. If the lady was pretty and alone in the room, Martin said, as he took his leave, that the ailing vicomte had instructed him to kiss the lady's hand in his place. If the lady was gracious enough to give him her hand, he kissed it longer than was necessary and let his lips stray gently over her wrist. Taking the count as his model, Martin wore fresh linen and shaved himself daily. The ladies seldom withdrew their hands and, once he had reached the wrist, it was not difficult to make further progress. Raoul smiled at Martin's successes but was pestered just as much as before, despite his brother's services. Martin was kept very busy, and when at last he received his suits, said with a laugh that they were no longer of such importance since he had had all the success he needed in his old uniform. But now came the great moment for him to be introduced to Paris society; the count had set his heart on this more than he himself had done.

One evening at nine o'clock, shortly before they set out, the count inspected the three young gentlemen whom he proposed to take with him to Mlle de Lenclos' salon. He himself was wearing a pale-grey silk rhinegrave; fair-haired Louis wore cinnamon; Martin a russet-brown suit, the colour of his eyes; and Raoul a dark-violet rhinegrave with metallic blue ribbons which matched his gleaming locks. The count suddenly discovered an ugly stain on Raoul's jacket.

'Hell, you've messed yourself up again in front.'

'Dominique did his best, Father. He cleaned it as well as he could, but he could not remove the stain.'

'You can throw it away and put on another.'

'Father, the only one that goes with the rhinegrave is also stained.'

'Is that really so?' jibed the count. 'And you say it quite casually. How do you usually appear at the Palais Royal?'

'Generally in this garb. The stain is quite recent.'

'Your lace is torn. Go and change from top to toe.'

'Father, I haven't a shirt or a better suit than this.'

'Why?'

Raoul did not reply.

'What do you do with your pocket money? Out with it!'

'The Chevalier de Lorraine forced me to gamble and I lost nine hundred livres.'

'A handsome sum but no excuse not to ask me for money. Make some real gambling debts next time and take my blue-grey rhinegrave and one of my shirts. Louis, your red stockings are appalling. Go and change them. The three of you can follow me later when you are presentable. I'll go on ahead.' The count put on his cloak, took his hat and left the boys alone.

Louis laughed. 'Naturally, from six pairs of coloured stockings I had to choose the wrong ones! I wish I had his taste. Come on, let's smarten ourselves up, Raoul.'

'I'm staying here.'

'You're staying here?'

'I refuse to wear his clothes.'

'Don't be so foolish,' Martin blurted out. 'You don't really have to be disgusted by one of your father's clean shirts.'

'You're right, but I won't wear anything of his.'

'Raoul,' said Louis, 'you are of the same build and I'm sure that his blue-grey rhinegrave will suit you.'

'Leave me in peace.'

'Your dislike of your father is unnatural.'

'I have plenty of cause. He made my mother unhappy and robbed me of a girl. Say that I have toothache. Goodnight.' Raoul left the room.

Louis turned to Martin. 'Has the count already spotted little Nicolette?'

'No, no,' laughed Martin. 'The vicomte is talking of a girl with whom he fell in love as a boy. He is in a bad mood because Nicolette has not appeared for three days. Her mother is ill and needs expensive medicines. It is easy to imagine where his pocket money goes.'

'Have you seen his fair one?' asked Louis.

'Yes, I caught a glimpse of her—a pretty ash-blonde creature, a snub nose and devilishly vivacious eyes. I would not trust her out of my sight.'

'That is why the vicomte is all the more faithful. Wait for me, I shall not be long.'

Louis returned in a few minutes wearing blue stockings. 'M. Saint-Jean, the vicomte is consoled; Nicolette is with him. We can go.'

Martin left the room at Louis's heels. The second coach was already drawn up in the entrance and the two young gentlemen climbed into it.

On the way, Louis said suddenly: 'M. Saint-Jean, I hope you will excuse me if I desert you for my friends in Mlle de Lenclos' salon.'

'Of course, Comte de Salvieux. Are you meeting a sweetheart there?'

'No, only one or two very influential people. The lady of my heart never leaves her house.'

'Is it true that she is old?'

'Yes, but she has three millions. As you know, I am poor and need someone to pay my tailor. You can laugh. I should advise you to look for a rich old mistress. You should really be more concerned about your future. If you knew M. de Brayonne's feelings for you, you would not feel so happy. The count's friendship is dangerous to you.'

'I am a soldier and I am used to danger. Could you not convince M. de Brayonne that I do not threaten his future in any way? We were enemies as boys but now there is no longer any reason why we should be so. Tell him that with my greetings. If it led to a reconciliation the count would certainly let us meet again.'

'M. de Brayonne envies you, and you know that envy can never be reconciled.'

'I control my envy through my reason,' replied Martin. 'Why should M. de Brayonne envy me?'

'He thinks that the count gives you presents in secret.'

'My God, the count has prodigious debts.'

'On your account perhaps.'

'On my account? I paid for my clothes with my salary and, apart from my weapons, I own nothing except a horse.'

'Did you sell your Lippizaner for a good price?'

'Yes, but the money is not at my disposal.'

Louis laughed. 'I wasn't trying to borrow any money from you, M. Saint-Jean. Did you recognise the crest on that coach we just passed?'

'I wasn't looking.'

'It belonged to the Grande Mademoiselle, the Duchesse de

Montpensier, the king's cousin. I know more than six hundred crests and the whole genealogy of the royal family.'

Coach after coach drew up outside Ninon de Lenclos' house. The famous yellow salon was filled to overflowing. Louis and Martin remained by the door to let their eyes grow accustomed to the bright light and to look for familiar faces. A smartly dressed young cavalier left his group and walked over to Louis, who went forward to meet him with a smile. Martin followed, expecting his friend to introduce him. Then he noticed how Louis slipped into the gossiping group and disappeared behind a hedge of acquaintances and other cavaliers. Martin felt a flush rise to his cheeks. The lights were beginning to make his eyes smart. He could move neither forwards nor backwards, and stood there, the object of many surprised glances.

Suddenly he saw the Comte de Racon at his side.

'Ah, there you are. Didn't you see me waving to you?'

'Monsieur, I do not belong in this society. Please allow me to leave.'

'Since when have you been so shy? Where are Raoul and Louis?'

'The vicomte sends his excuses because of a new attack of toothache, but the Comte de Salvieux is here.'

The count cast an eye round the crowd, caught sight of Louis and understood. With a laugh, he put his arm round Martin's shoulders. 'He's talking to the son of the Minister of War. The reason I'm speaking to you now is so that the people around should notice. I am one of our hostess's friends and was once lucky enough to mean more to her. One needs nothing but the natural grace of a lively spirit to be accepted here. You will find dukes, marshals, ministers and a host of important people rubbing shoulders with poor scholars and poets. Anyone who is received here can show his face anywhere and will be accepted. Don't worry, my boy. I did not bring you here to hold you up to ridicule, and I have no fears on your account. The Maréchal d'Humières is just taking his leave of Ninon de Lenclos. Come quickly. I'll introduce you to her.'

Martin followed the count past a dense group of standing gentlemen and seated ladies. Stools were pulled back, cushions offered and glasses handed to them. There was a murmur of laughter and voices; in one of the window bays a lute was being played, while a poet read a sonnet to an audience of three ladies. The men smoked and gambled. None of the gentlemen was drunk, no lady was bored, and the conversation never flagged. Martin suddenly found himself face to face with Ninon de Lenclos. She was dressed with startling simplicity, and her hair was still golden. From her chair, her bright eyes smiled up at the count. 'Is this your young friend whose handwriting I already know?'

'Yes, Mademoiselle, this is Martin Saint-Jean.'

'He bears a greater resemblance to you than do your other sons, and yet he's quite handsome.'

'You say "yet", and seem surprised,' laughed the count. 'As you see, nature occasionally produces a miracle.'

'In this case, Monsieur, I prefer to believe in the formative power of the character which can transform inherited features. Allow me a few words with the young man, so that I can make his acquaintance in conversation.'

The count bowed and left Martin with his hostess.

'Sit down, M. Saint-Jean,' she said, pointing to a chair. 'Tell me, how did this friendship between you and your father begin?'

'He accepted me as a friend after I admitted my love for him.'

'And when did that love begin?'

'I don't know. Possibly the first time I saw him. He was riding in the king's retinue and sat his horse more majestically than any of the cavaliers around him.'

Ninon fanned herself. 'One of the properties of love,' she said, 'is that it steals into your heart unawares. How do you spend your time here in Paris?'

'So far, committing follies, if I may be allowed to say so.'

'Follies can signify a great deal.'

'Mademoiselle, I am afraid that I shall not please you with my confessions.'

'Do your follies give you pleasure?'

'On yes, because they are a novelty to me.'

'M. Saint-Jean, I hope you are not referring to ladies.

'No, no, certainly not.'

Ninon threatened him archly with her fan. 'Go on telling the truth that was so apparent in all your letters and makes you so different from the rest, to your advantage.'

'Mademoiselle, what shall I do here in Paris?'

'Educate yourself.'

'I am a soldier and need no higher education.'

'There are marshals here tonight who know Caesar by heart.'

'Are they as successful as Luxembourg or Turenne?'

'Monsieur, now you place me in an awkward position for I'm afraid I cannot give you the answer.'

'Please forgive me, Mademoiselle. If there is a French translation of Caesar, I will read it.'

'Stick to your resolution and, above all, read Montaigne and the famous maxims of the Duc de La Rochefouchauld, who is here tonight among my guests. And how is the handsome Vicomte de Clarmont?'

'In indifferent health. He suffers from his teeth.'

'Poor boy, the pain must be terrible.'

Martin noticed that the lady's teeth were unusually white and gave her features the charm of eternal youth. At the same time he noticed two gentlemen standing behind her, obviously waiting to have an opportunity of talking with her.

'Mademoiselle, I do not know whether I have the right to keep others away from you by my presence. I do not wish to appear presumptuous.'

Ninon de Lenclos tapped him with her fan. 'M. Saint-Jean, the slightest suggestion of dismissal is the prerogative of the lady and never of the gentleman, particularly when the latter is a young greenhorn.'

'Forgive me, this is my first appearance in society.'

'How charming you are when you blush! Did you not have the entrée to the Comtesse de Racon's salon?'

'Yes, but until recently I was only the tolerated companion of the count's sons, and I have not yet grown sufficiently used to my new position to be able to behave like a gentleman.'

'To become a gentleman is a high goal, M. Saint-Jean, and there are few cavaliers to whom the term applies.'

'Is to be of noble birth one of the requirements?' he asked swiftly.

'Yes, nobility of birth must combine with nobility of character. But there are exceptions: many capable and noble characters are rewarded with a coat of arms by the perspicacious king and new gentlemen are created. Everyone has a right to expect much from the future but one should rely wisely only upon oneself. How your eyes light up! Does what I have just said please you?'

'Yes, Mademoiselle, for you give me courage.'

'You are a treasure. Tell me something to make me laugh so that I can learn the gay side of your nature.'

Martin thought for an instant and began: 'This morning I accompanied the Comte de Racon to Versailles. We gave our horses their heads, and as they galloped, we amused ourselves by looking up at the clouds. I spotted one with a nose and he pointed out one which looked like a hare. The nose turned into a broomstick and the hare became a greyhound which split into two. Are you amused?'

Ninon laughed: 'Yes, Monsieur, vastly. What happened to the two halves of the greyhound?'

'One turned into a plume and the other into a pig's head. Then we met two horsemen and had to end our game with the clouds.'

'M. Saint-Jean, you are even more adorable than your letters. Come and see me again on Friday.' She held out her hand to Martin and waved to a dandified nobleman to whom she introduced Martin as the Comte de Racon's young friend.

Martin walked off with his new acquaintance and soon found himself in a group of elegant youths of his own age who accepted him with respect. They were discussing a comedy and Martin was lucky to make a few apposite remarks. Someone mentioned that it was time to go and see the last act of *Phèdre*, and, before Martin was aware of it, most of the young men had disappeared and he found himself being introduced to a lady whom he knew well but had the presence of mind not to recognise. However, she offered him a seat which had just become free. Martin thanked her with some hesitation and sat down.

Then an elderly, elegantly dressed gentleman turned round, and, after a casual glance, began to observe him closely. Martin was once more introduced and the old nobleman said to him: 'Why have you come here?'

'Just to be here, Monsieur.' There was a ripple of laughter.

'What real reasons are you withholding in your answer?' enquired the old man.

'Please tell me why I arouse your distrust? Why should you suspect me of hiding something?'

The old man smiled, while the others laughed loudly, enough to draw the attention even of people sitting some way off. 'But what urged you to come here?' he persisted.

'It was the Comte de Racon's wish and my own personal curiosity.'

'And what do you hope to achieve by your presence here?'

'Nothing further, since Mlle de Lenclos has asked me to return on Friday.'

'And what do you expect from the second visit?'

'Nothing in particular, except that it will be enjoyable.'

'Why do you always avoid the issue?'

'Please tell me what motives you suspect in me?'

'You want to meet people here who will help you on in life.'

'Monsieur, that may be the Comte de Racon's wish, but it is certainly not mine. I want to succeed as a soldier and therefore the battlefield is more suited to me than the salon.'

'Are you really ingenuous enough to believe that?'

'I do believe it, Monsieur. I should be ashamed of myself if I had owed my lieutenancy to the personal goodwill of my superiors and not to my own actions. But I admit that there were soldiers who deserved my rank and did not attain it because they were unpopular with their colonels. I intend to help these unfortunate men as best I can.'

'To reap nothing but ingratitude?'

'Monsieur, I do not consider it noble to count upon gratitude.'

'Young man, the nobility of character which your words betray must be borne out by your actions.'

'Do you expect me to give you a list of my good deeds?'

'There is no good deed that does not hide some selfish motive, even if only to reserve a front-row seat in paradise one day.'

Martin looked confused. The lady of his acquaintance asked

his inquisitor: 'Is not the voice of conscience that urges one to do good, free from all baseness?'

The old gentleman turned to her. 'Yes, but a man is incapable of hearing its clear voice. If he hears it at all it becomes tinged with his own desire. He would ruin himself if he lived according to its dictates.'

'Please prove that to us,' said the lady.

'Madame, does conscience allow you to cause pain to fellow creatures?'

'No.'

'And yet our whole civilisation is based on evil actions, Madame. We live on the flesh of animals which we kill cruelly with our knives; we live in luxury which is paid for by the sweat of other men's brows; we defend our country by killing and maiming our fellow human beings; we enter convents and inflict the grief of separation upon the people who love us; we submit our wives to the pain of childbirth, and to our fathers we owe all our sufferings—our fathers to whom we owe our lives.'

An abbé, who had come up unnoticed and had only caught the end of the speech, said: 'Monsieur, you forget that pain has the task of purifying men's souls.'

The old man gave a subtle smile. 'I do not enter into disputes with the church.'

Martin recognised the abbé as M. d'Oubray and rose to greet him. The priest seemed delighted to see Martin and introduced him to his companion, who must have once been a very beautiful woman. In a whisper, Martin asked him the name of the distinguished old nobleman to whom he had just been talking. 'The Duc de La Rochefoucauld, the author of the famous *Maxims*.'

'I consider myself fortunate indeed to have been worthy of your notice,' Martin said with a deep bow. He was dismissed with a gracious nod. As he walked away with the abbé, he heard the duke say: 'The young man could not be drawn and seems to me to have more character than one usually finds today.'

D'Oubray and Martin were jostled into a window bay by the departing guests. The abbé asked for news of the countess, and Martin replied that she was in good health.

'I beg of you,' said d'Oubray, with a cautious glance at his companion who had just been greeted by two cavaliers and a lady, 'please remember me to the countess when you write and tell her that I am unchanged, although I may be wearing a priest's habit. She does not believe me.'

'Monsieur,' replied Martin, 'it is not my place to write letters to such a high-born lady.'

'Forgive me then for having importuned you with a wish which you cannot fulfill.' They bowed to each other and Martin was left alone.

At this moment the lady, whom he had to thank for his conversation with the duke, rustled up to him. A glove fell at his feet. Martin bent down at the same time as another young man, but was the quicker of the two. A slip of paper crackled in the glove. Martin secreted it and returned the glove. He read the note unobserved: 'Tomorrow, between midday and two o'clock.' Someone touched him on the back, and Louis' voice rang out: 'Congratulations, Monsieur, you have had the honour of speaking with some very exalted persons.'

'Has so much reflected glory from these people clung to me,' he replied over his shoulder, 'that you now consider it worthwhile speaking to me in public?'

'You disappeared suddenly before I could introduce you.'

'Please excuse me, Comte de Salvieux, there is someone I must greet,' said Martin, walking over to the Marquis de Chassigny.

Martin and Louis drove home in the same coach as the count. The count was in the best of moods and well satisfied with Martin. When he told him that Mlle de Lenclos had invited him to visit her on Friday, he said curtly that he would make Martin's excuses to her since Guy visited her salon that day. He did not wish M. de Brayonne and Lieutenant Saint-Jean to meet in the same place, and they would have to get used to this.

Next morning, when the count was already on his way to Court, Raoul proposed to Martin that he should accompany him to the Palais Royal. 'There is so much activity going on that no one will notice you.'

'Splendid, Raoul, I am bursting with curiosity. Can I go like this?'

Raoul examined Martin's sand-coloured costume. 'Of course, you are far more elegant than I am.'

'Why do you always affect such dark colours?' asked Martin. 'Your rhinegrave is almost black.'

'On my father's orders, because the dark material shows up my fair skin to advantage.'

'Of course. Now I understand why the count always wears light colours. François! I am riding with the Vicomte. Have Pluto saddled at once.'

In the Palais Royal, the menfolk were still abed while Madame was in her study writing to her German relatives. Raoul and Martin had an opportunity of walking at their leisure through the apartments where servants were sweeping and polishing. Martin was surprised at the broken glass and food lying on the floor, which was being carried away in pails. Raoul smiled in his weary, contemptuous manner. 'Monsieur prides himself on his roisterous board. Presumably he threw an apple of discord among his mignons. Hi, you,' he called to a red-liveried lackey. 'Did they start throwing plates again last night?'

'A soup bombardment, the roast went flying,
In a welter of scratching and biting and sighing.'

Martin laughed and the wag continued. 'Monsieur was content and peace was restored. Today, they all have sore heads, but Monsieur laughed.'

As Raoul walked on, Martin remarked: 'They seem to have very strange habits here, but tell me, how does Madame regard such behaviour?'

'Madame eats on her own.'

'Oh, like the Comtesse de Racon. Where are you going?'

'I want to show you the picture gallery. Monsieur wants to be the counterpart of his brother in all respects, and he is often successful. The king's household is dressed in blue livery, and, as you see, Monsieur's wears red. The king loathes Dutch painting, and Monsieur collects nothing else. The king loves women, and Monsieur loves handsome youths. The king is majesty personified, and Monsieur is a clown. The king's slightest displeasure brings danger, and Monsieur wouldn't hurt a fly. So there you are. These pictures are my only consolation. It is a pity that the morning sun is still shining on some of them. It spoils the pleasure of looking at them.'

They stood at the entrance of the huge gallery, the red silk walls of which were closely hung with pictures. Raoul tried to draw his friend's attention to one or two pictures, but Martin soon began to yawn.

'Look at this van der Velde landscape, Martin. What peace and depth!'

Martin pointed to another portraying fighting peasants. 'That's not bad. Does that serve as the model for Monsieur's pleasures of the table? Just look at those naked women. My God, aren't they fat? The count wouldn't like them ... All those rolls of fat and dimples! I'd like to slap their thighs.'

'That one is by Rubens, the famous Flemish painter,' said Raoul. 'He discovered how to paint the human skin, and so as to have plenty of it to paint he chooses plump girls as his models. Isn't that mother-of-pearl sheen beautiful?'

'Beautiful? I don't understand it. Tell me, do I have to look at all these pictures?'

'You're a barbarian, Martin,' Raoul said in despair, 'but I'll show you one of a battle-scene. That will certainly please you.' He led Martin on until they found one.

'Oh, that's wonderful!' cried Martin. 'That is what it's really like, but the horses are too thick and in real life would burst with so much oats in their bellies. But painters seem to like curves. How funny those helmets are. As though anyone wore things like that! The count has even discarded his hat because it's too heavy and wears his cap, but if I don't wear my helmet he curses me. I must be protected although he declines to be. Before the next battle I shall take a look at his hat, and woe betide him if he hasn't got the cap inside!'

'Do you really dare to quarrel with him?'

'Oh, I don't shrink from it in such cases. If I throw away my helmet he gives in. De Falleron is often bent double with laughing when we quarrel. Who is that coming?'

'Monsieur.'

They both bowed deeply as a group of men strolled towards them across the beautifully polished parquet floors. Philippe d'Orléans led the way on the arm of a remarkably handsome, fair-haired, blue-eyed cavalier, who quizzed Martin from a distance. Monsieur was very short in stature despite the thick soles and dangerously high heels on which he tripped gracefully. His rich suit was so overloaded with ribbons and lace that it looked more like a lady's dress than a cavalier's attire. His curiously feminine, but not unhandsome, face was painted, and a veritable cloud of perfume pervaded the gallery. A few pretty pages, who tittered and chattered together, followed the duke and his companion.

Monsieur came to a halt in front of Raoul. 'Ah, the handsome Vicomte de Clarmont. And how are your teeth?'

'Your Highness is more than kind to enquire about my health. I am better today, thank you.'

'You should bring yourself at last to trust my dentist, my dear boy. Who is the young man with you?'

'My half-brother, your Highness.'

'He does not resemble you. Have you come at last to ask a favour? Do you want a post for your brother? Oh yes, I know you. As usual, you are far too modest, although you know that I like rewarding small services. Well?'

'Your Highness,' Raoul began to stutter, 'we had no intention . . . Your Highness is too kind . . .'

'I wish I knew how to win your confidence. Young man,' he said, turning to Martin, 'you know your brother; tell me what are his wishes?'

'The vicomte has never confided any of his wishes to me, Monsieur.'

'And what about you, what do you wish?'

'I have none at the moment, if you'll allow me to speak the truth.'

'None at the moment,' he began to roar with laughter. 'Someone in my house who has no favour to ask of me. Did you hear that, Chevalier, the young man has no wishes? Magnificent, enchanting.' Monsieur clapped his hands with joy. His companion raised his eyebrows and looked at Martin with an amused smile.

'Let us hope he is right in the head.'

'Vicomte,' said Monsieur, rising on his toes and stroking Raoul's cheek with his soft, beringed fingers, 'you could become my gentleman of the bed chamber, with a pension of

20,000 a year! And I have a castle to give away into the bargain. What, is that not enough? So you want more? Do not hesitate to ask for it, you see that I am in a generous mood.'

'Your Highness,' replied Raoul, trembling with disgust, 'I beg you to give me time to think it over.'

Monsieur tapped him gently on the chin and then let fall his hand. 'How coy. Time for reflection! You have my indulgence but it is not certain that I shall always be in the same mood.'

Turning to his companion, he took his arm and said: 'Come dear boy.' The little group went on its way, while Raoul and Martin bowed deeply for the second time.

Raoul seemed to be blowing his nose as he wiped his face with a handkerchief. 'Who was the handsome fair-haired youth with Monsieur?' asked Martin.

'The Chevalier de Lorraine, Monsieur's great favourite, who at the same time dominates him. He is a man entirely without a conscience, greedy, lacking in honour, sly as a fox and dangerous to anyone who might win Monsieur's favour. I could curse my good looks. Promise, Martin, that you won't let my father hear of Monsieur's offer?'

'Naturally, I shall not say a word.'

'Thank you.'

'He would be quite capable of playing the pander.'

'Raoul, do not make your father out to be so evil. If you only took the trouble to appeal to his better nature I'm sure he would treat you as he treats me.'

Raoul put away his handkerchief and replied: 'Come, let's go back.'

Martin watched Monsieur and the chevalier disappear through a door at the far end of the gallery. Then one of the pages signed to them, ran across the floor, slid on the parquet and fell at Raoul's feet. Martin came to his help.

'Oh, thank you. I only hurt my backside. Can I join you gentlemen? Monsieur's morning rounds are too slow for me. I think today will be very dull. Madame is staying at home with a cold, and this evening they are giving *Le Malade Imaginaire*. Would the gentlemen like to see the comedy?'

'Not a bad idea,' said Raoul. 'Martin, do you know the play?'

'No, I've only heard that the great Molière died on the

stage while playing the part of the hypochondriac.'

'You are perfectly right,' piped the boy. 'What a witty death. I shall go and see it because it will not be given again for some time.'

'Good,' said Raoul. 'Let us go too; it will pass the evening, or have you other plans?'

'No,' replied Martin. 'I shall certainly be free from eight o'clock onwards. I should like to accompany you. I prefer plays to pictures.'

The page suddenly looked thoughtful. 'So long as Monsieur does not get angry because I ran away . . .'

'Monsieur never gets really angry,' Raoul replied with a smile.

'But he may do today, because you asked for time to think it over. I'd better go. I bid you good morning, gentlemen.' He sped away from them like the wind.

'The Duc d'Orléans is very peculiar,' said Martin, 'and yet his good nature is very winning. The count told me that he displayed great courage in the war and had he been given a stern upbringing would have become a hero. Cardinal Mazarin insisted on his being coddled to rob him of any desire to rule. You cannot therefore blame him for his effeminacy and should rather pity him. I should tell him quite simply that you are in love with a girl and that you regret you can offer him nothing but the deepest respect. He certainly will not show any rancour.'

'Martin, he knows my father and thinks highly of him. If he complains to him . . .'

'Let him complain. The count cannot possibly insist that you should debase yourself and become a minion.'

'He insists that I should reap advantages here.'

'What does he mean by that?'

'He never actually explains but I can quite imagine it.'

'But ask him, Raoul, keep on until he gives you a straightforward answer. If necessary, refuse to enter the Palais Royal again. With your father you only need to show courage and have confidence in him.'

'I lack that confidence.'

'Very well then, I'll speak for you.'

'I wouldn't hear of it.'

'Why not?'

'He would send for me, and the very sight of me would be enough to make him fly into a rage.'

'I'll remain in the room.'

'No, Martin, if you're my friend don't say anything, I beg of you. I will go and see him myself.'

'When?'

'Oh, don't torture me. I have a headache and I'm going to ride home. I want to be alone. Will you be silent?'

'Yes, of course.'

When the Vicomte de Clarmont and Martin left the theatre after the performance, they could not find their coach. Martin cursed while Raoul looked round for acquaintances who would give them a lift. He was so short-sighted that he could not see anyone. Coach after coach rattled away, litters passed and horsemen trotted off. Soon, the few less-prosperous theatre-goers had left the building.

An unknown servant came running up.

'Vicomte de Clarmont, M. le Marquis de Chassigny begs you to share his carriage. Follow me, Monsieur.'

Martin laughed, 'Fancy the Marquis de Chassigny being at the theatre! He must have come to see an actress and not the play.'

They followed the servant into a dark alley. 'Where is the coach then?' asked Martin. At this moment, human shadows slipped from the walls and there was a flash of steel.

'Raoul,' shouted Martin, 'they've lured us into a trap. Draw your sword!'

They drew their rapiers and fought like lions. Martin laid the first attacker low, disarmed the second with a slash and stabbed him through the chest. Windows hastily opened and a ray of light fell upon them. Men's and women's voices began to call for the watch. Their cries were taken up, and in the distance they heard an order being given. The cutpurses retreated and suddenly vanished. One of the wounded men was writhing in the mire, trying to stagger to his feet.

'Are you wounded, Raoul?' asked Martin.

'No, are you?'

'No, I'm all right. Hi, you there on the ground, why did you attack us?'

'Mercy! Spare me!'

'Answer me or I'll kill you.'

'Mercy, Monsieur, mercy! The Chevalier de Lorraine paid us well.'

'Silence him, Martin,' insisted Raoul. 'No one must guess that we know the instigator of this crime. Anyone whom the chevalier wants to thrust aside is lost. Here comes the watch. Go on, kill him.'

Martin did as he was bid before the wounded man could beg for mercy again, and Raoul hurried him away.

They ran through filthy ill-lit streets until Raoul had to stop to get his breath. He looked round. 'Are we being followed?' Martin listened attentively.

'I can hear horses' hooves. Start running.'

'I can't do it, Martin. Let's stand in that doorway.'

'Raoul, it's only a coach. I wonder if it's ours?'

The vehicle rattled up. Two grooms rode on ahead with torches, followed by four others. Martin waved and cried excitedly. 'Raoul, it's the count's coach. Stop! It's the Vicomte de Clarmont!'

The coachman and the groom stopped. Martin opened the door and the count pulled him inside. 'Martin, I've been given command of the Light Horse of the Guard.'

Martin was embraced, kissed and hugged, told to sit down, embraced again, while Raoul received a few unintentional blows. A lackey closed the door and the coach rolled on.

The count would not let either of them speak. 'Listen, you young ruffians, I have the right to create ten new officers. Give me your advice. Which of my officers shall I appoint to the Guards?'

'I congratulate you, Monsieur.'

'I asked you for advice, not for congratulations. Who is to be the first?'

'Du Lac.'

'Right. And the second?'

'De Falleron.'

'Right. And the third?'

'Perhaps . . .'

'No perhaps. Lieutenant de Clarmont is the third. Raoul,

you're coming into the Guards, and the fourth will be *you.*'

'Monsieur!' cried Martin.

'Yes, I need you to train the cadets. The king has agreed all the names, including yours. You will be the only lieutenant who is not of noble birth, but you will behave to the gentlemen with your usual respect and consideration and they will get accustomed to you. You won't be on guard in the Louvre or at Versailles, but you will come on manoeuvres. I have already sent two messengers to winter quarters. The Guards' quarters are at Versailles. Say thank you, you lucky fellow!'

Martin slipped from his seat to bend his knee, and the count caught him by the hair in his delight. 'You're pleased, eh?'

'Yes, Monsieur, but we have something serious and important to tell you.'

'Serious and important, what is it? Sit over there on the opposite seat. Raoul, come over here. Why were you on foot in the street?'

Martin described the attack and then their morning encounter with the Duc d'Orléans and his favourite.

'Did you give the chevalier occasion to envy you?' asked the count, turning to Raoul. 'Did the duke make you a gift?'

'Monsieur has always been particularly friendly to me, Father.'

'That means nothing.'

'Monsieur,' Martin asked quickly, 'can the vicomte continue to be in Madame's service once he is a lieutenant of the Guards?'

The count thought for a moment. 'Raoul, you'll remain at the Palais Royal until further notice, and visit the tailor tomorrow morning with Martin. Get measured for lieutenants' uniforms—scarlet with black facings and gold braid. Volin knows the requirements. The uniforms have to be ready in a week, for in a fortnight I am giving a banquet to all the officers of my new regiment and shall introduce my ten newcomers to them. I shall ask the Duc de Luxembourg and various commanding officers of the Guards. Here we are.' The coach pulled up in the doorway. They dismounted and learnt that the coachman, who had been waiting outside the theatre, had been ordered home in the name of the vicomte by a strange lackey. The count hurried up the steps and the half-brothers embraced each other. 'I am saved,' said Raoul.

'Yes,' replied Martin. 'He's got his command. Thank God for that.'

The following day the count visited Monsieur, with whom he was in favour, and casually informed him that the Vicomte de Clarmont was filled with undying love for his fiancée, a certain Mlle du Terne, and could hardly wait for the marriage which was due to take place at the New Year. Since his nerves were shattered, partly owing to his longing and partly to a nocturnal attack by cutpurses, perhaps Monsieur would be gracious enough to give him leave until after the marriage? Monsieur looked sour. He knew of the count's appointment and maintained that the new conditions would enable certain people to dispense with much that had hitherto been desirable, and hoped that he would soon see the handsome vicomte among his royal brother's courtiers. The count assured him that, in the spring, the vicomte would have to combine his duties with the Guards with his service at the Palais Royal. Monsieur shrugged his shoulders and replied that the Vicomte de Clarmont was not in his but in his wife's service, and that the count should address himself to her. In any case, there would always be a post open at any time for the vicomte in his personal service. The count thanked him profusely and visited Madame, who was about to leave with her retinue for the hunt. The Comte de Racon had always been anathema to her; as soon as he had made his request she replied in her coarse German manner that it was high time he took his son away from the Palais Royal, and she released the boy with the greatest pleasure.

From now onwards, Raoul had to accompany the count daily to the Louvre or to his new regiment. His happiness was short-lived, for his life had not only become richer in honours but more strenuous, and he could not slip away as he had done in the past. The count kept him constantly under his eye, laughed at his toothache, and flew into a rage when he complained that he was tired. What a forty-five-year-old man could do must be child's play to a twenty-year-old boy. Raoul had jumped from the frying-pan into the fire. The ladies of the Court pursued him, just as the ladies of the Palais Royal had done. The proximity of the king terrified him, and his service with the regiment was often beyond his powers of endurance.

The count postponed the already announced change of appointments and left the officers of the Light Horse of the Guard in the most painful uncertainty. Whoever questioned him on this subject received the reply that those who were capable need have no fear. Everyone made the greatest effort and no one dared be missing for a day, except two of the officers who had powerful relations. Some of them offered money, which the count accepted with smiling indifference, provided the sum was large enough.

As before, Martin was allowed complete freedom. He made new acquaintances every day and was invited to many salons. The count had decided that he should command his personal bodyguard (comprising twenty well-selected, magnificently drilled serfs) which was still on its way to the capital. Martin was to lead the troop in person to join the Guards regiment and be introduced to the officers on this occasion. Thus, Martin's preferential position was clear from the start, and no rancour would be felt against him since no nobleman would have to take orders from him direct. Later, he would take over the training of the ensigns, as Captain de Falleron's deputy. Martin was pleased with his duties and took great pains with the count's small pages who came to him nearly every day from the Hôtel de Brayonne, asking him for an hour's fencing lesson or an hour's riding.

One day, Raoul returned before his father from Court, suffering from one of his genuine headaches which grew ever more frequent, with their attendant fits of giddiness. He found Martin with Blanche who, to the young man's amusement, was frowning over her childish drawings; she was trying to sketch her monkey. 'Look, Raoul,' cried Martin, 'what our little artist can do. It really looks like a monkey.'

'Don't let me interrupt you. I'm going to lie down. The Court duties are a great strain on me.'

'I envy you, seeing the king every day.'

'I would rather give Blanche lessons.'

Martin laughed, 'That is a rather doubtful pleasure. Blanche is the apple in the Garden of Eden which you are not allowed to eat.'

The little girl quickly drew an apple and a question mark

beside it.

'Oh dear,' said Martin, 'now I suppose I shall have to tell her the story of Adam and Eve, for better or worse.' Raoul left the couple alone.

Towards nightfall, the count returned from Court and immediately sent for Raoul, who learned from Pierre that his father was in one of his worst moods. He had visited the Hôtel de Brayonne on the way home and there had been a great scene. With grave forebodings, Raoul entered his father's study. 'Why did you come home before me?'

'I had an appalling headache.'

'Is that true or are you lying?'

'It is the truth.'

'Before dinner, why did you only bestow a curt bow on the Grande Mademoiselle?'

'I did not know that the old lady was the Grande Mademoiselle, I took her for one of the Dauphine's ladies-in-waiting, who bears a close resemblance to her.'

'You ass, you confuse people all the time, greet them incorrectly and never notice when they look at you. They tell me that you ignored a gracious glance from the king.'

'Father, you know that I am short-sighted.'

'Well, find someone who can point things out to you at the right moment. There are plenty of poor devils who would be only too pleased to do it for money. Take Guy as your example. He never reads a book yet shines in every salon because he has taken in a poor student who keeps him informed of the contents of all the fashionable novels. You button your coat up far too high. There's a button missing here. Were you dressed like that at the reception?'

'I have just changed, Father.'

'You look dirty. Even if the king never washes you needn't take him as your model, for his Majesty can have any woman while we others have to court our women's favours. Don't think that your looks are enough; the most handsome man in the world will get nowhere if he stinks. You are as white as chalk. Are you constipated?'

'No.'

'Why don't you hold yourself properly?'

'I feel giddy, Father.'

'Well, sit down. What sort of giddiness? Do you often get these attacks?'

'No, only in the past few days.'

'And a headache as well?'

'Yes.'

'Are you feverish?'

'It is possible, Father.'

'Have you any other symptoms?'

Raoul became embarrassed.

'Yes or no?'

'Yes,' confessed Raoul at last.

'What kind?'

Raoul was unwilling to answer, but the count persisted until he was fully informed of his son's condition.

He went over to him and stood at his side. 'Do you know what you are suffering from?'

'No, Father.'

'You've got the Spanish pox.'

Two terrible slaps prevented Raoul from fainting in his terror. 'You secretive, lying toad. Why didn't you tell me? Why do you wait for me to find out? What women have you been with?'

'No one.'

Raoul protected his head with his arms too late. He received a blow from the count's fist. 'From whom are those letters you received? What is the lady's name?'

'Stop hitting me. I'll tell you.'

Raoul named one admirer after the other until the count called out at the mention of one name. 'Yes, she's poxed, but everybody knows that. How often were you with her?'

'Never. Martin was there. I never visited one of the ladies but sent him to all of them in my place.'

'Martin! Pierre, fetch Martin here at once.' Pierre popped his head round the door and hurried away.

The count banged his forehead. 'And I noticed nothing! I could break every bone in your body, you dog, you miserable dog. Where did you catch it then?' Raoul let his arms fall.

'A girl came to me once,' he said dully, 'a pastrycook's daughter who always fetches the washing.'

'Keep your paws off that girl, you understand?'

'Yes, I'll send her away at once.'

'Woe betide you if you continue with the trollop! I'll have you watched. Ah, here's Martin.'

The count immediately questioned him about Raoul's sick admirer. Martin admitted that he had once visited her.

'And how far did you go with her?'

'I did not even kiss her hand because she did not attract me.'

'You were lucky.' The count asked Martin a number of questions and it turned out that he was healthy. He ordered Pierre to fetch a doctor at once. The count sat down in a chair. 'The devil take all women. I should have found healthy mistresses for all of you, but I can't turn my house into a brothel. Guy plays fast and loose in the Hôtel de Brayonne. When I arrived he was making three naked strumpets play leap frog. What can I do with the three of you? Sit down, Martin.'

Martin obeyed and glanced anxiously at the vicomte, who was sitting on a chair with lowered head.

'Is Raoul sick?'

'He's caught the Spanish pox and will have to take a cure so that he will be fit to marry. I don't want a grandson who's a cripple or an idiot. Raoul, you've got to follow all the doctor's instructions down to the last detail. Martin, when you pay your gallant visits, never forget to question the servants as to the health of the lady. Those pourboires are money well spent. Could you, to set my mind at rest, confine yourself to one lady?'

'I don't know which one because all of them leave me indifferent.'

'Listen, Martin, I have an idea: I'll share Blanche with you. Could you then, for my sake, do without other women?'

Martin jumped to his feet. 'Is your offer serious?'

'Yes, then at least I should not have to worry about *you*. We often shared the same trollops during the war. I'll have a peasant girl brought from Grandval for Guy. Why are you blushing?'

'Monsieur, I have long since been in love with Blanche. I dream about her every night and can hardly bear to be in her presence. I love Blanche. Does that disturb you?'

'Not in the least.'

'Thank you, Monsieur. When can I go to her?'

'At once, as far as I'm concerned. I'm tired today.'

'Please give me leave to retire.'

'Stop, wait a minute. I want to see no tears and read no complaints. That must be a condition. The little girl is dearer to me than a mistress, although she is far too small for me. Be tactful and give her a present first.'

'Monsieur, I have nothing suitable and at this hour all the booths are shut.'

'I'll give you something for her. Wait a moment.' The count went into his bedroom, leaving Raoul and Martin alone for a few moments.

Raoul raised his head and turned his lustreless blue eyes on his friend, who was barely a few months older than himself. 'Aren't you ashamed of yourself, Martin?'

'Why should I be?'

'You read my mother's Bible. Should one covet another man's handmaiden?'

'Bah! Your ladies almost all live in a state of marriage and you had nothing to say when I visited them in your place. Your face is swollen. Did he recognise your sickness by that?'

'He struck me.'

'My God!'

Raoul staggered to his feet and held on to the chair to wait for the count.

'Here, Martin,' the count said as he entered. 'She is certain to like this coral necklace.'

'Thank you, Monsieur, can I go now?'

'Yes, go and enjoy yourself.'

Martin turned round as he reached the door.

'Monsieur, please be lenient with the vicomte.'

'You say you're in love and you bother about him?'

'Yes, because I'm leaving him alone with you.'

'You have nothing to fear.'

'Thank you.' Martin hurried away.

'Well, that keeps him busy,' said the count. 'Raoul, go to bed. I'll come and visit you with the doctor.'

'Father, can I go to Grandval for my cure?'

'No, old du Terne would hear of your arrival and learn of your condition. Keep your malady secret.'

Raoul shuffled out and closed the door behind him.

Martin washed, changed his shirt, put on a little perfume and carefully combed his hair. Then he asked the surprised old servant to let him in to Blanche. He entered the elegant bedroom where the little girl, apparently waiting for the count, was standing in the centre of the room in a new silver ballet dress. Martin bowed as though she were a lady of quality.

'Mlle Blanche, the count has allowed me to visit you. He is very tired today and, since I am his friend, he gave me this necklace for you. It is not a present from him but from me. May I offer it to you?'

Blanche's large brown eyes grew larger. She held out her hand for the chain and smiled with admiration. Martin kissed her white little hand and placed the necklace in it. Blanche curtsied to show her thanks, ran to the mirror, admired herself, clapped her hands, pirouetted and began to dance for joy. Martin's heart beat faster. Then she came to a standstill, curtsied again and pointed to the door.

'No,' said Martin. 'I have permission to remain with you. I love you, Mlle Blanche, and since I love you and the count loves me, he has offered to let me share from time to time his droits de seigneur over you. You were always gay in my presence and I have a feeling that you do not find me distasteful. Blanche, please make me happy.'

The colour disappeared from the little girl's cheeks. Martin went over to her and put his arm round her childish shoulders, lifting her trembling little face to his. 'Don't be afraid of me, Blanche. I am still very young but I can control myself and will not demand anything of you which might cause you pain. I will be very gentle with you, I promise Blanche. Perhaps more gentle than the count.'

He approached his lips to her full mouth and tried to read the expression in her startled eyes. The girl broke away, ran to the panelled door and fled into the count's room where Pierre was helping his master to undress. She flung herself at his feet and clung to him with such despair that he could not move. 'What is the matter, Blanche? Child, let me go. Hi, Martin!

Are you there?'

Martin entered, very embarrassed. 'Were you too rough with her?'

'No, Monsieur, certainly not, but perhaps too premature.'

'You've frightened her. Blanche, you needn't be afraid. Martin will stay by the door and not touch you. Stand up and stop that whining.' Blanche began to weep and clung more tightly to the man, who released her gently but firmly. 'Don't clutch on to my lace. I shan't fly away. Here, you can hold my hand. Martin, you obviously behaved like an oaf. Let us ask Blanche. Pierre, bring writing material. Well, little Blanche, now write why you were weeping.'

Blanche dried her eyes and took the quill. With unsteady hand she wrote the name of the count in huge letters and then in small letters the word Martin below it and struck it out so violently that the quill broke and the ink made huge blots on the paper. Turning her peony-red face to the two men, she brandished the sheet of paper, tore the necklace from her throat and flung it on the ground, so that the coral beads were scattered all over the carpet. The count roared with laughter. 'There we have her answer. Tell me, Blanche, can't you love my friend Martin?'

Blanche shook her head three times vigorously with disgust, began to tremble, laid the paper on the table and began to write with the broken quill. Pierre placed a new one in her hand. The count was given the question to read: 'Do I not please you any more?'

'Yes, Blanche, I only wanted to share you.'

Once more the quill scratched over the paper, and the next sentence read: 'I will die before you compel me.'

'I will not compel you, my child. You must not threaten me with dying. Strike out what you have written.'

Blanche obediently struck out the sentence and wrote: 'I will not belong to anyone except you.'

'Am I to believe that?' Blanche flung herself once more at the count's feet, tore open her silver dress and leaned her naked, childish breasts against his knee. The count picked her up and held her in his arms. 'Martin, I don't know why I deserve Blanche's love but at the moment there is nothing to be done. Now you've torn your dress. Aren't you sorry?'

Blanche shook her head. 'Pierre, bring her a blanket so that she can go back to her room.'

Pierre brought the blanket and the count wrapped her in it. 'My child, I shall always keep you with me as long as you are obedient and good. I don't like such outbursts. In future, write to me when something angers you, and send it to me in the correct manner. Torn clothes are an offence. Now, don't start crying again; I'm not angry with you. Go to bed.' Blanche kissed his hand and walked towards her bedroom door.

Martin barred her way. 'Mlle Blanche, I beg you to forgive me. I swear to you that I will never demand anything of you again and will never mention a word of my feelings for you. Please forget what offended you, and forgive me.'

Blanche stared at him half in terror, half in despair, and then glanced over to the count. At that moment a servant announced that the doctor had come and was waiting below. The count ordered Pierre to hand him his dressing-gown and swiftly left the room.

With a gesture, Blanche besought Martin to let her pass, but he stood firm and began once more to plead. 'Blanche, don't leave me like this, feeling ashamed of myself. Believe me, I now see quite clearly that it would be impossible for you to love anyone except the count. I love him perhaps more than you do and I can therefore understand your love. Can you not forgive me?' Blanche's huge dark eyes stared into Martin's entreating hazel ones. Pierre looked curiously at the couple standing there, and a grin began to spread over his face. Then Blanche, without taking her eyes off Martin's, nodded in token of her forgiveness. 'Thank you, Blanche, from now on I beg of you to look upon me as a brother and to let me treat you as a sister.'

Blanche took a deep breath and pressed her hand to her heart. Her breast began to heave and a smile lit up her face. She made a swift movement as though to go towards Martin, nearly lost her blanket, saved it in time and ran to the table, where she struck out what she had previously written and scribbled some new words. Martin stood there quietly until she came over and handed him a piece of paper. He read: 'M. Martin Saint-Jean is now my brother. I am his sister and I love him very much.' The young man clenched his jaws and bowed deeply with studied dignity. 'You make me very happy,' he said, 'and I thank you from the bottom of my heart.'

Shyly, the girl laid the paper aside and her smile faded. 'I must accustom myself to my new happiness, and I do not think it will be easy at first,' Martin said frankly. 'I bid you good-night. Please give me leave to retire.' Bowing deeply, they went their separate ways.

The count came in a moment later. There was a scowl on his face. Pierre handed him the paper. When the count read it he had to laugh. 'Apparently, I've just acquired a daughter. Actually, I often feel very paternal towards her. Anger is a great stimulant. I will sleep with Blanche.'

Martin had met the count in the corridor as he took his leave of the doctor and, despite the lateness of the hour, paid a visit to the vicomte, whom he found pale as death, lying in bed. He sat down on a chair.

'When will you be well again?'

'Perhaps in the spring. I wish I could die of it.'

'Raoul, such a thing can happen to anyone. There is no reason to despair. You should be happy that you know what the trouble is and that it can be cured. You will not have to go to Court now for some time.'

'No.'

'You see, that's already one advantage. You can read all day and forget your troubles.'

'I am disgusted with myself.'

'You must wash yourself frequently.'

Raoul could not help laughing. 'If only that would help! I'm disgusted with life. I feel that everything bright and beautiful is beginning to rot away from within. Look at the painted faces of the women, their beauty spots and their exquisite, panniered dresses. Underneath, they stink of corruption for everyone to smell, if they do not cover themselves with strong perfumes. Everything is powder and paint. Everything is done to deceive, but here and there the truth manages to creep through. Did you see the new chairs in the Palais Royal? Those entrails of gilt wood, those cancerous growths in silver! Look at those draped bedhangings, those billowing monstrous tumours. Look at me, Martin. I am a grub which is about to burst and from which the pus will flow.'

Martin laid a wet towel on Raoul's brow. The boy gave a wry smile.

'You think that my brain is sick, but I'm still quite lucid. Let us talk of something else and deceive ourselves with something beautiful so that we can forget the truth. Did you enjoy yourself with Blanche?'

'She rebuffed me.'

'How astonishing! I should have thought she would be delighted at the change from a satyr to a normal man. She will listen to you tomorrow.'

'No, she loves only the count. He probably behaved to her as he did to me. She never knew her mother, had a hard childhood and then sensed his goodness. But with this man it is dangerous to possess a female body. She is too small for him. Poor Blanche, if a mistress should come into the house . . .'

'Then he'll send her away,' replied Raoul. 'He never keeps two mistresses at the same time.'

Martin's eyes narrowed. 'He won't send Blanche away.'

'How do you know that, Martin?'

'He can't, because if he did he would lose my friendship.'

'Does your friendship really mean so much to him, that you would dare to threaten to leave him?'

'It's not a threat. Anyone who sent Blanche away would no longer be my friend.'

'Well,' said Raoul, 'you almost make me curious to know what will become of you. You have really lost your heart. I know what that means, but I no longer burn with passion for trollops.'

'Blanche is no trollop.'

'The Marquis de Chassigny had her before my father.'

'And if at this moment,' Martin blurted out, 'she was raped by ten Turks, it would not impair her chastity. Her body may be ravaged but not her soul.'

'In my opinion, body and soul are one.'

'The body is what the soul makes it.'

'Where did you get that idea?'

'You can see it all round you. The ageing Ninon de Lenclos is beautiful because of her natural disposition. Your mother is singularly beautiful, and your ugly father is sometimes more handsome than you.'

'You seem to wear glasses that enable you to see people as you wish to see them.'

'I see them as they really are.'

'Go on deceiving yourself if it gives you pleasure. One day you will *have* to see things as they really are.'

'You imagine that you are doing so now? But you can only see a short way into the truth. I see far deeper.'

'How deep?'

'Below the filth, which each man has in him, there is something bright. I was a swine for having tried to kiss Blanche.'

'It's a good thing you realise it.'

'By my terror, I saw that I was catching hold of her as though out of a morass, and I saved myself from that morass. My God! Raoul, my behaviour has been deplorable. I shall never be a saint, but I refuse to go on in the future as I have done in the past.'

'What a fine intention! What perception!'

'You need not mock me. I shall wait for Blanche. I shall protect her when the count has ceased to love her. Perhaps she will be able to love me then.'

'And what will you do until then?'

'I'll improve myself.'

'In what respect?'

'As regards women. I will try and take them more seriously.'

'Why don't you take a vow of chastity?'

'No, for I should become randy and begin to dream of naked women. That is perverse.'

'The whole world is perverse.'

'No, Raoul, there is a solution to everything.'

'How do you know?'

'My faith tells me there must be a solution, otherwise God would not be just. One day I shall be able to make love to Blanche, provided she returns my love. Then I shall ask for her hand and marry her.'

'How admirable!'

'Raoul, I swear to you that I will marry no other woman except Blanche.'

'We shall see.'

'You look repulsive.'

'I have good reason, Martin.'

'You should heal not only your body but your soul. You have utterly poisoned it.'

'No, someone else did that.'

'Don't put the blame on anyone else.'

'Martin, let me tell you something about my childhood.'

Raoul peered into the darkness and began: 'I was five years old, and was playing one day with a wooden horse at my mother's side. She was embroidering and talking to me. We were alone in the room and I felt happy. Then my father came in. I was not yet afraid of him and was only shy because he always ignored me. He ordered me to leave the room. As I did not want to leave mother, I ran over to her and looked at him. He stretched his hand out to seize me. My mother protected me from him, took me in her arms and said: "Raoul remains here with me." His eyes changed. "I wish to be alone with you, Madeleine." "But I do not wish it," she replied.

'I felt safe with her and thought that he would now leave. But he did not stir and said quietly: "Madeleine, send the child out." "No." Then he seized me, tore me from her arms and dragged me to the door. I screamed as if I had been on a spit. My mother tried to help me but father thrust her aside and pushed me out into the corridor. I tried to get back into the room but he had locked the door. I roared and screamed. I feared for mother, who was still there, unprotected, in his power. I beat my fists on the door and shouted even louder. Suddenly the door opened, my father put me across his knee and thrashed me severely. Then he left. My mother wept and tried to console me. Her hair was tousled and her lips were bitten through. Martin, how can a child, after such an experience, learn to believe in the good Lord? The world is full of horrors.'

'Yes,' replied Martin, 'but there is an antidote; one must love more.'

'I love no one except mother and you.'

'You should send your doctor to visit Nicolette.'

'It was she who infected me, and not I her.'

Martin whistled and said gravely: 'She can give the disease

to a host of men.'

'Why should that concern me?'

Martin looked at Raoul thoughtfully: 'Your love for little Lison passed from one day to the next. I saw her when I went to visit old Douranez at Grandval. She refuses to marry, although two farmers' sons are courting her. She has turned into a beauty, but she dresses too simply and is far too serious for her age. I think she nurses a secret sorrow. Perhaps she still hopes for you.'

'Must you revive old, unhappy things for me?'

Martin picked up the doctor's recipe. 'What names these medicines have! Let us hope the stuff will help you.'

Raoul had turned his face to the wall. 'Please leave me alone.'

Martin laid down the slip of paper and stood up. 'I hope you will sleep well, Raoul.' He left the room. It was past midnight and the house was silent.

Four days later, in bright winter sunshine, Martin accompanied the count on horseback to a little country villa a few miles outside Paris. A light layer of snow melted visibly before their eyes, and the count said with a laugh that by the time they arrived it would be spring. But when the two horsemen dismounted outside the villa, the count was told by the old servant that her mistress had been obliged to leave in a hurry, and bade their guests take some refreshment before riding home. The count, at first irritated, soon recovered his spirits and said to Martin that he could not be angry for long in his company. He invited him to eat with him at the expense of their absent hostess.

They were shown into a comfortable, well-heated room, where a table had already been laid. The count sat down and was about to eat, when Martin said: 'Monsieur, control your hunger. All these rumours about poisonings have made me feel nervous.'

The count pushed the plate away. 'You might be right, Martin. The husband is a jealous fellow and I've had no letter from her. I think it is time that this acquaintanceship was ended.'

'How casually you say that.'

'Our relationship was of a pretty casual nature. I am looking for a mistress of the right stature. Most of the women here are too small, and when they are tall they are too fat. Do you remember Bice? I met her recently at the theatre. That Italian plumpness! Not for me, thank you!'

Martin smiled. The count got up from the table. 'Du Lac is arriving today, or at the latest tomorrow, and the banquet is on Sunday; then I'm starting you on your duties. Would you like to leave Paris for a couple of days?'

'Monsieur, I prefer to be with you, but the vicomte would be very grateful if you would let him leave.'

'I know. Don't start pleading for other people and spoil my pleasure in your company.'

'Monsieur, you make the vicomte suffer.'

'I could say the same for him. I never have anything except trouble with the boy. He's no use for military service. After a lot of difficulty he served his prescribed year with the musketeers, where Guy is making a flourishing career, and could then have gone into service at Court. He implored me to spare him that. I tried to make him embark on a diplomatic career, like Louis. He travelled to Rome with Louis in the ambassador's suite. I questioned them on their return. Louis had made a host of useful acquaintances, while Raoul could not mention a single important name. He spent his time with French artists, watching them paint the ruins. At least, the picture he bought for me and sent to Grandval is in good taste. That Claude Lorrain is now the fashion. One of his landscapes hangs in almost every salon. So Raoul's sole success on his journey was a painting! I allowed him to study. He took a course in Latin but suddenly became interested in natural history. I said nothing till I discovered that he changed sciences as I changed my women, and that everything began to bore him. I lost patience and enrolled him in Madame's service. You know what success he had there! I made him a lieutenant of the Guards and took him to the Louvre. He did not stir a finger to court any favour, and now he is sick. And this unhappy creature is my son! Believe me, if I could exchange him for you, I should do so.'

'Monsieur, let him go to Grandval for two weeks.'

'No, Martin. There he would grow even more unworldly.

As soon as the doctor permits, I will take him with me to Court.'

'He has not seen his mother for three years and he misses her.'

The count banged his grey riding-boots angrily with his switch. 'She could come here and visit her son.'

'Monsieur, perhaps she is frightened of the life in your house, which is not particularly pleasant for anyone except me. Even Louis has now gone to stay with Guy.'

'He likes a change. If he found an opportunity of living with a duke, he would never return.'

'You've seen through him.'

The count stretched out his legs. 'Louis is like Guy. Both of them will go a long way. You can take my word for it.'

'Can't you be satisfied with Guy's ambition?'

'No. Stop discovering disagreeable topics. I am rested now. I'm inviting you to a pleasure jaunt which will take us back to Paris before dark.' The count stood up. 'Let's go before the smell of cooking tempts me to eat. We'll find an inn somewhere.'

The two friends were soon galloping under a pale blue sky, which reminded them of the still far-off spring.

On their return home that evening, the count found Colonel du Lac with Captain de Falleron and the six other officers who had been transferred from his former regiment, in the salon. He greeted them heartily, brushed aside their thanks and took du Lac and de Falleron to dine with the Marquis de Chassigny. Martin ate with the six officers and then retired to his room where, unknown to the count, he wrote a long letter to the Comtesse de Racon.

As soon as Martin had given the letter to François, he paid a visit to Raoul who was reading in bed by candlelight and thrust the book under the clothes in terror. With an embarrassed laugh, he took it out again and said: 'Oh, it's only you, Martin.'

His friend took the book from him. 'You must only read in the daytime.'

'In winter the nights are too long.'

Martin threw the book angrily on the table. 'These *Maxims*

again. Satan speaks out of the mouth of the old Duc de La Rochefoucauld, Raoul. You see the truth in a terrifying light . . . If only I could make you see the real truth. Nicolette has poisoned your body, the count your soul and the duke your thoughts. How can you be so weak and have no self-control?'

'Prove me the falsity of this maxim,' said Raoul with a forced smile. 'We often persuade ourselves that we love people who are more powerful than ourselves, whereas our friendship is merely based on self-interest. We frequent them not because we wish to do them a service but because we want some service from them.'

Martin's eyes flashed. 'That maxim is true,' he said curtly, 'when applied to love that is mere self-interest. Men have a different way of loving.'

'Do you think you know more about the human heart than the duke?' asked Raoul.

'I look upon things with a different eye.'

'How do you regard me?'

Martin paused for a moment and then replied: 'You are a man who is noble without any real warmth. You are in search of love without wanting yourself to love. You long for a simple country life as portrayed in the picture you sent to Grandval from Rome. You need a castle in a beautiful lonely spot with magnificent old trees, beneath which a shepherd boy sometimes plays his flute and tends his sheep. And you would find it pleasant to sleep in the arms of a shepherdess who loved you for yourself alone.'

'There is no love without self-interest, Martin. One is made happier by a passion one feels, than by the passion one arouses in the beloved.'

'That is another of those maxims.'

'Yes, and I agree with it.'

'Raoul, I have a request to make. Don't only read the maxims but read the gospels from time to time.'

'Have you become a heretic and are you trying to convert me?'

'I don't want to convert anyone. You can read your missal if you like, you understand Latin.'

Raoul heaved a sigh of boredom. 'I have never been able to see any sense in piety.'

'Then at least start to see some sense in life.'

'What is the meaning of life, my good Martin?'

'To do as much good as possible and demand nothing in return.'

'To what end?'

'So that the world will not become worse than it is, but better.'

'It is impossible to better it.'

'Oh no, it's not, if you begin with yourself.'

'Do you do that?'

'Yes.'

'Successfully?'

Martin wrinkled his nose. 'I visit only a charming widow who loves me more than I deserve, and who teaches me everything that can make a woman happy. I submit to her tuition and dispense with other women.'

Raoul laughed. 'How praiseworthy! Every other man is a ram when he's in love, but Martin thinks of his widow's happiness. You'll become a saint in due course.'

'I would rather remain a soldier.'

'Will the world become a better place if you kill your fellow men?'

'I serve my king, whom I honour.'

'It is easy to honour what you do not know. Please don't contradict me. All these conversations are pointless, although you understand my soul. Yes, Martin, I long for peace, in beautiful surroundings. I crave nothing more. I should like to sit at an open window for days on end and in a sunny land, looking out of the window from dawn to sunset. I should like to lie and sleep under tall trees, look up at the stars, without knowing their names or asking any questions about their course. I should like to be alone and have no memories and gradually forget myself. If I could only sleep!'

'I'll go, so that you won't have to remain awake any longer.'

'No, Martin, I did not mean that. All my nights are sleepless.'

'I'll send Blanche to you so that she can play you to sleep with her lute. Goodnight.'

Martin left the room and, at his request, Blanche visited the sick man. She sat down on a cushion in front of the fire and played a soft, lilting melody with a never-ending sequence of variations. Raoul fell asleep.

At midnight, the house was suddenly filled with noise. The count had returned with the Marquis de Chassigny, Colonel du Lac, de Falleron and a number of slightly intoxicated gentlemen, to be greeted by the six officers who were equally drunk. He sent a servant to fetch Blanche; she was to appear in her new ballet dress and dance. There was a great uproar when Blanche could not be found in her room. Martin was wakened and he went to Raoul who had woken up. Blanche was asleep with the lute on her arm in front of the fire, her head on the cushion. Martin woke her gently. 'Come, Blanche, put on your ballet dress. The count has company and you are to dance in the salon.'

Blanche raised her head and listened to the roars of laughter and the drunken voices. 'I'll accompany you,' said Martin. 'Don't be afraid.' She took his hand and led him to her room. Martin had to wait in the "zoo" while Blanche changed her dress with the help of the old maid in the room next door. Then she went downstairs with him and entered the salon on his arm.

The guests were drinking heavily. The foul-mouthed marquis lifted his glass and said: 'Yes, that's the little sparrow. Now help Comte de Racon to win his wager. He maintains that your value had gone up a hundred times.'

A few of the men made coarse jests and laughed obscenely. Wine was spilled over the tablecloth. Martin felt Blanche's hand grow cold and moist in his own. He noticed Louis de Salvieux among the guests, and greeted him, but Louis ignored him and stared as though spellbound at Blanche, whom he had never yet seen unveiled. Blanche had eyes only for the count, who tuned his lute and waved to her gaily. She would not release Martin's hand and began to tremble. The count played a lively dance but she did not stir. 'Dance, little Blanche,' encouraged Martin, 'I'll be close at hand. Don't you want the Comte de Racon to win his wager?' Blanche nodded, but her lower lip trembled ominously: 'Are you afraid?'

The little girl nodded again, and the first tear fell on the silver dress which was looped up and reached above her knees.

Martin saw the count's eyes narrow. He led Blanche firmly over to the seated man and whispered to him: 'Monsieur, please pull your chair into the middle of the room and then Blanche can dance for you under your protection.'

The count agreed, and Martin showed one of the lackeys where to place the chair.

'Ha, ha!' cried the marquis, 'we are to be given a performance. Who do you represent, Gaston?'

'I am Pan enticing the nymphs.' He sat down again and started once more to pluck the strings. Blanche threw a grateful glance at Martin, summoned up a smile and began to dance in the centre of the room. The noise suddenly subsided. Blanche's movements were so in harmony with the swift music that they might have been the notes which the count played with so light a touch. She was dancing for him alone, completely oblivious to her audience, until the marquis clapped his hands and a thunderous round of applause broke loose. Then she ran into the arms of the count, who laid down his lute and took her on to his lap with a smile.

'Gaston,' cried the marquis. 'You have won your wager. She is worth 10,000. Sell her to me for that sum.'

Blanche, her heart beating wildly, flung her arms round the count's neck.

'You won't get her for less than 20,000,' cried the count.

'I'll give you 20,000 for her.'

'Armand, my offer was only a jest. I would not part with her for less than 30,000.'

'You greedy wolf. I'll pay you 30,000 for her tonight.'

Scarlet with rage, Martin leaped up from his seat. 'Comte de Racon, I beg you to stop this jest or to take 20,000 from me.'

The count immediately retracted. 'Gentlemen, I do not seriously intend to put Blanche up for auction. I will not part with her to anyone and I am keeping her for myself. Don't cry,' he whispered into the little girl's ear, 'I won't let you go.'

But the consoling words came too late. Blanche had already soaked his lace cravat with her tears. He tried to release her arms from his throat, but abandoned the attempt for fear of hurting her. Then he tried to pacify her with caresses. As he bared the hair on her neck, a brown birthmark became visible.

Louis, who so far had not taken his eyes off Blanche, turned pale. He rose, walked round the noisy company to the count and said: 'Comte de Racon, I must speak to you urgently alone.'

'Wait until my guests have gone.'

'Yes, I'll wait.' Louis returned to his seat and began to question the Marquis de Chassigny about Blanche. He was only too willing to reply.

As soon as the count could manage to soothe Blanche and free himself from her, he sent her upstairs with Martin and joined his guests. As their drunkenness increased, he beckoned to Louis and slipped out with him unobserved.

In his study, the count offered Louis a chair, but the latter was too excited to sit down. 'Comte de Racon, Blanche is my sister. She was stolen from my parents as a three-year-old child eleven years ago, while we were on a journey. She was dumb from birth. I was immediately struck by her resemblance to my dead mother, whom I do not take after. Her dumbness and the birthmark on her neck, which I remember quite clearly, leave no doubt in my mind. Blanche's real name is Claire-Marie de Salvieux. I beg you to return my sister to me.'

'How do I know,' the count asked suspiciously, 'that you are not simply trying to get hold of Blanche cheaply?'

'There is a nurse in my part of the country who would recognise her.'

'I pay no attention to old wives' gossip.'

'Comte de Racon, as a boy, I often watched Claire-Marie being bathed. On her left cheek she has a birthmark very similar to the one on her neck.'

The count laughed. 'Our good Chassigny could have told you that.'

'No, Comte de Racon. I give you my word of honour.'

'Hm. And what do you propose to do with your sister now that she has belonged to the marquis and myself?'

'I propose to place her in a convent to save the honour of my house.'

The count frowned. 'By rights, you would have to challenge

the marquis and myself, Comte de Salvieux.'

'I am ready to fight a duel with both you and the marquis.'

The count was now serious. 'Am I to take you at your word, Comte de Salvieux?'

'Yes, you may.'

'Louis, I think you have stirred up a hornets' nest.'

'Monsieur, I have to avenge the honour of my sister.'

'You said nothing of that at the outset.'

'Because it did not seem necessary. Blanche was a foundling, and so neither you nor the marquis could be blamed.'

'Quite right. One can see the affair from different sides. Let us sit down. I want to find an amicable solution.'

'So do I, Comte de Racon.'

They sat down. Crossing his legs, the count said: 'I am quite convinced that your discovery is not a ruse, for you take the thing too seriously. A duel would expose Blanche's unfortunate position, and nothing would remain for the poor child except to retire for the rest of her life to a convent. That would be a pity because she is far too beautiful for a convent. I make you the following proposal. Let Blanche retire to a convent for a year and look for a husband for her. I am quite prepared to compensate you by giving her a large dowry. Do you accept?'

'Yes, if you give me your word of honour that you will never betray that Claire-Marie was in your house.'

'You have my word, Louis. I will make another proposal. I will give your sister to my son, Martin Saint-Jean, as a bride.'

'My sister is a countess.'

'She is no longer a virgin and has an infirmity. You cannot arrange a profitable marriage for her. Martin loves her despite her failings. I'll buy him a title one of these days and give him an estate on his marriage, with an income which will allow him to found a family with a lady of quality.'

'I know an eighty-year-old banker, as rich as Croesus, who would give a great deal of money to marry a wife from the nobility,' said Louis.

'Oh, I know that fool. He is a widower for the third time and is somewhat of a churl. I regret that I cannot outbid a banker, and hope that Blanche will soon bury him.'

'Monsieur, I beg you to lend me a coach that I may take my

sister from your house.'

'My dear Louis, until you bring me documents to prove the birth and disappearance of your sister, Blanche will remain in my care.'

'Comte de Racon, as her brother, I cannot allow my sister to live any longer with you.'

'I fully agree with you on that point. Tomorrow I shall instal her as an orphaned child of a distant relative with the Carmelites in the Faubourg Saint-Jacques. As soon as you have satisfied my demands, I will lay aside my guardianship.'

'Give me the key to my sister's room so that I can safeguard her from you.'

'Do you really think that one night, more or less, matters?'

'Certainly, you have now to treat the girl as a young lady of your own rank.'

'My memory is weak. I will remember her name again tomorrow morning and not spoil the farewell night.'

'I hope that you will make a sacrifice. Just now you were prepared to sell the girl to the Marquis de Chassigny.'

'You have no certainty of that. Please remember that you are my guest.'

Louis was about to reply, but thought better of it, and asked: 'When will my sister be leaving your house?'

'I shall let Martin deliver her to the Carmelites, punctually at eight o'clock. You can accompany the young lady if it relieves your mind.'

'Shall you inform M. Saint-Jean of my discovery?'

'Yes, for he would not tolerate the child's disappearance. He will give you his word of honour, as I have done, that no one will ever learn of Blanche's past. Are you satisfied?'

'Yes, up to a point.'

'Then let us rejoin the company.' The two men stood up and the conversation was over.

When Martin visited the count in his room the following morning, he was informed as to Blanche's future. Martin was flabbergasted. 'Does she already know?'

'No, she knows nothing. Louis will tell her in the coach. I have had enough of her scenes and want to avoid a farewell. Call Pierre so that he can fasten on my spurs. I'm going for a ride. You can greet Blanche from me. Tell her it grieves me to have to hand her over to her brother and I should like to congratulate her on her good fortune.'

'Monsieur, please tell her that yourself.'

'Why?'

'She will not believe either her brother or me, and she will think that you have bartered her.'

'The Carmelites will soon convince her. Pierre!'

'Monsieur,' said Martin, lowering his voice so that the valet, who was just entering, could not hear. 'Behave courteously to the child.'

'Do you want me to play a farewell scene?'

'Yes, of course.' Noticing Martin's stern face, the count ordered Pierre to ask the Comte de Salvieux and Blanche to wait upon him.

The couple soon appeared. The count bowed casually to Blanche, and began: 'Mademoiselle, the young gentleman at your side has recognised you as his sister who was stolen from your parents eleven years ago. Your name is not Blanche but Claire-Marie de Salvieux. You must put everything that has happened to you until today out of your mind. You will finish your education in a convent and marry an honourable man. No slur will attach to your name and you will become one of the best respected ladies in society. I congratulate you on your good fortune and take my leave of you.' The count bowed once more and walked swiftly from the room.

Martin looked anxiously at Blanche's distorted face. Then, from the colourless lips, he heard the clearly spoken word: 'No!' A second 'no' followed like a scream and the child sank to the floor. Martin lifted her to her feet.

'Blanche, little Blanche, control yourself.' Blanche tore herself away and in a flash, slipped through the door after the count. She ran down the stairs and into the street, where the count was just trotting away with two grooms.

She ran after him and screamed once more: 'No!' trying to catch up with his horse. The count turned round and saw Blanche stumble and fall. He turned his horse round, rode up, dismounted and helped her to her feet. She was mud-stained and kept repeating her desperate 'no!' The count took her firmly by the hand and led her back through the front door. A few women and a porter stared at them curiously.

As the count met Martin and Louis on the stairs, he hissed: 'I have you to thank for all this, Martin. Louis, please wait.' He disappeared into his study with the child. Martin leaned for support against the banister and fought back his tears. 'What have you done to the child, Comte de Salvieux?'

'The shock has loosened her tongue,' Louis replied calmly. 'She will learn how to speak, and later, no one will suspect that she was once the dumb girl. It is a lucky day for her although she cannot yet realise it. What is the count doing with her up there?'

'He will pacify her. You should be pleased that he is doing so.'

'Don't start weeping now.'

'We were like brother and sister.'

'M. Saint-Jean, please do not stay here on the stairs. I do not wish to arouse any attention. The servants are already beginning to stare.' Louis caught Martin by the arm and led him upstairs into a room. For a long time Martin tried to control himself. He slumped in a chair and covered his face with his hands. Louis remained at the door, opening it slightly from time to time and listening for any noise. Suddenly, the count entered with Blanche who was carrying her monkey and a little dog.

She was calm and controlled; she walked with composure towards Martin and bowed to him. Martin returned her bow. Thereupon, Blanche hurried back to the count, who ordered: 'Martin, you will ride to the regiment and start your duties. Take my bodyguard over the jumps. I hope you won't come home tonight with a long face. It is quite enough to have Raoul in the house with his constant lamentations. I am taking Mademoiselle personally with Comte de Salvieux to the convent. Come Louis.' Louis followed the count and his sister and Martin was left alone.

Blanche's departure had robbed Martin of any hope that he would one day possess her. He tried to numb his pain by plunging eagerly into his military life so that he would have no time left for thought. Long before dawn each day he was on his way to the regiment. He returned home late at night to make his appearance at some party or to visit Raoul's widowed former admirer who, despite her fading charms, still attracted him. She sensed that he was unhappy but did not ask him the reason to spare herself any premature pangs of jealousy. She enjoyed her love as though it was her last great passion, and gave herself body and soul to the handsome guards lieutenant who, now that he had no sweet dream as an ideal, was sometimes rather brutal to her.

Raoul recovered slowly and had much to bear. As soon as the doctor gave his permission, he had to go to Court, often returning home in a state of exhaustion. Nicolette tried several times to visit him, but the doorkeeper refused to let her into the house. Her father grew angry and stopped the count one day outside the house, demanding compensation for the ravaged health and lost innocence of his respectable daughter. The count cursed the pot-bellied pastrycook for a shameless pimp, threatened him with the law and ordered his grooms to thrash him in the open street. The incident was closed.

For a week, the count busied himself entirely with his regiment and the preparations for a huge banquet, which was to do him great credit. The Duc de Luxembourg appeared with all the regimental commanders, until the Hôtel de Racon resembled a headquarters. Guy, in his uniform of the Royal Musketeers, attended with his commanding officer, but was placed a long way from Martin at the table. After midnight, when the wine had gained the upper hand, Guy had to return home and Martin was sent to his room. Raoul remained until the Maréchal de Luxembourg left, and was only then allowed to leave the hall because he was ill.

The following day the count noticed how thin Martin had grown. He saw that he had no appetite and suspected the reason. On a drive to the Marquise de Sévigné's town house he dropped a hint that a certain future little banker's wife would probably soon be free again, thanks to an early widowhood. Martin replied curtly that a rich widow of noble birth was as much beyond his reach as a poor countess had been.

The count thereupon suggested that he could always hope for a secret love affair. This is how he had eventually consoled Blanche. Martin replied that Blanche's hopes concerned only the count and that he should not disappoint the future young widow, but the count said that he would guard himself against this. Martin made an angry retort, was reprimanded, jumped out of the coach and did not meet the count until next day on the parade ground. He was sent for, cursed for running away, and ordered to give riding lessons to the ensigns.

Louis de Salvieux had brought the count the necessary official confirmation of the disappearance of the small three-year-old Claire-Marie de Salvieux, together with a description of the child, which corresponded to Blanche's appearance. The count, with great relief, renounced the responsibilities he had undertaken in favour of Louis, who was no longer a minor, and gave his word that he would never visit Blanche. The child had implored the abbess to allow her a visit from the Comte de Racon, who was related to her, and during her minority had taken the place of her dead father. Louis was intelligent enough not to enlighten the unsuspecting abbess, but threatened his sister, when they were alone, that he would fight a duel with the count if she were ever to mention him again to anyone. Blanche was intimidated and did not ask for the count any more. She learned to speak with great difficulty and continued her music and dancing lessons with other elderly teachers. The good nuns lavished their affection upon her, gave her sweets and increased her little zoo by a family of ducks and a rabbit. Blanche spent much time with her animals, feeding each of them according to its needs. The monkey was her favourite. She christened him Gaston, as soon as she could utter the name, and forgave him all his naughtiness.

As soon as Colonel du Lac had established himself as the Regimental Commander's deputy, the count returned to Court and appeared at a levée, in the uniform of a general of the Light Horse of the Guard. The king was gracious, although a number of enemies had tried to bring him into disfavour. The count had the honour of holding the candlestick for his Majesty when he retired to bed. For a week, he went to the Louvre every day with Raoul, won the day in a Court intrigue and ruined an envious and dangerous enemy by a successful slander. He saw his place in the sun assured, and took Martin for a few days' relaxation on a long ride through the country.

Martin tried to appear gay, because he did not wish to be a burden to the count, but during their first night at an inn, his friend brought the conversation round to Blanche, releasing a storm of tears from the pent-up Martin. After two nights of inconsolable weeping, the young man, with a sigh of relief, sank on to his friend's shoulder and slept soundly.

The following morning at breakfast, Martin confessed that he now knew the meaning of unhappy love and was tired of whining. Did other men behave in the same way with their friends? Some were far more stupid, insisted the count. Martin laughed and said, quite seriously, that he would never forget Blanche and would expect nothing more from love. It was all over. The count looked dubious and advised him to go on yowling like a tom-cat, if he felt like it, for suppressed grief was bad for both the soul and the body. Martin found this axiom very amusing, embellished it with a coarse jest, and asked the count to throw a bucket of cold water over him next time it happened. The count promised. They set out on their return journey, visiting a few castles on the way.

At New Year, the count staged a full parade before the great manoeuvres, which the king honoured with his presence. Louis XIV, resplendent and majestic in gold, rode at the head of his princely escort along the lines of his grenadier regiments, halting on a slight eminence by the ladies' coaches. The march-past was magnificent: cavalry regiments of the guard with their drums, trumpets and victorious colours; black and grey musketeers in their red tunics and blue overcoats on mettlesome grey and black chargers; red gendarmes on chestnuts and piebalds; the light horse of the guard in scarlet tunics with white cockades in their hats on roans and chestnuts; glittering cuirassiers on massive percherons; pale-blue and white braided grenadiers on bays . . . The entire noble youth of France paid homage to Louis XIV on their silver-harnessed chargers to the stirring tones of martial music, the enthusiastic cries of the crowd and the admiring glances of the ladies. Martin, with Colonel du Lac's battalion at the head of the count's bodyguard, was so overcome by the majesty of his king that he could hardly turn his eyes away and very nearly broke the line. The be-jewelled women in the distance appeared to him as goddesses, and the glittering courtiers recalled some Olympian symposium. Raoul was far ahead with the Comte de

Racon's battalion; the comte with drawn sword, led his regiment past, without a stop, and rode with his troop to the prescribed position before manoeuvres could begin.

An enemy position was now captured, followed by a battle in which the Dauphin's infantry had to halt the attacking cuirassiers. Unfortunately, the latter rode into them, to the delight of the non-participants, but with disastrous consequences to those taking part. This trifling error, however, was quickly rectified by a musketeer regiment being brought up with great presence of mind, and the king, unaware of the altered programme, was loud in his praise of the mobility of his troops. Their advance, their wheeling and retiring, afforded a very impressive spectacle. Then a sudden snowstorm masked the view. The king ordered the manoeuvres to be postponed, got into his coach and drove off with the ladies. Some of the commanding officers were furious, because they had been given no chance of showing their prowess; others were delighted because they had already received a word of recognition from their sovereign. The count was satisfied with the performance of his regiment, praised the men and invited the officers to a banquet, which Raoul, although completely exhausted by the long ride and the cold, was forced to attend.

In the middle of carnival, just as the count was getting dressed to attend a masked ball with Martin and Raoul, Pierre brought him a letter on a silver tray. Recognising his wife's handwriting, the count opened it and read it. Martin was already looking at himself in the mirror. He wore a red domino over his ceremonial dress and was trying on various masks, none of which seemed comical enough.

'Martin!'

He turned round. 'Monsieur?'

'My wife is on her way to Paris. You asked her to visit Raoul and wrote to her without my knowledge. Explain yourself.'

'Monsieur, the vicomte's condition encouraged me to do this. I told neither of you, because I was not sure whether you would agree with me.'

The count threw the letter on the table. 'I should not have agreed. What should an ailing woman do in Paris at carnival time? You have no right to ask my wife to come to my house, behind my back. How many letters have you written to her?'

'Only two, Monsieur, I assure you.'

'Two letters. What was in the first one?'

'In the first, I asked her for the name of the village where you lay wounded after the battle of Seneffe.'

The count looked puzzled and Martin replaced the masks in their box.

'Martin, the first letter was justified, but the second was not quite in order.'

'I agree. I have behaved incorrectly to you, in an attempt to help someone else.'

'Someone you can't help, idiot, or else he would now stand up for you. Hi, you bundle of misery! What do you hope from your mother's visit?'

'I should be very pleased,' replied Raoul, 'if my mother stayed at the Hôtel de Brayonne, instead of here, and if you would allow me to live there as well.'

'For once you've given me a frank answer. When Martin is not here, you are not so forthright, but the Comtesse de Racon has to honour the Hôtel de Racon with her presence, and the Vicomte de Clarmont has to continue with his cure under paternal supervision.'

Martin approached the count. 'I beg you to forgive my independence.'

'I'll forgive you the two letters, but don't write a third.'

'I shall refrain from doing so, Monsieur.'

'Well, now get ready.'

Martin return to his box of masks and the count buttoned his sea-green domino. Raoul was wearing a black domino. 'Father, I should be very grateful if I could remain at home today. I am afraid of becoming giddy in the crowd and am overwrought at the thought of seeing my mother again.'

'I want to see you today at the Hôtel de Chassigny. Your withdrawal from public life gives rise to suspicions, which are not far removed from the unpleasant truth. Pull yourself together and pretend that you are healthy. If you are taken ill, come and see me in good time. I will exchange masks and dominos with you and take your place, so that no one will notice your disappearance. Then go into an empty room and rest until you can return to the revels. Comb your hair again, put on your hat and we can go. Martin, have you made your final choice?'

'I find this black nose amusing.'

'So do I. Raoul, you must wear a full mask like myself. Can you find one?'

Raoul rummaged in the box. 'Here is a green one.'

'It goes with the black. Come on. Off with you both.'

In his impatience, the count pushed the two boys through the door ahead of him.

The festivities had begun at the Hôtel de Chassigny. Everyone was masked and it was difficult to recognise an acquaintance. The count searched in vain for the marquis. Soon, Martin was pursuing a frail beauty through the crowded dancers. The dance should have been a minuet, but it became more and more involved. The dancing master, disguised as the king of hearts, tapped the floor in despair with his gilded staff. Vociferous love dongs drowned the orchestra. At this instant, a page jumped on to a table and cried in a shrill voice: 'The Marquis de Chassigny has the honour to entertain his guests with a troupe of gipsies.'

The crowd parted at the salon door, and four gipsy girls danced into the room with castanets and tambourines. The male guests did not watch their dance for very long, but started on the chase, until every woman disappeared in the crowd, on the arm of some cavalier. Everyone wanted to dance, but an old ragged gipsy came in with a huge bear, which he forced to stand upright with loud cracks of his whip. The bear growled angrily, and a few of the women screamed. The gipsy took his tambourine, rattled and beat it, while the bear lumbered in time, growling ever louder, to the delight of the gentlemen. Then the beast suddenly dropped on all fours, rose again with a savage roar, tore itself loose and ran with splayed claws among the spectators. There were screams and shouts; a table was knocked over and silver spoons rattled to the floor. The bear seized one of the ladies, who swooned immediately from terror. The gentlemen tried to hurry to her aid but they could not free themselves from their partners' grasps. The bear sniffed at its prey, obviously took it for a corpse, and relinquished it to the old gipsy, only to look round in search of another victim.

The Comte de Racon managed to free himself from the embrace of several importunate women; seizing a candlestick, he rushed at the bear, together with several other cavaliers. Swords flashed. The bear tapped its forehead, its head tipped backwards, and the red, laughing face of the Marquis de Chassigny appeared. 'Don't kill me, and don't singe my fur!' There was silence for a few seconds and then tumult broke loose. The marquis was applauded, cursed and fêted. Before he could get out of his bearskin, he was grabbed by the shaggy hide and flung to the floor, where he caught hold of a slender foot and brought the pretty girl to the floor on top of himself. Laughter increased at this coarse jest.

The bear's bride lost her mask; a cavalier quickly threw his domino over her, tore her from the monster's grasp and roared in his rage: 'Marquis, you have insulted my wife.'

The marquis struggled to his feet. 'You must punish the bear, if you want satisfaction. I'll leave you the skin.' With the help of two pages he got out of his costume, and the offended husband was persuaded by his friends that it was a harmless joke and was encouraged to join in the laughter. Sending his wife home, he continued to enjoy himself.

Refreshments were brought in at a sign from the host. The crowd split up into groups and those who wore full masks had to take them off in order to eat. Some of the guests noticed that Raoul was wearing the black domino, and Comte de Racon the green one. The colour of the hair, the face and voice of father and son were indistinguishable. The count enjoyed the joke and, calling Raoul over to him, stood with him facing the wall and began to sing a song. Then he asked which of them had sung, and no one could say for certain.

The musicians began to play another minuet. Raoul was invited to dance by a graceful mask, and was forced to comply. Martin caught hold of a lady a head and shoulders taller than himself. The Marquis de Chassigny approached the seated count from behind and slapped him on the shoulder. 'Now I know who nearly burnt my nose.'

'Oh, Armand, you old bear! Why aren't you dancing?'

'I'm still sweating.'

The marquis sat down so heavily that the chair creaked

beneath his weight. 'Gaston, I have a bone to pick with you. You would not sell Blanche to me, but you've sold her to someone else. Why?'

'He paid me 100,000 in cash.'

'Old Samuel told me yesterday that you still owe him 60,000 louis d'or. How does that fit in with the story?'

'Perfectly well. The Jew will have to wait.'

'Who is Blanche's new owner?'

'The Turkish Ambassador, who left the day before yesterday.'

'What a rogue you are to barter her to a heathen dog.'

'He may treat her better than you did.'

'You don't treat women, you take them and have your pleasure of them.'

'That suits you, bear.'

'Gaston, I'm furious with you.'

'Rubbish, the Turk was thin and a lightweight. You must crush your women.'

The marquis made a coarse reply. They both laughed, and two more cavaliers joined in the conversation. Behind their masks a few ladies listened curiously, until the count invited one of them to dance, and lined up for the minuet.

The minuet came to an end. The count saw Raoul, as white as a ghost, swaying towards him. He excused himself to his partner and went to meet Raoul.

'Father!'

'Come, do you want to lean on me?'

'Yes.'

The count led him swiftly from the salon, tugging at various ladies' hair as he passed. He opened a bedroom door, only to close it again swiftly. 'Hell, they might have locked the door! Do you want to vomit?'

'No, I'm only giddy, and everything is swimming before my eyes.'

The count found two more bedroom doors locked, and at last entered an empty room which seemed to be a study. 'Lie down on that bench. Here's a cushion for your head. Is it too low for you?'

'Yes, I'd rather sit.'

'No, stay like that. Keep your head up.' The count placed a

thick volume under the cushion. 'Is that better?'

'Yes, thank you.'

The count looked at the empty grate. 'How long will it take you to recover?'

'I don't know, Father.'

'I'll tell them to light a fire.' The count pulled a blue velvet cloth from the table and threw it over his son. 'Hell, I must change dominos with you. I'll help you out of it.' They exchanged costumes. 'This will be a real joke. I'll see if the women are really as wild about you as they say. Stay here until I come back, and hide your face if a pair of lovers disturb you. Do you want a doctor?'

'No, I only want to rest.' The count put on Raoul's green mask and left the room. Raoul turned his head to the wall. A servant came in quietly and lit the fire.

The count, aping Raoul's indolent attitude, leaned against a pillar in the salon and looked at the brilliant throng through the silts in his mask. He was noticed at once. A few ladies brushed past him as close as they could. Others followed, swaying their hips provocatively. The count drew the broad sleeve of the black domino over his hands so as not to be betrayed by his dark skin, and folded his arms as though utterly disinterested. Then an attractive figure came up to him, and asked in a lisping voice: 'Why aren't you dancing, Vicomte?'

Copying Raoul's tired voice, the count replied: 'I have danced enough, my fair one.'

'Can one ever have enough of dancing, Vicomte?'

'One finally wearies of everything.'

'Even of love?'

'Yes, even of love.'

'But why?'

'Because it is so repetitive.'

'But humanity has never tired of it.'

The count shrugged his shoulders and the lady withdrew. At this moment, a perfumed skirt brushed against him, and an obviously far older woman leaned against him. 'Oh, Vicomte, the heat in this hall! Where can I find a balcony?'

'I do not know my way about this house, but I will gladly ask one of the servants. Hi, you, take the lady to a balcony and then escort her back here.'

'Does one leave a lady to the tender mercies of a strange lackey?' she asked reproachfully.

'Madame, the Hôtel de Chassigny has an excellent reputation.' The lady withdrew in high dudgeon.

A tall slim figure, veiled in black, slipped from a group of revellers, and a gay voice said saucily: 'Vicomte, you are in black and so am I. That is why I would dance with you.'

'I have danced enough, fair mask.'

'Do you fear that I am ugly?'

'Your voice tells me that you are very young.'

'Voices can be very deceptive, Monsieur. Will you dance with me if I am beautiful?'

'Perhaps.'

The woman coquettishly lifted her tiny lace veil, and the count looked into the youthful face of a lady who had recently married. The veil was lowered, and she asked softly: 'Will you dance with me now?'

'A dance allows me only to touch your hand. That is why I will not dance with you, Madame.'

'What are you implying, Monsieur?'

'That I should not be content with your hand.'

The lady recoiled. 'I have been told that you are as bashful as a boy.'

'I am only very selective, my fair lady.'

The lady looked round, as though she wished to creep away into the crowd. At this moment, a tall harlequin caught her by the waist and tried to tear off her veil. The count came to her aid and said to the harlequin: 'Leave this mask in peace. I am protecting the lady.'

The harlequin burst out laughing. 'Raoul, have you been converted to love? I'm sorry for the lady. Have the decency to leave her to another.'

The count recognised the harlequin as his son Guy, and continued to play his part. 'Guy, I am protecting the honour of this lady and am taking her back to her husband.'

'He's kissing a marquise.'

'I don't believe you, because one does not deceive such a beautiful wife. In any case, I will not allow you to kiss this lady.'

'How determined you sound! I do not wish to quarrel with my elder brother. Where is the old man?'

'He has retired.'

'I have no wish to meet him because he forbade me to come here on account of his boy. May the vultures take the bastard! He'll pay for all this when the time comes.'

'Don't make yourself out to be so dangerous.'

'Raoul, I swear to you that the day Martin becomes a nobleman, my consideration will be at an end.'

'Who says he will become a nobleman?'

'The old man has it in mind. Louis de Salvieux told me. Don't tell anyone that I know.'

'I will keep silent.'

'You are a good fellow, Raoul. God protect your sweetheart. Adieu.' Guy ran off with a laugh.

'Vicomte,' said the lady, nervously clutching the count's arm, 'which marquise is my husband kissing?'

'Oh, one of them. It's permissible in carnival time.'

'But he forbade me to let anyone kiss me.'

'Every husband forbids his wife and no wife ever obeys.'

'I shall certainly obey him.'

'Then you must not speak to strange men. Do you know an elderly lady to whom I can escort you?'

'No, I don't want to know any.'

'Madame, I should be happy if you would allow yourself to be kissed.'

'What are you thinking of? Everyone would see.'

'Then come to a place where no one can see us.'

'Vicomte, had I known that you were so dangerous, I should have avoided your company.'

'There is still time to avoid me, but carnival will not last much longer. During Lent I follow the example of our honourable king and remain chaste. A lady over there has been looking at me for a long time. I do not like being stared at and shall retire. Do you wish to remain here alone?'

'No, I fear all these wolves in masks.'

The count took the lady's hand and she followed him with little resistance. 'Vicomte, now you can take off your mask.'

'Madame, I do not kiss in front of the servants. Come, my dark velvet moth, and seek the darkness with me.'

'Vicomte, I dare not disobey my husband.'

'Madame, you are the only woman who has been able to arouse my desire. Do not be cruel to me.'

'Vicomte, I had no intention of looking for an adventure with you.'

'I believe you, my angel. Careful, we are being watched. Quick, away from this corner. Here is a dark room. Inside with you, before anyone follows us.'

'Vicomte, don't shut the door. It is terribly dark.'

'Kiss me, then I will take you back to the salon.' The count pushed his mask aside and found a pair of lips quivering with greedy passion. He felt a soft carpet underfoot and, without taking his lips from hers, drew the young woman firmly but gently to the floor.

When the count returned to Raoul, the boy was still lying in the same position—half asleep on the bench under the velvet coverlet. The count touched him gently on his blue-veined brow. Raoul woke with a start and opened his eyes in terror. The count laughed at him. 'I have to thank you for a wonderful jest. You are to be envied, and now I am in need of rest. How are you feeling?'

'Better,' said Raoul, sitting up.

'Then come, do you want to play my part, or would you like your domino back?'

'I'd rather go home. I don't like this game of lies.'

'What do you really like?'

'To be alone, Father.'

'It's only one o'clock. Stay for another two hours. Here is your costume. Slip it on.' Raoul stepped aside. The count's eyes narrowed. 'Have I got to stand here holding your domino? Come on, slip it on.' Raoul obeyed in silence, and threw the green mask into the fire.

'Why did you do that?'

'Because they know me by my black domino.'

The count put on his own sea-green domino and they left the room together. On reaching the hall, Raoul left the count and looked round for Martin. A young, unmasked cavalier came up to him and introduced himself. 'You left the salon half an hour ago with my wife, and she returned ten minutes ago, alone. A valet told me that she was seen coming out of an empty room after you. Do you know the spot where the Paris road enters the Bois de Vincennes?'

'Yes, I know the spot.'

'Will you be there tomorrow morning at eight o'clock?' Raoul stared over the man's shoulder at the candles on the chandelier. A strange smile suddenly appeared on his face.

'Must I be more explicit, Vicomte de Clarmont?' asked the cavalier.

Raoul, still smiling, looked him in the eyes. 'I will be there tomorrow morning at eight o'clock.'

The cavalier bowed, and added: 'You and your seconds will be led along a path which ends in a clearing. You need not fear an ambush.'

Raoul bowed slightly with his usual grace, and said: 'Your name, Monsieur, is a pledge of your honour.'

The man left, and Raoul stood for a moment alone before the women began to crowd round him.

Martin had left the feast before the count and Raoul, and arrived shortly after them at the Hôtel de Racon. From the street he could see a light in Raoul's room, and, although it was half past three in the morning, paid him a visit.

Raoul was sitting at a table, writing, and turned round absent-mindedly to his visitor. 'Since when have people started writing letters at this hour?' Martin asked reproachfully.

'Are you going to start lecturing me?'

'Are you writing to a loved one?'

'Yes, to my mother.'

'But why, since she is on the way here?'

'There are things that are easier to write than to say.'

'What sort of things?'

'Martin, a gentleman should never be inquisitive. Please let me finish my letter.'

'Raoul, you need someone like my amiable widow. Look what she has just given me!'

Martin pulled up his lace cuff and held his wrist, adorned with a bracelet, before Raoul's short-sighted eyes. As he did this, he caught sight of a newly-sealed letter. 'To Lieutenant Martin Saint-Jean,' he cried. 'Well, here I am and that is your writing. What does this mean?'

Raoul seized it, but Martin tore the letter from his hands and ran over to a corner of the room. 'I want to read it.'

Raoul jumped up and hurried over to him. 'Martin, I was only playing a jest with you. You'll receive the letter tomorrow morning from Dominique. Please give it back to me.'

'Since when have you started to jest? The letter belongs to me, according to the address.'

'Martin, I beg you to give me that letter.'

'And I beg you to let me read it.'

'Martin, I implore you.'

'What ails you?'

Raoul swayed, and Martin caught him. 'Martin, things are growing black before my eyes.'

'I'll put you to bed. Try not to faint. Now, lie down.'

'The letter.'

'I'll give it to you at once, Raoul. It's over there on the floor.' Martin walked back, picked up the letter and broke the seal as silently as possible. He read:

MY DEAR MARTIN,

Tell my father that at last I have found the long-desired opportunity of honourably departing this life, which can bring naught but suffering to a weakling. I bequeath all my personal possessions to you. Take Dominique into your service and try to console my mother.

Your brother,
RAOUL

'Raoul, what have you in mind?' Raoul raised himself, only to sink back on the pillows. 'Confess, Raoul. Have you taken poison?'

'No, my body is sufficiently poisoned already.'

Martin seized him and shook him violently. 'Raoul, out with it, or I shall call the count at once.'

'I entreat you not to call him. Listen, and I'll tell you everything. By chance, I insulted a cavalier and now have to give him satisfaction. I am not a good duellist, because of my short sight, and shall presumably be killed.'

'Raoul, I will take your place, naturally. Your short-sightedness excuses you. What is the man's name?'

'He would not cross swords with you because you are not a nobleman, and I will allow no one else to take my place.'

'You father will fight in your stead.'

'I do not wish it, I tell you.'

'Raoul!'

'Martin, if you go to my father, I'll stab myself as soon as you are out of the room.'

'I'll take your weapons away and lock you in.'

'Then I'll throw myself into the street. I'm tired of being tortured. Everyone tortures me. I've had enough!'

'Raoul, your mother is on her way to you. She must find you alive, and she will know how to console you.'

'I cannot see her in this house. She must not even kiss me, because I am tainted. Can't you see that I must do it?'

'Your mother will not turn away from you.'

'But every hand that has touched the count revolts me. I had to lend him my domino and then put it on again. Take your hands off me.'

Martin quickly opened a window to let in the cold night air. 'Raoul, it's a starry night. Breathe slowly and deeply.'

'Martin, I looked at the stars from the new observatory and they made me feel giddy. It is true that the earth is only a star among myriads and that the sun is no more than a gleaming, fixed star in the universe. Space is boundless, ice-cold and black, an immeasurable abyss, pierced by glittering sparks! Man is as nothing on our tiny globe, a ridiculous whim of destiny, a vermin endowed with thought and sensitive to pain! Tell me why?'

'Raoul, you say appalling things. Has it actually been proved that the earth is not the central point of our universe?'

'It has long since been proved, so irrefutably proved that they have even ceased threatening scholars with the Inquisition. In another ten years not a soul will believe in the priests! In the universe there is no place for heaven . . . no place for the denizens of heaven. Man is composed of flesh that decays, and there is no resurrection.'

Involuntarily, Martin closed the window. 'Raoul, who created the universe, according to the scholars?'

'They cannot find the answer. Whoever ponders upon it loses his reason. It is all madness, Martin. Love is pure madness. Save yourself from my father; he would sell you for a piece of silver.'

'You are raving.'

'No, I am completely lucid. I can see the world, and my place in it, so clearly that I find it absurd to set the least value on a human life. In a hundred years no one will remember me, and men will be just as evil as ever and feel just as satisfied in their stench and their morass . . . And the stars in all their hosts will continue to glitter in infinity, even though the scholars may have discovered slightly more powerful lenses.'

'Raoul, there could also be an invisible world in this visible universe which has its place among the stars.'

'Look up into the sky, then you will banish such thoughts. Open the window again. Why don't you do it?'

'Because I do not wish to lose my new-found faith.'

'Martin, if you have the slightest respect for my honour, let me fight this duel.'

'Of what importance is your honour, Raoul, if you despise everything?'

'None, Martin, but I hope it is important to you. Anyone can say that he is short-sighted. I heard of a marquis who had to spend the whole of his life abroad because he avoided a duel on a similar pretext. I should like to spare my family that disgrace.'

Martin thought for a while, and Raoul observed him. 'Who are your seconds, Raoul?' he asked.

'Louis and Guy.'

'What did they say?'

'I sent Dominique with a letter to the Hôtel de Brayonne, and they told me they would accompany me on my ride.'

'What time are you leaving?'

'At half past seven in the morning.'

'Where to?'

'I refuse to tell you that.'

'Raoul, I'll make you a proposal. I promise that I will say nothing to the count of your intention, and will do nothing to stop you, if you tell me the scene of the duel.'

'You've thought out some plan.'

'Raoul, you have the choice.'

'I have to be at half past ten where the Rue de Paris joins

the Bois de Vincennes.'

'Thank you for your confidence. Goodnight, Raoul.'

Martin took the letter and left the room. Raoul lay there for some time, open-eyed. Then he stood up and finished the letter to the countess. He read it over to himself in a whisper:

MY BELOVED MOTHER,

I beg you to forgive me for the pain I am about to cause you. Forgive me, because at this moment, when I see my approaching end, I feel happier than ever before. I have come to the end of my strength and have but one desire—to rest. Do not be angry with anyone and do not try to find out who is to blame. Since my earliest childhood there has been a weariness in me which has grown into a longing for death. The whole of life leads to death, which for me will be redemption. Love Martin instead of me. He deserves your love a thousand times more than your son, who leaves his mother without being restrained by his conscience. Do not weep, I beg you! I have been incapable of living; at the most I have been a dreamer. If the world were like the painting by Master Claude, which I sent you from Rome, then I should like to be a human. But being a human was odious to me, and finally became a Hell. Adieu! My last thoughts will be with you.

Please forgive me.

Raoul signed the letter, strewed sand on it, blew it away, folded it and addressed it to the Comtesse de Racon, and sealed it. Then he rang his little bell for Dominique. 'Madame la Comtesse is to find this letter in her room. Lay out my blue riding coat and, if I should fall asleep, wake me punctually at five o'clock. Have my horse saddled for a quarter past five, and see that Monsieur le Comte is not disturbed by my departure. I need no breakfast and no groom. The moon will be bright enough.'

Martin had ordered François to wake him at seven, and was roused punctually at this hour. He went immediately to the count and woke him up. The count cursed and asked what was the matter. Martin said that if they wished to avert a tragedy they must be in the Bois de Vincennes before half past ten. He dared not say more because he had given his word. Martin's tone of voice, his look and excitement, had their effect; the count got up and dressed. Martin went downstairs to the master of horse. Two of the fastest horses were to stand in readiness immediately the vicomte left, but not before. Four grooms would suffice. The master of horse laughed and remarked jestingly that he regretted very much, but the vicomte had left with Monsieur de Brayonne and Comte de Salvieux shortly after five o'clock, so there would be some delay in saddling the horses. Martin shouted that this could not be true, and ran in a panic up to Raoul's bedroom.

Dominique confirmed his misgivings. Martin rushed into the study where the count had sat down to breakfast, insisted upon all speed, saying that it was perhaps too late. The count replied that he intended to ride to the regiment, and wanted Raoul to deliver an order to Colonel du Lac. Martin said that the vicomte was no longer in the house and had lied to him about the time. At this, the count jumped up and was down in the courtyard before Martin. The grooms could not saddle up quickly enough for him. He laid about him with his riding-crop and fastened his horse's girths himself. Then it was a wild gallop through the streets, speeding like lightning past the watch, through the inner city gate, so that the captain despatched his men to follow them, and the count had to show his pass at the outer fortifications.

The main road was obstructed by carts. The count and Martin used their whips to get through, for the frozen fields on both sides had been ploughed up. A groom's horse lost a shoe and had to return home. François's horse slipped on the ice, fell to its knees and went lame. He, too, had to turn back. It was nearly half past nine when they saw three horsemen riding towards them from the Bois de Vincennes; the one in the middle was wearing a bandage round his neck. An older man followed on a mule. The three men turned aside, and the count, together with Martin and the two remaining grooms, galloped past them.

On reaching the edge of the forest, the count ordered the grooms to wait, and asked Martin how far they had to go. Martin had no idea. Following the road into the undergrowth, they followed a snow-covered side path, which bore the fresh traces of horses' hooves. A horse neighed, and Guy came riding up. They stopped. Guy took off his hat and said that he was off to fetch a cart because Raoul had been mortally wounded. The count asked whether he was still alive, and Guy shook his head. The count crossed himself and ordered his son to tell the grooms that the vicomte had been the victim of highwaymen. They rode off in different directions.

Martin trotted off ahead of the count, following Guy's tracks, and reached the clearing where Raoul, guarded by Louis, lay on his riding-coat in the snow under two fine elms. Martin dismounted and ran over to the dead man. Raoul's shirt was open. Removing the loosely-tied bandage, he saw the fatal wound and covered it again. He cried that he had kept his word, but was to blame, all the same. That night he should have committed treachery. No one replied. With a piteous cry, Martin called out Raoul's name, but only a distant echo answered.

Louis de Salvieux went, hat in hand, to the count and began to give an account of the duel. The count listened, and insisted that Louis should conceal the truth and say that the Vicomte de Clarmont had been murdered by outlaws. Louis gave his word of honour. The count dismounted and gave Louis his steaming grey, mounted Raoul's chestnut and cantered back to the main road.

On his arrival he found only Charles, and called out, as he galloped past, that he should stand watch over the dead man in the clearing. After a mile, he met Guy returning with another groom and an ox-cart, driven by a peasant. The count did not stop. After speeding through the village, he reached the next hamlet and overtook the three cavaliers and the man on the mule, whom he had met on the outward ride. He reined in his horse, joined the gentlemen, and demanded to speak to the man with the neck wound, alone. The cavalier asked his companions to wait for him by the village pump, and remained behind with the count.

The count introduced himself, although the wounded man knew perfectly well who he was, and threatened to denounce the murder of his son to the Court, unless by midnight he had delivered two million livres to the Hôtel de Racon. The cavalier replied that he would deny it, and that his companions were bound by their oaths. The count replied that he knew all their names and that the rack would soon make them speak. Did he know what he could expect from the law? The cavalier swore by the Holy Virgin that his fortune did not amount to anything approaching two millions. He had avenged his wife's honour, and his victory could not be considered murder. The count replied curtly that he knew the financial position of a certain noble family, and offered the choice of the scaffold or poverty. The cavalier called him an infamous blackmailer. Ignoring the insult, the count declared, as he took his leave, that he would give him until midnight. The man controlled his rage and asked the count very politely to ride on with him. They could perhaps reach some compromise before they reached Paris. The count replied that one sword and two pistols would be of little avail against three swords and six pistols, and he considered it more prudent to wait here in the village for his escort. The cavalier now drew his pistol, but the count struck it out of his hand with his riding-crop and shot his horse. Before the cavalier's companions knew what had happened, the count had fled into a peasant's hut and bolted the door. After a short conference, the three horsemen tried to force an entry into the house, but the terrified peasants ran up with pitchforks and scythes. The three men preferred to take the count's horse and ride on with all haste to Paris.

The count gave the peasant a handsome pourboire and remained in the hut, where he enjoyed a country breakfast and sat by the window waiting for the cart and the three young gentlemen. As soon as they came in sight, he went out and ordered them to leave the dead man in the village church to be guarded by grooms. He proposed to ride on and, in order to avoid being conspicuous, he would send a coach from the Hôtel de Racon to fetch the corpse of the murdered man. Martin asked to be allowed to remain with Raoul in place of the grooms. The count gave him permission, and said that he must not reproach himself. Martin turned away and walked over to the cart.

The count mounted his grey, and Guy rode on his left as the new Vicomte de Clarmont. Louis rode behind, ahead of the grooms. On the way, Guy asked whether Martin was now

Monsieur de Brayonne, but his father replied that on the day of Raoul's death he forbade anyone to make such foolish jests. Martin Saint-Jean would become neither a Monsieur nor Marquis de Brayonne; and that Guy would sometime inherit all his father's titles, whereupon Guy insisted that the good Martin also deserved one. The count knitted his brows and did not reply. Guy then asked whether, as the Vicomte de Clarmont, he had the right now to live in the Hôtel de Racon as well as Martin. He received the curt reply that the count did not propose to make any changes before Raoul's funeral. Guy fell silent. They rode slowly back to Paris and reached the eastern fortifications just before midday.

The countess arrived two days later and was led to her son's open coffin, around which stood many weeping women. Paris hummed with the tragic end of the handsome Vicomte de Clarmont and the sudden ruin of a well-known noble family. The count made arrangements with the country police, and led his regiment to the Bois de Vincennes to look for the murderers. A few suspicious-looking ruffians were caught, put on the rack, and then hanged, drawn and quartered, after a confession had been wrung from them. The de Racon family travelled with the dead vicomte's lead coffin to the castle of Grandval, where the funeral was to take place with the greatest pomp.

THE STARGAZER

AT the banquet following the funeral of the Vicomte Raoul de Clarmont, Comte de Racon and old Baron du Terne came to an agreement, that Guy should marry the dead boy's fiancée as soon as the year of mourning had elapsed. The count promised to dissolve Guy's betrothal to the unsuspecting Mademoiselle d'Epponcourt, and took Guy into his confidence.

Guy showed no particular enthusiasm, but the count assured him that he was free to marry any lady of quality richer than Mademoiselle du Terne, if he could find one. The new tie did not have to be considered as indissoluble. Guy said, with a smile, that he would start looking for a wife at once, in order to escape Mlle du Terne. With her pockmarks she must be ugliness personified since her father had not brought her to the funeral of her former bethrothed. The count replied that her grief was so deep that she had not felt like making the journey.

While the guests watched a performance of Racine's *Bérénice*, in the salon, the new marriage contract was secretly signed in the study and Guy accepted his future father-in-law's invitation to visit his castle. Baron du Terne left next morning with Baron d'Epponcourt, and his daughter Marguerite was very offended when Guy took his leave of her and rode away with the old Baron. She considered that he might have travelled a little of the way in her company.

On the evening after the departure of the last guest, the count had two decanters of heavy burgundy brought up to his study and proceeded to drink glass after glass, in Martin's company. Martin drank in moderation and, after an hour, thrust his glass aside. 'Monsieur, you are doing your best to get drunk.'

'I want to be so besotted that I no longer know myself.'

'Why?'

'To stop thinking for a time.'

'Are you at last beginning to mourn for Raoul?'

'Don't talk to me about him. He was a good-for-nothing, and he is now at peace.'

'He was not a good-for-nothing, but he was too delicate for the life you compelled him to lead.'

'Are you reproaching me?'

'No, I'm reproaching myself, Monsieur. I should have helped Raoul to escape from your power, in spite of the fact that I might have lost your friendship. Raoul was my friend and I was not a good enough friend to him.'

'Stop talking like this. I don't want to hear anything about it. It is enough that Madeleine will no longer look at me. Complaints are useless, and remorse always comes too late. Something else worries me. I have wounded Guy's pride by banishing him on your account. He is travelling from the Château du Terne to Paris and will live in the Hôtel de Racon. His years of service with the musketeers end at Easter. He will take Raoul's place in my regiment and go to Court. Suggest to me now what I can do with you.'

'Monsieur, the vicomte was most cordial when I greeted him. He did not give me the impression that he was still my enemy. I should have welcomed a reconciliation, but I kept my promise and did not speak to him.'

'Did you lock your door every night?'

'Yes, but I am certain it was unnecessary. Everyone praises the vicomte. Tenelli says that Raoul's death has completely changed him. He distributed alms to the beggars, and was mild to the peasants and grooms. Don't you think that his malice may have been due to youth and that he has now changed?'

'No, Martin. I don't think so.'

'Shall I move to the Hôtel de Brayonne?'

'You will have to, Martin. Do you like being in the Guards?'

'Yes, Monsieur, very much. I shall not interfere with the vicomte because he is under Colonel de la Porte-Mury, while I serve under Colonel du Lac.'

'You are respected by all the officers and adored by the men. The ensigns would go through fire and water for you. You could eat every day at the Marquis de Chassigny's table now that you have turned his hunch-backed dwarf son into a good soldier, but because of your humble station I asked the Marquis to leave you where you were. As though you hadn't outgrown your station! I have committed one folly after the other.'

'Monsieur, what folly did you commit?'

'How did you tame the dwarf?'

Martin explained to him. 'Little Nicolas looked so hang-dog that I was sorry for him. I asked him what he could do, and he said he could cast lead bullets. That was a useful skill, I replied, and asked him if he had any of his ready-made bullets to hand. He showed me some. I chose a target and ordered him to fire. He hit the mark. I told him that a good sharp-shooter was already half a soldier. Did he know how to ride? He refused to reply. However, I overheard one of the ensigns say that the dwarf would be all right on a goat. When I asked him whether, at the gallop, he found it difficult to breathe on account of his hump, he admitted it. I sent for a docile horse, set him in the saddle and ordered him to trot round in a circle. I gave him the horse for his period of service, and said that I saw no good reason why he should not one day make a good soldier. I ordered the tallest and most aggressive ensign to protect the newcomer from any teasing, and allowed him to give vent to his coarseness. My foul-mouthed youth was delighted with his commission, and the dwarf was soon riding magnificently. I never saw any sign of his reputed malice.'

Martin began to hum a ditty.

'Our dwarf Nicolas,
Nicolas Coly,
Chassigny's Nicolas
Is the finest rider,
In the company.'

'He sings the song himself, Monsieur.'

'Martin, you could become a captain in de Chassigny's regiment.'

The boy gave a start. 'Monsieur, do you intend to banish me to the Pyrenees on account of Guy?'

'No, I shall not banish you.'

'Let me stay in the Guards. Let me stay in Paris. I beg you to arrange a reconciliation. I swear to you that I will never taunt the vicomte. I will treat him with the greatest respect. He will certainly have no cause to wish me dead.'

'Guy does not stop at wishes. You are a thorn in his side because your position is too high for a bastard.'

'Monsieur, I hope one day to command my own regiment and to acquire a title.'

'Never tell that to anyone.'

'Why?'

'It is always a bad thing to reveal your plans. Conceal your ambition, and don't be so eager in your service.'

'Monsieur, I have to do you credit. You must never regret that you found me a position in the Guards and introduced me into society. Please, Monsieur, reconcile me with the new vicomte and stop being anxious. I admit that sometimes I felt above myself and behaved too much like a nobleman. I will remember my origin every day and be as modest as I possibly can in the presence of the vicomte. Please reconcile us in Paris.'

'I will do it.'

'Thank you.'

'Fill up your glass.'

Martin obeyed, and the count drank two glasses of wine in quick succession.

'Monsieur, you're drinking too quickly.'

'I want to get drunk.'

'Can I go to bed?'

'No, you'll stay here.'

'Can I lie down in front of the fire?'

'Make yourself comfortable.'

'You will have a terrible headache tomorrow, and I shall say that it serves you right.'

Martin went over to the fire and lay down before it on the carpet.

The count drank in silence. About midnight he called: 'Hi, Martin!' but his friend did not reply. The count blinked owlishly towards him and muttered thickly to himself: 'He's asleep. I'll let him go on sleeping and tell him tomorrow. He'll beg me on his knees and deafen me with his wailing. I can't help him. He must leave the Guards.' The count put his elbows on the table. 'I'm mad about that boy. There's something about him which keeps me young . . . I'm becoming an old fool. The king is getting old, too. He's raised his bastard to Duc de Maine and no one in his wildest dreams dares to quibble. I command the Light Horse Guards, and quake before Guy. If I were to give the boy a permanent bodyguard of four men, I should make myself ridiculous and he would still not be safe! If only this wine helped! I shan't be able to say it to him tomorrow any better than today. I'll go on a journey with him and will tell him while we're away. He must know it before the day we return. I shall not come back until May . . .'

The count poured himself out another glass and it tinkled against the silver decanter. Martin woke up. The count did not notice and went on with his drunken monologue. 'I should never have believed it possible that I could be so upset. If I had only left him with Chassigny's dragoons, or at Les Chênes with the farmer. If only I had married Isabelle instead of Madeleine. She was just as rich, equally well-born, and nearly as beautiful. She had breasts like apples, and swayed gently when she walked. Her hips were smaller than her shoulders, and are now so broad that she looks almost like a peasant woman. Madeleine is still beautiful. I was always able to arouse her desire. Few women were as ardent as she, and now she is ill. Isabelle is healthy and at Court. She has borne her husband eight children; two of her sons already hold high positions and have distinguished themselves at war. What has Madeleine given me? All her children are dead, except Guy. Guy holds the title which should have gone to Martin. Guy will become the Comte de Racon and Guy will become Marquis de Brayonne. Guy will inherit Grandval, Brayonne and Fleury, and all the other properties. Isabelle told me that she was with child, but my head was full of Madeleine. Isabelle confessed on her wedding night and her husband was merciful. If only he had thrashed the child out of her belly! Now I have the boy round my neck and I cannot bear to part with him. If only I had never seen Madeleine! She fetched Martin to Grandval. I should have . . .'

The count suddenly caught sight of Martin at his side and set down his glass with a start. 'Comte de Racon!' cried Martin. 'What is my mother's name?'

'I was not speaking of your mother,' the count stammered.

'You're lying. You have lied to me from the very start. My mother was no bourgeois girl and she is not dead. She is a lady and she is alive! Her name is Isabelle! What is her other name?'

The count controlled himself and said: 'I swore to her husband that no one should ever learn the name of your mother. I forgot that you were here. Forget what you heard and leave me in peace.'

'Do you refuse to give me satisfaction?'

'I've already said too much and I am not saying any more.'

'I challenge you to a duel.'

The count blinked and tried to laugh. 'You are as drunk as I am and don't know what you are saying.'

He stretched out his hand for the glass, but Martin swept it and the pitcher off the table. 'I know what I'm saying. You have dishonoured my mother and abandoned her. You are a scoundrel, Comte de Racon!'

Pierre rushed into the room on hearing the breaking of glass. The count waved him away and said slowly, in an undertone, to Martin: 'Take back your insult or my hand will lose control.'

'Slap me then.'

The count rose heavily to his feet and struck Martin with all his might in the face, and at the next moment received a slap on the cheek, which made the scar flame fiery red. The two men stared at each other. 'Martin,' said the count quietly. 'I shall have you flogged.'

'That will be the peak of your villainy. Draw your sword! I will avenge my mother's dishonour.' Martin's sword gleamed in the flickering light of the candles. The count sat down.

'Can't you hold your wine?' jeered Martin. 'Or are you afraid, because I fence as well as you do?'

'Martin, your mother's present husband already fought with me for her honour. One does not fight one's father.'

'No, but one can fight with one's former friend. You have robbed me of all my rights. You could have married my mother, but you made me a bastard. I had to address Raoul and Guy by their titles, and they addressed me as a servant. Your sons were gentlemen from birth, and I had to work my way up from corporal to lieutenant, so that with this rank I could at least appear before your friends. No nobleman, when he has been arrogant, will fight a duel with me, and I have not the right to compel him. You can have me flogged because I slapped your princely snout, and I have no right to punish you for the same insult! You once had me flogged by your master of the hunt. It is lucky for you that you did not have it done by your jailer. I would now pierce you like a colander and would tear you to pieces like a wolf. Call your grooms! I will defend myself to my last breath, but no one is going to flog me while I am alive.'

'Put your sword away, Martin; I shall not summon anyone.'

'Are you hatching some ruse? Come on, I am trying to escape!'

The count jumped up and reached the door at the same time as Martin. 'I beg you, be reasonable. I threatened you just now in anger and would never have you flogged. How could you think such a thing of me? I intended to buy an estate for you and to petition the king to let you bear the title of a nobleman. You know that I had debts and was not in a position to carry out my plan. Then I learned that Guy is against your elevation to the nobility, and I began to fear for your life. I will help you to get a title. I shall do it somehow, but I must ask you to be patient.'

'Spare me your lies.'

'I am not lying, Martin. Ask Louis de Salvieux. When I asked for his sister's hand for you, I told him that you would be a nobleman with an estate of your own. He refused and betrayed my plan to Guy, but it will happen this year, in spite of Guy.'

'You expect me to believe that?'

'After Raoul's death I won a huge sum at gambling, enough to buy a marquisate. I'll show you the money if you doubt it.'

'I no longer doubt you.'

'I will recompense you in every way, Martin. You are already in the Guards and have a position which many sons of the nobility could envy. You are in society; you have the entrée everywhere, except to Court, and this will be granted to you as soon as you have a title. So you see that I have your interests at heart, and I shall continue to do so. I forgive your slap, Martin, and I beg you to forgive me.'

Martin walked over the broken glass to the table and sat on the oak top. 'Comte de Racon, I should be a dog if I allowed my honour to be bought. There is nothing between us to forgive. Allow me to take my leave of you, or will you deign to fight with me?'

'Martin, let us leave our decisions until tomorrow and sleep on it.'

'Nothing binds me to you any more.'

'Martin, since you have known me, have I ever offended your honour?'

'No, Comte de Racon.'

'Martin, I still respect your honour. I will accept your challenge and fight with you tomorrow.' Martin was speechless. 'I accept your challenge,' repeated the count, 'and will fight with you tomorrow. I shall leave behind a sealed letter, exonerating you from any blame, should I be killed. Will you remain here now?'

'Monsieur, I have done you an injustice by believing you to be worse than you are. When and where can we fight?'

'We will ride at seven o'clock.'

Martin slipped from the table and bowed. The count stood away from the door and let him pass.

When the count stepped into the courtyard at seven o'clock, Martin was already on his horse. The count mounted his grey and they rode into the country. The early morning sun battled with the mist and bore down on it until the blue February sky shone on the treeless forest. In the shaded spots the snow still lay.

The count galloped towards the trees and trotted along a narrow path to a concealed clearing, which was still half covered with snow. The brown grass was wet with dew. A few firs raised their heads to the sun above the beech trees.

'Have you not changed your mind, Martin?'

'No, Comte de Racon.'

'Is the place to your taste, M. Saint-Jean?'

'I find it eminently suitable.'

The two men dismounted and tethered their horses to the trees. They took off their coats and the count looked up at the sun. 'Stand over there, M. Saint-Jean.'

'Comte de Racon, this is a duel to the death.'

'I am at your service, M. Saint-Jean.' There was a clash of swords.

Martin suddenly leapt back and cried. 'You're not attacking, you're merely trying to disarm me.'

'I have no wish to murder you.'

'Defend yourself.'

Steel clashed against steel. The count retreated step by step to the edge of the clearing, but Martin was in a towering rage. 'Attack, damn you. This is no duel, Comte de Racon.'

'I don't care what it is.'

'I will drive you into the bushes and stick you like a pig.'

The count withdrew his left arm, as though he could already feel the branches, thrust Martin's blade, quick as a flash, into the air, ducked, and ran under it into the centre of the clearing. Martin pursued him. 'You will not succeed a second time.' The count parried each blow and tried to force Martin to turn until he had the sun in his eyes, but Martin realised his intention and forced him round in turn by standing slightly to one side and continuing his fierce sallies. He managed to wound the count in the arm.

'Touché.'

The count changed hands and his right sleeve began to turn scarlet.

'My aim will be better next time,' laughed Martin. But the count began to take things seriously and defended himself well with the left hand. The blood ran from his lace cuff and dripped into the trampled grass and the snow.

Then Martin stumbled and fell. The count hurried to the centre of the clearing and waited for him. 'M. Saint-Jean, give me time to bind up my arm.'

'Do so.'

Taking off his waistcoat and shirt, he made a bandage from

his shirt. 'I am ready.'

'Tie the sleeves together so that you won't lose the bandage.'

'I cannot do that on my own.'

'I'll help you.'

Martin stuck his foil into the earth and went over to the count. 'Are you bleeding badly?'

'I don't know.'

'Put on your waistcoat so that you won't catch cold.'

'You are making me warm enough, M. Saint-Jean.'

Martin caught sight of the scar on his hairy chest. 'Monsieur, show me your arm.'

'Why?'

'I want to see if you are seriously wounded.'

'Not seriously enough to abandon the fight.'

Martin unbuttoned the loose shirt-sleeve and untied the bloodstained linen. 'The stab must be deep, for the blood is oozing out very dark. I will bandage it more firmly.' Martin took a long time over it.

'What are you playing at?'

'I can't fight with you any more.' Martin turned his eyes away and suddenly fell to his knees. 'Forgive me!'

The count raised him to his feet. 'Forgive me, too.'

'I must not forgive you,' said Martin, tearing himself away with a sob and running blindly towards a fir trunk. The count followed slowly. Martin laid his face against the bark, and remained leaning against the tree. The count placed his hand lightly on his shoulder. 'Don't touch me,' shouted Martin.

The count walked away, put on his waistcoat and hung the coat over his shoulders. Then he sat down on a tree-stump and waited.

At last, Martin approached him. 'Monsieur, there is only one solution for me. I must say farewell to you for ever.'

'What have you in mind?'

'I can go to Canada or enter the service of a foreign power.'

'Is that the truth?'

'Why should I always speak the truth?'

'Martin, I am your father. Are you courting your death?'

'I shall find it somewhere.'

'Have I got to remain for the rest of my days in anxiety and uncertainty as to your fate? Spare me that, and rather put a bullet through your head before my eyes.' Martin turned round and went over to the horses. The count jumped up, ran and caught him, just in time to prevent him taking a pistol from its holster. 'So you really want to kill yourself?'

'You wanted it to happen before your eyes?'

'No, Martin.'

'Where then?'

'Have you no thought for what you are doing to me?'

'You never gave it a thought when you left my mother.'

'I have bitterly regretted it.'

'Remorse always comes too late.'

'And what of your remorse?'

'I shall give myself no time for regrets.'

'Are you fully determined?'

'Yes, Comte de Racon.'

'Martin, until yesterday you loved me and you were my friend.'

'Yes, by God, Comte de Racon, it is terrible for me to have had to wound you. Had you only kept silent! There is only one way out, my honour demands my death.'

'Yes, I can see that and it is beyond my power to stop you, but I beg you, think over your decision today and let me know tomorrow morning. Think matters out calmly and try also to see these things with my eyes. Can you grant me that request?'

'Yes, if that is all you ask.'

'I ask nothing else and I trust you, Martin. Help me into my coat.'

'You'll never get that bandaged arm into it.'

'Hell, how shall I manage?'

'I don't know, Monsieur.'

'Fetch my cravat.'

Martin obeyed and brought it to the count. 'Monsieur, get on your horse. I will fasten the coat over your right arm. Are you capable of riding to Grandval alone?'

'Won't you accompany me?'

'I must not meet anyone, Monsieur.'

'Oh, we'll say we were attacked by robbers, and play a real comedy.'

'I am in no mood for comedy.'

'You take everything too seriously.'

'That is my way. I will accompany you as far as the courtyard and will remain until tomorrow with Farmer Douranez. Do you agree?'

'Yes, M. Saint-Jean.'

Martin helped the count and both of them prepared to leave; they rode in single file through the forest, over the melting snow.

As soon as Martin had left the count at the castle gates, he rode across country for a few hours and arrived for the midday meal at Les Chênes. He learned that Lison wanted to enter a convent and refused all offers of marriage. The peasant cursed, but the mother took the girl's part. Martin barely listened to their chatter and rode away during the afternoon. The early-spring day waned with a rosy sky, giving place to a starry, frosty night.

At dawn, Martin reached Grandval and made his way to the count's bedroom. Pierre was already making the bed and told him that M. le Comte was waiting for him in his study. Martin entered and found the count, despite his wound, fully dressed and sitting in a chair. His heavily bandaged arm was in a sling and the right half of the black velvet coat hung loose over his shoulders. His face bore all the traces of a sleepless night. Rising from his chair, he walked towards Martin. 'Good morning, Martin. What have you to tell me?'

'Nothing new, Monsieur. My honour impels me to abide by my decision.'

The two men summed each other up. At last, the count asked softly: 'Is there nothing that overrides your honour?'

'No, unless you could name anything higher.'

'Have a word with Father Tulier.'

'Monsieur, I know that suicide is against the Christian doctrine, but I cannot continue to live since both my parents are of noble birth with the stain of the bar sinister and no possible remedy. I have to avenge my mother's dishonour on my father ... and that too, is impossible. Guy has often dubbed me a bastard. To suffer undeserved abuse for the rest of one's life is intolerable, Comte de Racon.'

'Martin, I have decided to break my oath and tell you the name of your mother. I am not doing this so that you can reveal your maternal origin. Your mother would have to deny you for the honour of her husband and her children, and her husband would have to bring me to court for slander. Do you want it to come to a trial in which we must inevitably lose our honour as slanderers?'

'No, Monsieur. I do not desire that. I am in the same position as Raoul. But he went willingly to his death. I shall be thrust out of life by my shame. There is no other way for me.'

'Martin, have you thought carefully of your whole past?'

'No, only the most recent events, Comte de Racon.'

'I beg you then, review your life from the beginning until today. Ask yourself whether there could not possibly be something which would make it worth while your continuing to live. You are an officer and the king needs every soldier.'

'You mean that I should sacrifice my honour to the king and wait for another war? I already intended to seek my death on the battlefield, but yesterday you did not wish that, Comte de Racon.'

The count tried to laugh. 'We have ridden a hundred times together against the enemy and I have never feared for you so much—not even when I saw you unhorsed in that mêlée.'

'Monsieur, I have thought out the following solution. I intend to make an end of it near Grandval, so that you will be spared further uncertainty. You expressed the wish that I should review my whole life from the beginning. I will do that, and beg you not to have a search made for me before tomorrow morning at dawn, at the scene of our encounter. Please do not ask for any more postponements, and grant my wish.'

'I will grant it.'

'Monsieur, you have shown me many favours in the past, and I thank you.' Martin was about to seize the count's left hand, to kiss it as he left, but the count calmly raised it almost pontifically in the air. Martin looked puzzled into the black, slanting eyes, which were entirely devoid of expression. The count turned his back and returned to his bedroom. It took Martin some time to recover. Then, clenching his teeth, he left the study by the other door.

At midday, the count was told that M. Saint-Jean's horse

had returned alone. The count asked whether the pistols were still in the holsters, and was told that they were empty. He gave the strange order that no one was to look for M. Saint-Jean until the following morning, and, despite his wound, rode off in company with two grooms. He galloped along the glittering river, through the sunny valley, before returning to Grandval. The severe pain in his arm, aggravated by the ride, had compelled him to grow calmer. After he had rested for a while, he sent Pierre to ask his wife whether she would prefer to see him now or later. The valet returned to say that the countess would see him at once in her salon.

The countess received her husband with icy dignity. Her black mourning veil framed the frozen beauty of her pale face like a dark cloud. 'Monsieur, what brings you here?'

'I intend to travel. Your long periods of loneliness seem to affect you. If it would please you to invite some guests, you need not in future consider yourself under constraint.'

'Monsieur, you know that, apart from the du Ternes, the village children are my only guests.'

'Madame, I occasionally met M. d'Oubray in Paris. As you probably know, he now wears a priest's habit. If you have no objection, I will invite him to stay at Grandval. I am quite certain that he will accept my invitation, for since he dabbles in alchemy, his name is mentioned more than he would like in Paris, in connection with the poison rumours. He will be glad to escape the gossip by a stay in the country, and I hope that during my absence he will manage to convert you. It is known at Court that you are a Huguenot, and that does me more damage than you would suspect. Nor is it in Guy's favour. If you would be of use to your son, then become converted. May I invite M. d'Oubray in your name too?'

'Monsieur, I would never renounce my faith.'

'Then discuss philosophical questions with your friend.'

'What do you mean by that?'

'Madame, I can expect no more children from you and I give you your freedom. I do not know what your condition permits, and merely ask that you should protect my honour before the outside world.'

'Are you giving me my freedom?'

'Yes, Madame, I should have done it long ago. Do you accept?'

The countess sat down and pointed to a chair, but the count remained standing. 'Monsieur,' she said, looking up at him, 'what am I to understand by your offer? Do you intend to reward me or to ruin me?' The count did not reply. 'Monsieur,' she went on intensely, 'were I to accept, I should be more in your power than ever. You could at any time accuse me of adultery and banish me on these grounds. If you want to get rid of me in order to bring home a healthy wife, then you need not have recourse to these machinations. I would gladly die of grief after a glass of wine.'

'Madame, I have no possible cause to wish you dead. Your son Guy is my heir.'

'How I always feared for Raoul, and now I am afraid that Guy is in danger.'

'From whom?'

'From Martin or from you.'

'Madame, tomorrow you will see that Martin is no threat to Guy.'

'Tomorrow, what do you mean? Your face is ashen pale!'

'My wound pains me, that is all.'

'Monsieur, Martin's horse returned alone, and you forbade anyone to look for him before tomorrow. Is it true that you have quarrelled with him?'

'There is a glimmer of truth in every rumour.'

'What is the matter with Martin?'

'I cannot tell you.'

'There is something sinister about you. Please leave me.'

'Madame, I shall invite M. d'Oubray without your consent, so that I shall be solely responsible. I repeat, I give you your freedom. You can consider yourself in secret as divorced from me.'

'Monsieur, life holds nothing for me now. Nevertheless, I thank you. Write to M. d'Oubray what you will, but please let no one atone for any of your changes of heart, except myself.'

'Madame, I hope that you will find consolation.'

The countess arranged her veil with trembling fingers and said: 'Good evening, Monsieur.'

'Good evening, Madame.' He bowed and left.

The count sought out the priest and dictated a letter to M. d'Oubray. Father Tulier cautiously expressed his joy at the prospect of soon having an aid in this difficult task of spiritual guide to the de Racon family. The count exchanged a few polite words with him, took the letter and said farewell. Back in his study, he ordered Pierre to have the letter delivered and to fetch Dr Borel. The old man changed his bandage and retired. The count paid a visit to Martin's room, which had recently also been on the first floor. Among the young man's few possessions, he found Raoul's books and weapons. The count sat down and turned over the pages of a book, but soon closed it and left the room. Walking along the corridor, he made his way down the spiral staircase in the south-east tower, to the dining-hall.

The evening sun cast its mote-filled beams into the sumptuous, unheated room and came to rest on the tapestries, depicting bacchantes and satyrs. The count went out on to the bright terrace and then returned to the hall. He shouted for a lackey and ordered him to bring in a table and some mulled wine. Sitting down opposite the gay coloured arras, he began to drink. Pierre wanted to have the fire lit, but the count dismissed all the servants. The sun sank, turned scarlet and began to cast dark shadows. A few marble figures still gleamed in the park. Pierre brought in a fur coat and a fur-lined sleigh-rug and lit a few candles. He helped his master into the cloak, covered his knees and stole from the room. The count continued to drink goblet after goblet of the wine, which gradually cooled. Outside it was a clear, frosty night. The valet returned and asked whether the count intended to eat in his study. He received a vacant stare, and a stiff hand pointed to the door. The count's breath steamed in the cold. Pierre replaced the coverlet, which had slipped from his slender knees, and, with an anxious expression on his face, left the room.

About two o'clock in the morning, there were steps on the terrace and the tall french windows opened with a rattle. Martin entered and walked over to the seated man. The count tried to rise to his feet, but fell back in his chair. 'Martin,' he said thickly.

'Yes, Monsieur, it's Martin.'

'I want to go into the park and can't get up.'

'What do you want to do in the park?'

'To put my head under the fountain.' Martin helped the drunken man to his feet and supported him.

'Monsieur, it is winter and none of the fountains is playing.'

'Martin, you are terribly cold.'

'So are you, Monsieur. You must go at once to your bedroom. Can you walk?'

'Not yet.'

'Then you had better sit down again.'

The count fell back into his chair. 'Bring me some cold water.'

Martin peered into the corridor, caught sight of a lackey and sent him to carry out the count's order. He took the pitcher and brought it in. 'Here is your cold water, Monsieur.'

'Pour it over my head.'

'Must I?'

'Yes.'

'Bend over to one side.' The count did as he was bid and Martin drenched him.

The count shook himself like a dog and leaped into the air. 'Ah, that was good. It's running down my back. Well, what have you decided?'

'I'm staying with you.'

The count pushed back his damp hair. 'So you no longer want to die?'

'No,' replied Martin with a smile, 'otherwise you would become a real drunkard.'

'What is the real reason for your return?'

'I'll tell you as soon as we get into a warm room.'

'Call Pierre, and help me upstairs.'

Martin called the valet and they helped the staggering man up to his bedroom. 'Monsieur,' said Martin, 'sleep off your intoxication and we will discuss things tomorrow.'

'Are you staying in the castle?'

'Yes, Monsieur, for certain.'

'Will you still be alive tomorrow?'

'Yes, Monsieur, for certain.'

'Promise me, Martin!'

'I promise you.'

Martin had to assist Pierre once more, because the count had to be put to bed like a child. Martin retired to the study next door, and, despite the lateness of the hour, ordered a copious meal.

The count slept until midday and woke with a throbbing head. He caught sight of Martin talking to Dr Borel; they came over and immediately changed his bandage. When he asked them to leave him in peace they left the room. That afternoon, he was feverish and was ordered to remain in bed. Martin sat down by his bedside and wiped his brow from time to time. They exchanged no words, and Pierre, who had kept his ear to the keyhole during the previous night's quarrel, listened in vain.

When the count was woken up by the early morning sun, he found Martin lying on the bed next to him, fully dressed. At first he was too shocked to touch him; but then he noticed that Martin was breathing peacefully. He seized him by the hair. 'You!'

Martin gave a start and opened his eyes. 'What's the matter?'

'You gave me a great fright.'

'Why?'

'I thought you were dead.'

'I only needed a little rest and I must have fallen asleep.'

'Tell me how you came to change your mind?'

Martin stared up at the canopy and began his explanation. 'When I finally left you, I felt as though I were the guilty one, for you turned your back on me and did not say goodbye. Over and over again I assured myself that you were to blame, but my inexplicable feeling of guilt continued to grow and I was powerless to shake it off. When I reached the clearing, I sat down on a tree stump—where you sat the other day—and looked back on my past as far as my memory would reach, and then once more from the beginning until our duel. However I looked at it, I could find no other solution than the one I had decided upon, and yet I could not free myself from that feeling of guilt. There were bloodstains all over the snow. I bitterly regretted having wounded you, and tried to persuade myself that you were angry with me because of your wound. I then thought of returning and once more asking your forgiveness, but I considered myself foolish and was afraid that I could be accused of cowardice. You forgave me in the clearing, and you have never nursed any rancour in the past. I sent my horse home to banish any idea of a return, despatched all my thoughts to the devil, and decided to make an end of it all. But when I placed the pistol to my temple I seemed to see your raised arm, and I did not press the trigger.

'I saw you as clearly before me as on that morning, and could not make out the expression in your eyes. I was pleased at our bargain that I was not to be looked for until morning, and suddenly decided to wait until nightfall. I felt terribly hungry and began to be annoyed with myself. At last it grew dark, and then, to my hunger was added the cold, and still I had not found the answer. The first stars began to glitter. I remembered my last evening with Raoul, when he had spoken of the godless infinity of the universe, and I suddenly felt a desire to test the truth of his theory.

'I left the clearing and climbed a hill, where the trees had recently been felled, leaving only stunted thorn bushes. I stood there and looked up at the stars, and imagined that the earth was only one star in the firmament. I felt as though the ground had slipped from beneath my feet, but I clung to my idea. And then I found that I was insignificant, unimportant, meaningless and small. Of a sudden, honour, suicide and disgrace meant nothing! I had to laugh at myself. Raoul was right. What is a man, when he considers the stars? Now it would have been an easy matter to make an end of things, but I had left my pistols below by the tree stump. To amuse myself, I thought once more of my own insignificance and of your strange farewell and merely wanted to go down and laugh at your insignificance as well.

'But then the stars were remote again and my feet were on solid ground. And suddenly, the darkness was dispelled from my heart and my love gleamed within me like a sun. I saw with devastating clarity how abominable my intention was, and returned to Grandval. I took a short cut and climbed over the park wall. I belong to you, Monsieur.'

Silence reigned in the room, until a fly began to buzz by the sunny window. Then, without looking at his friend, the count asked: 'Were the stars a dream?'

'No, it was real, and you were right to be angry with me.'

'I was not angry with you.'

'What then?'

'I don't know, Martin.'

The count felt something soft touch his ear, and rubbed it. 'Have you really forgiven everything?'

'Yes, everything, Monsieur.'

The count turned to him. 'And what about your honour?'

'There are higher powers than my honour,' Martin replied calmly. 'It is satisfied, because you fought with me as though I were a nobleman, thereby respecting me for what I am according to my birth, and what, one day, through your grace, I shall also be before my fellow men.'

The count turned his head away once more. 'Incidentally, my wife also knows that your unknown mother is a lady of quality.'

'Who else knows?'

'No one. What cannot be proved, is seldom believed.'

'I will remember that.'

'You would be well advised to do so, Martin. Would you like to travel with me?'

'Of course, Monsieur. Where do you wish to go?'

'To Italy.'

'It must be wonderful there, but what about the Court?'

'The Court has grown dreary since the king gave up dancing and no longer laughs at coarse jests. His bastard's beautiful instructress preaches a virtue in a gentle voice and he likes to dally with her. The Montespan is now in the same position as the dreary La Vallière once found herself in and is puce with rage.'

'She deserves it.'

'I shall inform the king that the sudden death of my eldest son has distressed me so much that I have fallen ill; the doctors have ordered me to visit an Italian spa.'

'Monsieur the Comte de Racon has to take the waters,' laughed Martin. 'Do you remember the bath you took in Brayonne?'

'I shall never forget it. Colonel du Lac can easily deputise for me until June.'

'Shall we be away so long?'

'Yes, and then I shall buy you an estate and ask the king to raise you to the nobility.'

'That will be wonderful. I hope they will not torment my dwarf. I shall write on his behalf to Captain de Falleron and ask that he be given leave until my return.'

'Don't you think we should get up now?' asked the count.

Martin slipped from the bed and tidied his clothes. 'How is your arm?'

'I can hardly feel it. For some strange reason you didn't kick me once during the night.'

'You must stay in bed. I'll send Pierre for Dr Borel.'

Pierre stuck his head through the door, and Martin blushed. 'Monsieur, the fellow has been listening.'

'He always does. Keep your mouth shut, Pierre.'

'M. le Comte, I'm off to fetch the doctor,' said Pierre with a grin.

THE ITALIAN JOURNEY

THE count's arm did not fester badly, but the wound did not heal for several weeks and it was not until the beginning of April that they could set out on the Italian journey they had planned. They left Grandval with little baggage, four grooms and two servants. Hardly had they left the boundaries of the estate than the hitherto rather solemn friends grew so exuberant that their escort almost lost respect for them. But they knew the couple from the war, and wisely maintained their military bearing at the rear of the column while their masters rode ahead, chasing each other and knocking off each other's hats.

The count did not stay in the same place for more than two or three days, but pressed on impatiently to the south. Occasionally they travelled in company, escorting the coaches of ladies of quality and fighting with robbers as they had fought against the enemy in the war. Martin was enchanted by the bright countryside of southern France, and as excited as a child by the unexpected novelty and the colourful transformation of spring. He spoke of Raoul, as though he were with them in spirit, and often insisted that he was looking forward to Rome because his dead friend would have been so happy there.

Then a fast messenger overtook them, bringing a letter from the countess. His wife wrote that he should return with all possible speed, because Baron d'Epponcourt had arrived with his second wife and Marguerite, and refused to recognise the dissolution of the marriage contract. He had the law on his side and maintained that the contract was valid and binding. The count made light of the matter and wrote a letter to his wife, telling her to engage a lawyer, and insisting that the contract was now no longer in force since it affected M. Guy de Brayonne and not the Vicomte de Clarmont. He sent his regards to the Abbé d'Oubray, since the countess had announced the arrival of her guest, and despatched the messenger back to Grandval.

They reached the sea at the end of May, and Martin was wildly excited by the brilliant blue and the warmth of the water. As Martin did not wish to leave the coast, they travelled as much as possible along the shore so that Martin could bathe whenever he felt inclined. The count bathed only at midday, and usually sunned himself while Martin splashed about among the rocks or in the sand. Martin did not wish to disturb the count, but he had discovered that it was a joy to wrestle with the elder man. At every opportunity he insisted on a trial of strength. Despite their difference in build they were equally matched, and the outcome of the contest could never be foreseen. The count suggested that, for a change, Martin should wrestle with some of the grooms, but the dirty creatures smelt so strongly of garlic that he refused to wrestle with anyone except the count, who in vain pleaded his forty-six years. When he was recovering from a hard-won victory or a swift defeat, Martin looked for starfish, mussels and crabs, swam about in the sea or joined some fishermen to help them pull in their heavily-laden nets and admire the catch. Sometimes he would put to sea with them, and was once caught in a storm. He had to suffer the anxious count's anger and was forbidden to go out in a boat again.

Martin said he was now twenty-one and a major, and could perfectly well look after himself. They argued the matter, with the result that Martin was allowed to go out in a sailing boat, while the count, and two girls who had now joined their escort, rode along the shore. Martin stayed in the boat until the cliffs grew steeper and the rocks prevented his landing whenever he pleased. The friends then followed a mule track, were inseparable once more, and spent but little time with the girls whom the count dishonestly but politely called 'our ladies', while Martin simply referred to them as 'our necessities'. The two girls made no further attempt to arouse any deep feelings in their patrons and managed skilfully to find their own enjoyment.

They continued their journey along the coast to the south, and reached Rome at the height of summer. The city had been abandoned by society to the broiling sunlight. The count wanted to travel further south, but Martin gave him no peace until he had at least visited the most famous churches and had bestowed a pious kiss on St Peter's bronze toe. He asked the count for the return of part of his loan, secretly made a contribution to St Peter's, and hung his most valuable sword, as an offering, on the church altar. The count pointed out to him the beauty of the fountains and the statues, and this began to arouse a feeling for art in the young man. Then came news of an outbreak of typhus, and they fled from the city to the sea. The count was fortunate enough to buy two magnificent Arab horses. The friends were busy for some days schooling them, and kept postponing their journey from day to day.

On the white sandy beach at Ostia, between the pines and the rolling sea, the two friends raced at full gallop, naked, bareback, their hair flying in the wind. They kept as far as possible to the small strips of sand between the pools, which gave their horses' hooves a firm surface, jumping over the shallows, throwing up the silver spray and encouraging their beasts with wild cries. Not until the race had been clearly won by the count, and Martin could no longer make up the ever-increasing distance between them, did the victor rein in his sweating horse and look over his head with a flashing smile. 'Monsieur,' said Martin, 'Pollux is the better horse.'

'I told you so. Shall we exchange mounts?'

They dismounted, and the count handed Martin the snaffle of the winning black stallion. 'There, he's yours, my friend.'

'Monsieur . . .'

'I don't want any protests . . .'

'Your gift is too princely. Please remember that, to the outside world, I am still only the bourgeois Lieutenant Saint-Jean. With such a magnificent steed I shall be embarrassed by being taken for a nobleman of your rank.'

'And do you think it would be pleasant for me to see you riding about like a poor lieutenant? You are my ambulant guilty conscience.'

'I don't want to be that.'

'But you are, whether you like it or not.'

'Please disassociate me from your conscience.'

'How can I?'

'Forget that I am your son, and look upon me only as a friend.'

'Do you no longer want to be my son?'

'Monsieur, I should have the same feelings for you if we were not related. Let us throw our relationship to the winds for the duration of our journey.'

'That is a crazy idea.'

'As far as I'm concerned, there are many things far more crazy. Have you never thought that many an aristocrat must have been sired by a handsome lackey or a lusty stable lad? One sees and hears a great deal in Paris.'

'Are you casting a slur on our female ancestors?'

'No, I didn't mean it like that. I only wanted to curb the exaggerated stress you lay on origin, so that you won't continue to be troubled by your conscience.'

The count stretched out his hand. 'Give me your reins. Thank you.' He swung himself up on the second horse and rode at walking pace to the pine wood, making for home. Martin lengthened the stirrups of the black horse and trotted after the count.

'Are you offended, Monsieur?'

'No, not if you accept Pollux.'

'Thank you very much for the horse, then,' Martin replied quickly. The count bowed, but there was no smile on his face. The horses loped along. They stretched their necks, were reined in once more and champed gently at their bits.

'Very well,' said the count. 'I will forget our relationship and permit you, as my friend, to use the familiar form of address as is customary.'

Martin gave a start. 'No, no. There's no reason for that.'

'The familiarity will only hold good for the journey.'

'I beg you to spare me this temporary honour.'

'Say "tu" to me whenever you feel inclined.'

'For how long does that hold good?'

'For ever.'

'Very well. I am happy to use it, my friend.'

They embraced each other; the horses reared and had to be quieted. Martin trotted in a circle, returned to the count and said: 'I'd like you to give me the rest of my money this evening, so that I can give you a present in return.'

'What do you want to give me?'

'You'll see.'

'I'll give you your money.'

'Oh, I'm so delighted with Pollux,' cried Martin. 'Let's ride into the sea.'

The count laughed and patted his mount's gleaming neck. 'You go for a swim on your own. This heat arouses my desire for my lady.'

'I will accompany you to her castle.'

They turned towards the sea and galloped along the wet sand, which left no trace of their horses' hooves. Upon nearing Ostia, they turned off into a pine forest where their servants and the girls were lying contentedly in the shade. Charles and François took their horses, the count led his girl into the bushes, while Martin ran across the hot sand into the glittering ocean. He flung himself into the waves, dived and began to swim like a fish.

That evening, the count and Martin visited a cardinal, whose villa was the meeting place of every art connoisseur. He owned magnificent antique sculptures and a collection of rare, precious gems, which he was only too pleased to show to visitors. Martin found an opportunity of having a few private words with this ancient prince of the church, and asked him the address of an honest jeweller. The cardinal smiled at the ingenuousness of this request, and said that with a connoisseur every jeweller was honest but sold imitation stones to the others. Was he thinking of buying a piece of jewellery? Martin acquiesced and named the sum he wished to pay. The old cardinal said that, in such a case, he must be very wary. The following day he was to visit the Holy Father. If the lieutenant cared to accompany him, he would show him a jeweller's on the way. Martin was only too pleased to accept his invitation and arrived punctually the following morning. The cardinal offered him a place in his coach next to a deacon, and condescended to discuss all manner of worldly affairs with him.

The young man's intelligent honesty delighted him, and he laughed loudly when Martin confessed that he could see nothing beautiful in marble buttocks when everything else was missing. Why did they not at least restore the broken-off noses to the heads? 'Because no one knows where the noses are,' replied the priest.

In Rome, the cardinal stopped at a jeweller's, entered with Martin and ordered the merchant to bring out his most valuable wares. Martin chose a ring with a single large diamond, and as soon as the cardinal had tested the genuineness of the stone, the deal was made. Martin thanked him and wanted to ride home, but the old gentleman enjoyed his society and took him to the Vatican, where Martin, together with a band of pilgrims, received the papal blessing.

Late that evening, he returned to the count and handed him his gift. The count was speechless, and took the jewel, which fitted the ring finger of his left hand perfectly. Martin said that it was the right place, and that the diamond went well with his signet ring. The count examined his be-jewelled hand and let the precious stone play in the candlelight. Martin suddenly grew anxious that his present might not be in good taste, but the count assured him that the ring was so beautiful that he would never again take it off. He made every effort to hide his emotion and thanked Martin profusely. But the latter suspected that it was too valuable a present, and the count realised that his friend had read his mind.

Now they travelled further south. France was forgotten. The count sang Italian airs to his lute. Martin also tried to sing but he was seldom in tune. In vain, the count begged him to spare his sensitive ear, but Martin insisted that the only way he could express his pleasure was by making a noise. The count thereupon bought him a flute, and on some sunny rock at dawn, or in the evening, tried to teach him how to play it. Martin blew for all he was worth, but had so little ear that the count soon lost patience and gave up his lessons. Then, one morning, he surprised the count by playing a solemn air based on only four notes. The count listened for a long while unobserved, and when Martin noticed him, asked where he had learned the melody. Martin admitted that it was his own composition and that he was playing it in honour of the sunrise. The count suggested that he would do better to practise a shepherd song. Martin insisted that too many notes confused him, and that he played as best he could. The count said no more.

They arrived at Naples. With a large party of ladies and gentlemen, they climbed Vesuvius, and Martin was convinced that he was looking at the gateway to hell. In his curiosity, he approached as close as possible to the crater and returned to the count coughing violently, only to receive a cursing for his irresponsibility. The ladies present, however, regarded Martin as a hero and made a fuss of him at the Neapolitan Court, where the count was presented by the French ambassador.

After a round of gaiety, sailing and hunting, the friends wanted to be alone again and travelled leisurely along the coast to the south, until one day they reached some ruined Greek temples by the flat sea shore. The count said that they were more beautiful than Rome and Venice, and Martin swore that he did not wish to go any further.

That evening, the two friends sat on the warm, mossy steps of the largest ruined temple, the honey-coloured Doric pillars of which still bore a pediment, and watched the sunset. On the horizon, a violet veil of mist descended upon the spangled water, towards which the sun slowly sank. A star appeared high in the blue sky, and the torrid heat of the day died. Martin stood up and, in a sudden outburst of melancholy, cried: 'I cannot bear this vastness.'

'What do you mean by that?' asked the count. 'Did you stay too long in the sun today?'

'No, the magic is now past.'

'What kind of magic?'

'A moment ago you were still everything. What a pity we are humans and have to remain imprisoned in our bodies! I feel like yelling until I could be heard in Africa!'

A smile appeared on the Pan-like face. 'Hold fast to the evening star and lean against me.'

Bewildered, Martin looked for the star, moved down one step and laid his head against his friend's knee. The count laughed silently, and asked as seriously as possible: 'Can you pull yourself together, or must I help you?'

'Lay your hand on my hair.'

The count tugged it. 'Can you still spy the evening star?'

Martin raised his head and looked up into the mocking brown face that contrasted darkly with a yellow pillar in the light of the setting sun. 'Won't you be my father again for a moment?'

The count said with great dignity: 'It is a dangerous thing when a hermit crab slips out of his house. Then he is vulnerable and without protection. I offer him a fine, new, speckled house and guard him while he changes shells.'

Martin had to laugh. 'Please go on talking.'

'I'll tell you a fairy story:

'Pan once took a fancy to a goatherd and taught him to play his pipes. The lad loved the music and asked the god for the instrument. But Pan would not give it to him and returned to the forest. Since then, the shepherd cried: "Come to me, Pan," and neglected his herd. I am afraid that one day, when you get back to France, I shall hear you say: "I wish I had never gone to Italy." '

'No, Pan, you will never hear that from me,' Martin contradicted him eagerly. 'Every morning since we left Grandval I have been amazed that heaven allowed me to go on such a wonderful journey. It would be ungrateful and unreasonable of me if I did not want to return to France.'

'Why the melancholy then?'

'Because I cannot discover the peak of our friendship. Have you no knowledge, or are you concealing it from me?'

'I am no hand at philosophising.'

'That is why you are as wise as the pagan god Pan, and know better than I what is worth your while and good for me.'

'You may be right, my boy.'

The count removed a tiny red blossom from Martin's hair; it may have fallen from the luxuriant weeds on the pediment. 'When you are quiet and peaceable, I never feel better than with you. Make yourself comfortable.'

Martin turned round, raised himself and rested against his friend's knee. 'Can I stay like that?'

'Yes, now you can watch the evening stars.'

He stared at the glittering sea. The sun had drawn close to the horizon and was now a fiery golden ball.

'I had given up hoping for perfect happiness,' whispered Martin, 'but now I have found it. The bright serenity of the stars banishes all confusion. I feel that we have sloughed our skins and are part of each other. I am at peace.'

The sun set, and the after-glow tinged the sea with scarlet. A cool breeze sprang up, making the grass on the shore bow its head, and whipping the calm sea into silver spangles.

Martin felt a slight movement on the part of the count. Without looking up he said: 'Is something amusing you?'

'I'm waiting for a mosquito to sting me or a flea to bite me,' replied the count, 'for happiness always seems to end in that way.'

'Mother of God,' shouted Martin, jumping into the air. 'Just listen to him. It's the man's own fault that I love him madly once again!'

After a short while the count rose to his feet: 'What do we do now?'

'I should like to go and eat,' said Martin gaily. 'Then we could come back and see the temple by moonlight and sleep between the pillars.'

'We'll do that if it is not too damp.'

They left the temple. Overhead, the stars had appeared in all their hosts, and they walked along the sands to the fishermen's huts where they found their horses, the servants and the girls. The last purple gleam vanished on the sea.

The next morning, while the temple still lay in the milky light of the sun's first rays, they set out on their homeward journey. Before reaching Naples, they made the acquaintance of two gentlemen from Wurttemberg who spoke abominable French; they asked the count whether they could travel in his company for safety's sake. They were fond of a good jest and were both hard drinkers. The count gambled with them, won their money but as the result of Martin's constant reproaches, let them win back a part of their losses. They parted company in Rome and it was obvious that the gentlemen from Wurttemberg were very pleased to be rid of the two volatile Frenchmen.

The count knew several princely families in Rome, made a round of visits, and was invited every day to some palace or other. Although he was not particularly cultured, he was a past-master at holding a witty and amusing conversation with those whom he wished to impress, and the French embassy soon had to thank him for some very useful information. Despite his ugliness, he had even more success with the Italian ladies than with the French, and had to fight two duels with younger rivals, behind the Roman tombs. Martin landed in the maternal arms of a somewhat faded beauty and was annoyed when, for some reason, the count suddenly decided to leave in a hurry. Their departure seemed in the nature of a flight, and they rode almost without a halt to Milan, arriving there in the last days of August. The count wanted to cross the Alps into France before winter, but could not tear himself away from Italy. He rented a villa on a beautiful lake, so that he could spend a few more carefree days there with Martin.

One warm, late summer night, Martin rowed the count out to the centre of the lake and then shipped his oars. The count, who had settled down comfortably in the bottom of the boat, pricked up his ears. 'I hear music.'

'It comes from the brightly-lit villas over there,' replied Martin.

'Yes, but I can't make out the tune.'

'Would you like to go to a party?' asked Martin.

'No. I have enough of them ahead of me in Paris and Versailles.'

The count sat up. 'I've been thinking things over in the past few days. Old du Terne gets richer every year because he supplies the army with corn. But he's been unlucky with his new stud farm because he understands too little about horses. That's something you understand. Do you think you could run a stud farm on my estates if I gave you some experienced help?'

'Yes, Monsieur, but I am sure that your experienced people would not need me.'

'Well, I need an honest overseer, so that they can't get up to any mischief.'

'Do you think that a lieutenant of the Guards would enjoy being an overseer?'

'I shall ask for leave for you until next autumn, and should be very grateful if you would organise my stud farm during that time.'

'I don't want to go to Grandval but to join the Guards.'

'I am sending you officially to Grandval.'

'On duty?'

'Yes, on duty, and there is no argument, for the stud is to provide the army with remounts. I forbid you to leave the de Racon county.'

'Monsieur, that means banishment.'

'Please do not raise your voice. I have little hope of bringing about a successful reconciliation between you and Guy, and I want to feel assured of your safety. During your stay in the country I shall buy you an estate which carries a name and a title, but I must ask you not to betray my intentions to anyone, so that my plan cannot be thwarted. If you are questioned, you need only reply that, in the lifetime of the first vicomte, I had intended to ennoble you at his request, but that on his death I changed my mind, so that you now have no hope of receiving a title. Say it rather sadly, so that no one can suspect you of harbouring any dangerous ambitions. Your elevation must be a complete surprise. No, don't interrupt me. If a reconciliation is brought about—which I very much doubt—you shall serve for a year with the Guards. If it does not succeed, I shall pull strings to get you a high military post in a frontier garrison. Reconcile yourself to both these alternatives, and console yourself with the prospect of an estate and title.'

'Monsieur, is my future to depend upon the favour or disfavour of your son?'

'I have to make it dependent upon that because the Vicomte de Clarmont is my heir. As soon as war breaks out again, you will naturally ride at my side in the field.'

'Won't the vicomte go to war?'

'Yes, but not under me. He will serve as an engineer officer on Vauban's staff.'

'Is that certain?'

'Yes.'

Martin looked up at the sky. 'Monsieur, I believe in a God who made all these stars and who embodies the entire world. He will not let me fall, yet I wish we were at war today.'

'Be patient. Louis will soon set the land aflame. He thirsts for fame, and the peace of Nijmegen brought him great advantages but no decisive victory. The king needs victories to slake his thirst for glory.'

Martin lowered his oars into the water. 'It's time to row back,' said the count. 'I'm shivering, there is dew on my coat.'

Martin rowed in silence and the count returned to his place in the stern of the boat.

At that moment, a small, well-lit galley put out from the shore. Martin paid no attention to the elegant ship and merely checked his course from time to time. The galley approached slowly and they heard a French air. 'What an enchanting voice,' said the count, raising his head. 'It sounds like a boy's, but I'm certain it's a woman singing.'

'It may be a castrato,' said Martin.

'No, castrati only sing in the theatre. It is a young but unhappy voice. I should like to see the singer. Make for the galley.'

The song died away as Martin obeyed. The count sat on the thwart, took his lute and began to sing.

'*Sailing girl, come sail to me,*
Silver fish I catch you see.
Many a silver fish have I,
Turn your ship, and then come nigh.
A gold and silver fish I'll give thee,
And even my ship, if you're sweet to me.'

Their boat had now drawn close to the galley, and a small figure jumped to its feet on the foredeck. Bright jewels gleamed in her modish dress and her pretty locks were ablaze with diamonds. A pair of huge, dark-blue eyes, set wide apart, peered into the night. 'Blanche!' said Martin, letting go both oars. The oarsmen in the galley drew closer. Blanche recognised the count in the boat and fell back on her yellow silk cushions, deathly pale. A wizened old man anxiously caught hold of her hand, which she swiftly withdrew. Louis de Salvieux and a young lady bent over her anxiously. Then the galley passed, and the two men in the rowing boat could only see its stern light.

The count was the first to break the silence. 'The four of them are on their honeymoon, and the old man has to pay the piper. So Louis got his countess. Quite a pretty creature.'

'Who was the old man?'

'Boquelin, the banker.'

'Louis has sold his sister to him.'

'That is the fate of pretty sisters.'

'My God, my God!'

'Don't be so miserable and row me to shore. I'm freezing.'

'Monsieur, the galley came from the Villa Silvani. The banker must be living there. I will visit Louis tomorrow.'

'All right, but be careful. Louis will know whom you want to see.'

'He will have to introduce me to Madame Boquelin.'

'Yes, and he will be obliged to pay me a visit. I should like to meet his young wife.'

'Monsieur, Blanche is now setting her hopes on you.'

'I hope that you will succeed in ousting me from her favour without the old man putting poison in your soup. Lovers are inclined to lose their heads. Be careful, Martin.'

Martin rowed with all speed to the bank, and crashed the boat into the stone steps. 'Hell, was that really necessary?' asked the count. Martin did not reply and was the first to jump ashore. Lackeys secured the boat and the two men went up to the brilliantly lit salon, between their two rooms, which occupied the entire front of the villa. Martin bowed to the count and retired to his room without a word.

At this moment, in France it was raining. The Comtesse de Racon sat by the fire in her salon playing chess with the Abbé d'Oubray. She watched impassively how her opponent hesitantly withdrew his castle, only to return it to its former position. D'Oubray noticed her attention and asked with a smile: 'Since when have you watched my moves with such eagerness, Madeleine? Do you really find this game so interesting?'

'I was only looking at your hand.'

'Don't you know it yet?'

The countess picked up a lost chessman and placed it on her knee. 'Don't ask me, Etienne.'

'Why, Madeleine?'

The countess frowned. 'Must I continually tell you that I can't answer you?'

'I merely asked you if you did not know my hand yet.'

'But you always ask the same questions.'

'And you never reply.'

'Etienne, do not force me.'

'Madeleine, I promised that I would lay aside my habit for love of you. Would you listen to me if, to outward appearances, I belonged to the world once more?'

'I can promise you nothing. I do not like to think that you would lay aside your habit for the sake of a woman. Do not become an apostate on my account.'

'Madeleine, parting from you made me decide to become a priest.'

'It should have been a vocation, Etienne. I'm afraid you are even less serious than Gaston . . . and perhaps less honest.'

'That is very unkind of you.'

The countess placed the piece back on the table. 'You have almost converted me to Jansenism, which differs little from my own faith. But when I asked you to take me to the Port-Royal convent, so that I could have an opportunity of speaking to those scholarly nuns, you told me that neither the king nor the Pope looked kindly upon Jansenism, and that it had long since been declared a heresy. I was to take a few more steps under your guidance before reaching the true faith. You were playing with my soul.'

'No, Madeleine. I was trying to lead you by a roundabout way to salvation. The paths to truth are seldom straight.'

'Etienne, we have agreed not to quarrel any more about our faith. I have recovered my inner convictions by reading the gospels, and need no authority apart from God and my own conscience.'

'A christian must not be proud but humble; even Protestantism asserts that.'

'Gaston has never taken my pride amiss.'

'He asked me to convert you.'

'Yes, because he would reap great benefit from my conversion.'

'Madeleine, I hoped to be your saviour.'

'My need is not as great as you think.'

The countess smiled gently at the abbé's disconsolate face and leaned her head against the chair. 'Can you hear the rain? I have listened to it for many years. It is soft and peaceful and often comforts me. You sit beside me and your foot brushes mine, yet there is a glass wall between us and I am as lonely as ever.'

'Shall I break down the glass wall, Madeleine?'

'You may try, Etienne.'

'That is a challenge.'

'Yes, but I will commit neither treachery nor sin.'

'He gave you your freedom.'

'That is true, and he looked terrible when he did it. I think he had just fought a duel with Martin Saint-Jean, whom he loves. He looked like a lost soul. What did I matter to him then? Now Martin is his friend again and I'm not sure that he would willingly part with me to someone else. It is a problem which I spend my life trying to solve.'

'The most enigmatical men are often the shallowest, Madeleine.'

'I would give a great deal to be with him now,' she replied softly. 'I would ask him whether he is really indifferent to me.'

'I am absolutely convinced that he is. Everything base wishes to deny the existence of the sublime, or, if that does not work, to forget it. He would find your presence unwelcome.'

'Yes, it might be so, unless I confessed my lies. Your dead sister advised me to. If only I had followed Angélique's advice. In those days he would perhaps have forgiven me. Today he would no longer do so. I am irrevocably caught in my network of lies and they will weigh heavily upon me to the grave.'

'But you told me the truth.'

'Yes, but you are not my husband.'

He tried to take her hand, but she recoiled

'Don't touch me.'

'What is the matter?'

'I cannot love your hands!'

Terrified by her own words, she placed her hands on her lips. D'Oubray rose to his feet. 'I shall leave tomorrow, Madame,' he said with a bow, and left the salon.

The countess sat there as though frozen to stone. She began to tremble. Then she laid her head on the table, beat her forehead against the chess board and began to weep desperately.

In Italy, Martin lay wide-awake in his moonlit bedroom. The count came in, approached hesitantly and stood there for a moment. 'Martin, I have not come to tell you anything new.'

Martin merely moved his lips and then compressed them more tightly. 'You'd better try and get some sleep.' Martin nodded. He tried to catch the count's eye as he stood there with his back to the moon. 'Perhaps I should have told you of my decision before we left France,' he said unsteadily. 'I could not suspect that you would see Blanche today.' Martin's face quivered. 'Do you want to be alone?'

'Don't leave me on account of Guy,' Martin said with an effort.

'I shall never leave you. Even if we had to part, I shall always meet you again somewhere.'

'Swear that to me on your honour.'

'Yes. I swear it to you on my honour.'

In the Villa Silvani, Blanche was kneeling at her bedside, praying fervently. From the next room echoed the loud snores of the old banker who, on account of his asthma, had to sleep in an armchair. Through the tall, open window the little waves could be heard lapping against the stone steps.

At about ten o'clock next morning, Martin rode to the Villa Silvani and found the occupants at breakfast surrounded by a menagerie of dogs, cats, parrots and monkeys. Louis de Salvieux seemed pleased, and courteously introduced his boyhood friend to the company. Martin was offered a chair, which he accepted. A puppy immediately started to nibble at his shoe, and Gaston, the little monkey, climbed on to his shoulder.

Blanche removed him with a smile. The unaccustomed sound of her voice made him tremble. He found her more beautiful than ever and took the greatest pains not to stare at her constantly. Louis asked after the health and whereabouts of the count. Martin replied as simply as possible, asking questions in return, while the old man looked at him suspiciously. Martin noticed that the young Comtesse de Salvieux was very friendly to Blanche, and that Louis was at his sister's beck and call. She took a plate of fruit from his hands, fed the monkey with some grapes and then expressed a wish to go and pick roses.

The company finished their meal and, surrounded by a swarm of animals, went into the well-tended garden where a few roses were still in bloom on the stone walls. Blanche picked a bouquet. The monkey imitated her, pricked his paw on the thorns and began to whimper. Blanche handed the roses to her brother and bandaged the animal's little paw with a silk ribbon. Louis never left her side, thus preventing any word being exchanged between her and Martin. The banker followed with the Comtesse de Salvieux, sweeping the dead leaves from the parapet into the water with his ivory cane. The lake was calm, and resembled a sky-blue mirror.

They returned indoors and Blanche sent for a vase. When she began to arrange the blossoms on a beautiful mosaic table, the monkey once more tried to help. Blanche lifted the vase to display its beauty, and accidentally let it fall on the flagstones. The tinkle of broken glass frightened the monkey and it fled up one of the curtains. Martin hurried over and, as he bent down to pick up the roses, Blanche whispered the count's name. As he returned the flowers to her, Martin whispered that he would come that night by boat to the smaller staircase. The girl gave him a grateful look and made a great fuss about the broken vase. The old banker promised to replace it with a silver one. Martin took his leave, and Louis de Salvieux saw him to his horse.

That afternoon, Louis de Salvieux paid a courtesy visit to the Comte de Racon and, in the name of the banker, invited him and Martin to supper. The count said mockingly that he had to think it over whether the good Boquelin should be saddled with this extra burden. Louis laughed, and said with glee that the old moneybags was mad on entertaining noble guests and was still rich enough to buy himself a duchy. The count accepted the invitation.

The three men rode to the Villa Silvani and were given a princely reception. The table was decorated with the rarest blossoms; the most expensive delicacies had been provided for their enjoyment, and the ladies glittered in all the splendour of their jewels. The count immediately began to pay gallant court to the young countess. Louis watched him closely and had no time to keep an eye on his sister, who was thus able to exchange a few harmless words with Martin. Blanche almost lost control of herself and looked far too often at the count; when he serenaded the young countess after the meal, and took his lute and sang, she turned so pale that M. Boquelin thought she had been taken ill. He called for her maid and tried to loosen her bodice, but she struck his gouty fingers with a silver spoon and recovered her composure. Martin had the presence of mind to say that the count loved play-acting. The girl sighed with relief and gave him a grateful smile. The conversation then turned to the poison trials which had been taking place in Paris since April. One case brought to light another hundred, and the highest in the land were indicted. Paris was in terror, and even the king quaked at Versailles. It was whispered that he had to protect the Montespan from the chief of police, who spared no one and was incorruptible. The count left at ten o'clock. As he took his leave, he kissed the hand of the Comtesse de Salvieux, and then the hand of his hostess, who once more turned pale.

On the ride home, he remarked to Martin that the Comtesse de Salvieux had sweaty hands and a blotchy skin, and that Blanche's behaviour had been most embarrassing. He would not visit the Villa Silvani again, and they would be leaving next morning. Martin replied that he had some business to attend to, and that the count should wait up for him. 'Why?' asked the count. To avoid answering any further questions, Martin rode over with François to a fisherman and ordered the lad to hold the horses. Hiring a boat, he rowed in the shadow of the bank to the Villa Silvani.

The count was playing his lute in his bedroom when he heard a sudden splash of oars on the lake. He went into the dimly-lit salon and, a moment later, Martin appeared with a small, veiled figure. The count looked displeased. 'What does this mean, Martin?'

'Monsieur, you have a visitor.' There was such a pleading expression in Martin's brown eyes that the count bowed to the lady. 'Madame, you are too reckless and you must return to your husband immediately. Martin, I took you to be more intelligent.'

Martin took Blanche by the hand and tried to say something, but suddenly became tongue-tied. The count had to laugh and, with as much severity as he could muster, said: 'You're standing there like a couple of naughty children. Get back to your boat immediately.'

'Monsieur,' said Martin. 'You have a promise to keep to this lady. I will come and fetch her later.'

'What are you thinking of?'

'Monsieur, you must not disappoint Blanche. You really mustn't.'

A sound of shrill girlish laughter came from the back rooms, and then Pierre's raised voice. The count drew Blanche into his bedroom and swiftly closed the door. The girl unveiled her pale face. 'Madame,' the count said angrily, 'do you realise what great danger you are in? You have jeopardised your good reputation. The old man can throw you out, and your brother would have to challenge me.'

'Monsieur, I have come to you because you told me that I could do so after my marriage.'

'No one takes such things seriously, Madame Boquelin. You are a lady and know what that entails.'

'I am only Blanche.'

'You are a silly child. Veil yourself and come with me,' he said, cautiously opening the salon door. 'Martin!' But his friend was nowhere to be seen. The count looked out at the lake, but the boat had disappeared. The sound of splashing died away along the bank. 'Martin!' There was no reply. The count returned to his room and offered Blanche a chair.

'The boy's gone. You will have to wait for him. Take my lute and play on it to pass the time. Goodnight.' He was about to leave the room when Blanche fell to the floor with a cry. He turned round, lifted her up, carried her over to the bed and, after a moment's hesitation, sat down beside her.

'Be reasonable, my child. I can't steal you from the old man.'

'I know that, Monsieur. I thought that you, too, would have been pleased to see me. Please forgive my mistake.'

'When were you married?'

'In June.'

'Have you given yourself since then to any other admirer?'

'I have been waiting for this moment.'

The count observed her white face, the large pathetic eyes and the pale lips. 'One sees by your mouth that it has long remained silent. Does the old man kiss you?'

'Only my hands and feet. I allow him nothing.'

'Doesn't he insist upon his rights?'

'If he makes the slightest gesture I behave like a mad woman. I have my own bedroom and he is not allowed to come near my bed.'

'This marriage cannot be easy for you.'

'Oh yes, he does everything I wish.'

'Yes, as long as he doesn't suspect that any man is hanging around you. Dotards can become very malicious.'

'That's what Louis always says. I am careful.'

'Supposing your absence tonight is noticed . . .?'

'My maid is lying in my bed. Her hair is dark like mine and she promised to lie on her stomach. He sometimes looks in at me when he cannot sleep.'

'Let us hope he can sleep tonight.'

'Do you really wish that?'

'Yes, because I'm sorry for you.'

'Thank you, Monsieur,' said Blanche, with a sob in her throat.

'Please don't start to weep.'

'I am not weeping. I know that you don't like it.'

'Blanche, why don't you love Martin? He is still as much in love with you as he was before.'

'Martin is only my brother.'

'I should have looked upon you as a daughter.'

'Then I should have thought that every man was like the

Marquis de Chassigny! I was happy with you and I still belong to you. That is what I wanted to say to you tonight. There is much I wanted to tell you, now that I can speak.'

Blanche clenched her fists and bit her lips.

'What did you want to say to me?' asked the count.

The girl summoned up a smile. 'I wanted to tell you that you were very good to me. When I came to you, I thought that you were more terrifying than the marquis. I tried to hide, but you found me immediately. You laughed, took me on your lap and asked me whether I could crack nuts with my teeth; then you said that you had bought a nutcracker for me and would give it to me next day. Did I like nuts? I was terrified, and you said that my heart was beating too fast for such a small creature, and you set me down on a chair. Do you remember, you went out and returned with the monkey? That was the nutcracker, and he did his work perfectly. The monkey was very like me, you said, but I found that it also resembled you a little. You fastened it to the foot of the table with a chain. I plucked up courage and gave it a cushion. Then you laughed again, wished me a restful night with my new pet and left the room. I waited a long time to see if you would return, but you didn't.

'Next day, you said that the monkey stank appallingly and that I must keep it in my living-room. Then, because of the stench, you took me into your own bedroom and had your will of me. You were not terrifying like the marquis. You always pacified me when I was frightened and I lost my fear. Your friendly words made me love you. Please say something . . .'

'You tell charming stories.'

'I remember everything, Monsieur. When you fell asleep, you sometimes laid a hand on me and I fancied that you did it to protect me. You were never brutal or pinched me when I did not understand at once what you wanted of me. My brother and my sister-in-law are both friendly to me, and M. Boquelin gives me costly presents, but no one finds me droll and laughs at me, and there is no one whom I can cling to. Are you angry with Martin for bringing me here?'

'Yes, I am.'

'He only carried out my wishes.'

'He does not have to do what you want.'

'But I am very grateful to him.'

'I shall make him pay for it.'

'No, Monsieur, please don't. Without his help I should not be here.'

'You don't belong to me.'

'To whom then?'

'I don't know, my child.'

'Can I come to you when M. Boquelin is dead?'

'I am married, Blanche.'

'So you were in Paris.'

'At that time you were a toy, and now you are a lady.'

'I am still a toy, but M. Boquelin is not allowed to play with me. Can I come to you when he is dead, Monsieur?'

'Your brother would not allow it, and I do not want you as a mistress.'

'Would you allow me to be your wife's companion? I only want to be with you.'

'You can come as a guest, if your brother agrees.'

'He will have to agree, or I'll threaten to tell the story of my past. He is afraid of that. Promise that you will take me in when I come to you as a widow.'

'But M. Boquelin is in the best of health.'

'That can quickly be remedied, Monsieur.'

'What do you mean, Blanche?'

'I have procured something that will not agree with him.'

'Weren't you listening, Blanche, when M. Boquelin spoke about the poison trials? The chief of police lets no one escape and even indicts princesses of the blood.'

'M. Boquelin is a monster.'

'And you are thinking of becoming one. A murderess loses her charms.'

'Is that true?'

'Yes. You know the rumours about the king's mistress. She is the most beautiful woman in France, but the king has long since turned away from her. You were far sweeter when you were with me, and I feel no desire to kiss you.'

'Did you read my thoughts?'

'Not quite, but for some reason you no longer attracted me.'

'But, Monsieur, suppose M. Boquelin lives to be ninety?'

'Let him live to be a hundred.'

'I could not bear it.'

'As long as you can keep him at bay, it won't be too difficult.'

'I don't want to grow old with him.'

'At sixteen, you have plenty of time before you.'

'I am fifteen, Monsieur.'

'So much the better.'

'Monsieur, I will not harm my husband, but if I can't come to you any more, I'll take the poison myself.'

'Promise me that you will spare M. Boquelin.'

'Yes, I promise you.'

'Will you keep your word?'

'Yes, by my love for you.'

'Give me your hand on it, Blanche.'

Blanche gave him her hand and he held it tightly. 'Now you please me once more.'

Her face lit up. 'When can I come to you again?'

'Next winter.'

'Truly, Monsieur?'

'Yes. When there is no danger for you.'

'Monsieur, it will be easy in Paris. Louis is renting a house in the city and I can visit him there. He will have to keep silent when I slip out of the back door. We are travelling to Rome, but I shall be back at Christmas.'

'Will M. Boquelin be able to stand the winter journey?'

'I'll wrap him up in twenty fur coats.'

'You would do better to fall in love in Rome.'

'I know whom I love, Monsieur.'

'You understand nothing about love. You need a more suitable lover.'

'I need nothing except to be in your presence once a year. I am happy now, Monsieur. I only want to visit you now and then, and I will not stay long. I should like to go now.'

The count stood up. 'I'll go and see if that boy has returned.' He walked into the dark salon and called, 'Martin!' and then repeated his call to the water below. There was no reply. 'I'm sorry, Madame,' he said on his return, 'but you will have to wait. I should like to go to bed.'

Blanche immediately rose to her feet. 'You can call your valet, I can easily hide behind the curtains.'

'And when Pierre has left, what then?' he asked with a smile.

'I'll sit down on a chair and wait for Martin. I can play you to sleep with your lute.'

'Would you like to deputise for Pierre?'

Blanche blushed. 'Oh, yes.'

She stood on tiptoe to help the count out of his coat. To tease her, he stood erect to make things more difficult for her, and let himself be undressed. Blanche hung the jacket and waistcoat on a hanger, placed the shoes near the door and laid his hose and stockings on a chair. 'Do you want to take off anything else?'

'Not for the moment. I'll attend to you.'

'Oh, Monsieur!' Blanche was overwrought and began to cry.

The count sat down on the bed and took her on his lap like a child. 'You know I should never forgive myself if I missed such an opportunity.'

'Oh, Monsieur, I'm so glad that I didn't listen to any of those dandies.'

'Have you had many proposals, Blanche?'

'Yes, Monsieur, but none of them was like you.'

'How can you know if you did not try them out?'

'Monsieur, they were all either frankly insolent or terribly serious.'

'And what about me?'

'You are between the two. There is a twinkle in your eyes which is your saving grace. I'm quite content as long as you are fond of me; I am happy as long as I love you.'

'You dress is too ostentatious to be in good taste, and your perfume is too strong.'

'Shall I wash it off?'

'Yes.'

'Where is the water?'

'Over there in the bowl.' He let her stand up and removed the dress. Blanche hopped out of the gay brocade, slipped like a squirrel out of the three red silk petticoats, tiny shoes and pale-blue stockings and fine cambric shift, and placed them in a pile on a chair. Then she turned round and announced: 'Monsieur, I bathed in hot water and I am spotless.'

'Really!'

'It's true.'

'I believe you.'

Blanche washed her breasts and throat, and dried herself on her shift. 'Can you still smell the perfume?'

'Hardly. You have a good soap in the Villa Silvani.'

Blanche gave him a bright smile. 'Because I know that you lay store by it. What do you want me to do now?'

'Give me a kiss first.'

'But, Monsieur, you're still laughing and I shall only come up against your teeth.'

'I'll close my mouth.'

Blanche knelt at his bedside and embraced him, slipping her hands under his dark hair. When she kissed him he laughed aloud. 'You've learned nothing in the meantime. Oh, Blanche, how can one be so pretty and so faithful?'

'Do you want to kiss me now?'

'Yes, but lie down here first.'

'Above or under the blanket?'

'Above. I can hear the boat.'

'Do I have to get dressed?'

'No, there's plenty of time.'

'Are you pleased that I'm here now?'

'If I said so, I should compromise myself.'

'No, no, you would. I'm so happy, Monsieur.'

'I'm delighted to hear it. But aren't you afraid you might have a child?'

Blanche shook her head. 'The doctor said that I should probably never have one. Louis did not trust me and sent me to a doctor when I had a sore throat at the convent. I can't bear doctors.'

'Nor can I. Now be as quiet as a mouse.'

'Last night you sang a pretty little song, and I recognised your voice immediately. You sang about little ships and little fish.'

'If you don't keep quiet I'll bite your pretty lips. No, don't be afraid. Come on, I'll only kiss you. Close your eyes, Blanche.'

Blanche closed her eyes and made no further sound.

It was long past midnight when Martin knocked softly at the bedroom door. No sound could be heard from within. He knocked louder. Then he heard the count swearing sleepily. 'Monsieur, your visitor must leave now.'

'Wait, she's coming in a minute.'

Martin waited patiently, until Blanche appeared, weeping bitterly. 'Give me your hand,' he said with a bow, 'so that you don't fall.' He led the girl down the steps to the boat, helped her in and rowed along the bank. Blanche continued to weep a little, and then suddenly said quite gaily: 'I'm looking forward to Christmas in Paris. You'll bring me to him again, won't you?'

'I shan't be in Paris this winter.'

'Why not?'

'I have to set up a stud farm for him in the country.'

'Who will bring me to him, M. Saint-Jean?'

'He has reliable servants.'

'Will he send them to fetch me?'

'I don't know what you've arranged with him.'

'Please, M. Saint-Jean, remind him of me sometimes in your letters.'

'I will do as you ask. Speak more softly, Madame. Voices carry a long way on the water. There is no light burning in your house.'

'Then they're all asleep and they haven't missed me. Thank you, Monsieur.'

'Please be quiet.' The boat glided almost without a sound in the black shadow of the bank, past gardens and villas. Noisy, drunken laughter came from one of the palazzos. When Blanche began to tremble with cold, fear and exhaustion, Martin took off his coat and wrapped it round her. The stars paled and the first gleams of daybreak appeared in the east.

Martin stopped by some steps. The timbers of the boat scraped against the weatherbeaten stone. Blanche slipped off Martin's coat and hurried up the steps. Martin listened until he could no longer hear her soft steps. Then the steps returned. 'M. Saint-Jean!' she whispered anxiously.

'What is it?'

'There's a watchman outside the door.'

'I'm coming.' Martin tied the boat to a painted oak pillar, jumped out and drew his sword. Blanche pointed out the direction. He made every effort to be as quiet as possible, and soon caught sight of a figure in front of the side-door. He stopped and rustled his foot on the gravel. The watchman did not stir, and Martin discovered that he had mistaken an ornamental cypress for a man. He led Blanche past the tree to the door, to which she had a key. Martin opened it carefully and said. 'Madame, where is your room?'

'In the front, looking on to the lake.'

'Please throw something in the water, if you are undiscovered, to set my mind at rest.'

'Yes, M. Saint-Jean. Many thinks.'

Blanche slipped into the house. Martin returned quietly to the boat, untied it, and rowed slowly away. The, in the first gleams of dawn, he saw Blanche's bright figure by an open window, and heard a splash in the water as though a fish had leapt.

The count set out next morning on the homeward journey, as he had planned. Martin paid a short farewell visit on his behalf to the Villa Silvani; he did not see Blanche, who was still in bed. Louis was obviously relieved. The banker regretted that his latest noble acquaintance was leaving so soon, and expressed the hope that the Comte de Racon would honour him with a visit at the end of the year in Paris.

The two friends rode through the beautiful late-summer landscape and crossed the steep passes into France, which was already a blaze of autumn tints. No trace remained of the exuberance they had displayed on the outward journey. Martin was silent and reserved; the count was serious, though friendly. When they rested, he gave Martin lessons on the flute, showing admirable patience with the false notes played by his untalented but eager pupil, until eventually Martin could play a few simple airs without a mistake. The music seemed to bring him consolation.

They reached Paris in September, and learned, on their arrival at the Hôtel de Racon, that the Vicomte de Clarmont had left with the Court for Fontainebleau. This news both surprised and delighted the count. He found a pile of letters waiting for him, including a very recent one from his wife. He opened it and read:

MONSIEUR,

I hope that your whereabouts will be known at the Hôtel de Racon, and that this letter will reach you. Two of your previous letters came from Naples and Rome respectively. You wrote that you would be returning in August and I informed the Baron d'Epponcourt of this, since he pestered me with his enquiries. He arrived here with his wife and daughter on the 1st August, determined to settle a matter under litigation with you personally. I suggested that he should ride and meet you in Paris, but apparently his finances will not permit him to stay in the expensive capital. He continues to insist on the validity of the contract, and although he lost the first case against me, to his great expense, he insists upon lodging an appeal unless you give way. I should be very grateful if you would free me of these uninvited guests, because, on account of Guy, I am worried about my dead friend's child. He is in dire financial straits and comes here every two weeks to extort money from your steward with threats. I have pawned half my jewellery on his behalf. I hope that, on your return to France, you will come to Grandval as soon as you can.

MADELEINE

The next letter contained an invitation to his hunting lodge from the Marquis de Chassigny. The count read his correspondence, and was informed of the latest events by the steward. He learned that the Vicomte de Clarmont, in his father's name, had invited the Duc de Luxembourg to a large banquet, after which two silver knives and three gilt spoons were missing. He was speechless at Guy's bold enterprise and sent him a large sum of money to Fontainebleau. Then he wrote to his wife that he would shortly be returning home, and sent his most affectionate greetings to Baron d'Epponcourt, his wife and daughter.

Colonel du Lac was summoned to a long conference. The count rode with him and Martin to the regiment, spent four days on the parade ground, meted out rewards and punishments, and returned with Martin, whose leave was prolonged, to Paris, where he ordered himself clothes of the latest cut and called upon the Maréchal de Luxembourg to express his gratitude. Then he packed, and, in foul weather, rode with Martin to Grandval.

THE VICOMTE'S GREAT DANES

ON his arrival at Grandval, the count greeted his uninvited guests with the greatest courtesy and asked his wife for news of the Abbé d'Oubray. The countess replied that he had left six weeks before and would probably not be returning. What did that mean? Their outlooks were so different that a friendship would not possibly be of long duration. Had the friendship been of an intimate nature? The countess denied this, trying to read the expression in his black eyes, and the count refrained from any more questions. He remarked that the Baron d'Epponcourt's second wife looked like a black gipsy, and that the sixteen-year-old Marguerite had turned into a beauty. A conversation with the baron cleared the air. The baron was prepared to waive the contract if the count would agree to pay him a considerable sum in damages. As the fiancée of M. de Brayonne, Marguerite had refused several favourable offers of marriage, but at the moment had no prospects of a husband of her own rank, thus causing her parents great anxiety. The count made no objections to the baron's demand, but considered the sum he asked to be too high. Pitiless bargaining now began, which lasted for days on end.

Knowing his guests's passion for gambling, the count took every opportunity of inviting the baron to play cards. He paid his losses on the spot and contented himself with written acknowledgments of his winnings. The baron, in his excitement, and terrified by his second wife, who strongly opposed his vice, began to cheat without due care. Finally, the count handed him a pile of promissory notes and demanded immediate payment. The baron begged for time, because the sum involved was enormous. The count maintained that he had a dangerous creditor and could not wait any longer. The baron asked him to deduct it from the damages and, after two days, was only too pleased to be let off his gambling debts in full settlement.

The count forced him to make a written renunciation of his son-in-law and any damages, and announced to the baroness that he intended to give a banquet in her honour for all the local gentry. During the preparations he tried to win Marguerite's affections, but the girl found him so repulsive that he finally gave up his efforts.

Martin was constantly on the road, exploring the county for a favourable site for a stud farm. He rode from farmstead to farmstead, until he discovered an ideal spot near Château Fleury, and could then return to Grandval. The count was satisfied with his choice, and gave orders for the dilapidated stables to be repaired and additional stalls to be built. Martin asked the bailiff for builders, and wanted to live at Fleury so as to be able to supervise everything on the spot.

The count, however, invited him to the banquet, which was to be in the nature of a farewell feast, and Martin was pleased to be able to spend this short time with his friend before his departure.

The guests arrived in full complement. There was gambling, dancing and hunting. Martin renewed his acquaintance with Marguerite, who graciously let him ride at her side, and obviously preferred him to Baron du Terne's youngest unmarried son. The girl's pretty face and white skin reminded him of Blanche, and although he missed Blanche's dark eyes, he found the arrogant little lady's mocking grey eyes and her wealth of ash-blonde hair very charming.

On the fourth morning of the festivities, the horns sounded for the hunt. The count led his guests to their horses and coaches, and personally saw to the comfort of the most noble ladies. They suddenly noticed a group of horsemen in the avenue approaching at a swift trot. The leading and most resplendently dressed of the eight riders was none other than the Vicomte Guy de Clarmont, accompanied by five enormous Great Danes. He waved, set his horse to a gallop, careered past a coach into the courtyard, making some of the ladies flee to the steps, performed an impeccable levade, jumped out of the saddle and bowed twice, with courtly elegance, to the entire company. Martin saw him kiss his mother's hand, embrace his father and introduce his guests, who, in the meantime, had dismounted. The newcomers expressed a wish to take part in the hunt, and the count ordered fresh horses to be brought. The gentlemen mounted and the coaches got under way. The count trotted with Guy at the head of the procession. Martin rode beside the countess's coach in which several ladies were riding.

When the riders turned off across the stubble and galloped away, Martin spurred Pollux and rode up on the count's free side. He bowed to the vicomte. The count turned to him and said: 'What do you want?'

'Monsieur, where am I to stay while the Vicomte de Clarmont is at Grandval?'

'Stay here for the moment. I'll send for you this evening.'

'Guy, have you trained your dogs to hunt stag?'

'Yes, all types of quarry, except birds.'

Martin retired. The count cast a critical eye over the vicomte's elegant attire.

'That costume is too luxurious for travelling and is unsuited to the hunt.'

'It is very simple compared with my party clothes,' replied Guy.

'You offend good taste.'

'One only stands out if one shines.'

'But one should never want to shine.'

'Monsieur, hasn't everyone noticed that Saint-Jean rides a better horse than you do?'

'He won it in a wager. Are your debts very high?'

'I do not want to spoil your hunting by giving you a complete list of the items.'

'I'll discuss them with you this evening. Oh, there's Grouchet! I wonder what he has laid on. If a stag escapes into the heronry, I will have the beaters flogged. Can you hear the pack? Come on.' Spurring their horses, they galloped ahead of the other riders towards the beech forest where the foliage had already turned a russet-brown.

Martin joined the younger people, among whom was Marguerite on a dappled grey, at the side of du Terne's youngest boy. She scowled. The handsome young nobleman lent over to her and said: 'Mademoiselle, you deserve a far more handsome bridegroom. However fine his coat may be, his face is hideous. Leave him to my sister.'

'I don't grudge her anything, except his title.'

'Do titles mean so much to you then?'

'Yes, for without rank and money one has no entrée at Court.'

'Mademoiselle, your words have aroused my ambition.'

Martin said that he was *de trop* and sought other company.

The hunt progressed with varying success, and the toll of stags was heavy. The party breakfasted in a hunting lodge and did not return until nightfall to the castle, where an hour and a half was spent in changing clothes and titivating. The company eventually sat down to supper and, during the meal, enjoyed the songs of two Italian actresses. After supper, the elder guests played cards while the young began to dance. The count beckoned to the Vicomte de Clarmont, and the two men slipped unnoticed from the brilliantly-lit salon.

Once in his study, the count took Guy over to the fireplace and opened the conversation by saying: 'How high are your debts?'

'260,000, Father.'

'Isn't that rather a lot for a lieutenant of the Guards?' he replied calmly.

'I agree with you, Father, but I had to uphold your prestige by keeping up appearances at Court.'

'My prestige?'

'Your long absence harmed not only you, but me. There were whispers that you had been banished, and in some quarters I was cold-shouldered. I could think of no other alternative than to copy your handwriting and write my own recommendations, which finally procured me the entrée at Court. I'm convinced that I acted as you would have done, for, after my brother's death, you promised to introduce me at Court as your heir.'

'Yes, I promised you that.'

Guy bowed without rising from his seat. 'It is kind of you to remember it. I have the copies of your, or rather of my letters, so that you will not contradict me before the people in question. I chose the names of several spas at random, and hope that your health is now completely restored.' Guy took a bundle of letters from his gold-embroidered brocade coat and handed them to the count.

'One of the secretaries of the French Ambassador to the Court of Naples put me in the most invidious position on your account,' he continued. 'At Versailles, he told me the story of a diabolical-looking Comte de Racon who, with an equally crazy companion, climbed Vesuvius in order to see the poor souls sizzling in hell fire. The devil blew sulphur fumes from his nostrils and the whole company was carried down to the valley, half suffocated, by charitable monks. The Comte de Racon alone had suffered no harm from the smoke, for the devil had recognised him as his peer and spared him with infernal consideration. There was loud laughter. I pretended to be in despair at the rashness of my father who had barely recovered and whose next letter gave me great cause for anxiety. He had had a bad relapse and had to return to the springs.'

'I'll remember your story,' the count replied with a smile.

'I have just come from a funeral,' continued Guy, 'at which the king with all the marshals and various colonels of the guards were present. The Duc de Luxembourg deigned to mention your return to his Majesty. The king raised his eyebrows and said: "Oh, is the Comte de Racon back? I hardly remember him." Do you know what this means?'

'Who has died?'

Guy named a marshal, and continued: 'Shortly before the old man's death, I asked for the hand of his daughter through Colonel de la Porte Mury, and received the reply that the marshal did not favour an alliance with the house of Racon. The colonel was furious with me and maintained that he had disgraced himself on my account.'

'I will clear you with him.'

'Monsieur, the maréchal's daughter will receive a far larger dowry than the scarecrow you found for me.'

'I would not have agreed to your choice, either.'

'Why not?'

'I have my reasons.'

'That is a poor answer.'
'It must suffice.'
'Monsieur, tell me why the widow would not receive me when I wanted to pay her a formal visit of condolence?'
'You must have behaved badly somewhere, and she got to hear of it.'
'That is a fabrication.'
'How much did the banquet, which you gave to the Duc de Luxembourg, cost?'
'Just 7,000, Father.'
'Guy, I am very pleased with you, and shall see that you are promoted to captain.'
'Thank you.'
'To what extent are you able to pay your debts yourself?'
'Pay them myself?'
'Yes, don't look so surprised.' Guy shuffled in his chair and flicked a speck of dust from his sleeve.
'Well?' asked the count.
'Father, you must have spent the hour before supper questioning my grooms.'
'You used that hour to bribe Pierre.'
'I admit it. After my brother's death, you acquired wealth in some mysterious way, and during the journey you usually shared a room with your bastard.'
'Because it was cheaper. I lived very sparingly.'
'Sparingly? You have a new diamond ring.'
'That was a present.'
'Are you trying to make me believe that you still receive presents from ladies at your age?' said Guy with a laugh.
The count let the ring glitter in the firelight and said: 'You tried to make out that you are without means, although you have two full chests hidden in the Hôtel de Brayonne.'
'I thought that my servants were incorruptible. Give me leave to render the men in question harmless.'
'Any servant can be bribed.'
'And can therefore be dangerous, Father.'
'Why dangerous?'
'I was forced, by lack of money, to commit a murder with robbery.'
'The fellow did not tell me that.'

'Shall I tell you the story?'

'Yes, but first look and see if Pierre is in the next room.'

Guy looked into the bedroom and found it empty. 'Do you remember Constant du Fayel?' he asked, sitting down once more. 'You brought him seven years ago from Brayonne to Grandval, with Louis de Salvieux.'

'Yes, I remember.'

'Constant du Fayel,' Guy went on, 'was presented at Court by one of his wife's relations, and was unfortunate enough to win 120,000 livres in one night at Fontainebleau. I was in the direst need of money and offered him my protection for the return journey. We rode together and I suggested a short cut. When we came to an inn, I made his servants drunk. I ordered four of my grooms to disguise themselves as robbers and attack us shortly after we left. They captured the mules, and would have got away with the booty had not that stupid Fayel, relying on his strength, pursued the robbers into the forest. As a nobleman, I had to give him my support, and rode after him. We found the robbers, who in their bewilderment forgot to shoot, and Constant killed a groom. The other three cried that they were servants of the Vicomte de Clarmont.'

The count completed the tale. 'And that cost the Vicomte du Fayel his life. Were the servants content with your hush-money?'

'Yes, but I should have preferred to silence them for good.'

'Did anyone suspect you?'

'The three surviving robbers threw away their disguises and masks and transformed the dead robber into a shot groom, so that everybody believed my story of the fight.'

'Guy, those three fellows must disappear, for your own safety. Do they know of your cache in the Hôtel de Brayonne?'

'No.'

'Give them a false hiding place and order them to bring the coffers to Grandval. You must unload their pistols before they start and leave the rest to Master Grouchet. We'll discuss the details tomorrow. I'll make you an offer. I'll pay you double the amount of your debts if you become reconciled with Martin.'

'I have no quarrel with the boy,' replied Guy, feigning surprise.

'Let us not delude each other, Guy. Anyone who can attack and kill a boyhood friend would certainly not shrink at doing away with an uncomfortable half-brother. What must I give you to spare him?'

'The marquisate of Brayonne.'

The count buttoned up his coat, although he was sitting by the fire.

'You only use the title "Comte de Racon",' said Guy, 'and could easily dispense with the income from the marquisate. I should not then have to ask you for more money.' The count reflected for a few moments. 'Guy, I shall remain Marquis de Brayonne, but I will transfer to you the usufruct of the marquisate for the duration of Martin's life. If he is killed, or disappears, the income reverts to me, or, in the event of my death, to my cousin Gérard de Montignon, to whom I shall entrust the administration of Brayonne from the day of my demise until your unborn children's majority.'

'You intend to bequeath Brayonne to my future children and not to me?'

'Yes, I have decided to do that to safeguard Martin.'

'You are an extremely crafty old fox. Can't you make me a better offer?'

'No. Do you accept? '

'Yes, in God's name, Father. Will you pay my debts as well?'

'I will pay them after deducting the amount you have blackmailed out of my bailiff.'

'You are very generous. When shall we sign the contract?'

'At this very moment.'

'And when will you send a copy to your cousin Montignon?'

'I have no intention of sending him a copy; it would only make him hope for Martin's death and mine. I shall write and tell him that, after my illness, I made a new will in which I remembered him. On my death he should communicate with you, with the district officer, the governor and the Marquis de Chassigny.'

'So, you will send copies to various people for safe keeping?'

'Yes, I shall do that. You could maintain, after my death, that I had drawn up the will while not in my right mind, but I very much doubt if you would win a case against my cousin, because Gérard de Montignon is the wiliest member of our family.'

'When will you send your messenger?'

'Early tomorrow morning. I shall entrust it to Grouchet.'

'Please don't forget that you proposed Grouchet for another little job.'

'Send your grooms early tomorrow to Paris.'

'I will do so and unload their pistols now,' said Guy, standing up. 'May I withdraw, Father?'

'Go, and send your mother and the priest to me. There's plenty of time for the pistols.'

Guy bowed and left the room. The count rang for a servant and sent a message to his master of the hunt that he was to report to Grandval immediately with his most reliable men.

A little later, the countess appeared in a grey velvet dress. Since she was in half-mourning, she wore only her pearls. Guy arrived a few moments later with the priest. They sat down. Turning to his wife, the count said: 'Madame, I have just bought Martin's safety from Guy by handing over to him the usufruct of the revenues of Brayonne. I wanted you to know this, and that is why I sent for you.' Father Tulier's face remained impassive, but the countess stared at Guy in terror.

The latter said regretfully: 'Mother, unfortunately, Father believes me capable of perfidies which have never entered my mind. I bear no feeling of hatred for Martin.'

'Monsieur, do you consider Guy capable of murdering his brother?' asked the countess.

'No, Madame, but people lose their heads in anger. As boys, Guy and Martin were enemies.'

'But many years have passed since then.'

'Certainly, Madame, I have kept them apart until today, but now I have removed the ban. Be so good as to write what I dictate to you, Father.' The priest went over to the table, and the count dictated the contract.

'My son, has something happened recently to justify your father's decision?' the countess asked Guy.

'Nothing at all. Since Raoul's death he seems to have immoderate fears concerning Martin. My God, I didn't dare arouse his anger by contradicting him.'

The countess listened to her husband's dictation. 'So he proposes to by-pass your inheritance in favour of Gérard de Montignon and your off-spring?'

'Please do not contradict him. His anger is dangerous to everyone.'

'You are very young. Do you think you will be able to administer such large revenues intelligently?'

'I shall be able to do just as well with the income as he does,' laughed Guy.

'Oh, Guy, now that you are my only child, I worry constantly about you. I regret I sometimes preferred Raoul to you, and feel that my maternal love for you has awakened from a deep sleep, growing ever stronger.'

'Do you want to satisfy an unwanted, ill-favoured child's hunger for love?'

'Forgive me, Guy.'

'Madame, the unexpected gift of your love makes me forget all the sorrows of my childhood. May I kiss you?' Guy went over to the countess's chair, bent down and kissed his mother. She shuddered imperceptibly. 'How strange you are! I should like to know your heart.'

'I do not know it myself, Mother. I shall take great pains to be worthy of your love, and hope in time to enjoy a beautiful, mutual understanding.' She offered him both her hands; he caught them and kissed them.

The count produced the finished document. 'Here, Guy, read the contract. Where's Martin?'

'He is dancing energetically in the salon,' replied the countess.

'Father Tulier,' said the count, 'my master of the hunt will wait upon you for the copies. You can use one of my bailiff's secretaries.'

'Comte Gaston, in spite of my age, I am still capable of making five separate copperplate copies.'

'Thank you. Please send a lackey to fetch Martin.'

'Certainly, Comte Gaston.'

'I am satisfied with the wording,' said Guy, handing the paper to Father Tulier, who left the room with a curt nod. 'Father,' said Guy, with a bitter smile. 'You are taking precautions as if there were assassins in your house.'

'Experience teaches one caution, Guy. I now intend to reconcile you formally with your half-brother, Martin.' The countess was about to say something, but Guy made her a secret sign. She remained silent and stared into the flames. There was a knock at the door and Martin entered. He bowed and remained at the door, pale with excitement.

'Martin,' said the count. 'The Vicomte de Clarmont wishes to be reconciled with you. Forgive each other, once and for all, for the injuries you did each other as children and try to be friends.'

Martin hurried over to Guy with outstretched hand. 'I have long wished to be reconciled,' he said eagerly. Guy shook his hand and, in a friendly tone replied: 'There is more need for forgiveness on your side than on mine. I admire your generosity and look forward to being friends.'

The embraced each other, then Guy turned to the countess while Martin went over to the count. 'Monsieur, will this reconciliation have favourable consequences for me?'

'Yes, Martin. You will accompany me to Paris, live in the Hôtel de Racon, and continue to serve as a lieutenant in the Guards. I no longer need the stud farm.'

Martin could not repress a cry of joy, but the count rebuked him. 'You can thank me tomorrow morning.'

'Monsieur, why are you so serious?'

'I have ensured this reconciliation in writing and handed over the income of Brayonne to the vicomte.'

'What does that signify?'

'That I am nervous and suspicious. Tonight you will find two huntsmen keeping watch outside your door. Ask no questions, you imbecile. Go and enjoy yourself.' Martin bowed, in his confusion, and left the room in the best of spirits.

'Madame,' said the count, 'I have letters to write.'

'Will you allow Guy to accompany me?' asked the countess, rising to her feet.

'Yes, I do not need him any more.' Mother and son left the study and the count remained alone.

Baron d'Epponcourt was so infuriated at the resplendent arrival of the Vicomte de Clarmont that he refused to gamble, retired to bed and ordered the servants to pack. He forbade his wife and daughter to take any further part in the festivities, but the two women, hearing the music and the gay chatter mounting from the salon, laughed at him and hurried downstairs. Marguerite joined an ebullient group of young people, who were practising the latest dance-steps. The black-haired baroness, who was still a young woman, managed to attract the attention of two elderly gentlemen and was invited to dance by both of them. She gave her hand to them in turn, laughed and joked and paid no attention to her daughter.

When the Vicomte de Clarmont entered, Marguerite tried to take her revenge on him in a purely feminine way, by leaving the dancers and mincing past him on the arm of the youngest du Terne, so that her silk dress brushed against his gold-brocade coat. Guy looked round, followed her and asked for a dance. She refused, and danced twice with the young du Terne. When a minuet struck up, Guy repeated his request and the girl at last accepted. Since he knew all the figures, it was not difficult to pay her a compliment each time they met in the dance. 'Mademoiselle, you have developed into a beautiful rose.'

'And you have become a beanstalk. I understand that your bride is as withered as you are. Is that true, Monsieur, or have they slandered her?'

'It is not quite correct, my beautiful Mademoiselle. You are very heartless to me.'

'Why?'

'You are taking a delight in reminding me of my gloomy future.'

'Gloomy? You should long for your bride.'

'I felt an ardent desire for my first bride and suffer the tortures of the damned.'

'Is that why you are so thin?'

'Probably.'

'You poor creature!' laughed Marguerite, giving her hand to her opposite partner. Guy waited for the next encounter, and whispered, as he bent towards her: 'I still hope, Mademoiselle.'

'For what, Vicomte de Clarmont?'

Guy replied with a look. Marguerite blushed and took a false step, which upset Martin's partner. 'Mademoiselle d'Epponcourt is tired,' Guy said apologetically. Taking hold of the girl's arm, he led her past the card tables into a temporarily empty room where refreshments stood on a table. 'Mademoiselle, I spoke to my father after supper and begged him on my knees to change his mind. His greed is appalling. I begged and wept in vain.'

'Why should that concern me?'

'Be truthful, Mademoiselle. Would you like to be mine?'

'It would not displease me, Vicomte.'

'Then I am saved.'

'Saved?'

'Marguerite, I have loved you since my childhood. I love you passionately, and shall love you for ever.'

'Will you kindly release my arm?'

Guy obeyed, and said hurriedly: 'Marguerite, now there is nothing to stop us. You need only have the courage to marry me in secret and you will become Vicomtesse de Clarmont, Comtesse de Racon and, in addition, Marquise de Brayonne. The claims of the church are all-powerful in France. Even my father has to bow to them.' Marguerite was speechless with surprise.

'Say that you will, before we are disturbed,' insisted Guy.

'You have my promise.' Guy put his arm round her and kissed her on the lips. 'I do not care for kisses. We are leaving tomorrow. Accompany us, and marry me on the way. My parents would gladly give their consent.'

'Mademoiselle, my father has ordered me to remain here.'

'I despise you if you are afraid of him.'

'Give me a proof of your love and I will find the courage to defy him.'

'I will give you nothing before the wedding.'

'You are abominably cruel.'

'What do you demand, Vicomte de Clarmont?'

'An open door.'

'Monsieur, I am no lady's maid.' Marguerite took a sweetmeat from a silver bowl, nibbled it, and turned away, her head in the air.

Guy controlled his anger and remained standing behind her. 'Well, have you changed your mind about the wedding?' she asked over her shoulder.

'Mademoiselle, I have an idea. We will ride tonight to the village church. I will talk the half-crazed old parish priest into marrying us.'

'I like your proposal.'

'You are a heroine.'

'When shall we leave?'

'As soon as everyone is asleep. I'll have two horses brought to the gate in the park and wait for you there.'

'I shouldn't dare to walk in the park alone.'

'Then I'll meet you below, in the uninhabited part of the castle by the north-east tower.'

'Do you expect me to cross the bridge over the moat where the watchdogs are kept? They are certain to bark.'

'We shan't cross the bridge but slip along to the south-east tower where there's a little gate leading to the orchard.'

'Then we shall have to pass occupied rooms.'

'I'll send my dogs on ahead. They'll growl at anyone and warn us in time. Someone's coming! Will you meet me by the north-east tower?'

'Yes, Vicomte de Clarmont.'

'Mademoiselle, tomorrow you will be the Vicomtess de Clarmont, and I shall have married a goddess.'

Guy's travelling companions rushed into the room with Martin. 'Ah, there's the vicomte. Look, he's caught a little bird. Can we carry off the little lady for a dance?'

Marguerite looked from one to the other, sizing them up, and pointed to Martin. 'He's the best dancer. Monsieur, you have the honour.'

Martin looked delighted. 'Mademoiselle, today is my lucky day. The Vicomte de Clarmont is at peace with me. The most beautiful lady in the party has singled me out as her partner, and I can return to Paris with my friend and join the guards regiment.' He led Marguerite quickly into the salon where the music had just stopped. Nearly everyone was seated and there were no chairs available. Martin removed a cushion from under a page and laid it on the floor, next to a table where some elderly people were gambling. 'Won't you sit down, Mademoiselle?' Marguerite made herself comfortable and Martin sat down beside her on the floor. 'Is it true, Mademoiselle, that you're leaving tomorrow?'

'That was my father's intention, but there may be a change tomorrow. Can you keep a secret?'

'I have always been able to do that.'

Marguerite bent down to him. 'The vicomte is marrying me tonight.'

'Which vicomte?'

'The Vicomte de Clarmont.' The girl whispered the plan to Martin and clapped her hands. 'Isn't that wonderful, Monsieur?'

'Mademoiselle, in Heaven's name, do not embark on an adventure with Guy!'

'You are jealous, my friend,' she laughed.

'Who are the witnesses?' asked Martin.

'He never mentioned anything about them.'

'Mademoiselle, take one of his friends as a witness and choose a second gentleman yourself.'

'Isn't a marriage without witnesses valid?'

'No, Mademoiselle.'

Marguerite jumped up.

'Wait here. I will ask him at once.' She looked round and hurried from the ballroom.

The ballet master announced a solo dance. The young people gathered round to watch the beautiful Comtesse de Racon dancing with a duke's son. Martin stood up as Guy came over and said: 'Mademoiselle d'Epponcourt has expressed great confidence in you and wishes your presence at a certain place.'

'I have entirely forgotten the matter,' replied Martin, 'and beg you to demand of me no service that might lose me the friendship of the Comte de Racon.'

Guy placed his hand on Martin's shoulder. 'That is just the reply I would have expected from you, Monsieur. The silly goose took my jest seriously and has put me in a very awkward position. I am sneaking away, and beg you to tell the young lady that I cannot keep my promise.'

Martin looked nonplussed, but could not help laughing. 'I do not much care for your commission, Vicomte de Clarmont,' he said with a frown.

'Consider that you are doing me a favour, M. Saint-Jean.'

Martin looked into Guy's slanting green eyes and replied:

'I will comply with your wishes, but I shall refuse to render you similar services in the future.'

'I appreciate your kindness and hope that I shall soon have the opportunity of doing you a similar service. She is waiting in the antechamber.' They bowed to each other and went off in different directions.

Martin found Marguerite eating sweetmeats and surrounded by admirers. She called out to him exuberantly: 'Monsieur Saint-Jean, are you looking forward to our little jest?'

'Mademoiselle, actually the whole thing *was* a jest and we both took it seriously.'

She hurried over to him and caught his sleeve. 'What was a jest?'

'The Vicomte de Clarmont's proposal.'

'That is not true!'

'He has asked me to tell you so.'

'He has lied to me!'

'Mademoiselle, the gentlemen are looking. Show your pride and let us laugh at our credulity, which has now been punished.'

'I shall slap him!'

'He is hiding from you.'

'The coward! Go and find him and avenge me!'

'One does not resort to a rapier where a jest is concerned.'

'You are a coward, too!'

'Madame, tomorrow morning your anger will have vanished and you will see me in a new and better light.' He retired with a bow.

The party broke up after midnight and everyone retired to their rooms, apart from a few gentlemen who continued drinking and gambling. Martin found two huntsmen outside his door. One of them grinned at him and said. 'Monsieur, there is a little page waiting inside for you.'

Martin entered the room and came face to face with Marguerite wearing a riding-habit and carrying a bundle under her arm. 'M. Saint-Jean,' she said, her cheeks aflame with excitement, 'the vicomte was not joking. He made his excuses to me in person and said that he had confused you because, as the friend and favourite of his much-feared father, he does not trust you. I promised to meet him down below by the north-east staircase, but I have not the courage to go along these corridors alone. I trust no one except you, and, although he mistrusts you, I am asking you to accompany me.'

'Mademoiselle, your future husband might not approve.'

'Please come.'

'Who are the witnesses?'

'Two of his friends.'

'Did you speak to the gentlemen yourself?'

'No, M. Saint-Jean.'

'Have you informed your parents?'

'No, the vicomte was opposed to it. He advised me to tell my father on the homeward journey that I was now the Vicomtesse de Clarmont. He wanted to avoid any quarrel between my father and the count and will only tell the latter three days after the ceremony.'

'Mademoiselle, I will go with you. Your choice of costume was wise. You will be taken for a page in the dark.' Martin opened the door for Marguerite, and left with her. By the tower-staircase he stopped to whisper: 'Go down on your own and do not say that I am here; we must not offend the vicomte. I will follow you at a safe distance and protect you in case of need.'

'Could I be in any danger?'

'Perhaps. I can hear footsteps. Stay where you are.' Martin walked away.

Guy came up the stairs with his five Great Danes, and called out: 'Who is there?'

'I,' replied Marguerite, stepping forward.

'Mademoiselle, I waited for you below.'

'I was just on my way down.'

Guy caught her hand and led her down the spiral staircase. 'What are you carrying under your arm?'

'A dress for the ceremony.'

'That is unnecessary.'

'But I'm wearing riding-breeches.'

'Why?'

'I always ride astride, Monsieur.'

'I did not know that. I ordered a lady's saddle. My friends will not be here for an hour. You have plenty of time to change.'

'I don't want to change.'

'Do you refuse to obey me until after our wedding?'

'I always do as I please.' They had reached the lower corridor. 'Where are you going?' asked Marguerite.

Guy entered a room where a fire was burning in the grate. 'I had the fire lit,' he explained, 'so that you would not get cold waiting. Sit down. This room belongs to my father, but he seldom uses it and will certainly not come here tonight. Down!' The dogs obeyed.

Marguerite looked round and caught sight of a fully-made bed. 'Does your father sleep down here sometimes?'

'Yes, when he exercises his *droits de Seigneur* on the servants and the village maids.'

'I want to leave.'

'You will change here.'

'I refuse.'

'Where will you change then?'

'In the vestry before the ceremony. Leave my buttons alone! I have not yet given you permission to use the familiar form of address to me, and please remember my station.'

One of the dogs raised its ears and growled. 'Down!' said Guy.

'Lead me to the horses,' said Marguerite.

Guy laughed. 'Mademoiselle, do you still not suspect that a silly goose is to be plucked in this room tonight?'

'Help!' Guy seized her by the hair.

'If you utter one scream, I'll hit you across the mouth so that you'll be unrecognisable tomorrow. There, that's the jacket gone. Don't worry, I'll handle your damned hose. Ah, so you'd scratch and bite! You just wait. I'll soon put a stop to that.'

Marguerite struggled desperately, but Guy seized her and pulled her breeches tight to spank her. At the first slap, the five dogs jumped up and approached.

Guy stopped. The door opened noiselessly and Martin entered. Marguerite sank to the floor. 'Vicomte,' Martin said politely, 'I think Mademoiselle has been punished enough for her frivolity. Call off your dogs so that I can help her to her feet.' Guy whistled to his dogs. Martin held out his hand to

Marguerite and lifted her to her feet. She was too terrified even to weep; she tore herself free and ran for the door. Martin caught her and said: 'Mademoiselle, please calm yourself. The vicomte only wanted to teach you a lesson.'

'Challenge him to a duel!'

'No, Mademoiselle, you deserved the fright you have received, and in future you won't be so credulous. Vicomte, I suggest that we should take Mademoiselle back to her room.' Guy did not answer. Martin helped Marguerite to tidy her clothes and picked up her little bundle.

'M. Saint-Jean,' said Guy. 'I now understand why my father employed you to teach the cadets. You have a wonderful talent for education.'

'So have you, Vicomte.' The three went upstairs.

Marguerite did not utter a word until they reached her door. Then she turned round and hissed: 'Vicomte, I shall tell my father everything and he will challenge you, since M. Saint-Jean is too cowardly to do so.'

She was about to slip into her room, but Guy caught hold of her and whispered: 'Mademoiselle, if you do not keep silent I shall tell the assembled guests that I thrashed you like a page because you tried to force me to marry you.'

'You are a fiend.'

'But if you remain silent, I will do the same.'

'The young du Terne will not be such a coward as Martin Saint-Jean,' sobbed Marguerite.

Martin nudged Guy and said seriously: 'Mademoiselle, I have changed my mind and will challenge the vicomte to avenge the offence.'

'Ah, so you've found your courage. Fight it out in the moonlight. I will watch from the window.'

'Bravo!' laughed Guy. 'M. Saint-Jean, our little lady wishes to see blood. I suggest the fencing-room as the location. The moon shines into that, too, and we shall not be seen by anyone. Do you agree?'

'Yes, if Mademoiselle does.'

'Up to the fencing-room then,' cried Marguerite.

'Hush,' said Martin, 'we must not be caught. But where can we find seconds?'

Guy intervened: 'Mademoiselle will act as second.'

'Isn't that against the rules?' asked the girl.

'No,' said Martin, 'not in this case.'

'Then forward, Gentlemen!' They climbed up to the second storey followed by the five Great Danes.

The fencing-hall, which faced east, was only half-lit by the moon. Guy ordered his hounds to lie in the corridor in front of the door, and prepared for the bout. Martin also drew his sword. 'A serious wound will suffice,' said Marguerite graciously. Martin laughed and flashed his teeth.

'Mademoiselle, please give us the sign to start.'

Marguerite counted, and the rapiers clashed. Suddenly, Martin sprang back. 'I am wounded in the shoulder. Mademoiselle, please fetch a bandage.'

'Oh, M. Saint-Jean, why did you not wound the vicomte? I shall be back immediately.'

She hurried out and Martin sat down, roaring with laughter, on the bench by the window. 'Vicomte, I'm afraid I must make a show of wounding you. Please pretend that you are in pain so that the little pest will finally go to bed. Let us hope she does not ask to see my imaginary wound.'

'You fight well, M. Saint-Jean.'

'So do you, Vicomte.'

Guy whistled.

'Why are you whistling?'

'I'm only calling my dogs.'

The corridor sprang to life. The latch clicked and the five Great Danes sprang into the room. Guy stroked their powerful backs, let them lick his hand, and said: 'M. Saint-Jean, you have robbed me of a pleasure because it offended your virtue. You have shown yourself courageous, tactful and intelligent; nevertheless you have annoyed me. I will neither allow myself to be dictated to by a bastard nor to be cheated by my father. His cunning contract will never be signed, because his darling was injudicious enough to place himself in my power on this very important night. I have waited for years to be alone with you and my five dogs. At him, Leto! At him, Midas! At him, Sultan! Thetis! Caesar!'

Martin saw his way to the door barred, and a hideous end in store for him. He ran the first dog through with his rapier, dropped the hilt and seized two practice épées, with which he started to fight the four remaining assailants. His cries for help were drowned by the wailing of the mortally wounded beast.

Guy ran out of the fencing-hall and shouted down the corridor: 'Help! Help! My dogs have gone mad.'

Martin managed to climb on to the bench and then on to the window-sill, still fighting off the leaping beasts; then, one of the monsters bit through his shoe and tried to drag him down, while two others got the épées between their teeth, and the fourth tore a piece out of his coat. Martin thought himself lost, but the dog released his foot and retreated for the next leap. Martin let go the épées so suddenly that the snapping hounds fell against the attacker. Then, in a flash, he opened the window and jumped down blindly from the second storey. The thwarted dogs leaped up wildly against the sill, and the watchdogs began to bay from the moat below.

Martin had somersaulted in his fall and landed just behind the orchard wall on a heap of dry leaves, which lay there ready to be carted away. He realised that he was safe and sound, worked his way out of the rustling heap, rushed in to the park and up the terraced steps, opened the french windows and stormed into the dining-hall, where the remaining gamblers stared alternately at him and at the other door, from which the Vicomte de Clarmont entered, shouting: 'My dogs have gone mad and are tearing Martin Saint-Jean to pieces.'

Shouting with rage, Martin rushed at Guy, flung him to the floor and began strangling him. Chairs were knocked over, the gentlemen hurried up, and the count tried to pull Martin away from his victim. The Vicomte de Clarmont, already purple in the face, was saved in the nick of time. Martin was restrained and held by three cavaliers, while the count, with the aid of two lackeys, laid the vicomte on a bench. Guy fought for breath while Martin continued to roar: 'He set his dogs on me! They were not mad!'

'The Vicomte de Clarmont's mad dogs are to be shot at once,' cried the count. 'Take the vicomte up to his room and lock him in. Four huntsmen are to stand guard outside his door and not to let him leave the room, under penalty of death.' Guy was carried upstairs. The count went over to Martin. 'Keep your mouth shut and calm yourself at once. Gentlemen,

I thank you for your support. You can release the young man now. Martin, come with me and tell me everything, calmly. Goodnight, Gentlemen.'

'Comte de Racon,' cried Martin, beside himself with rage, 'you protect the vicomte although he set his dogs . . .'

'Be silent,' roared the count, 'one more word and you will regret it!' By the expression in his eyes and his pale face, Martin realised that the count was prepared to strike him before all the guests. Pale as a ghost, he limped from the hall, followed by the count. The whole castle was in an uproar, shots rang out, dogs howled, women screamed and lackeys ran shouting to and fro.

The count made Martin sit down in his study and stood before him listening to his account of what happened. The boy's voice often faltered when he looked up into the dark, frozen face, and a growing fear made him tremble. When he had finished, the count sent Pierre for Dr Borel and stood at the fireplace with his back turned to him. He did not change his position, even when the doctor entered to bind up Martin's injured foot. Not until the physician had left, did the count turn to him. 'No contract can protect you against Guy. You must leave tomorrow. I will give you 200,000 livres in cash and we will never see each other again.'

'Monsieur!'

'Please remain seated. I have always been afraid that it would come to this, and now the time has come. Guy is Vicomte de Clarmont, and my heir. You have to go, not he.' Instead of replying, Martin groaned so piteously that the count took a step towards him. 'Martin, there is no point in making our parting more difficult. I know how much you love me and you know how devoted I am to you. But we are not women who are unable to give something up. We must end our friendship. Life offers plenty to make one forget.'

'Where shall I go?'

'Out of the country. Fight against the Turks, or help the king found a colony in Canada.'

A faint smile appeared on Martin's face: 'Monsieur, only your presence counts for me; your words are meaningless. I don't believe what you are saying.'

'You must believe.'

Martin shook his head with a smile.

'Don't be a fool,' said the count.

'Monsieur, I should be mad to think you could cast me off. You'd rather murder me.'

'Martin, unless you leave tomorrow of your own accord, I shall be compelled to have you removed by force.'

'Monsieur, if you carried out that threat you would no longer be the man I know. You say things for which you cannot answer. Remember what you promised me in Italy.'

The count knitted his brows. 'Believe what I say now, and there will be no need for me to threaten you.'

Martin rose. 'Monsieur, whatever may have happened between the vicomte and myself, you should not throw me out. You may banish me, as you decided to do in Italy, although I am innocent. I would suffer that, but do not force me to part from you for ever. Even you could not justify that.'

'Martin, Guy looks upon all my possessions as his inheritance and says, quite rightly, that I damage him if I support you. So far, you have cost me little, but a property and a title are expensive.'

'I renounce both of them.'

'Nobody except myself would believe that.'

'Monsieur, I will swear verbally and in writing that, from today, I will accept no presents from the Comte de Racon and that I will hand over everything he might give me to the Vicomte de Clarmont. I shall use the name of Saint-Jean to the end of my days. I will be like Colonel du Lac and live in barracks on my pay, but I wish to keep your friendship.'

'Say that to Guy and he will laugh at you. He will look on you as an idiot or a sly fox in a monk's cowl, who by hypocrisy extorts money from fools. Men such as you are rarely understood. They make enemies because they are uncomfortable and disturb the existing order. I have supported you until today, but cannot do so in future. Guy knows he could risk murdering you in my arms without being punished. I have decided on his favour.'

'Monsieur, you could not discard me for a man whom you know to be evil.'

'I must and will do it, Martin.'

'You must? The hideous ambition that Guy aroused in you is now speaking. Guy's resplendent arrival has dazzled you. He is a great lord with a brilliant future and I am destined to be a servant, despite my origin. But you need a man like me and you need me more than I need you. I beg of you to keep your promises to me and not to succumb to temptation.'

'Martin, your efforts are in vain. I am forced to sacrifice one of my sons. What would you do in my place?'

'I would sacrifice Martin if I could improve Guy.'

'That means that I must sacrifice Guy because he is unregenerate. Unless I had him hanged . . . Would you feel happy then, Martin?'

'No.'

'That is the reply I wanted to hear. It is easier for you to suffer as the innocent party than to have a constant feeling of guilt. Now you know enough.'

Martin ran towards him and seized him by the shoulders. 'I can't leave you.'

'Martin, it is time for us both to be rational. The whole Italian journey was folly on my part. I should have remained at Court. Now I shall find it difficult to get back into favour and re-establish my position. Let me go; I do not like being constrained.'

'If you banish me, I will kill myself.'

'If you love me you will not do that. I want your promise, Martin.'

'Yes, I promise you, I promise you anything, but I'm not leaving.'

The count shook him off. Martin stammered: 'Say that it is not true, say it, speak to me, answer me! You see how terrified I am.'

'Leave my cravat alone and don't behave like a woman.'

'Is your lace worth more to you than me?'

Martin tore off his lace cravat and flung it, in ribbons, on to the floor. The count thrust him away. 'Stay where you are. It's enough for one of us to stand here in rags.'

Martin looked involuntarily at his coat which had been ripped to pieces by the dogs. He pressed his hand to his face and turned away. 'Forgive my behaviour. I should leave, but I cannot.' The count's face softened, but he controlled himself and went into his bedroom.

Martin heard the door close gently and fell to his knees. He wept in his despair until he had no tears left, then looked round and saw the torn lace cravat on the floor. He picked it up and dried his eyes. Then he put the damp rag under his waistcoat and stood up. Limping to the window, he pulled aside the heavy brown curtains and opened it. The moon had hidden her face behind a cloud. Here and there, a star twinkled above the tree-tops. Martin folded his hands and his lips began to move. The damp air entered the room.

When Martin had closed the window and turned round, the count was standing there. 'Do you see now that you have to leave?'

'Monsieur, I am reconciled to my fate.'

'You have changed. Have you anything to say to me?'

'I kept repeating my Pater Noster,' Martin replied calmly, 'because no other prayer occurred to me, and the weight of the hour was suddenly lifted from me. My heart is lighter now.'

'You have already withdrawn from me.'

'You yourself wanted it.'

'Am I losing your love too?'

'I wonder, my friend. I do not think that you have lost any of my love. There is something between us that does not belong to this world. Something that may be waiting for us in the beyond.'

'What?'

'I haven't bothered to ask. Perhaps we should be satisfied.'

'Satisfied with what?'

'With all that was between us. What has been remains, and what will be does not concern us now.'

'Whom does it concern?'

'Possibly our guardian angels. May I leave now?'

'Tell me more about us?'

'I can't tell you more, Monsieur.'

'Are you sure?'

'Yes, tomorrow I must start a new life, and I do not even know how to begin. Perhaps someone else needs me.'

'Do you now feel free of me?'

Martin smiled. 'If I had to carry you round the world on my

back, I would gladly do so.'

'Even with that bandaged foot?' asked the count, trying to jest.

'In any condition, Monsieur.'

'I believe you.'

'Because you know me, my friend!'

'Martin,' said the count, 'it will be better if, now and again, I behave unreasonably. I will meet you in the spring and we will make a journey together. I will contrive to meet you from time to time, unknown to Guy, as we did in Italy. I shall have to accustom myself to the fear that, one day, Guy will discover you and murder you. I will meet you in the spring.'

'Monsieur, now I feel as though a hurricane had flung me at your feet. Now everything is as it was before.'

'Yes, and you will obey me for the present.'

The count drew Martin close.

'Monsieur, why are you so terrible?'

'Forgive me.'

'I forgive you everything.' With an almost imperceptible movement, the count released Martin and said: 'Come and see me tomorrow morning. I shall have time to consider where you can spend the winter and where I can meet you. Go and sleep now, my friend.'

Martin bowed and limped from the room. Outside the door, his knees suddenly gave way and he had to lean against the wall for support.

When Martin entered the count's room next morning, he found him at breakfast. 'Good morning, Martin. Sit down. Pierre, lay a second place. How's your foot?'

'I can't put on either a shoe or a riding-boot.'

'And I don't know where to send you.'

'What about a campaign against the Turks?'

'Are you serious?'

'More or less, Monsieur. As far as I know, the king would be pleased if the Turks pinned down the emperor's troops in the east.'

'Hm!'

'Monsieur, you look as you sometimes did in the war when you were planning an attack and were not quite sure of your tactics. Why do you avoid my eyes?'

The count looked him full in the face. 'Do you know a suitable spot for your winter quarters?'

'No, I leave the choice to you.' The count attacked his breakfast. Martin took a few bites then asked: 'Where shall we meet in the spring?'

'I can't tell you yet. You must go to the frontier at least.'

'Am I to serve with the Marquis de Chassigny's dragoons?'

'No, Guy would find you there.'

'What do you propose to do with Guy?'

'Nothing. I shall not even refer to yesterday's encounter.'

'Is that just?'

'No, but that is all I can do. Promise, for my sake, that you will spare him, should you ever have an opportunity of taking your revenge on him.'

'I will spare him, for your sake. I give you my word of honour, Comte de Racon.'

The count nodded. 'Do you realise that you are in danger from Guy for the rest of your life?'

'Monsieur, I was long enough in the war not to mind whether a bullet came from the front or from behind. Why should I worry about death? Only God knows the hour of my end.'

'You always have an answer ready.'

'Monsieur, where will you take me in the spring?'

'I can't say yet.'

'But it will be in the spring, won't it? It mustn't be in the summer.'

The count cut himself a slice of cold meat. 'If nothing interferes, it will be the spring. I will let you have news.'

'What can prevent it?'

'Service at Court.'

'Monsieur, that is a daily routine and you never stood it for very long. You often slipped away to one of your friends' castles, or hunted at Grandval or Brayonne. Instead of this you will meet me.'

'I will do it.'

'In the spring?'

'Yes, to Hell with you. Now leave me in peace!'

'Please promise me.'

'That's not necessary.'

'Yes, for you are begging the question.'

Pierre came in. 'M. le Comte, M. le Baron d'Epponcourt asks whether you could loan him a groom who, if need be, could act as master of his horse. His own master of the horse has entered the service of one of your guests.' Pierre obviously had something else to add, but the count gave him no time.

'Please inform him that, unfortunately, I have no suitable groom at the moment.' Pierre left.

'Now give me your promise.'

'What promise?'

'That you will meet me somewhere in the spring.'

'I promise you.'

'Thank you. May I write to you?'

'No, Guy could intercept the letters and learn of your whereabouts. Now I know where I can hide you! Ride to the Lord Lieutenant of Provence, whom we visited on our journey. I will give you a letter of introduction to him, and shall write to the Marquise de Sévigné. He is her daughter's husband, and I hope that she will recommend you to him; he knows how to keep silent. Now Pierre, what do you want?'

'M. le Comte, M. le Baron has ordered his horses to be harnessed and wishes to take his leave of you.'

'Wait for me,' said the count, as he left the room. Martin put his aching foot on the empty chair and finished his breakfast.

A few moments later, Pierre came in: 'M. Saint-Jean, the count wishes you to visit him in the baron's room.' He passed Guy's door, where four huntsmen stood on watch; they stared as he passed.

The count and the baron broke off their conversation as Martin entered, and offered the young man a seat. 'Martin,' asked the count, 'would you be prepared to give the baron's children riding lessons during the winter?'

'Monsieur, I thought I was going to the Lord Lieutenant of Provence.'

'As an officer of the king, you'll not be safe enough. Every passing traveller visits his wife and would recognise you from the Paris salons.'

'I invite you with the greatest pleasure, M. Saint-Jean, to be a guest at my castle,' said the baron. 'I lead a very rustic life and very rarely have guests.'

Martin bowed. 'How old are your younger children?'

'Six. Two strapping twin boys, and my daughter Marguerite needs a companion on her rides.'

'I accept your invitation, and thank you for your confidence in me.'

'I am delighted. I have heard nothing but good of you.'

'Don't tell anyone where you are going,' warned the count. 'Mount by the kennels, ride round the park and meet the baron on the main road.'

'Why this detour?'

'Guy's window looks out on to the courtyard and I could not take away his pistols. Have you packed?'

'I gave orders to Dominique before I came to see you.'

'Good. Hurry then. I'm riding with the baron and I shall see you again.'

'Monsieur, I should like to take leave of Madame la Comtesse.'

'Well, make it brief.'

'As brief as possible, Monsieur.'

The countess received Martin in bed, for she was indisposed. 'Oh, M. Saint-Jean, what terrible things have happened once more! You must curb your hatred.'

'Madame, the vicomte's dogs were not mad. He set them on me. Forgive me for telling you this, but I cannot bear that you should reproach me unjustly.' The countess covered her face with her hands and turned her face to the wall. 'Madame, I have promised the count not to take my revenge on your son. You need have no fear for the vicomte. I shall never return to Grandval, and I am taking my leave of you for ever.'

'Guy lied to me!'

'Madame, I beg you to think of me kindly when I am gone. I have looked upon you as more than a mother.'

'My poor Martin!'

'Madame, I shall have the consolation of meeting the count in secret, occasionally. I beg you to tell no one.'

'What is your destination now?'

'That, too, is a secret. I am spending the winter as Baron

d'Epponcourt's guest and assistant master of horse.'

'M. Saint-Jean, I am worried about my dead friend's child. The baron idolises Marguerite and completely neglects her education. Please be chivalrous to her.'

'I shall naturally be that, Madame. Could you suspect me of anything else?'

'I was under the impression that the girl found favour in your eyes.'

Martin blushed. 'She is very like the woman I love. That is all, Madame.'

'May heaven grant that it remain so. Farewell! I pity you, and regret that I have not a son like you. It grieves me to lose you. Remember me in your heart as a maternal friend.'

Martin knelt down and kissed her proffered hand. 'You fetched me to Grandval and, by so doing, enabled me to find a father and a friend. I thank you for your generosity and your kind words. Thank you, Madame!' Martin rose, bowed deeply and limped from the room.

When Martin, accompanied by François on the second mount, and old Dominique on the pack-horse, rode out of the wood, he caught sight of the baron's coach bowling along the road with two outriders. The count galloped up with two grooms and rode at his side. 'What did you say to my wife?' Martin repeated the conversation word for word. 'Promise me that you will never visit her in secret when the vicomte and I are absent.'

'I shall never return to Grandval. This answer must suffice, if you do not wish to offend me at our parting. How far are you riding with me?'

'I'm leaving you here.'

'Monsieur, I shall look forward to the spring. Please greet Madame Boquelin for me when you see her, and be friendly to her.'

'Have you any more instructions to give me?'

'No, but Blanche loves you truly, Monsieur.'

The count took out a purse. 'Here, Martin, take this. No arguments, now! Farewell! And remain exactly as you are.'

'Thank you. What I don't use I will return to you in the spring, the rest as soon as possible. Au revoir, Monsieur!'

They embraced. The count gave the nervous Pollux a blow with his switch and galloped off with the reins slack on his horse's neck.

When Martin finally pacified Pollux and looked round for the count, he saw him disappearing behind the village houses, far ahead of his grooms.

PART THREE

IN EXILE

MARTIN was still looking back at Grandval when Marguerite's voice rang out: 'M. Saint-Jean, are you coming with us or do you want to turn back too?'

'Mademoiselle, it is not seemly for you to wait for me.'

'Your right cheek is bleeding.' Martin wiped it with his glove. 'Is your valet clumsy when he shaves you?' asked Marguerite.

'Yes, occasionally.'

'You should dismiss him. You look funny with a bandaged foot and no riding-boot. It is not very elegant.'

'Mademoiselle, your jacket is not elegant either. It is too short in the sleeves.'

Marguerite blushed. 'I can't help it if father never has any money,' she said peevishly. 'It is the gambling devil in him. Last autumn the Comtesse de Racon gave him my mother's jewellery, which was part of my dowry, but whenever I asked him about it he either evaded the question or said that some rogues had stolen it during the journey. You will be surprised at the conditions at home. The park is overgrown with weeds, the tapestries in the castle are falling to pieces and most of the furniture is broken. The twins still whimper and wet their hose, and every day one of the maids runs away.'

'Oh, it can't be as bad as all that.'

'It is far worse. My stepmother is having an affair with Baptiste, the groom, and her youngest child resembles him. Father is the only one who doesn't notice it. I am frightened of my stepmother. She once dragged me across the room by my hair; but you can get along with her provided you don't contradict her.'

'Mademoiselle, if everything is as you say, I shall not remain long as your father's guest.'

'No, you must stay a long time and keep me amused. I am often bored.'

'Have you no governess to give you lessons?'

'Madame Rambert has been with another family for two years now. I should have gone to a convent until my marriage, but I refused and father kept me at home. He always lets me have my own way unless my mother incites him against me. He promised me this morning that he would marry me to one of his boyhood friends, a recently bereaved marquis.'

'Then you'll have a husband of a certain age.'

'I don't know him, but father says he will certainly grant me all my wishes. I want magnificent clothes and a coach with gilt mouldings, four greys and lackeys as tall as the Comte de Racon.'

'Why are you laughing, M. Saint-Jean?'

'At the idea of your tall lackeys. Please start trotting so that we can catch the coach up.'

'I would rather ride alone with you.'

'Mademoiselle, your parents would not like that.'

'But I like it. I shall continue at walking pace.'

'Mademoiselle, as your master of the horse, I shall drive your horse a little.'

'No, it would run away with me.'

'Then start trotting.'

'You are very forceful, M. Saint-Jean.'

'Only occasionally, Mademoiselle.' Martin's crop swished through the air and Marguerite quickly put her grey into a trot.

'M. Saint-Jean, your foot was bitten by a mad dog. Could you have caught hydrophobia?'

'The dog that bit me was not mad, but I don't know whether I shall be able to bear a second day's riding. My foot hurts terribly.'

'I am sorry for you.'

'You are very kind.' Marguerite did not stir from Martin's side until the midday halt, and continued to gossip until he knew every detail of her family life.

As Martin had feared, he was unable to ride next day. The

baron offered him a seat in the coach and he sat opposite the married couple with his foot up, in ever increasing pain. Marguerite kept siding up to the coach and enquiring after his health through the window, until the baroness said that her questions would certainly not help to cure the master of the horse. The following day the pain had become unbearable, so that Martin, with a high fever, had to be left behind at a wretched village inn, since the baron did not wish to increase his travelling expenses by a longer stay. Dominique sent François in search of some old herb woman, and the capable lad returned with an old shepherdess, who actually managed to cure the blood-poisoning which had set in.

While he lay on his sick-bed, Martin kept re-enacting the nightmare scenes of the past few days. To calm himself he played his flute and began to read *The Meditations* of Marcus Aurelius—one of the books he had inherited from the first Vicomte de Clarmont. But the high moral precepts of the noble Roman Emperor were soon obscured by the image of the count. He tried in vain to overcome his doubts. Not until his foot was almost healed and he could set out again on his journey did his fears and sorrows vanish and his natural gaiety return.

In good spirits and full of curiosity, Martin arrived at the baron's castle, to find that it conformed exactly to Marguerite's description. Baptiste, the groom, had taken the place of the steward who had left for lack of pay; with pride and dignity he wore his predecessor's livery, which was too tight for him. When the baron was absent, he served the morning chocolate to his mistress in bed, and the maid Annette, who had been in the service of the late baroness, knew how to make herself important in the servant's kitchen with insinuations.

The naughtiness of the six-year-old twins surpassed the bounds of imagination. When, for the first time, he put them on the ponies which the baron had bought for them immediately on his return, he discovered that the seat of little Claude's hose was warm and damp. He pulled him off the horse and said that the little 'wet breeks' should quickly put on another pair and ride on his nurse's lap rather than on a pony. Claude stamped his feet and began to scream, whereupon

Martin locked him in an empty loose-box and did not let him out until André had finished his lesson. Claude ran to his mother who abused the new master of the horse as a brute and a fiend. Before the second riding-lesson, however, both the children's pants were dry. The twins obeyed Martin implicitly, and soon grew so attached to him that they followed him about like little pages. They woke him early in the morning, hopped on to his bed and were furious if they found his bedroom door locked and were told to run away and play. This usually happened when he forgot to send Jacqueline, the maid, back to her room before falling asleep.

The black-haired, amorous girl had fallen in love with him and threatened to scratch the eyes out of any other girl who dared to look at him. Martin ignored her sentiments and took her for granted. This pleased Marguerite who knew everything that went on in the castle. She looked on Martin as her cavalier and was jealous even of her brothers. She went out riding with him and the twins every day, and was furious if he paid more attention to the boys' seat than to her chatter. The youngsters had no nerves, and the baron was delighted when he saw their progress. He thanked Martin profusely for taking such pains, and constantly tried to make him gamble, but Martin was adamant and refused to touch a card.

At the beginning of January, when the baron was absent again and the baroness recovering from a successful confinement, an antiquated but luxurious coach, with several grooms and pack-horses, arrived. From it descended the baron's long-expected boyhood friend, to ask formally for the hand of Mlle Marguerite d'Epponcourt. Marguerite happened to be out riding with Martin, and the baroness had to receive the old marquis alone. She offered him refreshment and said in a gentle, rather plaintive voice, that he must be a little indulgent with her stepdaughter. The untutored child refused to behave like a young gentlewoman and despite all reprimands, constantly roamed the neighbourhood with a young officer whom, unfortunately, the baron held in high esteem and had engaged as master of the horse. She, herself, feared for the girl's virtue and prayed to God that she would preserve her innocence until her marriage. The marquis asked coldly why the young lady had not been sent to a convent like every other young lady of her standing. The baroness then began to complain of the foolish weakness of her husband, who could not bring himself to thwart the child. Marguerite had refused to go into a convent. The marquis looked thoughtful, and the baroness begged him once more to be indulgent. At this moment they heard horses' hooves in the neglected courtyard, and the marquis saw Marguerite returning with Martin from her ride.

The baroness sent Annette to Marguerite, who appeared in a dress she had outgrown with soiled, crumpled lace. On catching sight of her, the baroness complained to the marquis that he could see for himself how little store the girl set by her appearance, and how painful it was that nothing could be done about it. The old man paid Marguerite a few casual compliments, and remarked to the baroness that he was only passing through and hoped shortly to pay another visit, for he wished to see his boyhood friend again. He took his leave after the midday meal, without having made a marriage proposal, and drove away with the greatest possible speed. Marguerite was very upset, and the baroness accused her reproachfully of having driven her prospective bridegroom away. Marguerite flew into a tantrum, screaming that it was not her fault that she had no beautiful dress and a stepmother who was only interested in her own children. With a dangerous flash in her eyes, the baroness replied that this was natural and that Marguerite should leave the room politely, or else woe betide her precious hair. Marguerite fled weeping to her bedroom.

A little later, a lackey chewing onions sidled up to Martin, who was teaching the twins to draw, to inform him that Mademoiselle would like to ride with M. Saint-Jean. The twins started to scream with rage. 'M. Saint-Jean,' shouted Claude, 'you left us for the whole morning after our riding-lesson. Please stay with us.'

'Draw a horse next to the soldier,' insisted André. 'You promised!'

'Be quiet, so that the onion-eater can hear what I say. You there, if you don't immediately swallow what you have in your mouth and stick the remaining onions in your pocket, you'll get a taste of my fist.'

The lackey swallowed in amazement and pocketed his onions. 'Tell François that I shall be in the courtyard in ten minutes,' ordered Martin. 'I'll ride Mira.'

'Very good, M. Saint-Jean,' replied the lackey, hurrying away.

'Now, I'll draw you the horse,' said Martin. The twins watched him intently. 'Move your heads, I can't see the paper. I can't draw a plaited mane, I'll give it a flowing one and you can decorate the saddle-cloth yourselves.' Martin completed a picture, which looked like a sausage on legs, but the boys were satisfied. He dismissed them with the piece of paper to the nursery, put on his coat, since the sky was overcast, and went down into the courtyard where an impatient Marguerite was waiting for him.

Hardly had they left the gate than Marguerite said in a voice quivering with excitement: 'The marquis has left without asking for my hand.'

'My heartfelt sympathies.'

'He had such a beautiful coach.'

'And a head like a radish with that pointed beard.'

'Yes, but husbands are never handsome.'

'Particularly when they slip out of your clutches.'

'Why are you so disagreeable to me, M. Saint-Jean?'

'Mademoiselle, if I were a marquis, I should not ask for your pretty hand.'

'Why not?'

'Because you are dirty and unkempt.'

'That's what my stepmother says, but I can't help it. Nobody washes my linen. The babies' napkins always have to be washed, or the maids have something else to do. Your shirts are always clean because Jacqueline is in love with you. While my nurse was here my clothes were always in order, but Barbara quarrelled with my stepmother and had to return to her village.'

'Why don't you ask your father for a lady's maid?'

'More than once he has picked a maid to wait on me, but no one obeys him and the girls only do what my stepmother wants.'

'Why don't you leave and visit relations?'

'I have only a great-uncle, a bishop, who looks after my dowry, and my uncle d'Oubray who is always travelling round the world and has now taken Holy Orders. All my other relatives have quarrelled with my father.'

'Go into a convent then until they find another husband for you.'

'Never, M. Saint-Jean. I won't set foot in a convent, for once I was inside they would never let me out again. My stepmother often says to my father that the best thing for me would be to become a nun.'

'It looks to me as though your stepmother has her eyes on your dowry.'

'That's quite possible. She often complains that her children have to grow up in poverty, while I have been well provided for. She once wrote to my great-uncle asking him to send money from my dowry so that she could give me a trousseau, but he never sent any.'

'He was right.'

'What shall I do?'

'Darn your hose when you get home. The seam is coming apart at the knee.'

'I should like to gallop,' Marguerite replied, blushing. Beneath a grey sky, they raced across the damp meadows and fallow-land to a clearing where logs were being carted away. 'Look,' said Marguerite, 'that is how my father has to pay his gambling debts. If he goes on like this we soon shan't have any firewood left.' Martin did not answer. They skirted the pathetic patch of logs and tree-stumps and turned into a young beech wood where the bare branches were tangled like undergrowth.

'They ought to be thinned out,' said Martin. 'Why doesn't your father send his labourers to attend to it?'

'Because no one would go if he were sent. The wood thieves prefer thick trunks.'

'Your father must engage an energetic bailiff, and the sooner the better.'

'He had one who grew rich and then gave notice.'

'Why don't you take on the post?'

'I?'

'Yes, you've nothing else to do.'

'Do you expect me to deal with peasants and serfs? I never speak to them since one of them was insolent to me.'

'Shall I make them respect you? I would gladly be of assistance.'

'Thank you, M. Saint-Jean, but this dilapidated estate is no concern of mine. I am a girl and I have no wish to work for the benefit of my stepmother's children.'

'But you could do it for your own good name.'

'I want to marry and get away from here. If you were of noble birth you would please me.'

'But perhaps you wouldn't please me,' laughed Martin.

'Wouldn't I? I know very well you find me attractive.'

'You may be wrong.'

'No, I'm not.'

'You were grievously wrong over the Vicomte de Clarmont.'

'He wanted me though.'

'There you're right.'

'So you see!' The path grew narrower and Marguerite rode on ahead. Laying her head on her horse's neck, she held on to overhanging branches until they sprang back into Martin's face. Each time she was successful, she laughed.

The path ended at a tumbledown hunting lodge; a sapling had sprouted from one of its windows. 'I'm tired and I should like to take a rest here,' said Marguerite, dismounting. 'Tie up my horse.' Martin obeyed. Marguerite went into the lodge and trampled about in the dry rustling leaves.

'Put your coat down here, M. Saint-Jean, so that I can sit down.'

'Do you want me to freeze?'

'No, I'll take off my cloak and then we can sit close to each other.'

'Mademoiselle, I do not wish to sit too close to you.'

'Why not?'

'Because I might find it too warm.'

'We're in January, M. Saint-Jean. Take off your coat if you are a cavalier.' Martin did as she asked him. They sat down and wrapped themselves in the second coat.

'Well, now we're sitting down and soon we shall have cold feet,' said Martin.

'My feet are warm. Please entertain me.'

'Mademoiselle, you will ruin your reputation if you ride too often alone with me. You should always take a groom with you.'

'M. Saint-Jean, I feel perfectly safe with you.'

'Your confidence does me honour.'

'Why are you such a pillar of virtue?'

'Because green little girls leave me cold.'

'What do you mean by "green"?'

'Had I interrupted the Vicomte de Clarmont a little later, you would no longer have been green.'

'Who told you that I am?'

'Mademoiselle, it would be discourteous of me to doubt your virtue.'

Marguerite sighed. 'Oh, this virtue! If I only knew whether it were worth while.'

'I can assure you that it is,' replied Martin, hiding a smile, 'since you may want to be respected by your future husband.'

In mock despair Marguerite protested: 'I wish tomorrow were my wedding day! Afterwards I could do as I please.'

'And what would please you after your wedding?'

'A lover who really attracted me.'

'Do you propose to follow your stepmother's example?'

Marguerite struck Martin's knee with her whip. 'You insult me. I never look at stable lads.'

'Mademoiselle, if you hit me again I shall give you tit for tat.'

'You would not do such a thing. There!'

She struck him again and Martin used his whip. 'Ow! You are unkind to me, M. Saint-Jean.'

'I warned you.'

She tried to slap him but Martin caught hold of her arms. 'Mademoiselle, please try and behave yourself. It's time for us to return, otherwise anything might happen.'

'Let me go!'

'Promise me first that you will be good.'

'Apologise to me, M. Saint-Jean.'

'Very well, I apologise.'

'I will behave.'

Martin released her and Marguerite rubbed her wrist. 'You are hateful, M. Saint-Jean.'

'I am very sorry.' Marguerite began weeping. 'Why are you weeping, young lady?'

'Because I'm unhappy.'

'Console yourself. There are plenty of old rakes like the marquis. You will be sure to find another.'

'I thought life was beautiful, and really it's all so disgusting. Even my mother had an affair with your father, the Comte de Racon. Annette told me so . . . And she died while he was sleeping at her side.'

'Does that obscure the image of your dead mother?'

'Yes, M. Saint-Jean, the Comte de Racon is so ugly.'

'Mademoiselle, your mother loved him, and so he must have qualities that make him lovable. Forgive your mother.'

'Oh, M. Saint-Jean, if there were someone I could care for.'

'Claude and André are very nice little boys.'

'They only like you.'

'That is your own fault. You are only loved if you are worth loving.'

'I have not noticed that you are,' she mocked.

'I did not say that I was; I meant that you should try to be.'

Marguerite dried her face on her sleeve. 'My nurse, Barbara, told me fairy tales and said that one day I should marry a handsome prince, but I was too poor for the Vicomte de Clarmont and too dirty for the marquis. I won't wait much longer.'

'What do you mean?'

Marguerite plucked at the dead leaves. 'My virtue is a millstone round my neck.'

Martin burst out laughing. 'Mademoiselle, only your Father Confessor should hear that!'

'No, for he would give me a heavy penance. I don't want to atone.'

Martin looked through the paneless window into the tangled branches. 'Mademoiselle, I should like to tell you something now. Would you like to hear it?'

'Yes.'

'At the age of fourteen I began with an actress, and since then I have had a host of trollops and ladies.'

'Ladies of quality?'

'Yes, those too. I loved none of those women and merely satisfied my greed, like a starving man. Then I fell in love with a woman who will never be mine. An unhappy love is hell on earth, but at least it allows one to suspect something of the glory of true love. Love is divine, and whether hidden or visible, its glow reflects a shining light from heaven. You will find it in the caresses of a mother, in charitable monks who tend the sick, in the rule of a noble, upright prince, in the tenderness of lovers and in the blessings of priests. There is nowhere in the world it does not want to dwell.'

'Could it dwell here, too?'

'Yes, it could. You must open your heart so that love can enter into it, and be careful not to obscure it. Not everyone understands that. I was loved by a noble widow and was attached to her, but with the best will I could not bring myself to return her affection. When I visited her before leaving for Grandval, after the death of the first Vicomte de Clarmont, she embraced me at parting with such tears of despair and such burning kisses that, later, I was ashamed of having been everything to her, whereas she had meant almost nothing to me. I was suddenly ashamed of her gifts, and intentionally mislaid them. I shall never visit her again. I hope that she will find a friend who returns her love and who is worthy of her. I cannot love two women.'

'Does Jacqueline's love also make you feel ashamed?'

'Yes.'

'Then why do you allow her into your bedroom?'

'Because I am too used to women to be able to do without them. Preserve your virtue until you find a bridegroom of suitable standing. In the meantime, rest assured you will not miss anything.'

Marguerite lay back on the leaves. 'M. Saint-Jean, I think you are cheating. I am probably missing a great deal, or else would Jacqueline visit your bedroom and my mother fall in love with your father?'

'Be careful you don't get any ticks,' warned Martin. Marguerite sat up immediately and brushed the leaves from her hair. Martin helped her, suddenly stood up and pulled her to her feet. 'Mademoiselle, you must not stay here any longer. It would be a pity if you flung yourself, without love, at a man incapable of fully appreciating your qualities and one who would thus have to feel more ashamed than you.'

'M. Saint-Jean, you are an idiot.'

'That may be. I know a lady who visited the Comte de Racon, uninvited, without degrading herself in the least, since she truly loved him. You are incapable of such a love.'

'Thank God for that, M. Saint-Jean.'

'Yes, thank God!' Martin picked up Marguerite's cloak and shook it. 'Now, slip into this.' Having done so, Marguerite left the building with a contemptuous shrug of her shoulders. Martin put on his cloak as he walked, untied the horses and helped her into her saddle. He proceeded to ride once more behind her. Marguerite did not utter a word, and this time she did not try to make the branches spring back into his face.

On their return home, Martin accompanied the girl into the castle and then went to the kitchen where Jacqueline, the poultry maid, was crumbling stale bread in an earthenware pot for the hens. He acknowledged the greeting of a few grooms who were warming themselves by the stove, and asked Jacqueline when his shirts would be ready. 'They won't dry, Monsieur, so I shan't be able to iron them today.'

'I need them the day after tomorrow, because I'm leaving.'

The maid looked crestfallen as she replaced the pot on the oven. When Martin left the kitchen she ran after him into the pantry. 'Why are you leaving, Monsieur?'

'Because I don't like it here. The castle is falling into decay, and so are the occupants. The children are still all right, but it is a disgrace for an officer of the king's guard to ride about with a young lady as badly dressed as a lousy page who has lost his master in the war and has to fend for himself. I've had about enough of your master's hospitality. I'm packing tomorrow.'

'Oh, Monsieur, do stay.'

'No, I refuse to go out riding again with your dirty Mademoiselle.'

'Monsieur, I can wash Mademoiselle's linen and repair everything.'

'Can you?'

'Of course, Monsieur. I always darn your stockings and your

underclothes, so why shouldn't I be able to attend to women's linen?'

'I didn't think you capable of doing it because you are here to look after the poultry.'

'I should like to have been a lady's maid, Monsieur, because I have a gift for that, but Annette will not let me near Madame, and Madame gives anyone who does something for Mademoiselle another job to do. But I will ask her for her linen, steal some soap and wash and iron it in secret. Believe me, Monsieur, by Sunday Mademoiselle will look quite different . . . so please stay here.'

'I'll stay until Sunday, and if you have spoken the truth, I'll stay until the spring. I saw your woodcutter today. He obviously still loves you fervently, for he gave me a very black look. You should listen to his proposals instead of hanging round me.'

'I won't have anything to do with him as long as you're here. I may return to him then.'

'Be careful he doesn't find some other girl.'

'No one here is as ardent as I.'

'Are you so sure?'

'Was one of the housemaids with you last night?'

'No, you witch, I wanted to be left in peace.'

'Did you hear me knocking?'

'Don't bother to knock. When the door is unlocked, come in. Otherwise stay outside. On your way!' Jacqueline curtsied and returned to the kitchen.

On Sunday, everyone noticed that Marguerite's clothes were clean and tidy for a change. Marguerite was delighted with Jacqueline's industry and gave her a necklace. Martin rewarded the maid with a contented smile and the observation that he had no intention of leaving for the present.

The baron returned with a certain M. de Riberac, learned of the marquis's abortive visit and was almost in despair. He cursed Marguerite and kept whining that he had to find a husband for an ill-bred daughter and knew of no nobleman who would make a suitable son-in-law. That evening, as he sat at cards with M. de Riberac, his guest suddenly asked for Marguerite's hand. The baron was amazed, because M. de

Riberac possessed nothing but his horse and the clothes he stood up in and was notorious throughout the whole neighbourhood as a gambler and a drunkard who was an expert at running up debts for drink and preying on people from whom he could win a little money at cards. He was still young, not unpleasing in appearance, and a useful swordsman. He liked to boast of the campaigns in which he had fought, but it was whispered that his numerous scars could just as easily have been received in brawls.

The baron turned red, threw down the cards and was about to turn down the offer with contempt, when the baroness looked up from her book and said that Mademoiselle d'Epponcourt was too good a match for the gentleman, and if his offer were serious he would have to be content with half the dowry. M. de Riberac replied that he was quite agreeable, for he had not made his offer out of greed but out of love for the enchanting young lady. The baroness cast a glance at her husband, which silenced him, and told their guest that they would think over his offer until the following day. Then she returned to her book and the gentlemen shuffled the cards.

Next morning, Marguerite was summoned to her parents and introduced to M. de Riberac. This was her bridegroom, and she should be delighted in future to be able to live so near her parents, for the large diary farm which was hers could be converted into a country seat for her. When Marguerite replied that the house was dilapidated, that she refused to live in it, and that M. de Riberac did not attract her, the baroness gave her the choice of becoming an old maid or of entering a convent. Her reputation was already so bad that she would have to abandon any hope of getting a rich husband. Marguerite was thunderstruck, and when M. de Riberac flung himself on his knees before her and implored her to accept his offer in her confusion she accepted. The baroness immediately drew up a marriage contract in her own hand, whereby M. de Riberac relinquished half the dowry in favour of his parents-in-law. A notary was sent for and Marguerite appended her signature. A letter was then sent to the bishop asking him to hand over the dowry.

The same evening, Marguerite came weeping to her parents and, with the courage of despair, threatened that if the contract were not torn up she would refuse to give her consent at the altar. As usual, the baron could not resist her tears, and would easily have been persuaded to alter his decision had his wife not intervened and in a soft voice explained to Maguerite that the marriage was a long way off, and that there was enough time to consider the matter at leisure and to cancel or amend the contract if necessary. Marguerite was pacified and retired to her bedroom.

The baroness easily succeeded in persuading her husband to agree to the marriage plan by mentioning his debts, which he could pay with half the dowry. Then she had a tête-à-tête with M. de Riberac, spoke touchingly of the girl's frightened innocence and advised him not to shrink from making use of his marital rights before the marriage so that the girl, overtaken by events, would be only too willing to consent in church. M. de Riberac promised to follow her broadminded advice at the next opportunity, but never managed to find Marguerite alone. She would only suffer his company in Martin's presence on their rides, and bolted her door at night. March 1st was the date secretly arranged for the wedding, and yet, by the middle of February, M. de Riberac had approached no nearer to his goal.

One evening, when Martin was having his boots removed by Dominique, there was a sudden wild knocking at the door and Marquerite's terrified voice asking for admittance. Martin hastily put on a pair of shoes; Dominique pulled back the bolt and left the room. The girl was tousled and out of breath. Martin pushed forward the single rickety chair and asked her to sit down. 'M. Saint-Jean,' she cried, 'M. de Riberac has behaved in the most shameless manner. When I tried to enter my bedroom he caught hold of me, dragged me to my bed and tried to violate me, as the Vicomte de Clarmont wanted to do. Challenge him and kill him on the spot! I hit him on the shin with the heel of my shoe; he let go and I managed to run away, but he kissed me and tore my dress. Avenge me!'

'Mademoiselle, M. de Riberac is in love with you, and one must be indulgent with one's bridegroom.'

'I implore you to free me from this fellow.'

'I have no desire to cross swords with M. de Riberac. I will advise him to mend his manners.'

'Kill him!'

'I am no murderer, Mademoiselle. Allow me to take you to your room.'

Marguerite sat down on the wobbly chair. 'M. Saint-Jean, you have not changed for the better recently. You are off-hand with me and only laugh when you play with the twins. Have you become jealous?'

'No, I'm waiting for news from the Comte de Racon, because spring will soon be here. This long wait is becoming a nightmare. I no longer belong to the light horse of the guard and shall presumably have to serve with a shoddy line regiment somewhere on the frontier. I cannot go to Paris and am compelled to hide for the rest of my life from the Vicomte de Clarmont's hatred. Have I any reason to be gay?'

'Certainly not, M. Saint-Jean, but my position is no better and my future is possibly even blacker. Your suspicions that they had designs on my dowry were correct. Half of it will almost certainly go to my parents, I should have shown more courage with father, but I am too afraid of my stepmother. You must save me from this Riberac.'

'They will only find another adventurer for you. If I owned a property, would you become my wife?'

'No, for you are not of the nobility.'

'And if I possessed a bought title?'

'I don't hold with new titles. I can muster seventy-three noble ancestors! Help me to find a nobleman and I will reward you after my marriage.'

'Is that a serious offer, Mademoiselle?'

'Yes, you are my only hope.'

'I will help you without expecting any reward. I will take you to your uncle, the bishop.'

'Anything but that, M. Saint-Jean. He wrote to me at Christmas that he was praying to God that he would be granted the joy of arraying me in a nun's heavenly bridal veil. My great-uncle would put me in a convent.'

'There you would be safe from importunity. Does the idea of bearing a child each year to a husband you do not love attract you then?'

'I have never given the matter a thought.'

'The Comtesse de Racon bore one child after the other until she was an incurably sick woman. Isn't a convent better than that?'

'My stepmother continues to bear children and is none the worse for it.'

'I wish you the same health as she enjoys.'

Martin began to pace up and down the room. 'Some of my comrades in the regiment are bachelors,' he remarked suddenly. 'I could write to one of them. He is the third son of a marquis, a capable, honest youth and not entirely without means. Perhaps he is still free.'

'Write to him!'

'Must I do so at once?'

'Yes, I beg of you.'

'I will ask your father for writing material,' replied Martin with a smile, 'and accompany you to your bedroom door.'

'No. I'll wait for you because I should like to read the letter.'

'And what of your reputation?'

'My stepmother says that it is already irreparably lost.'

'Mademoiselle, that is only because you persist in riding alone with me.'

'But, M. Saint-Jean, nothing has ever happened.'

'Surely you know that people always suspect the worst?'

'I'll wait for you all the same.'

'As you please. Close the door behind me, and don't reply to Jacqueline if she tries to come in. I will call you by name so that you will know it is I.'

Martin found the baron playing cards with M. de Riberac. 'Ah, M. Saint-Jean,' cried the baron, 'won't you join us?'

'No, thank you Monsieur, I've only come to ask you for some writing material and to inform M. de Riberac that he has frightened Mademoiselle. She came to me in distress.'

The embarrassed baron began to rummage in the drawer for quills and paper. 'M. Saint-Jean, how did I frighten Mademoiselle?' asked de Riberac.

'You should know better than I. Please be patient until the

marriage, so that I shall not have to protect your bride against her bridegroom.'

'I have no idea what you mean.'

'Then there must be some mistake, and there is no need for me to warn you. Thank you, Baron. Could you find me some sealing wax?'

'Here it is, M. Saint-Jean.'

'Thank you.' Martin picked up his writing material, bowed curtly and left the room.

'Monsieur,' said de Riberac in a sudden outburst of anger, 'tell me why you tolerate this young greenhorn here?'

'He is the illegitimate son of a count who paid me well for keeping the boy here.'

'Is he Marguerite's lover?'

'No, certainly not. I have often asked her, and each time she says that he will have nothing to do with her. I would gladly forbid her his company, but even less can I let her ride out with the grooms, and he is very good with the children.'

'Well, now I can ride with her.'

'My dear Riberac, I am indebted to the young man's father and wish to avoid any unpleasantness. I have quite enough troubles as it is. Let's continue with the game.'

Marguerite let Martin into his room and watched him as he began to write. As soon as he had written the address, he laid the pen aside and asked:

'Mademoiselle, do you constantly have to brush against me with your dress? You are very pretty and I beg you not to lead me into temptation.'

'Bah! You are a saint and resist every temptation except Jacqueline, the maid.'

'Go and sit on my bed and don't come over here, or else I won't write to my regimental comrade.'

Marguerite pouted but did as she was told. 'What does he look like?'

'He is taller than I, has beautiful wavy hair and is very gay.'

'Then he is obviously nicer than you.'

'Let us hope so. And now don't disturb me any more, please, because I want to write legibly.' Marguerite kept quiet and Martin's quill began to scratch once more. 'I've finished now,' he said at last. 'Would you like to read it?'

'No, you read it to me.'

'MONSIEUR,

Presuming you to be still unmarried, I should very much like to present to you a young lady from a very ancient family; she is very beautiful and finds herself in a predicament as a result of the second marriage of her father, the Baron d'Epponcourt. They are trying to force the girl against her will to marry a man who is prepared to renounce half the dowry, which would certainly be paid in full to a suitor from a respected family of equal standing. On account of my origin I cannot, unfortunately, be considered. If you care to come here, you can convince yourself of the lady's charms and, at the same time, you will have the opportunity of making a favourable impression. Your visit will not bind you in any way, for you could use me as a pretext, saying that you were passing through and wanted to see your regimental comrade again. You will probably not find me here, but that won't affect matters or disturb anyone. Should you see the Comte de Racon, please do not mention this letter and please do not betray my address to anyone. As you probably know, the Vicomte de Clarmont is my bitter enemy and I am forced to keep my whereabouts a secret from him. Trusting in your silence and loyalty, I hope that this letter will be well received and I remain, with respectful greetings, your former regimental comrade,

MARTIN SAINT-JEAN

'Are you pleased with this letter, Mademoiselle?'

'Yes, but why did you not describe me in greater detail?'

'I have never learned the art of extolling my wares, and, in any case, my suggestion makes me feel like a huckster. If the young cavalier did not know me he would probably take me for a pimp. I can only hope he will come and rescue you from your plight.'

'M. Saint-Jean, please add a postscript that my dowry amounts to 200,000 livres in cash.'

Martin did as he was asked and remarked: 'In any case I

have warned your bridegroom. Your father seemed ashamed of his son-in-law. I hope he will give him a piece of his mind.'

'He would only do that with the consent of his wife. If only I could be under your protection day and night.'

'Shall I order Dominique to sleep in your closet?'

'That would be kind of you, M. Saint-Jean.'

'Gladly, but don't give me away, and tell no one that you applied to me for a guard. Old Dominique cannot harm your reputation.'

'M. Saint-Jean, I am grateful to you. Please send that letter off tomorrow. I shall tell my father that I refuse to marry M. de Riberac, in any circumstances, and will give him no peace until the fellow is gone.'

'Mademoiselle, you must not aggravate the baroness. Hold your peace and wait. You can always refuse to accept at the altar, or flee to your great-uncle. You know you can rely on my support.'

Marguerite stood up. 'You are my knight and I trust you.'

Martin called Dominique and ordered him to sleep as a guard in Marguerite's closet. The old man scowled, but lit Marguerite to her room.

Next day, just before the midday meal, while Martin was practising on his flute, seven horsemen and two pack-horses trotted into the castle courtyard, which had become a barnyard. They were led by Comte de Racon's master of the hunt who as soon as he had dismounted asked to speak to M. Saint-Jean. With four huntsmen, carrying two coffers, he was shown up to Martin's room.

Martin, who was engrossed in his playing and had not noticed their arrival, jumped up and cried with joy:

'Master Grouchet, you've brought me news of the Comte de Racon! Where am I to meet him?'

Grouchet turned to his four men. 'Go and rejoin the others.' The men set down the coffers and left the room. Grouchet took out a thick, sealed letter from his coat and handed it to Martin, who recognising the count's writing, seized it eagerly. Breaking the seal, he found several pages and began to read while the master of the hunt opened the coffers.

To My Son, Martin Saint-Jean,

Circumstances have forced me to make a new decision which is final and irrevocable. I am indispensable at Court and will shortly be travelling in the king's suite to Marly. The Vicomte de Clarmont is my constant companion and, as his father, I am in duty bound to support him in every respect and to further him in all his undertakings. I am no longer in a position to gratify my own personal pleasures. My inclinations have to take second place to my duties. I shall never meet you again and forbid you to come in search of me. I should refuse to recognise you.

On my orders, Grouchet is bringing you 10,000 livres in cash. I have bought you an estate in Brittany with a yearly income of 6,000 livres. You will find the deed of conveyance enclosed. In future, call yourself after the name of your property, Saint-Jean de Beauvois. According to the custom in the country, you will be respected everywhere as M. de Beauvois, which is almost tantamount to a patented title. I can no longer bother about the title promised to you because, as a result of my long absence last year, I am still partially in disgrace. I have ordered Grouchet to bury 50,000 livres for you in Beauvois, in the hinder-most cellar to the left of the steps leading to the fountain.

You will also find letters of recommendation to two regimental commanders, one of whom is in command of a fortress in Flanders, and the other of a grenadier regiment in the Vosges. Since I have not shrunk from giving the real reason for your dismissal from the guards, you will certainly be accepted by one of these gentlemen and you can thus continue with your military career. You will also find a letter of recommendation from the Marquis de Chassigny. Do not forget to use the name of your property, so that the name 'Saint-Jean' will be forgotten.

If you wish to render me a last service, apply to serve abroad. The Elector of Brandenburg engages soldiers from all countries and would eagerly accept a French lieutenant who had taken part in the battles of Seneffe and St Denis to train his troops. I give you one piece of advice: see to the administration of your estate first. You can always sell it any time if you want to buy another property elsewhere.

Look upon this estate as an assurance for your old age and as a home for your children.

Try to realise why I had to break my word, and say to yourself that a man of twenty-one must be wise enough not to ask more of the world than it is prepared to offer. Give Grouchet a receipt, and travel with a large enough escort because of the money and the deed.

GASTON,

COMTE DE RACON, MARQUIS DE BRAYONNE

Martin placed the letter on the table and folded the remaining papers together, unread.

'M. Saint-Jean,' said Grouchet, 'here are the keys to the coffers. Please count the money.' Martin looked at the master of the hunt uncomprehendingly. 'M. Saint-Jean, I need a receipt from you in writing that I have delivered the money to you in full, together with the deed of conveyance.'

'A receipt?'

'Yes, for M. le Comte.'

'I could not write to the count.'

'I have been ordered to ask for a receipt and will not return without one.'

'What have I to sign for?'

'That you have received the deed and that the coffers contain 10,000 livres. Please count it before nightfall. I will report to you later and leave tomorrow morning. Please give me leave to retire.'

'You may go, Master Grouchet.' Left alone, Martin sat down on the rickety chair and stared into space. His face was expressionless, as though his spirit had been completely numbed. He sat there motionless until Dominique came and reminded him that it was time for supper.

Martin went down to the dining-hall where the baron's family were already at table. Marguerite's face was tear-stained and the baron was as red as a turkey-cock. 'M. Saint-Jean, M. Saint-Jean,' cried the twins, 'six fine huntsmen came to you, and a master of the hunt with silver braid! Are they taking you away?'

'No, they have not come to take me away.'

'M. Saint-Jean,' cried the baron, 'do you expect me to feed seven men and nine horses, in addition to your valet, your groom and your own five horses?'

'No, I will pay for them. They are leaving tomorrow.'

'Good, and kindly do not incite my daughter against her bridegroom.'

'I have incited no one, and I shall be leaving tomorrow too.'

'M. Saint-Jean, it was agreed that you should remain until I acquired a new master of the horse.'

'You have had long enough to look for one. I have broken-in all your horses, and your six-year-old boys ride as well as ten-year-olds. I see no good reason why I should stay here.'

'I have a master of the horse in view and beg you to remain until he arrives so that you can test him before you leave and see that I do not engage an oaf. I think very highly of your horsemanship.'

'Baron, can you afford a master of the horse?'

'I am bound to give my daughter a brilliant wedding, and urgently need new servants. I should very much like to borrow yours for the banquet.'

'So that's it! And when is the marriage to take place?'

'Next week.'

Martin noticed Marguerite's look of entreaty. 'A week more or less makes no difference, Baron. I will remain until the marriage.'

'I am delighted.'

'M. Saint-Jean,' cried the twins in unison, 'you mustn't go away. We want to learn fencing, jumping and how to play the flute!'

After supper, Martin found Grouchet in his room. 'I have been waiting for you. Can I have the receipt?'

'Take the money and the deed with you. I don't want to know anything about it.'

'Are you out of your mind?'

'That is possible. Here, take the key.'

'No, M. Saint-Jean.'

'Master Grouchet, can you read?'

'Yes, a little.'

'Then read this letter.'

Martin took the count's letter from his pocket and handed it to Grouchet. The master of the hunt tried to decipher the writing with his long-sighted eyes. His grizzled red moustaches quivered. Martin waited until he cleared his throat and returned the letter. 'M. Saint-Jean, you should be very grateful.'

'Master Grouchet, I am not sensible enough for that. I was always a fool. Take the coffers and leave me alone.'

'M. Saint-Jean, I must take a receipt back to M. le Comte.'

'I won't write a word to him.'

'Then at least write to Madame la Comtesse.'

'Yes, I can do that. Sit on my bed and wait for me. I'll write at once.' He fetched the borrowed writing material and sat down at the table.

There was a knock at the door and Marguerite entered. She drew back as she caught sight of the master of the hunt. 'What do you want here?' Martin asked gruffly.

'I have an urgent request to make, M. Saint-Jean.'

'And I have an urgent letter to write. Sit down next to Master Grouchet.' After a moment's hesitation, Marguerite sat next to the master of the hunt while Martin carefully composed the following letter to the Comtesse de Racon:

> MADAME,
>
> Today, Master Grouchet, on orders from the count brought me two coffers containing 10,000 livres and a deed of conveyance confirming me as the owner of an estate. I take the liberty of sending both to you, since I do not want them, and am enclosing the letter I received; it will answer all your questions. I am dismissing Dominique and beg you to look after him. He has served me faithfully, as he served the late vicomte, and is too old for an unsettled life.
>
> With my deepest respects,
>
> MARTIN SAINT-JEAN

Martin folded the letter and enclosed the letter from the count, the recommendations and the deed. Having placed them carefully in an envelope, he sealed them with his iron seal. He retained only the Marquis de Chassigny's letter of recommendation, which he put in his pocket. 'There, Master Grouchet, now you have your receipt. Take Dominique and the coffers to Grandval.'

Grouchet stood up, took the package and the keys. 'I will fetch the coffers. Farewell, M. Saint-Jean.'

'Farewell, Master Grouchet.' The master of the hunt left the room. Martin rose to his feet. 'And now, Mademoiselle, what do you want of me?'

'M. Saint-Jean, my father insists upon my marrying M. de Riberac, because without half my dowry he faces ruin, and my great-uncle will not pay out the money until after my marriage. My stepmother ordered me just now to give M. de Riberac a bridal goodnight kiss. I refused. Everyone laughed, and when Riberac kissed me in spite of my struggles, I ran to you. I won't have a child by this man. Kill him, or elope with me. You must save me.'

'But why me?'

'Because you are my only friend.'

'I am not your friend and I am tired of rescuing you. Only idiots are noble. The woman I loved was in my power and, like a true retriever, without demanding the least favour, I took her to her lover. I would never do that again. I am sorry for you but I warn you to beware of me. I could catch fire and flare up like straw since you have aroused my passion. This Riberac is no worse than myself. Write to the bishop, your great-uncle; he alone can save you. François will take your letter to the post. Write tonight. Hurry. And please do not come to my bedroom in any circumstances in the future without an escort.'

'Did the Comte de Racon's master of the hunt bring you bad news?'

'Get out and don't ask me any more questions.'

'I don't want to write to my great-uncle. I shall wait for your regimental comrade. Until then, protect me!'

'Mademoiselle, neither you nor I know if he will come. Leave my room.'

'Don't shout at me. Why are you trembling like that?'

'Hi, Dominique!'

The old servant appeared. 'Accompany Mademoiselle and pack your things. You're riding back to Grandval with

Grouchet. I want to be alone. Get out, or I shall lose my temper.' Martin's face had undergone such a terrible change that both the girl and the servant almost fled from the room.

Four huntsmen came in and carried the coffers out with all speed. Martin flung himself, fully dressed, on the bed. When Jacqueline, the maid, put her head round the door and spoke to him he flung the candlestick at her. She fled. The extinguished candles rolled under the table. Martin tossed and turned, tore the pillows and spent a sleepless, tortured night. He did not weep. Just before dawn he heard the master of the hunt ride away with his men.

When Martin descended into the courtyard at nine o'clock, Marguerite and M. de Riberac were already on their horses. 'Ah, here's the master of the horse,' cried de Riberac. 'I cannot persuade my bride to stir without your escort.'

Martin mounted Pollux and said, 'M. de Riberac, I see that you are riding the baron's best horse today.'

'Yes, thanks to Dame Fortune who smiled on me at the gaming table.'

'You seem to be a very lucky man.'

'I am, M. Saint-Jean, but Venus has not yet smiled on me. How are the gods disposed towards you?'

'Not particularly amiably.'

They trotted through the castle gate. 'What purpose had your recent visitors?' asked de Riberac.

'They brought me greetings.'

'So, it's a secret. The men rode magnificent horses. The master of the hunt gambled with us but he refused to speak. He played for very low stakes and I did not win anything from him. He curses better than I do. Obviously he was once a soldier.'

'Yes, he was.'

'Did he bring you money from your father?'

'No.'

'But that is what is being rumoured, M. Saint-Jean. Will you gamble with us tonight?'

'I never gamble, M. de Riberac.'

'I'll wager the baron's horse.' Martin did not reply.

Marguerite turned off into a fir plantation, and they rode

through it until they came to damp meadowland bounded in the distance by bare, rust-red woods. The pale, early spring sky grew bluer. Marguerite scanned the empty fields then followed a track, which disappeared among a few solitary hazel bushes at the edge of the dense forest. At last she reined in her horse. 'M. de Riberac, I have something to tell you. You are obviously blind and deaf since you still have not noticed that M. Saint-Jean is my lover. Go on being deaf and blind and take that for your disgusting kiss.' A rapid blow with her riding crop hit the astounded cavalier in the face. Marguerite led her horse behind Martin's and roared with laughter.

'By the hounds of Hell,' de Riberac screamed, 'I'll make you pay for that! You first Saint-Jean, and then you, well-born whore. Dismount, Saint-Jean, and draw your sword. Go on laughing, you trollop, until I have run him through . . . then you won't laugh any more!'

The men jumped down from their horses, tethered them to the hazels, took off their coats and drew their swords, Marguerite looked down from her horse as the duel began. Martin's lips tightened and his eyes were mere slits. At this moment he looked like his father, and Marguerite cried: 'M. Saint-Jean, you have the Comte de Racon's head on your shoulders!'

Martins eyes flashed dangerously. He parried with ease and attacked with ever-increasing speed. M. de Riberac was a skilful swordsman but Martin was his superior. Marguerite shouted with glee as she watched her bridegroom growing terrified, changing over to the defence and trying in vain to gain some respite with leaps and feints. Martin drove him as he pleased in a circle round the horses, until they had returned to their point of departure. Then de Riberac screamed and fell to his knees. Martin had run him through the vitals. Instead of withdrawing his blade, he tore the sword from the vanquished man and thrust at him over and over again, until the screaming victim died in the direst agony. Then he turned round.

Marguerite, terrified by his distraught face, spurred her horse and tried to flee. Martin rushed at the grey, caught hold of the reins, tethered it to a bush and pulled the girl out of the saddle. 'Well, you little liar, is your thirst for blood satisfied? Are you shuddering now, or do you want me to kill someone else for you?'

'Let go of my clothes.'

'No, I won't let go. Now you're going to pay me my reward. Defend yourself and scream . . . I feel like screaming even louder. Your screams are better than blood . . . You're like strong wine. You make me forget his broken word!'

Marguerite defended herself desperately and screamed for help, but Martin tore off her garments one after the other and, in his unleashed savagery, had his will of her. After he had given rein to his passion he stood up, suddenly sober. He threw the torn clothes over the quivering girl, untied his horse and galloped straight across the greenish-brown meadows to calm down.

Returning in a wide circle, he found Marguerite lying in the same piteous position on the ground. He dismounted, tied up his horse, took a piece of her shift and wetted it in a puddle. Wiping her face clean, he tried to help her dress. But her worn-out clothes were so torn that he had to give up his efforts and finally wrapped her in his coat, which reached down to her riding-boots.

'Marguerite, tell me, are you feeling better?' The girl began whimpering and weeping. 'Marguerite, I cannot understand how I could commit such an atrocity and would willingly atone with my life. I will take you home and report to your father. He can deliver me to the hangman.'

'And then what will happen to me?'

Martin did not reply. The girl caught hold of his shirt and screamed. 'M. Saint-Jean, what will become of me? What will happen if I have a child?'

Martin gave an imperceptible start. 'You won't have a child!'

'Is that true?'

'Yes, it's true.'

'But how do you get children then?'

'A girl can't have a child from the first time.'

'Are you sure?'

'I'm quite sure.'

Marguerite shuddered in utter disgust. 'I no longer want a husband. Write and put off your comrade. I don't want him any more!'

'Yes, I'll write to him, and you write to your great-uncle and confess.'

'M. Saint-Jean, I refuse to enter a convent.'

'There is nothing left open to you if you don't marry.'

'I want to remain in the world, away from my parents. Help me! You have dishonoured me and you must not abandon me.'

'I shall be broken on the wheel, Mademoiselle.'

'No, I still need you.'

'Do you wish to conceal my crime?'

'I will conceal my shame. No one must learn of it. M. Saint-Jean, you must not breathe a word to my father. In God's name, save yourself!'

'Anyone who sees you will easily guess what has happened.'

'No, M. Saint-Jean, they must not guess. Fetch me some clothes.'

'That can't be done without arousing attention, Mademoiselle. But I could say that I left you, at Riberac's request, and then heard your cries for help and returned just in time to save you. What do you think of that?'

'Yes, say that M. de Riberac tore my clothes. Can they punish you for running him through?'

'Yes, if they look upon it as a murder.'

'You mustn't be punished.'

'If the baron vouches for me, nothing will happen. Have you no wish to take your revenge on me?'

'I will forego it if you swear to me that you will never again do to me what has just happened.'

'I swear it.'

'Raise your hand and swear by God and the Holy Virgin.' Martin raised his hand and swore. Marguerite wiped away her tears. 'M. Saint-Jean, swear one more oath. Swear that you will never desert me!' Martin swore once more. 'Now put me on the horse in front of you and take me home.'

Their arrival caused great excitement in the castle. The baron said that a third prospective bridegroom had been lost, but that at least he had got back his horse. Their story was believed. The baroness alone doubted Marguerite's providential rescue, and told the others that it would now be more difficult than ever to find a husband for her of her own standing. Riberac was placed in a coffin. Marguerite retired to bed with a fever; Martin wrote to his comrade in the regiment that Mademoiselle had changed her mind and he should not visit her.

On the evening of the same day, the baron came to Martin's room, thanked him for saving his daughter's honour and protested that her dislike for Riberac had weighed on his concience, and that the result of the duel was almost a relief to him. What did Martin propose to do in the immediate future? Martin said that he could not decide whether to go and fight against the Turks or to enter the service of the Elector of Brandenburg, for the Vicomte de Clarmont's enmity barred any chance of his promotion under the French flag. He had nothing against remaining master of the horse for some time, because he was fond of the twins. The baron seemed delighted and blurted out: 'Does my daughter appeal to you?' Martin turned red and said that, since he was not of noble birth, Mademoiselle did not esteem him. The baron replied that he needed a son-in-law of some means. Equality of birth was less important. Martin replied that he had returned to Grandval the money which the master of the hunt had brought. 'For safe custody?' Martin hesitated and finally acquiesced. The baron asked how high the sum was. Martin mentioned the figure and also the deed of conveyance which he had also returned, adding that he had no intention of settling down in Britanny and wished to sell the estate as soon as possible.

The baron rubbed his hands and asked whether Martin would like to live on the property which belonged to Marguerite. Martin replied that he would have to think it over. At this, the baron began to speak of Marguerite's dowry and the amount which he would have to deduct in view of the fact that Martin was not of the nobility, and finally tried to borrow a little money from him to pay a pressing debt. Martin said that he had no cash at his disposal, and offered to supervise the spring sowing on the rest of the baron's properties for three months, so that Mademoiselle could have time to decide one way or the other. Without Marguerite's consent to the marriage he would not pledge his money. The baron agreed to this proposal, and the following day Martin took over his duties as bailiff.

When Marguerite learned of her father's new marriage plan, she found an opportunity of speaking to Martin alone, asking him if he had become swollen-headed and really imagined that she would give him her hand. Martin denied it, and explained calmly that he had only accepted the baron's proposal in order to have some grounds for granting her wish that he should remain close at hand. It was uncertain how long he could keep up this pretence, but he would do everything in his power to avoid being parted from her. The girl sighed with relief, said she was convinced of his good intentions, and allowed him to play the role of a serious suitor in front of her parents.

Martin became the terror of the lazy servants and the salvation of the peasants. He fought for every cow the baron tried to sell in order to gamble away the paltry proceeds. He had the meadows irrigated and forced the baron to dispose of a horse to make up a deficiency of seed. He put the builders to work on the repairs to Marguerite's country house. By replacing the worn-out harrows and ploughs, he succeeded, by April, in bringing under the plough again the fields which had been neglected for years.

The baron sighed under his bailiff's tyranny and soon refrained from contradicting him. Martin was in the saddle from morning till evening and began to look like a thirty-year-old man, although he was only just twenty-two. He saw Marguerite very seldom because she was often confined to bed with stomach-ache and could no longer ride.

One morning at the beginning of May, when Martin had ridden off to see how work was progressing at the country house, he found a number of strange servants, two coaches, and two carts laden with household utensils drawn up in front of the building. When he asked the meaning of this, he was told that the property had been sold to a nobleman who wished to take immediate possession. Martin returned at the gallop to the baron's castle, only to find that the gentleman had just left. Martin pursued him and gave him a piece of his mind through the carriage window. The baron excused himself by saying his creditors had threatened to impound his castle, and started to whine. Martin refused to listen any longer and rode off in a rage.

Two days later, when Martin lay on his bed reading *The Meditations* of Marcus Aurelius by candlelight, he heard a strange rustling outside his door. Lifting his head, he asked:

'Who's there?'

Marguerite's weak voice called out his name. He jumped up, opened the door and found the girl lying, deathly pale, on the floor. He lifted her up, carried her over to the bed and bolted the door.

'What is the matter? Why have you come here?'

'Those drops are killing me.'

'What drops?'

'My stepmother has forced me to take drops for my stomach trouble, for a week now, but each time they make me vomit violently and, instead of getting well, I feel much worse. To-night, in her impatience, she gave me a double dose and it made me choke so badly that I thought I should suffocate. I broke out in a cold sweat and became terrified. Since I was alone I came to you. You must protect me from my stepmother. I am so weak that I cannot refuse to take the drops. You must forbid her to give me any more.'

'You are soaking wet. I will carry you to your room and send for Jacqueline.'

'No, no! Jacqueline will do nothing for me now that you are supposed to be marrying me. I am terrified of my stepmother. My father has left and now she is constantly urging me to go into a convent. I am to give half my dowry to my family. I have a dreadful thirst.'

'Lie there and I'll bring you something to drink.' Martin covered Marguerite with his cloak and went down to the castle kitchen. It was deserted. On searching the larder he discovered a pail of milk, filled a jar and carried it up to his room. When he entered, Marguerite was leaning over the side of the bed retching without being able to vomit. Martin gave her the first glass of milk to drink and the result did not disturb him. She managed to keep down the sixth glass. Then he laid her back on the pillows, took a dirty shirt to wipe the floor and threw it out into the corridor. When he felt Marguerite's brow, he found it moist and icy cold. Without losing any time, he undressed the half-unconscious girl and rubbed her with a clean towel until her circulation returned and he himself was sweating profusely; then he put her under the blankets and saw, to his relief, that she was asleep. He left the room.

After closing the door and hiding the key, he crept as softly as possible to Marguerite's room, saw a phial gleaming in the moonlight, removed the stopper and sniffed at the contents. The liquid had a medicinal smell. Martin returned with his booty to the kitchen, ferreted in the larder and poured the contents into a plate of soup. Then he took the plate, threw the remains of the roast into it and went into the courtyard, where he whistled for one of the dogs and placed the food before him. The dog ate greedily, while Martin kept the others at bay with stones. Hardly had he licked the plate clean than a terrible change came over the animal. Its legs splayed; with raised hackles it began to choke, and suddenly fell with a howl on its side, foamed at the mouth and died. Martin ran back to the castle, threw the empty bottle out of Marguerite's window into the weed-choked garden, where it broke on the stones, and returned to his room.

Marguerite was sleeping peacefully. Martin sat down, rested his head on his hands and waited hour after hour for the striking of the clock in the big hall, which could be heard through the floor. He woke the girl at four o'clock.

'How do you feel?' he asked.

'I'm thirsty, M. Saint-Jean.'

He gave her some more milk and laid her gently back on the pillow. 'Do you feel sick?'

'No, the milk has done me good.'

Martin pulled his chair closer to the bed, and sat down and said: 'Mademoiselle, your stepmother's drops are doing you harm. I have thrown the bottle out of your window and beg you to say that you did it yourself. Don't tell anyone that you came to see me tonight. Are you well enough now to listen to me?'

'Yes, M. Saint-Jean, but I would rather sleep.'

'You must keep awake. Where does the old nurse you once told me about live?'

'In a village, four days' journey from here.'

'Have you ever visited the woman?'

'No, why do you ask me that?'

'You must tell the baroness tomorrow morning that you intend to visit your nurse with me.'

'I don't want to live in a dirty peasant-house.'

'A peasant-house is no dirtier than your bedroom, Mademoiselle.'

'Why should I go? I'm far too ill.'

'Mademoiselle, would you prefer to let yourself be killed with poisons?'

'Killed?'

'I gave the drops to one of the dogs and he's dead.'

'M. Saint-Jean!'

'Don't scream!'

Marguerite tried to catch hold of Martin's hands, but he withdrew them. 'Mademoiselle, I will not abandon you. You must escape from your stepmother. Have you any jewellery?'

'Only what I wore as a child, but tell me . . .'

'Keep quiet. I'll tell you what is important for you to know. Tomorrow, early in the morning, pack all your valuables. I'll take you to your nurse. From there you can write to the Comtesse de Racon and ask her to find you, as soon as possible, a position as lady-in-waiting or companion in some house of quality. The countess was devoted to your mother and will certainly help you.'

'I have no wish to be in service.'

'Mademoiselle, you have no other choice unless you prefer to enter a convent.'

'M. Saint-Jean, my father tells me that you are rich and own a property. Buy me a small house in Paris. Give me a few thousand livres as compensation and then say farewell.'

'I do not possess a few thousand livres, mademoiselle. I lied to your father so that he would not throw me out. I am as poor as a beggar, if you must know.'

'But the Comte de Racon's master of the hunt brought you two coffers full of gold.'

'I did not accept that money, Mademoiselle.'

'Why not?'

'I refuse to tell you. Now will you leave with me tomorrow

morning and go to your nurse?'

'Yes.'

'Very well. Pretend that you are feeling worse than you are, and ask for a coach.'

'I want to ride. A coach jolts too much.'

'Then I will ride slowly with you.'

'M. Saint-Jean, my second habit is even smaller than the one I wore on the day of M. de Riberac's death. Lend me one of your coats. You are not much taller than I, and not too small round the hips. My clothes are too tight at the waist, although I have grown much thinner recently, for I always went to bed unlaced. Take me to Grandval to the Comtesse de Racon, instead of to my nurse's village.'

'That is out of the question.'

'Why?'

'I am banned from Grandval. I'll take you to your nurse.'

'No, M. Saint-Jean, my stepmother could come and harm me there. If Grandval's forbidden to you, take me to another of the Comte de Racon's castles where he won't be. I don't want to meet either him or his son.'

'Mademoiselle, you demand too much.'

'Nothing is too much after what you did to me.'

'You are right. I'll take you to one of the tenant farms in the Racon county, but no further.'

'That will suit me.' Marguerite bestowed a gracious smile upon him. 'And what other plans have you in mind?' she asked.

'I shall ride to Austria and fight for christianity against the Turks.'

'Yes, go and fight against the Turks. I feel sick again.'

'Here, vomit into this basin.'

'Why didn't you hold it for me last time?'

'Because I didn't think of it.'

'You are stupid, M. Saint-Jean, and I don't want to vomit now.'

'Mademoiselle, you must tell everyone that you are going to visit your nurse, so that no one will know your real destination.'

'Yes, I will do that. It will be amusing to run away.'

'Can you stand up?'

'No, because I have nothing on. Why did you take off my shirt?'

'Because it was wringing wet. Do you want to put it on again?'

Martin picked Marguerite up in her blanket, carried her to her room and laid her down on her bed. 'Where are your shifts?'

'Over there in the chest.'

'It's full of dirty linen.'

'I haven't anything clean.'

'Look for something yourself and give me my blanket.'

'Look the other way.' Martin looked away, stretched out his hand behind his back for the blanket and ran out of the room, for he had heard the twins chattering next door. Dawn broke.

Marguerite slept soundly until nearly midday, causing Martin great anxiety. He passed her bedroom several times without hearing a sound. Shortly before the midday meal he saw the baroness enter the room, heard her scolding and raising her voice. Then he packed his belongings. That afternoon, on the pretext of the girl's illness, he visited Marguerite and found her alone. Weeping bitterly, she told him that her stepmother would not allow her to go and visit her nurse and had tried to make her drink some more drops; she had knocked the spoon out of her hand, however, and gone down to the kitchen to fetch milk and food herself. Martin said that she must not lose courage now and be ready in the courtyard to leave at daybreak. He thrust a rolled-up riding-coat into her bed, bowed and took his leave.

Marguerite was at their rendezvous at the break of dawn, and Martin helped her to mount her grey. François was already in the saddle, holding Martin's second charger and a pack-horse. Martin mounted Pollux, ordered François to give him Mira's reins and called up to the castle eaves, where a sleepy maid's head appeared at a dormer window, saying that Mademoiselle had left to visit her nurse. With a pressure of his thighs he set Pollux into a trot and the little troop left the castle gates.

Martin soon turned off the road, across the fields, and broke into a gentle canter. The sun rose over the green countryside.

Marguerite rode happily at Martin's side, but her strength soon failed her and they stopped by a brook under some weeping willows to rest for an hour. Marguerite was then lifted on to Pollux, because he had a smoother action than her grey. Before midday, however, they had to halt again outside a village. Martin left the girl at a farmhouse in François' care, rode with the grey into a nearby town and was lucky enough to sell the too conspicuously coloured beast for a good price. He returned to the farmstead and informed Marguerite of the sale, but she was too exhausted to reply. Martin made her ride in front of him on Mira, who was still fresh, and they continued their journey in this way, with François riding Pollux and leading the pack-horse.

That evening, Marguerite had come to the end of her strength, and when, before curfew, they reached a town, Martin noticed that she was unconscious. They found a modest inn; Marguerite was introduced as Martin's wife, and for economy's sake they shared a bedroom. François slept in the stable and Martin sent for the doctor. The landlord's servant arrived with a venerable dotard, to whom Martin whispered at the door that he was not to tell his young wife the truth about her condition unless it was nothing worse than a disordered stomach. The old man replied, with a smile, that he knew the danger of fear and excitement and would take care not to frighten the patient with a careless word. While he visited Marguerite, Martin retired into the dark background of the oak-panelled room. Marguerite refused to let the doctor touch her, but Martin persuaded her of the necessity of an examination and she gave in. The doctor did not take long to examine her.

Martin took him outside, and learnt that his wife was three months pregnant and was in urgent need of a few weeks' care and rest. He paid the old man's fee and told Marguerite that she was suffering from a slight poisoning and would soon be well again. She must let him take her to a convent where she would be free from pursuit and she could write at once to the Comtesse de Racon, who would be certain to come and fetch her in a coach. Marguerite began to scream and rage like a madwoman. Martin had deceived her and was in league with her stepmother to make her disappear into a convent.

In vain Martin insisted that he only had her interests at heart. She refused to believe him, threatened to beat her head against the wall or to jump out of the window on to the flagstones below. At last, he gave way and said he would continue to escort her, but the ride would be agony for her because they would be unable to take very much rest. The baroness would certainly notify the police if she were not found in her nurse's village. They must use side paths and spend the nights in the forest. Marguerite agreed, and maintained that she would rather arrive dead at Grandval than alive in a convent. They left before dawn and rode as fast as the horses would allow. On the second day, François' mount was in such bad shape that Martin had to decide to sell most of his baggage, so that the valet could continue the journey on the pack-horse.

That afternoon, they met a regiment of light horse riding at ease in small groups. François pointed to the soldiers and remarked slyly to Martin: 'That would be a good opportunity of rejoining our own kind.'

'If you want to enrol,' replied Martin, 'at least wait until Mademoiselle is brought to safety.'

'Monsieur, do you think you will ever reach the emperor if you lose our horses one after the other? I have no wish to go and fight the Turks on foot. How would it be to introduce yourself to the officers? It's no guards regiment, and looks a bit ragged, but at least we should not need to carry muskets. You could take Mademoiselle to that fine castle over there on the hill.'

Marguerite moved her head feebly on her protector's shoulder. Martin loosened his grip and turned to François: 'I can hear the cry of a decoy but I must turn a deaf ear. My conscious demands that I should take Mademoiselle to the Comtesse de Racon. Will you continue to be my groom for another few days at twice your pay?'

François looked embarrassed. 'Monsieur, I have long since realised that you have no money and I will accompany you to the Racon county without extra pay, but if we don't meet another regiment I'll join the outlaws and let you march to the emperor on your own.'

François jogged along on the former pack-horse behind the faster mounts, until one morning the powerful beast was found lying dead on the straw. Martin searched once more for a horse dealer who, sensing his plight, asked the most shameless prices for his worn-out nags. Martin tried desperately to haggle but was eventually glad to buy a tough soldier's hack at the price of a horse three times better.

From now on they slept in the open. The May weather was dry and mild, but neither of them had an eye for the landscape which had donned an almost summery garb. Martin saw that the double burden was too much for his thoroughbred horse, and what he had always feared now happened. Three days from the Racon county he had to shoot Pollux and buy a second horse. He now rode more slowly, keeping to the forest as much as possible; taking his bearings from the sun, he followed the old woodcutter's trail through the pines and the pale-green beech undergrowth.

They reached the Racon lands at last. In spite of Marguerite's protests, Martin took a day's rest. He washed himself carefully in a stream and appeared shaved and washed before Marguerite, who noticed that he was wearing his last clean cravat, which she had wanted to borrow for her arrival. She insisted that she could not appear looking so dirty before the countess, and that Martin should lend it to her immediately. Martin replied that he intended to keep it himself because he would have to see the countess personally and would beg her to send some fresh linen for the girl. Marguerite insisted that if he now intended to set foot in Grandval, he should have the courtesy to deliver her in person. That was impossible, said Martin, for he would have to creep into the castle like a thief. The girl cursed but he turned a deaf ear to her.

They reached Les Chênes as darkness fell. When the dogs began to bark, Douranez appeared with a lantern. Martin dismounted and greeted the peasant, who looked surprised and asked the reason for his visit. Martin begged him to take in Mademoiselle d'Epponcourt for the night and not to mention it at the castle. Maurice Douranez told him that the count and the Vicomte de Clarmont were at Grandval and that in three days' time the vicomte was marrying Mlle du Terne. Martin gave a start, and the farmer, realising his terror, volunteered that he would not mention his presence to anyone. François was hidden in a barn so that none of the farm hands should recognise him. Martin hurriedly took leave of Marguerite, who mockingly wished him luck at Grandval and in the Turkish war, and galloped off. The farmer led the girl into his house and ordered his son-in-law to attend to the horses.

IN THE THICKET OF LIES

By the faint light of the crescent moon Martin galloped across the flowering meadows, skirted Grandval and pulled up at the little back gate to the park, where he tethered Mira to a bush. Jumping over the wall, he hurried along the gravel path between the hedges to the castle. On the ground floor, the only lights to be seen were from the dining-hall window. Faint chinks of lights gleamed through the curtains at the countess's window. With a thumping heart, Martin made his way on to the terrace and peered into the dining-hall. The count and the Marquis de Chassigny were sitting there drinking their wine. The marquis looked sleepy and the count was staring into space. By his pallor, mottled cheeks and swollen eyelids, Martin could see that, in contrast to his former way of life, he was on the way to becoming a drunkard. Next to the pitchers of wine stood what looked like a bottle of spirits. Martin left the terrace and leaned against the stone balustrade of the steps. Then the french windows opened suddenly and a noisy troop of young men and women, who must have come from inside the castle, stormed out and ran down the steps to the park. Martin just had time to hide behind a hedge.

As soon as the cries and laughter of the young folk had died away in the distance, Martin made his way through the orchard to the northern courtyard and crossed the bridge into the building. Feeling his way from door to door, he reached the south-eastern spiral staircase and climbed it.

He stopped on the first floor. Ahead, near the new stairs, sat a lackey with a lamp. Martin walked swiftly past him, and was already at the door of the countess's antechamber when the lackey recognised him and jumped up with a cry: 'M. Saint-Jean, I will announce your arrival.'

'No, keep your mouth shut!' He threw the man his last few silver coins, which fell with a tinkle to the stone floor. Old Denis put his head out of the door. 'Is Madame la Comtesse alone, Denis?' Martin asked hastily.

'Yes, M. Saint-Jean.'

'Take me to her at once and don't tell anyone that I'm here.'

The servant let Martin enter, called out his name in the salon and let him pass.

The countess had risen to her feet in surprise. The young man fell to his knees before her. 'Madame, forgive my temerity, and forgive me for having come. It is not on my own behalf. I fled here with Mlle d'Epponcourt to save her from being poisoned by her stepmother. Mademoiselle is at Les Chênes and seeks asylum with you.'

'M. Saint-Jean, could you not have sent someone to tell me this? Your life is in danger. The Vicomte is at Grandval. Flee as quickly as you can!'

'Madame, I cannot stand up before confessing to you that I have seduced Mademoiselle. She is with child by me and does not yet know it. I sent you a deed of sale and the money which the count sent me. I beg you to ask that the estate which was intended for me be given to Mademoiselle so that she will not be in want. I cannot protect her any longer as I intend to leave France.'

The countess drew back and sat down in her chair. 'My God, how could that happen to the unfortunate child? M. Saint-Jean, I begged you to behave chivalrously to Mademoiselle.' Martin remained on his knees and did not raise his head. The countess rose to her feet and bolted all the doors. 'M. Saint-Jean, you are safe with me. I will send Denis to my husband. You shall make your request to him.'

Martin jumped up. 'No, Madame, don't send Denis to him, I beg you . . . I implore you!' Flinging himself once more at her feet, he caught the hem of her dress. 'Don't send for the count! I will face any court but do not compel me to speak to him. Plead with him for Mademoiselle and allow me to go.'

'M. Saint-Jean, I dare not ask my husband for a large sum of money or a property in your name. I pleaded with him twice on Guy's behalf, and I tremble when I think of his anger.

He never mentions you and he has forbidden your name to be uttered in his presence. It has been hell in Grandval since he has been here making preparations for the wedding. For the slightest mistake he has the servants flogged, and he had a maid, who tried to flee in her terror torn to pieces by the dogs. Appalling things must happen in his room below and in the torture chamber, for one hears ghastly screams rising from there. Fortunately, the Marquis de Chassigny arrived with Guy and this has somewhat curbed his cruelty. Oh, M. Saint-Jean, you were his guardian angel, and now you too have fallen from grace. Stand up! It is for you now to plead for the girl. I shall send Denis to him.'

'No, Madame, no!'

'Do you wish me to bear the brunt of his anger?'

'No,' groaned Martin in despair.

'Please release my dress. I have thought of a solution. Write him a letter.' Martin rose to his feet and the countess opened her *escritoire*. 'Sit down here, M. Saint-Jean. Here is a quill, ink and paper.'

'Madame,' said Martin, taking up the quill, 'I do not know how to address him.'

'Do not bother about the address.'

'What shall I write?'

'Write: "I have seduced Mlle d'Epponcourt and beg you to transfer to her the gifts you sent to her father's castle, which I have returned to you" . . . and then just sign your name.' With compressed lips, Martin wrote as he was bid. The countess looked over his shoulders until he laid down the quill. 'That will do,' said the countess. 'Do you love Mademoiselle?'

'No, Madame, not in the slightest. She wishes what has happened to remain a secret because she does not suspect that it must come to light. What will happen to the child if it survives?'

'It will be put in the care of strangers without the name of its parents being revealed. I shall see to it that no one ever knows and that Mademoiselle's honour will be preserved.'

'Mme la Comtesse, Mademoiselle is in a very perilous state. Please send her a coach and fresh linen as soon as you can, so that she need not feel ashamed when she arrives.'

'I will send Emilie at once with my coach and linen. Do you

need anything yourself?'

'No, Madame, nothing.'

'I would gladly give you money for your travelling expenses.'

'Madame, please do not shame me.' The countess opened the drawer and counted out some coins into a purse. 'Madame, please save yourself the trouble, I refuse to accept it.'

'M. Saint-Jean, in spite of your lapse, I have not lost my respect for you. I should not like to reproach myself later, and beg you therefore at least to take this small purse.'

At this moment there was a knock at the door and Denis announced: 'M. le Comte!'

They both turned white with terror. The countess was the first to recover her composure. 'I must open to him; hide yourself!'

But Martin remained as though frozen to the spot. The countess unlocked the door and the count staggered in. He was drunk.

'Ah, there's the boy! Madame, since when do you lock your doors? Come, out with it! How many visits have there been before today?'

Instinctively, the countess ran over to Martin, who stepped forward. 'Comte de Racon, this is the first time I have come and it is not on my own account.'

'I find you in my wife's salon, and you have the insolence to approach me!'

Martin picked up the sheet of paper, went swiftly over to the count and handed it to him. 'Read that, Comte de Racon,' he said, and then returned to his place.

The count read it and gave a malicious laugh. 'Ah, so the offspring follows in his father's footsteps. Not bad; and now one humbles one's pride and comes to beg. One wants to live on an estate and found a family. Very pretty, Martin. It does you honour.'

'Comte de Racon, I will not touch a single penny of your money. Mlle d'Epponcourt is no longer my concern and I am riding to Austria to fight the Turks under the emperor's standard.'

'So you're riding to Austria? Will that purse be enough to get you to the frontier?'

'I will not accept any money,' shouted Martin.

'Oh, yes you will, after I've gone. I have resold the property at a very good profit . . . perhaps there will be something left over for Mademoiselle. I will think it over and see that you leave Grandval this instant, unharmed. Do not let me find you with my wife again.' He turned away to the door.

'Comte de Racon,' cried Martin, 'stay where you are!'

The count turned round and leered with contempt at Martin, who turned even paler but did not flinch before the look in those bleary eyes. 'Have you any other request?'

Martin unbuttoned his coat and took a brownish rag from beneath his shirt. 'I have always worn this until today.'

'What is it?'

'The strip I once tore from your cravat.'

The black eyes became glassy and lost their sneering expression. 'Why do you show it to me?'

Martin was no longer capable of speech and, with trembling hands, restored the strip of lace to its former place. 'Does that mean that in spite of the fact that I broke my word to you, you still love me?'

Martin began to gasp for breath, and the countess stretched out her hand anxiously to him. The count did not notice.

'Martin!'

The young man ran towards him and flung himself into his arms. The countess's eyes opened wide with surprise. Martin wept like a child and the count held him close and murmured in his drunkenness: 'Martin, I will make good what I have done to you and I won't send you away again. I have never been able to forget you. Whatever I may do to stifle the memory of you, no crime can equal the breaking of one's word as I have done, and no intoxication prevents me from suddenly remembering it. Since I have been here, I drank down there in the hall and kept waiting for you to come through the french windows. Why did you come here instead of to me?'

'I did not know that you still loved me.'

'You ass, you ridiculous clod. I was as big a fool as you.' The count hugged Martin even tighter and buried his face in his son's hair, trying to stifle sobs which shook his frame. Despite his drunkenness, he soon recovered his composure and said with determination: 'Martin, no dictates of reason will again keep me from you. I will go with you to Austria. I will hand over the marquisate of Brayonne to Guy and allow him to administer Grandval. We will fight together against the Turks and never return to France. We'll leave tomorrow morning. Guy can get married without me. Do you hear me, Martin?'

'Yes, I hear you,' said Martin, looking up. 'You want to ride with me to Austria.' He raised his head and kissed the count's old scar.

'Don't do that, Martin. I stink of spirits.'

'Monsieur, I can now leave with a light heart. I will fight for christianity, which means more to me than the king of France. Please don't gainsay me. You are drunk, and tomorrow you'll realise that your place is here.'

'Martin, I will not let you go. You will sleep in my room tonight. Why must you be foolish? I'll stay here until the marriage is over. You will live in the hunting lodge under Grouchet's protection, and then we'll ride to Austria together. Here, take my handkerchief and dry your face.'

They released each other and Martin wiped away his tears. At this moment, he caught sight of the countess and went over to her. 'Madame, have no fear. As soon as he is sober he will alter his decision and remain here. He already sees that he must be present at the vicomte's marriage, and he will then realise that he cannot give up his position in the army and at Court. Thank you a thousand times for the bounty you have shown to that unfortunate girl, and allow me to take my leave.'

The count caught hold of him. 'My head is quite clear enough to know what I am saying, and woe betide you if you run away from me.'

Martin smiled at him. 'It would be too great good fortune for me, my friend . . . more than I have ever deserved.'

'I don't know whether I bring you good fortune. I doubt it. Tomorrow I will give you the money for the girl.' The count made his way to the door, opened it, stepped back a little and took up his position in front of Martin.

Guy crossed the threshold and lowered his two cavalry pistols. 'Father,' said Guy, after a slight nod to his mother, 'I regret to tell you that I am determined not to let your bastard leave this room alive. I have brought my grooms. Do not try and save the fellow. All the advantage is on my side and I should prefer to avoid a quarrel with you.' For a few moments there was complete silence, except for the crackle of wood in the grate.

'Can you show good reason for your conduct in front of your parents?' the count asked calmly.

'Yes. Last autumn, Martin Saint-Jean tried to strangle me before witnesses. If I kill him, I am not only taking my legitimate revenge but protecting myself from him.'

'Guy, Martin gave me his word of honour that he would not take his revenge upon you. You can rely on his word. Put your firing irons away! Close the door and let us discuss matters peacefully.'

'Father, you are trying to buy the life of your favourite with promises. Out of fear, you will probably offer me the marquisate of Brayonne; you would then divert further large sums to your favourite and eventually do great damage to my inheritance. I ask you, once more, to stand aside so that I shall not have to call my servants.'

'Do you dare to raise your hand to your father?'

'Only if you compel me to.'

'Guy, your mother is a witness that I have decided to leave with Martin to fight the Turks, to get him out of your way once and for all. I will transfer to you this very night the marquisate of Brayonne and the rights of administration over all the Grandval estates.'

Guy roared with laughter. 'So, you're off to fight the Turks! You look like it. Can you tell me another fairy story?'

'I will prove to you that I am perfectly serious about my offer,' the count replied calmly.

'You need not trouble to prove anything; I no longer believe your word. You swore to me last autumn that you had broken for ever with Martin and that he would never return. It is now May and, lo and behold, I meet Martin in Grandval two days before my marriage!'

'Martin came here of his own accord, unexpectedly.'

'You lie more ingeniously than I do,' jeered Guy, 'and

always break your word for some unpredictable reason. If one thinks to have gained your support in some plot and is about to succeed, you will have given up your role and disappeared into thin air.

'You do the same at war. The Duc de Luxembourg told the king that there was no better cavalry leader than you, but none who was more of a lone wolf. When you were given orders to make a frontal attack, one never knew whether you would attack from right, left, the rear, or whether in fact you would attack at all. The consequences were a matter of indifference to you. The king laughed at his comments but you can be quite sure that he will never give you a big command. I'm telling you this merely to show you that no one can ever rely on you.

'Morever, you are growing old. You are nearly fifty and your debauches have worn you out. If you are serious about the Turkish campaign, you are perhaps suffering from some disease that causes the brain to soften; that may account for your misdeeds, which have made you hated throughout the whole countryside. You are no longer in possession of your faculties and therefore a danger to me. I have every reason to fear that your offensive love for your bastard will one day outweigh your paternal love for me. I am not motivated by any desire to murder, but am acting in calculated self-protection when I insist that your bastard must die. I ask you for the last time: Stand aside!'

The countess went over to Martin and gave him a sign, whereupon, under her protection, he made for her bedroom door, pushed home the bolts and was out of range of Guy's pistols. Then, by the faint light of the fire, he saw the vicomte's three grooms facing him with drawn swords. Martin drew his own rapier; swift as lightning he ran the middle one through and, calling for help, defended himself against the thrusts of the other two. The count rushed in, banged the door against Guy, closed it and placed his back against it. The countess could be heard calling for help and Guy summoning his servants. At the sight of the count, Martin's opponents retreated and took to their heels. The count ran the nearest man through the thigh, kicked him into the maid's room and locked that door too.

'Are you wounded, Martin?'

'No.'

'Bring me the dead man's pistol.' Martin obeyed, while the count opened wide the window, leaned out and shouted with all his might: 'Armand de Chassigny! Armand de Chassigny!' The drunken voice of the marquis replied from his window. 'What is it, Gaston?'

'There are rebels in my house. Call my grooms and come to my aid. Send for master of the hunt Grouchet. Hurry, Armand!'

At the same moment, the door to the salon was burst open. The count turned against the intruders and shot the leading man. Martin saved himself by jumping to one side as Guy fired both his pistols. Now Guy also drew his sword. The count roared at the servants: 'The Marquis de Chassigny is on his way. I will have you all broken on the wheel and hanged! Take that, you swine! Out with you!' Another groom sank to the ground. The others were awed by the sight of the master of the castle, who would not let any of them pass. After the count had wounded two more, the others fled over the bodies by the door and rushed blindly through the countess's salon, to be met in the antechamber by the marquis and his armed men.

When the countess entered her bedroom she found Guy and Martin engaged in mortal combat before the fireplace, while the count watched for an opportunity to part them. The countess was at her wits' end. 'For the love of God, don't murder each other! Help, Marquis! Part them, Gaston!'

The giant shadows of the two men danced on the walls and over the countess who had fallen to the ground, watching, as though numbed, the outcome of the duel. When the count noticed that Martin, true to his promise, was only defending himself and being ever more hard-pressed, he seized Guy at a favourable moment from behind, in an attempt to fling him on the ground. But Guy gave him such a thrust with his elbow in the stomach that he fell against the mantelpiece and had difficulty in rising. Noises and shouts came from the salon. 'Martin,' cried the count, 'you are almost with your back to the wall!' Martin lunged; Guy leaped back and parried. The count flung himself between them, took the rapier from Martin's hand and flung it on the canopy. Taking up his position in front of the disarmed man, he shouted at Guy: 'Put your rapier away and don't dare to threaten me.'

'Put yours down first,' said the son, 'instead of waving it about in front of my nose.'

'Surrender, Guy! Your servants have all fled and the Marquis de Chassigny is already in the salon.'

But Guy refused to be thwarted and tried instead to reach the disarmed man by getting round the count. His father followed the turn with rapier pointed. Guy lowered his sword and said with icy calm: 'Father, I refuse to consider the game lost, for I shall never have such an opportunity again. I now propose to ignore your sword. I shall not look at it any more. I know that your threat is only pretence and that you do not intend to wound me. You have the choice! Guy de Clarmont or Martin Saint-Jean. Lower your sword or you will run me through.'

'Guy!' shouted the count, 'keep away from me! You're mistaken. Keep away from me, Guy. I cannot sacrifice Martin for you. Martin, get away!'

Martin turned towards the door of the maid's room but, at the same moment, Guy attacked again and ran straight on to the count's sword. With a terrible scream he tumbled backwards and slumped beside the kneeling countess, who with her remaining strength drew him towards her. 'Guy, my son Guy! Guy, my only son!'

Guy struggled, and a stream of blood poured from his mouth. The countess tried to hold his head high, but the mortally wounded man writhed, tore himself from her lap on to the carpet and drowned in his own blood.

The Marquis de Chassigny, in his nightgown, entered the room. 'Hi, Gaston! Are you still alive? Bring light. Who is that on the floor?'

One of his lackeys brought a candlestick and the marquis saw what had happened. Martin was leaning against the wall with his face in his hands; the countess lay unconscious next to the dead vicomte.

The count could hardly stand erect.

'Armand, he is past help.'

'Who stabbed the vicomte?'

'He ran against my sword.'

'Is that true, Gaston?'

'Yes, Armand, I was protecting Martin, for my heart was stronger than my head.'

'M. Saint-Jean,' the marquis cried, turning to Martin, 'hand me all the weapons.'

Martin picked up Guy's and the count's swords from the carpet and handed them to the marquis, who examined them closely. 'These diamonds on the hilt belong to the Vicomte de Clarmont, and this blood-stained blade belongs to my friend. Where is your sword, Saint-Jean?'

'On the canopy.'

'What?'

'I will fetch it down for you.'

Martin climbed on to the bed and brought the marquis his sword. 'M. Saint-Jean, confess the truth. You fought with your father's sword.'

'No, Monsieur, but I am to blame for the misfortune.'

'You admit your guilt.'

'Yes, Monsieur, I am guilty.'

'Give me your word of honour that you will not leave Grandval, and I will return you your sword.'

'Marquis, I give you my word that I will remain in Grandval.'

Without a word the marquis handed back the weapon and turned to the count, who in the meantime had lifted his wife on to her bed. 'Gaston, is she still alive?'

'She is unconscious. Call her maid and Dr Borel. Let me pass, Armand, so that she won't see me when she recovers consciousness.' The marquis stood aside, and the count, followed by Martin, went into the salon where his servants had collected. They made way for him and he passed them without so much as a glance. The narrow corridor was full of people who also stood aside to let him pass unhindered. No one dared ask a question and not until the door closed behind them was there a rustle and a whisper.

The count stood motionless in his study, staring at the brown curtains as though he could see out into the night through the velvet. For a long time Martin did not dare to betray his presence, but at last he said gently, 'Monsieur!'

The count turned round. 'Come and see me when I send for you, and now get out of my sight.' Martin left the room. He met four young officers from the guards regiment who had come from Paris with Guy. They recognised each other and exchanged greetings in passing. As he walked away, they turned round and stared as he disappeared without a candle along the dark corridor. Martin opened a door somewhere in the north wing and entered a room where simple beds had been prepared in readiness for the expected guests. He took off his riding-boots, flung himself on the nearest bed and slept like a log.

In the meantime, the marquis, as the count's deputy, was giving orders, while old Borel attended to the countess. Emilie emerged from her corner, trembling with fear. Denis and Pierre had been found bound and gagged in their rooms. The rebel grooms were locked in the dungeons and the dead laid out in the court-room. The Vicomte de Clarmont's corpse was carried to the chapel while all traces of the recent conflict were removed. Everyone was busy but no one spoke above a whisper. Horror seemed to be increasing, although outside the dawn was breaking.

Next morning, at about ten o'clock, farmer Douranez arrived at the castle at the behest of the impatient Mlle d'Epponcourt. He had already learned in the village of the terrifying events of the night, and asked Denis to obtain a coach from the countess for Marguerite. The countess gave orders and the farmer returned to Les Chênes riding on the box next to the coachman. He released François from his hiding-place so that he could accompany the girl to the castle. Marguerite cursed Martin because her fresh linen had been forgotten, and drove in his best riding-coat to the castle. She was received by the countess's new lady-in-waiting because she herself was in the chapel by the dead man's bier. François wandered from room to room looking for his master, until he finally discovered him asleep. He woke him and asked where he should put his baggage, only to be told that Martin did not know himself. Mira was tethered outside the park wall by the little gate and was to be taken to the stables. He would eat in the park by the statue of Flora. Pierre was to be informed so that his whereabouts would be known.

Martin, served by François, ate a meal on the stone bench at the feet of Flora in the shade of the light green box-hedge. The meal was served on silver plates with magnificent dressings, and the rare wine sparkled in a gilt goblet. As soon as Martin had satisfied his hunger he told the servant to clear away, and lay down on the gravel where he again feel asleep.

He woke up at a light touch, to see the count standing in the bright sunlight before him, dressed in black. 'Come, Martin, let's go for a short walk.' Martin jumped up and accompanied the haggard man past the bright flower beds. 'Where did you spend the night?'

'In a room which had been prepared for guests.'

'I have now chosen a room for you and given orders for the funeral. The servants have all lost their heads and I cannot afford even to get drunk. I have sent messages to the neighbours and informed Baron du Terne that his daughter must put on mourning instead of her marriage finery. It will suit her ugliness far better than flowers and bright-coloured brocade. Why do you look at me out of the corner of your eye?' Martin flushed and did not reply. 'Do you find it unpleasant to walk behind a man who has murdered his son?'

'Monsieur, you are mocking me. I am to blame for the tragedy.'

'You admitted your guilt to the marquis, and now he doesn't believe me when I tell him that the vicomte fell by my hand. I have come to tell you that you must admit the truth to everyone. Do you think I want to have your death on my conscience too? Don't start lying to me!'

'Monsieur, I admitted my guilt because I came of my own accord to Grandval and thus caused the vicomte's death.'

'Explain that to the marquis, but don't mention a word about assaulting the girl.' Martin tried to turn back to the castle but the count stopped him. 'Walk with me a little further. There is no hurry for your explanation. I want to ask you a question. Why do you want to abandon the girl?'

'She herself wants to be rid of me.'

'Why?'

'Because I raped her.'

'You're incapable of such a thing.'

Martin bit his lips. 'Did you really rape her?'

'Yes.'

'Were you randy for lack of women?'

'No, I had plenty of them.'

'Then what possessed you to do it?'

'I don't know.'

'Was my letter to blame?' Martin looked away. 'Come on, out with it! Did you rape the girl before or after you had received my letter?'

'After.'

'How many days after?'

'Next day.'

'Now I know for certain . . . it was my fault that you came here. That is a consolation to me.'

'Monsieur, there was no excuse for my crime.'

'Whatever you may think, we have turned each other into beasts, with more fortunate results for you than for me. Forgive me, that was only a jest.'

'Monsieur!'

'Don't get excited. For me, you have that halo round your tousled head again, and even if it is a little tarnished it doesn't disturb me in the least! Otherwise I should fancy myself too black compared with you.'

'I don't understand how you can still jest.'

'My humour is that of a man who jests on the scaffold. How do you feel about it?'

'Desperate.'

'I can imagine that.' The count stopped and felt in his pocket until he found the key. 'Let's go out into the forest.'

'Monsieur, I promised the Marquis de Chassigny to remain at Grandval.'

'The forest belongs to Grandval. In any case, we shall be back in an hour at the latest. The guests who live the furthest away arrive today, and I shall have to receive them. My wife has put the little d'Epponcourt in Guy's bedroom and has recovered quite well from the shock. Let us hope she does not collapse until the guests have gone.'

The two men came to the gate and the count unlocked it. Martin walked at his side through the woods, with no eye for the beauty of the spring day. The count looked up at the birds twittering in the treetops and fluttering in the undergrowth, and took a sunny path that led up gently to an eminence. From the top of the sandpit the view extended across the river and the valley to the wooded heights on the horizon. The count sat on the embankment, dangled his legs and patted the ground with his hand. 'Sit down, Martin.' Martin did as he was bid. The count stared at him until he turned his head away and began to tear up clumps of grass.

'Martin, I think it best that we should be completely frank. You cannot replace the dead Guy for me. I have committed an irreparable folly and, so to speak, removed the wrong man. That is what my reason says, but my heart speaks differently, and therefore I have lost my bearing. Had my wife not been a witness I could think up enough lies to save both of us, but she will not let slip the opportunity of freeing herself from me. She will clearly see that I am a danger to her and will indict me as the murderer of my son.'

'But why is your wife in any danger from you?'

'Do you think that I would remain married to a barren woman as long as I am capable of siring a new heir to succeed me? Look at this countryside! My cousin de Montignon will not inherit it, I assure you.'

'Monsieur, do you intend to murder your wife?'

'No, I intend to make a second marriage. I shall not be condemned to death, because Guy incited his grooms in open rebellion to kill you. I expect to be imprisoned for a few years. My position at Court and in the army is finished. I hope that Chassigny will keep you on as a lieutenant. I have given Grouchet 100,000 livres, which he will hand to you as soon as everything is settled here. Buy yourself a property somewhere and come and visit me from time to time.'

'Monsieur, I shall give your 100,000 livres to Mlle d'Epponcourt and remain with you as long as you want me. You will be allowed a servant to keep you in good health and prevent you from brooding. But you know that I am in duty bound now to warn your wife against you.'

'I know it, my boy,' replied the count with a smile. 'Persuade me to see salvation in folly and I will remain my wife's husband, renounce an heir, and not regret having sacrificed my bad son to my good bastard.'

Martin gave a start. 'My God, how can I demonstrate to an unbeliever the necessity for leading a christian life!'

'Well, if you can't, then let me do what seems reasonable according to my lights and remain my friend, as before, so that you don't make me wish you dead and Guy alive once more.'

'Monsieur, I will take instruction from a Jesuit and demonstrate to you as soon as possible that by each evil action you only commit yourself to a deeper hell.'

'I don't want to hear anything about hell, because I believe neither in heaven nor hell. You must prove to me by wordly canons the necessity for leading a noble life. Think well! I cannot bear this constant conflict in my nature and will decide in favour of reason if you fail in converting me to folly.'

'Monsieur, give me your word of honour to spare your wife until I can supply you with the proof.'

'Martin, here is my watch. It is a quarter-past-two. Either you have convinced me by three o'clock or you will have to forgive me in advance for any crimes that I may yet commit.'

'My God, what can I say?' cried Martin in even greater distress. 'Can't you see that evil only breeds more evil? You abandoned my mother, and thus Guy came into the world to become my enemy.'

The count's faun-like face broadened into a grin. 'Guy became your enemy because my noble wife, in her compassion, brought you to Grandval, and secondly, because out of paternal love I made you my sons' companion. Thus compassion and love gave rise to evil, and you are confuted. I could confute you, my friend, with yet another example. Out of my evil letter came evil, for you raped the girl. Then out of nobility of character, you brought her here and, you see, I killed Guy. Thus, once more, out of good came evil. Is that true or not?'

'It is true and at the same time untrue, for you do not mention what happened to you. For my sake you renounced much cruelty in the war.'

'Which I usually regretted later.'

'Monsieur, don't begin to torture me in revenge. Punish me some other way for I have confessed my guilt.'

'Do you really know nothing which would make me see the light?'

'No.'

'Do you give me up?'

'I can do no more. May God forgive me.'

'Try once more.'

Martin looked out over the fair, green valley. 'Over there, Monsieur, are cultivated fields. When I received your letter, most of the baron's fields lay fallow. I had trained all his horses and taught his children to ride, so there was no further reason why I should stay with him, and yet, since I had wronged his daughter I did not want to leave the girl to the mercy of her stepmother, and acted as the baron's bailiff. They were not my fields and I knew that next spring they would once more lie fallow, to be sold eventually or left to go to ruin. But when the green corn began to sprout I was overjoyed, and it was the same during the war when I carried wounded men out of the gunfire, even though they died later from festering wounds. For me, there was always something to do which made life worth living. Even yesterday I had a desire to join the Turkish campaign, for my life would once more have a purpose and my guilt concerning the girl, which oppressed me, would have become bearable.

'But now, all the crimes you commit in the future will weigh upon me because I have failed in this hour. Each time you murder a man I shall become a murderer, and, even if you do it in secret, I shall have to bear the guilt. Since I cannot even atone for my own crime, how shall I be able to make reparation for your future misdeeds? You will pile guilt upon guilt on me, until I stifle under the load, or perhaps until one day I succeed in convincing you of the need for leading a good life. God grant that it will not then be too late and that you will still be capable of doing so.'

'I did not expect to hear such words from you,' said the count after a prolonged silence. 'You maintain that an innocent man can be made guilty by a guilty person. Can you at least prove to me the truth of this statement?'

'Yes, Monsieur, I can give you an example. Let us imagine that a young man had seven years to build up his bodily strength by exercise, and neglected to do so. Then, one day, he comes with his friend to a slope, far steeper than this pit at our feet, and the friend takes a false step and falls so that the other can only hold him by the arms. The young man would like to pulls his friend up, because he has not kept his body in trim he lacks the strength. He holds him for a while and then lets him fall, and is thus to blame for his death. I had many years in which to educate myself, and was too lazy, because I was happy in my ignorance. That is why I have failed today and have to bear all the consequences.'

'Martin, my demand was not serious.'

'Yes, Monsieur, you were serious. Out of compassion you now want to remove the burden you have laid upon me.'

'I give you my word of honour that I will spare my wife.'

'You will bitterly regret having given your word.'

'I shall have to get used to such regrets.'

'What do you mean?'

'I mean that, for your sake, I shall have to try as hard as I can to live unreasonably so that your halo will not be blackened beyond repair.'

'I don't understand you.'

'But I understand you. I never really knew what you were like, but now I think I have your measure. You have often borne burdens which were too heavy for you and I have therefore overestimated your strength. Do not worry about me. Even if I'm too foolish to find my own salvation, I can find yours, my boy, and that should suffice for a man like me.'

Martin stared at the man in utter amazement, until the black eyes began to smile and he suddenly understood his friend's words.

As they returned through the little gate in the park, the count said that he would like to remain out of doors since the weather was so fine. Martin was to go to the castle and ask whether any guests had yet arrived. He would wait by the statue of Flora. They parted, and the count made himself comfortable on the sunny stone bench by the statue. Martin soon returned and reported that no one was there, except a troupe of strolling players which had been ordered for the marriage. The count sighed with relief and said that any reprieve was now welcome. Martin sat down beside him and, with a beating heart, asked for news of little Madame Boquelin. The count replied with a smile that Blanche had visited him several times during the winter and had played the lute for him, as David once played for Saul, but that he had not hurled anything at her.

Towards nightfall, the first carriages passed the castle gate and the courtyard was filled with horsemen. The count joined the Marquis de Chassigny and his late son's friends in the salon, and greeted each guest with great dignity. He walked as far as the foot of the staircase-of-honour to meet his most important guests, and escorted them from there to join the others. A horseman, dressed in black, had been posted at the spot where they entered the avenue, to warn each guest of the disaster. Thus the first surprise was over before the greeting, and the count received no exclamations of horror but merely excited questions, which he dismissed with the same words: his house had suffered a great misfortune and he begged his guests to stay for the funeral.

The gentlemen crowded round the Marquis de Chassigny, who told them of the rebellion and its consequences, always insisting that the vicomte must have been the victim of an unfortunate accident which, unhappily he had been unable to witness. The ladies sought out the countess and shed many tears in her salon. The countess had sufficient strength to maintain the same poise as her husband, and rose, with her own inimitable grace, to greet each new lady as she entered the room. She had locked Marguerite in Guy's room, so that there could be no gossip. Marguerite, in one of her hostess's high-necked dresses, looked sulkily out of the window down on to the busy courtyard and would have been only too pleased to join the other ladies. Emilie sat sewing at her side, and consoled her with the repeated assurance that her dress for the funeral would be ready in time and would suit her admirably. She said this only to pacify her, because she had received strict orders from the countess not to complete the dress until the last guest had left.

Martin, too, was alone in his room, but when he learned that Colonel de la Porte Mury, Captain de Falleron and the Comte de Salvieux had arrived, he went down to greet them. He paid no heed to the whispering that went on behind his back and was soon surrounded by a group of younger officers, who embraced him warmly and asked how he had fared during his banishment. He told them of his winter quarters at the Baron d'Epponcourt's castle, and of his return in the service of a lady. He did not mention the recent tragic events.

The guests retired to their rooms to change and, at nine o'clock, the company sat down to dine. At about eleven o'clock, in a solemn procession, wearing black ribbons, they paid a visit of honour to the dead vicomte in the chapel, walking in pairs, the ladies ahead of the gentlemen. The countess led the Marquise de Chassigny by the hand and the count walked beside the marquis. They walked in silence round the sumptuous coffin between rows of tall candles, while four lieutenants stood in silent vigil. Then the cortège returned past the last visitors to the salon, where each guest offered his condolences to the dead man's parents. Finally they all retired to rest.

The following afternoon, while the guests on the terrace were watching a ballet called *Orpheus and Eurydice*, there arrived in quick succession Baron du Terne with his wife and weeping daughter, the old governor of the province, and Comte Gérard de Montignon with his three sons and their respective wives. The count personally escorted these guests to their apartments. To the ugly, inconsolable bride, he remarked that he had looked forward to seeing her smile by the light of the marriage candles, and was deeply distressed that he now saw her tears flow at the dead man's bier. The poor girl, in so far as her grief would allow her to speak, said that she had a terrible feeling of having brought misfortune to his sons, and had decided to spend the rest of her life in a convent.

Comte de Montignon, as Comte de Racon's cousin, demanded to know the exact cause of the tragedy, and the same question was asked by the governor of the province, who, to the displeasure of the count, had brought a bourgeois secretary from the district office. Since the rest of the guests were enjoying themselves in the park, the count decided to answer their questions immediately. He invited them to his study. Comte de Montignon insisted that both his eldest son and the bastard, Saint-Jean, should be present, and the governor made the same claim upon the Comtesse de Racon. The count realised that they proposed to hold a court of enquiry, and for his part asked permission for his friend, the Marquis de Chassigny, to attend. His request was granted.

The gentlemen entered the study according to precedence, and made themselves comfortable while waiting for the countess. The old governor, who owed his high position not only to the fact that he belonged to one of the oldest titled families in the land but also to his fidelity to the king in the days of the Fronde, sat by the fire while his elegant secretary took up his place behind the chair of the unobtrusive, black-clad district officer's secretary. A second chair facing them remained free for the countess. The Comte de Racon sat on the right of the governor, then came the Marquis de Chassigny and the count's cousin, the Comte de Montignon, whose sharp though handsome features clearly betrayed a certain family resemblance. Among the elder gentlemen, the Comte de Racon was the only one without a wig. Martin stood behind the count's chair, while the Comte de Montignon's son sat behind his father's.

When the countess entered, everyone rose and bowed to her. She returned their greeting with a nod of her black-veiled head, sat down on the armchair by the fire and folded her hands in her lap. Martin noticed the count's hands clutch the arms of his chair as he sat down.

The old governor cleared his throat and began: 'As a friend of the late Comte de Racon, who died in '54, it grieves me deeply to mention in this company a suspicion which ever more urgently requires elucidation. There are rumours that this was no tragic accident but the murder of the Vicomte Guy de Clarmont. I call upon you, Comte de Racon, to tell us all the events that led up to the misfortune.' The count responded immediately and gave a true account without once faltering. When he had finished, the governor turned to the Marquis de Chassigny:

'Marquis, have you anything to add to your friend's statement?'

'Yes, your Excellency. The vicomte's attack was open rebellion against his own father and regimental commander. The servants of both the count and the countess were overpowered beforehand and later found tied up in their rooms. The vicomte's grooms had orders to murder Martin Saint-Jean, and the assassins had been promised a reward of 300 livres. Furthermore, they were ordered to spare only the life of the count and to have no consideration for his servants. Anyone who doubts my words can question the vicomte's surviving servants.'

'Had the Comte de Racon's illegitimate son—his name escapes me—also armed grooms with him?' asked the governor.

'No, your Excellency,' replied the marquis, 'I did not see his groom until the following morning in the castle.'

'I have been told,' the governor went on, 'that Comte de Racon dismissed his illegitimate son last autumn and that the young man returned unexpectedly. What was the reason for his return? I want to hear the answer from the young man himself.'

Martin stepped forward from behind the count's chair. 'I brought a lady to Grandval to hand her over to the countess for protection.'

The governor beckoned to his secretary, who handed him a paper. After reading it, he turned his eyes back to Martin and said: 'A certain Mlle Marguerite d'Epponcourt was abducted from her father's castle by a lieutenant of the light horse of the guard named Martin Saint-Jean. What have you to say to this accusation?'

'I rescued the young lady from her stepmother who was trying to poison her.'

'Can you prove your accusations against the baroness?'

'The baroness compelled her stepdaughter to take drops of some medicine that made her vomit. I gave the liquid to a dog, which immediately died.'

'Have you any witnesses?'

'No.'

'Did the girl see the dog die?'

'No.'

'Have you exploited the girl's credulity for your own ends?'

'I beg your Excellency to tell me what this question implies.'

'Did you invent the story of the poisoning attempt to make the girl elope with you?'

'No!'

'Are you having a love affair with the girl?'

'No.'

'Then why did you court the danger of being indicted as the girl's seducer?'

'Because I felt it my duty to rescue her.'

'Why did you feel bound to do this?'

'Out of compassion. The young lady was treated worse than a servant wench by her stepmother.'

'That is quite true, Excellency,' interrupted the countess. Everyone peered at her face which was half hidden behind her black veil.

'M. Saint-Jean,' continued the governor, 'do you deny having killed M. Charles de Riberac in a duel?'

'I do not deny it.'

'Are you aware that the king has decreed the severest penalty for the survivor of any duel in which one of the parties is killed?'

'I know, but I killed M. de Riberac after hearing Mademoiselle's cries for help, because during the ride he used violence upon her.'

'Tell me what occurred.'

'I went riding with Mademoiselle and M. de Riberac. He sent me home. Then I heard cries for help, rode back and found Mademoiselle struggling with the man. I freed her and was forced to fight with M. de Riberac.'

'Let the girl be brought here.'

Martin made for the door but the governor called him back. 'You are to remain here.' Martin returned to his place behind the count's chair and the governor's secretary left to carry out the order.

Marguerite appeared in the countess's altered dress, bowed gracefully and looked round with a saucy smile. Comte de Montignon's son rose and offered her his chair which was graciously accepted. 'What is required of me?'

'Tell me how M. de Riberac came to be killed,' said the governor.

Marguerite blushed. 'M. de Riberac behaved insolently to me and M. Saint-Jean came to my aid.'

'Was it not perhaps the contrary, my charming Mademoiselle? Did not M. Saint-Jean behave insolently and M. de Riberac come to your aid?'

'Certainly not, Monsieur. M. de Riberac was a monster and M. Saint-Jean rescued me.'

'M. de Riberac was your fiancé.'

'The more reason for him to be a real monster, Monsieur.'

'Did you incite M. Saint-Jean to murder him?'

'I often incited him but he always refused, until on our ride he could not help it.'

The marquis and young Montignon laughed loudly, but the old governor frowned. 'Gentlemen, I must ask you to be serious. You have heard Mademoiselle's admission that she incited Saint-Jean to commit a murder. Mademoiselle, you have admitted yourself to be guilty of the death of M. de Riberac, and you will have the opportunity of bewailing your guilt in prison.'

The countess rose so quickly that she was the first to reach Marguerite as she swooned. With astonishing strength she lifted the girl from her chair, held her in her arms and, raising her veil, said with flaming anger: 'Your Excellency, it would be a monstrous injustice in God's eyes to imprison this child who does not know what she is saying. If M. Saint-Jean killed M. de Riberac, he did it to save the girl's honour. Riberac was a penniless adventurer and it was a crime to have betrothed him to the girl. She was promised to him, provided he relinquished half her dowry in favour of her parents. The child foresaw a terrible fate and knew of no other way to save herself than by M. Saint-Jean's blade. I insist upon a pardon for this seventeen-year-old girl.'

Marguerite recovered consciousness and clung to the countess. The governor intervened. 'Madame, I beg you and Mademoiselle to sit down again so that I shall not be forced to rise.'

The countess, however, with flashing eyes, replied: 'I shall not be seated before your Excellency promises the pardon I have just demanded.'

The old man rose, with the help of his ivory cane, and everyone present followed suit. 'Mlle d'Epponcourt,' he said, 'are you capable of speaking?'

'Madame, what does he want of me?'

'Answer, Marguerite. You will not be sent to prison.'

'Mademoiselle, do you love Saint-Jean?'

'No.'

'What would you say if we were to make it impossible for you ever to see Saint-Jean again?'

'I should be grateful! He brought me here and now he can go.'

Once more there was loud laughter. 'Why would you be grateful for his removal, Mademoiselle? Has he not behaved impeccably towards you?'

'Yes, de Riberac behaved badly. M. Saint-Jean saved me from him. I have written to my father. I am remaining here with the Comtesse de Racon and will not return home.'

'Why do you not wish to return there?'

'Because my stepmother ill-treats me. She gives me no clothes, makes me ill with medicine and tries to force me into a convent. But I won't go to a convent.'

'What do you want then?'

'A nobleman with a castle.' Everyone laughed, except the countess and Martin.

'Mademoiselle,' said the governor, 'you may leave the room.'

'And you will not send me to prison?'

'No, Mademoiselle.'

'Is that certain?'

'I give you my word of honour,' said the old man with a smile, 'that I will protect you against any accusation.' Marguerite freed herself from the countess's arms, curtsied swiftly and made her exit. The countess walked to her chair and sat down, whereupon the gentlemen followed suit. The district officer's secretary bent over the governor's chair. 'Will you allow me to make an observation, your Excellency?'

The old man turned to the official: 'What do you wish to say?'

'I will start investigations at the castle of Baron d'Epponcourt to find out whether M. Saint-Jean's accusation against the baroness has any foundation. Mlle d'Epponcourt's testimony clears M. Saint-Jean so completely that, in the name of the Chief of Police, I take it upon myself to revoke his arrest, provided he can prove himself innocent of the death of the

Vicomte de Clarmont.'

'Gentlemen,' interrupted the countess, 'I understand that you are disposed to doubt my husband's evidence. As the sole witness, I can assure you that every word he has spoken is the truth. The vicomte fell at the hand of his father, after he had disarmed his illegitimate son, and was forced to stand in front of him to protect him. The vicomte did not believe in my husband's serious intention to defend himself, although he tried to convince him in a loud, clear voice. The vicomte was of the opinion that my husband would countenance fratricide rather than use his sword against his own heir. I myself wanted to warn him and cry out, but I was numb. So the vicomte ran to his death, and I, his mother, for the sake of justice, say that the blame for my son's death rests neither with my husband nor with M. Saint-Jean, but that it was entirely his own fault. My husband had to choose between two sons and, before God, had I been in his place I should have been forced to behave exactly as he did.'

There was a deep silence, broken only by the sound of the fire crackling in the grate. 'Madame, before I put a question,' said the governor, 'it is my wish that you spend three weeks in one of my castles as my guest and under my personal protection. There you will be questioned about the death of your last remaining son, and fear of your husband will not prevent you from speaking the truth.'

'Your Excellency will forgive me,' interrupted the Comte de Montignon, 'if I add a few words. After her stay with your Excellency, I offer the countess asylum for the rest of her life in one of my castles, so that it will be impossible for her husband ever to take his revenge upon her.' The governor nodded in assent. 'Thank you for your offer, Comte de Montignon. It makes my task considerably easier. I ask you now, Madame, in view of these changed circumstances whether you wish to contradict your evidence?'

'No, Excellency. I reject any suspicion that my husband has threatened me! After my stay with your Excellency I shall continue to live at Grandval, unless my husband decides differently.'

The count's left hand trembled so violently on the arm of his chair that Martin bent down and laid his small sinewy hand over it. This calmed the count for the moment, but everyone noticed Martin's gesture. The district officer's secretary whispered something to the governor, but the latter shook his head and said aloud: 'I will use all my authority to see that no use will be made of torture.'

'If anyone is to be tortured,' said Martin, 'then I beg that it may be me.'

'And why you?' asked the official.

'Because I have good nerves.'

The governor tapped on the floor with his ivory cane. 'The testimony of the dead man's mother dispenses with the need for torture.'

But the district officer's secretary bent down once again and whispered in the governor's ear, whereupon he asked, much against his will: 'Comte de Racon, in what circumstances did your elder son die?'

The count gave a start. 'He was set upon by robbers. What has that to do with the death of my second son?'

'General enquiries have been made about you,' replied the official, 'and it has come to light that your eldest son, when in the company of his younger brother and the Comte de Salvieux, was murdered in the Boise de Vincennes. I believe that the Comte de Salvieux is a guest here in your castle. Let him be fetched.'

The governor's secretary left the room. The count began to tremble again, but this time Martin did not place his hand on his.

Louis de Salvieux came in, bowed casually and tossed his fair hair from his brow with an arrogant gesture.

'What is required of me by this grave assembly?'

The district officer's secretary replied: 'Comte de Racon has just told us the truth about the death of his eldest son, with whom you were at the time. Who killed the Vicomte Raoul de Clarmont?'

'Why ask me what you already know from the Comte de Racon?'

'As an eye-witness, you could give us a more detailed account.'

'Well, I was riding with the late brothers when some outlaws fell upon us, and the vicomte was fatally run through.

The fellows were caught later. They confessed under torture and were broken on the wheel.'

'Comte de Salvieux, the count's version does not agree with yours.'

'Yes, it does,' interrupted the countess.

Louis bowed to her. 'Gentlemen, I do not understand what type of parlour game is being played here. May I ask for an explanation?'

'I must ask everyone except the Comte and Comtesse de Racon and the Marquis de Chassigny to leave the room,' said the governor. Comte de Montignon tried to protest, but the old man replied firmly that his presence was unnecessary for the moment. Gérard de Montignon rose and, with his son, preceded Louis de Salvieux and Martin from the room. The two secretaries, taking their presence for granted, remained behind the governor's chair. The governor took a letter from his pocket, unfolded it leisurely and, turning to the count, said:

'Comte de Racon, the king's chief of police handed me this letter, which was addressed to him, requesting me to check the truth of its contents on the occasion of your dead son's marriage. Let me read it to you.

> 'Driven by my fear and my conscience, I appeal to the royal authorities for aid against my father, Comte Gaston de Racon, Marquis de Brayonne. Last autumn he dismissed his bastard, with whom he had unnatural relations, and since then has changed in a terrifying manner. As I do not know the whereabouts of the bastard, I live in constant fear of being murdered by this dangerous fellow, who has several times treacherously attempted to kill me in order to gain my father's sole favour. Two years ago, on the same grounds, he had my brother murdered by hired assassins in the Bois de Vincennes, a crime which I have concealed out of consideration for my father.
>
> 'I have been for fourteen days with my father in Grandval to help him with the preparations for my approaching marriage. He is now often in a condition that makes me believe that I have sometimes a madman before me instead of a father. Not only did he have some poachers flogged and hanged, but, in spite of their confessions, had them tortured

in the cruellest manner for days on end, until they died of their injuries. He had a maid, who tried to flee after committing a trifling offence, torn to pieces by the dogs, and brought two of his female serfs into a physical state approaching that of a tortured person. I am beginning to fear for the life of my mother, whom he has forbidden to approach him and who trembles day and night for fear of him. Fear of my father now outweighs my filial love for him, and this fear must be my excuse for appealing to the authorities to investigate conditions at Grandval. I have hopes for the interdiction of my poor ailing father who is *non compos mentis*, and end this letter with complete confidence in the justice of the high representative of the royal power.

GUY, VICOMTE DE CLARMONT'

The governor handed the letter to the count, who was incapable of receiving it, and the district officer's secretary had to take it from the old man.

'Comte de Racon, do you recognise your son's handwriting?' he asked.

'Yes.'

'Are you in a position to deny the crimes attributed to you by your dead son?'

'No, Excellency.'

'What have you to say in your defence?'

'Nothing, except that I was in fact in a state bordering on madness.'

'What was the cause of this condition?'

'The absence of my illegitimate son, Martin Saint-Jean. I had no hopes of ever seeing him again.'

'But you yourself dismissed him.'

'Yes, Excellency, but not because he threatened the vicomte; on the contrary. Seven years ago, my son Guy locked him in a dungeon in an attempt to suffocate him, set his five Great Danes on him last autumn, and his servants the day before yesterday. Martin Saint-Jean is innocent of the death of my eldest son, with whom he had a close friendship. Martin is innocent of the death of my sons. I beg you to spare my son, Martin Saint-Jean, and to believe my words.'

'Comte de Racon,' said the official, in an icy voice, 'it will be necessary to submit M. Saint-Jean to torture in order to learn the truth about the death of the Vicomte Raoul de Clarmont, for on this subject you may possibly be mistaken.'

'No mistake is possible. My son Martin is incapable of committing a murder. I know him, Gentlemen, better than I know myself. My son Guy hated him and has accused him falsely in order to ruin him. Guy was jealous of him and did not trust me. He did not believe that I could dispense with Martin. Excellency, my son Guy lied in order to seize my estates for himself, and he wished to be rid of both me and my bastard. Read the letter once more. It is self-evident.'

'Be silent, Gaston,' said the marquis. 'You are losing your head. Excellency, allow me to give you my judgment on Lieutenant Saint-Jean. The young man served under me as a corporal, for a year and a half, and his behaviour was impeccable during that period. I would place my hand in the fire that he is innocent. The late vicomte, on the contrary, was a gallows bird, despite the impression he made at Court, and his letter to the chief of police is a proof of his vicious character.'

'Yes, Marquis,' interrupted the countess, 'my unfortunate son Guy was not a noble character and did not behave in a brotherly manner to Martin Saint-Jean.'

'Madame,' cried the governor, 'you are accusing your own son.'

'Yes, Excellency, in the cause of justice. Like the Marquis de Chassigny, I am convinced of Martin Saint-Jean's innocence of the death of my eldest son, and beg you not to part my husband from Martin. My husband committed his crimes half unwittingly, and will not repeat them as long as Martin is with him.'

'Are you countenancing your husband's crimes?'

'No, but I stand by my testimony.'

'Madame, your words carry very great weight. Are you prepared to commit them to paper and swear to them on oath?'

'Yes, your Excellency.'

'Let writing material be brought. Comte de Racon, you may leave the room.'

The count stood up and took a few hesitant paces towards his wife, who calmly turned her deep blue eyes on him. The district officer's secretary hurried over and placed himself between the couple. The count made for his bedroom door and the proceedings continued without him.

Martin waited a long time in his bedroom for news, and when no one appeared made his way at random to the count's room, where he found his friend sitting in a chair before his disconcerted valet. 'Monsieur, what will they decide to do with us?'

'I don't know, Martin. Guy had written a letter to the chief of police, which is a heavy indictment against you. You are supposed to have had Raoul murdered by hired assassins. They want to torture you.'

'Let them do it. I shan't say anything foolish.'

'Try and flee.'

'No, I won't abandon you. Don't worry, the Marquis de Chassigny and your wife will speak in our favour.'

'Yes, Madeleine defended both of us. I had not dared to hope for that.'

'Monsieur, pluck up your courage. Come down with me to the guests.'

'I can't stand up, my knees would give way.'

'Here, give me your hand.'

'No, Martin, I cannot face them. A district officer's secretary cannot be bribed. Guy wanted to have me declared irresponsible for my actions. He wrote to the police. But I am not mad. Guy's mouth has not yet been entirely stopped. The circumstances of Raoul's death could come to light, and the source from which I obtained my new wealth. We should have gagged him better, but now I can't touch him. Martin, you must go into hiding. Pierre, leave the room. Martin, let us think of a good hiding-place.'

Martin called the valet back and said to the count: 'You must go to bed and recover your strength. The guests will have to fend for themselves, and I'm sure your wife has done everything in her power. I hear voices next door; I'll go and ask where we stand.'

'No, Martin. Stay here.'

'I shall not be a moment.'

The count tried to stand up, but remained as though

chained to his chair.

Martin knocked at the door of the study and entered. The governor looked at him in amazement, but the countess, in her exhaustion, did not even notice him. The two secretaries were writing industriously at the table, but the marquis called out in his booming voice: 'Come in, M. Saint-Jean. Everyone, apart from the district officer's secretary, is convinced that you are completely innocent of the Vicomte Raoul de Clarmont's death. It is astonishing what crimes the dead man attributed to you. Captain de Falleron has just been here and cleared your father and yourself from any suspicion of an unnatural relationship. When did you share a camp-bed with your father?'

'When he was frozen.'

'That is what de Falleron said. Your father also mentioned that the vicomte had set his Great Danes on you, and the countess added that, in his defence, Guy had maintained the dogs were mad. Did they bite you?'

'Yes, on my feet, Monsieur.'

'That proves they were not mad; otherwise you would not be here today. You see, your Excellency, how every statement of that damned Satan's spawn—forgive me, Madame—turns out to be a lie.'

'M. Saint-Jean,' said the governor, 'please give us a full account of that murderous attempt on your life.'

'May I first of all inform the count what sort of sentence he can expect?'

'This is not a court of law,' replied the governor. 'Here we are only making enquiries to see who, if anyone, is to be indicted. A court of law has other methods.'

'Will either the Comte de Racon or myself be arraigned before a court?'

'That is not for me to decide, but for the district officer who has police powers. Now tell us your story, M. Saint-Jean.'

Martin began his tale calmly, in simple language, and answered all the questions that were put to him. The light was failing.

Strains of music could be heard from the dining-hall. There, the Comte de Montignon was acting as host, as though Grandval were already in his possession, and his eldest son's wife acted as hostess for the countess. The veiled bride wept in the chapel by the dead body. Marguerite, who had come uninvited to join the guests, was flirting with three lieutenants at the same time.

The old governor adjourned the session when one of Comte de Montignon's lackeys came in and asked what time the gentlemen proposed to eat. Martin returned to the count, and did not hear the governor tell the countess that she would find guards outside her apartment, with orders to forbid her husband entrance.

Martin ran into Pierre. 'M. Saint-Jean, M. le Comte is not well. Look at him sitting there.' The count was sitting in the same position as before.

'Monsieur, things look favourable for us,' said Martin, hurrying over to him. 'I don't think we shall be summoned to the Courts. Nothing will be decided until tomorrow.'

'Are you still safe and sound?'

'Yes, quite. Did you think they would torture me?'

'You were away a long time.'

'Monsieur, you must overcome your fear and keep your poise. Lie down for an hour and then go downstairs. Remember your duties as a host. Please stand up.' With Martin's help the count rose to his feet only to collapse again. Pierre leaped forward and the count was carried to his bed. 'He has no fever,' said Martin, feeling his pulse and reassuring the valet. 'He will recover.'

Pierre took off his master's coat and shoes, and Martin loosened his remaining garments. 'M. Saint-Jean,' he said anxiously, 'he's beginning to shiver.'

'That's only the excitement.'

'Monsieur, I shall remain here for the night. Do you think he has the ague?' asked Pierre.

'No, I left him too long alone, that's all.'

'But why doesn't he speak?'

'Go, and close the door behind you.' The valet left. The count caught hold of Martin's hands and felt his fingers.

'What are you doing, Monsieur?'

'There are no traces of the thumbscrews.'

'Monsieur, if I tell you I'm safe and sound, it is so.'

'What about your back?'

'Shall I pour some cold water over your head?'

'Martin, I should lose my reason if they tortured you.'

'Monsieur, if it ever comes to my being tortured, which I do not now believe, I shall look upon it as a judgment from Heaven.'

'Which you have not deserved!'

'Which I have deserved.'

'No.'

'Let us not quarrel. I will not betray the duel, so that Louis de Salvieux will not be punished and our honour preserved.'

'Martin, put your arms round me until this shivering stops. Thank you. That's better. I'm glad you're here, for now my reason also tells me that I did not kill the wrong one.' Beginning to recover, the count added: 'Martin, your presence works wonders. My cowardice is passing. Look, my hand is steady now. If you only knew how quickly my courage is returning, you'd start roundly abusing me.'

'Abusing you? Why?'

'Don't ask. I'm going downstairs.' The count sat up and slipped off the bed.

'If you get up like that you'll lose your hose. Call Pierre.'

'Pierre!' The valet came in and dressed the count, but as Martin was about to leave the room with him, he caught hold of a chair and said: 'I still feel giddy. I'll wait until they finish eating. We'll dine up here.'

'Lay two places, Pierre,' ordered Martin.

The count sat down. 'Martin, tell the governor's secretary that I wish to have a conversation with the gentlemen. Perhaps his Excellency will be good enough to name the time and place.'

'Monsieur, do you also want to speak to the Comte de Montignon?'

'The devil take that damned vulture!'

'Monsieur, please don't do anything foolish. You are in very bad shape and you are still shivering a little. Shall I tell the governor's secretary that you are slightly feverish and would like his Excellency to pay you a visit?'

'You mean that I should report sick and see the governor alone?'

'Yes, that is what I mean, my friend.'

After a few moments' reflection, the count replied: 'Please

ask the governor to come and see me, and do not linger. I shall wait here for an answer.' Martin left the room. Servants brought in the supper. Pierre drew up the table and served his master. But the count did not touch the food.

'His Excellency asks me to inform you that he will visit you after supper,' said Martin, entering the room.

'Thank you.'

'Aren't you hungry, Monsieur?'

'No.'

'Monsieur, you must have something to eat. An empty stomach gives one black thoughts. I have an enormous appetite. May I begin?'

'Yes, enjoy your food.' Martin sat down and ate like a ploughboy. They heard a noise in the study and the count gave a start. There was a knock at the door and one of the governor's equerries looked into the room. 'His Excellency is here.' The count rose to his feet. 'Pierre, shut the doors and sound the alarm if anyone tries to force his way in. Martin, you wait for me.'

'I will wait and will enjoy my dinner, Monsieur.'

The count strode firmly into the study, where the governor had just seated himself by the fire.

'Thank you, Excellency, for your kindness in coming to visit me.'

'Your son told me that you were ill.'

'I have recovered.'

'Sit down, Comte de Racon, and tell me what you wish to discuss.'

The count sat down opposite the old man and asked:

'Do they still intend to torture Martin Saint-Jean?'

'The district officer has that intention, but not the governorship. I take it that you know where the power lies.'

'Excellency, I have decided to tell the truth about my son Raoul de Clarmont's death. He fell in a duel.'

'Who killed him?'

The count revealed a name.

'Who were the seconds?'

'My son Guy and the Comte de Salvieux.'

'Comte de Racon, this means a year in the Bastille for the

Comte de Salvieux, and the scaffold for the murderer. The truth of your confession will be checked.'

'Excellency, it will be discovered that I ruined the murderer's family. I blackmailed two million out of him as the price of my silence.'

The old man stared at the count and said in a voice of utter contempt: 'Your confession then also means a heavy punishment for you, Comte de Racon.'

'Yes, your Excellency, but Martin Saint-Jean's innocence is proved. Will torture now be necessary?'

'No, provided the several evidences do not conflict. I advise you to inform the Comte de Salvieux how things stand.'

The governor stood up and the count followed suit. 'Excellency, may I keep Saint-Jean with me until his fate is decided?'

'Yes, the Marquis de Chassigny has vouched for both you and your illegitimate son.'

'Can I rely upon that?'

'On the marquis?'

'No, that Martin will not be taken away from me.'

'The district officer's secretary is questioning all your servants. Be patient until tomorrow. Your testimony alters the position. You will be informed tomorrow.'

'So you cannot give me full assurance!'

The old man leaned on his ivory cane. 'The district officer's secretary will certainly give it to you. I'm amazed that you should sacrifice your position, your fortune and your honour for this bastard. It is a good thing that your father did not live to see this day.'

'Your Excellency, Martin's mother was a lady of my own standing. She had to conceal his birth.'

The old man's expression grew milder. 'Now your confession becomes more comprehensible. It never entered my head that the young man could be of noble birth.'

'Your Excellency, I cannot give his mother's name, even if you want proof.'

The governor tapped his stick on the ground. 'Every son must vouch for his father! Your confession is inspired by an infatuation, an almost effeminate weakness.'

'Your Excellency, I educated Martin more harshly than my

legitimate sons. I never spared him in the war. He was wounded in the thigh and the shoulder. I forced myself to throw him out, but I refuse to see the marks of the branding-iron on him . . . no dislocated limbs, no crippled hands. I will not allow him to be maimed for the rest of his life. I would rather shoot him.'

The old man sat down in his chair again and beckoned to the count to do likewise. He stared into the flames, and a long silence ensued. At last without looking away from the fire, the governor said: 'Comte de Racon, had I the true power of a veritable representative of the king, I would hand you over to justice. But since I possess but a mere semblance of power, and since in reality I am no more than the most respected nobleman in the province, I will admit to you that the French nobility, by its loyalty to the king during the past twenty years, has gradually been reduced to the painful situation of having to tremble before bourgeois officials. The district officer of our province is a cloth merchant's son, and each time I want to issue a decree I have to ask his permission beforehand. It is true that certain of the gentry still behave with great brutality to their servants. In the old days this was punished by the Assize courts, but it is surely intolerable when the district officer's secretary can threaten a son of the Comte de Racon with torture on a mere suspicion.

'Your downfall would mean a triumph for the king's officials at the expense of the nobility. As a representative of that nobility, I feel in duty bound to have consideration for you as the son of my dead friend. I shall therefore remain silent about your confession and only reveal it if there is no other way of averting the danger of your son being tortured.

'But, should the district officer doubt your wife's testimony and haul Saint-Jean before the courts as the murderer of the Vicomte de Clarmont, then I will lay down my office. The mistress of Grandval stands so high by her rank and her impeccable reputation that it was a disgrace to every nobleman present to see her being questioned by me in front of that pinchbeck lackey of the cloth merchant's son. I have served my king since my youth and I shall remain true to him to the grave, but I refuse to allow myself to be a slave of his minions.'

The old man rummaged for his gold snuff-box, took a pinch, waited for the effect, then turned and looked the count full in the face. 'Comte de Racon, I shall speak to the Comte de Salvieux myself and make every effort on your behalf. I advise you to rest your nerves until after the funeral. Remain in your apartments until I have left the district secretary and your wife. I will send you intelligence in good time so that, if need be, you can flee the country.'

'Your Excellency, I can find no fitting words to thank you.'

They rose, and the count escorted his guest to the door. He bowed low, and the old man went into the corridor where two of his equerries were waiting for him.

Martin had ended his meal when the count entered the room. He jumped up and hurried over to him. 'Monsieur, how dreadful you look! Did the conversation turn out badly for you?'

The count flung himself on the bed. 'I don't want to hear or see any more. Pierre, undress me.' The valet did as he was bid. Martin busied himself round the fire, where he had kept the soup warm. He took a full plate over to the bed, but the count refused it, ordered the room to be aired and said that they should let him sleep until the following day. Then he turned his face to the wall.

Viscomte Guy de Clarmont's funeral took place next morning, without the Comte de Racon. The countess preserved her composure during the service and the subsequent burial, and tried to comfort the weeping bride. During the funeral banquet she sat between the governor and Baron du Terne, and only later, when the ladies tried to follow her into the salon, did she ask permission to retire for an hour.

The count slept the whole day and the following night, and was unaware of the guests' departure and a visit from the Marquis de Chassigny, who, with his wife and niece, were the only ones to remain in Grandval. The countess had left with her lady-in-waiting and her maid in the governor's coach, after leaving Marguerite d'Epponcourt in the care of the marquise. The gay creature still had no idea of her condition and innocently believed that her expanding waistline was due to the richness of the castle's food. She soon noticed, however, that the witty marquise liked writing letters and novels and found her charge a tiresome bore, and that the marquis's niece prefered to be alone with her uncle. Marguerite often went for drives on her own, for, on the countess's instructions, Dr Borel had forbidden her to ride. She usually met Baron du Terne's youngest son, who would talk to her from horseback or enter her coach. The coachman and the grooms grinned behind their backs. Sometimes Marguerite stopped and went for a walk through the woods with her escort. He had the impertinence to call her Princess Fatty, and she in return called him a coxcomb, but she allowed him none of the liberties which the servants imagined and turned a deaf ear to his complaints of her cruelty.

The count was confined to bed for several days with a fever. Martin sat engrossed in a book, with him, but did not mention what he was reading for he did not want his friend to know that, with a certain purpose in mind, he was ploughing through a French translation of Aristotle's *Ethics*. His silent presence had a soothing effect on the count. The fever abated and he made a quick recovery. He sent for Master Grouchet to discuss the matter of the imprisoned grooms and ordered his master of the hunt to sell the rebels as galley slaves.

As soon as the condemned grooms had been marched off, the count went for a stroll with Martin, who carried his lute. They left the sunny park by the little back gate and followed the winding path that led to the sandpit. The count unbuttoned his cravat. 'We should have ridden, boy. Walking still tires me.'

'Monsieur, the wounded men will certainly die on the march.'

'That will save them from the galleys. It gives me a sneaking pleasure that the chief of police cannot accuse me of cruelty this time. I am procuring oarsmen for the king's ships, and shall receive a sum for them which will perhaps pay our travelling expenses to Austria.'

'Monsieur, you have all the makings of a liberator of christendom.'

'Why not? I'll behead the Turks and leave it to you to

convert them.'

'Monsieur, I think that a Turk would be easier to convert than you, for he believes in a God and a devil, whereas I have to impress upon you the need for leading a good life without being allowed to refer to either. Still, I think I could do it now. Do you feel like listening to me?'

'Not particularly, but I might, out of respect for you. Find a sunny place where I can lie down.'

'There are the sandpits,' said Martin, pointing ahead. 'Would you like to climb up there, so that a certain conversation can be continued at the same place?'

'No, I don't want to climb.'

'Then sun yourself on the sandy slope.'

'Yes. It will be nice and warm there.'

'On reaching their goal, Martin sat down on the gold and yellow sand and offered his friend his knees for a cushion. The count made himself comfortable, and Martin began his speech: 'Everyone knows that a monarch will strive for peace and order in his country, so as to reap the utmost benefit from his kingdom. You do precisely the same, for that reason, in your county. You demand industry from your peasants so that there will be good harvests, and honesty from your officials so that you can increase your revenues. You demand fidelity and reliability from your servants. In short, you impress every virtue into your service because you know full well that lazy peasants will ruin the crops, dishonest bailiffs will cheat you, corrupt judges will work for their own profit instead of for yours, and that, without a reliable staff, the house will fall to rack and ruin. You demand from your soldiers implicit obedience, for a rabble will not submit to orders and will fail in battle. Have I made myself clear so far?'

'Yes, but I'm getting tired.'

'Please hear me out. You strive for advantage in every field whether you are dealing with subordinates or superiors. The king demands capable servants, so you are a capable general and an impeccable courtier. You have to improve yourself for your own good. You know that one does not trust a liar, so you make every effort to appear honest.' The count was about to stop him, but Martin held him firmly by the arm. 'I haven't finished. You have to appear as a man of honour and display loyalty, generosity, courage and charity, if you wish to be respected by your fellow men, for it is in the nature of men to love the exalted and to hate the base. I have nearly finished! To reap every advantage you need a healthy body and a healthy mind, for a sick man can neither lead a regiment in the field nor enjoy worldly pleasures, and an imbecile is utterly useless. Now the body wants nothing better than moderation in eating, drinking and in traffic with women, and nothing suits the mind better than a study of science and the arts. Thus, in my opinion, I have proved to you the need to lead a good and, by the same token, a reasonable life.'

Weeks passed and no word came from the countess. The count remained inseparable from Martin, who displayed neither fear nor impatience but the serene indifference of a stoic. They fenced and hunted together, lay in the sun, wrestled, broke-in young horses and went off on a two days' journey. When they returned they found the Marquis de Chassigny in despair, for he thought they had fled to Austria. The count swore by all that was holy that he harboured no thought of flight. He only wanted to enjoy his freedom to the full while he was still able, and the marquis must allow him this. The marquis forgave him, but was less pleased when the count discreetly began to give his niece presents. Why did he not look round for a mistress? That was no easy matter from a country estate. It would have taken little to make the marquis challenge the count, but then Pierre opportunely brought an appetising girl and peace was restored.

A letter came for the countess, which her husband opened, as was his custom. Baron d'Epponcourt wrote in a trembling hand, thanking the lady for her generous acceptance of his unfortunate daughter, and begged her to keep Marguerite until he was in a position to come and fetch her. He was seriously ill and could no longer hope to recover without the devoted care of his wife. The letter ended with regards to the count and greetings to Marguerite, who should repent her flight and pray for her father. The count showed the letter to the girl and she shed a few tears.

Finally, on the 12th June, one of the governor's bodyguard announced the arrival of the Comtesse de Racon, and that evening the viceregal coach arrived in the castle courtyard with an escort of twenty horsemen. Everyone was present to greet her, but the countess merely offered her hand to the marquis, looked in horror at Marguerite's shapeless waist, bowed to the rest of the company and retired at once to her apartments. The count controlled his impatience and, instead of following her, invited the Marquis de Chassigny to play cards with Martin and himself in his study. His guests accepted, and the three gentlemen took their leave of the ladies.

The marquis had just won the third game of lansquenet, and was shuffling the cards with a grin when Pierre announced the countess. The three gentlemen stood up as she entered. She was wearing a new black silk dress and a flimsy black veil over her beautifully waved hair. In her left hand she held a snow-white lace handkerchief, and in her right an open letter. Greeting the marquis with a formal bow, she turned to her husband: 'Monsieur, my own statements and the written testimony of the marquis have been accepted and you have been condemned to a moderate fine for the cruelties you have inflicted upon your peasants and maids. You will find the sentence in this official document.

'M. Saint-Jean, no suspicion attaches to you any longer, and your accusations against the Baroness d'Epponcourt have been confirmed in the cruellest manner. The baroness was in communication with one of the poisoner Voisin's assistants and will pay for her crimes on the scaffold. She has poisoned her husband, Marguerite's father. M. Saint-Jean, since my husband no longer has an heir, your future is assured. I bid you to ask for the orphaned girl's hand in marriage forthwith. Go to her, M. Saint-Jean.'

Martin bowed and stammered: 'On your orders, Madame,' and left the room.

'Marquis,' continued the countess, 'I still have something to discuss with my husband.' Her guest also bowed and left the room. The count took up the document and laid it on the table next to the cards. 'Please be seated, Madame.'

'I shall be brief, Monsieur. I have given great thought to your son, Martin Saint-Jean, and request you to let him marry Mlle d'Epponcourt. I suggest that you should apply to the king for his legitimation.

'Madame!'

'Monsieur, if his mother is still alive and you were to explain your case to her, I am sure she would be prepared to reveal her secret to the king for love of her child. If the king learns of Martin's origin he will certainly restore him his rights and a title, provided you are prepared to ask him for this favour. Good evening, Monsieur.'

'Madame, I beg you to remain for a little while.'

'Have you anything to ask me?' said the countess, turning to him again.

He took a step forward, stopped, and, taking great pains to control himself, asked as calmly and formally as possible: 'Madame, have you really decided to accept Martin as your son?'

'I love him as a son.'

'Madame, I have not deserved this!'

'Martin deserves it, Monsieur.'

'Guy was killed on his account.'

'That was God's will.'

'Madame, you bring me news that I am a free man and you present me with a son!'

'I am only doing my duty before God.'

'Madame, I am incapable of thanking you!'

'Do not revert to your insane cruelty. The district officer sends you that warning.'

'The district officer of the province? But were you not the governor's guest?'

'I went to see the district officer.'

'You, a countess, visiting a cloth merchant's son!'

'He is one of the king's high officials and behaved more courteously to me than many a nobleman.'

'Who else did you meet?'

'Half a dozen lawyers. I attended no festivities and had plenty of leisure to weep for my last son.'

'Madame, I shall travel to Paris at once.'

'Is Martin's mother still alive?'

'Yes, Madame. She is a widow. Her husband died last autumn. I will write to her. Martin must come with me, but I shall tell him nothing, and I beg you to say nothing in case the plan misfires. I shall leave in two days.'

'Monsieur, I request that you let your son marry Mlle d'Epponcourt before you leave.'

'Madame, that would not be seemly so shortly after the vicomte's death.'

'The girl is expecting a child.'

'I know that, Madame, but the marriage will not take place until my return.'

'You want to thank me, and yet you postpone the marriage!'

'Martin's marriage has to be a brilliant affair, whether he obtains his legitimacy or not. The girl must be patient.'

'Is that your last word?'

'Yes.'

The countess bowed her head, crumpled her handkerchief and left the room without saying goodnight. The count quickly picked up the official document, read it, flung it on the table and cried: 'Pierre, bring wine. I'll fetch the marquis myself. And see that the table is brightly decked and that there is music. Fetch my Court dress and start to pack. We're leaving for Paris in two days' time. Here you are, you old robber, go and get drunk.' He threw a handful of silver to the valet and closed the door behind him.

In the meantime, Martin had been announced to the Marquise de Chassigny, where Marguerite was to be found. He asked permission to speak to the girl alone, and Marguerite followed him outside.

'Have you a secret to tell me, M. Saint-Jean?'

'Mademoiselle, I beg you to come with me into the park, because I know no suitable room where we could be undisturbed.'

'How do you come to use the word "we"?'

'You'll learn that in a moment.' They crossed the dining-hall into the park, hurried along the arboured walks and came to a halt by the statue of Flora. The sun had not yet set. The head of the smiling goddess was gleaming in a russet-gold light, and her white limbs were already bathed in cool, blue shadows. 'Please sit down, Mademoiselle.' Marguerite did as she was bid, and Martin stood before her. 'I beg you to give me your hand in marriage.'

'What?'

'I am asking you to marry me.'

'Are you completely out of your mind?'

'It is the countess's wish, Mademoiselle.'

'Then I'll tell her that I would not dream of taking a bastard for my husband.'

'I am no longer without means and shall return to my father's regiment of guards as a lieutenant.'

'Go wherever you like. I look upon your offer as a jest.'

'Mademoiselle, I should never have dared to ask for your hand were you not about to bear my child.'

'That is not true!'

'I learned it from the doctor who examined you during our flight and Dr Borel has confirmed it to the Comtesse de Racon.' Marguerite sat on the stone bench as though overwhelmed. She had turned so pale that Martin, fearing she was about to faint, stretched out his hand to her, but she rose to her feet and thrust him aside.

'Monsieur Saint-Jean, you assured me that your dastardly behaviour would have no consequences.'

'I lied in order to reassure you, for there need not necessarily have been any. I beg you to forgive me.'

'Liar!' A hail of slaps rained down on the young man's cheeks until he could neither hear nor see. He did not defend himself and kept his hands to his sides. Marguerite did not stop until she was exhausted. She slumped on the stone bench and began weeping.

'Will you accept now, Mademoiselle?' Martin asked.

'Never! I'll drown the brat. To me, it is as though I had a cat in my womb. I loathe you. Go, leave me. Leave me at once!' Martin returned to the castle and sent Emilie to look after the girl.

The count and the marquis were in the hall. The former caught hold of Martin, embraced him and shook him wildly. 'Boy, we are indeed lucky. Go to my wife, thank her and kiss her hand.'

'At once, Monsieur. Mlle d'Epponcourt refused my offer of marriage.'

'So much the better for you! I'll get you a princess who won't leave the marks of her fingers on your cheek.' The marquis laughed uproariously and Martin hurried to the salon.

The countess accepted Martin's grateful hand-kiss and listened to his tale. 'You frightened Marguerite and it's quite understandable that she should spurn you now, but I am convinced that she will accept your second or third proposal. I expect you to observe patience, endurance and loyalty.'

'I will not disappoint you, Madame, because my conscience demands it.'

'Can I rely on your conscience this time?'

'Yes, Madame, please.' Martin blushed.

The countess proffered her hand, which he kissed once more. 'Monsieur Saint-Jean, I will hold your child over the font.'

'Madame, you are like the Madonna in your compassion.'

'I am beginning to look upon you as a son.'

'My life belongs to you, Madame,' said Martin kneeling at her feet. For a moment he leaned his face against her black silk dress, and then rose hastily to his feet.

'Go now,' she said, 'and do not forget your good intentions.'

Martin bowed and left. Hardly had he left the room than the countess was summoned by Emilie to Marguerite, who, in her despair, was hysterical.

The count completed his preparations for the journey at the greatest speed, and begged the marquis not to take it amiss that he was leaving without him. At every crossroads the coaches would lose a wheel, the ladies would feel ill and have to rest for hours, and they would never reach Paris. The marquis was offended, but the count knew how to compensate him by promising him a shapely wench and by presenting the marquise with a pair of earrings, glittering with diamonds.

The countess waited until she was alone in Grandval with Marguerite before breaking to her the news of her father's death. Marguerite was too preoccupied with her own misfortunes to feel any grief at this further blow. She maintained that his death had saved her from becoming a beggar, and that it was a relief to her because she would never see her parents' house again. The countess tried to interest her in baby clothes and napkins for the baby, and praised Martin, which merely aroused the girl's contempt. She would not touch any sewing and lay abed half the day in the finest weather. When the Baron du Terne's youngest son tried to visit her she locked herself in her room, but wrote him a letter next day. She received a reply and, from then onwards, two grooms were constantly underway between Grandval and the du Terne Castle. The countess sighed and said anxiously to Dr Borel that matchmaking, even with the best intentions, was a difficult task. And an unrewarding one, the old man insisted.

THE STRUGGLE FOR LEGITIMATION

MARTIN and the count rode so fast that they might have been bearing a message for the king. They reached Paris and stopped outside Tailor Volin's shop, where the count ordered a new uniform and three suits for Martin, carefully choosing the material himself. Then they went to the Hôtel de Racon, alarming the servants by their unexpected arrival. While waiting for a hastily prepared meal, the count wrote a letter to Colonel du Lac and ordered Martin to deliver it to the regiment. As soon as Martin had left, the count wrote another letter which caused him considerable difficulty. He wrote:

MADAME,

You will be surprised to find that this letter is unsigned. The writer begs you most humbly to see no offence in this omission, but a precaution, so that the letter will not be thrown unread into the fire. May your eyes be gracious enough to read it to the end, for the happiness or misfortune of an admirable young man depends upon it. As his spokesman, I beg you to recall your sojourn in a convent many years ago. There you made the acquaintance of a lady who told you of a boy named Martin. This Martin has become the favourite of his father, whom God has punished with the loss of his two legitimate sons, with no hope now of another heir.

Martin knows of his doubly-noble origin, without knowing his mother's name. In public, he ranks as the bastard of his father, the count, and is pledged never to reveal his half knowledge of his aristocratic mother, lest, for lack of evidence, he should become an object of ridicule. Possibly you can imagine the agonies of a young man who is magnanimous enough never to make the slightest reproach to his father, and who, despite his simple name, is appreciated in society owing to the virtues he has inherited from his mother.

Madame, the writer knows that he could never ask the slightest favour of Martin's mother, but he dares to address you with a plea for Martin: Would you be gracious enough to speak on his behalf and, with your gentle words, arouse the maternal feelings in the heart of that lady who, twenty-two years ago, held the little Martin in her arms? Call to your aid the sweet memories of your own maternal happiness to move a justifiably irreconcilable woman to compassion. Tell her that she alone could put an end to the spiritual suffering of the young man and ensure his material future. Tell her that it lies in her hands whether the rich estates of this man, whom fate has robbed of his children, will pass to distant relatives or to his subsequently legitimised bastard. Tell her that, to procure this legitimacy, only a secret confession to the king is required. As soon as the king—and no one but the king need know of it—learns of the young man's maternal origin it will be possible, by the king's grace, to procure Martin's legitimation, thus enabling him to become his father's heir and successor.

I beg you to dissuade the lady of your acquaintance from taking a cruel revenge by ignoring my plea. Together with the guilty party, she would condemn an innocent person to eternal misery. Please ask her whether it would not be the action of a noble soul to make one who has deserved it happy, and by her generosity to shame eternally another who deserves no joy. May a compassionate God inspire your lady to follow the dictates of her heart, rather than of her pride. Madame, be compassionate enough to give a sign to one who is filled with remorse and punished by the loss of all his legitimate heirs. By breaking your silence, either restore his hopes or shatter them. He is ready to atone in any way and waits with bowed head for your answer.

The count waited until nightfall, borrowed Pierre's cloak and hat in order not to be recognised, and took the letter, under cover of darkness, to a certain elegant town house.

Asking to see the steward rather than the doorkeeper, he gave the man a large *pourboire* to hand the letter to no one but Madame la Maréchale.

In his impatience for a reply, the count did not stir from the Hôtel de Racon for three whole days, but no messenger appeared. Then he went to Versailles, and by his well-rehearsed portrayal of a grief-stricken father, aroused the compassion of all the ladies. The king deigned to say a few words of condolence. By virtue of his brilliant talents the dead Vicomte de Clarmont had been an adornment to the Court, and his death was thus a loss to the whole of France. The count replied that this epitaph, from the mouth of the wisest of all rulers, made him realise, on the one hand, the enormity of his loss, while, on the other hand, it brought him the consolation that he had once more merited the king's attention. Louis smiled graciously, and the count hastened to let a new expression appear on his pock-marked face, indicating recovery from his inconsolable grief.

A protracted melancholy would have seemed unseemly, for Louis liked only gay faces around him and abhorred the sight of mourning. The count discarded his black coat and confined himself to a few dark ribbons, displayed in such excellent taste that they became the fashion at Court overnight. He sang songs to the ladies on his lute, heaving the deepest sighs which could have been addressed equally well to his dead son as to the wayward heart of a beautiful woman.

At home, however, the count's behaviour was abominable, for the longed-for letter did not arrive. Martin fled and stayed with Colonel du Lac, who instructed him in the way a regiment was administered. His comrades gave a large banquet to celebrate his return, and the dwarf, Nicolas de Chassigny, on hearing the news rejoined the regiment. One hot mid-summer day the count appeared unexpectedly to find the whole regiment bathing and his offspring acting as swimming teacher. His anger fell like a hailstorm on all the officers. Training was immediately resumed and continued for four days. Three men caught sunstroke, a horse dropped dead and then the martinet was gone. They could take a breather.

Upon his return to Paris after nightfall, the count learned

that a stranger had been asking for the Comte de Racon for the past two days. He flew into a rage and cursed the steward for not having pressed a *pourboire* on the visitor. The man's attempts to justify himself only increased his anger, and he was just about to resort to violence when the doorkeeper announced a stranger, who entered in cloak and hat, handed the count a letter, without a word of greeting, and turned swiftly to the door. The count bade him wait, broke the seal of the letter and read by the light of the staircase lantern:

> A mother's love has proved stronger than any oath. A private audience has been requested. Please do nothing before receiving a further letter. On the occasion of a drive to Versailles tomorrow morning, one wishes to observe a young man from a distance.

The count crumpled the letter, stuck it under his coat, felt for his purse, gave the messenger twenty pistoles and ordered the doorkeeper to send a groom to fetch Lieutenant Saint-Jean from the regiment. Then he ran up the stairs to his room and ordered Pierre to bring the little wife of the banker Boquelin, if the lady could find some way of leaving her house in secret.

Pierre carried out his mission with his usual sly skill, and just before midnight a hired litter drew up in the entrance of the Hôtel de Racon. The girl's delight was boundless when the count told her of Martin's return. The count was more tender and kind to her than ever before, and when Martin arrived at daybreak he met on the stairs a small veiled lady, who embraced him with a little cry of joy and hurried away, leaving him quite confused.

Blanche's absence this time, however, had been too prolonged. At two o'clock, the ancient banker had been unable to sleep and had looked in on his wife, who, although in bed as usual, seemed to have suddenly grown larger. The old man became suspicious and pulled back the bedclothes, to discover the maid lying there in place of his wife. He was on the point of losing his reason, and when, just before dawn, Blanche slipped unsuspectingly into her bedroom she came face to face with her infuriated husband. He tore off her veil, abused her in a voice shrill with excitement, calling her the most unflattering names, and pulled her by the hair round the room. Blanche screamed for help but no one dared to come to her aid. By scratching and biting she managed to free herself at last, and a wild game of catch-as-catch-can ensued through the rooms of the luxurious house.

Blanche's host of small dogs, yapping gaily, joined in the fun, and several times nearly brought their mistress to the ground. Suddenly, as the mad chase pursued its course round the table, the old man collapsed and lay glassy-eyed on the floor. Now the lackeys hurried in and shouted for the banker's house physician. The old man was placed in a chair, and it was found that he had just had a stroke. The doctor immediately bled him. Blanche, surrounded by her pets, stared in terror at this hideous operation. Yet, strangely enough, M. Boquelin recovered visibly under the doctor's care and asked in a thick voice where his wife had spent the night. Blanche fell to her knees, at a safe distance from him, begged his forgiveness and said that no power on earth would force her to betray where she had spent the night. M. Boquelin began to utter a stream of incomprehensible words, but the doctor removed him unceremoniously from the sight of his adulterous wife and carried him into the bedroom.

In her terror, Blanche wept hysterically and, towards midday, fled on foot with her favourite pet to the Hôtel de Racon, where she found neither the count nor Martin. Pierre hired a coach for her and she was driven to the house of her brother, who had left Paris with his wife. The old steward must have had his own thoughts when the terrified girl asked him for protection and accommodation. He had his mistress's apartments made ready, and Blanche retired with her puppy to the Comtesse de Salvieux's bed.

In the meantime, the count and Martin were on the way to Versailles. The young man was wearing his new bright-red, gold-braided lieutenant's uniform which fitted him like a glove and suited him admirably. A white ostrich feather waved from his black hat and his jabot and cuffs were of the costliest Mechlin lace. He was riding a thoroughbred chestnut and was chattering gaily to the count, who was in an excellent mood and looked at him from time to time with appraisal. 'Monsieur, why are you not in a hurry today? I cannot remember a single occasion when you did not gallop to Versailles.'

'Today I have plenty of time.'

'Can't we at least overtake that coach in front, because we are getting all its dust? My fine coat's getting quite grey.'

'Very well, let's overtake it.'

The count and Martin galloped past it. 'Monsieur, why did they not greet us? The two fat old aunts inside stared as though they knew us.'

'Did they? Well, let's wait till the coach draws near again—perhaps they are two ladies of high station. One must always keep on the right side of the ladies, and even more so when they have reached the rank of fat old aunts. Can you make Darius do a perfect levade?'

'Of course, Monsieur!'

'I should like to see you do it.' Martin left the road with his chestnut and proceeded to display his horsemanship on the meadow. The count pretended to watch, keeping his eye on the heavy rattling coach with its gleaming gold studs which bore on the panels the crest of a late Maréchal de France. The four powerful black horses were black-plumed, and the servants and outriders wore black livery. The count turned to one side in order to give the occupants an unhampered view of Martin. The young man performed a perfect levade and shouted triumphantly: 'You couldn't have done better yourself!'

To his dismay, he noticed that the count had ridden off. He blushed with embarrassment, doffed his hat to the ladies and trotted after his friend, who was waiting for him and laughing.

'Monsieur, you disgraced me before the "aunts".'

'You disgraced yourself. You should have paid more attention.'

'I don't like being shamed.'

'Nor do I.'

'I'm furious with you.'

'Well, take your revenge.'

Swift as a flash, Martin tore off the count's hat, so that his wig fell awry, and galloped off with his booty. The count adjusted his wig and set out in pursuit, overtaking the grooms he had sent on ahead and several dust-veiled coaches at full gallop. He managed to catch Martin, who laughingly returned his hat. As good friends, they rode on towards the king's palace. Its rose-red façade was already beckoning at the far end of the straight, wide avenue.

A few days later, the count received a second letter from the mysterious messenger. It read as follows:

> The audience was satisfactory. Compose a petition and, as soon as possible, try to obtain a private audience. You have been forgiven now that one has seen a very fortunate young man. But one wishes no sign of gratitude and no further meeting.

The same night, the count drew up the petition and travelled early next morning to Versailles. There he took the requisite steps to procure a private audience. With gold and promises he tried to gain the favour of some influential courtiers, and handed Maréchal d'Humières a sealed letter for the king, with the request that he should hand it to the sovereign in person.

Four weeks later, the king was gracious enough to receive the count in private audience. Louis showed himself to be well-informed but had the matter once more explained to him in detail. At last, he said that he would think matters over. The count knew that this phrase was ambiguous, but that it would not be prudent to ask for a more definite reply. He thanked the king profusely for his favour and was dismissed with a stern glance.

The king's scowl gave him food for thought. He made some enquiries as to His Majesty's private opinion of him, and finally discovered that he had been described to the pious Madame de Maintenon as an insolent free-thinker. From now on, he attended all the services when the king was present and spoke on every occasion of the miraculous consolations offered by the Christian faith, which the blows of fate had revived in him, enabling him to begin a new life.

In the meantime, the countess waited week after week at

Grandval for news. Her letters to her husband remained unanswered and Martin gave no sign of life, although she had written to him twice reminding him of his obligations; she did not suspect that the count purloined the letters. At the beginning of August, she wrote to the Marquise de Chassigny asking whether she knew the whereabouts of the Comte de Racon and his son. The marquise replied that she had met the count several times at Court, but since she had retired to her country estate she had not seen him again, and could give no news of Lieutenant Saint-Jean.

The countess had hoped to see Marguerite married before her confinement, and now these hopes were dashed. Marguerite no longer left her room, in order to conceal her condition from the servants. The countess's attempts to console her only increased her hatred for Martin, whose behaviour now, with the best will in the world, could not be excused. Neither woman was aware that Martin had frequently asked the count when he could marry Mlle d'Epponcourt, and that he had always been given an evasive answer.

One broiling day, when Martin returned from his regiment through the streets of the capital, he saw, to his amazement, the count's charger and his grooms outside a church portal. He trotted up and asked Charles whether the count was inside. Charles nodded assent, and Martin said he should not try to make a fool of him. Nevertheless, he dismounted and entered the church.

As soon as his eyes had grown accustomed to the cool twilight of the aisle, he saw the count kneeling some way ahead near the altar, engrossed in prayer. Martin hurried up to him and touched his shoulder. 'Monsieur, what has come over you?' The count gave him a curt look, shrugged his shoulders impatiently to show that he did not wish to be disturbed and rattled his rosary. Martin, greatly offended, stood for a moment behind his friend's back and then also fell to his knees. The minutes passed. Four old women were mumbling their prayers. Martin said six Pater Nosters and nudged his friend, only to receive a hard nudge in return. He tugged at the count's rosary.

'Pray, you oaf,' hissed the count, growling a Pater Noster

under his breath.

'Why should I pray?' whispered Martin.

'To save your lousy soul from the fires of hell.'

'Monsieur . . .'

'Be silent.'

Martin grew angry and started to pray so noisily that his voice enchoed through the nave. The four old ladies turned round. Martin relapsed into an embarrassed silence. The count continued to pray. A good hour passed. Then the four old ladies rose to their feet and shuffled to the exit. As they opened the door the sunlight streamed for a brief moment into the church. 'Ugh!' said the count, sitting down on the footstool of his *prie-Dieu* and stretching his legs. 'Another hour and I should never have been able to stand up again. God bless Master Volin for having provided me with knee-pads. How did you manage to survive?'

'Monsieur, for God's sake tell me what you hope to achieve by those prayers.'

'Only this, my boy: I am trying to get back into favour, so that one day the king will decide to raise you to the nobility. Did you see those four cross-eyed crones? They are the most dangerous of all the gossips at Court, and at the same time the most useful if they ever say a kind word about you. I recognised them as they got out of a coach in front of the church and followed them in. They will help to give me a reputation for piety. Did I look pious or like a Pharisee?'

'You're a hypocrite.'

'You should be grateful to me.'

'I'm ashamed of you, and I don't want to get a title that way.'

'Don't be so sanctimonious. Guy would have laughed himself silly and thanked me from the bottom of his heart.'

'I'm not like Guy, and beg you to drop that mask; it is unworthy of you.'

'I will not discard anything which might be to my advantage. A free-thinker cannot hope for advancement today. Others have already adapted themselves to the new rarefied air of sanctity and have stolen a long march on me, with which it will be difficult enough to catch up. Tell Colonel du Lac that he must order the fellows to attend mass regularly, and he is to hold an open-air service in the field before the big manoeuvres. Help me to my feet.'

Martin did as he was bid. The two men walked to the door.

'Monsieur,' asked Martin, 'is there no more dignified way of getting on by one's own merits?'

'I don't know of any.'

'I beg of you, do not make too great a sacrifice for me.'

'At least the sacrifice furthers my own ambition; and now I want to get out into the sun.' On the ride home the count related all manner of racy stories, but Martin did not pay him the compliment of laughing. Just before they reached the Hôtel de Racon, the count suddenly losing his temper, ordered him to rejoin his regiment.

The count had correctly summed up the impression he had made on the old women in the church, and soon had the reputation at Court of having been brought back to the fold, Relying upon this reputation, he plucked up courage one day during a ride humbly to ask the king whether he had come to any decision upon a certain secret matter that was still in abeyance. The king replied that important decisions should never be hurried. Various aspects were being given due consideration and he would see. Thus the count had made no progress. So great was his disappointment that he almost committed the folly of begging the monarch to hasten matters. But he was shrewd enough to control himself and to protest that all his hopes rested with the king, and that he was convinced that one day there would be an end to his painful uncertainty. Louis did not reply, and the count, with a deep bow, fell back among the troop of followers.

After the ride with the king, the count paid a visit to the country house of his friend Ninon de Lenclos, whom he begged to remind the Marquise de Maintenon of his petition should an opportunity arise. Ninon promised to do everything that friendship demanded and prudence allowed. In token of his gratitude, the count gave her a costly trinket, rode back to Paris, and would have started to drink heavily during the next few days had Blanche's frequent visits not taken his mind off his hopes and fears.

The girl had returned to the house of the banker, who, since his stroke, had been paralysed down the right side and had neither the strength nor the authority to punish his unfaithful wife. Blanche slipped out of the house almost every night, ignoring the repeated warnings of her brother to leave for the country with her husband on account of the heat. The count had ballet dresses made for her and she danced for him as she had done years ago. Her figure had remained so child-like that she still did not look more than sixteen.

Martin suffered terribly from his unrequited love. The count did not object to his watching Blanche's dances or listening to her lute-playing, and did not dismiss him until the presence of a third person became embarrassing. At the outset, Martin could only be driven from the room by repeated requests. But then he could no longer bear Blanche's gaze, and tried to deaden his grief by strenuous service with the regiment. The count, on the other hand, visited his troops very occasionally and was constantly either at Versailles or visiting various acquaintances outside the capital.

In September, the count travelled to Blois. One day, during a stag hunt, the king beckoned the Comte de Racon to approach. From a safe distance the courtiers were watching the massacre of a host of game, and the king, who for once was bored at the sight of this carnage, was gracious enough to walk a few steps apart with the count and to say that since the Racon estates were so considerable it would be a pity if they were to pass to the wealthy house of Montignon. But, in order to legitimise a certain young man born out of wedlock, it would be necessary to obtain the consent of the Comtesse de Racon, even though she still clung to her Huguenot faith.

Trembling with excitement, the count replied that the legitimation of his son, Martin Saint-Jean, had not been his own idea but his wife's, who loved the young man as a mother. Would His Majesty allow the lady to address a letter to him? Louis shook his head and said that he would like to speak to the countess in person. The count asked whether she should come to Blois, whereupon the king smiled and said that the route to Versailles was shorter, and even if the lady possessed winged shoes she would not be able to join the Court at Blois, since they were returning to Paris in three days' time. The count was about to fall to his knees and thank him, but the monarch waved him aside with a gracious gesture. The count did not miss an opportunity of boasting that he knew the date of their departure, and for the rest of the day was in the best of spirits.

At the end of September, a fast messenger arrived at Grandval, and the countess received a letter from her husband requesting her to travel to Paris immediately in order to sponsor Martin. The countess went to her desk and wrote:

MONSIEUR,

I shall be unable to grant your request until after Mlle d'Epponcourt's delivery, when mother and child no longer require my presence here.

MADELEINE.

The countess sent her letter by ordinary post, and the count raged when he finally received it. He despatched a second fast courtier and threatened to come and fetch his wife personally. The countess was unmoved. With Martin he began to plunge into a round of pleasure and parties and to look round for a good match for his future heir. He interviewed various wealthy fathers and respected ladies of quality, compared the various dowries, connections and physical features of the girls in question, and occasionally took Martin into his confidence. The young man, however, always replied that he was under an obligation to marry Mlle d'Epponcourt, and that he intended to do so. The count flew into rages, but Martin was adamant and fled to the regiment when his demands became too insistent.

At the beginning of November 1680 Marguerite gave birth to a lusty boy. Her delivery was difficult, but the young mother made a speedy recovery when the countess suggested taking her to Paris. After three weeks, they set out without bothering to inform the count. The youngest du Terne suddenly put in an appearance and could not be persuaded to leave the lady's carriage. He hovered around the coach until the countess explained that Mlle d'Epponcourt was betrothed to another, and that it was not seemly to turn her head just before her marriage. This banished the gay cavalier, and Marguerite complained the journey was now a bore. The countess consoled her with the thought of Paris and the parties she would be allowed to attend. The girl then recovered her gaiety and the young cavalier was forgotten.

The countess sent Denis on ahead to the uninhabited Hôtel de Brayonne, with orders that the steward should make all preparations to receive the ladies. The servant was given strict injunctions to see that the count did not learn of their arrival; consequently they still believed at the Hôtel de Racon that the countess was at Grandval, although she had already been three days at the Hôtel de Brayonne. The countess was carrying out a well-devised scheme of her own. Fearing that Martin might have been caught in some other love-toils, she hoped to surprise the young man with Marguerite's enhanced beauty, and to win him. She had the most beautiful dresses made for the girl, and ordered new dresses in the latest Paris fashion for herself and her lady-in-waiting. Then she sent her slyest lackey in disguise to the Hôtel de Racon to spy out the count's and Martin's movements for the next few days. She learnt that a fête was to be given by the Marquise de Sévigné at the Hôtel Carnavalet, and this seemed suitable for her purpose. In the evening, she ordered her lady-in-waiting, shy old Mlle de Lange to stay at home, and drove with Marguerite to the marquise's hotel.

While the Marquise de Sévigné was reading to a select audience the last letter from her beloved married daughter, Martin spoke to little Madame Boquelin, who had arrived with her brother and sister-in-law. Blanche was wearing a blue-green dress with a host of diamonds in her hair, which had been arranged in curls. 'Madame,' Martin said with a smile, 'he has to pretend to be listening to the marquise, whether the letter interests him or not. I'm sure he will not come and sit beside you today because your stern brother is here.'

'M. Saint-Jean, I'm so afraid that he may fall in love with his mistress.'

'He has already dismissed her.'

'Oh, M. Saint-Jean, is that really true?'

'Yes, Madame. He grows more difficult to please every day and is never satisfied.'

The girl lowered her head. 'Yes, he is never quite satisfied.'

'Madame, he will never tire of watching your dancing. You are always a charming new toy for him.'

Blanche blushed with pleasure, but her mood changed to one of anxiety. 'And what will become of me?'

'How can I tell? Anyhow, you have in me a friend who is prepared at all times to protect you from danger.'

Blanche gave him a shy, grateful smile. 'I am already terrified of returning home. M. Boquelin looks so repulsive. One side of his face has dropped, and his valet is the only one who can understand him when he talks. The doctor says that a second stroke would kill him. If only I knew how long he would live!'

'What would you do then, Madame?'

'Louis will never allow me to become your father's mistress and will simply look for a new moneybags for me. But I shall escape. Would you hide me if your friend would not take me?'

'I would buy a little house for you, Madame, and give you a bodyguard composed of grim veterans.'

'Would you really do that?'

'I would do anything for you. You have only to command.'

'Is there no way in which I could constantly remain near your father without being recognised?'

'No, Madame, unless he acquiesced.'

'He would never agree,' she said, lowering her head once more.

'Who wouldn't agree, and to what?' asked a man's voice. They looked round and caught sight of Louis de Salvieux. 'M. Saint-Jean, for a long time I have wanted to talk with you. Do you know whom my sister visits in secret?'

'I know no more than you do, and I'm not your sister's keeper.'

'Could you not convert Claire-Marie to virtue?'

'Would *you* remain true to a withered old crone?'

'M. Saint-Jean, is it true that you are to be declared legitimate by the king?'

'What? It is the first I have heard of it.'

'I have it on very reliable authority.'

'I will ask my father at once!' Martin hurried over to a group of people standing round the Marquise de Sévigné, and took up his position behind the Comte de Racon. The Marquise de Chassigny noticed him and smiled. 'Why do you smile, my dear friend?' asked Madame de Sévigné.

'Look over there! The masculine counterpart of you and your daughter.'

'Oh, yes. But could one compare M. Saint-Jean with my daughter?'

'No human being could ever be compared with her,' teased the marquise.

'Don't say that again or I shall begin to believe it.'

'As if you have not always done so!'

'Oh, no. I guard against such nonsense, which would put me on a level with any peasant woman. The ugliest old crone looks upon her brat as the greatest miracle of creation.'

'Unjustly so,' said an abbé. 'Whereas no one hs the right to question you, Marquise, if you hold such an opinion.' His hostess contradicted him, and an amusing argument began.

Martin whispered a question in the count's ear. 'Who said so?'

'Louis de Salvieux.'

'Oh, I submitted a petition but have heard nothing definite yet. When you're not certain about something it is better to keep things to yourself.'

'But have I really cause to hope?'

'Yes, go on hoping and spend sleepless nights. My wife has to give her consent.'

'I am sure she will do that.'

'Comte de Racon, what does this cryptic conversation mean?' asked the marquise.

'You must forgive me, Madame, but I cannot answer your question. The boy has forgotten his manners.'

Martin excused himself swiftly and returned to Louis and Blanche. 'Comte de Salvieux,' said Martin, trying to curb his excitement, 'we are waiting for the king's decision, but nothing is known for certain yet. Madame, just think what it would mean to me to be of equal birth to all these ladies and gentlemen. Excuse me for a moment, I should like to get a breath of fresh air.' Martin left the salon and went out into the dark courtyard. It was raining heavily. He took refuge in the covered way that cut the courtyard in two halves. The coachmen from the many coaches had collected there in groups, to gossip. Martin leaned against the pillar. The cool night air and the darkness refreshed and calmed him.

After a while, he returned to the house and met Louis in the doorway 'M. Saint-Jean, I should like to speak to you. I know on good authority that the king is disposed to grant your father's wish. My sister will shortly become a widow. I offer you her hand in marriage because I know your feelings for her.'

'Unfortunately, I am no longer free, Comte de Salvieux,' stammered Martin.

'Are you betrothed?'

'Yes.'

'To whom, if I may ask, M. Saint-Jean?'

'To a girl who has had a child by me.'

'Do you only wish to marry her because of the child?'

'Yes, Comte de Salvieux.'

'Has the child already been born?'

'I imagine so.'

'Would you be free if it were still-born?'

'I had not thought of that. Yes, I should be free then.'

'Good, M. Saint-Jean. Let me know when you have further news. Can I count upon your love for my sister?'

'By my devotion to your sister you can be assured of that. I fear, however, she will listen to no suitor.'

Louis smiled. 'I should like you for my brother-in-law, M. Saint-Jean, because it would solve one awkward problem at least.'

'What do you mean?'

'I imagine that you would be able to come to terms with your father.'

Martin did not immediately understand the significance, and then flushed scarlet. 'Come, let us go indoors, Comte de Salvieux.' Louis walked on ahead with a smile.

Martin found Blanche surrounded by a host of admirers. He felt no desire to compete with these gentlemen and retired to an alcove where he could be alone with his thoughts. The musicians suddenly began to play a dance, and Blanche fled from her admirers and hurried over to Martin. 'M. Saint-Jean, will you be my partner?'

'I, Madame?'

'You are the best dancer and my favourite escort after the Comte de Racon.'

'But why the favourite among so many others?'

'Because you are still my brother Martin, M. Saint-Jean.'

'Oh, Blanche, do you know what your brother has in store for you?'

'Do you mean yourself or my real brother?'

'I mean the Comte de Salvieux.'

'What has he in mind?'

'He wants to marry you to me as soon as M. Boquelin is dead. Don't be afraid! I am betrothed to a girl of noble birth whom I shortly have to marry, but there is faint hope that I may be able to get out of it honourably. Then I should be free and I should make a proposal to you, which I now wish you to hear in advance. I love you, my sweet Blanche and I know whom you love. I would marry you without making any demands on you. I would leave you freer than you are now. I would make it possible for you to be near the one we both love. Would you marry me, under these conditions, Blanche?'

Blanche's dark eyes stared into Martin's hazel ones. 'You are an angel, M. Saint-Jean.'

'Unfortunately not, since although I am loth to admit it even to myself I still refuse to give up hope. I shall not despair as long as you visit my friend.' At this, Blanche covered her face with her hands. 'Madame, have I offended you? Have I hurt you? I beg you, speak to me, Blanche.'

'Oh, M. Saint-Jean, why do you love me and why do I have to love him? Why is it all so complicated?'

'He is very fond of you,' Martin said gently, 'and things are well as they are.'

'How do you know that all is well?'

'My heart tells me so.'

Blanche turned to him. Her eyes were moist in the candle-light. 'M. Saint-Jean, I should like to give you all the diamonds in my hair and all the flames from these candles! While I can still continue to look upon you as a brother, I am not so terrified of life.'

'Do you still want to dance with me?'

'Yes, M. Saint-Jean, but the minuet has already begun. I will dance the next one with you.' At this moment Comte de Racon came up. 'You must leave each other. You look like a pair of lovers. Madame, your sister-in-law awaits you.' Blanche glided away. 'Do try and behave a little more discreetly, Martin. Someone has just remarked that widows today become betrothed before their husbands are nailed down in their coffins.'

'Thank you, Monsieur!'

'Why?'

'For wanting to make me your son.'

'That is only natural. Confine your attentions to Blanche when you are in my house, but not before Paris society. Do you see that girl over there in the light yellow dress?'

'The little slim one who keeps smiling?'

'Yes, that's the one I mean, Martin. Her father is a relation of the late Duc de La Rochefoucauld. She has a dowry of 500,000. Why don't you pay her some attention?'

'I don't feel in the mood for frivolity tonight.'

'Martin, that is no answer. I expect legitimate grandchildren.'

'I'm afraid you'll wait in vain.'

'Are you being obstinate again?'

'Why shouldn't I be, when my father Pan shows his cloven hoof?'

'Shall I tear out your ears?'

'Then you would have a pair of donkeys' ears in those famous, beautiful hands of yours.' The count was about to reply but there was a sudden stir among the seated ladies and gentlemen.

The steward announced to the hostesss that two well-born masques requested admittance. The marquise gave orders that they should be admitted and the company rose to its feet, expecting that some princess, or even Madame de Maintenon, had come to pay an unexpected call. The dancing couples stopped and looked expectantly towards the door. The Comtesse de Racon entered with Marguerite d'Epponcourt. Both were wearing black velvet masks. The countess's severe black velvet dress was embroidered with silver at the bodice and adorned with pearl-grey ribbons and white lace. Marguerite's white dress was woven with gay flowers which enhanced her youthful grace.

Martin had immediately recognised the two ladies. Not so the count. He stared at his wife and suddenly gave Martin a dig in the ribs. 'Do you know the lady?'

'Which one, Monsieur?'

'The tall one with the dazzling white bosom.'

'Do you mean the one in the black mask?'

'Yes, the one with the magnificent figure. By her proud bearing I should take her for a Spaniard, but then her decolletée would be concealed by lace. She is wearing no jewellery except her pearls. That wonderful mouth! Do you know her, Martin?'

'As little as you do.'

'Ah, now the marquise has hidden her from view. These damned obtrusive fashionable hair-styles! But I saw enough. This woman is a beauty. She must be thirty-five, and in a short time will begin to wilt. She is unhappy. I can see that by the expression of her mouth. If only I could see her eyes! There she is again! She's still wearing her mask. Now she's turning round. I've never seen such a neck.'

'Monsieur, could you be falling in love?'

'Are you blind to such beauty?'

'Your jealousy is dangerous.'

'Admit that she's beautiful.'

'Yes, incredibly beautiful.'

'Martin, I must meet her.'

The count forced his way through the gossiping guests to the newcomers, to whom the marquise had just offered chairs. The countess remained standing and glanced at the count. 'Madame,' he said turning to the marquise, 'would you be good enough to introduce me?'

'You wish to be introduced?' The marquise could not help laughing and turned to the countess. 'Madame, I am to introduce you to this gentleman! Monsieur, you'd better handle this yourself.' She slipped aside with a peal of laughter. The count looked non-plussed and suddenly recognised his wife.

'Madame!' The next moment he tore off her mask. 'Madeleine, how dare you?'

'I wanted to surprise your son with his bride.'
'You have surprised me.'
'That was not my intention.'
'Where have you come from?'
'Direct from the Hôtel de Brayonne.'
'Where did you get that dress?'
'From an excellent dressmaker. I have incurred debts in your name and can produce the bills.'
'How long have you been in Paris?'
'Exactly four and a half days.'
'And I knew nothing about it!'
'Now you know almost everything. Martin has a son. Where is he hiding, Monsieur?'
'Over there by the window. Come to the Hôtel de Racon with me immediately!'
'Why immediately?' Martin approached, greeted the countess and then Marguerite, who had taken off her mask and was responding with provocative laughter to the many admiring glances of the men. The Marquise de Sévigné told a few of her close friends that the Comte de Racon had begged her to introduce him to his wife. There was renewed laughter. The Comtesse de Salvieux was anxious to introduce Blanche to the countess, but little Madame Boquelin pleaded a sudden indisposition, began to weep and left the building without taking leave of her hostess.

Next morning there was a stormy scene in the Hôtel de Rason. The count wanted to leave with his wife for Versailles at once, but the countess insisted that Martin and Marguerite were to be betrothed beforehand. The marriage festivities could take place later at Grandval. The count grew violent but his wife was adamant. Martin, who had already proposed once more that morning to Marguerite and been accepted, in view of his future rank, was waiting in the antechamber to receive his father's belated permission.

The count tore open the oak doors. 'Come in, you idiot!' Martin entered the study but the countess had gone, and all that remained was a trace of her perfume. In a towering rage, he caught Martin by the shoulders. 'Is it true that you've proposed for the second time to that stupid goose?'

'Yes, and Mademoiselle accepted.'

The count raised his hand to slap Martin but the young man drew back. 'Monsieur, I beg you not to forget yourself. It would demean you to strike me.'

The count lowered his arm, controlled his temper and asked in a calm voice. 'Are you determined to thwart my wishes?'

'In this instance I must do so, Monsieur.'

'Very well, my little prince. Wait for me here!'

'Where are you going?'

'I'm going to queer your pitch.'

The count tried to make for the door but Martin barred his way. 'Monsieur, I beg of you, think of my honour.'

'I am thinking of it. The family name of d'Epponcourt has been disgraced by the execution of the baroness.'

'The girl was completely innocent.'

'That does not alter the point.'

'Monsieur, you want grandchildren, and I shall have children.'

'I can dispense with your first offspring and shall look forward to your second.'

'Monsieur, I will not allow my son to be brought up by strangers.'

'You were with strangers as a child and you survived.'

'Monsieur, you know nothing about the beatings from morning till night! What do you know about the cruel mockery of other children? "Byblow", they shouted at me, "scullion", "street-sweeper", "Prince Bastard". I had no mother and father. No one was kind to me except an old woman who mistook me for her own son, Jean. I prayed to my patroness and to the Holy Virgin that for once in my life I should be allowed to see my benefactress who sent me the money, none of which was ever given to me. I was hungry and shivered with cold. I ran about barefoot, even in winter. It was hell, Monsieur!'

'All right, you can keep the brat.'

'Monsieur, I do not wish to repeat my own life with my son!'

'Were things so bad for you in Grandval?'

'Good or bad, my child has to be legitimate.'

'Until today,' the count said slowly, 'I thought it was your wish to replace the vicomte for me.' Martin looked down at the floor. 'Martin,' he continued in a very gentle tone, 'is your love for me so trifling that you cannot bear your own guilt?'

Martin put his arm on the count's shoulder. 'I beg you to help me.'

'You saved the girl from being poisoned and asked me for money for her, which I willingly gave you. You have done enough, Martin. A husband will be found for the girl and your son will be brought up at Grandval. I release you from a responsibility from which, in these circumstances, any court of law would release you. Believe me when I tell you that.'

'My conscience says otherwise.'

'You can't live according to its dictates.'

'Monsieur, you know that you like me to have a kind of halo round my head.'

The count laughed and ruffled his hair. 'Yes, that is what I want, my boy. I will see to it that you are not to blame if the silly goose rescinds her acceptance.'

'Monsieur, what have you in mind?'

'I must go and see my wife.'

Martin released him. 'Please let me come with you.'

'I would rather you waited here.'

'Please, Monsieur!'

'Come then, you obstinate creature.' They left the salon together.

Mlle de Lange retired through a side door as the two gentlemen entered. The countess was drying her eyes. Marguerite sat on a stool, peeling herself an orange. 'Madame,' said the count with a bow, 'I regret that I gave vent to my anger just now. I have spoken to Martin and have changed my mind. You made the condition that you would only recommend Martin's legitimation to the king if Martin and Mlle d'Epponcourt were betrothed beforehand. I had intended to find another husband for the girl, and should have been prepared to look after her until then like a daughter, and to deprive her of no pleasure. As my wife's protégée, I should have introduced her to the salons, thus setting a noble example of Christian charity. The ladies would have been eager to show the girl that an executed stepmother would leave no stain on an innocent stepchild. All the gentlemen would have extolled the girl's beauty. She would have had a possibility of choosing the best of several suitors and would not have been forced to take for her husband a fellow who had mortally wronged her; but I see now that I cannot persuade Martin to behave dishonourably to a lady. I have given him permission to fetch a priest so that the wedding can take place this very morning.'

'Monsieur,' cried Martin, 'thank you, thank you from the bottom of my heart!'

'Stand up.'

Martin obeyed and the countess tried to interrupt, but the count continued in an even sterner voice: 'I have made a sacrifice which both you, Madame and Martin, are apt to overestimate. I will not have my house made intolerable by the presence of a daughter-in-law whose mother ended her life on the scaffold. I wish to conceal my son's marriage from the world and insist that my daughter-in-law remain for the rest of my life at Château Fleury, which I forbid her to leave.'

Marguerite leaped to her feet. 'You want to lock me up in a country castle?'

'Yes, Mademoiselle. You have understood me perfectly. Pack your things as soon as you are married to my son.'

'I won't leave Paris.'

'Mademoiselle, do not forget that within a short space of time you will have to treat me as your father-in-law. I order you to prepare for the journey. Martin, what are you waiting for? Why don't you fetch a priest?'

'Monsieur, it would be cruel to banish my wife to Château Fleury.'

'She will be free after my death. I am already forty-eight.'

'Monsieur . . .'

'Martin, I have come to the end of my patience. None of my late sons would have dared to propose such a daughter-in-law to me. After your legitimation I shall permit you to visit your wife in Fleury, and for this purpose will grant you six weeks leave, so that you will have an opportunity of adding a second offspring to your first.'

'No,' screamed Marguerite, 'I don't want another child.'

'Mademoiselle, I insist that you provide me with five lusty grandsons. My son knows what he owes me and will behave accordingly.'

'I want to enjoy myself and to postpone the marriage.'

'Mademoiselle, either you marry my son now or you will take back your word.'

'Mademoiselle,' cried Martin, 'don't let him frighten you into changing your mind. I will fetch the priest for the ceremony and then put you in the coach myself. Be of good heart and travel to Fleury. I promise you I will not rest until the count grants you your freedom. I shall soon be able to bring you back to Paris.'

'No, no, I won't go to Fleury! Your father may have me murdered there. Madame, protect me!'

'Monsieur,' said the countess, 'I beg you to let me take Marguerite with me to Grandval after Martin's legitimation.'

'No, my daughter-in-law is to live at Fleury so that the neighbours will never catch sight of her.'

'Then I'll accompany her to Fleury.'

'Madame, I forbid you to change your residence.'

'I shall refuse to obey you.'

'Grouchet will see that my orders are carried out.'

'Are you going to place your master of the hunt above me?'

'Yes, and he will also act as custodian to my son's wife.'

'M. Saint-Jean, speak to your friend.'

'I will do so later, Madame.'

'You are a coward, M. Saint-Jean,' cried Marguerite scornfully.

Martin hurried over to her side. 'Mademoiselle, please leave the room with me quickly before anything unfortunate happens. Quick, quick, you are in danger!'

'I will not leave my benefactress.'

'Marguerite, I am your protector.'

'I am not yet "Marguerite" to you. Help!'

The count laid Martin low with a blow from his fist, strode over to Marguerite and asked: 'Do you believe me now that I will impose my own will on him, or do you want further proof? Must I thrash you to teach you how to obey?'

'No.'

'Will you accept your banishment without further argument?'

'No.'

'Will you marry Martin?'

'No.'

'Why not?'

'Because I don't want a father-in-law of whom I have to be afraid. I want to enjoy my life and be gay, and not be locked up to bear one child after the other!'

'Will you take back your word?'

'Yes, if you promise to let me stay with your wife and treat me as a daughter.'

'Very well, I will keep you as a daughter and leave you with my wife.'

'Then I release your bastard.'

'Marguerite,' cried the countess, 'you don't know what you're saying.'

'Yes, Madame, I know perfectly well,' said Marguerite, turning to her. 'I do not need this Martin, for I shall certainly find a husband of noble birth who will treat me with respect.'

'But think of the child.'

'You are welcome to it, Madame.'

Martin stood up and looked in bewilderment from one to the other. 'Is your head singing?' asked the count.

'What has been decided?'

Marguerite laughed and replied gaily: 'You are free of me, M. Saint-Jean.'

'Is that true, Madame?'

'Yes, M. Saint-Jean,' the countess replied.

'Is there to be no wedding?'

'No,' said the count, 'so I'll invite you and the young lady to the theatre this evening.'

'Monsieur, then we are reconciled,' said Marguerite, clapping her hands.

'Madame,' said the count, going over to the countess, 'take an example from your protégeé and do not weep.'

'I only wanted to do the best for Marguerite and Martin,' replied the countess, sobbing into her handkerchief.

'Make them both happy in a different way. Let Marguerite enjoy herself as your gay companion, and speak to the king on Martin's behalf.'

'I will speak to him.'

'Thank you, Madame,' said the count, quickly leaving the room.

Martin staggered across to Marguerite. 'Mademoiselle, can I have my child?'

'Do whatever you like with the brat, but keep its mother's name a secret and don't compromise my future.'

'I will keep my counsel.'

Marguerite placed a slice of orange in her mouth. 'You can go, Monsieur.' Martin bowed to the ladies and also left the room. 'Will you take me with you to Versailles?' Marguerite asked the countess who was still in tears.

'No, my poor child.'

'Why not?'

'That would be quite impossible.'

'When will you take me into society again?'

'I don't know yet.'

'Madame, you mustn't weep. I'm glad that things have turned out this way for I never trusted the count, and Saint-Jean looked as though he was determined to present his beloved father with a new grandson every year. I am in no hurry to marry, and I absolutely adore the theatre. Are you coming with us?'

'No.'

'A pity, Madame. Are you taking me for a drive?'

'In an hour's time.'

'Not until then? What am I to do in the meantime?'

'I'll lend you a novel written by the Marquise de La Fayette. You can read it in your room.'

'Oh, that boring Princesse de Clèves with her hidebound virtue! My stepmother had romances which were far more exciting.'

'Marguerite, I beg you to leave me alone for a few minutes.'

The count had retired to his study, where Pierre was showing him two slightly worn suits. 'M. le Comte, they're not worth repairing any more. The trimmings have long since been out of fashion.'

'Have you found a new sweetheart for whom you wish to look like a coxcomb?' asked the count, sitting down in his chair.

'M. le Comte, rags are only fit for an old-clothes dealer.'

'And I suppose his name is Pierre?'

'You're mistaken, M. le Comte. His name is Samuel Goldfuss.'

'Cut the buttons off and keep the rest of the booty.'

'Thank you, your Grace. What am I to do with the black ribbons on your other clothes?'

'They have to remain on till next May.'

Pierre looked bewildered. 'Are mourning ribbons now worn at a marriage?'

'There'll be no marriage, you old Paul Pry.'

'Pity. M. le Comte, can I show you a couple of pairs of riding boots which you haven't worn for more than a year?' There was a knock at the door and Martin entered. 'Well, it's nice of you to come,' laughed the count. 'I thought you were offended and on your way back to the regiment.'

'Comte de Racon, I have a question to ask you.'

'Lieutenant Saint-Jean, I should like to point out that I am in no mood to talk about closed incidents. If you start annoying me I shall order you to return to Colonel du Lac.'

'My question will not annoy you.'

'What is it then?'

'Tell Pierre to leave the room.'

'All right. Off with you Pierre!' The valet left with the clothes.

Martin began speaking without taking a chair: 'Yesterday Louis de Salvieux offered me the hand of his sister, Claire-Marie, who will shortly be a widow. I accepted in the event of my becoming free. Would you allow me to marry Blanche?'

'You can have her, as a mistress, any time you like, but you will never have her as a wife.' Martin turned even paler. 'Blanche is sterile, my boy,' explained the count.

'But perhaps it's only with you that she cannot bear a child?'

'Nearly every woman has a child by me. I know her better than you do. Moreover, she was dumb. That can be passed on to the children. Leave it to me to find you a wife.'

'I shall marry Blanche, or no one.'

'That is a pity, Martin. I should like to have entrusted the future of my race to you to save myself the trouble.'

'What do you mean?'

'We are getting ourselves into deep water. If you don't marry, I shall. My wife has been ill for nine years and has lately grown visibly weaker.'

'You promised to spare your wife.'

'I do not keep all my promises.'

'But you know that every day people are being executed, and that any poisoning now comes to light.'

'Not all of them, Martin, provided you guard against traitors.'

'Monsieur, even the Duc de Luxembourg was thrown into the Bastille and banished to a fortress.'

'You can be quite sure that the duke will return to favour. He is the last great commander with the Turenne touch.'

'Monsieur, the many tombs in Grandval are filled with old bones. What do they care for living heirs? What do dead souls care? Your father's spirit lives as little in you as yours does in me. You insist upon having grandchildren. Aren't you chasing a shadow?'

'Spare me a second sandpit sermon. In order to save you, I once threw my entire reason to the wind and nearly lost my estates, my position and standing. I came out with a limp, and that was a warning.'

'Do you know whom you resemble?'

'No, whom?'

'Jesus of Nazareth, who said: "Leave all and follow me".'

'I refuse to let my name die out because I refuse to abandon my idea of life. You were more dangerous to me, boy, than all my enemies while you were still my idol. Now you will be my son and your divinity will have gone. You will have lost your freedom as soon as you become the Vicomte de Clarmont, and from now on, like Raoul and Guy, you have to fall in with your father's wishes.'

'I will remain the bastard Saint-Jean!'

'Then you'll be a murderer.'

'You are a monster.'

'Don't excite yourself. One marries for intelligent reasons and not for love and decency. Acts of violence are soon forgotten and infatuations soon pass. Wives are never instruments of pleasure. They are constantly pregnant or indisposed when you want them, or they become offended and refuse you their charms.'

'I beg you to give me Blanche and to spare your wife.'

'I won't grant you both. Which do you choose?'

'I renounce Blanche.'

'That is as I expected. Lift up your chin! You won't die of a broken heart. The more you snivel the sooner you'll enjoy yourself again. Go and howl your eyes out somewhere, then come to the theatre this evening.' Martin turned on his heel and left the room.

In the meantime the countess had ordered her coach, and drove with Marguerite and Mlle de Lange to the convent in the Faubourg Saint-Jacques to visit the Duchesse de La Vallière who, as a Carmelite under the name of Sister Louise of the Compassion, was making reparation for the sins of her youth. When the countess alighted by the convent gate, Marguerite asked to be allowed to wait in the coach in spite of the winter cold. The countess left her in the care of Mlle de Lange and went into the building alone. A sister led her to the bare visitors' room, where she sat on a stool in front of the grille and gave rein to her thoughts.

After about half an hour she heard a slight rustle. A pale, black-veiled nun appeared behind the grille and asked in a gentle voice: 'Now, where did I meet the Comtesse de Racon?'

The countess rose to her feet. 'Madame, it is many years since you were my guest with various persons of exalted rank in the country, and you may perhaps recall the conversation we had that evening. Before that you often spoke to me at Court.'

'You are Madeleine de Racon.'

'Yes, Madame.'

'What brings you here?'

'My longing for peace.'

'Peace is to be found in God, Madame, not in the world.'

'You have abandoned the world. Have you really found true peace here?'

'Yes, my soul is at peace. My sinful heart burns with a constant and consuming flame for God. My repentance has given me absolution.'

'Sister Louise, I am surrounded by sin and am myself a disconsolate sinner. Where shall I find the strength to live a godly life in the world?'

'In the world it is impossible to remain free from guilt. Sin is rife there. I fled from the world and have found the love of God. Come and join me.'

'I dare not escape.'

'Who is to forbid you?'

'My conscience.'

'Oh, I know the blandishments to which our conscience sometimes resorts. They stem from Satan, Madame. He tried to foil me with maternal duties, with pleas from childish lips, but God gave me strength to free myself and I left my chains behind.'

'Has one the right to free oneself while others remain in bondage?'

'God must mean more to us than anyone else.'

'And if you sacrifice yourself on behalf of others?'

'One must sacrifice to no one but to God.'

'But does not God also reside in other human beings?' asked the countess.

'God is remote from sinners,' replied the nun.

'But Christ went down among them.'

'Madame, who dares compare himself with the son of God?'

'I am a Huguenot, Sister Louise.'

'And you come to question a nun?'

'Forgive me!'

'Madame, I will pray that you may find the right path that will lead you back to God.'

'I thank you.'

The nun bowed calmly and retired.

The countess left the convent and found three cavaliers on horseback by her coach, in animated conversation with Marguerite. A lackey jumped down from the box. 'Make way for Madame la Comtesse!'

The men doffed their hats and the countess climbed into her coach and drove away. 'Mlle de Lange,' she said angrily, 'why did you not send those gentlemen away?'

'Madame, I was not allowed to say a word.'

'Marguerite, have you so little pride that you converse with strange gentlemen from your coach?'

'All three of them are of noble birth and will visit me to-morrow.'

'But, Marguerite, you cannot invite people without my consent. What will the gentlemen think of you?'

'That I am beautiful.'

'And that you are frivolous.'

Marguerite gave a shrill laugh. 'I'll show them. I'll lead them by the nose and then laugh behind their backs!'

After his last conversation with the count, Martin left the house and wandered swiftly and aimlessly through the streets on foot. He was crossing a narrow alley between houses built on a bridge and noticed a flapping silver fish which an excited boy with a line dangled about his companions' heads. While Martin watched the game a pickpocket stole his purse. Then he went slowly on his way until he came to an open square.

Ahead of him lay Notre Dame, its two squat towers rising to heaven like an unassailable citadel of God. For the first time, Martin noticed the stone miracle of its ornate façade. His sharp eyes could make out the monsters on the central piers, and the grimacing faces of the high gargoyles under the cloudy sky, looking across the town into the country. Then a flight of doves masked his view and settled on the heads and hands of the saints above the doors. Martin entered the church, going out of the bright sunshine into the darkness.

A few candles cast their gleams on the mighty pillars which disappeared in the impenetrable darkness above. And yet, in this gloom, the stained-glass windows reflected the daylight from outside. Martin advanced slowly, hat in hand, into the soft depths of twilight, and knelt down by a side-altar with his head against a stone pillar. From an altar near the choir came the voice of a priest praying; it echoed and died away in the vastness. A beggar, whose eyes were accustomed to the darkness, crept noiselessly between the figures to old, kneeling women and approached Martin, who had laid his hat down on the flagstones. A grab, and the hat disappeared as though spirited away by the hands of a ghost. Two o'clock struck from the tower.

Martin felt a slight touch, turned his head and caught sight of Blanche in the reflection of a candle held by her old maid. 'M. Saint-Jean!'

'Oh, Madame.'

He stood up while the old woman placed the candle before a small statue of the madonna on one of the huge stone pillars. 'M. Boquelin is in great pain,' Blanche explained, 'and I have a guilty conscience. I have come to offer a candle to the Virgin Mary.'

'Madame, all is lost.'

'What is lost?'

'I could marry you but he will not give his consent.'

Blanche caught Martin by the hand. 'Come into the shadow over there and kneel at my side. Catherine, give me my cushion.' The old woman handed Blanche a silk cushion and she knelt down, well away from the light of the candle. 'M. Saint-Jean, did he think that you would make demands of me?'

'No, he wants strong, healthy grandsons. You are too frail and too weak. I did not tell him that I would have married you only in the eyes of the world, for he would have laughed at me.' Since Blanche made no reply, Martin continued: 'I am glad you're here, Madame. I've been here a long time trying to pray, but my thoughts refused to obey me, however much I tried to say my devotions. I can see him now standing in front of me, talking to me, and my heart almost stops beating in horror.'

'M. Boquelin's gaze is horrible. What do you find horrible?'

'Madame, I have never yet allowed his evil power to terrify me, for I always considered it something irrelevant, like his ugliness, as long as I was deceived by what I mistook to be his underlying kindness. Now I am forced to see him as he really is. Blanche, he is ugly to the core!'

'No, Martin, no!'

'Madame, there is no act of violence of which he is incapable, and perhaps no crime that he has not committed a score of times. If you knew him as well as I do, you would never visit him again.'

'M. Saint-Jean, remember that he sacrificed a son to you.'

'I have to replace that son for him now. I shall become the third Vicomte de Clarmont to be harried to death by his father.'

'No, M. Saint-Jean, he is not as evil as you maintain.'

'He is a thousand times worse,' shouted Martin. 'If I were a stonemason I would sculpt a gargoyle with his grinning face, and place it next to the others on this cathedral, so that it could spit water and bird droppings, a memorial to the monster whom destiny decreed should cross my path. I used to love this man! My heart burned for him and my love was as insatiable as a giant flame, it was more than a human frame could endure, a constantly rising flood. I was completely happy in Italy. Hardly a day passed when we did not see each other. Who can define friendship, Blanche? I know no one who had such a friend as I had. He understood me better than I will ever do. I cannot tell you what he meant to me and what I thought I meant to him. Love compels us to look for perfection in the object of our love and leaves us with the black emptiness of an extinct volcano. But I can never love that man again.'

'Martin, you must not abandon him or me.' There was a tremor in Blanche's frail voice.

'I will never abandon someone who needs me. I will produce healthy issue for him and protect you until everyone cries "enough" and gives me back my freedom. I really thought that he loved me.'

'He does love you, Martin. I know it. And I know how much. He is only fond of me, but he really loves you.'

'If only that were true, Blanche.'

'It is true, M. Saint-Jean. Last winter he was like a sick man because you were no longer there. He forbade me to mention you and yet he spent whole nights discussing you. He told me stories about you while I played my lute to him. He once said to me, as he began to grow tired: "Your presence soothes me, but his is better. You calm me, but he brings me peace. My treachery is beginning to consume me." '

'Did he use precisely those words?'

'Yes, those very words. And on another occasion he told me that I loved him too much. One should never give one's heart to anyone or else, after the parting, there remained an open wound which never healed; and he groaned as though in pain.'

'Yes,' said Martin bitterly, 'he cannot stand pain, but he

does not care about the pain he inflicts on others.'

'M. Saint-Jean, don't you think that he is sad now because he knows that you are unhappy?'

Martin could not help laughing. 'He was cheerful enough when I left.'

The muffled sound of chanting came from the depths of the nave.

'M. Saint-Jean, how can I console you?'

'I cannot be consoled, Blanche. On your account I wept on the shoulder of a friend who knew how to comfort me, but there is no one with whom I can weep now for that friend, and I have no tears left.'

'M. Saint-Jean,' whispered Blanche, 'it is very dark here. If you would like to lay your head on my knee, no one would see.'

'Sweet Blanche Claire-Marie!'

'I love you as a brother,' whispered the girl.

'Madame, the world would not believe that. I will not endanger your reputation but try to pray from my own prie-Dieu. You should pray for that dying old man.'

'Yes, M. Saint-Jean.' The crystal beads of her rosary tinkled softly. The darkness began to hum with their prayers and the bright glow from the windows increased. Then, from a side-chapel, rose the responses of the Litany, filling the great cathedral, until the murmur grew to a wild rhythmic cry of 'Ora pro nobis', rising to the very rafters. Blanche's clear voice rose above Martin's head like a bell in a storm, and did not weary of its plea.

When the Litany came to an end, Martin said to her: 'The saints are listening but they give no sign.'

'Did you pray, too?'

'No, I could not bring myself to ask for anything. I kept repeating the name of God in my innermost heart. That is all I could do. This cathedral is miraculous. God must dwell here more than elsewhere. If the darkness were suddenly to break, we should see the radiance of His face and all our grief would be at an end.'

At this moment the wandering beam of a candle lit up a human face, which still had rotting tooth stumps but neither nose nor lips. From the gaping hole they heard a croak: 'Alms in the name of the Holy Virgin!' Blanche searched for a coin and put it into the diseased and wasted hand, which retreated like a mouse into its clotted rags, only to emerge again and pluck Martin by the sleeve. 'Alms . . .'

'Away from me, you scum!' The flame of the candle went out and Martin's arm hit the air.

'M. Saint-Jean, remember that her place is here in church. Have pity on her!'

'Yes,' said Martin, 'her place is in the church. You spoke the truth, Blanche!'

'What do you mean, M. Saint-Jean?'

'Madame, I cannot find my purse. Please lend me yours. I will return it. Please give it to me quickly!' Blanche handed him her silk purse. Martin leaped to his feet and hurried after the ghostly beggar-woman whom he saw lighting her candle at an altar. 'Here, catch! Buy yourself spirits and a ball dress, and don't get your purse stolen!' Martin returned to Blanche and knelt once more at her side. 'How much was there in your purse, Madame?'

'About twenty gold louis.'

'I will return them to you the next time we meet. May I accompany you, or do you wish to stay here longer?'

'Tell me why you gave the beggar-woman such princely alms?'

'Because she revealed to me the truth which was constantly before my eyes but I had not noticed until today. Blanche, this cathedral is a picture of the world and of men. Inside, the most resplendent colours gleam and the most hideous cripples slink; outside, the hierarchy of angels glides above the portal and dragons spit from its towers. He is made of the same stuff. I only loved what was fine in him. But he is like the world.'

'No. M. Saint-Jean, he is not as evil as the world.'

'Blanche, the world is neither good nor evil. It is Heaven, Hell and everything.'

'I never heard that said before.'

'Nor have I, Madame, but today I have seen it, and now I know it.' After a silence, Martin added: 'Just now, I abused the Comte de Racon. Now I am ashamed of myself and beg you not to despise me.'

'M. Saint-Jean, there is no one I respect more than you.'

'Madame, you take me to be nobler than I really am. Please do not believe that I love you without self-interest. I would have married you without demanding the merest trifle of you, but I should never have abandoned the hope of your love and should have made it difficult for you to meet other men. But I swear to you, Madame, that in the future I will fight against my selfishness.'

'Will you not be able to love your friend again?'

'Yes, I shall really love him from today onwards.'

'You make me happy.'

'Madame, I have failed in many respects, but I shall make up for it. Sacrificing the second vicomte to me was too much for him. In return it is my duty to do more for him than nature normally affords. Now it is a matter of breaking down the barriers.'

'What barriers, Monsieur?'

'The barriers of one's character!'

'Can one do that?'

'He has done it countless times when, for my sake, he has refrained from doing evil. My God, and I abused him! Please never tell him what I said.'

'I will not tell him. Are you now consoled?'

'Yes, Madame. I am.'

'Then please console me, M. Saint-Jean. I have such a guilty conscience. M. Boquelin is suffering terribly.'

'For that he has to bear a large proportion of the blame,' replied Martin, 'because at his age, he married you against your will. I am to blame, your brother is to blame and so is the Comte de Racon. Finally, a fifth of the blame is yours.'

'M. Saint-Jean, do you think that a partial guilt weighs less heavily than the whole?'

'Yes, of course. You are the only one of the five who feels any remorse.'

'What shall I do?'

'Pray for him.'

'I prayed a whole Litany for him and for you. Isn't that enough for today?'

'You must know that yourself, Madame.'

'I will say one more rosary for him. Will you wait with me?'

'Gladly, Madame.'

They knelt side by side, and since Blanche was tired and her knees hurt from the flagstones, she leaned gently against Martin. A man suddenly cleared his throat and a deep voice boomed: 'Is that the way to pray?' They both gave a start. Martin recognised a priest's habit. 'We are brother and sister, your Reverence.'

'Leave the church immediately. Aren't you ashamed of yourselves? Out with you, or I shall send the verger with his staff.'

As Martin stood up he noticed that he had lost his hat. 'Forgive me, your Reverence, but I must have mislaid my hat somewhere.'

'Then leave it for St Anthony's pig to eat. People don't lose their hats in church.' Blanche fled from the just wrath of the priest and led Martin out of the cathedral.

Outside in the daylight her fear vanished. 'M. Saint-Jean, today he caught two innocent people.'

'Where is your coach, Madame?'

'Over there, M. Saint-Jean.' Martin accompanied the lady to her carriage and kissed her hand.

'Farewell, Madame, and take my eternal gratitude with you. I will go and look for your maid and send her to you.' Blanche climbed into the coach and sat there while Martin returned to the cathedral. He discovered Catherine among some praying women and told her that her mistress was already in the carriage. As he sprinkled himself with holy water from the stoup, on leaving the church, a priest passed. 'Reverence,' said Martin, 'would you be good enough to explain to me why such hideous water-spouts were used on such a fine building?'

'No,' replied the priest in his deep voice, 'I will not be good enough, but I will ask you something: if the devil's brood is allowed to roam about the church, why shouldn't they be outside too?'

Martin laughed and swiftly took his leave.

That evening, the count took Marguerite and Martin to a performance of Molières *Le Misanthrope*. During the intervals he left them and visited the other boxes. On his return he found the remaining seats occupied by boisterous, gossiping young men and Martin standing behind an empty chair. The count sat down. Marguerite laughed shrilly at the sallies of Célimène and the anger of Alceste. A strange cavalier offered her sweetmeats and flirted with her. When the count dropped his glove, Martin picked it up. Then he leaned over the rail, pointed to the stage and, turning to his son, asked what Lieutenant Saint-Jean thought of the misanthropist. Martin replied amiably that a misanthropist did not know true love and was therefore to be pitied. His father tried to read the expression in his face, met his hazel eyes and turned away to the stage. Shortly after this he left to pay a visit to a lady in the Grande Mademoiselle's box.

In order to be on time for mass in the Court chapel, the count left with his wife for Versailles next morning, long before daybreak. Martin had been told by the countess to keep an eye on Marguerite. His protection turned out to be necessary, for, by midday, five gentlemen had appeared to pay their respects to the lady. Martin had their names announced and dismissed two whose reputations were notorious throughout the capital. Marguerite chattered gaily with the three other youths, ignoring the presence of the silent but attentive Mlle de Lange, to whom Martin spoke from time to time for the sake of politeness. The visitors stayed on, but since, to Marguerite's annoyance, Martin did not invite them to the midday meal, they were compelled to take their leave.

The count was fortunate at Versailles. His benefactor, the Maréchal d'Humières, drew the king's attention to the Comtesse de Racon as he walked along the corridors. Louis beckoned to the pair. He asked the countess whether it was of her own free will that she had agreed to recognise one of her husband's illegitimate sons as her own. What had led her to do this? The childlessness of her husband, and her malady, which had made her barren for some years. The king looked at the beautiful woman in surprise and said to the count that he would expect him next day, together with his wife and son, after his ministerial conference.

When the couple returned that night from Versailles, they found Marguerite helped by Emilie, busy trying on the countess's clothes in the salon. The countess was annoyed but too tired to scold her. Martin had retired to bed. The count had him woken and gave full rein to his exuberance, embracing and shaking the patient Martin. He suddenly asked whether he had hurt him. Martin shook his head and said that the Comte de Racon's joy was always a hailstorm which his shoulders were broad enough to bear. He was well tousled by the time he was allowed to return to bed, and Pierre began to grumble because M. le Comte had not removed his fragile court wig before starting his horseplay.

VERSAILLES

At four o'clock in the morning Martin was woken by Dominique. The old valet shaved him and helped him into his green and silver Court dress. He was barely dressed before Pierre knocked and announced that his master was ready and growing impatient. Martin hurried to the study, where the count had just finished breakfasting by candlelight.

'Ah, there you are at last! It's a fine day. We can ride and shall arrive with clean boots. Show me how you bow to the king.'

'Like this, Monsieur.'

'Is that so? If you did it like that they'd string you up.'

'Show me.'

The count rose, assumed a look of reverence, bent almost double and, without raising his eyes, slowly drew himself up to his full height. A broad grin, which the count noticed, appeared on Martin's face.

'What do you find so funny?'

'Monsieur, you are a wonderful sight. I have never seen you so servile.'

'The king only tolerates slaves. Come on, copy me!'

'Monsieur, I should only laugh.'

'I advise you to restrain your mirth. Come on.' Martin bowed as deeply as the count had done. 'Wipe that pride off your face. Imagine you have Jupiter in front of you.'

'Jupiter was a pagan god and means nothing to me.'

'Keep those answers for another time. Put on an act, you oaf.'

'Very well, I'll put on an act.'

'That was better. Remember that face.'

'I'll remember it.'

'Have you had breakfast?'

'No, not yet.'

'Then eat with my wife in the coach.'

'Pierre, is Madame la Comtesse ready?'

'Yes, Denis has just come to say that she is. The coach is at the gate and the grooms are already mounted.'

'Come on, Martin. Downstairs with you!' Pierre helped his master into his cloak and handed him his hat, while Martin ran out and collided with Dominique who was bringing his. Outside it was still dark and misty. The heavy coach rattled and lumbered over the cobblestones through the ill-lit streets to the city gate. The countess shivered in spite of her furs. Her long period of standing on the previous day, and her unaccustomed short rest at night, had tired her. Martin was hungry but refrained from eating in the dark for fear of staining his coat.

At last, day began to break. The trees flitted past like ghosts. Martin noticed that the countess was watching him and shyly took some bread and meat from the basket on the back seat next to Emilie. 'Madame, may I have some food?'

'Yes, please do.'

Martin began to eat, and from time to time threw a chicken-bone through the window. 'Madame,' he said at last, 'thank you for letting me ride with you. I should like to get out now and ride with the count.'

The countess smiled. 'You will shortly have the right to call him father.'

'I hope, Madame, that I shall still be able to address him as before.'

'As before? Why, M. Saint-Jean?'

'Because he is a stern father and was a kind friend to me.'

'But you will be pleased to be able to appear before the world as a nobleman.'

'The world has shown quite enough respect for the bastard.'

'Did you not suffer under your name?'

'I was an imbecile to have suffered as long as I did. One can be noble without having a noble name, and an oaf although bearing the title of duke and possessing an age-old family tree.'

'Aren't you happy today?'

'Happy, Madame?' cried Martin in amazement. 'Happy with a motherless child . . . Happy without the right to marry the woman I love? Happy with a future which will make demands perhaps beyond my strength? Madame, I must be content with the fact that I am not unhappy.'

'Can I help you, M. Saint-Jean?'

'No, Madame, you are speaking on my behalf today before the king and I shall owe you my gratitude for the rest of my life. May I leave you now?'

'Tell the coachman to pull up.' Martin, however, opened the door and jumped out into the street where François immediately hurried up with his mount. He mounted and galloped up to the count, who in his impatience had pressed on ahead.

As they approached Versailles, a few rays of sunshine broke through the grey, wintry sky, tinging the clouds. Squat on its tortoise-like hill the rose-pink palace stood in majestic beauty. The blue and gold railings gleamed, vying with the gold braid on the red uniforms of the guards who were drawn up in front of each wing. Coaches and horsemen seemed insignificant in the vast courtyard, and the host of bright coloured soldiers and blue and silver-liveried lackeys looked like ants to the riders as they approached.

Martin, who had hardly addressed a word to the count on the entire journey, suddenly asked whether the throne room lay behind the window of the central wing. The count replied with a grin that this was the bedchamber of the king of France, from which it could be deduced that even in the royal palaces the bedroom was one of the utmost importance. Martin wanted to ask further questions, but the count greeted a few riders who passed them and then looked round and scowled because he could see his wife's coach in the far distance behind a host of others. Then he recognised the Duc d'Orléans' coach, galloped up, doffed his hat, bowed and accompanied Monsieur to the inner railing, before returning to the outer railing where Martin was watching the guard being changed to a roll of drums. At last, the countess's coach arrived and pulled up at a side-entrance. The countess alighted, left her furs inside the coach and entered the palace with Martin and her husband.

It was still some time before Mass. The count walked on ahead, up the gleaming marble staircase to the Hall of Mirrors, where a host of ladies and gentlemen were waiting outside the king's apartments for their sovereign to appear. Martin followed modestly, trying to avoid attention, for the count suddenly began to treat him as though he didn't exist. Two elderly ladies enquired after the countess's health. With a sympathetic expression on his face the count listened to the self-reproaches and complaints of a gentleman-in-waiting, who could not forgive himself for arriving at the levée too late. Two younger gentlemen, telling risqué stories with their handkerchiefs to their mouths, were suddenly disturbed by the Comte de Racon who thrust his devil's head between them and began preaching a sermon. Martin was astounded to recognise several phrases he had used to the count in the sandpits at Grandval. Many of those present had coughs and colds which made it difficult to hear what was said. Martin, noticing that several people were looking him up and down with interest, began to observe them obliquely in the mirrors which reached to the ceiling. He admired the flowers blooming in silver holders, as though it were midsummer, the huge silver candelabra, the crystal chandeliers, the carpet, statues and inlaid tables on which stood gilt baskets of fruit.

Then the crowd parted, and through a side-door entered a few superbly dressed ladies, one of whom stood out by her youth and extraordinary beauty. Golden locks framed a fresh, young face and a pair of pale green eyes looked arrogantly at the assembly. The courtiers pressed forward to greet her, bowing almost to the floor. A fat old woman near Martin disturbed the adoring admiration of a bow-legged old courtier by saying: 'The Duchesse de Fontange grows more beautiful every day. Is it true what people have been saying about her since last Friday?'

'People are saying nothing,' replied the old man in a hushed voice, 'but we all share her joyful expectancy.'

'And what has the marquise to say?' asked the count.

'Which one?' asked the old man with a sudden twinkle in his eye.

'I mean the present one, of course.'

The old man raised his eyes to the painted ceiling and murmured, as if over-awed: 'The marquise is pleased for all upon whom God bestows His grace.'

Martin turned to a page who was carrying a cowering lapdog. 'Who is the present marquise?'

'The Marquise de Maintenon of course. Where have you come from that you didn't know that?'

A pair of folding doors opened wide and the king stepped from the antechamber of his sleeping apartments, followed by Monsieur, the Dauphin and other high dignitaries and ministers, wearing the ribbons of their orders. The king doffed his white plumed hat from his billowing chestnut wig, greeted the ladies and strode forward to the chapel. The crowd surged forward because everyone wished to be noticed by his Majesty during Mass, and was therefore eager to obtain a prominent place. Martin lost sight of the count and joined the countess, who begged him to remain near her.

After Mass, the Court strolled behind the king through countless royal apartments to the tall, inlaid bronze doors of the study, into which the sovereign retired for a conference with his ministers.

The count, fretting with excitement, finally joined the Maréchal d'Humières, who began to describe some battle. A few women, with a host of beauty patches on their faces, tried to convince the countess that her bosom would look even whiter if she were to adorn it with little black patches, a ladybird or a true star. Martin stared at an elaborate silver clock which recorded not only the hours but the days, the nights and even the months. Every quarter of an hour a *carillon* sounded, a ball fell and Father Time moved his scythe.

At midday, the courtiers sat down at table in various rooms. The count took up his position, with his wife and son, outside the door of the study where the king was in council. A few gentlemen, who were also waiting for an audience, looked askance at him. Thereupon he asked one of the worst backbiters to explain a difficult point in the morning's sermon. Martin brought up a stool for the countess, but the count growled that when one was waiting for the king it was not seemly to sit down. Martin replaced the stool and asked a lackey for the whereabouts of the closet, but the man merely grinned and did not reply. Martin strolled off on his own to look for it and, to his amazement discovered that people were relieving nature in odd corners of remote corridors, and that, out of courtesy, the few closets had been left for the use of the women.

When he returned he found the count in a furious temper because of his absence. 'Boy, the king's council meeting can be over at any minute.'

'Monsieur, I won't stir from your side again. Shall I get your wife some refreshment from that table over there?'

'Are you out of your mind? Is she to have her mouth full when the doors open?'

'M. le Comte,' mocked one of the courtiers, 'you have brought a restless flea with you.'

'What do you mean by "a flea"?' retorted the count. 'He's dressed in green and is therefore a tree-frog.'

The doors opened. Backs were bowed but only the ministers appeared. The king's private secretary brought up the rear, looked round and announced: 'His Majesty will receive the Comte and Comtesse de Racon.' Martin saw them disappear behind the double doors.

'Young man,' asked one of the courtiers, 'are you really only a tree-frog?'

'Yes, Monsieur, if the Comte de Racon said so.'

'Is the count expecting some favour?'

'A tree-frog could not possibly know that.' Martin retired to an alcove and looked out on to the park and the bare trees. The pennants were hanging limp from the gondolas on the canal. The rain streamed from the grey sky, making little ripples on the water in the fountain basins.

The king sat alone in his study at a table covered with a violet-blue Persian cloth worked in golden thread. The count bowed in the prescribed Court manner, while the countess curtsied gracefully in her black velvet dress. The king's white, ringless hand waved them to their feet. Louis was wearing a brown velvet coat, beneath which gleamed the bejewelled ribbon of an order, and a costly embroidered blue waistcoat; diamonds glittered from the pommel of his sword and garters.

After a moment's silence, while his brown eyes leisurely admired the countess's beauty, he deigned to address the count:

'Comte de Racon, since your son, Martin Saint-Jean, is the

issue of an illegitimate liaison with a noble lady known to me, and you are childless, I grant you leave to bestow upon him your name and your coat-of-arms. For his maternal arms he may use a count's coronet *or* on a field *sable*. I hereby declare him to be your true and rightful heir. Martin Saint-Jean will become M. de Racon but, anticipating the whims of fate, I decree that M. de Racon shall hold the rank of a younger brother with regard to any future sons born to the Comte Gaston de Racon in wedlock. You will find the gist of my words, Comte de Racon, in this document dictated and signed by me to supply evidence of my favour.'

The king picked up a sealed letter from the table and handed it to the count, who fell to his knees and accepted it. 'Your Majesty makes me the happiest of all mortals by your infinite kindness. May God grant me strength to repay at least a part of my everlasting debt of gratitude and to contribute on the battlefield to the glory of my great and gracious king.'

'Call your son,' ordered the king. The count rose to his feet and retired backwards with bent shoulders and lowered head to the door, as though loth to leave the majestic sight of his sovereign. Then, after another deep obeisance, he raised himself to his full height.

'Madame,' said the king, turning to the countess, 'you have afforded us a fine example of married love. Your conduct has been admirable in the extreme, and yet I am convinced that your splendid action will be surpassed by one of even greater merit. Have you the courage to renounce a faith which, in the light of truth, has been proved to be a sad error?'

The countess turned pale. 'Sire,' she said, trembling, 'your Majesty's request is a command, but my heart is incapable of making such a vital decision in so short a time. I beg your Majesty to be considerate.'

'Madame, I saw your husband at Mass, but not you. You should listen to the sermons of our enlightened Bossuet.' The countess was so confused that she could find no answer. The king suddenly noticed the count and Martin: 'Come closer, young man. I have just presented you with a father and a mother.'

Martin walked swiftly towards the king and knelt before him. 'I thank your Majesty most humbly for the benevolence you have shown to the Comte de Racon.'

'M. de Racon, until now you have served as lieutenant in your father's regiment and accompanied him to war. From tomorrow you will serve for a year in my second musketeer company, in which your half-brothers once served. Here is your commission. You may rise.' Martin, still kneeling, took the document and rose to his feet, stammering words of thanks. 'Comte de Racon,' the king continued, 'the Maréchal d'Humières will present your son to the Court.'

Dazzled by the overpowering majesty of his sovereign, Martin did not hear the count's reply and, like a sleepwalker, suddenly found himself in the king's retinue. The courtiers were grouped in a golden-white compartment round a square table, at which the king, served by the highest in the land, ate in public. Martin watched the monarch drink three plates of soup, one after the other, eat a whole pheasant, half a partridge, a bowl of salad, two slices of ham, mutton in garlic sauce, a plate of pastries, fresh and candied fruits and, finally, three hard-boiled eggs. The ceremony surrounding this feat appeared to the young man so god-like that he did not realise how hungry he was. After finishing his meal, the king rose from the table and retired to his council chamber where his ministers awaited him.

While the king was working, the Court spent its time gossiping. The count and Martin appeased their hunger at a well-laden buffet. This called forth the amusement of Monsieur, who came up unexpectedly. 'Ha, ha! My royal brother's appetite seems to be infectious. Why did you not eat at my table?'

The count swallowed a morsel. 'I was received in audience. Your Highness is really too kind.'

'Yes, too kind and desperately bored. Come and see me one night in Paris. They tell me that your conversation is still spicy, although you've recently joined the ranks of the pious.'

'Your Highness must consider that one loses one's habits very slowly.'

'Thank God, Comte de Racon.'

The Maréchal d'Humières came up, bowed deeply to Monsieur and asked with a smile:

'Is your Highness already aware that the Comte de Racon, by the king's grace, has once more a son and heir in the person of this young man here?'

'No, I did not know, but I congratulate you sincerely. A legitimation, was it not?'

'Yes, your Highness,' the count replied with a bow.

'So,' Monsieur chuckled, 'you have cocked a small snook at death and your dear relatives. The young man is good-looking, but not nearly so handsome as the first Vicomte de Clarmont. Has he any particular interests?'

'No, he is as normal as a stable-boy.'

'What do you intend to do with him?'

'In my gratitude I feel it my duty to let him serve in the king's household.'

'Very right and proper. What is your name, young man?'

'Martin de Racon, at your Highness's pleasure.'

'Go on eating. I hope to see you soon, Count, and please do not bring any of your new piety with you to the Palais Royal.' They took their leave and the Duc tripped off on his high-heeled shoes, smelling at his pomander.

Martin seized a chicken in aspic and tore off a wing. 'What shall we do with him, Comte de Racon?' asked the maréchal. 'Shall we leave him to his chicken or shall we introduce him to a few of the nobility.'

'He can eat his fill later.'

Martin threw the half-eaten chicken wing back on the plate, licked his fingers clean, wiped his mouth on the back of his hand and hurried after the maréchal, who was making his way with the count towards a group of bejewelled ladies. The countess was among them.

The new M. de Racon was well received on all sides and aroused the particular interest of the elderly ladies with marriageable daughters. The maréchal invited the count to a party of ombre, but the count excused himself on the pretext of Monsieur's invitation and left the palace about four o'clock.

The paving stones of the broad courtyard were still wet although the rain had ceased. The horses were swiftly brought up. The count distributed silver coins to his grooms and announced to them that they were now in the presence of his son, M. de Racon. François let forth a shout of joy, dug Charles in the ribs and cried: 'Now I'm as aristocratic as you!' Martin mounted. His eyes caught those of the countess, who was watching the horsemen through the window of her coach. The young man rode up to her. 'Please forgive me, Madame, for what I said to you on the way here.'

'I only wanted your happiness, Martin.'

'I know that, Madame and you shall not regret your noble action. I will do my duty and, if possible, not disappoint anyone again.' He doffed his hat and galloped off to join the count, who was riding ahead, to be met with the impatient question:

'How do you feel now?'

'Not very different from before, Monsieur.'

'Admit that you are happy, my boy.'

'I am delighted that *you* are.'

'Don't start to spoil my day.'

'I don't want to spoil anything for you, my friend.'

'Yes, remain my friend.'

'Were you afraid that I could not remain so?'

'I make you Marquis de Brayonne.'

'The name Brayonne does not have a pleasant ring in my ears. I will bear the name which the king gave me.'

'You want to punish me.'

'To punish you?'

'Don't be a hypocrite, Martin.'

'Monsieur, shall I let the cat out of the bag?'

'Please do so.'

'You are doing everything you can for me and I have every intention of making the best of it.'

'What do you mean by that, Martin?'

'To be a pleasant husband to the woman you may choose for me, to be an admirable courtier without becoming an oaf, and to try and become a general in the army.'

'Give me your hand, Martin.'

'Here is my hand on it.'

'Thank you, my friend. Let us gallop on ahead.'

The two men galloped at the head of the column along the straight road, which stretched as far as the eye could see in the direction of the capital.

MADELEINE'S SACRIFICE

THEY reached Paris at nightfall. Martin did not accompany the count and countess to the Hôtel de Racon, but rode to his tailor to order a musketeer's uniform and cloak. The count joined his wife in the coach and helped her to alight when they drove into the entrance. He ordered the horses to be changed, because he was shortly leaving for the Palais Royal, and escorted his wife up the steps.

Pierre was waiting for him. The valet bowed and reported: 'There is a lady waiting for you, M. le Comte.'

'Where?'

'In your study.'

'Is she a very small lady?'

'Yes, M. le Comte.'

'Then tell her she must come some other time, and get out my violet-grey Court dress.'

'Monsieur, are you showing a lady the door?' asked the countess coldly.

'Madame, she keeps importuning me with a request that I am not in a position to grant. She wishes me to find her rather backward son a post in my regiment. Will you permit me to join you in your salon? I wish to avoid meeting her.'

'Please do so.'

Hardly had they sat down in the salon than the door burst open and Blanche entered in a black dress without a cloak. 'Monsieur, M. Boquelin is dead! All his sons, daughters and near relatives are in the house, quarrelling bitterly. Louis has engaged three lawyers to represent me.'

'Madame,' said the count rising to his feet, 'what transpires in your house is no concern of mine.'

'But I cannot stay there.'

'Then move to your sister-in-law's in the Hôtel de Salvieux.'

'Louise will sell me again.'

'Please pay more heed to your choice of words, or no one will take you for a lady of the nobility.'

'Monsieur, didn't Martin Saint-Jean come home with you?'

'He has gone to his tailor.'

'Please let me wait for him.'

The count frowned.

'Madame,' said the countess quickly, 'come and sit over here. How long have you known my husband, since you are on such good terms with him?'

The count left the room.

Blanche took a chair next to the countess and looked at her appealingly. 'I belonged to the Comte de Racon because he once bought me. Then the Comte de Salvieux recognised me as a long lost sister and married me off to the old banker, Boquelin. Now he wants to marry me to M. Saint-Jean, but the Comte de Racon is opposed to it. M. Saint-Jean is a very kind man. He is even prepared to marry me without compelling me to be unfaithful to his father. Now they will start looking for another rich husband for me. I hoped the count would protect me, but he does not wish to be bothered with me.'

The girl began weeping. 'Have you no parents, child?' asked the countess.

'No, I am an orphan.'

'Have you not relatives, apart from your brother, who would take you in?'

'No, Madame, my brother wants to profit from my future.'

'Do you love my husband?'

'Yes, Madame, I love him dearly.'

The countess took off her gloves. 'It is all very sad and very strange,' she said wearily.

'Oh, Madame, the Marquis de Chassigny owned me first and sold me to the Comte de Racon. Your husband was very kind to me and I should like to remain faithful to him. But, if I am forced to belong to a third man, my soul will be torn to pieces. Each of them takes a fraction of it, but fortunately nothing remained with the marquis, and the banker was too old to insist on his rights.'

'But how could my husband protect you?'

'I don't know, Madame. I hoped he would hide me for a few days until M. Saint-Jean had thought of something. He always helps me.'

'He will be here soon, child. Will you have supper with me tonight?'

'Madame, you are very kind to me.' The countess rang a bell. When Denis appeared at the door, the countess ordered him to lay three places, and asked: 'Why has Mlle d'Epponcourt not waited on me? Where is Mlle de Lange?'

'They have both gone to see a comedy. Mlle de Lange asked me me to inform you that she feared she was able to afford but little protection against the young lady's numerous admirers.'

'Denis, the steward is to fetch Mlle d'Epponcourt and Mlle de Lange. Ask M. de Racon to wait on me as soon as he returns.' Denis left. The two black-clothed ladies sat in silence. Two lackeys laid a handsome little table with food for three people and placed it between the countess and Madame Boquelin. 'Do start,' the countess said to her guest, 'or the food will get cold.'

Blanche helped herself and the countess told her of the great event of the day. Denis announced M. de Racon, and Martin entered the room. The countess, observing his surprise, said amiably: 'Would you care to have supper with me if you have nothing better to do?'

'Thank you, Madame. With the greatest pleasure.' Martin greeted Blanche with a bow and took a stool facing her. The ladies were already eating the sweet when he began his meal. The three-branched candelabra lit up the faces of the company: the even features of the countess, the large, child-like eyes of the little widow, and the young man's frank, open face. To break the silence, the countess asked Martin as gaily as possible:

'When do you start your service with the musketeers?'

'Tomorrow, Madame.'

'Are you looking forward to it?'

'Yes, Madame, because, after my year's service, I shall join my father's regiment on an equal footing and shall no longer have to bow and scrape to officers of my own rank because of their noble birth. Anyone who has served in the guards has the right to buy a regiment and command it.'

'I congratulate you, Monsieur,' Blanche said shyly. Martin bowed.

'May I ask the reason for your mourning?' he asked politely.

'M. Saint-Jean . . . I beg your pardon, M. de Racon . . . my husband is dead and I do not wish to return to his house or to my brother Louis.'

Martin wiped his hands on his napkin and replied, after a moment's reflection: 'Madame, I advise you to return to your brother's house immediately. Tell him you wish to mourn M. Boquelin for a year in the Carmelite convent where you have already spent some time. He cannot refuse you. As a guest of the convent, you will not have to observe the rules of the order and you can go out every day at your pleasure. You will have more liberty than heretofore.'

'The Mother Superior is very strict and does not allow visits from gentlemen.'

'Do you want to receive gentlemen?'

'No, M. Saint-Jean, but what shall I do when my year of mourning is over and my brother wishes to marry me off again?'

'Give me the name of the gentleman he finds for you and I shall have a few words with him.'

'What will you say to him, M. de Racon?'

'That he will have to fight a duel with me before he can obtain your hand.'

The countess gave a start. 'You go too far, M. de Racon. The king has forbidden duels.'

'They are fought all the same, Madame. I should be a poor cavalier indeed if I allowed Madame Boquelin to be delivered up to another moneybags. But it is a long time till next winter and she has nothing to fear during her year of mourning.'

Blanche sighed with relief. 'M. Saint-Jean, you have helped me once again. Thank you, Monsieur.'

'I think it is time the young widow left,' said the countess. 'Madame, come and see me whenever you feel in need of an older friend.'

Blanche blushed and turned her head away. 'Madame, you make me feel ashamed.'

'There is no need to feel ashamed. Your fate excuses you, and your frankness arouses confidence and compassion.'

Blanche groped for the countess's slender hand and pressed her lips to it. 'Madame, could I not be your guest until tomorrow?'

The countess was speechless and withdrew her hand.

'Madame,' said Martin quickly, 'will you allow me to see Madame Boquelin to her litter? I shall give her four grooms for protection. Let us go, Madame.'

But Blanche slipped from her chair and fell on her knees before the countess. 'Forgive me, Madame, please. I was tactless and immodest.'

The countess still did not reply and Martin intervened: 'Madame Boquelin, your hostess meant visits in the daytime and you will be received gladly tomorrow.'

'Is that true, M. de Racon?'

The countess had recovered her composure. 'Yes, my dear child.'

Martin helped Blanche to her feet and said apologetically: 'Madame, she is distraught by the death of her husband. Come, Madame Boquelin.' Taking the arm he offered her, Blanche bowed once more to the countess and the young man led her quickly from the room. Pierre was outside the door. 'Monsieur, M. le Comte wishes Madame Boquelin to wait in his study until he returns.' Blanche gave a little cry of pleasure, hurried along the corridor and disappeared into the study. 'Pierre,' said Martin sharply. 'If anyone should ask for Madame Boquelin, she is the guest of Madame la Comtesse. Do you understand?'

'Yes, Monsieur.'

'Tell the master of the horse to send four grooms with Madame Boquelin to the Hôtel de Salvieux.'

'Your orders shall be carried out.'

Martin had not gone two steps before Denis caught him up. 'Monsieur, Madame la Comtesse wishes to speak to you.' Martin returned to the salon.

The table had been cleared and removed. The countess was obviously agitated. As soon as the lackeys had left and Martin had sat down beside her she began: 'Martin, this morning you said things to me in the coach that I still find disturbing. The little widow confessed her love for my husband and told me you wanted to marry her without insisting upon your rights. Is she the woman you love but cannot marry?'

'Yes, Madame.'

The countess stared at him in utter amazement. 'How can anyone be so unselfish?'

'What else is there for me to do, Madame? You cannot force someone to love you, but you can help whenever you are needed.'

'You know how to help.'

'Yes, I pride myself on that.'

'Martin, I too need help.'

'You, Madame?'

'I must confide in you with veiled words. I once lied in order to save my life and now I regret that lie. Is it permissible, in the service of God and in order to help another, to yield to baseness?'

'Certainly, Madame, as long as one remains oneself.'

'But is that possible?'

'Yes, Madame, I think it is.'

'Martin, what is the source of your spiritual strength?'

'I sensed the godliness in man.'

'But is there any godliness left on earth?'

'There are flashes from time to time. Did you not find the little lady charming just now?'

'I beg you not to jest.'

'Madame, on rainy nights I have often gone riding. Below me the mud splashed up from black, slimy puddles, but on clear nights the stars above were reflected in those same puddles. You see, Heaven can be seen in puddles.'

'Do you go often to church?'

'No more than anyone else, Madame.'

'Do you pray?'

'Sometimes.'

'Martin, suppose that to save another you leaped into a marsh and were drowned?'

'Then you would be drowned in a bid to rescue someone.'

'But do you not imperil your soul in so doing?'

'I have never bothered about my soul's salvation.'

'But don't you want to be counted among the sheep on Judgment Day?'

'Madame, when you want to give help to someone you forget your own salvation. Since we have all to pass through purgatory, a few years more or less do not worry me. When a soldier in battle tries to save his life, he is later made to run the gauntlet.'

'Martin, the harshness of life is sometimes intolerable.'

'Only sometimes, Madame, and then you must give a good account of yourself or be disgraced.'

'But you failed on one occasion,' the countess said softly.

'Yes, Madame, very badly, and there is nothing left there to save.'

'Monsieur, I must ponder your words. Goodnight, M. de Racon.'

'Goodnight, Madame.' Martin rose, bowed and left the salon.

It was only with great difficulty that the steward, who had been sent by the countess to the theatre, and Mlle de Lange could prevent Marguerite from going on to a ball with one of her admirers. By the time she reached the Hôtel de Racon the countess had already retired to bed. Next morning she was given a long lecture on morals and had to promise not to go to the theatre in future without permission. The girl pouted and admitted quite frankly that she intended to amuse herself rather than die of boredom, and did not care two pins for the conventions. The countess just managed to control herself and said that her husband was shortly giving a banquet to celebrate the legitimation of his son, and that the girl would be certain to enjoy herself on that occasion. Marguerite was pacified.

The preparations for the banquet had fully occupied the count for several days. It was attended by more than two hundred ladies and gentlemen come to congratulate the happy father and young M. de Racon. Among the guests were the Marquise de Sévigné, the Marquis de Chassigny, his wife and sons, Ninon de Lenclos, the Maréchal d'Humières and the Comte de Montignon. They sat at table from early afternoon until late at night, constantly changing places and dancing between the courses. Marguerite was courted by at least ten cavaliers and could hardly escape from the toils of her partners. But the countess's beauty overshadowed the charms of all the other women. Men, dotards and youths, paid her homage and showed her the steps of the latest dances. The count grew jealous and danced with his wife three times in succession, and by so doing made himself a laughing stock. The Maréchal d'Humières asked for the next dance with the much-courted lady and said jestingly that one must be prepared at times to dispense with a permanent possession. The count had to yield but grew annoyed. Hardly had the Maréchal returned his wife than Martin asked permission to dance with her. Once again the count was forced to agree and was teased by the old soldier for never taking his eyes off her.

The Marquise de Sévigné laughingly declared that her next letter would undoubtedly amuse her daughter in the country, and Ninon de Lenclos insisted with mock sadness that she had discovered too late that the embers of love best endured in marriage. Her *bon mot* was immediately repeated, and that same evening Ninon received two offers of matrimony which she rejected on various flighty pretexts, promising to cherish them in memory. The Marquis de Chassigny handed the count her latest poem, celebrating Hercules's acceptance by the gods, a charming allegory on Martin's legitimation. The count read half-way through the long poem, found it very beautiful, handed it to the hunchbacked Nicolas de Chassigny to read, and sent a page to tell his wife that she should come and listen to it at her husband's side. After Nicolas had read it with great eloquence, everyone assured the Comte de Racon that his son was a perfect nobleman and, as a young war hero, fully deserved comparison with Hercules. Even Comte Gérard de Montignon, who had listened with his wife and son, professed to be charmed by Martin's personality. The legitimation had come like a bolt from the blue, but he managed to conceal his disappointment and anger and to congratulate his cousin most cordially.

Next day, the count took Martin to Versailles to the headquarters of the musketeers. Marguerite, who had drunk too much, stayed in bed with a headache. The countess read her

Bible and gave orders that she was not to be disturbed.

That evening, the count and Martin returned home within a few minutes of each other. They dressed and left the house immediately, the count to dine with the Marquis de Chassigny and Martin to meet his new regimental comrades who, according to tradition, had prepared all manner of practical jokes to play on him.

The count found the marquis suffering from an attack of gout, and the marquise writing a novel, the most beautiful passages of which she wanted to read to her guest. The prospect of a literary evening caused the count to complain suddenly of a stomach ache and, bent double, he took his leave with a thousand apologies, returned home and ordered a copious supper in his study.

When the table had been cleared and the count was making up his mind whether to go out or remain at home, Pierre announced the countess. The count rose to his feet in surprise as his wife entered. She was wearing a simple black dress and no jewels. 'Monsieur, I have a question to ask you and beg you to give me an honest answer.'

'What is the question?'

'If you had the possibility of further issue, would you allow M. de Racon to marry according to the dictates of his heart?'

'Yes, but why do you ask?'

'Would you allow M. de Racon to marry Marguerite d'Epponcourt or Madame Boquelin?'

'Yes, whichever he preferred.'

'Is that true, Monsieur?'

'Yes, certainly, but since the occasion will never arise, please spare me such useless questions.'

'Monsieur, if you promise me that you will not punish Borel, I will make a confession.'

'A confession? Yes, I promise I won't harm the old man. What have you to tell me?'

'Monsieur, I have lied to you for nine years. I am as healthy as you are.' The count was speechless. The countess took advantage of the silence before the inevitable storm and said swiftly: 'I have made this confession for the sake of your son. You can ignore it if you like. Good evening, Monsieur.'

'Stay here! Stay where you are.' The countess did not move.

'Madame, you were ill when I returned from Brayonne in '72 after being wounded.'

The countess turned scarlet and looked down at the floor. 'That was merely from terror, Monsieur.'

The count drew near and said quietly and clearly: 'It would have been better had you made this confession five years ago. You are now thirty-nine.'

'At that time I saw no reason to make a sacrifice.'

'Madame, you have Martin to thank that you are still alive. I often toyed with the idea of poisoning you in the classic manner, and now I should be glad to know to what gentleman you have accorded your favours in the past?'

'To no one, Monsieur.'

'Do you expect me to believe a confessed liar? The first, I'm sure, was M. d'Oubray. Am I right?'

'No.'

'Please continue to be honest!'

'I have belonged to no man except you.'

'You are the most splendid liar I know. I should like to tear your dress off and thrash the truth out of you. How often has d'Oubray possessed you?'

'Never. Not once.'

The count took his riding crop. 'Not once?'

'Monsieur, remember that in Martin I have presented you with a son!'

The count threw his riding crop into the fire. 'Why didn't you yield to M. d'Oubray?'

'Because I could not love his hands.'

'Why not?'

'I found them unpleasant.'

'And had they not been unpleasant, Madame?'

'Then I should have refused him nothing.'

'That sounds honest. So, I have to thank his unpleasant hands for your fidelity.'

'Yes, Monsieur, his hands alone, because nearly two years ago you had a whim to set me free.'

'I remember. Did I not immediately cancel that offer?'

'No, you did not.'

'And you expect me to believe that you have not made use of your freedom?'

'I never met a man sufficiently attractive and lovable.'

'Not even Martin?'

'Monsieur!'

'Madame, I could believe you, were you not so astonishingly beautiful.'

'I beg you to believe me.'

He caught her by the shoulders. 'Madeleine, are you trying by this confession to hide your guilt? Are you expecting a child by someone else?'

'No. I have never deceived you with a man.'

'Shall I lock you up for a few months?'

'Do with me what you will. I have told you everything.'

'Are you aware that I love you?'

'There is hatred in your words.'

'You drive me mad, Madeleine. I feel an almost irresistible desire to bite that neck which someone else has kissed.'

'No one has kissed it.'

'You are sacrificing yourself for Martin. Do you love him so much that on his account you will deliver yourself to a beast?'

'You are a human being.'

'Not at this moment. You deserved a man of Martin's worth rather than me. How deeply do you love him?'

'I love him like a mother.'

'Since when, Madeleine?'

'Since the night he came back in secret and you found him in my salon. I saw when you embraced him how much you loved him.'

The count removed his hands from his wife's shoulders. 'I did not ask about myself but about Martin. By rights you should hate him because he was the cause of Guy's death.'

'Hate is pointless and stifles all consolation.'

'Yes, you are right. There is no sense in distrust either, when the person under suspicion knows well how to defend herself. I should wait for three months, but I cannot be patient for another day. Expect a visit from me at about ten o'clock.' He escorted his wife to the door.

The countess hurried through her salon into the bedroom. 'Emilie!'

Her maid laid aside her sewing and curtsied. 'Madame la Comtesse?'

'Emilie, I am going to retire now. Bring some warm water, get fresh bed linen and make the bed.'

'It was changed on the day of your arrival.'

'Do what I tell you. Why don't you hurry?' Emilie slipped out of the room. The countess opened a drawer and took out a fresh night-gown. She unfolded it, discovered some torn lace, threw it on the floor, unfolded the next and continued to reject one after the other because none was immaculate. In her despair, the distraught woman sat down in a chair and began weeping.

Emilie came in with the bed linen. 'What is the matter, Madame?'

'My nightgowns are all torn.'

'The lace is worn out, Madame, but you always insisted that they would still last for a long time.'

'I can't put on any of these. How late is it?'

Emilie looked into the salon. 'A quarter past nine by the wall clock.'

'Heavens, where is the water?'

'It's being heated.'

'Make the bed. My God, there are stains on the silk coverlet.'

'You spilt your chocolate on it, Madame.' The countess fumbled with her bodice and tore at the strings. 'Please wait, Madame la Comtesse. I'll help you.'

'You attend to the bed. Look out my best nightgown. Send Denis to the kitchen and tell them to send up the water at once. Sprinkle scent on the pillows.'

'Immediately, Madame la Comtesse.'

The countess stepped out of her dress. 'Leave the blankets alone! I need the water first.'

'Madame la Comtesse, are you feverish?'

'Don't be so foolish, just do as I say! I will make the bed myself.'

The countess hurried over to the bed in her grey silk petticoats and changed the pillowcases. At last, the two pitchers of water arrived. 'Emilie, wash me from top to toe.'

'Madame, you will catch your death of cold.'

'It doesn't matter. Unfasten my petticoat.'

'Madame, you've knotted it.'

'Take a pair of scissors . . . Warm the towels by the fire . . .' Emilie hurried as fast as she could without understanding the reason for all the flurry. When she had washed her mistress before the fire and dried her, the floor was drenched with water and one of the carpets wringing wet. 'Now give me the best of those nightgowns. Get one of the maids to wipe up. Emilie, these ribbons are torn too.'

'They are all worn out, Madame la Comtesse.'

'What shall I do? What shall I do? What is the time?'

Emilie ran into the salon and back. 'It's twenty minutes to ten.'

'Impossible!'

'Please look at the clock for yourself.'

'Emilie, I can't put this nightgown on as it is.'

'Why don't you wear your négligé over it?'

'No, that's quite worn out too.'

'But no one sees you at night.'

'Emilie, I'll put on my new black velvet dress. Bring me a shift.'

Emilie stood there open-mouthed. 'Is Madame la Comtesse expecting a visitor tonight?'

'That is no concern of yours.'

The maid brought a new cambric shift and helped her mistress to put it on. 'Which bodice and petticoats do you want to wear with it?'

'The cream-coloured petticoat with the gold embroidery, and the pearl-grey bodice. The black-and-gold shoes . . . And my pearls. That's all. Hurry, hurry! It must already be a quarter to ten.' Emilie scurried about the room like a weasel and sent Denis to fetch the maids. The bedroom was tidied while the countess laced herself. As soon as they had gone she looked at herself in the mirror. 'Emilie, untie my hair and rearrange it. Remove the entire head-dress.'

'Madame la Comtesse, the curls need attention . . .'

'There's no time now. Give me a black silk ribbon and a veil. No, take the curls away . . . Don't tug like that.'

Emilie arranged the gleaming, chestnut-brown hair partly with a ribbon and partly with a flimsy veil which fell loose from the temples. 'Madame la Comtesse, you look very beautiful like that but it will not hold.'

'It does not matter.' The countess put some rouge on her lips and cheeks, then wiped it nearly all off until only a vestige of colour remained. There was a knock at the door. She sprinkled herself with scent and rose to her feet. 'Leave the room, Emilie.'

The girl ran out of the room. There was a second knock at the door, but the countess made no sound.

The count entered wearing a pale-grey silk dressing-gown. He was freshly shaven and his hair was well combed. His costly snow-white shirt was open at the neck. They stood there contemplating each other. 'Madame, do you realise that you have allotted me a hideous role in your quest for martyrdom?'

The countess clutched the strings of her bodice. 'I was unaware of it.'

'Madeleine, I have no desire to play the hangman and should, if possible, like to rob this night of its ugliness. I am glad you chose that dress. Play the part of the unknown woman I took you for when you entered the Marquise de Sévigné's salon masked, and let me in turn play the role of a stranger who has come to see you. Could you do that?'

'I will try, Monsieur,' the countess answered in a toneless voice.

'Sit down on your bed. You are ailing and I have come to pay you a visit. Imagine that I am wearing my new costume . . .'

The countess sat down on the bed and turned her huge, dark-blue eyes on the man as he approached. 'Madame, were you not expecting me today?'

'Yes . . . No . . .'

'Madame, you are confused. I should have allowed you more time. May I sit by your side?' The countess made no reply. 'Madame, you have no grounds for fear. A single cry will fetch your servants and I am lost.' He sat down at the far end of the bed. 'I was told that you were ailing but I believe that your illness stems less from a disorder of your body than from a heart in distress. There is no better cure for an ailing spirit than a conversation with an understanding friend. Have you such a friend?'

'No.'

'Madame, I have no right to wish to be your friend. I have known you too short a time to have deserved your confidence, but I saw you at that party and I believed that I had discovered your secret grief at first sight. You are lonely, Madame. What do you long for?'

'I do not even know myself, Monsieur.'

'Did you know it before you were married?'

With a tremor in her voice the countess whispered: 'Young girls always have childish dreams . . .'

'And those dreams never came true,' he continued.

'Perhaps in Heaven,' she said wearily.

'Madame, do you believe in a heavenly love capable of replacing an earthly love?'

'Yes.'

His black eyes twinkled with amusement. 'Do they understand how to kiss in Heaven?' he asked.

'I am not very good at such jests, Monsieur.'

He immediately became serious again. 'I certainly did not wish to offend you, Madame; I merely doubt in your trust of heavenly consolation, for had you really believed in such a consolation you would long since have grown resigned and adopted that calm, tolerant smile, which is so attractive because it forgives human frailties. But you look as stern as though you still endowed men with the capacity for perfection and expected it of them.'

'No, I do not demand that,' the countess replied firmly.

'Is that true, Madeleine?' She nodded her head and looked away. 'Madame, I know that I am ugly. My hands alone are beautiful. And my nature is exactly the same—almost entirely black, with only a bright patch here and there. I would willingly lend you my brightness if I could to lighten your loneliness a little. Was M. d'Oubray incapable of consoling you?'

'Yes, he was even blacker than you because he was not honest with me.'

'Am I being honest with you now?'

'It would seem so, Monsieur.'

'Have you any wish it is within my power to grant?'

'No, I wish for nothing now.'

'Nothing at all?'

'Monsieur, let us prolong this moment for a while.'

'Madame, I have a question to ask you: could you love this hand?' The countess averted her eyes. 'I beg you to give me an answer.'

'Once I could have done so.'

'But I was no different then.'

'*I* was different, Monsieur.'

'Would you thrust my hand away if I were to touch you?'

'I should not be permitted to.'

'Please do not forget your role. I am a stranger and in your power. You can have me arrested.'

'I do not care to go on with this game.'

'Why not, Madeleine?'

'You are the cat and I am the mouse. Please make an end of it.'

'What kind of an end?'

'You still ask me that!'

'Please don't start weeping.'

'I could scream!'

'Please don't do that!'

'I'm going mad.'

'No, Madame, you are not. I will call your maid and you will sleep alone as usual.' He stood up. 'I will come tomorrow evening at the same time.'

She caught hold of the sleeves of his dressing-gown. 'Don't go! I could not bear the suspense of a whole day.'

'Madame, it will be easier for you than for me.'

She released him. 'You are mocking me.'

He went to the door. 'Good night, Madame.'

She ran after him. 'Gaston!'

He turned round. She was on the point of fainting and he put his arms round her. 'Madeleine, tell me, do I horrify you?'

'Oh, don't go, Gaston.'

'Do you really know what you're saying?'

'Please stay here.'

'Madeleine, I do not wish to accept a sacrifice.'

'It is no sacrifice.'

'No sacrifice?'

'No!'

'What is it then?'

'I don't know, Gaston.'

'Madeleine, you are completely overwrought. Your brow is burning-hot. I am really not worth getting feverish about. Please rest until tomorrow.'

She clung to him. 'Gaston, for the love of God, don't leave me alone now.'

'Shall I continue to play the understanding friend?'

'Think of Martin and be human to me.'

'I would rather be tender to you, Madame. Your hair is coming undone. May I remove the bow?'

'Yes, untie it.'

He took her head and said pleadingly: 'Madeleine, I hope that in spite of everything I have done to you, you are too magnanimous to make me an executioner. I am waiting for you to thrust my hands away.'

'I want your hands!'

He released her and stepped back. 'You want these hands?'

The distracted look vanished from the countess's face and suddenly she was calm and miraculously transfigured. She stood up, self-composed. 'Yes, Gaston, I want your hands.'

'Can you love them?'

'I have always loved them.'

By eight o'clock next morning everyone in the Hôtel de Racon knew of the new state of affairs, although the count had retired to his own room in the early morning. The countess rose at nine o'clock and was dressed to the accompaniment of soft music which could be heard through the closed door of the salon. As she sat by her dressing-table, Emilie showed in the coiffeur who, with a host of preparations, began to arrange her hair in the latest fashion set by the Duchess de Fontange. The steward called for his orders, and Mlle de Lange was ordered to buy cambric and lace. Marguerite paid her a visit and was delighted to watch the edifice of ribbons being crowned with a starched lace cap. Martin came in, wished her good morning and took his leave immediately because he had to report for duty. Denis served chocolate, and Marguerite, on the countess's orders, was served with a cup. Two young dandies were received graciously; one of them presented Marguerite with a bottle of scent and the other entertained her with witty jests and the latest gossip.

A little later the count entered wearing his Court dress and wig.

'Are you not ready yet, Madame. We shall be very late at Versailles.'

'Monsieur, I must beg you to excuse me today.'

'You do not wish to accompany me?'

'I do not wish to give the reason before an audience.'

The count turned to Marguerite: 'Mademoiselle, I must ask you to take the gentlemen into the salon. Everyone is to leave the room.' Chatting and laughing, the young people took their leave. The coiffeur raised his eyes to heaven, for he had to break off his work before the 'fontange' had been completed. He followed Emilie out through the side door.

The count stood behind his wife's chair and observed her face in the mirror. 'Will you give me your reasons now?'

'Gaston, may I wait for a week?'

'A week? What does that mean?'

The countess felt for his outstretched hand and looked entreatingly at his bewigged face in the mirror. 'Gaston, it has taken me twenty-two years to come to you . . .'

'Nine years, Madeleine.'

'No, twenty-two. I was parted from you ever since Raoul was born. Allow me a few days of happiness until something else estranges us again. Be a little patient.'

'What could possibly estrange us? The Court certainly could not, Madeleine.'

She pressed his hand to her face. 'Gaston, could you perhaps wait two days?'

'You intrigue me. Are you keeping something from me? Speak, Madeleine!'

'The king expects me to renounce my faith. He told me so in the council chamber when I was alone with him. You had gone out to fetch Martin. I am frightened of Versailles.'

She felt the grip of his hand relax and tenderly touch her cheek. A quiver ran through her body. 'Are you afraid that I might insist upon your conversion? I shall not do that, Madeleine.'

'Do you allow me to remain a Huguenot?'

'Yes, for as long as you like . . . Since you prefer to be burnt at the stake rather than renounce your faith. My hypocritical piety must suffice the Court. But since they are beginning to persecute the Huguenots again in some of the provinces in spite of the Edict of Nantes, I shall take precautions. I shall make the excuse that you take religious matters so seriously that you insist upon studying the works of the church Fathers and other holy books, so that you may know the exact nature of the religion you are about to exchange for your own. I will procure those books for you and have them arranged on shelves in your salon. You will soon have the reputation of being a scholar and the pleasure of attacting various spiritual advisers. Do you agree?' She pressed his hand to her lips.

He sat down on the left arm of her chair. 'Did the king pay you any compliments?'

'No, he recommended me to listen to Bossuet's sermons.'

He bent down and kissed her in the shadow of his wig, crushing several ribbons of her unfinished *coiffure*.

'You are more beautiful than yesterday, Madeleine, and there is a new note in your voice.'

'That is no wonder Gaston,' she said, radiant with happiness.

'It is a great wonder to me. In the old days, even after the most passionate nights, you showed me an icy face in the morning. Was everything forgotten each morning when you woke up?'

'At night you robbed me of my reason.'

'Have you not yet recovered it today?'

'My love has taught my reason a lesson.'

'Truly?'

'You wish to tease me.'

'No, but I should like to see your face once at the moment it freezes. I have always missed that moment. I will close the doors, arouse your ardour and watch you when you become unapproachable once more.'

'Monsieur, you are dressed for the Court!'

'I shall not go to Versailles today.' He placed his Court wig on the silver chocolate tray. 'There is nothing more enticing than to put you out of countenance. The more embarrassed and confused you become, the more beautiful and feminine you are.' He stood up and bolted the doors. The countess also rose. 'Monsieur, please remember that this is my visiting hour.'

'Madame, in my house I can do as I please. If it pleases me to take the midday meal in bed with you, I shall do so.'

'Gaston . . .'

'Madeleine, a woman like you cannot renounce tenderness for nine long years.'

'I did not permit myself to think of tenderness.'

'I will kill you if you are lying!'

'I am too unafraid and too proud to lie.'

'That is a good answer. If you were only a little more vivacious and natural in company you would become one of the most prominent women in no time and I should burst with jealousy. Though your manner of speech is sometimes precious, and the precious has long since gone out of fashion.'

'Why do you talk to me for so long if you find me old-fashioned?'

'Tell me whether you really loved me last night, or whether I merely robbed you of your reason?' She turned her head away. He stood close behind her. 'Madeleine, I am madly in love with you and cannot free myself of doubt! You wanted to sacrifice yourself. Was it a sacrifice?'

'What can I say to you if you don't trust me and cannot feel my love?'

'What I take for love may mean only that I aroused your senses.' She turned, took hold of his head and ran her lips over his scar. When he made no move, she repeated the caress. 'Madeleine, Martin used to do that sometimes.'

'I learned it from him.'

'From Martin?'

'Yes, he did it when you embraced him in my salon before Guy's death.'

'Must you try and arouse new doubts in me at every instant?'

'Forgive me, Gaston.'

He removed the shawl from her shoulders. 'Madeleine, I believe you love me.'

'My bodice!'

'Please, Madeleine.'

'The sun!'

'It's not too bright for me.'

'Gaston, I am no longer young.'

'Do not remind me of that. You have cheated me of a thousand nights for which I shall never be able to make up. When I saw you in the Marquise de Sévigné's salon I took you for thirty at the most. Where did you get that blue mark on your shoulder? A man must have embraced you there. Hypocrite! That is why you were afraid of the light.'

'It was you, Gaston.'

'No, it was not I. I am never rough with the women I love. Who was the fellow?'

'Have you forgotten how you behaved to me in your study?'

'Forgive me!'

She kissed him in her soft, sensuous way and her kisses were returned wildly, passionately. 'Gaston, my knees are trembling.' He drew her to the bed and she fell back on the coverlet.

There was a knock at the door. 'Silence out there!'

They heard Denis's voice crying, 'M. le Comte, the Comte and Comtesse de Montignon are in the salon.'

'I am coming at once. My wife is not feeling well. Madeleine, the relatives will have to wait.'

'Gaston, my hair, my dress!'

'You fainted and I had to loosen your dress. Hell, now you are really freezing. I could wring Gérard's neck.'

'Don't be angry with me, Gaston.'

'Tears, that's the end! Calm yourself. I will leave you in peace. I hope you will not be indisposed this evening?'

'No.'

'Good then!'

'Gaston!'

'What?'

'Gaston, I would die for you.'

'Bless you for that. Emilie, bring me some vinegar and smelling salts!'

The maid replied from outside the door:

'M. le Comte, my door is locked.' He opened the maid's

room, strode across to the door, unlocked it and made his way into the salon.

Contrary to all expectations, the happiness of the Comtesse de Racon endured. Her beauty blossomed into an ultimate mellow glow. The count found in her a body that might have been created for him, and a new personality; in short, everything he had sought elsewhere in vain and had found partially or imperfectly only in the women who had attracted him. His passion increased with the countess's love; she granted all his wishes without making the slightest demands on him. Realising that it was beyond her power to understand his nature, she discovered to her surprise that her strict morality was not offended by his ruthless desire. He roused her from her torpor and made no attempt to intrude into the lonely world of her spirit. He never asked what she was thinking, but when he felt so inclined he knew instinctively her innermost feelings; and then, by a gentle caress or a tender word, he could bestow upon her a happiness which seemed to flood her with a wealth of light.

They spent Christmas in Paris. Every fourth day the count rode to Versailles and was a constant guest of the Duc d'Orléans at the Palais Royal. Martin was enjoying his life as a musketeer and had soon made a number of friends of his own age. He avoided the Hôtel de Racon for fear of rousing the count's dangerous jealousy, and spent his leisure with comrades from his own regiment or from the Horse Guards who were stationed not far from his own quarters.

The countess and Marguerite often went into society. They usually left the hotel without the count, but generally returned in his company for he would turn up unexpectedly just before the end of the party in whatever salon his wife happened to be. He wished her beauty to be admired, but for the merest unfounded trifle constantly made the wildest scenes of jealousy, so that finally, to pacify him, she asked for a second lady-in-waiting as guardian of her conjugal fidelity. He remembered an impoverished widow, one of his distant relatives, sent for her, found her old and respectable enough, gave her strict injunctions and, to everyone's relief, was delighted with the detailed reports she gave him. Marguerite was vexed that Mlle de Lange now had an ally; and with her admirers played all manner of tricks on the two 'dragons'. To save himself endless complaints, the count locked her up from time to time in her room.

In society everyone laughed at the Comte de Racon who, after twenty years of marriage, was as enamoured of his wife as a young suitor, and some of the ladies teased him openly. Then one evening, in the Marquise de Sévigné's salon, he confounded the mockers by declaring that he been previously so dazzled by the light of stars that he had been forced to turn away from the sun. Now that age had begun to dim his eyes he could perceive only the brilliant sun, which outshone all the stars. Mockery was immediately silenced. From then on, there was no more talk of ridiculous infatuation but only of the astonishing love of the Comte de Racon, until the gossipers turned their attention to other events and other characters.

With her brother's permission, Blanche was now living with the Carmelites and wrote to Martin every two or three days, asking when she could visit the Comte de Racon at his home. Martin put her off with polite excuses and out of consideration for her, told the most atrocious lies. Blanche grew suspicious and drove one afternoon, on chance, to the Hotel de Racon, where the count was waiting in angry impatience for his wife who had gone to visit the ailing Marquise de Chassigny. When Pierre announced Madame Boquelin, the count shouted that he was not at home and said to Martin, who happened to be present, that he was in love and as long as this condition lasted he had no further interest in Blanche. Martin suggested that he should treat the girl more like a child and, out of consideration for his son, the count agreed.

The little widow was received in his study, and the two gentlemen, to amuse themselves, taught her to play lansquenet. Blanche was quite happy, but slow-witted and kept asking Martin for advice. Martin asked the count to invite Mlle d'Epponcourt to join the game and the count sent for the girl, who because of further disobedience to Mlle de Lange, was under house arrest once more. She appeared looking sulky, but soon brightened up and, for the benefit of the two gentlemen, started impersonating an uncouth soldier, banging her fist on the table and, to Blanche's horror, giving vent to the most appalling oaths. The count began to cheat, was caught by Martin, and told by Marguerite that certain people who did not behave properly had no right to keep others confined to the house. This impertinence flabbergasted the count, but he swiftly collected his wits and said sternly that he had only been testing Martin's sharpness. Martin laughed, and Marguerite laughed even louder. Blanche frowned in despair turning from one to the other and asked Martin whether she could lay some of her cards in her lap because there were too many to hold. There was a further outburst of laughter.

At this moment the countess entered. Her husband invited her to play instead of Madame Boquelin. She replied that she would prefer to be an onlooker, and sat down between Martin and Blanche. The count threw down his cards and left the room in a sudden rage, banging the door behind him. The countess followed almost immediately. Marguerite said that she could foresee a terrible scene of jealously. Blanche wanted to know why, and learned from Marguerite that the count was one of the most uxorious husbands in Paris. The little widow gave a start and the cards fell from her hand. Martin hurriedly escorted her to her litter which was waiting in the entrance, and whispered, as he helped her in, that the count still felt paternally towards her. With his volatile character he would be certain to receive her again within a few weeks. Blanche sobbed and said that she had never wished to be anything else than the count's daughter, although she knew only too well how little use he had for one. Martin saw her litter disappear in the twilight and retired to his room. He wrote a letter to the count and handed it to Pierre. Then he left the house to keep an appointment with Nicolas de Chassigny.

As a result of Martin's letter, the count wrote a few lines to the little widow Boquelin. Overjoyed, Blanche read:

MADAME,

My son has acquainted me with the pathos of your position and bade me bring you a little joy. My house is open to you whenever you need maternal or paternal consolation. I send you my regards and those of my wife, and beg you in return to give mine to your sister-in-law and your brother de Salvieux.

GASTON, COMTE DE RACON, MARQUIS DE BRAYONNE.

From now on Blanche spent much time with the Comtesse de Racon, to whom she had been attracted from the first moment and soon loved like a daughter. Blanche could read all her wishes in her eyes, and in society was often taken for one of the countess's ladies-in-waiting. Marguerite mocked her for her servility and treated her with cold disdain. Blanche was afraid of Marguerite's tactlessness, and at pains not to hear her wounding remarks. One day, when she was alone with the countess, she suddenly burst into tears at her feet and begged for forgiveness. The countess understood, raised her to her feet and said that such a charming child as Blanche could never cause her sorrow.

Contrary to the countess, the count regarded the period of mourning for the second Vicomte de Clarmont to have long since ended, and enjoyed himself at masked routs and balls. He suddenly remained away for days and nights on end and had money brought to a dancer's house. The countess told herself that a woman of her age could not expect her belated happiness to last forever and consoled herself with a secret hope which she mentioned to no one. But she had been mistaken in this unpredictable man. He returned to her arms more in love than ever, and when, on Ash Wednesday—she had waited for this day in order to sweeten the period of Lent he abhored—she told him that she was pregnant, he almost strangled her with delight. She begged him to allow her to return to Grandval because the atmosphere of the crowded salons would not be healthy for her. He told her that she could leave whenever she liked and he would escort her on the journey. She smiled happily and sighed. He sent for the most famous doctors in the city to confirm his wife's surmise and the same day bought her diamonds worth ten thousand livres.

Martin was on guard duty at Court and did not get home that night until four o'clock. Dominique lit him along the corridors to his room. The count was just leaving his wife's room when he recognised Martin, beckoned to him and cried:

'You can marry your silly goose or an old woman on crutches as far as I'm concerned. I don't want any children by you. I'm going to have some myself!'

Martin was thunderstruck. 'Monsieur!' he shouted and flung his arms round his father's neck.

BLANCHE CLAIRE-MARIE

NEXT morning, after a long conversation with the count, Martin had himself announced to Mlle d'Epponcourt. Marguerite, who was having her hair curled by her grumbling old maid, greeted him coldly and offered him a stool. Martin remained standing. 'I wish to speak to you alone, Mademoiselle.'

'Then you must exercise a little patience, Monsieur.' Instead of sitting on the stool, Martin took a chair, sat down and crossed his legs. The maid continued curling her mistress's fair hair and then combed it out again. 'How do you like my "harum scarum" hair-style?'

'You look like a poodle.'

'You're very flattering. You seem to share your father's opinion in everything.'

'I don't know what he thinks of the "harum scarum".'

'He forbade Madame Boquelin to adopt that style.'

'Really!'

'The countess also has her hair arranged to his taste. I would never do that.' Martin dangled his legs and looked out of the window at a cat walking along the tiles. 'M. de Racon,' said Marguerite, 'you are the most boring cavalier in the whole of Paris.'

'You will probably change your mind after your maid has left the room.'

'Have you any new gossip?'

'Yes, Mademoiselle.'

'Fasten my ribbons, Babette, and then you can go.' The maid sniffed, tied the ribbons and left.

Martin rose to his feet. 'Mademoiselle, the Comte de Racon gave me permission yesterday to marry the woman of my choice, since he has hope of further issue. I am now proposing to you for the third time.'

'Could you guarantee that your charming father would not poison me one day?'

'I can fully guarantee your safety.'

'What else have you to offer me?'

'On my wedding day the count is giving me Château Fleury with all its meadows, fields and woods, and the dairy farm which brings in a revenue of eighty thousand.'

'Livres or louis d'or?'

'Livres.'

'That is not very much.'

'No, but I can buy a regiment and horses for a stud farm.'

Marguerite thrust out her lower lip. 'I have no interest in a stud farm. Ask for the Hôtel de Brayonne instead of the meadows and the forest.'

'As you know, Mademoiselle, I have acquired the status of the Comte de Racon's youngest son, for my lifetime, and have no right therefore to pose as the Vicomte de Clarmont or M. de Brayonne. If the countess is fortunate enough to present her husband with two sons, I shall in future be only a simple country squire who, like all superfluous sons, must seek his fortune in the war.'

'And do you propose to tolerate that?'

'Naturally, Mademoiselle.'

'You are an ass.'

'Thank you!'

Marguerite reflected for a moment. 'Do you know what they have in mind for me if I refuse your offer?'

'Yes, Mademoiselle. They will raise your dowry to fifty thousand livres and look for a suitable husband for you. So far, your suitors have declared their love but no one has asked for your hand in marriage.'

'Monsieur, I have almost too many strings to my bow.'

'Mademoiselle, I beg you to marry me for the sake of the child.'

'What store you set by that byblow! I will marry you on condition that you promise me complete freedom in my marriage.'

'Do you mean by "freedom" that, even as Madame de

Racon, you will be allowed to dally with good-for-nothing gallants?'

'Yes, M. de Racon.'

'You demand too much.'

'I consider that you owe me some compensation.'

'Mademoiselle, if the wife I marry were to make a mockery of me in the eyes of the world, she would never do it a second time.'

'How so, M. de Racon?'

'I would cure her of the habit as soon as we were alone.'

'In what way, may I ask?'

'I would use my hands.'

'So you threaten me with violence?'

'All asses are violent.'

'So I have discovered. I will see that I do not fall into your power once more. I will not marry you, M. de Racon.'

'Mademoiselle, please try to be reasonable. It is quite obvious that I would not begrudge you a secret lover if our marriage, despite our efforts, proved a failure, but I should insist that you behaved like a lady in public.'

'I *am* a lady.'

'The Comtesse de Racon is a lady, Mademoiselle. I should treat any woman with consideration and respect who made even a small effort to resemble her.'

'I do not trust you to show either.'

'Mademoiselle, I came to you with the most honest intentions.'

'I do not believe in your honour, for you lied to me after you raped me.'

'I beg you to forgive me now.'

'I shall never forgive you. I hope that you will suffer ten times the pain I had to suffer at the birth of your child.'

'Your wish might easily be granted if there is another war.'

'I hope it will be!'

'Mademoiselle, you now have an opportunity of taking your revenge, for by accepting my offer you would rob me of any hope of ever being able to marry the woman I love.'

Marguerite laughed. 'Revenge is sweet, but all the same I will not fall for your bait. Good day, Monsieur.'

'Good day, Mademoiselle.'

Martin bowed and left the room.

In the corridor he met two silk-clad fops who were waiting upon Mlle d'Epponcourt. With courteous bows they passed each other and Martin reached his bedroom door. As he opened it he heard Blanche's clear voice below, bidding a friendly good morning to the door-keeper. He stood still for a moment and listened as the light, rapid steps mounted the stairs on their way to the countess's apartments. Martin waited until the salon door closed, went into his room and donned his uniform.

That evening, when Martin returned from the parade ground, Dominique announced that Madame Boquelin was waiting for him in the salon. As Martin entered he found Blanche weeping at the feet of the countess and hiding her face in the elder woman's lap. 'Good evening,' said Martin. The countess replied to his greeting and Blanche raised her head.

'Can I be of service?' asked Martin, after kissing the hands of both ladies.

'Yes, we want advice once more and help from you,' replied the countess. 'Madame Boquelin wishes to accompany me to Grandval, but her brother has forbidden her to make the journey. She was unwise enough to mention before him that my husband was travelling with me. I prefer Madame Boquelin to all the ladies I know and should be very grieved if tomorrow I should have to be parted from her for a long time.'

'Madame,' asked Martin, 'will you allow me to have a few words alone with Madame Boquelin?'

'Certainly, Monsieur.' The countess rose and retired to her bedroom. Blanche wiped away her tears.

Without approaching the girl, Martin asked: 'Madame, do you know that the count has given me permission to marry any woman I please?'

'Yes, the countess told me so.'

'Mlle d'Epponcourt has released me, Madame. The Comte de Salvieux would not forbid my future bride to be the travelling companion of her future parents-in-law. You could pretend to be betrothed to me.'

Blanche looked down at the floor and her lips quivered. 'You want to do too much for me.'

'I am ready,' continued Martin, 'to go now, or tomorrow

morning, to your brother and sign a marriage contract. As soon as you have left I will cancel all the arrangements. This will be easy when I admit to your brother that I shall probably not be my father's heir. At the moment we can let your brother think that the Comtesse de Racon is still ailing and barren, and that one day I shall come into the title of Comte de Racon. If it is your wish to remain constantly within reach of my father, then I beg you to agree to a formal marriage with me before your brother finds out the true state of affairs. Do you agree to a betrothal?'

'Monsieur, you suggest all this as though it were a mere trifle! You have repeatedly said that you would marry me without making any claims, but I should have been wicked to accept such an offer. In sacred matters one should never be frivolous, and certainly not for the purpose of conniving at something which is a sin before God and men.'

'Madame, since when has your love become sinful?'

Blanche sat down in the countess's chair and her black eyes stared past Martin into the shadow of the faintly-lit room. 'Monsieur, I respect the Comtesse de Racon and love her like a mother. She is too noble to be jealous, but I have noticed that she suffers when her husband flirts with other women. I implored God to remove my love from my heart, but God would not listen. Then I confided in the Mother Superior. She told me I was a sinner and should repent so that I might be worthy of loving the saints and the Holy Virgin in place of the Comte de Racon. I replied that they were so remote, but the Mother Superior said I must lift up my soul. I asked her if there was anything heavenly that was somewhat nearer than the saints and the Virgin Mary, and she replied that God was everywhere, both near and far. Then I asked her if the little angels, portrayed as winged children in the sacred pictures, really existed, and the Mother Superior replied that every man has a guardian angel and that I should love mine. I promised to do so and I was given remission.

'But I did not know what my guardian angel looked like and since I could not imagine him to be smaller than myself—for how could a little winged child protect me?—I thought of my angel as a handsome youth in bright, heavenly robes, with snow-white wings, hovering above my head. I raised my soul to him and began to love him. Then I realised that I could also love someone else's angel and it would not be sinful. I imagined his guardian angel other than mine, dark and strange, with sable wings and a gold robe and piercing eyes. I love his angel more than mine, and since all guardian angels have to watch over their charges and be loyal to them, I look on him as if from above, through his angel's eyes, and love him truly from afar. In this way I can love him. Since we played lansquenet together, the most he does is to pinch my ear and call me his little monkey. Gaston is dead.'

'Which Gaston?'

'The monkey he gave me. The nuns loved it and gave it too much food until it got colic.'

Martin did not laugh. 'Madame, the count will one day remember his former toy.'

'Monsieur,' said Blanche turning to him, 'I should like to go to Grandval with the countess and help her look after the peasant children, to feed and clean the little ones. I should like to see your little son who apparently resembles you very much. Dr Borel wrote and said that he has scabies. That comes, I'm sure, from neglect. None of my puppies gets the mange because I bathe them every day. I should like to bathe the little one and put ointment on him and the scabies would soon go.'

'You want to adopt my child?'

'Yes, for he has no mother. Martin, I should like to have him. Please have him sent here to me at the Carmelites.'

'One doesn't send little children to anyone, Madame.'

'Let Dominique fetch him in a coach. I will look after him.'

'I intend to keep him myself.'

'You? You're a man and know nothing about children.'

'What would your brother say if you adopted my bastard?'

'He would be pleased, because if I had the boy I should pay no more visits to the Hôtel de Racon.'

'Is that so?'

'Yes, Monsieur, that is my suggestion.'

'Madame, I'm afraid you'd soon be homesick for the count.'

'I'm used to that. Will you lend me your son?'

'I would rather leave him with the Comtesse de Racon, otherwise he would also be overfed.'

'No Martin. No one else would be allowed to feed him.'

'My child remains at Grandval.'

'And I have nothing!'

'Accept my offer and then you'll have everything: the countess, my child and the count.' Blanche made no reply. 'Madame, why are you suddenly silent? Have you no confidence in me?'

'Yes, I trust you, Monsieur, but I cannot go through with this fake betrothal.'

'Please do it, Madame. I would willingly render you any service.'

'That is untrue, Monsieur. You have just said that your son is to remain at Grandval.'

'I said that because I feel responsible for both you and my child.'

'If you really loved me you would give me the child.'

'Madame, I will not give my child to anyone. Please allow me to withdraw.'

'No, Martin.'

'Why do you want me to stay?'

'Help me!'

'You won't allow yourself to be helped.'

'Is there no other way?'

'I know of none.'

Blanche lowered her head.

'Little Blanche,' said Martin, moving nearer to her, 'I know how much you love him and how much you suffer when you do not see him for a long time. You want to make a sacrifice out of consideration for the countess. You cannot do that, Claire-Marie.'

'Yes, I can, Martin, because I love him in a new way and because, after what has happened, I am nothing without him. First there was my terror of the Marquis de Chassigny, until he freed me of that fear and protected me by his kindness. Something intangible still clings to me from his caresses and his hands, and that is enough, Monsieur.'

'No, it is not enough.'

'Then give me your son.'

'You could adopt him if you became betrothed to me.'

'Martin, your intentions are good and I should like you to

come to my aid, but you cannot and must not do it. Have compassion on me and please do not be angry.'

Martin fell to his knees before her. 'Please be my fiancée until you find someone you like better than my father. I will always remain your brother and will give you your freedom at any time. Please let me ask your brother for your hand.'

'No, Martin, that would be deceitful and unjust to you.'

She slipped from her chair into his arms. 'Martin, I only want to weep with you.'

He held her in his arms with the greatest tenderness. 'Weep your fill if it helps you.'

'Martin, let me stay with you like this until tomorrow.'

'That is impossible. We're in the countess's salon.'

'The countess is bearing him a child.'

'And you shall have mine if only you are willing, Claire-Marie. It is also from him, although it arrived by a roundabout way.'

Blanche raised her head. 'But you are also his child, Martin.'

'Yes, Claire-Marie.'

The girl stopped weeping. 'How strange that is!'

'What is strange about it?'

'I have always known and yet never realised it. You belong entirely to him, don't you, Martin?'

'Yes, because he is my friend.'

'Because he is your friend,' repeated Blanche. 'Martin, now I am consoled, although a moment ago I was still sad. Must you really become engaged to me?'

'Yes, if you wish to remain with us. A mock betrothal is not as bad as a deceitful marriage. We need not marry.'

'Do you mean that I shall not be committing a sin before God if I pretend to be betrothed to you?'

'I mean that you have already used so many ruses that you can easily afford another one.'

'But I can never repay you!'

'Give me a kiss on the lips, Claire-Marie, in gratitude.'

Blanche granted his wish. 'You have a far softer mouth,' she said in surprise.

'I am slightly different from him.'

'Now you are laughing exactly as he does. I can only see your teeth because it's so dark in here.'

'Will you become my fiancée?' Martin asked.

Blanche took his left hand and began to fondle it. 'His hands are far more beautiful than yours. Yours are small and firm. He was often good to me and you have always helped. You are very wise and very kind. Do what you think is right, Martin.'

Martin pressed her hands. 'Thank you, Blanche. May I kiss you before you leave, as you have just kissed me?'

'I shall be your fiancée in name alone.'

'I know. I won't kiss you.'

'Are you sad?'

'Not really.'

'You must not be sad. Give me a farewell kiss.'

'Now or tomorrow?'

'Now if you like.'

He embraced her more tightly and kissed her, trying at the same time to control himself. She closed her eyes and instinctively nestled up to him. He felt her lips surrender more and more to his and, in a flash, a burden was lifted from his heart. He released Blanche, who stared at him with terror in her eyes. 'Martin!'

'Yes, Claire-Marie?'

'What has happened to me?'

'I gave you a farewell kiss because you are accompanying the count and countess to Grandval.'

'I want to go home now.'

'I will escort you to your litter.'

'No, no, I'll go alone.'

She jumped up and ran out of the room. Martin waited until he heard the gate close. A few moments later, with four grooms carrying torches, he was on his way to the Hôtel de Salvieux.

Louise de Salvieux was at first surprised and then delighted by M. de Racon's late visit. It was arranged that the marriage contract should be drawn up next morning at the Hôtel de Racon, and that the betrothal should be celebrated. Martin knew that for his sake the count would willingly postpone the journey to Grandval, and he was not mistaken. The count was delighted that the Comte de Salvieux had been outwitted. He ordered the servants to unpack, and prepared for a small celebration. The countess drove to the convent and fetched the strangely disturbed little widow. The marriage contract was then ceremoniously compiled by two lawyers in the count's study, signed by the Comte de Racon, the Comte de Salvieux and the engaged couple. During the ceremony Blanche looked neither at her brother nor at Martin.

That evening at the party, which was suitably modest because of Lent, Blanche sat pale and silent at Martin's side and took scarcely a bite. She kept looking shyly at the count, who pretended not to notice. Next day, with two puppies on her lap, she left the capital in company with the countess. Martin accompanied them part of the way on horseback, and the count trotted on ahead with Marguerite who chattered gaily to him. When Martin bent down from his horse and held out his hand to say farewell, Blanche did not offer hers but merely looked at him without a word and turned away to the countess. Martin galloped off. The pained look in those dark eyes lingered in his mind.

Until Easter, 1681, Martin lived alone at the Hôtel de Racon. He took his midday meal with the Marquis de Chassigny or other friends of the count, who were pleased to have him as a guest. Usually he supped at home, with two or three musketeers of his own age, and then went into society. He had no mistress, and spent all his spare time with the count's regiment because he did not wish to leave the hunchback Nicolas de Chassigny unprotected. This double duty was strenuous and he was a prey to tiresome doubts.

He received no news from Grandval, nor did he write any letters, although he was often tempted to take up a quill and ask his friend for news of his beloved. But as long as the girl still belonged to the count he refrained from doing so. Blanche's kiss and her glance as she left had told him enough, but he had not the courage to woo the little girl's heart away from him. He reproached himself for having confused her, but was at the same time full of hope. A few ladies guessed that he must be unlucky in love and tried to console him. His calm, gentle manner, his stocky, unusually powerful build, his self-composure, made him attractive to experienced women. But even when a pair of lips were offered, he confined himself to a polite hand-kiss.

A week after Easter, Martin took advantage of a rainy day when he had no duties to visit Colonel du Lac and Captain de Falleron. The colonel took him into the orderly room and pointed out to him that the current account books and personnel lists revealed all manner of discrepancies, for which the regiment's commanding officer was personally responsible. The colonel's detailed explanations appalled Martin because, for the first time, a regimental inspection had been ordered by the minister of war and no one knew the exact date. Martin asked the colonel to send a speedy messenger to Grandval, and was relieved to hear that the count had already been notified fourteen days before and had replied that he would appear as soon as possible. The colonel asked Martin to help him convince the count of the seriousness of the position, to stress the importance of certain obligations and make him understand that they had decided to tell the truth to the commissioner, whatever the consequences. Martin promised to do what he could and asked to see Captain de Falleron. He was told that the captain, with several other officers, had been sent on furlough to purchase new equipment. Martin took his leave of du Lac and left the barracks.

While he was mounting his horse in the wet barrack courtyard the croaking voice of the dwarf, Nicolas de Chassigny, rang out from an open stable door. 'Good morning, M. de Racon.'

'Ah, good morning de Chassigny. Are you on stable-duty?' There was loud laughter. Martin rode over to the stable and found several ensigns, who rose to their feet from a pile of straw. 'What are you doing here, Gentlemen?'

'It's like this, Monsieur,' replied de Chassigny, 'we were to have an hour's riding, but both the covered courses are so full that you couldn't make a turn on your hindquarters. The colonel would not give us leave and that is why we are sitting here.'

'Why don't you practise in open country?'

'It's too risky in this wet going.'

'Gentlemen, in war you have to ride in all weathers. Where is Corporal Dallieux?'

'He's gone drinking.'

'How long are you on duty?'

'Until midday, M. de Racon.'

'Well, it's now ten o'clock. I'll take over for Dallieux and give you a couple of hours' practice. Get mounted.'

'Do we have to take orders from a musketeer?' asked one of the ensigns.

'You certainly do,' replied Martin. 'I am still a lieutenant of the Light Horse of the Guard. What is your name?'

'De Vitry, M. de Racon.'

'When did you join the regiment?'

'At Easter.'

'Let me see how quickly you can get into the saddle.' This challenge acted as a spur to both the young gentlemen and the troopers. One horse after the other was mounted in the courtyard. Little de Chassigny managed to be second. 'Was that fast enough, M. de Racon?'

'Yes, Nicolas, but your left stirrup is still twisted. Eight men. Is that all?'

'Yes, M. de Racon.'

'In pairs behind me, forward!' Martin trotted through the puddles out of the courtyard, followed the muddy road for a while and then turned off across the fields at such a brisk gallop that the rain lashed and stung his face. On uneven moorland Martin made them practise turns at the gallop, and Nicholas de Chassigny was particularly skilful. 'Nicolas, you will soon be one of the best riders in the regiment. Your horse appears to turn with you instead of you with the horse.'

'I'm only doing what you taught me,' croaked the little hunchback. 'I use the weight of my hump; according to whether I shift it to the left or right, Toto obeys. Look, M. de Racon!' Nicolas trotted to and fro, delighting the spectators with a little ditty:

'Friend Toto,
Do it so!
Yes, Toto
That's right so!
Clever fellow, Friend Toto!'

But one of the ensigns sang:

'Oh, Toto, oh, Toto!
Whoever can your rider be?
Your rider is a little flea!'

Nicolas took this amiss, wheeled, brought his Toto up to a magnificent levade and threatened the scoffer with a cavalry pistol. 'Who's a flea?' The astonished ensign could find no reply. Nicolas fired and a damp plume fell to the ground.

'Chassigny,' shouted Martin, 'ride back to your place! If I were on duty here I'd make you pay for that quip with a few days under arrest. At the gallop up that slope to the firs! The first to arrive is the winner.' Nicolas sped off. Lighter than the others, he crouched in the saddle like a cat, screaming at the top of his voice: 'Oh, Toto, come Toto,' and arrived two lengths in front of Martin on the fir-clad height. The others followed at various distances. 'Gentlemen,' ordered Martin, 'now down there at the steepest spot, one after the other. Let your horses slide. Lead the way, Chassigny.' Nicolas slid down to perfection. The others followed, except one, whose horse pranced nervously among the firs. 'Ensign Vitry,' called Martin, 'do you ride badly or have you a particularly unruly mount?'

The ensign gave his black horse a thwack with the switch. 'He's a rogue, M. de Racon.'

'All right, I'll change horses with you. Dismount.' They exchanged horses. Martin trotted round a few firs and found that the black horse was as docile as a lamb. Then he shouted down to the young gentlemen who had pulled up below: 'Circle in single file. Now get down with you,' he added, turning to Vitry. 'Loosen the curb and pull lightly on the snaffle. The grey is quite sure-footed. Bend back or forward as you like. I'm not so insistent on riding regulations in open country; the main thing is to keep a straight back.'

'M. de Racon,' said the ensign. 'are you doubting my ability to ride?'

'I'm doubting your courage and am giving you an opportunity of proving you're not a coward. Get down with you.' De Vitry leaned back and the horse slid down the slope. Martin followed, leaning forward on his obedient black horse. 'Stiffen your back, ensign. You're upsetting the grey. Loosen your reins or he will throw you. Steady Phoenix, steady Phoenix!' Calmed by its master's voice, the grey recovered its confidence but as soon as it reached level ground it leaped forward wildly and sped to the other horses, broke the circle and, bucking viciously, threw its rider. The other ensigns burst out laughing and caught the grey. Martin dismounted. 'Hallo, Vitry! Come and get your horse.'

Covered with mud, Vitry picked up his hat which had fallen off and found himself obliged to lead the snorting grey back to Martin who, in turn, handed him the reins of his black horse. 'Ensign, I advise you to report to Colonel du Lac today and ask him to transfer you to the new grenadier company.'

'But I am a nobleman, M. de Racon,' stammered de Vitry.

'The king also demands that his nobles should serve in the infantry, and as a foot soldier and a musketeer I had to do a lot of marching in spite of my rank. You will become an infantryman.'

'That is not up to you to decide, M. de Racon.'

'Vitry, you are an exceedingly poor horseman. I do not wish the reputation of the regiment to suffer as a result of your cowardice and inefficiency.'

'M. de Racon, for this twofold insult you must give me satisfaction.'

Martin's eyes narrowed. 'Ensign, every soldier must be prepared to accept a service reprimand. In consideration for your rank I did not voice my opinion before the others. If you will take your horse once more up the slope and bring it down, I will accept your challenge.' De Vitry clenched his teeth and the two gentlemen mounted their respective horses. The ensign dug his spurs into his mount so viciously that it shot up the slope like an arrow. Shortly before reaching the top it bucked, and a struggle began between the rider and his mount.

The other ensigns laughed uproariously once more. One of them cried: 'The black horse knows what it's all about. That is why he's bucking.'

Nicolas hopped up and down in his saddle with joy. 'Hi, he's lost both his stirrups. He's off!'

'Right about face!' shouted Martin. 'In twos at the trot.' Taking his position at the head of the column, they returned to barracks.

It was not long before the riderless horse caught up the laughing ensigns at full gallop. 'He's reporting,' croaked Nicolas. Martin looked round and saw ensign de Vitry limping after the column, and turned off on the main road. It was now raining harder.

At this moment a troop of light horse came towards them. With a cry of joy Martin spurred his grey, galloped through the puddles and drew up in front of the Comte de Racon, who greeted him surlily: 'Ah, so you're still alive, Lieutenant de Racon.'

'Monsieur, for a number of reasons I could not write, but I am delighted that you are back. How are the ladies?'

'They are well. Get your nag out of the way. I don't want to get soaked through.'

'Are you riding to Paris?'

'No, to Rome, as you see.'

'So much the better. I'll ride with you to Rome. Gentlemen, ride back on your own and tell the corporal I shall be here on Friday, at eight o'clock, on duty.' The ensigns trotted past and saluted. Martin took up his position on the count's left side.

At this moment they caught sight of the limping, mud-stained de Vitry. 'What is the meaning of this, Martin? That's de Vitry.'

'That's right, Monsieur.'

'Why do you allow him to return on foot through the mud?'

'It was his own fault and he deserves nothing better.'

'One of the others should have let him ride behind him. He belongs to a very noble house and his father paid me an enormous sum for his position.'

'Even if his father paid you a million, he would never make a light horse officer . . . maybe a dragoon.'

'Attend to your own duties with the musketeers and don't interfere with my regiment.'

The count turned round. 'Charles!'

'M. le Comte?'

'Take the pack-horse to the ensign over there. Tell him to get on it and return it tomorrow to the Hôtel de Racon.'

'Very good, M. le Comte.'

The count trotted on again swiftly. 'Martin, Colonel du Lac

is delighted with you, but I'm not. You must be polite to your peers.'

'I refuse to consider either their rank or their wealth, Monsieur. Whatever I do is in your interest. How do you stand with the forthcoming regimental inspection?'

'To hell with Louvois! Du Lac wrote me an urgent letter to Grandval. The minister of war's impertinence to the nobility surpasses all bounds. A pox on the lying swine!'

'In any case,' Martin replied curtly, 'Louvois is a capable servant of the king. Without him the army would consist of lazy country squires and dishonest colonels who would keep back their men's pay or put down on paper the names of more soldiers than they really possess. Do you propose to catch fifty-two vagrants and thrash them overnight into light horsemen, or are you going to turn your grooms into men of straw?'

The count pulled a wry face. 'You seem damned well-informed.'

'I am, Monsieur. Du Lac took me into the orderly room, showed me various lists and account books and implored me to pester you until all these discrepancies were put right. Everyone fully realises that you will look for a scapegoat if the inspection turns out badly for you, but du Lac is not prepared to be a scapegoat and cannot be bribed.'

The count was speechless. 'Half your officers,' continued Martin, 'turn up for duty three times a month at the most. All the work is left to the colonel and the corporals. Where will that end? I have noticed this for some time now, but since it is like that in all the regiments in peace-time I have never mentioned my vexation before. You must put matters right immediately. It's different with the musketeers; every man is at his post and the slightest unpunctuality is heavily punished. Can I be of any assistance in collecting the fifty-two missing men?'

'No, thank you, Lieutenant de Racon. Chassigny will lend me fifty-two dragoons.'

'He will be taking a risk if he does so.'

'Don't worry. The war minister's commissioner has already visited him.'

'But suppose he recognises the heavy dragoon horses?'

'For God's sake, keep your mouth shut!'

'When are you going to pay the men the money which has been owing since February?'

'I've attended to that.'

'Thank God! Did you make Grouchet impress some recruits from your estates?'

'Yes. The fellows are on their way here on foot.'

'Monsieur, I could turn them into horsemen in fourteen days if I were seconded from the musketeers.'

'I have plenty of corporals who can teach them to ride.'

'Have you given the colonel enough money to renew the harness and uniforms?'

'Yes.'

'Really enough, Monsieur?'

'Another word and I'll clip you across the ear!'

'I've outgrown your methods of education.' Martin trotted as though by chance through a puddle, so that the count was splashed.

'Clumsy oaf!'

'I'm sorry, Monsieur.'

'From tomorrow I shall be with the regiment every day and train them myself,' said the count. 'Is it true that you recently took the Falleron squadron over the jumps in wet weather and lost a couple of horses?'

'I only lost one horse Monsieur. The other recovered. I replaced the injured horse at my own expense.'

'Are you in debt?'

'No, there was no reason for it. I can easily last out till June.'

'You're becoming an unbearable paragon of virtue, Martin.'

'Only to compensate for you.'

'How did the mistresses fare during Lent?' asked the count.

'The Maintenon came through with flying colours but Montespan will soon be finished.'

'That's good. How long is your leave?'

'Until five o'clock tomorrow morning. My company has to accompany the king on a hunt.'

'I'm glad you told me. I will join the company and wait upon the king.'

'I thought you intended to be with the regiment every day.'

'And I thought to find a pleasant friend in you and not an unpleasant schoolmaster.'

'Monsieur, on your account I have been terrified by this regimental inspection.'

'The danger is not nearly as great as you imagine.'

'Are you sure?'

'Absolutely.'

'Thank heaven!'

'It's pouring down for all it's worth,' said the count, shaking the rain from the brim of his hat.

'Monsieur, stop at an inn in the next village and wait until it stops raining. It's growing brighter over there.'

'That's a good idea, Martin. Except for my backside, I'm wetter than the wettest field-mouse. Hi, Pierre! Ride on ahead and order something for us to eat in the next village.'

As soon as the count had changed his clothes in the warm parlour of the inn, he sat down with Martin by the fire at a table on which the landlord had already placed a pitcher of mulled wine. They both drank several tankards, while half a sheep was turning on the spit. The count leaned back and stretched out his legs, 'I feel fine now, my boy. Tell me what you do when you're off duty?'

'What they all do in Paris in Lent.'

The count's eyes began to glitter. 'Have you been observing the latest fashion of fasting?'

'No more than you have.'

'You look as if you've got the wasting sickness. Have you yearned for your pretty little bride?'

'Monsieur, it is stale news to me that I always appear foolish to you. Let's talk about something else.'

'I'll talk about what I like. Blanche gave me a letter for her future bridegroom.'

'Give it to me,' said Martin, flushing.

'I don't know where I put it.'

'Pierre!' called Martin. 'Bring M. le Comte's wet coat.' The valet put down the glass and obeyed. To the amusement of the count, Martin searched the various pockets without finding the letter. 'You've lost it, Monsieur.'

'No, I put it in the pocket of my hose.' It was found in his wet breeches and Martin read the unsealed letter:

MONSIEUR,

Your little son no longer has the scabies and is the prettiest child in the world. Everyone here takes me for his mother. I have seen to this so that the child need not be hidden away. This is agreeable to Mlle d'Epponcourt, the Comtesse de Racon and the count, and presumably will be to you. If it isn't, I am very sorry. It is far more beautiful at Grandval than in Paris. We call your boy Léon, unless you decide on another name for him, because he roars like a lion. The countess says that none of her children ever made such a din and none was so lusty. She sends you her regards, and I send mine as Claire-Marie-Blanche.

Martin put the piece of paper in his coat.

'A sweet little letter, isn't it?' asked the count.

'An enchanting letter. How long is she remaining at Grandval?'

'Until your marriage, my boy.'

'Don't talk rubbish.'

'Talking of rubbish, there's the salad. Let's eat.'

'Monsieur . . .'

'Don't ask me until I've eaten. I have something to tell you.'

'What?'

The count stuffed his mouth with salad and a soft-boiled egg.

'You're trying to put me off.'

'Hm!'

'You gobble your food like a wolf.'

'Hm!'

'You might at least leave some for me.'

'Here you are!' No sooner had the salad bowl been emptied than Martin repeated his question, but the landlord brought in the soup. This was followed by a dish of mutton and cold ham. The count's hunger was now appeased and he wiped his mouth. 'Well, my boy, I won't tease you any longer and I'll tell you what you want to know. You are aware that I have fallen in love with my wife. That I am still in love with her must be something of a novelty to you. I would have brought her here had not old Borel raised the very devil. All right, let her recover. I went through all this once before at Grandval, and suddenly remembering the delicious widow to whom, in your chivalry, you have become betrothed, I paid her a late visit . . . Why have you turned so pale?'

'I haven't. Please go on.'

'I wanted to take my pleasure with her, but she would not let herself be kissed and begged me to do anything provided I spared her lips. I thought she must have bad teeth, but it was nothing of the kind. I grew suspicious, then obstinate, and asked for an explanation, until the tears began to flow, and you know how much I care for that, and then out came a confession. Can you guess what she said?'

'How should I know?'

'Have you no inkling?'

'You are a malicious devil.'

'She said that you had kissed her when you said farewell and that she could not forget it. I must not be angry with her, and so on and so forth, and she did not know what was the matter with her. Well, I knew all right and I told her.'

'What did you say to her?'

'That she was in love with you.'

'She opened her eyes like cartwheels and refused to believe me.'

'What then?'

'Then? Are you really interested in the "then"?'

'Very much so.'

'I've nothing more of any importance to tell you.' Martin caught the count by the arm.

'What did you do to the girl then?'

'That couldn't possibly interest you. Let go my arm!'

'Monsieur, if you do not tell me immediately what you did with my fiancée I'll throw you off that bench on to the floor.'

'Oh ho!' The table fell over and the innkeeper rushed in. Roaring with laughter the count ran out into the rain, followed by the infuriated Martin. The count let himself be caught beneath the roof gutter and pushed Martin under the spout. 'Are you cooled off now, my boy?'

'You're the basest knave I've ever met.'

'Please don't push me in the mud before you know whether

you're in the right. I treated the little girl like a daughter and finally put an end to our old relationship.'

'Is that really true?'

'If you don't believe me, I'll put it in writing.'

'Monsieur, you're the best friend a man could have!'

'And I'll have you know that you're the most stupid.'

'Forgive me.'

'I shan't forgive you the epithet "basest knave" until to-morrow.'

'No, now!'

'Well, come inside, it's too wet out here. Let's have some wine.'

After they had sat down at the table again and paid for the broken crockery, the count continued his story. 'I fled from Grandval because I couldn't cope with three beautiful females. The d'Epponcourt girl has all the local males on a string and will not allow Blanche a single admirer. That must please you! Blanche and Madeleine are hand in glove. The whole castle is teeming with children. Each time I entered the salon I could be certain that children were flitting about behind the curtains. They squatted under the tables and oozed out of every door. If I grew angry I was treated as a brute. Blanche began whimpering and Madeleine started weeping.

'Finally, one day, Blanche was playing the lute to me in the park; Madeleine sat beside her sewing babies' napkins, and six lackey's brats were leading your offspring round in circles. Only one thing remained, flight. But had I not received a letter from our good du Lac, I should still be at Grandval today. What can you know of the sweetness of a full-blown woman? Each night is precious because each day she grows a little older. And I, ass that I am, sit here! I disregarded her lips for nine long years! Martin, I'll send for her, or I shall ride back to Grandval. If Pierre doesn't find me a handy trollop this evening I shall lose my wits.'

'You seem to have lost them already.'

'I admit it. What about you? How do you feel without Blanche?'

'According to what you told me, she's still unaware that she loves me. I must wait.'

'How can you stand that?'

'You have accustomed me to a lot.'

'I?'

'Yes, Monsieur, you. You are a devil's spawn, but on occasion you can be wonderfully decent and I would let myself be flayed alive for you.'

'And in the meantime you call me names. Come on, let's be off to Paris. Mount your horses, lads.'

But the count had no occasion to send for his wife or to visit her at home. His regiment came through the inspection with flying colours and was immediately despatched to the eastern frontier. Martin's company of musketeers also received its marching orders. No one knew the king's plans and the entire Christian world turned its eyes uneasily towards France, where the most brilliant army in Europe was massing.

Then, at the end of September, 1681, Louvois suddenly appeared with 20,000 men and heavy guns before the city of Strasbourg, and on the 30th of that month occupied the obsolete fortress without a shot being fired. Law was on the side of the king, too, for his legal advisers had discovered that in the olden days Strasbourg had belonged to France.

The emperor and the princes of the empire held a different opinion. Europe trembled. Was his most Christian majesty a greater menace than the Turks? Did he intend to restore the realm of Charlemagne and set himself up as the emperor of Christendom? Fear made the princes join forces. Louis insisted that he had no further territorial claims and was careful not to launch a war prematurely, but he held Strasbourg and withdrew only part of his army from the frontier.

On 1st December 1681, Martin's year of service with the musketeers ended and, at his request, he was released to join the Comte de Racon's regiment, which he reached after many detours. The count was on his way to his new winter quarters in the formerly Spanish Franche-Comté. He was delighted when Martin arrived, and since, in his opinion, the regiment could do without him, he decided to ride to Grandval via Paris. He left the dependable Colonel du Lac in charge and, for the two of them, the successful but bloodless campaign was over.

In Paris they found a pile of letters which, because of their constant moves, had not been forwarded. The countess's last letter to her husband contained the words: 'You will be delighted when you come home.'

The count, in addition to his own, read Martin's letters from Blanche, without learning what he longed to know. Blanche kept Martin informed, like a true guardian, of his son's progress, never forgot to send her regards to the count as his devoted little daughter, and always insisted that she was completely happy at Grandval. Four long letters told of Marguerite's brilliant marriage to a nephew of the Comtesse de Racon, a Huguenot, who, after the ceremony, sold his estates and left France with his wife and fortune to join the army of the Elector of Brandenburg. Martin gave a sigh of relief. The count took him to Court, where the king bestowed an order upon General de Racon and promoted Lieutenant de Racon to captain in his father's guards regiment.

The 3rd January 1682 was drawing to a close when one of Master Grouchet's huntsmen sped through the village of Grandval in the direction of the castle. The road was ankle deep in snow. A horseman awaited him at the entrance of the avenue. The huntsman shouted that the count was on his way, and the horseman spurred his mount and galloped off to the gate. The huntsman rode towards the forest and gave his chestnut a rest. It had begun to snow.

A little later, the count and Martin reached the village. On their fast horses they had outstripped their grooms by a couple of miles. 'Martin, if they haven't learned of our arrival in the village there will be hell to pay.' At the first house they met an old man carrying a bundle of straw. 'Hi, you there! Don't you recognise me?'

'M. le Comte is back!'

'How are things at the castle?'

'Well, M. le Comte, well.'

'What does that mean?'

'Things are well, we are told to say.'

'Who the hell gave you orders to say that?'

'Madame la Comtesse ordered it.'

'How is Madame's health?'

'All is well, M. le Comte. All is well.'

The count raised his riding crop. 'Stop,' cried Martin, 'can't you see they are preparing a surprise for you at the castle,

Monsieur? The missing huntsman obviously had orders to announce us. Curb your impatience and let us ride on.' The count spared the old man and spurred his dappled grey into a gallop. 'Slow down, Monsieur,' laughed Martin, 'or we shall take the ladies by surprise.'

'All right, you slow down, you cold-blooded fish.'

The count sped along the long avenue and was obliged to halt at the closed gate. Martin found him cursing and threatening the watchman, who blamed the early darkness and cautiously opened the gate. The count galloped up to the steps, dismounted and, entering the hall before Martin, stood there as though dazzled.

The countess, surrounded by children carrying candles, came slowly down the steps in a gold brocade dress. She was carrying a cushion, and out of its white lace a baby's dark head could be seen. A few steps behind her came Blanche in a silver lace dress, a twelve months' old child dressed in red in her arms. He crowed and gurgled as he stretched his little hands out to the flames. The bright light of the candle merged with the bluish dusk, lending a softness to all their faces. The count rushed up the steps: 'Madeleine, what have you brought me?'

'Your son, the Vicomte de Clarmont.'

Martin had remained in the hall. He saw Blanche look at the happy couple, turn her blushing face to him and approach carefully with her burden. He went towards her. 'Is that my child, Claire-Marie?'

'Yes, this is Léon.'

'Can I hold him?' asked Martin. The baby began to kick.

'Yes, Monsieur, but you must take your cloak off first because it's full of snow.' Martin cast aside his grey cloak and Blanche handed him the child, who immediately clutched at the gold braid on his uniform. 'He's not in the least afraid of you. Isn't he beautiful? He has your eyes and mouth, and under that bonnet he has light brown curls which stand up from the forehead like yours. I look after him entirely on my own.'

'Thank you for your letters, Madame.'

'Why did you only write me six letters?' she asked.

'I did not know whether you would care to read my letters,

and I found all yours together on my return to the Hôtel de Racon.'

'Oh, that is a pity.'

'Yes, Madame, a great pity. I should have liked to write to you far more often.'

'So should I, but I was afraid that my nursery gossip might have bored you. Were you often in danger?'

'Not once.'

'Oh, and we trembled so much for you.'

'I thought of you every day, Claire-Marie,' Martin said gently. Blanche turned round.

'Martin, they have gone and I did not even greet him.' The lighted candles still stood on the white flagstones and the lower steps. Through the tall windows the twilight gleamed a tender blue. Then old Denis appeared on the landing with a candle. 'Monsieur Martin, M. le Comte asked me to tell you that he will eat with his wife in the salon.'

'Thank you, Denis.'

'Goodnight, Monsieur. Goodnight, Madame.' The old retainer disappeared.

'We've been locked out, so to speak,' said Martin with a smile. 'Where shall we eat tonight?'

'I don't know. I've always eaten with the countess. There is no fire in the dining-hall.'

'Madame, may I suggest that you eat with me in the count's study?'

'Monsieur, Léon has begun to cry.' Martin quickly held the child away from him. 'Léon,' cried Blanche, 'you are a naughty boy. Martin, we must get him in the warmth. It is far too cold for him here. He very rarely wets himself.' She took the child from him. 'Come Martin. I'll show you his little cot.'

Martin followed her as she hurried ahead of him up the stairs into a room which, with its yellow bed-hangings and luxury, unconsciously reminded him of the actress Amaryllis. A canary was whistling and hopping about in a brass cage. In front of the fire stood a carved gilt cradle, a little copper bath and several silk cushions from which Blanche's puppies jumped up.

Blanche silenced her pets, laid Léon on his cushion and

proceeded to undress him. 'Martin, isn't it a beautiful cradle? When he's a little bigger Gaston will use it, for the moment he has an even smaller cot. Look, Léon hasn't got a blemish. Doesn't he look like an angel?'

'Yes,' said Martin, far more interested in Blanche's charming activities.

'Please be careful that he doesn't crawl over to the fire. I'm going to fetch clean clothes for him.' Martin knelt down beside the small pink child, who smiled up at him. The baby caught hold of his hand and began to crawl up his leg. 'If you hold him steady,' Blanche cried, 'he can walk already.'

But Martin put the little boy down and stood up. 'Madame, I should like to change. Will you excuse me for a moment?'

'Gladly, Monsieur. Wait a moment, would you like to eat here tonight with your little son? I have no salon, but this is a beautiful room and my table is large enough for two.'

'Have you often received guests here?'

'No. Whatever makes you think that? I always receive my visitors, as Mlle d'Epponcourt does, in the salon, and Madame la Comtesse is always present. I did not think you would object.'

'What should I object to?'

'To eating in this room. Would it not be seemly?'

'Why shouldn't it be?'

'You look so stern,' said Blanche shyly. 'Perhaps you'd better give orders where the meal is to be laid.'

'Please have the table laid here, Madame. I shall be delighted to be your guest.'

Since the servants had not yet arrived with the baggage, Martin returned after an hour in a riding-coat. Blanche was sitting by the cradle. 'Please remain seated, Madame. I heard you singing. What was the song?'

'Only a lullaby, M. de Racon. My darling is already asleep and the food is over there. I have fed him and bathed him and now he's asleep.'

'I should like to hear the lullaby. Please sing it again.'

'Yes, but you mustn't look at me, it makes me shy.'

'I'll look at Léon.'

Martin sat down on the other side of the cradle and noticed

that the bird-cage had been covered with a cloth. Blanche began to sing:

'Go to sleep my baby,
The donkey's asleep in its stall
Sleep has closed the brown cow's eyes
Baby please close yours!

Go to sleep my baby,
Maria's rocking the Jesus child
Rocking it in a lily cup
Baby close yours too!'

The canary, under its cover, blithely trilled an accompaniment to the song.

'You have such a tiny voice,' said Martin, 'that it seems to come from afar, from over there where the stars are twinkling.'

'Monsieur, supper is served.' They sat down at the table by the light of a three-branched candlestick. Blanche tried to serve Martin, but he would not permit it.

'Madame, I will help myself. May I give you this piece of breast?'

'No, I prefer the drumstick.'

'You'll get greasy behind the ears.'

'I will be very careful, Monsieur.'

'Where are your puppies? Here is something for them.'

'I've given them to my maid. He did not like dogs in the bedroom.'

'I am not he, Claire-Marie.'

'Shall I call Chou-Chou and Cymbeline?'

'No, don't trouble. This partridge is good. 'Neither of them spoke for a while. Blanche ate very little but Martin was ravenous. When he had satisfied his hunger, he took his napkin and turned to his hostess. 'Madame, will you allow me to wipe your face?'

'I have just tried to do so myself.'

'You haven't been very successful. Please keep still.' Martin moistened his napkin and cleaned Blanche's cheeks. 'Now that you're clean again, may I give you a kiss of greeting?'

'No, you'd better not. Martin, he did not even notice me,

but tomorrow I will kiss him on both cheeks as well as on his hands.'

'Yes, as his daughter you can do that.'

'Thank God.'

'Claire-Marie, what is the matter all of a sudden?'

'Oh, nothing.'

'Why the tears then?'

'Martin, you can't imagine how happy I've been.'

'And now your happiness is over,' he added, 'because it was too great.'

'Yes, Martin.'

'That's often happened to me. It doesn't hurt for long.'

'It hurts terribly.'

Martin took a pastry from the dish, only to replace it immediately. 'Madame,' he said, 'he told me that you loved me. I will tell him he was mistaken, and one day he will visit you again.'

'No, Martin.'

'Yes, Claire-Marie.'

'He knows me as Blanche.'

'Claire-Marie suits you better. You carried my child down the steps as the Virgin Mary would have carried the Infant Jesus.'

'Madame la Comtesse looked like the madonna, not I.'

'You were my madonna and you will always remain so for me.'

'I wanted to bring something too.'

'For that I thank you, Madame.'

Martin looked over to the cradle. 'I should now take my leave, but please let me stay a little longer.'

'Forgive me,' whispered Blanche.

Martin went over to her. 'What have I to forgive?'

'That I cannot make you happy.'

'Does that grieve you?'

'Yes, Martin.'

'Madame, for my sake, try not to be sad.'

Blanche's face puckered and her lips began to quiver. 'Martin, I am torn in two.'

'What do you mean?'

'Perhaps he was not mistaken.'

'In what respect?'

'That I love you.'

'You!' Martin's plate clattered to the floor.

'No, Martin, no!'

'Please, Clarie-Marie, give me your lips, your lips only, for I shall know by them whether you love me or not.' Blanche began to hit Martin with her small fists until he recoiled. His eyes were clouded with pain and his features distorted by passion. Blanche bit her fists and cried as if she herself were in pain: 'You mustn't look like that.'

'Madame, forgive me. It will soon have passed.' He tried to pour himself out a glass of water and inadvertently knocked over the glass. Blanche picked it up.

'Martin!'

His eyes, now calm, met hers. 'What is it?'

Blanche's face was as white as the tablecloth. 'Martin, I must know for certain. Please kiss me.' A few seconds passed before he took her in his arms again. He gave her a long kiss as he had done in Paris, and, as before, her lips began to yield and soften to the touch of his. When he released her she clung to him. 'Martin, Martin, don't send me away. I shall die if you send me away.'

'I will marry you, Blanche.'

Blanche gave a start. 'Martin, I am being unfaithful to him. I thought I should still love him, as though from heaven, but now I remember what he did to me and it no longer affects me.'

'Blanche, my little Blanche!'

She buried her face in his lace jabot and, nestling against his shirt, became aware of the scent of his linen and grew calmer. He made no attempt to disturb her. At last she said in a bright, very clear voice: 'Martin, you can do with me what you will.'

'Do you really mean it?'

'Yes, Martin.'

'Claire-Marie, as things are today you must promise me one thing.'

She looked up at him. 'What, Martin?'

'That in the future you will only look upon my father as a daughter and that you will be faithful to me.'

'I will never deceive you. and I will be the Comte de Racon's daughter.'

'Give me your hand on it.'

Blanche sat upright in her chair and offered him her small hand which he grasped, only to release it immediately. 'And now, Claire-Marie, shall I go or stay?'

'Stay! Tell me what I must do?'

'Do?'

Blanche grew embarrassed. Rising to her feet, she said: 'Let me clear the table.'

Martin also stood up.

'I will help you, Blanche.' They put the crockery outside the door and returned to the room.

'There is a terrible smell of food in here,' said Blanche. 'Can I let in some air, or do you think it will be too cold?'

'Yes, let us have some air. In the meantime I will stoke up the fire.' Martin bent down to the grate, poked the embers and laid a beech log on them. Blanche opened the window and then began to rock the cradle. When Martin stood up he caught sight of Blanche's huge, gleaming eyes.

'I have a new ballet dress and have practised a new dance without a teacher. Shall I dance for you, Martin?'

'No, please don't.'

Blanche lowered her eyes. 'I wanted to dance in the salon for him after supper, and now we are here.'

'Blanche, am I such a bad substitute?' Blanche looked up again. Her dark eyes were moist and frightened.

Martin went over to her. 'Blanche, be honest with me. Would you prefer to be with him now?'

In her fear she held fast to the cradle. 'Yes, now that you ask me.'

'Blanche, I cannot drive him out of you! Let us be brother and sister again and kiss no more. Let's say goodnight now, Blanche.'

'Martin, Martin . . .'

'Blanche, we're torturing each other. It's ridiculous.'

'Martin, why didn't you tell me what to do?'

'My God, Blanche, what am I to say to you?'

'He always told me. I shall certainly disappoint you if I do not know what I have to be like, and that makes me afraid.'

'I only want you as you are,' Martin said softly.

'What am I like?'

Martin peered into the cradle at the sleeping child. 'Blanche, I shall have to wait until you're grown up and can give me your hand like a queen in a beautiful regal dress and in a church full of burning candles.'

'Last summer I had my seventeenth birthday.'

'That is too young for marriage.'

'But the countess was sixteen when she had her first child,' said Blanche with surprise.

'Then she also was too young, and so was I when I had my first experience of women. I desired their bodies and understood nothing of their hearts; and in the Comte de Racon you were looking for a tender father, not for a man. You could only bear the man because of his kindness, even though you grew accustomed to his passion.'

'How do you know that, Martin?'

'I am already twenty-three,' said Martin with a smile.

Blanche looked at him with boundless respect. 'If you prefer, I will gladly wait until I am twenty so that I can love you as a grown-up woman.'

'And until then will you renounce all tendernesses?' Martin asked, as seriously as possible.

'No, not all of them. He allows me to sit on his lap and kisses the tip of my nose. Will you kiss me from time to time?'

'As a second papa?'

'No, as my brother.'

Martin laughed loudly, caught Blanche by the shoulders and kissed her heartily on both cheeks. 'Blanche, you silly goose, why should we turn our backs on our past? A moment ago I did not kiss you as a brother, and you were not a little sister nestling against my shoulder. Let us love each other as best we can.'

'But you said . . .'

'Blanche, in a few years you will become my queen, whether you are my little mistress or my sister.'

'Martin, the snow is blowing into the room.' They hurried over to the window and were enveloped in a cloud of whirling snowflakes.

Martin closed the window and tried to draw the curtains,

but Blanche caught him by his hands. 'Please leave it open, otherwise it will be quite dark in the early morning. It does not grow light until after seven. What shall I . . .'

'You must do absolutely nothing, but we will now undress for a wager. The winner is the first to be in his nightshirt.' Martin was quicker than Blanche and leaped with a cry of triumph on to the bed, while Blanche was still unfastening her last petticoat. He took off his shirt, made himself comfortable and said gaily: 'Do you want any help?'

'No, Martin.'

Blanche kept on her shift and placed Martin's clothes in a tidy pile.

'Will you finish your tidying before dawn?'

'Martin, I've suddenly got so many things on my mind.'

'Come here and tell me about them.'

Blanche approached hesitantly and sat down on the end of the bed. 'Martin, in the Marquis de Chassigny's castle there was a picture of a fair-haired girl sitting next to a sunburned youth on the grass. The boy had wings like an angel, and a butterfly had settled on the girl's hand. I always wanted to sit like that one day with a friendly boy, and often stood in front of the picture. One day the marquis found me standing there, caught hold of me and carried me off. After that, I could not bear to look at the picture and no longer hoped for the boy. His face was rather like yours and he had broad shoulders like you. I'm afraid I'm not pure enough for you.'

'I have been a far greater sinner than you,' replied Martin calmly.

Blanche's expression was full of entreaty. 'Martin, I should like a lot of candles and sanctity and Father Tulier's blessing, so that I could come to you without sin.'

'Are we not sanctified by our love?'

Blanche did not avert her eyes. 'I want all the sanctity there is.'

Martin suppressed a sigh. 'Blanche, I will ask the count to arrange a most sacred marriage for us as soon as possible. If I know him, he will invite a lot of guests and the preparations will last two months. Can you wait as long as that?'

'Yes, if you agree.'

Martin swallowed his disappointment. 'Fortunately, I'm

rather tired. May I sleep here?'

'You can always sleep here,' said Blanche with a blush.

'Thank you for the honour. I will only do so again on the night of our marriage.'

'Are you angry with me?'

'If I did not know you, I might think you were making me dance on a string. But I know you. Goodnight, little Blanche-Claire-Marie.'

'Martin . . .'

'Please don't speak, I'm tired.' Martin settled down to sleep and Blanche lay down beside him. She listened to his breathing and sensed that he had now fallen asleep. Her wide-open eyes stared into the room. The candles on the table had half burned down; the gilt carving on the cradle gleamed like metal. The silver lace dress hanging on a hook shone as though spun from moonlight. The fire crackled and spluttered, throwing up red sparks and gradually subsiding into embers. Somewhere in the castle a clock struck eleven. The silk curtains of the magnificent bed billowed like a yellow cloud.

Then Blanche sat up carefully and bent over the sleeping man. Martin had turned his face to the wall. She could hardly distinguish his features and his brown hair looked almost black. Blanche ran her finger through a few strands, bent down lower and smelt his hair. Martin moved and turned more over on one side. In the faint light of the candle Blanche could see the scar on his shoulder, and could not refrain from stroking it. His skin was warm, dry and smooth and the scar was slightly prominent. Blanche removed her hand as though she had burned it, slipped away to the edge of the bed and tried to sleep. She changed position several times without being able to get comfortable, and inadvertently brushed Martin's leg with her foot. She drew back with a start, settled down at last and found that the rhythm of their breathing was in harmony. She began to enjoy the echo and followed the sleeping man's breathing until she grew calm and finally fell asleep.

Towards midnight a faint cry came from the cradle. Blanche awoke, stood up and looked over at Léon, who was kicking happily and babbling in his baby tongue. The canary was twittering in reply. Blanche felt his napkin and tidied the bedclothes. Léon gurgled with contentment and began to suck his thumb. She rocked him a little and then glanced at the sleeper.

Martin was lying as before, half turned to the wall. Blanche took a small silver candlestick, lit it from another candle and knelt on the bed with the light in her hands. The beam of the candle lit up Martin's handsome face; one ear was peeping out of his brown healthy hair. She observed him for a long time and forgot to pay attention to the candlestick. A drop of hot wax fell on the arm of the sleeper. Martin opened his eyes and looked in surprise at Blanche, who was numb with terror and embarrassment. He rubbed his arm and went back to sleep. Blanche knelt there motionless for a while, before replacing the candle on a stool at the end of the bed. Then she lay down cautiously beside Martin and nestled close to him. 'Why are you doing that, Blanche?' he asked. She could find no reply. Martin turned towards her. 'Why did you lean against me?'

'I was drawn towards you.'

He chucked her under the chin. 'And yet you want to wait until our marriage.'

'I only wanted to feel you near me as I went to sleep.'

'Blanche, your warmth disturbs me, we can't remain like this. I should like to make up for what has been done to you and would rather do it now than wait till Spring.'

'Martin, if I get passionate the snow will soon cool me down.'

Martin laughed aloud. 'Oh Blanche, I shall have to join you in the snow, because I am beginning to burn. I will return to my bedroom.'

She put her arms round his neck. 'Stay here, Martin.'

'I can't, Blanche, otherwise I shall burst into flames.' Gently he tried to release himself from her arms, but she would not let him go.

'Martin, I cannot be alone.'

'Blanche, it is wrong to torture someone you love.'

'You only arrived today and you mustn't leave already.'

'Please, Blanche, let me go. I shall certainly be more than two weeks at Grandval and I will take you out every day in a sleigh and we'll ride to Château Fleury. I will teach you how to ride.'

'I don't want to wait any longer.'

'Is this night holy enough for you?'
'Yes, Martin, yes.'
For a few moments he peered intently into her eyes to test the truth of her reply, and his restraint melted.
'Martin . . .'
'What is it?'
'Oh, Martin, how can you ask?'
'Tell me what you want to say, Blanche?' he whispered into her hair.
'Ever since I was born I have been waiting for you.'
'I know that, Blanche.'
'You know it?'
Beneath her enchantment he felt her desire surge towards him and lifted his head so that he could see her face. She was radiant in her surprise. 'You are as handsome as before, your face has not grown dark. You are still gentle and you love me as I love you.'
'Now you are happy.'
'Martin, you are an angel.'
There was a twinkle in his eyes. 'No, Blanche, angels don't do such things.'
'Everything seems so right, you and the night and myself.'
'Yes, Claire-Marie.'
'Oh, Martin, to think that this could be!'
Martin, wholly intent upon giving Blanche the most perfect happiness, succeeded, in spite of his youth, thanks to his strength matched by exquisite self-control.

The count laughed heartily when he heard of the betrothed couple's happiness. The countess considered that their conduct was unseemly and begged for a speedy wedding. But the count insisted that he did not like things done in a hurry. He advised Martin to end his nightly visits before dawn, if possible, and to steal back to his room without a light. He sent for a builder to start on the alterations to the façade and interior of Château Fleury, and supervised them himself. He invited guests, enjoyed his hunting and was preoccupied with preparations for a magnificent feast, purposely forgetting the Court and his regiment of light horse.
Louis de Salvieux paid a surprise visit to Grandval, offered

his congratulations on the birth of the Vicomte de Clarmont and, in view of the changed conditions, demanded that his sister's betrothal to M. de Racon be cancelled. Blanche appeared on Martin's arm and declared that she recognised his guardianship, as before, but should he make any difficulty she would not shrink from admitting publicly that she already had an eighteen-months-old son by her future bridegroom. Louis was terrified of public malice, knowing that any damaging rumour would be believed, although there was no proof. He gave his consent once more, but took his revenge by considerably reducing the dowry. This infuriated the Comte de Racon. Martin, seeing the danger of a squabble between the two men, threatened that he would renounce the dowry entirely, whereupon the count immediately became reconciled with Louis.

On 14th May 1682, in the early morning, the five hundred guests left the castle hall by the terrace on which the sun had cast its first rays. Through the flower beds in full blossom they made their way across the park to a huge open marquee, where the altar from the castle chapel gleamed with a host of candles. The Comte de Racon led the bride, whose white dress glittered with diamonds, to the altar. The Marquis de Chassigny escorted Martin. The jubilant voices of the choir joined the orchestra in solemn hymns, and the music mingled with the twittering of birds and the firing of the small cannon presented as a wedding gift to Captain de Racon by the ensigns of his regiment. When Father Tulier in a moving voice pronounced his blessing Blanche swooned, overcome by the solemn magnificence of the occasion. Martin carried her through a press of women to a flowery arbour where, bedded on cushions, she soon opened her eyes.

Martin left her to recover with her maid and Mlle de Lange, and returned with the ladies to the open-air church to attend the christening of the young Vicomte de Clarmont. The baby, who was given the name of Gaston Louis by his father and his godfather, the Maréchal d'Humières, behaved better than little Léon who, a fortnight before, had been privately christened Léon Gaston and had yelled at the top of his voice.

After the ceremony, the parents and the happy couple received the congratulations of the guests on the terrace. Blanche clung to Martin when the Marquis de Chassigny, after kissing her hand, maintained that she was the loveliest bride he had ever seen, but that he could not understand how it was possible that she bore such a striking resemblance to a little dumb girl whom her husband had also known. Martin replied with a smile that nature was occasionally pleased to jest. The resemblance did not disturb him, but it could not be very pleasant for his wife to be compared to a girl who had been bought and sold. The marquis apologised and made way for the Comte de Montignon, who was waiting to congratulate them next and had meanwhile been listening attentively.

Strains of music could be heard from the dining-hall, and after the last congratulations had been offered, the Comtesse de Racon gave her hand to the Maréchal d'Humières to open the ball. Blanche was still feeling weak after her fainting fit but, like the countess, who was once more expecting a child and since April had constantly suffered from fits of giddiness and vomiting, did not dare display weariness. The count had ordered both ladies to be present for the duration of the feast, and considered the fact that his daughter-in-law had swooned as an intentional breach of good manners. He was tireless in entertaining the guests and delighted in giving them surprises. They sat down to eat in the dining-hall while lightly-clad nymphs, to the delight of the gentlemen, splashed in the fountains and were chased by brown-skinned fauns from which they fled in terror. The Marquis de Chassigny ate standing up, in order to have a better view of the performance, and was delighted when one of the fugitives tripped out of the park into the hall and asked him of all men, for protection against the savages. All the gentlemen roared with laughter and their host was delighted at this successful jest.

At two o'clock in the afternoon, everyone drove or rode to the river and sailed in brightly painted, beflagged barques downstream to Château Fleury, which stood, pink and white with its gilt weather-cocks, on the steep bank. Filled with curiosity, they climbed up to the terraced gardens, admired the beautiful panorama, and were received at the gate by a host of pretty farm children offering drinks and pastries. The count showed his guests the five newly appointed rooms and received many compliments on his good taste and appreciation of the fine arts. The ladies were asked to decorate the brightly coloured bridal apartment with spring flowers which stood there ready in baskets. The gentlemen were encouraged to enjoy shooting pigeons which were released from cages from the upper terrace. Wagers were laid and everyone admired the skill of the hunchback Nicolas de Chassigny who never missed a bird.

The horns sounded the departure and the guests found their horses and coaches ready. The count ordered the coachmen to drive as quickly as possible and galloped on ahead with some officers of his regiment. Martin rode his grey beside the coach containing his wife and the countess. The road had been so well laid that no coach-wheel broke and the ladies hardly felt the jolting. A maypole had been erected in each village through which they passed. Children ran after the procession as far as they could, or fought for the silver coins which little Madame de Racon threw to them from a basket. The fruit trees were in bloom; the evening breeze bore away their scent and ruffled the corn and the treetops. The peaceful river glistened brightly in the setting sun.

At Grandval they sat at table until late into the night, and later watched a ballet and a fireworks display. Then the couple were escorted by a host of slightly drunken gentlemen and rather shrill ladies, with torches and lanterns, to a two-seater coach. Martin lifted his bride into it, seized the reins and, followed by a troop of grooms, drove through the dewy night to Fleury.

THE LADIES OF GRANDVAL

THE count had given orders that the guests were to be received by the newly married couple the day after the marriage, at Fleury, and to be given a banquet. The barques were ordered for half past ten and the coaches and horses for eleven o'clock.

The young couple rose early in order to supervise the preparations. Tables were laid on the garden terraces and swings erected. The count's cook with his assistants came from Grandval, and hurled a copper kettle against the wall because the pots were not large enough and the firewood was too green. A fast messenger rode back to Grandval. Blanche did her best to console the steward's wife, who had completely lost her head. Martin quarrelled with the gardener, who refused to cut down the box hedges on the centre terrace, and explained to him that five hundred people had to have room to eat. Tempers rose, but by ten o'clock everything was ready.

Martin joined his wife on the upper terrace. Wearing a brightly coloured dress, she watched for the arrival of the barques. 'Come down to the river, Madame. We shall be less disturbed there.'

Blanche reflected for a moment. 'He wants to see us walk down the steps to receive the guests.'

'We'll run up the side steps,' replied Martin, 'as soon as the trumpets sound. Come, Claire-Marie.' She gave him her hand and climbed down the many steps from terrace to terrace to the river stairs, which descended into the sunlit water. They sat down together on the grass. Blanche leaned against Martin and sighed. 'I wish the guests were not arriving until this afternoon.'

'You should be pleased that we do not have to return to Grandval tonight. Has your maid started to pack?'

'Yes, Martin. Last night, little Gaston was slightly feverish and the countess was terrified. Léon screamed when I went to see him. His bath-water was far too hot. Those nursemaids are all so stupid! What'll happen if Gaston is seriously ill?'

'Don't excite yourself before you know what is the matter with him. Perhaps he's well again already. He was admired far too long by the ladies and handed from one to the other. Small children cannot stand that.'

Blanche bent down and picked a drifting branch of blossom from the water. 'Martin, the countess asked me to come to Grandval should the children need me. For Gaston's sake I would willingly wait for the departure of the guests and follow the count two days later.'

'I will ask his permission.'

Blanche pressed his hand. 'Martin, after Gaston's birth the countess said that I was her support and solace. Can she do without me in her condition?'

'Don't you want to go to Court with us?'

'I want to be with you always, and also near the countess. She could have forbidden me her house the first time I met her at the Hôtel de Racon. I have a duty to her and I love her very much.'

'Blanche, you won't be so selfish as to wish to remain at Grandval?'

'No, but without me she fears for Gaston. Léon was much sturdier at his age. Gaston is as thin as an eel and simply will not put on weight.'

'He takes after his father,' laughed Martin.

'That's what I said, but the countess is perpetually worried. She trembles if he only sneezes. Following my example, she wants to put on his napkins and bathe him herself; she fusses over him far too much. As soon as she picks him up he gets moody and angry. I'm afraid that if I go to Court I shall constantly have a bad conscience.'

'And if you were to remain here?'

'Then I should constantly be longing for you. What shall I do?'

'Must I give you my advice again?'

'Yes please, Martin.'

Martin threw a pebble into the water. 'If you had learned to ride, I should say: come with me and ride on a fast horse to Grandval in my company from time to time, but since you are so timorous and won't trust yourself on the most docile horse I advise you to nurse your bad conscience, for the countess would not be able to bear a whining daughter-in-law.'

'But would you like to have a wife with a bad conscience?'

'Don't let me see it.'

'Martin, I acted as a counterweight to Dr Borel when you were both at the war. He kept saying that he could no longer take the responsibility and needed a younger doctor to give him a hand. As though the count would ever tolerate a younger doctor in the house! The old man's fear was infectious and made everyone tremble. Apart from me, she only had gloomy creatures about her: the two old ladies-in-waiting, Madame d'Ouville with her asthma, Father Tulier who preached her a sermon every evening, and Dr Borel with his spectral dotard's face. I was the only one who had the courage to banish those croaking ravens from her room.'

'You're a little queen!'

'I'm only afraid of horses, Martin. Won't you let me stay with the countess till winter?'

'Blanche!'

She slipped down a step and embraced his knees. 'If I can't bear it any longer without you, I'll come to Paris under Master Grouchet's escort.'

'No, I forbid that, for the king does not remain the whole year at Versailles but travels with the Court to Fontainebleau, Blois or Marly. You must not follow me about like an adventuress. I would rather remain parted from you for months on end.'

'Can't you visit me every few weeks for a few days?'

'Have you seriously made up your mind to remain?'

'Yes, Martin.'

'I have even greater cause to be grateful to the countess than you have,' said Martin, looking over the glistening river. 'I will visit you as often as the count allows. Come and sit at my side again so that the hem of your dress won't get wet.'

Blanche did as she was bid and asked softly: 'Can you give me any advice as to how I can be happy without you?'

Martin hesitated for a moment. 'I'll tell you something

about my life,' he said at last. 'The count gave me his friendship when I was fourteen. I loved him so much that I always wanted to be with him. He did not care for that and sent me for a winter to Master Grouchet at the hunting lodge, and for a year and a half to the dragoons. At first I could hardly bear it for homesickness, but then I helped myself by directing my love to soldiering. I told myself that I was a soldier for his sake, and my melancholy left me. I wrote him many letters.'

'I'll do the same, Martin. I will look after the children and, in my love for you and them, the world will remain bright as it is now and the countess will be happy.'

A blast of trumpets rang out. They jumped up quickly and ran up the steep, shadowy steps. When they reached the castle and saw the gaily-beflagged barques drawn alongside, they descended hand-in-hand, with all the dignity of a princely couple, to receive their guests.

The day passed to the complete satisfaction of the Comte de Racon, and Martin plucked up courage to inform him of Blanche's request. He showed understanding, gave his consent and allowed his friend to spend a week with his wife at Fleury. They both thanked him and asked the countess whether she and the children would stay with them for this period. The countess agreed and on the following day, after the guests had gone, accompanied by Dr Borel, Emilie, the nurse, the nursemaids and the children, she drove to Château Fleury where she received an enthusiastic welcome and was given the magnificent room with the balcony.

A month later, Martin, as a captain of the light horse of the guard, took over a squadron composed of twenty-five well-born ensigns. Following in Raoul and Guy's footsteps, he appeared at Court and took the greatest pains never to disappoint his friend and father. Although by nature he was no courtier, by his intelligence, charm and understanding of his fellow men, he managed to find favour in high quarters and was universally respected. He kept away from all intrigues, never divulged secrets, banished boredom, and disarmed malice by a friendly jest. The Maréchal d'Humières described him as a perfect gentleman whose rise could be prevented only by insufficient ambition.

The Comte de Racon was aware of this failing, but for some strange reason never showed any displeasure. He used to say that it was enough for an ordinary mortal to be recognised at Court and to remain in favour; everything else lay in the hands of God. Martin knew that this hypocritical remark concealed the count's considered intention not to lay a heavier burden on his son's shoulders than he was capable of bearing. Remembering the sufferings of the first Vicomte de Clarmont, Martin was very grateful to his father.

One hot August morning, Blanche sat in the park at Grandval with little Léon in a wicker hammock slung from an elm branch. A liveried boy pulled the rope, so that the hammock swung higher and higher, and Léon began to scream with delight. Blanche's flimsy dress flew in the air. Her feet touched the branches and her shadow travelled over the gravel. The boy suddenly shouted: 'Here comes M. de Racon.' Blanche let forth a little cry. The boy brought the swing to rest, hoisted Léon on his shoulders to give him a pickaback and make him forget his interrupted pleasure. But Léon began to scream until he could be heard at the main gate.

The travel-stained Martin ran to his wife, who in turn ran through the maze of flower beds until he sprang over the last hedge that parted them and took her in his arms. 'Blanche, he has sent me here for a whole month on duty!'

'For a whole month, Martin!'

He kissed her. 'I have brought my squadron of twenty-five ensigns, who will all pay Court to you. Where is the countess?'

'Over there in the arbour.'

'Take me to her. Is that Léon yelling?'

'Yes, but it's only temper. I know him. Do I have to greet the gentlemen immediately?'

'No, they haven't arrived yet. I'm at least five miles ahead of them and I almost killed my horse getting here. You're prettier than ever, although I've covered you with dust. Take my arm. As soon as I've carried out my commission I'll wipe the dust off your dress.' Blanche took his arm and they walked over to the arbour. The countess stepped out. Martin bowed and handed her a letter with her husband's greetings. When the countess asked to be allowed to read the letter on her own,

Martin took Blanche away. Léon had stopped yelling because his nurse had begun to swing him again. The countess broke the seal of her husband's letter, and read:

MADAME,

I regret that I cannot greet you in person, and hope that you and the Vicomte de Clarmont are in good health. You will be having soldiers in the house, for Martin is riding to Grandval with his twenty-five ensigns to train them in my woods. Furthermore, ten Huguenot weaver families will be arriving; they were forced to leave Chassigny's villages. I do not intend to give them a permanent asylum, but I am expecting to reap a benefit from them. They are to teach my serfs cloth-weaving, but at the first sign of a Huguenot persecution they must disappear from the county.

I forbid you to have any personal contact with your co-religionists but you may give them some monetary aid. Above all, I wish you to behave as though the arrival of these exiles came as a surprise. You must take them in as though without my knowledge. The thought of employing them as weavers is your idea, not mine. On your instructions, the steward will buy looms and install them in the barns. Should you meet with any resistance, Martin will see that your orders are obeyed. He has been informed. Discuss the matter with no one. The Huguenots came to you on a mere rumour. They heard of a compassionate Huguenot, the Comtesse de Racon, and will beg you to give them shelter. Make what arrangements you like. I am expecting letters from you and Father Tulier, which I shall answer forthwith. I shall agree to your proposal of using the weavers as instructors. Destroy this letter, and go on making every effort to come to terms with the Catholic faith.

I am waiting impatiently for the Autumn, and shall then visit you as soon as you are well again. Each line you write gives me pleasure and, despite our long parting, I think of you with tenderness. Why were your last letters so formal? Have you heard anything about me which has offended you? Do not believe any rumours, or else forgive me. Please go on entrusting your thoughts to me. It is possible that I understand more than you would give me credit for, and do not understand much that you believe me capable of doing. Even when you are close to me you remain unattainable. Draw closer to me by your letters and do not cease to love.

YOUR GASTON.

The countess kissed the signature and hid the letter in the folds of her gown. She left the arbour and walked along a pergola, where she found her two old ladies-in-waiting. She asked Mlle de Lange to go to the castle and order twenty-five beds to be arranged in ten guest rooms. There would be twenty-six more places required in the dining-hall, and a banquet was to be given that evening in honour of M. de Racon. Mlle de Lange walked away and the countess continued her stroll with her second lady-in-waiting. She passed a lawn surrounded by flower beds, where little Gaston was sleeping under a parasol. The nurse was sitting some way off in the shade, sewing. The countess then followed a little gravel path that led to the statue of Flora. Then she saw the branches of some bushes moving slightly in the still summer air and turned off along another path with a smile.

Martin was kept busy in Grandval until the end of September, and did not return to the count's regiment with his ensigns until after the looms had been installed and little M. de Brayonne had arrived. The countess was so weak that, on Martin's earnest representations and written pleas from Blanche and Dr Borel, the count cancelled his planned visit and did not return to Grandval to inspect his estates until Spring 1683, when the countess had already left for a spa. Blanche took the place of the absent châtelaine with great grace and dignity. The count called her the little lady of Grandval and was delighted every morning to receive her greeting because, without paying the slightest attention to his mistress, she embraced and kissed him with all the naturalness of an affectionate daughter.

Deprived of her husband's ardent attentions the countess made a speedy recovery, thanks to invigorating baths, continual rest, and the pleasant knowledge that her children were under the care of a daughter-in-law who understood more of the little ones' health than the most experieced nurse. Once her strength had returned, she was able to travel at midsummer to Brayonne, from where the count rode out to meet her. Dr Borel implored her to deceive her husband as to the state of her health for at least six months. She pretended to acquiesce, but his advice fell on deaf ears. They remained for the hunting in Brayonne, drove back to Grandval and from there to Paris. On Christmas day the countess announced that, since October, she had been expecting a third child, and the count showered her with presents.

These years of peace had done much to increase the prosperity of France. Louis XIV was at the height of his power, while the crumbling empire was now hard put to it to resist the attacks of the Turks. On 12th September 1683, however, Vienna was liberated by the Polish King Sobieski, and Louis saw his secret ally faltering. With swift determination he invaded the Spanish Netherlands with a well-equipped army, taking one fortress after another.

One fine afternoon in June 1684, when the count's regiment of the light horse had reached the fortress of Luxembourg, the two ladies of Grandval were busy writing on the castle terrace under a canvas parasol. The countess, propped up by cushions, lay on an upholstered bench, while Blanche sat in a high chair at the table. Nearby stood a little wooden pen, in which the eighteen-months-old M. de Brayonne was crawling about with his toys. A lackey was driving the four-year-old M. de Fleury, the three-year-old Vicomte de Clarmont and three small servant's children round the fountain in a pony cart. Two of the nursery-maids were laughing and gossiping. In the distance, Father Tulier could be seen engrossed in his breviary. Blanche was writing to Martin with a white goose quill:

> DEAREST MARTIN,
>
> I pray for you each day to your guardian angel, and to his angel for him, and to the Holy Virgin for the Comtesse de Racon. I do not fear for either of you, although you are at war, but my fear for the countess grows each day, and yet she must not be allowed to see it. If only you could have been with us when little Armand came into the world! You

have such a soothing influence. Now everyone is afraid. Prayers are being said for the countess in all the village churches, and Father Tulier says two Masses every day. Dr Borel creeps about the castle like a bird of ill-omen. When I ask him if the countess's constant fluxes are dangerous, he merely shrugs his shoulders. If I leave the children too long with her, he looks so angry that the little ones begin to whimper. The countess must always recline, whereas, before Armand's birth, we were allowed to drive her about. I am very disturbed. Recently, she has had to use a litter which looks like a stretcher. A "reclining litter", they call the contraption. What do you think of that?

And yet she is gay, and seems to grow gayer each day. Her eyes shine as they have never done before. If only I could take away at least a part of the pain that lies in store for her. Do you remember the way she once clutched your hand in terror? What am I to say when she asks for you? Why does she have one child after another and I have none? Can you understand the will of God?

I have all manner of things to confess to you. I have given Father Tulier my entire dowry to build a church, so that he can fulfil his life's wish and leave the countess in peace. He has been very stern since he received a letter from his bishop. He said to her, in my presence, that the bishop had asked whether he was making progress with her conversion, and he deeply regretted that he would be forced to reply in the negative. The Edict of Nantes afforded almost no protection any more to the Huguenots, and in many places there was a law disinheriting children of mixed marriages. She could see, therefore, that her heresy not only imperils her soul but threatens the earthly happiness of her children. They were terrible words! She turned pale and began to tremble. I asked the priest to leave, and accompanied him out of the room. I told him that he had frightened the countess in her condition and that it was an evil thing to have done. He replied that when it was a question of saving a soul, one could have no consideration for a body. He could have said many things which would have terrified her even more. Then I offered him my dowry for building his church and this seemed to pacify him. He promised to write an evasive letter to the bishop and to spare the countess. When I returned to her bedside, I found her calm and resigned. She said that she had recommended her children to God and feared no more threats. God would protect her children.

Persecution of the Huguenots has started throughout the province, but it is still calm in the Racon country. In Grandbourg a Dominican monk was flogged when he tried to preach against the Huguenots. Father Tulier fears the direst consequences. Each day refugees beg for protection and work at the looms. I give the people money and send them on their way. Father Tulier says that the count would have them chased off the property with dogs. That, he added, would be cruel but more intelligent. The reception of the Huguenot weavers had been a great sin, although the count had only given his consent out of avarice. Every unrepented sin would bring its own retribution.

Father Tulier wants to use a meadow between the elm avenue and the castle village for his building site. He has commissioned an architect to draw up the plans and is sending three preliminary sketches for the count's approval. Martin, the count must give his consent to the building of the church, and bear half the cost. My dowry is only enough to pay for the architect, to buy the stone and build the foundation walls. Stones are being brought here and wood is being cut in the forests. Tell the count that this is vital for his sons' succession rights. I know that he will curse and pay. Please ask him to forgive me for being so independent. I am doing it for his wife and children. I know that you won't be angry with me!'

Yesterday evening, the countess, with a calm expression on her face, told Father Tulier that he should exercise a little patience. After her delivery she would free herself from the ties of her church. Father Tulier congratulated her, and said he could see by her serenity that she was on the verge of true salvation. He would inform the bishop and add a prayer of thanksgiving to his prayers for her health.

Martin, I know that you cannot come here and I do not wish to sadden you with useless pleas, but it would be so much better if you could be with us at this time. Everyone seems to rely on me. When I laugh, every face brightens;

when I am serious, they are all clouded. I must constantly appear to be of good cheer and radiate calm.

The three boys are my joy. Since Léon likes spinach, I recently gave Gaston a spoonful. He looked furiously at me out of his slanting eyes and instead of swallowing, blew out his cheeks and spat it out all over my dress. I shall never give him spinach again! Imagine the countess finding him more beautiful than fat little Armand, whose chubby angel-face is far more engaging! She constantly asks: 'What is Gaston doing? How is Gaston?', and she finds his great naughtiness charming. Léon's nostrils are still quite round, I'm afraid that one day he will stick peas or stones in them and I never let him play on the gravel. At the moment he is driving with Gaston in the pony cart. Now he wants to splash about in the fountain. That is forbidden, and he has begun to yell and to hit his nursemaid. Madame looks anxious. My God, now Gaston has begun to scream. Farewell, I must go to the children . . .

Blanche placed her silver inkwell on the letter, so that the wind would not blow it away, jumped up and ran down the terrace steps. The countess's eyes followed her and noticed her giving Léon a slap and picking up the Vicomte de Clarmont. The screaming ceased. Blanche sang a little ditty. The nursemaids took Léon by the hand and began dancing with him and the other children. Blanche danced with Gaston and then with all the others together.

The countess smiled and looked at the pen where the little M. de Brayonne was now sitting peacefully on a pale green cushion. She waved to him and calmly re-read the letter she had just written:

MONSIEUR,

Father Tulier will be writing to you about me, so I shall refrain from mentioning the subject he will discuss. Instead I must thank you for the great patience you have always shown as regards my faith. Through Emilie I have heard of their conversion methods, which would fill me with fear and disgust did I not know that nothing can happen to men unless it be God's will. We should not pity the martyred but those who torture them. I know what you are capable of doing, and my gratitude knows no bounds. Before our marriage you promised me that you would respect my faith and you have always kept that promise to me. Your patience has now begun to bear fruit. I will confess to you that I have begun to free myself from the rigidity of my belief. I began to wonder why people consider creeds so important. I have come to reflect much and look on some matters as trifling, while others are of supreme importance. Christ is more than any creed, more than the Bible, and everything resides in God. Monsieur, I would not say this to anyone except to you. Possibly it is heretical. I have heard and read so much about divinity that my head is in a whirl, and now I have to discard it all before I can hope to realise what I really believe.

The boys are well-behaved and healthy. Claire-Marie is as happy as a little bird. She checks the account books for me, so that I have hardly any work left to do, and has recently been sleeping in the next room to mine so that she can be near should anything untoward happen.

My period of waiting is sweet. It means waiting for your letters and waiting for the birth of your child. You write that you fear for me and beg me to forgive you. What have I to forgive you, Gaston? My happiness? I do not understand you, and will tell you something which perhaps, in turn, you will not understand.

I have realised that one can only be just to a human being if one takes the trouble to judge each case on its own merits. When two different people commit the same misdemeanour, one sins differently from the other, he sins more or less, or does not sin at all. Then good deeds, too, weigh differently in the balance. When a spendthrift drops twenty francs, into a beggar's hand, it is little. If a miser parts with a few copper coins, it is much. If a robber spares a man, he is credited with having done a good deed; whereas it is taken for granted that a just man should behave generously. Perhaps you will by now have discovered in me a talent for preaching? Anyone who has to listen to two sermons a day must finally be able to preach.

Gaston, I beg you never to worry on my account. Since I

found you again in Paris I have become happier every day. I feel that I am on my way to a happiness that is growing too great for me. Recently I came across an heirloom, a Venetian goblet, and wanted to drink golden-yellow wine from it, but when I filled it it broke. It made me smile, and I shook the drops off my hand into the air.

Farewell! And grant me a place in your heart when you think of me from time to time. Those are your own words, Monsieur, and because they are beautiful I close with them.

YOUR MADELEINE

At this moment, Blanche came up the steps carrying a bunch of roses. 'Madame, the children have been taken into the shade because they were getting too hot.' She bent over the pen, took up the little boy and called to the nurse from the dining-room.

'Dorette, Armand has soiled himself. How often have I told you that you should keep your eye on him? When he gets red in the face you must put him on the pot. Take him indoors with the cushions, clean him and then bring him back here.' The nurse disappeared with M. de Brayonne.

Blanche sat down on her chair. 'Madame, I am going to write a few lines quickly. Shall I send your regards to Martin?'

'Yes, greet him affectionately from me.'

'Madame, "affectionately" would be a dangerous word to use, for the count always purloins my letters from Martin's coat when he is asleep.'

The countess smiled. 'I will send him my regards in my own letter. When are Grouchet's men leaving?'

'Tomorrow, before daybreak.'

'Have the shirts been wrapped up in double canvas?'

'Yes, Madame. I have perfumed them well, so that the scent will remain until they are unpacked. May I go and seal my letter?'

'Yes, my child.'

'Madame,' said Blanche, 'Martin will find a rose-petal this time. Would you care to send one in yours?'

'No, Claire-Marie. Such pretty thoughts do not suit a woman of my age.'

'But you are loved so ardently.'

The countess blushed a little. 'All the flowers in the park would not suffice if I could send them to him in the field.' Blanche went into the castle with her letter and the bunch of roses. The countess folded her hands and listened to the voices of the children behind the hedge in the park. Then she heard a slight rustle, turned her head and caught sight of old Borel standing in his black, shabby robe in the doorway, looking pale and fragile. With a smile she told him that she had no need of a restorative. He bowed deeply and retired. The pregnant woman looked out again across the bright park. Red roses were blooming in all the beds and arbours. The fountains glittered in a spray of diamond drops. The limbs of the statues gleamed as though made from snow, against a green background of trees and cut hedges.

Four days later, Blanche was in her bedroom writing to Martin. In spite of a handkerchief held to her eyes, the tears dripped on to the paper.

MARTIN,

The Comtesse de Racon died early this morning. Please, Martin! Please, Martin, come home!

I will tell you everything. After she had given birth yesterday to the little boy, she asked to see him. The child was washed and shown to her; she touched him, called to me and said: 'Claire-Marie, this child is to be christened Martin, and Martin is to hold him over the font.' I was full of hope, but Dr Borel was whiter than wax and immediately sent for new bandages. She began to bleed. Martin I could not help. I ran to Father Tulier and made a vow. The priest came to her room, but Dr Borel stood outside the door and shouted that he would admit no black crow, even if they burned or excommunicated him. He was like a madman in his drooling terror and would not stand aside. I begged Father Tulier not to take his words amiss, for, after all, it was his duty to do everything in his power to save his mistress. He had to spare the countess the least excitement. Father Tulier said that he, too, had his duties and was sorry for the Comte de Racon's children. At this he turned on his heel and left.

I went with Dr Borel into the countess's room. She was awake and asked the meaning of the quarrel outside the door. The doctor said it was nothing. When she insisted upon knowing the truth, I told her. She looked kindly at Dr Borel and thanked him for his services. As long as hope remained, she said, right was on the side of the doctor. When hope began to fade, the claims of the priest would take precedence. Father Tulier could come in, and she asked that her daughter-in-law and Dr Borel should be present. I sent Denis for the priest. Dr Borel remarked that he had given me credit for more loyalty. The countess overheard him and begged me to sit on her bed. I wept. 'Do not grieve too much on my account,' she said. 'Believe me, the moment I cease to breathe will be the right moment, decreed by God. I can die in peace for I have left the man I love three living children who will be cared for by a beloved daughter and protected by a beloved son.'

When Father Tulier entered she turned her bright blue eyes on him and said, in a weak but clear voice: 'I told you that after my delivery I would free myself from the bonds of my former faith. I now cease to be a Huguenot, and confirm to you in all earnest my true belief as a Christian. I believe in God and his justice. I believe in the crucified and the resurrected Christ and in his support. I believe in the Holy Ghost who illuminates man with the truth. You decide for yourself, Father Tulier, whether my creed complies with the demands of your church. Do not demand any oaths or vows of me. You have known me and you know of my life. Weigh in your own mind what you remember of me, and leave it to God to judge my sinful soul.'

'Do you dare to die in a state of sin?' boomed Father Tulier. 'I trust in God's compassion,' was the answer. 'He will punish me beyond my strength.' The priest stood there like a tower, tall, stout and black, and looked down at her. I trembled for her. 'Have you nothing more to say to me?' he asked. Her face lit up with a smile. 'Yes, Father, just this: the light appears in the darkness and the darkness grows aware of it.' Father Tulier did not reply. He made the sign of the cross over her, turned away from the bed and ordered candles to be lit, then slowly left the room.

Emilie and the ladies-in-waiting came in and wept. The countess spoke to them: 'My dear friends, Madame de Racon will care for you.' They both came over to me. I embraced them and bade them be calm. Then I caught sight of Dr Borel. He could hardly stand up. I led him to a chair and said that he had the right to sit down. The countess asked for a drink and Emilie brought her some fruit juice, which she drank. Then she wished to say farewell and ordered the doors to be opened. The candles were lit. Father Tulier came in in his robes and stood by her head. Everyone filed past to catch her eye, and went away weeping. Until evening the serfs and tenants with their wives and children, many from the remotest villages, came to see her. Dr Borel had to close the doors several times and, on each occasion, to re-open them at her request. I brought her the children and allowed them to stay there as long as they kept quiet.

When it grew dark she fell asleep, and the doors were closed. Dr Borel did not dare disturb her rest. Father Tulier prayed loudly until she opened her eyes again. She whispered the names of her dead children and no longer recognised me. The priest asked her if she were now ready to die in the true faith. She moved her lips and fell once more into a doze. Father Tulier administered the last rites then left the room. At midnight I heard drops falling to the floor. When I saw blood seeping under the bed I lost consciousness. Dr Borel revived me. I prayed until the sun rose. Then in my heart I felt a tiny stab, and, when I looked up, Dr Borel said: 'Madame la Comtesse is dead!'

Martin, I cannot write to the count. Tell him that his three little sons are well. I shall wait for you.

CLAIRE-MARIE

Once the Luxembourg fortress had fallen to the arts of Vauban and the courage of the French troops, Louis deemed it advisable to let the terrified countries of Europe revert to peace once more. He proved his wish for peace by offering armistice terms, but his generosity met only with distrust and irreconcilable hatred. The negotiations dragged on till August. Louis lost patience and threatened new terms far harsher than the previous ones. The princes then accepted the first offer in all haste. His demands were met and a part of his troops withdrew to France.

Martin and the count returned to Grandval at the end of August, and found many changes. Blanche and the two ladies-in-waiting were in mourning. The Comtesse de Racon's coffin stood in the crypt between the large and the small coffins of her children who had died in infancy. Dr Borel was no longer alive. He passed away in his eighty-sixth year, a few days after the death of his mistress. Father Tulier had grown thinner and led the life of an anchorite. He told the count that he had informed the ecclesiastical authorities that the countess had died in the true faith. He had been offered a living, but had refused to accept any reward. The count promised to complete the building of the church without delay, and returned Blanche's contribution to Martin.

The Comtesse de Racon's funeral took place with great pomp, in the presence of many guests. On the following day, the ceremonial baptism of the third little son took place. Martin held the child over the font. Baptising the little Martin was the last office performed by Father Tulier. He begged the count to appoint his successor, and never left his room again. The count remembered d'Oubray, discovered his whereabouts and offered him the vacant post. The worldly abbé immediately travelled to Grandval and became confessor and spiritual adviser to the de Racon family. His tolerance gained him the favour of his patron and the sympathy of M. de Racon. Father Tulier died that winter and was buried beneath the altar of the new church, which had already been given a roof. The count toyed for some time with the idea of marrying again but, since his three late-born sons were obviously flourishing, and little Madame de Racon showed herself capable of carrying out the duties of a châtelaine, he contented himself with beautiful mistresses, whom he changed with great frequency. He deemed it necessary to inform the Court of his late wife's conversion, and accepted congratulations and condolences with an expression perfectly befitting each emotion.

At Fontainebleau, in October 1685, his most Christian majesty solemnly revoked the Edict of Nantes, and by so doing ratified a general witch-hunt against his Huguenot subjects, who had so far only been subjected to local persecution. His object was to reinforce the political unity of his kingdom with a single Christian faith. The sudden revocation of the edict fell upon the unsuspecting Huguenots like a bolt from the blue. Many of them were so terrified that they renounced their faith at once, but others, despite the royal ban, tried to escape to protestant countries. Thousands managed to flee, thousands were forced by torture to recant, and thousands died for their faith.

The Comte de Racon commissioned a picture for the altar in the new church of Grandval, portraying the conversation of his wife by the late priest beneath an enthroned madonna. The Comte de Montignon, however, did not remain idle and quite openly expressed his doubts as to the lady's conversion, in order to seize the succession rights for his sons according to the new law. The Comte de Racon was quite prepared for such an attack, and wrote to his cousin that he was willing to take the matter before the Courts. He thought it only fair, however, to inform him that he had written proof of the dead woman's conversion, that he knew of the Montignon's Huguenot grandfather, and that he himself had a youngest son in M. de Racon. The latter had been legitimised by the king; his well-born mother was a catholic by birth and he could, therefore, by the king's favour, at any time become the Vicomte de Clarmont. Gérard de Montignon assessed his own position in comparison with that of his cousin, had qualms about his ancestors, and forthwith admitted in writing that his suspicions had been sadly ill-founded.

The Marquis de Chassigny left the service when ordered to use his dragoons to convert stubborn Huguenots. Martin had the incredible audacity to mention to the king the 'dragonades' he had with his own eyes seen carried out in a village. The monarch was outraged. He had been led to believe that the conversions had taken place at the subjects free will and as the result of real conviction. Louis issued orders that the dragonades were to cease immediately, and that the distasteful matter was never to be mentioned in his presence again. His order was carried out in places where the interest of the authorities coincided with his will, and ignored elsewhere. The atrocities continued.

Martin saw himself suddenly surrounded by enemies at Court and suspected of being a free-thinker. He was incapable of defending himself against the sly insinuations of his accusers, received a scowl from the king, and approached his father for support. The count ordered him to make public atonement. Martin refused. The count sent him to Brayonne and told the Court that he had banished his disobedient son to a lonely hunting lodge, where the stern spiritual adviser of the house of Racon would drive the youthful fantasies from his head. Martin travelled by way of Grandval and then, with his wife, the four children and M. d'Oubray, to Brayonne. He spent a few happy weeks there until the count summoned him back to Paris and to his regiment.

IN THE BLACK FOREST

WHEN Louis XIV saw that his enemies, who had gained in strength in their struggle against the Turks, were about to ally themselves against him once again, he decided to anticipate their moves and to prepare for war. Louvois introduced the bayonet to replace the pike used by the infantry, and foresaw a great success for his innovation. By September 1688 the king's armies were in complete readiness; a strong force, commanded by the dauphin and the Maréchal de Duras, launched a surprise invasion of their opponents' unprotected frontiers. They made quick progress, as the enemy troops were still largely engaged in fighting far from home in the Turkish war.

Late one evening, in a downpour of rain, the light horse, serving as vanguard to the infantry regiments, reached their headquarters in a Black Forest village. General de Racon sat down to table with some of his officers in the parlour of a farmhouse, and after the meal discussed the next day's march over a map. Colonel du Lac expressed a wish to give the tired horses a day's rest, but the general replied that he wanted to leave the rain-soaked forest as quickly as possible since it afforded no protection against an ambush. Colonel de la Porte-Mury shared the view of the regimental commander. Du Lac said sourly that he hadn't seen a glimpse of an enemy, but if the Comte de Racon wanted to play for safety it would be advisable to rest for a day, so that the grenadier regiments could catch up with them. The distance between the vanguard and the main army was five miles too great.

De la Porte-Mury replied that du Lac had presumably forgotten that the king had ordered his army commanders to carry out the operations with the utmost despatch. Du Lac, swallowing his anger, replied calmly that on manoeuvres one gave precedence to the gentry, but in war-time one listened to the advice of old campaigners. The general brought the argument to a close by saying that they would have a rest in two days' time. He added jestingly that he knew Colonel du Lac from many bloody campaigns and was looking forward to seeing the Vicomte de la Porte-Mury under fire. The last campaign with its interminable sieges had afforded little opportunity for battle.

The two colonels were reconciled. The count ordered a double chain of sentries to be posted round the village, gave the password and ordered Captain de Vitry to attend to the supplies of oats and hay. At five o'clock in the morning the trumpets would sound the advance.

After the officers had taken their leave, the count retired into the kitchen of the commandeered house where Pierre had erected his camp-bed near a roaring stove. The regimental doctor rose from a stool. 'Listen,' the count said to him, 'your pills are muck. The pains in my back are no better, and if I can't get on my horse tomorrow I'll have you hanged.'

'I beg your Grace to have patience. It takes some time to get rid of lumbago. I've ordered you rest and warmth, but your Grace insisted upon riding in the rain. You could easily get inflammation of the kidneys.'

'I already have pains in my kidneys and I'm freezing cold. Where's the mulled wine?'

'Spiced wine is very dangerous because it heats the kidneys. I've had an infusion boiled for you.'

'A tisane? That would be the last straw! Pierre, go and find Major de Racon. Listen, you quack. Tell me the truth: am I seriously ill, or not?'

'Your Grace is ill and you need rest.'

'Stop talking to me about rest. Give me some stuff to take away these pains.'

'There is no such thing, your Grace.'

'Go to hell then!' The doctor retired. The count paced up and down, until Pierre returned with the news that the gentleman was still busy finding billets for his squadron. The count asked for his lute, but when Pierre took it out of the haversack both the wood and the strings were found to be damp. In his annoyance the count returned to the smoky room, while Pierre prepared the wine the doctor had forbidden.

Soon, Martin entered with François, who retired after taking off his master's damp cloak. 'How are your pains, Monsieur?'

'Better, my friend.'

Martin placed his sword and pistol on a stool, removed his red coat and said: 'You have a hellish fire there. One could roast an ox on a spit over it. Does it have to be so hot, or can I open a window?'

'I can't stand an open window.'

'And I can't stand the heat.'

'Are you annoyed about anything?'

'Monsieur, once again you've sent Vitry to requisition, although you know that he ferrets about for hidden gold and incites the men to look for booty. We should win over the populace instead of infuriating them.'

'Martin, your eternal grousing against Vitry is getting dangerous. He thinks I refused to promote him to major because of you.'

'Monsieur, I should find it very strange if an inefficient man were allowed to jump a rank which capable officers had honourably held for many years.'

The count sat down stiffly on his bed. 'Remember, you were appointed captain and subsequently major of the guards by the king in person, whereas Vitry's father paid for his son's commission.'

'A major's rank cannot be bought!'

'I shall agree to Vitry's promotion so that, with his powerful connections, he won't be a danger to you after my death.'

'Don't talk as though your death were imminent. You're looking for another bribe, that's all.'

'Martin, we're not alone.'

'Monsieur, Pierre is mulling the wine and cannot hear.'

'My boy, don't take it amiss that I have no money to spare to help your further advancement. I want to keep you near me for a while. As soon as you're a colonel I shall lose you.'

'So that's it! But I have always longed to command a regiment.'

'Patience, my boy. In this campaign I shall offer you an opportunity of distinguishing yourself in front of the

Maréchal.'

'Really, Monsieur?'

'Do you really think I will disgrace myself with Vitry?' With a sigh of relief, Martin sat down on a chest. 'You needn't begrudge him his title,' added the count with a smile. 'As soon as he commands his own regiment as a colonel, his inefficiency will become so apparent that it will earn him an honourable discharge.'

'I shall look forward to that,' replied Martin. 'Pierre, what are you brewing in that peculiar pot?'

'A tisane for M. le Comte, according to the doctor's recipe.'

'Is mulled wine so harmful for you, Monsieur?'

'Harmful or not, I'm going to drink it and I'll leave you the tisane.'

'Then let Pierre rub your back.'

'Martin, you know . . .'

'I know everything. Drink up your infusion and I'll go and prepare the ointment.'

The count stood up, went over to the oven, pushed Pierre aside, poured himself out a silver tankard of wine, emptied it at a gulp, refilled it again, emptied it once more and laughed. 'Now Martin, you can put on the ointment.'

'What have you just been drinking?'

'The tisane of course, my friend.'

'Pierre, what has M. le Comte been drinking?'

'I don't know, Monsieur. M. le Comte pushed me aside.'

'Martin,' said the count, sitting down on his camp bed, 'without wine this forest depresses me. I have never seen anything so sinister as these huge dripping firs. Every valley looks like an entrance to the underworld. The farmsteads are like rotten fungi. Give me a rub and be friendly. I'm in terrible pain.'

Martin made no reply but emptied two tankards of wine in succession, then sent Pierre out with the jug and rolled up his shirt sleeves. 'Well, Pan, now lie down nicely on your stomach.'

The count was lying on his back and said: 'Help me turn over.'

Martin looked down at him gravely. 'I hope you haven't anything worse than lumbago. I must ask the regimental surgeon.'

'No, don't ask him anything. I'm not going home, in any case.'

'Has it come to that?'

Martin helped the count turn over and greased his back in the painful places. 'You are feverish and will have to go down the line.'

'And let du Lac reap my laurels?'

'No, so that you don't kill yourself.'

'I shan't do that. They tell me the Neckar country is beautiful. It's covered with vineyards. Do you believe that?'

'Why not?'

'Have you finished rubbing me?'

'Does it hurt?'

'No, but that's enough. Help me over. Thank you! I'm cold without blankets.'

'You couldn't be cold in this heat.'

'You are only warm from rubbing me.'

Martin called the valet. Pierre piled blankets on the count, made him as comfortable as possible, and François made M. de Racon's bed. Martin made himself comfortable, dismissed the servants, took Blanche's last letter from his shirt and began to re-read it.

The count interrupted him with the question: 'Do you remember whom I ordered to check the sentries?'

'You forgot to detail an officer, and that is why I took it on myself.'

'You always have to shoulder everyone else's duties. When are you going off?'

'About two o'clock.'

'Martin, I'm freezing cold on the unheated side.'

'Shall I bring you a feather bed?'

'I shall suffocate under it. Lie down with me.'

Martin put Blanche's letter away, stood up and lay down at the count's side. 'You should be like old King David and get two girls. One could warm you then on each side.'

'Thank you for the sleepless nights.'

'Don't pretend that in your condition you would be fit for any amorous games. If you must know, you're seriously ill.'

'I know it.'

'Think about going home, my friend.'

'If you'll come with me, I'll go.'

'Monsieur, I have to remain with my squadron.'

'I'll give you leave.'

'That would stain my soldier's honour. You are excused because you are ill.'

'I'm riding on with you.'

'Monsieur . . .'

'You won't be rid of me. I propose to die in your arms, and I hope that I shall succeed.'

'Are you beginning to rave?'

'No, but I won't let you go to sleep. Talk to me so that I can forget my pains.'

'Do you think that the king will be able to keep this barbaric country occupied?' asked Martin.

'He can only hold it until the enemy brings his troops back from the east.'

'That means that the king will bring the Turks into Europe.'

'Yes, I'm curious to see when we shall come up against resistance.'

'Monsieur, if the Christian princes of the empire, Protestants and Catholics, are united against the Turks, our king should join them instead of attacking them in the rear. When we have conquered them we shall meet the Turks.'

'Presumably, my friend, Louis will then become the liberator of Christendom and we shall then have our Turkish campaign.'

'The king has bad counsellors,' said Martin. 'He should change his Minister of War and his Father Confessors.'

'Do you propose to commit a second folly at Court?'

'I shall refrain from doing so.'

'I hope so.'

Martin drew Blanche's letter once more from his shirt. 'Stop rustling that paper,' growled the count.

Martin refolded the letter and replaced it with a sigh. 'You are a pest, Pan.'

'And you are as hot as one of these stoves in which they put the fire in these parts. Open the window and lie down on your own camp bed.'

Martin stood up. 'I shall leave the window shut.'

'Am I to sweat?'

'Yes, sweat out all your malice.'

The count uncovered himself. Martin piled more wood on the fire and said: 'Remain uncovered if you like.' He lay down again.

'Martin?'

'What is it?'

'I should like to have read Madeleine's farewell letter again but I left it at Grandval. Write to Blanche and tell her to send it to me.'

'Must I do it at once?'

'Yes . . . No. Spare yourself the trouble. What I can't have immediately will be too late and of no further interest to me.'

'Monsieur, please grant me a couple of hours' sleep.'

'Martin, I sometimes ask myself what would have happened to Madeleine had she been still alive.'

'Such questions are idle.'

'Yes, but I can't get rid of the idea. I cannot see her on her knees. She would never have become a catholic. I killed her and at the same time saved her life. I wish her alive, and at the same time I'm glad she's dead. A pox on the king!'

'Do you hate the king?'

'Yes, for he revoked the Edict of Nantes. He should have allowed the nobility the privilege of choosing their own faith. His tyranny goes too far. Madeleine believed in my patience. Hell, I still believe that a countess should be allowed to believe in what she wants. I should like to roast all those black crows of priests in a drum of oil over the fire . . . with the exception of Father Tulier.'

'Monsieur, you will have to pay for that wish in purgatory,' said Martin sternly.

'Do you seriously believe that?'

'I believe in retribution after death, Monsieur.'

'I spit on such a belief.'

'You are delirious.'

'I'm infuriated with the stupidity of the world. Is there anything more ridiculous than a God before whom an ever-increasing congregation of souls sings hallelujahs for all eternity, while a similar number of sinners wail interminably in the depths of hell? There he is on his throne and has to listen to all that! And you believe in such a thing?'

'Your wife believed it too.'

'No, I don't think she believed it. She was more intelligent than you. You only think when you have to. When I was alone with her she was shy in conversation. Once in the last few years, when I felt bored with her, she said on the verge of tears: "I cannot jest with you, like Martin does." Nevertheless, once in a while, in her letters, I came across a humorous remark . . . I spoke too little with her . . . I loved her inordinately and caused her all manner of pain. Martin, I am burning with remorse.'

'At the most you are burning with fever.'

'No, not only with fever. I should be ready to believe in God and his retinue if he gave me an opportunity of making retribution to Madeleine. He could let me return to the world in a hundred years, perhaps as her brother, so that I could find an opportunity of lending her my support in some distress. If I could do that I would willingly roast in hell-fire. But what use is a stupid God? Why should one atone when one cannot make reparation?'

'You're blaspheming. I beg you to stop talking in this vein.'

'Martin, I cannot forget Madeleine. A few months after your legitimation I gave a coin to some little peasant brat at Grandval. I caught her eye and, at that moment, felt that she was mine completely for the first time. It infuriated me so much that I could have killed the little urchin. The devil take it all.'

Martin yawned and said sleepily: 'Become charitable so that you will bring your wife joy in the next world.'

'Stop your jests. You are lucky with Blanche and see all your wishes fulfilled. You're growing fat and boring and you don't need my friendship any longer.'

'I'm not getting fat.'

'Yes, you are. You have thighs one could beat a drum tattoo on, and your nose is getting thick.'

'I don't mind. It's still more handsome than yours.'

'Don't get angry. I'll see that you lose weight.'

'You're still talking rubbish.'

'Only to keep you awake, my boy. I'll leave the education of my three sons to you and will make you pay for it if they turn out no good. I don't understand anything about education.'

'I'll accept your commission, Comte de Racon,' said Martin.

'Thank you, M. de Racon. You need some knotty problems to solve, otherwise you'll get rusty. A rival would be good for you. I shall return to Grandval tomorrow and let Blanche nurse me back to health. She has softer hands than you and will rub my back more gently.'

'Are you really returning home?'

'Yes, my boy. Tomorrow. You can remain with your squadron.'

'Monsieur, do you want to alienate my wife's affections?'

'No, that would not be noble. During my last visit to Grandval I had the misfortune to fall in love with Blanche. She has changed so completely since your marriage that I should love to know what her caresses are like now. Would you withdraw your friendship if I presented you with a pair of horns?' Martin did not reply. Trying hard to conceal his glee, the count asked seriously: 'Can I try?'

'Yes, try.'

'I'll take you at your word! It'll be your fault if I win.'

Martin rose.

'Have you drunk so much that you need to relieve yourself?'

'I'm going to write to Blanche.'

'Tonight?'

'Yes.' Martin fetched writing materials, sat down, and thought carefully before writing each sentence in his fine, neat hand. As soon as he had signed it, he read the letter, folded it and held a piece of sealing wax to the fire.

'Show me the letter before you seal it,' demanded the count.

Martin looked over to him. 'Aren't you ashamed of yourself?'

'Don't grudge me the pleasure. I want to know what precautions you have taken against me.' Martin handed him the letter. The count unfolded it and read:

Sweet Claire-Marie,

Thank you for your letter of the 19th September. I have kept all your sweet words in my heart and they sing there like happy children. We are in a gloomy forest. The cold rain pours down from the inexhaustible clouds which lie thick and heavy on the black crests. There is no rain in Grandval comparable with this. The men stick their hair under their hats and look like champanzees. No enemy could be waiting for us here, so you can be reassured. Beyond the Black Forest lies unprotected open country, with wealthy cities which we shall enter, unless God wills otherwise.

Things are not well with the count today. He has pains in his back and is feverish, and as a sick man he will bring this letter to you. He needs rest, warmth and entertainment and a woman who loves him. He knows that you entertain a child's love for him, but he will try to court you. Give him what your love will allow you to give. He will demand nothing of you because he is my friend, but he has a way with him that hardly anyone can resist. He is like a burning summer, bewitching and enchanting women until they become oblivious of their past and future. He is like Pan who plays his flute in the noon-day heat. We are in Autumn now, but I cannot imagine that he will ever grow old. I shall understand if you prefer to listen to his lute-playing rather than read a letter from me. I have only words, while Pan has music at his command.

There is nothing I would not forgive you, but when I return I shall ask you which of us has the affections of your heart. I will give you to him or take you back, but I will not share you. I hope that I shall find you my unimpaired property, but I leave you free to follow the dictates of your heart at any time.

I shall never forget the look in your eyes when you said that for you I was the sun. When the sun shines the day is bright, and you were like the pale crescent moon at midday who offered herself to the sun like a little ship to be borne on part of the way. Blanche, if only I could be with you, if only I could feel how you loved me at this moment.

Claire-Marie, you know my heart and will not be angry if I, with my happiness in jeopardy, do not beg for your eternal fidelity. I can see you wrinkling your brow as you read these words. You will be a trifle bewildered. Your thoughts will strive for clarity, and if you know the answer you will write to me. My little queen will take a white goose quill and will perhaps begin like this. 'Monsieur, you have given me a hard nut to crack! I'm certain that I shall crack it, but I still do not know what I shall do with the kernel.' Madame, you will know when the time comes.

Tell little Léon that I will bring him a trumpet if he stops yelling for one whole day. Anyone who beats the drum must himself remain silent, or else the din would be too great. Tell M. d'Ouville that, instead of a pony, the Vicomte de Clarmont should from now onwards ride a horse, which will not bear the touch of the whip and will throw him off if he takes fright. Part him for a time from Léon so that he cannot be tyrannised by him. Make Léon the protector of little Armand, and allow Gaston to give little Martin a pickaback. In future, I shall give you more instructions of this nature because the count has asked me to supervise the education of his sons. Please give me a lot of news of the children, and teach Léon to write to me. Farewell,

MARTIN DE RACON

The count tore the letter in two. Martin rushed over and managed to retrieve the scraps. The man looked up at him with his black, fever-wracked eyes and said amiably: 'You are the biggest idiot the world has ever seen. Anyone who rates Pan above Apollo will be given asses' ears like Midas. That, at least, you should have added as a warning. Be silent!'

'Monsieur . . .'

'Did you really consider me so puerile that, at fifty-five, I should pay court to a lady who is perfectly happily married to a thirty-three-year-old man, and who, incidentally, belonged to me before her marriage? Do you think that Blanche is incapable of making a comparison? I should never have any success with a woman whom you have once made happy, for you are far more considerate and stronger than I am.'

'You are saying that only to pacify me.'

'Ask Blanche, if you doubt me.'

'Monsieur, there are things I do not ask my wife.'

'Martin, I see that I have cooked something up for myself. I only wanted to jolt you a little out of your composure because you were sleepy and I could not sleep. I swear to you that I had no intention of leaving my regiment and that under no circumstances will I return home.'

'But you must, because you're ill.'

'If I return, I will let myself be nursed to health in Brayonne and not at Grandval.'

Martin turned away, threw the shreds of the letter into the fire and said, without looking round: 'Monsieur, I am now going to make the rounds.'

'Send your lieutenant.'

'I'm going myself, unless you order me officially to remain. Do you need anything?'

'Yes, Martin. Make it up with me.'

'Monsieur, you led a donkey on to thin ice, because in your eyes he was too happy. You merely wanted to make him slip, but the ice was too thin and broke.'

'I'll pull you out by the ears!'

'See that in your gallant attempt at a rescue you don't fall in after me.'

'Martin, I might say that you should not have credited me with such vile intentions.'

'And I could say that one should not make such malicious jests at the expense of one's best friend.'

'I am ready to make any amends you wish.'

Martin looked over his shoulder. 'Are you serious?'

'Yes.'

'Then drink your tisane.'

'You are a swine.'

'Goodnight!'

'Martin!'

Martin remained by the oven, filled a cup with herb-tea, turned round and asked with an impassive face: 'Yes or no?'

'Do you want to take your revenge and make me look ridiculous?'

'You'll know that once you've swallowed the tea.'

'Well, give me the stuff.' The count raised himself with great difficulty and took the cup. 'Drink with me to our reconciliation.'

'It is up to you to atone, not me.'

'Martin, a pious Christian always has something to atone for and to forgive.'

Martin laughed, filled a second cup and said: 'To your health.'

They both drank and Martin made a grimace. 'Ugh. Would you like some more?'

'No, thank you very much!'

Martin fastened his belt, went outside and returned with two cloaks.

'Monsieur, our overcoats are dry. I'll lay them over your feet so that you can cover yourself when you start shivering.'

'You'll need yours.'

'No, it's stopped raining.'

'I can hear it dripping.'

'It's only dripping from the roof.' Martin left the kitchen.

The count could not sleep, and waited. When the fire died down he gave a shrill whistle with two fingers, whereupon Pierre appeared with brushwood and logs which he laid on the embers, and disappeared. Martin returned at last, to be asked by the count: 'How many did you catch?'

'Two from the inner ring.'

'Tell me their names.'

'That won't be necessary, Monsieur. I have punished them on the spot. One had crawled under a hayrick and will be suffering from bruises for fourteen days.' Martin removed his boots and unbuttoned his coat.

'I hurried off because of you. How are the pains?'

'I can hardly feel them now.'

'Can I ask a favour of you?'

'What do you want?'

'That you return tomorrow to Grandval and, instead of a series of mistresses, take yourself a second wife as quickly as possible.'

The count laughed. 'Pan is being sent to look for a wife so that he cannot commit any disturbances in the park of Grandval.'

'I didn't mean it like that.'

'I know. Is Blanche to be given any more children to look after?'

'She'll bring up a dozen for you, my friend.'

'Three boys are enough for me.'

'Wouldn't you be happier with a wife than with mistresses who deceive you?'

'No wife could love me as Madeleine loved me. I shan't marry again. Great events never repeat themselves, and the little ones never vary. When one grows old every pleasure seems to lose its charm . . . the war, the Court, gossip in the salon and women . . . I will not build a house in Versailles and shall cancel the purchase of the ground.'

'As soon as you're well again,' said Martin, lying down on his camp bed, 'your melancholy will pass and the world will appear more beautiful than ever.'

The count stared into the fire. 'I would rather be talking with Madeleine now than with you. Perhaps . . .' At this moment they heard shrill cries from outside. Martin leaped to his feet and put on his boots. The count said with a grin: 'I have an idea that the fellows have found three or four ill-concealed girls.' Martin did not bother to put on his overcoat, but seized his riding crop and hurried out. The screams increased and then suddenly died.

Next morning, contrary to expectations, the weather had improved. The count could hardly move and had to be lifted on to his horse by two soldiers. Martin watched. 'Well, my boy,' said the count, as he took the reins, 'wasn't that fine?'

'Monsieur, an old woman would have been quicker in the saddle.' The officers and men standing by laughed, and Martin hurried away to his squadron.

The regiment marched swiftly through the misty valleys under the dripping firs. The sky grew bluer. Martin could no longer remain with his squadron and galloped to the head of the first battalion, where the count was trotting between Colonel de la Porte-Mury and Lieutenant-Colonel de Falleron, ahead of five staff officers and an ensign.

'Have you anything to report?' the count asked sourly.

'No, Monsieur. I came to enquire after your lumbago.'

'That is no concern of yours.'

'Have you any pain?'

'Falleron,' said the count to his companion on the left, 'isn't he a plague?'

'You'll forgive him soon enough for calling you an old woman,' said the colonel with a smile.

'Not that soon. Major de Racon!'

'At your orders, Monsieur.'

'Return immediately to your squadron and do not let me see your face for three hours.' Martin doffed his hat, bowed and galloped back at full speed, as though the enemy were at his heels.

'Well, I'm rid of him for a while,' said the count. 'I don't like the look of those red cliffs ahead.'

'The road must be very narrow there,' remarked de Falleron. 'Has Captain de Vitry posted a squadron up there?'

'He said nothing about it. His patrol was four miles ahead and did not catch sight of a single pike.'

'Monsieur. I can't see a single red coat. If the rocks are unoccupied I would send de Vitry to the infantry, although the advance guard passed the place unmolested.'

'Perhaps he forgot to report the occupation.'

'Forgetfulness on service should be punished,' said Colonel de la Porte-Mury.

'Falleron,' ordered the count, 'send the ensign to de Vitry.' The colonel obeyed, and the count slowed down his horse to walking pace. He loosened his neck-band and rubbed his back.

'I cannot imagine,' said the Vicomte de la Porte-Mury, 'that we shall reach the Neckar without a battle.'

'I am counting upon small skirmishes,' replied the count, 'because the Duke of Württemberg has called up his last men. This evening we shall have the forest behind us. Shall we wager on the number of days before we are in Stuttgart?'

'Rather let us wager how long the siege will last. The duke will not receive us as guests.'

'Who knows! Perhaps the king has offered him some diamond studs.'

The officers laughed at his jest. 'It struck me,' said de Falleron, 'that there were no young men in the village. Perhaps they are massing in the woods. The greybeards looked rather grim.'

'Undrilled peasants are no soldiers,' replied Colonel de la Porte-Mury contemptuously. Captain de Vitry came up at the gallop with the ensign who had been sent to fetch him. He tried to ride close up to the count, but his horse tugged savagely on the bit, reared and threw its rider to the road. There were roars of laughter. The ensign caught the horse; de Vitry picked himself up, covered with mud, and reported to the count on foot.

'Have you occupied the rocks ahead?'

'No, Monsieur.'

'Why not?'

'I did not think it necessary.'

'You've no brains in your head, Vitry! Because of you, the advance guard was insufficiently covered. Return to the rear and report as a lieutenant to Colonel du Lac.'

The degraded man looked foolish. The ensign flung him the reins of his horse and said politely: 'Here's your pretty little mount, Lieutenant.' De Vitry mounted and rode away.

'Monsieur, who is to occupy the rocks until the infantry arrives?' asked de Falleron.

'Lieutenant de Chassigny.'

The colonel despatched the same ensign with the order.

'Monsieur,' asked de la Porte-Mury, 'will you wait here, according to the rules, until the Chassigny squadron has reached the top of the cliff?'

'That will take too long. Come! At the gallop, Gentlemen.' The seven officers put their horses into a gallop at the same time as their commanding officer. The distance between the eight officers and the rest of the battalion rapidly increased. When the count arrived with his companions under the sandstone cliffs, there was a thunderous roar overhead and a deadly hail of iron and stones rained down on the horsemen.

The leading squadron turned back. Shots rang out all round. Horses reared and wounded men screamed. The cry was raised: 'The General has fallen!' Colonel du Lac rode up from the rear and managed to get the situation in hand. 'Dismount! Take cover! Storm the heights!' he roared. The hunchbacked Lieutenant de Chassigny was the first to scramble up the steep slope. Martin galloped into the throng, lashing out with his riding-crop. Colonel du Lac stopped him. 'Major de Racon, no man is to advance until the cliffs have been stormed. Dismount like the others.'

'I must go to the Comte de Racon.'

'Obey me, or I will have you court-martialled for insubordination in the field.' Martin spurred his horse and knocked a man over. Du Lac pulled him out of the saddle. 'Your father would not wish you to rush headlong to your death.'

Martin saved himself from the horses' hooves, ran along the road between the firs, fought his way through the dry branches, tearing his clothes, and came face to face with a bearded fellow with a gleaming club. He shot him, hurried on, ducked in time to avoid a shot, and heard cries for help. He plunged into the fray, wrestled with a fair-haired youth, tore the knife from his hand and stabbed him, freed himself, was attacked once more and rescued by the soldiers. He reached the road again and found it jammed with horses. He was still a long way from the cliffs.

The storming of the heights was achieved with heavy losses. The peasants fought like lions, but suddenly retired at a horn signal from their leader and disappeared into the impenetrable forest. The light horsemen came face to face with age-old bronze guns and looked down upon a tragic scene below.

By the time Martin reached the scene of the disaster, the maimed and mangled horses had already been dragged away and the dead men covered with flags. Officers and soldiers stood round in a silent circle. Martin looked from one to the other, did not dare to ask a question, lifted the corner of the regimental flag and let it fall again immediately. In his mind's eye, he saw a starry night on the steps of a southern temple as he looked up at the count sitting above him, his dark, tanned face against a honey-coloured column. He saw the count rise drunkenly to his feet in the dining-hall by night; saw the black mane of a black charger before him, and the count's fine hand on his dirty peasant shirt feeling for his heart beats. Then darkness fell upon him.

Du Lac took over the regiment as its acting commander. He ordered three days' rest, took up his quarters in the next village, and on the fourth day had the dead buried with military honours near the red cliffs. He promised M. de Racon that he would see to the transport home of the count's mortal remains. But it was in the depths of winter, after a heavy rearguard action, that they returned to the scene of the ambush, and at the spot marked by a white armlet on a crucifix they found beneath the frozen earth and snow only the corpse of a mangy dog. The other graves had also been robbed of their dead. They searched by the roadside and round the cliffs, only to discover a few human bones of various origin which had been buried in a common grave.

The rage of soldiers and men alike was boundless. They put to death twenty prisoners in the most gruesome manner, set fire to three villages and massacred the inhabitants. Major de Racon begged Colonel du Lac to put a stop to the atrocities, since the souls of the dead were not bound to their transitory remains and would certainly not feel disturbed because their bones were left to rot on the mossy ground of the Black Forest instead of in the bosom of the earth. Du Lac asked him if the thought of his father's corpse being eaten by wolves and foxes did not make him shudder. Martin replied that the wolves and foxes only did what nature intended them to do; while men who murdered sinned against their own divinity. He could not avenge his friend by hatred; he could only show his gratitude by good deeds. Du Lac, remembering that the general had so often listened to his son's pleas, ordered Major de Racon to call the regiment to order and to punish any lack of discipline with the utmost severity.

THE END

FORTUNE'S WHIRLWIND
by JOHN JAKES
The American Bicentennial Series Volume 1

The spellbinding saga of the proud, passionate men and women who took a handful of colonies and made them a nation.

This vibrant novel of romance and adventure introduces a stunning new historical figure: Phillipe Charbonneau. Illegitimate son of an English Nobleman, Phillipe joins the turbulent struggle that is the beginning of the American Experience. Through his struggles, his loves and his courage the reader is caught up in the maelstrom of events that are to shape the destiny of a mighty nation.

0 552 10004 8—**65p**

TO AN UNKNOWN SHORE
by JOHN JAKES
The American Bicentennial Series Volume 2

'The Americans are the sons, not the bastards, of England!' But the English King, 'German George', had other ideas. And Philip Kent finds himself plunged into a storm of events—including a blazing battlefield struggle that would bring him face to face with his hated halfbrother, Roger . . . a tempestuous romance with the daughter of an American revolutionary . . . and a series of exhilarating encounters with a little band of radicals and patriots who authored one of the most revered documents of all times—The U.S. Constitution.

TO AN UNKNOWN SHORE—the second volume in an exciting series of novels celebrating America's two years of independence.

0 552 10005 6—**65p**

THE TREES
by CONRAD RICHTER

Sayward Luckett was only fifteen when her mother died and she had to take the woman's place in the family, but she grew up quickly. They had many dangers to face—not only the Indians and the wild animals but the threat of the endless forest itself . . .

This is the story of Sayward's long life on the frontier, a life full of the hardship and the joys that faced every family in those pioneering days.

Sayward's story is continued in Conrad Richter's other two novels THE FIELDS and THE TOWN.

0 552 10116 8—**60p**

THE FIELDS
by CONRAD RICHTER

'Oh, it was a strong country out here. The woods died mighty hard. No soft living like back East. It had slews of work and plenty varmints, beasts and humans. But they couldn't keep folks from clearing and plowing, hunting and sugaring, visiting and celebrating some public day if they wanted. Life went on much the same out here, she reckoned, like it did back in the Bay State.'

Frontier life was slowly settling down as Sayward Luckett Wheeler began a new chapter of her life with children of her own, but she still needed every ounce of her fighting spirit to face the dangers that every day in the young country brought . . .

This is the second novel in Conrad Richter's great trilogy which ends with THE TOWN.

0 552 10117 6—**60p**